Pleasures
of Music

Jacques Barzun

$2.25

Pleasures of Music

Pleasures of Music

A Reader's Choice
of Great Writing about Music and Musicians
from Cellini to Bernard Shaw

≫≫ ≪≪

EDITED WITH AN INTRODUCTION BY

JACQUES BARZUN

1344

Published by The Viking Press
NEW YORK

COMPASS BOOKS EDITION

ISSUED IN 1960 BY THE VIKING PRESS, INC.

625 MADISON AVENUE, NEW YORK, N. Y. 10022

DISTRIBUTED IN CANADA BY

THE MACMILLAN COMPANY OF CANADA LIMITED

FOURTH PRINTING NOVEMBER 1966

The editor's acknowledgments to holders of copyright and publishing rights are made in the list of Sources and Acknowledgments, pp. 611–17.

PRINTED IN THE U.S.A. BY THE COLONIAL PRESS INC.

FOR

A. R. B.

TABLE OF CONTENTS

The Musical Life

POLITICS AND PATRONAGE

APROPOS OF INSTRUMENTS

Fantasies and Confessions

Correspondence

Maxims and Good Stories

Pleasures of Music

"Nobody is ever patently right
about music."—VIRGIL THOMSON

INTRODUCTION
Music and Words

JACQUES BARZUN

I

Anyone, with or without a musical ear, who has learned to read words, can understand everything in this book.

It is necessary to say this at the outset, because many educated people are known to harbor an odd prejudice against literature that deals with music. Whereas the ordinary reader courageously tackles the slang of thieves, the jargon of psychiatry, and the ever-changing vocabulary of war, he balks at the supposed impenetrability of discourse on music. He will plunge in boldly and make out for himself what "flak" and "gremlin" stand for, he will tackle *Finnegans Wake* or thread his way through cookbooks laced with French, but will retreat baffled before such dread technicalities as "first violin," "accompaniment," and "repeat."

There is modesty, no doubt, in this shying off, and perhaps the germ of a true principle, which is that words are no substitute for musical sound. All the books on "appreciation" and all the program notes in the world are powerless to reproduce the experience of music —of the simplest music as of the most complex. But the pleasure proposed in an anthology such as this is not the pleasure of music; it is the pleasure of reading. To many it will bring reminders of past musical pleasures, but to all it can yield the pleasure of beholding the many forms and roles of an art which is as old as man, and which modern means of communication have made all-pervasive.

Music nowadays, whether we like it or not, is interwoven with the texture of our lives from morning till night. Music resounds for, with, and through everything; it is canned and broadcast, recorded and rebroadcast; it is, so to speak, piped into our houses at the very time when it has virtually ceased to be piped within them. Hence to read how music comes into being, how it is played and received, argued about, paid for, and judged, stands on a par with any other literary experience. The stories, critiques, confessions, and human documents collected in the pages that follow show us a portion of life which it takes no special knowledge to respond to. But one's expectations must be just: no one expects to be shot while reading a novel of war; similarly, no one must expect to hear lullabies while reading about music. The world's great literature, regardless of subject, is taken in through the imagination.

"But," it may be objected, "that is precisely the difference. It takes no learning to imagine the horror of being shot down in a plane, whereas it takes musical learning to follow a writer who describes, say, the conducting of an orchestra."

To which the rejoinder is, "Not if he is a good writer." Turn to pp. 277 and 601 of this book and you will find that both Debussy and his British confrère who deals with Sir Thomas Beecham make you see without effort the conductors they describe. At the same time, they make you feel quite differently about their identical subject, and differently about themselves as critics. And you will observe that the writers do not even tell you precisely what is being played—much less the secret of how it is done. Their words describe the antics of Man, not the technique of the baton.

Surely it is absurd to pretend that only in reading about musical matters does pleasure demand complete mastery of detail. You may read an endless series of historical novels, a mass of present-day reportage or science-fiction, without ever really knowing the simplest things known by the real or imaginary participants. Gripped though you may be by the recital of war in the air, what do you know about the caliber and power of the projectiles you are dodging? Can you distinguish the altimeter from the oil gauge? Not unless your author helps you. Yet reading about it is neither worthless nor intellectually reprehensible. By reading you enter into the feelings of your fellow man, and by imagining situations from a minimum of detail you make your own the best part of what is common to him and you.

Similarly with music, which is, above all, a social art and by any standard a sizable concern—hence a lavish dispenser of pleasure, prestige and profits. Historically, music has been a partner of religion, war, royal pomp, and ostentatious leisure. As an independent art no less than as handmaid of civilized life, it is a breeder of passions, great and little, and thus a source of both comedy and tragedy. To say all this is to say that in its domestic and foreign relations music is bound to be the subject and starting point, if not the inspiration, of great literature—as I believe that the present sampling will show.

Given these facts, my standard of selection was obvious and simple. Setting aside all writings whose purpose was chiefly instructive or theoretical, or whose interest was solely that of association, I had to choose classic expressions of as many different moments of the musical life as possible. And musical life, let me say it again, was not to be taken as meaning exclusively the concert hall or the composer's study. It might, for example, mean music at meals, which Chesterton makes the occasion for a characteristic onslaught upon modern culture (see p. 161). It could also mean the wrangle of voices debating the duty of the artist to society and to utopia—a subject that occupies one whole section of this volume. The only difficulty in making an anthology answering to this definition was to resign oneself to omitting good things.

As to what constitutes a "classic" expression, judgments are bound to differ; nor was it possible to apply a uniform standard to genres as unlike as private letters, tales of fantasy, and biographical anecdotes. But I tried to bear in mind three tests—the representative worth of the sample, the greatness of the mind that conceived it, and the felicity of the prose. I cannot pretend that all the pieces I have selected show all these qualities in equal degree; but I venture to say that these selections compare favorably, as literature, with corresponding collections about a single subject—great letters or speeches, state papers, or rhapsodies about horses and dogs.

One reason this claim may be advanced is that within the last two hundred years many musicians of genius have also been masters of the literary art, while not a few literary masters have lent their good ear to music and become first-rate critics. Rousseau, Hoffmann of the Tales, Schumann, Berlioz, Wagner, Nietzsche, Hardy, Shaw, Tolstoy, Samuel Butler, Debussy, Hugo Wolf, to name but a handful, have cast their knowledge of music—and of music-in-life—into the form of stories, essays, maxims, or satires. What seemed the freshest and truest of these will be found in the pages to follow.

Still other men, making no pretense to literary art but pursuing careers as composers, performers, or newspaper critics, have also been moved by music to admire, to despair, or to envy *on paper;* they have left letters, memoirs, epigrams, or anecdotes that deserve a place in a reader's musical "companion." Finally, there exists an oral tradition or "proverbiage" of music, which has handed down a number of possibly unfounded but often well found stories that clearly belong in a treasury of what is characteristic as well as entertaining about the art.

For no piety should make us overlook the fact that music and the making of music are admirable subjects for comedy, high and low. The first response to any really strange music is laughter—the Javanese conceal well-bred smiles on hearing Beethoven, and we grin shamelessly at their love songs accompanied by nose-blown flutes. Even within our own culture, so-called classical music will arouse honest laughter in the untutored, and it takes only a few wrong notes at a rehearsal to turn, for all concerned, a funeral dirge into a joke. The more sublime an art can be, the more perilously it skirts the ludicrous. It is therefore no accident that the literature about music is so predominantly hilarious. Nor should we forget that the playing of most instruments is inherently as farcical as love-making. It is mere habit, born of a felt necessity and a pragmatic sense of results, that makes us think otherwise. Consequently the sportings and disportings of tenors, trombonists, cellists, horn players, drummers, and even of the plangent pianist and swaying violinist, are fair game for the satiric pen.

As against the Rabelaisian laugh, the eulogies of the poets seem tame. It would be easy to fill several volumes with verses in praise of music, but, barring a few brief lines, they would, if put side by side with the right piece of prose, fail to carry conviction. Shakespeare was at least honest in hedging: "*If* music be the food of love, play on." (Otherwise, be quiet.) Browning, to take a more recent instance, was a good amateur pianist, but when he came to write "Abt Vogler" (about the man who taught both Weber and Meyerbeer) he filled the poem with such a clatter of miscellaneous musical terms as to cast suspicion on his knowledge of their meaning. No doubt he used them just for sound, "musically," but that is only another way of saying that he cared more for his poem and his drama than for music. On this ground I have excluded all poetry, except of course the lines that happen to be quoted in the chosen stories or essays.

For a kindred reason I have left out the ancients. What we truly know about their music could be written on the back of a visiting card, and what they say of it must remain either mysterious or incredible. By way of illustration and résumé, I include a short passage from Robert Burton's *Anatomy of Melancholy;* the reader who is tempted to enter the labyrinth of speculation about ancient harmony can look up the authors whom Burton cites. He may then be cheered by the discovery that Plato's hospitable feelings toward musicians came late in life. In the earlier *Republic,* the philosopher was inclined to consider their freedom a menace to the good society—on which point see George Sand two thousand years later (p. 371).

One more word about the text of the selections: except for those originally in Russian, all the translations into English are mine. In some cases no earlier translation existed; in others they seemed to me inexact or stilted. Whenever I found a good English version I consulted it and borrowed its happy turns of phrase, as I hope latercomers may do with any lucky hits of mine. But the principal reason (besides greater readability and my enjoyment of the task) for supplying some of these classic pieces in a new English dress was to permit condensation. Wherever possible I have of course preferred to give a narrative uncut—a whole chapter if detachable from a book; but often in autobiographies and articles from nineteenth-century magazines extraneous matter was present in such bulk as to preclude reprinting *in extenso*. It would have been a pity to omit the story of Jenny Lind in America just because P. T. Barnum lacked concision; or to deprive the reader of De Quincey on "whistling Waterloo" because it forms a digression within a long essay. Usually my omissions are of entire paragraphs or sections, and are indicated by the conventional dots or white space. Only in one or two essays did it prove necessary to do finer surgery on sentences, and hence to refrain from using the dots, which would have plagued the reader to no purpose. Anyone seeking the full original will find it listed among the sources at the back of the book, with an exact reference to the pages drawn on for the selection.

In many of those books, moreover, the reader whose interest has been aroused by the single excerpt will find much to repay his curiosity —other essays or letters, full-length memoirs and novels, or an ingenious series of fables and tales.

II

Though it is no surprise that the art of music should have generated a body of readable literature, it should perhaps astonish us that the bulk of that literature has been written since 1800. To be sure, we have been keeping more blackened paper since 1800: this is called the historical sense and it makes for bulk. Then again, the nineteenth century was a great age of music, and whatever was played or sung was written about, and the writing published. Finally, it could be maintained that we find truest and best what is nearest to us, and therefore favor the recent past. But if we compare the words of, say, Luther or Milton—both true devotees of music as well as men who could write—with those of Robert Schumann or Bernard Shaw in a later age, we see that something has happened to writings on music. We are tempted to add that something has happened to our feelings about music; for it is inevitable that when our experiences are put into words for us by literary artists the emotional associations and their cause alike take on new qualities. When Adam had named the Tiger, it was a fiercer animal than before.

Now judging from prose accounts, it would seem a fair generality that until about two hundred years ago music evoked only the broadest, vaguest feelings even in thoughtful men. They were perhaps no less deeply moved by sounds than we are now, but they were seldom roused to delve into and discuss their delight. Here, for instance, is the role and the praise that Milton assigns to music in his little essay on education, under the heading of Exercise:

The interim of unsweating themselves regularly, and convenient rest before meat may both with profit and delight be taken up in re-creating and composing their travailed spirits with the solemn and divine harmonies of music heard, or learned; either while the skilful Organist plies his grave and fancied descant in lofty fugues, or the whole Symphony with artful and unimaginable touches adorn and grace the well-studied chords of some choice composer; sometimes the Lute, or soft organ-stop waiting on elegant voices either to Religious, martial, or civil ditties; which if wise men and prophets be not extremely out, have a great power over dispositions and manners, to smooth and make them gentle from rustic harshness and distempered passions.

This is enough to convince us that Milton understood music and enjoyed it, but not even the grand rhythm of the prose can conceal the conventionality of the sense. Like Luther and Shakespeare and Burton, Milton repeats the cliché about the power of music to make men good and gentle, and he says this right after an allusion to "martial ditties." One wonders what those about to be massacred by Cromwell's armies thought on this point as they heard the Roundheads advance to the chant of a godly hymn. It is not until the nineteenth century that we find an ironic observer such as Flaubert, who puts down in his *Dictionary of Platitudes*: "Music—makes a people's disposition more gentle; e.g., 'The Marseillaise.'"

This contrast of times and men does not warrant the conclusion that by the nineteenth century people had stopped writing nonsense about music. They hadn't, as some of the following pages will show (e.g., pp. 68–69). Precisely because music acts so powerfully on those who like it, there is a natural affinity between nonsense and music. To expect anything else is like expecting love letters to be models of sobriety and worldly prudence. But just as there are great love letters, which do convey wisdom—the wisdom of passion—so there can be great musical literature which not only conveys musical enthusiasm with accuracy but also extends our understanding of music itself.

It is important to assert this and keep asserting it, for many good people are so deeply revolted by nonsense that they deny the possibility of even talking about music. And these would-be censors of free speech are reinforced by the diffident "literary people" who, like poor Emerson (p. 600), feel awash as soon as the stream of sound begins to flow—though they lack his candor in turning the deluge to account. Both groups maintain that music is an experience apart, which words can never reach; and when challenged about this dogma, they argue that criticism is possible only in literature and the plastic arts because both of these deal with objects that may be pointed to. Music, not being made up of objects nor referring to objects, is intangible and ineffable; it can only be, as it were, inhaled by the spirit: the rest is silence.

The first thing these persons fail to see is that it is precisely their obscurantism that encourages inflated nonsense and *Schwärmerei* about music. For until a proper language has been established by the efforts of talented men, the common intelligence is at the mercy of folly—its own and that of others. It is a mistake to suppose that the language of criticism about literature arose of itself, or that it is fully satisfactory even now. Still more mistaken is the assumption that literature (or painting) deals with objects and is therefore more easily discussed, as if words had a special grip on that one portion of reality.

The truth is that although literature *uses* words, no one has yet given any generally accepted account of what the art itself consists in. What poetry is, no one has unmistakably defined. What happens in a work of literature remains a subject of endless debate—there are

thousands of books to tell you what goes on in *Hamlet,* and no two
of them agree. To be sure, one can give the plot of *Hamlet* in a few
words that a child can understand, but the difference between the
play and the paraphrase, between the child's understanding and
Shakespeare's conception, is exactly the intangible substance, the
ineffable meaning of what we call literature. This difference can be
illustrated even on the smallest scale. Take the line,

> Absent thee from felicity awhile . . .

Supposing any man in the street to understand this at sight (which
is a generous supposition), ask him to explain it. He will probably
suggest that it means, "Give up having a good time for a while." Then
ask whether the original line is simply a dressed-up version of the
same idea, a fancy way of putting a common thought. If the answer
is yes, you know that you have before you a man who not only takes
a low view of poetry, but one who is also insensitive to meanings. In
short, words are not fixed devices that firmly grip our perceptions,
feelings, memories, and visions. They are on the contrary shifting
symbols, whose relations among themselves and to our individual
minds are infinitely subtle and difficult to trace. When we know how
subject to varied interpretation legal documents may be, we can
confidently say that literature as an art is a "music of meanings," and
that criticism frequently fumbles in trying to transfix it—just like
the criticism of music.

The parallel with painting is clear enough: what Cézanne uses as
a starting point for a picture may be apples, but they are not *what*
he paints in the sense in which the advertising artist employed by
the fruit-growers' association might assume, nor does any serious
discussion of Cézanne's work involve the term apples except as a
quick way to refer to a part of the painting.

In music, of course, this sort of quick reference to a passage is
difficult or impossible for the untrained, but it is easy for those who
have learned the terminology as they grew familiar with the substance
of the art. Such terms as "the recapitulation," "the second subject,"
"the hidden octaves between the outer parts" may seem very recondite,

but they are no more so than "the dangling participle at the top of the page." The chief difference between the amenability of music to this sort of verbal discussion and that of literature or painting is the difference between a knowledge of terms which is taken for granted as part of the educated person's equipment and a knowledge which is still deemed "special." The awe-struck attitude of the literary man in the face of musical jargon is nothing more than the awe-struck attitude of the illiterate before the man who can read.

But the force of the parallel does not stop there. It has long been recognized in literature that true criticism does not consist in the exclusive analysis of an author's grammar and syntax. A poem is not judged or explained by listing the metaphors, constructions, and idioms which it employs. Even the latest attempts at "pure" literary criticism, which tries to keep out everything not in the work itself, find it necessary to discuss the multiple meanings of words, and this brings the critic plump into historical research, psychology, and the experience of life.

Similarly, the so-called technical criticism of music is not criticism at all. Immensely useful as it is for teaching—like grammar and rhetoric to the writer—it *adds* relatively little, even to the trained reader who understands it. At its best it is something more than parsing; it corresponds to a résumé of plot, a paraphrase of intentions, or a thematic analysis, such as are used in the criticism of literature. But in neither art does mere analysis re-create or refresh one's sense of the passage to which it applies. Sometimes, indeed, the analysis is so abstract and removed from the object that we are not reminded of the work at all. In this, the technical type of music criticism resembles its opposite extreme, the "poetic" type, about which the complaint is that it might fit any piece of the same general character. But since a piece of music can be built on a common pattern in the same way that a comedy can be built on a common plot, the complaint applies equally to both types. And if the critic pushes the technical description farther into particulars so as to identify the work unmistakably, he necessarily falls back into grammar and syntax; so would a literary critic who tried to identify a poem by saying that "the second stanza begins with a periodic sentence containing a split infinitive and rimes *a b b a*." All this, once again, is most useful for teacher and student, but it is not criticism in the larger sense of the word.

What then is criticism in that sense and how does it deal with music? In answering this it would be unwise to limit the genre by saying that criticism must follow the model set by Shaw or Berlioz or Schumann. Each critic has his language and his special purpose or characteristic bent. The present volume will show a wide variety of styles and modes of attack. Nevertheless, the "higher" criticism as a whole has certain recognizable features, of which the most fundamental is that it is addressed to the laity—not an ignorant or inexperienced laity but an unspecialized one; the same laity for whom all art is intended; the laity without whom some of the greatest artists would still be unknown, carefully shielded from the rigors of fame by a tight phalanx of professors and technicians.

In the second place, criticism must offer general ideas. This is not to say vague or commonplace ideas, but, on the contrary, ideas of the utmost precision, which yet have a bearing elsewhere than at their point of origin. This is the meaning of Shaw's assertion: "I believed I could make musical criticism readable even by the deaf." When, to take an example from this book, Apthorp draws out the analogies between a full-course dinner and a sonata, we are wittily reminded that the element of form is not limited to art but discoverable in all human activities, while at the same time we are given an entertaining lesson in the comparative method.

Analogy and comparison are in fact at the root of all criticism worth the name. With real art available, no one wants to read a secondhand discourse that solely and vainly tries to reproduce experience by offering us its skeleton. Tolerable discourse must be live enough at least to throw out a few feelers into surrounding country. A more ambitious criticism must weave back and forth between the work of art and the rest of life, which includes other works of art as well as the reader's fund of common ideas. In this way, and only in this way, can the work, new or old, be knitted into the fabric of our perceptions and into that of culture at large. In this way, and only in this way, can we come to know with reasonable fullness what we think and feel about an artist and his work.

For all judgments are comparative, and the best judgments take in a greater multitude of considerations than can be made, all at once, conscious and explicit. As Mr. Vernon makes brilliantly plain in one of the essays in this book, a musical work is never perceived, by anybody, as purely an experience for the ear. While listening we properly concentrate on the sounds—just as we are all eyes before a painting —but the receptive mind, and later the reflective, should ideally embrace nothing less than the universe. What good criticism does, while reviving the memory of the work, is to associate it with some corner of the universe that we do not know or might not think of. In short, what criticism ultimately aims at is the utmost extension that is compatible with the utmost refining of the *esprit de finesse* described by Pascal.

III

As regards music, it seems significant that the development of this sort of critical thought very closely follows the rise of opera. In the extract I have chosen from Monteverdi we can see a pioneer attempt to connect his technical innovations with poetry, drama, and psychology. The oversimplification is obvious and unconvincing, but the tendency is clear. From that moment on, wherever opera flourishes, there flourishes also an abundant literature of polemic, praise, and would-be musical philosophy. The eighteenth century produced a vast quantity of writings in these forms, all about opera, and they so thoroughly popularized the twin ideas of the seriousness of music and the necessity of music drama that the nineteenth century only had to believe the one and create the other. When we recall, besides, that throughout the period since Monteverdi the interchange of styles and devices between opera and "pure" instrumental music, and between both of these and "sacred" music, has been contant and fruitful, we are forced to the conclusion that it is by virtue of its hybridization in opera that music in all its forms has achieved its present status as an art worth talking and arguing about. Today even those who fidget under music and resent what they cannot grasp would be chary of echoing the contemptuous challenge of the French philosopher Fontenelle: *"Sonate, que me veux-tu?"*—"Sonata, what do you want with me?" The new order of things may lead to hypocrisy and secret self-torture at intimate series of Bach recitals, but among the dispensers of noble pleasure and profundity music has come to stay.

Nor is this all. These same three hundred and fifty years have also seen the rise of the musician in both the social and the intellectual scale. The trade has become a profession, and the professional—unlike the charlatans we shall see satirized in Molière—is now a man of ideas: he is educated, reads books, studies physics, and writes about aesthetics. The State itself fears his opinions and takes cognizance of his chord progressions to see that they are progressing in the right direction. It would be a bold man who would still give vent to the prejudices against "fiddlers" or "bad company" so freely uttered by Lord Chesterfield, or even more recently by Emerson and Byron.

It was of course to overcome the bad associations of the name musician that Beethoven called himself a "tone-poet" and spoke of composing as *dichten*—a nomenclature which brings us back to the question, How shall music be written about once its substance and meaning have become as thoroughly "dramatized"—i.e., impregnated with ideas—as in the modern world?

Beethoven himself speaks of "those senseless terms—allegro, andante"—because, as he says, "the music often expresses something quite different" from their original meaning of "joyful" or "walking." He and many of his successors have tried to remedy this defect by peppering their scores with more particular descriptions of the mood, feeling, or action intended. But whether applied once to a single passage, or adopted by musicians generally, any words used are bound to be metaphorical, not literal. Stop and consider the "sour" note: the term is a verdict and an image without being a description. An andante movement does not walk, it merely suggests the pace of a man walking. The "movement" itself is not a movement; it is either many movements, made by the performers as they blow and scrape, and by the particles of air they disturb, or it resembles motion only in that it takes up a certain amount of time. Yet no one would dream of ruling out these convenient transfers of meaning. No one had better dream of it, for the objection, if enforced, would mean the end of civilized language itself. All speech, even the most commonplace, is inescapably metaphorical, and very few words can be said merely to denote; few, that is, fail to set off the overtones we call connotations.

Hence the search for a critical vocabulary in which we may speak of music by strict denotation is quite absurd: not even the conventional notes and signs of a score can precisely denote the sounds that we hear—they are merely broad hints to the performer. But since each art uses certain materials and methods of its own, it is bound to use a number of terms that are special without being technical—for instance, the names of the instruments—and that an educated reader can pick up as readily as the lingo of any hobby. These terms should "denote" as much as possible and should be used with rigid fidelity—the critic who despairs about drums on a later page shows what happens when this strictness is not observed.

But beyond this point the language of criticism is to be neither special nor strict; precise, yes; but not strict in the sense of inflexible, for its role is to mediate between common experience and the characteristic means or effects of the given art. And it is here that the criticism of music has lagged behind that of literature; the fault lies not in the nature of things but of men: music critics have taken refuge in technicalities instead of devising the phrases that would enlighten "even the deaf." They have frightened the common reader, and in both these ways neglected their art and their task.

Note incidentally that the same charge may be laid against the critics of the plastic arts. Where, for instance, are the great essays about the masterpieces of sculpture? For the same reason, who can stand more than a page at a time of the currently accepted criticism of painting? Until Ruskin came along and taught the world how to write about buildings, what could one read about architecture—always excepting the manuals full of dates and floor plans? This deplorable scarcity proves once more that it is not the fluidity of music that makes discussing it difficult. A statue is not fluid; it has readily namable parts from head to toe, and is evidently a man, a horse, a woman, or a child. What is wanting is the prose with which to discern and discriminate. The problem is literary, which is why we are dependent, for whatever criticism we have, upon geniuses who are not only inspired but also articulate in the presence of art. And this in turn is but another justification for reading literature about the several arts, including literature itself: our power to "express an opinion," for relief or persuasion, springs from other men's verbal inventions.

Perhaps we can now draw the several threads of the discussion together: it will, I think, automatically suggest the proper speech for exchanging ideas about music. Criticism in any art, it was said, should compare and make analogies. Again, most of the fundamental operations of the musical art are expressed in analogies: allegro, andante, repeat, retard, recapitulate. Finally, the great development of music in modern times has taken place under the stimulus of contact and mixture with the other arts. Analogy, similarity in difference, is thus the great rule to follow, in perceiving and in criticizing.

To put it another way, the subject matter of all the arts is a unity, even though the expressive means and the relative powers of the several arts differ. Music cannot paint, nor literature yield colors, nor architecture have a beginning, a middle, and an end. Yet as time goes on and techniques keep pace with desires, the legitimate analogies multiply. There is "tone color" in music—this quite apart from that other eighteenth-century invention, the color-organ; there is "rhythm" in painting, and "dissonance" in architecture—the asymmetric use of two alternating details so that they periodically clash; there is, long has been, word-music in poetry and prose; there is sculpture marked with pictorial effects, and painting full of plastic sensations. All of these arts, moreover, may be associated with one another's nominal "subjects" and may be rightly characterized as dramatic, serene, gay, sinister—as well as by a thousand other qualities.

We may, that is, use any of these expressions about music when we know how to apply them without serious ambiguity. No one is deceived by being told that Mozart's harmony "flows" smoothly, that the Ninth Symphony is a "massive" work, or that Haydn wrote a "Clock" symphony. The trouble comes when the excitement caused by the work of art gives rise to an outburst of unexamined metaphors —I refer the reader once more to the account of Sir Thomas Beecham's conducting. Precisely because music and its rhythms act immediately on our deep-lying fibers, because these rhythms and sounds suggest physical motion and are associated with social rites—from dancing to wars and burials—talk about music is likely to be painfully elemental. Hence the difficulty is not, as the Know-Nothings pretend, that music has no "content" and therefore defies comment, but rather that it has too much and therefore is all-suggestive. Whence the wild comparisons of the sound of trumpets with the color scarlet, of solemn chords with the gates of heaven opening, and of a famous duet with sexual ecstasy.

Clearly the critic or speaker must choose among all the suggestions thronging into his mind, including the technical and formal if he happens to be a professed musician. And the test of all such comparisons, analogies, associations, and transfers of sense-perceptions is pragmatic: let them be subjective or objective, concrete or abstract, secular or religious, physical or metaphysical: those which, after repeated use and repeated reading, serve well because they fit—because they lead to significance—are good. The rest are follies or curiosities, which should no more discourage the effort at precision than does the book-reviewing which finds a "poignant masterpiece" in every week's supply of novels.

Only, in order that music criticism shall catch up with the literary, there must be a public interested enough to read and criticize the critics. None but the public can say which of the ideas or expressions hazarded about the art are ultimately the most fitting, and worthy of becoming part of the traditional vocabulary of criticism. Moreover, this public must within the bounds of social intercourse be critical of its own remarks: if after a recital the performer is criticized behind his back as "lacking in inner warmth," the question must somehow come up, What does this mean? Is there an inner and an outer warmth? And is warmth the right image? Possibly it is intelligence that is lacking, or breadth of tone, or range of loud and soft—for one must first keep an eye on the object and then illuminate it by classing it under a general head.

Above all, the citizen who likes to air his views about music must be principled in talk, that is, not simply tell the truth but reject and resist the ever-present cant of ready-made opinion, which seems at the time so witty, so subtle, so superior, but which is often nothing more than a new version of an old fallacy. The same responsibility, in short, should attach to the words spoken about art in ordinary society as to comparable remarks about the latest process for extracting sunshine from cucumbers. And just because sense and sensibility about art are more elusive, it is useful as well as agreeable to familiarize oneself with earlier writings on the same themes.

Of these, the ones concerned with music are more abundant and varied, they occur in more unexpected places—as this selection shows —than one is accustomed to think. Though only sampled in these pages, they take in the whole circle of possible experiences connected with music as an art and a profession. Why this great body of wisdom and amusement is not common property, like the lore about painters and poets—the cinquecento and the Mermaid Tavern—would be a mystery except for the fact with which we began, namely, the fright of "literary" readers and the growls from the musical dogs-in-the-manger.

It is high time this segregation should cease. The record album has made the nonmusical man obsolete, and meanwhile printed books and free public schooling have forced the musically gifted to become literate. It remains for both groups to overhaul each other's manner of addiction to their respective arts. Whether one goes to writings about music for intellectual profit or solely for pleasure is a wholly personal matter. But the most casual reader who is by way of hearing musical talk—over the radio or in the flesh—cannot help being struck by the difference between the prevailing tone of that talk and the language of the great composers and true connoisseurs, even in their most trivial moods. The gap is like that between the lives of the composers and the movies concocted about them. In the reality, as one might expect, there is more zest, more passion, more courage, more insight, more naturalness—and of course more suffering; and if one brings formal discussions into the comparison, there is more truth (and more fun) embodied in the few pages of a letter by Mozart, in a jotting by Delacroix, or a portrait by Romain Rolland, than in the combined utterances of ten generations of "sober judges" and "competent musicians."

To say this is not to sound a call for incompetence and inebriation, but to urge that we borrow, for our own sakes, a little of the sacred fire from the spot where it is really burning. Failing this, we run the ignoble risk—despite all the long-playing records and the six hundred and fifty-nine orchestral societies scattered across the land—of deserving the scornful words that the philosopher Lucentio applies to the pigheaded performer Hortensio in the *Taming of the Shrew:*

> Preposterous ass! that never read so far
> To know the cause why music was ordained!

Fiction

E. T. A. HOFFMANN

➤➤➤ ⫷⫷⫷

A Tale of Don Juan
(As It Happened to a Traveling Enthusiast)

Composer, critic, novelist, and civil servant, Ernst Theodor Wilhelm
Hoffmann (1776–1822)—he changed the initial *W*. to *A*. out of admiration for *A*madeus Mozart—wrote much besides the famous tales and
greatly influenced the course of music. Wagner, to name but one bene-
ficiary, said that he gathered more congenial instruction from Hoffmann than from his teacher of music.

An ear-splitting bell and the shrill cry, "The show is on!" woke me
from the sweet sleep into which I had fallen. The double basses
were humming in chorus, a stroke on the drum, trumpet calls, and
then the oboe played a clear long-drawn-out A. The violins took
the pitch. I rubbed my eyes. Was the ever-busy Satan playing me
tricks in my cups? No. I am still in the room of the hotel where
I stopped yesterday half-dead with fatigue. Just above my head
hangs the magnificent bell rope. I give it a violent pull, a waiter
appears.

"In the name of heaven, what is the meaning of this confused
sound of music so near me? What concert is being given here?"

"Your Excellency,"—I had ordered champagne with my table
d'hôte—"Your Excellency perhaps does not know that this hotel connects with the theater? This covered door gives on a passageway
which takes you to box twenty-three—the strangers' box."

"What do you mean, theater? Strangers' box?"

"Yes, a small box with two seats only; three at most can sit there.
It's reserved for distinguished guests. It is close to the stage, up-
holstered in green, and shut off with grillwork. If Your Excellency
wishes—they are giving today the *Don Juan* of the celebrated Herr

21

Mozart of Vienna. The price of the box is one and eight. It can be put on the bill."

He was already opening the door of the box as he said these last words, for at the very name *Don Giovanni* I had quitted the room and hurried down the corridor. The theater was large for a medium-sized town, decorated with taste and brilliantly lighted. The boxes and stalls were filled. The opening chords of the overture convinced me that the orchestra was excellent; even if the singers were only competent, I would be enjoying the full delights the masterpiece affords.

In the andante I was seized by the dread of the fearful subterranean "realm of all woes." Terrifying anticipations of the Unspeakable shook my soul. Whereupon the gay fanfare in the seventh measure of the allegro resounded like the exultant cries of a criminal. I thought I was seeing demons stretching their glowing claws from deepest darkness to seize the careless mortals dancing on the thin edge of the bottomless pit. The struggle between the nature of man and the cruel, unknown powers that lure him to destruction was presented clearly to my mind's eye. Finally the storm subsided and the curtain went up.

Chilly and disgruntled in his cloak, Leporello walks up and down before the pavilion in the starless night and begins:

> Night and day, toil and toil . . .

In Italian, say I to myself, even here in this German town! *Ah, che piacere!* [1] It means I'm going to hear all the recitatives, everything just as the great master conceived and felt it!

Don Juan bursts upon the stage, and behind him Donna Anna, clutching the transgressor's cloak. What a spectacle! She might have been taller and more lithe, or more majestic in her stride, but what a countenance! Eyes flashing love, hate, anger, and despair; as a burning pyre throws off sparks which—like Greek fire—consume everything in their path. Her dark hair fell upon her neck in loose ringlets, the white nightdress revealing charms that no one

[1] "Oh what fun [it will be]!" An allusion to Masetto's song in the opera.

could behold without danger. Still under the shock of the frightful deed, her breast heaves spasmodically. And what a voice! Listen to her sing:

Have no hope unless you kill me . . .

Through the tumult of the orchestra her accents—as if cast of unearthly metal—startle like lightning. In vain does Don Juan seek to be rid of her. Does he really want to? Why does he not brush aside this mere woman with his powerful hand? Why does he not flee? Has the crime of which he is guilty sapped his courage, or is it the conflict within him between love and hatred that holds him paralyzed? The old father has paid with his life for the folly of fighting in the darkness against this dreaded duelist. Don Juan and Leporello come forward, talking in recitative together. The Don casts off his cloak and stands there in his superb suit of crimson velvet embroidered with silver—a noble and vigorous figure. His countenance is manly, a high-bridged nose, eyes piercing, lips softly molded. The strange play of a muscle above his brows gives him momentarily the expression of a Mephisto. It makes one shudder involuntarily without its weakening the impression of beauty. It seems as if he could fascinate by a magic like the snake's, as if the women who fell under his gaze were unable to tear themselves away from him and were strangely compelled to bring about their own perdition.

Tall and dried-out, Leporello trips all around his master. He is dressed in a red-and-white striped vest, a short red jacket, and a white hat with a red feather. His features curiously combine the expression of good nature, rascality, covetousness, and ironic impudence. In contrast with his graying hair and beard, his black eyebrows stand out strangely. This old rogue is obviously the man to serve Don Juan. They have in fact scaled the wall and taken flight. Torches: Donna Anna reappears with Don Ottavio, a dressed-up, foppish, dandified little man of one-and-twenty years at most. He apparently is living in the house as Anna's fiancé, since he can be called out so promptly. He must have heard the fracas from the beginning and could certainly have helped the father save himself, but no doubt he had to dress carefully first and he is probably careful about stepping out at night.

> What, O ye gods, do my eyes perceive! O dreadful sight!

More than despair over a violent murder is expressed in the horrified, heartbreaking accents of this recitative and duet. Don Juan's bold deed, which put his life in jeopardy while cutting off that of Anna's father, would not suffice to draw forth these tones of anxiety from a human beast; only a more threatening, a more fatal conflict within could produce them.

Now comes the tall, haggard Donna Elvira to complain also of the traitor Juan:

> Thou nest of deceit . . .

Her beauty must have been great but is now past its bloom. The not unsympathetic Leporello was remarking that she spoke like a printed book, when I thought I heard someone near or behind me in the darkness. It was quite possible that someone had quietly opened the door behind me and entered the box. This distressed me utterly. I was so happy to be alone in my enjoyment of this superb performance of the masterpiece; I wanted so much to embrace it with the tentacles of my finest perceptions, and to withdraw into my innermost self. A single word, which could so easily be a foolish one, would snatch me in the most painful way out of my poetic and musical enchantment. I made up my mind to take no notice of my companion and rather appear so enthralled as to preclude any sign or glance on his part. With my head resting in my hand and my back turned to him, I gazed engrossed upon the stage.

The performance kept to the standard of excellence set by the opening. The infatuated, wanton little Zerlina offered the good-natured dolt Masetto the comfort of her endearing words and ways. Don Juan spoke out without reserve from his innermost lacerated heart, expressing his contempt for the human pygmies who surround him, who exist for his pleasure and whom he catches only to destroy. All this appears in the wild air:

Now their heads are hot with wine . . . ,

the play of his brows being even more expressive than before.

Now come to his feast the guests wearing masks. Their trio is a prayer rising to heaven in shafts of pure light. Whereupon the mid-stage curtain goes up on a scene of gaiety. Glasses clink, masqueraders and peasants dance together in abandon under the encouraging eye of the Don. The three who have sworn revenge appear and all grows solemn, until the dance begins anew. Then Zerlina is rescued, and to the mighty thunders of the finale, Don Juan bravely defies with drawn sword the enemies ranged against him. He strikes out of the bridegroom's hand the fancy-dress dagger and makes his way through the rabble like a doughty Roland scattering the army of the tyrant Cymort, while they comically fall over one another and let him reach the open.

Several times I thought I had felt behind me a gentle warm breath, heard the rustling of a silken garment, and suspected the presence of a woman in the box. But lost as I was in the poetic world of the opera I paid no further attention. Now that the curtain had come down, I turned to see who my neighbor was. No, words fail to express my astonishment. Donna Anna, in the very costume she had worn on the stage, stood behind me, staring intently at me with her great expressive eyes. I stared back speechless. Her lips (or so it seemed to me) parted in a gentle, ironic smile in which I could read my own ridiculous expression of face. I felt as if compelled to address her and yet from sheer amazement could no more manage to find my tongue than if I had been paralyzed by fright. At last, at long last, my words came out almost mechanically. "How can this be? That I should see you here?" To which she replied, in the purest Tuscan, that if I did not understand and speak Italian she would have to forgo the pleasure of conversing with me, for she spoke no other tongue.

Her words were to me like music. Speech heightened the expressiveness of her dark blue eyes, and every flashing light therefrom sent a stream of fire through my veins, making my pulse throb and my whole being tremble. She was Donna Anna—of that there could be no doubt. It did not occur to me to wonder how she could possibly be on the stage and in the box with me at one and the same time. As in happy dreams what is strange seems natural, and then by pious faith one understands the supernatural, connecting it easily with the so-called natural events of daily life, so did I fall into a kind of somnambulism under the spell of this marvelous creature. All at once I felt there were secret bonds linking me so closely to her that she could not be parted from me even by her appearance on the stage. How I should like, my dear Theodore, to impart to you all the remarkable things that passed between the Signora and me. Only, when I try to set down in German what she said, every word seems dull and stiff, every sentence seems awkward and impotent to reproduce what she so easily and gracefully uttered in Tuscan.

When she spoke of *Don Giovanni,* of her role, it was as if she revealed for the first time to my gaze the true inwardness of the masterpiece, and I could now begin to witness and understand the fantastic phenomena of an alien world. She said that her true life was in music and that she thought she could grasp by the act of singing many otherwise hidden secrets of the self that no words could manifest. "Yes, I see it all then," she went on with burning eyes and agitated voice, "but everything about me is dead and cold, and when I am applauded for a difficult roulade or a happy trick, it is as if icy hands clutched my glowing heart. But you, you understand me, for I know that you too are at home in the wondrous romantic realm where dwell the heavenly powers of sound."

"But how do you—you miraculous creature—know anything about me?"

"How? Did not the magical frenzy of love and eternal longing pour from your being when you wrote the part of —— [2] in your latest opera? I understand you. Your soul was laid bare to me in

[2] Which part in which of Hoffmann's eleven operas is not stated, but the date excludes the best known, *Undine* (1816).

song. Yes"—here she called me by my first name—"I have sung you; what your melodies are, that I am."

The bell rang to end the intermission. A sudden pallor drained the color from Anna's unrouged face; she put her hand to her heart as if in sharp pain, but saying quietly, "Unhappy Anna, your darkest moment is upon you," she vanished from the box.

The first act had delighted me, but after my remarkable experience the music affected me in a new and extraordinary way. It was as if the long-deferred fulfillment of unearthly dreams were being granted in real life; as if the hidden intimations of an enchanted soul had been transfixed in sound and forced to assume the most wonderful, tangible shapes. In Donna Anna's scene I found myself enveloped by a warm, soft spirit; its intoxicating breath passed over me and I trembled with bliss. My eyes closed involuntarily as a burning kiss seemed to be imprinted on my lips. But the kiss was like a long held note expressive of endless passionate longing.

The finale had begun in wanton merriment:

Now the table has been laid . . .

Don Juan sits there between two girls, popping one cork after another to permit the fermenting spirits to escape from their prison and achieve dominion. The room was small; it had a tall Gothic window at the back, through which one could see into the night. Even while Elvira reminded the faithless lover of his vows forsworn, one could see occasional flashes of lightning and hear the dull rumbling of the approaching storm. At last the mighty bolt fell. Elvira and the other girls flee as the marble colossus, heralded by the terrible chords of the subterranean spirits, enters towering over the dwarfed but dauntless Don Juan. The floor quakes under the thundering strides of the giant. Don Juan cries through the storm, through the thunder, through the demonic howls his terrific "No!" The hour of damnation has come. The statue disappears. Thick smoke fills the room, horrible specters emerge, under whose torments Don Juan twists and turns. He is seen and lost and mixed with their evolving shapes. An explosion, as if a thousand bolts converged: Don Juan and the demons have vanished, one knows not how. Leporello lies in a dead faint in one corner of the room.

What a relief now to see the remaining characters appear, vainly seeking Juan, who has been snatched by the powers of Hell from the grasp of earthly revenge. It is as if one had also escaped for the first time from the circle of diabolical spirits. Donna Anna looks altered: a deadly pallor is spread over her features, her eye is dimmed, her voice quivering and uneven. Yet even so the effect of her short duet with the sweet little bridegroom is very moving. He is eager to celebrate their nuptials, now that Heaven has conveniently relieved him of the perilous duty to execute revenge.

The final fugal chorus had splendidly rounded off the masterpiece, and I hurried back to my room in a state of exaltation such as I had never known. The waiter was just then summoning me to the table d'hôte and I followed him mechanically. Owing to the Fair, there were distinguished people in town, and their talk turned to the afternoon rendering of *Don Giovanni*. All praised the Italians and their gripping performance, but little remarks dropped now and then with facetious intent showed that probably none of the speakers had any notion of the true meaning of this opera of operas.

Don Ottavio was generally liked. Donna Anna, on the other hand, had struck one gentleman as too passionate. On the stage, he felt, one should moderate oneself prettily and avoid aggressive display. The scene of the old man's dying had really upset him. Here the speaker took a pinch of snuff and gazed with indescribably stupid shrewdness at his neighbor. The latter replied that the Italian diva was none the less a fine figure of a woman, only, too careless in dress and make-up. Why, in the scene just referred to a strand of her hair had come loose and made a shadow on one side of her face! At this point another guest began to sing between his teeth, "Now their heads are hot with wine," whereupon a lady remarked that the

Don had been the least satisfactory of the cast. The Italian had been too somber, too intent, and had failed to take the frivolous, carefree character as lightly as it should be played. But the final explosion was much admired. Having stood as much of this chatter as I could, I hastened back to my room.

In the Strangers' Box, No. 23

I felt cooped up, stifling in that narrow musty place! At midnight I thought I heard your voice, dear Theodore; you clearly spoke my name, and there was a rustling behind the tapestried door. What was there to keep me from revisiting the scene of my wonderful adventure? Perhaps I shall see you as well as her, the one who occupies all my thoughts. How easy it would be to carry in the small table, two candles, and writing materials! The waiter brings the punch I have ordered, finds the room empty, the tapestry swung back. He follows me into the box and looks at me with a suspicious eye. At my nod he sets the drink down on the table and takes his leave with a question still on his tongue, glancing back as he goes.

Turning my back upon him, I lean over the edge of the box and look about the deserted house. Lighted fantastically by my two candles, its interior shows a fairyland, a magical architecture of quivering, glimmering members. The curtain sways in the draft. What if it were suddenly to billow up and reveal Donna Anna terrified by hateful demons? "Donna Anna!" I call her name hardly knowing what I do.

My cry is lost in the empty hall, but it brings to life the spirits of the orchestral instruments—a mysterious note that issues from them seems to whisper forth the beloved name. I cannot help shuddering, but it is a thrill of pleasure that shakes my nerves.

I recover my self-possession and feel doomed to impart to you, dear Theodore, some idea at least of my conviction that I now understand for the first time the true character of the divine master's work. Poet speaks only to poet: only a romantic spirit can penetrate the Romantic, only an exalted artist soul undergoing initiation within the temple of art itself can understand what the initiate utters in his exaltation.

If one considers the poem of *Don Giovanni* without ascribing to it any deeper meaning, but only as a history, it is very hard to imagine how Mozart was able to conceive and compose the music that he did. A debauchee who likes wine and women to excess and who cheerfully invites to his rowdy table the stone statue representing the old man whom he struck down in self-defense—really there is but little poetry in that; and to tell the truth, such a man is hardly worth being singled out by the powers of Hell as a prize specimen for their collection; nor does he deserve that the Stone Man, transfigured by a spirit from on high, should dismount from his stone horse in order to exhort the sinner to repentance in his last quarter hour, just before the Devil provides his best henchmen as escort for the trip to his domain.

We must rather believe, Theodore, that nature fashioned Juan as she does her favorite children, giving him all that brings man close to Divinity, raises him above the crowd, above the factory products which leave the workshop as nonentities, as zeros, unless a true figure is placed before their numbers. All this made him destined to conquer, to lead: a strong, handsome body, a breeding of the kind that generates in the human breast the enkindling sparks of sublime feelings, a profound sensibility, a quick comprehensive intellect. But it is the fearful consequence of the fall of man that the Fiend retains the power to seduce men, and especially to place pitfalls in that striving toward perfection which manifests their divine nature. This conflict of the godlike and the diabolical forces constitutes the essence of the earthly, just as the hard-won victory gives us the concept of supernal life.

The demands upon this life which Don Juan's body and soul required him to make exalted him, but the insatiable, burning desire coursing through his veins drove him greedily, restlessly, to seize upon all the phantasms of this world in the vain hope that they would quench his lust. There is indeed nothing on earth more exalting to man's true being than love. It is love that works so secretly and powerfully to upset and transfigure the constituent parts of Being. No wonder, then, that Don Juan hoped by it to still the yearnings that ravaged his breast; no wonder this was the means by which the Devil slipped the noose around his neck!

In Don Juan's soul the Hereditary Fiend cunningly implanted the thought that through love, through the enjoyment of woman, he could attain on earth that which dwells in our breast as a heavenly promise only, that very longing for the infinite which links us directly to the overworld. Fleeing restlessly from one beautiful woman to another more beautiful, beyond the point of satiety, and drinking his fill of their charms until he found drunken, degrading intoxication; believing himself always deceived in his choice, yet always hoping to discover the utopia of final satisfaction, Juan was doomed to find earthly life dull and shallow to the end; and while he despised mankind generally, he revolted against the delusion which, seeming to be the best that life could afford, had ensnared him so bitterly. The enjoyment of woman was not even any longer a satisfaction to his senses, but merely a cynical mockery against Nature and the Creator.

He was driven onward by a deep contempt for the common features of life, to which he felt superior, and by sardonic laughter at men who expected to find in happy love and its homely community of feeling the fulfillment of the highest wishes that Nature has treacherously planted in our hearts. He was forced to rebel against the thought of any such relationship, and to wreck it wherever he found it, while he fought the unknown Being who decides our fates, a Being who seemed to him as one maliciously rejoicing in the misery of the creatures whom he makes and sports with as in a cruel game.

Every betrayal of a happy woman, every stout blow struck at lovers' joys, every irremediable grief brought by Don Juan upon some loving pair, was a glorious victory over the Enemy, raising the doer above our narrow life, above Nature, above the Creator! He wills himself even higher than life, only to sink deeper into

Hell. The seduction of Anna and its involvements is the summit of his achievement.

Donna Anna is in all natural endowments Don Juan's counterpart. Just as the Don was originally a wonderfully strong and handsome man, so is she a godlike woman. Over her soul the Devil has no power. All the arts of Hell contrive only her earthly ruin. As soon as Satan has compassed this ruin, in keeping with the heavenly decree, the carrying out of vengeance can no longer be postponed. Don Juan mockingly invites the statue of his dueling victim to a gay supper, and the transfigured spirit, for the first time recognizing Juan as the Fallen Man and grieving over him, does not disdain to visit him, though in terrifying guise, and exhorts him to repentance. But so corrupt is Don Juan's soul that not even a beam of heavenly grace can pierce his heart with hope and kindle him to save himself!

You have undoubtedly noticed, dear Theodore, that I have spoken of Anna as seduced, and I shall try to tell you in a few words, as well as I can at this late hour, when the thoughts that well up within me outrun utterance, how I feel that the music alone, quite apart from the text, conveys the tragic conflict between these two antithetical natures, Don Juan and Donna Anna. I said above that Anna was Juan's counterpart. Had Anna been destined by Heaven to let him recognize his own divine nature in the love which, Satan aiding, ruined him, what then? Suppose she had tried to swerve him from his own despairing effort at self-destruction? No! It was too late. When he first saw her he had reached the height of infamy and could only feel the devilish urge to corrupt her. She herself could not be rescued. When he fled the deed was done. The fire of a superhuman sensuality—a glamour from Hell—had been infused in her and made her powerless to resist. Only he, only Don Juan, was capable of rousing in her this erotic madness, with which she in turn enveloped him—he who sinned with the overpowering destructive rage of Hell.

The deed once done, he wanted only to flee. But for her the thought of her ruin was like the embrace of a horrible death-dealing monster. The memory of her father's death at Juan's hands, her betrothal to the frigid, unmanly, commonplace Don Ottavio, whom she once thought she loved—even the love consuming her soul with devilish ardor, the love that in the moment of ecstasy had flooded her being and now burned like the annihilating power of hate—all this racked her breast. She feels that only Juan's destruction can bring peace to her fatally tortured soul, while this same peace requires her own earthly destruction. Hence she incessantly prods her languid bridegroom to revenge; she herself pursues the betrayer, and recovers calm only when the subterranean powers have dragged him down into the pit.

And now she will not give herself to the eager bridegroom:

> Allow, oh, dearest, another year for my heart to mourn . . .

But she will not survive that year. Don Ottavio will never embrace the woman whose true piety saved her from being Satan's dedicated bride.

How vividly I felt all this in the first devastating chords of the recitative and narration of the duel by night! And again in Donna Anna's scene in the second act—"O cruel one"—which superficially refers only to Don Ottavio but which speaks in subtle overtones of that state wherein the soul is bereft of all earthly happiness. What else do those strange words mean which the poet perhaps unconsciously threw in:

> Some day, perhaps, heaven will once more pity me!

The clock strikes two! A warm, electrifying breeze envelops me. I recognize the fragrance of the Italian perfume that first apprised me yesterday of my fair neighbor's presence. I am seized by a blissful feeling that I could express only in music. The breeze blows stronger through the hall, the strings of the piano in the orchestra vibrate audibly. Heavens! As from a great distance, borne on the floating, swelling tones of an ethereal orchestra, I think I hear Anna's voice:

> Tell me not, oh, beauteous love!

Open out, oh, distant, unknown realms of spirit! Open, miraculous land of Djinns, where inexpressible, heavenly pain, akin to unutterable joy, brings to the enchanted soul raptures beyond all earthly promises! Let me enter the circle of your cherished apparitions, and may my dreams—now terrifying, now soothing like a friendly embassy to mankind—gently guide my spirit while my body sleeps in leaden bonds, and let it roam the Elysian Fields.

Midday Conversation at the Table d'Hôte, by Way of Epilogue

CLEVER MAN, *taking out his snuffbox and tapping emphatically on the lid:* It is really a nuisance that we shan't have any more good opera for a while. That is what comes of overdoing things.

MULATTO-FACE: Sure, sure. I have told her again and again. The role of Donna Anna always took her peculiarly. Yesterday she was like one possessed. During the whole of the intermission, they say, she lay unconscious in her dressing room, and in her scene of the second act she nearly had a nervous seizure.

NOBODY IN PARTICULAR: You don't say!

MULATTO-FACE: I do say: a nervous seizure and they couldn't get her away from the theater.

MYSELF: Merciful heavens! I hope it was nothing serious. We shall soon hear the Signora again, I trust?

CLEVER MAN, *taking his pinch of snuff:* Hardly! The Signora died this morning at two o'clock sharp.

TALES OF FANTASY (1813)

BERNARD SHAW

❧ ❦

Mr. Jack, Composer

The year after began with a General Election, followed by a change in the Ministry, a revival of trade, a general fancy that things were going to mend, and a sudden access of spirit in political agitation, commercial enterprise, public amusements, and private expenditure. The wave even reached a venerable artistic institution called the Antient Orpheus Society, established nearly a century ago for the performance of orchestral music, and since regarded as the pioneer of musical art in England. It had begun by producing Beethoven's symphonies: it had ended by producing a typical collection of old fogies, who pioneered backwards so fast and so far that they had not finished shaking their heads over the innovations in the overture to *William Tell* when the rest of the world were growing tired of the overture to *Tannhäuser*. The younger critics had introduced a fashion of treating the Antient Orpheus as obsolescent; and even their elders began to forebode the extinction of the Society unless it were speedily rejuvenated by the supersession of the majority of the committee. But the warnings of the press, as usual, did not come until long after the public had begun to abstain from the Antient Orpheus concerts; and as the Society in its turn resisted the suggestions of the press until death or dotage reduced the conservative majority of the committee to a minority, the credit of the Antient Orpheus was almost past recovery when reform was at last decided on. When the new members of the rejuvenated committee—three of whom were under fifty—realized this, they became as eager to fill the concert programs with new works as their predecessors had been determined to exclude them. But when the business of selecting the new works came to be considered, all was discord. Some urged the advisability of performing the works of English composers, a willful neglect of which had been that one of the practices of the old committee of which the press had most persistently complained. To this it was objected that in spite of the patriotic complaints of critics, the public had showed their opinion of English composers by specially avoiding the few concerts to which they had been allowed to contribute. At last it was arranged that an English work should be given at the first concert of the season, and that care should be taken to neutralize its repellent effect on the public by engaging a young Polish lady, who had recently made an extraordinary success abroad as a pianist, to make her first appearance in England on the occasion. Matters being settled so far, question now arose as to what the new English work should be. Most of the committee had manuscript scores of their own, composed thirty years before in the interval between leaving the academy and getting enough teaching to use up all their energy; but as works of this class had already been heard once or twice by the public with undisguised tedium; and as each composer hesitated to propose his own opus, the question was not immediately answered. Then a recently elected member of the committee, not a professional musician, mentioned a fantasia for pianoforte and orchestra of which he had some private knowledge. It was composed, he said, by a young man, a Mr. Owen Jack. The chairman coughed and remarked coldly that he did not recollect the name. A member asked bluntly who Mr. Jack was, and whether anybody had ever heard of him. Another member protested against the suggestion of a fantasia and declared that if this illustrious obscure did not know enough about musical form to write a concerto, the Antient Orpheus Society, which had subsisted for nearly a century without his assistance, could probably do so a little longer. When the laughter and applause which this speech evoked had subsided, a good-natured member remarked that he had met a man of the name of Jack at somebody's place in Windsor, and had heard him improvise variations on a song of the hostess's in a rather striking manner. He there-fore seconded the proposal that Jack's fantasia should be immediately examined with a view to its performance by the Polish lady at the next concert. Another member, not good natured, but profes-sionally jealous of the last speaker but one, supported the proposal on the ground that the notion that the Society could get on high-and-mightily without ever doing anything new was just what had brought it to death's door. This naturally elicited a defiant state-ment that the Society had never been more highly esteemed than at that hour; and a debate ensued, in the course of which Jack's ability was hotly attacked and defended in turn by persons who had never heard of him before that day. Eventually the member who had introduced the subject obtained permission to invite Mr. Jack to submit his fantasia to the committee.

At the next meeting an indignant member begged leave to call the attention of his colleagues to a document which had accompanied the score forwarded in response to the invitation by which the Antient Orpheus Society had honored Mr. Owen Jack. It was a let-ter to the secretary, in the following terms:

Sir: Herewith you will find the instrumental partition of a fantasia composed by me for pianoforte and orchestra. I am willing to give the use of it to the Antient Orpheus Society gratuitously for one concert, on con-dition that the rehearsal be superintended by me, and that, if I require it, a second rehearsal be held.

The member said he would not dwell on the propriety of this com-munication to the foremost musical society in Europe from a minor teacher, as he had ascertained Mr. Jack to be. It had been suffi-ciently rebuked by the secretary's reply, despatched after the parti-tion had been duly examined, to the effect that the work, though not destitute of merit, was too eccentric in form, and crude in har-monic structure, to be suitable for public performance at the con-certs of the Society. This had elicited a second letter from Mr. Jack, of which the member would say nothing, as he preferred to leave it to speak for itself and for the character of the writer.

Church Street, Kensington, W.

Sir: Your criticism was uninvited, and is valueless except as an illustration of the invincible ignorance of the pedants whose mouthpiece you are. I am, sir,

Yours truly,
Owen Jack

The most astute diplomatist could not have written a more effective letter in Jack's favor than this proved. The party of reform took it as an exquisite slap at their opponents and at once determined to make the secretary smart for rejecting the work without the authority of the whole committee. Jack's advocate produced a note from the Polish lady acknowledging the receipt of a pianoforte fantasia and declaring that she should be enchanted to play for the first time to an English audience a work so poetic by one of their own nation. He explained that having borrowed a copy of the pianoforte part from a young lady relative of his who was studying it, he had sent it to the Polish artist, who had just arrived in England. Her opinion of it, he contended, was sufficient to show that the letter of the secretary was the result of an error of judgment which deserved no better answer than it had elicited. The secretary retorted that he had no right to avail himself of his private acquaintance with the pianist to influence the course of the Society and stigmatized Jack's letter as the coarse abuse natural to the vulgar mind of a self-assertive charlatan. On the other hand, it was maintained that Jack had only shown the sensitiveness of an artist, and that to invite a composer to send in a work and then treat it as if it were an examination paper filled by a presumptuous novice was an impertinence likely to bring ridicule as well as odium upon the Antient Orpheus. The senior member, who occupied the chair, now declared very solemnly that he had seen the fantasia, and that it was one of those lawless compositions unhappily too common of late years, which were hurrying the beautiful art of Haydn and Mozart into the abyss of modern sensationalism. Hereupon someone remarked that the gentleman had frequently spoken of the works of Wagner in the same terms, although they all knew that Richard

Wagner was the greatest composer of that or any other age. This assertion was vehemently repudiated by some and loudly cheered by others. In the hubbub which followed, Jack's cause became identified with that of Wagner; and a motion to set aside the unauthorized rejection of the fantasia was carried by a majority of the admirers of the Prussian composer, not one of whom knew or cared a straw about the English one.

"I am glad we have won the day," said Mr. Phipson, the proposer of this motion, to a friend as the meeting broke up; "but we have certainly experienced the truth of Mary's remark that this Jack creates nothing but discord in real life, whatever he may do in music."

Jack at first refused to have anything further to do with the Antient Orpheus; but as it was evident that his refusal would harm nobody except himself, he yielded to the entreaties of Mary Sutherland and consented to make use of the opportunity she had, through Mr. Phipson, procured for him. So the negotiation proceeded; and at last, one comfortless wet spring morning, Jack got out of an omnibus in Piccadilly and walked through the mud to St. James's Hall, where, in the gloomy rooms beneath the orchestra, he found a crowd of about eighty men, chatting, hugging themselves, and stamping because of the cold; stooping over black bags and boxes containing musical instruments; or reluctantly unwinding woolen mufflers and unbuttoning greatcoats. He passed them into a lower room, where he found three gentlemen standing in courtly attitudes before a young lady wrapped in furs, with a small head, light brown hair, and a pale face, rather toilworn. She received them with that natural air of a princess in her own right which is so ineffectually striven for by the ordinary princess in other people's rights. As she spoke to the gentlemen in French, occasionally helping them to understand her by a few words of broken English, she smiled occasionally, apparently more from kindness than natural gaiety, for her features always relapsed into an expression of patient but not unhappy endurance. Near her sat an old foreign lady, brown skinned, tall, and very grim.

Jack advanced a few steps into the room; glanced at the gentlemen; and took a long look at the younger lady, who, like the rest, had had her attention arrested by his impressive ugliness. He scrutinized her so openly that she turned away displeased, and a little embarrassed. Two of the gentlemen stared at him stiffly. The third came forward and said with polite severity, "What is your business here, sir?"

Jack looked at him for a moment, wrinkling his face hideously. "I am Jack," he said, in the brassiest tone of his powerful voice. "Who are you?"

"Oh!" said the gentleman, relaxing a little. "I beg your pardon. I had not the pleasure of knowing you by sight, Mr. Jack. My name is Manlius, at your service." Mr. Manlius was the conductor of the Antient Orpheus orchestra. He was a learned musician, generally respected because he had given instruction to members of the Royal family, and, when conducting, never allowed his orchestra to forget the restraint due to the presence of ladies and gentlemen in the sofa stalls.

Jack bowed. Mr. Manlius considered whether he should introduce the composer to the young lady. Whilst he hesitated, a trampling overhead was succeeded by the sounding of a note first on the pianoforte and then on the oboe, instantly followed by the din of an indescribable discord of fifths from innumerable strings, varied by irrelevant chromatic scales from the woodwind, and a doleful tuning of slides from the brass. Jack's eyes gleamed. Troubling himself no further about Mr. Manlius, he went out through a door leading to the stalls, where he found a knot of old gentlemen disputing. One of them immediately whispered something to the others: and they continued their discussions in a lower tone. Jack looked at the orchestra for a few minutes and then returned to the room he had left, where the elder lady was insisting in French that the pianoforte fantasia should be rehearsed before anything else, as she was not going to wait in the cold all day. Mr. Manlius assured her that he had anticipated her suggestion and should act upon it as a matter of course.

"It is oll thé same thinks," said the young lady in English. Then in French, "Even if you begin with the fantasia, Monsieur, I shall assuredly wait to hear for the first time your famous band perform in this ancient hall."

Manlius bowed. When he straightened himself again, he found Jack standing at his elbow. "Allow me to present to you Monsieur Jack," he said.

"It is for Monsieur Jacques to allow," she replied. "The poor artist is honored by the presence of the illustrious English composer."

Jack nodded gravely as acknowledging that the young woman expressed herself becomingly. Manlius grinned covertly and proposed that they should go upon the orchestra, as the band was apt to get out of humor when too much time was wasted. She rose at once and ascended the steps on the arm of the conductor. She was received with an encouraging clapping of hands and tapping of fiddle backs. Jack followed with the elder lady, who sat down on the top stair and began to knit.

"If you wish to conduct the rehearsal," said Manlius politely to Jack, "you are, of course, quite welcome to do so."

"Thank you," said Jack. "I will." Manlius, who had hardly expected him to accept the offer, retired to the pianoforte and prepared to turn over the leaves for the player.

"I think I can play it from memory," she said to him, "unless Monsieur Jacques puts it all out of my head. Judging by his face, it is certain that he is not very patien— Ah! Did I not say so?"

Jack had rapped the desk sharply with his stick and was looking balefully at the men, who did not seem in any hurry to attend to him. He put down the stick; stepped from the desk; and stooped to the conductor's ear.

"I mentioned," he said, "that some of the parts ought to be given to the men to study before rehearsal. Has that been done?"

Manlius smiled. "My dear sir," he said, "I need hardly tell you that players of such standing as the members of the Antient Orpheus orchestra do not care to have suggestions of that kind offered to them. You have no cause to be uneasy. They can play anything— absolutely anything—at sight."

Jack looked black and returned to his desk without a word. He gave one more rap with his stick and began. The players were attentive, but many of them tried not to look so. For a few bars Jack conducted under some restraint, apparently striving to repress a tendency to extravagant gesticulation. Then, as certain combinations and progressions sounded strange and farfetched, slight bursts of laughter were heard. Suddenly the first clarinetist, with an exclamation of impatience, put down his instrument.

"Well?" shouted Jack. The music ceased.

"I can't play that," said the clarinetist shortly.

"Can *you* play it?" said Jack, with suppressed rage, to the second clarinetist.

"No," said he. "Nobody could play it."

"That passage *has* been played; and it must be played. It has been played by a common soldier."

"If a common soldier even attempted it, much less played it," said the first clarinetist, with some contemptuous indignation at what he considered an evident falsehood, "he must have been drunk." There was a general titter at this.

Jack visibly wrestled with himself for a moment. Then, with a gleam of humor like a flash of sunshine through a black thundercloud, he said, "You are right. He *was* drunk." The whole band roared with laughter.

"Well, *I* am not drunk," said the clarinetist, folding his arms.

"But will you not just try wh—" Here Jack, choked by the effort to be persuasive and polite, burst out raging, "It can be done. It shall be done. It must be done. You are the best clarinet player in England. I know what you can do." And Jack shook his fists wildly at the man as if he were accusing him of some infamous crime. But the compliment was loudly applauded, and the man reddened, not altogether displeased. A cornist who sat near him said soothingly in an Irish accent, "Aye, do, Joe. Try it."

"You will: you can," shouted Jack reassuringly, recovering his self-command. "Back to the double bar. Now!" The music recommenced; and the clarinetist, overborne, took up his instrument and, when the passage was reached, played it easily, greatly to his own astonishment. The brilliancy of the effect, too, raised him for a time into a prominence which rivaled that of the pianist. The orchestra positively interrupted the movement to applaud it; and Jack joined in with high good humor.

"If you are uneasy about it," said he, with an undisguised chuckle, "I can hand it over to the violins."

"Oh, no, thank you," said the clarinetist. "Now I've got it, I'll keep it."

Jack rubbed his nose until it glowed like a coal; and the movement proceeded without another stoppage, the men now seeing that Jack was in his right place.

But when a theme marked *andante cantabile,* which formed the middle section of the fantasia, was commenced by the pianist, Jack turned to her; said "Quicker, quicker. *Plus vite*"; and began to mark his beat by striking the desk. She looked at him anxiously; played a few bars in the time indicated by him; and then threw up her hands and stopped.

"I cannot," she exclaimed. "I must play it more slowly or not at all."

"Certainly, it shall be slower if you desire it," said the elder lady from the steps. Jack looked at her as he sometimes looked at Mrs. Simpson. "Certainly it shall not be slower, if all the angels desired it," he said, in well-pronounced but barbarously ungrammatical French. "Go on; and take the time from my beat."

The Polish lady shook her head; folded her hands in her lap; and looked patiently at the music before her. There was a moment of silence, during which Jack, thus mutely defied, glared at her with distorted features. Manlius rose irresolutely. Jack stepped down from the desk; handed him the stick; and said in a smothered voice, "Be good enough to conduct this lady's portion of the fantasia. When *my* music recommences, I will return."

Manlius took the stick and mounted the desk, the orchestra receiving him with applause. In the midst of it Jack went out, giving the pianist a terrible look as he passed her, and transferring it to her companion, who raised her eyebrows and shoulders contemptuously.

Manlius was not the man to impose his own ideas of a composition on a refractory artist; and though he was privately disposed to agree with Jack that the Polish lady was misjudging the speed of the movement, he obediently followed her playing with his beat. But he soon lost his first impression and began to be affected by a dread lest anyone should make a noise in the room. He moved his stick as quietly as possible, and raised his left hand as if to still the band, who were, however, either watching the pianist intently or playing without a trace of the expert offhandedness which they had affected at first. The pleasure of listening made Manlius forget to follow the score. When he roused himself and found his place, he perceived that the first horn player was altering a passage completely, though very happily. Looking questioningly in that direction, he saw Jack sitting beside the man with a pencil in his hand. Manlius observed for the first time that he had an expressive face and remarkable eyes and was not, as he had previously seemed, unmitigatedly ugly. Meanwhile the knot of old gentlemen in the stalls, who had previously chattered subduedly, became quite silent, and a few of them closed their eyes rapturously. The lady on the steps alone did not seem to care about the music. At last the flow of melody waned and broke into snatches. The pianoforte seemed to appeal to the instruments to continue the song. A melancholy strain from the violas responded hopelessly; but the effect of this was marred by a stir in the orchestra. The trombone and trumpet players, hitherto silent, were taking up their instruments and pushing up their mustaches. The drummer, after some hasty screwing round his third drum, poised his sticks; and a supernumerary near him rose, cymbals in hand; fixed his eye on Manlius, and apparently stood ready to clap the head of the trumpet player in front of him as a lady claps a moth flying from a woolen curtain. Manlius looked at the score as if he did not quite understand the sequel. Suddenly, as the violas ceased, Jack shouted in a startling voice, "Let it be an avalanche. From the top to bottom of the Himalayas"; and rushed to the conductor's desk. Manlius made way for him precipitately; and a tremendous explosion of sound followed. "Louder," roared Jack. "Louder. Less noise and more tone. Out with it like fifty million devils." And he led the movement at a merciless speed. The pianist looked bewildered, like the band, most of whom lost their places after the first fifty bars; but when the turn of each player came, he found the conductor glaring at him and was swept into his part without clearly knowing how. It was an insensate orgy of sound. Gay melodies, daintily given out by the pianoforte, or by the string instruments, were derisively brayed out immediately afterwards by cornets, harmonized in thirds with the most ingenious vulgarity. Cadenzas, agilely executed by the Polish lady, were uncouthly imitated by the double basses. Themes constructed like ballads with choruses were introduced instead of orthodox "subjects." The old gentlemen in the stalls groaned and protested. The Polish lady, incommoded by the capricious and often excessive speed required of her, held on gallantly, Jack all the time grinding his teeth, dancing, gesticulating, and by turns shshsh-shing at the orchestra or shouting to them for more tone and less noise. Even the lady on the steps had begun to nod to the impetuous rhythm, when the movement ended as suddenly as it had begun; and all the players rose to their feet, laughing and applauding heartily. Manlius, from whose mind the fantasia had banished all prejudice as to Jack's rank as a musician, shook his hand warmly. The Polish lady, her face transfigured by musical excitement, offered her hand too. Jack took it and held it, saying abruptly, "Listen to me. You were quite right; and I am a fool. I did not know what there was in my own music and would have spoiled it if you had not prevented me. You are a great player, because you get the most beautiful tone possible from every note you touch, and you make every phrase say all that it was meant to say, and more. You are an angel. I would rather hear you play scales than hear myself play sonatas. And"—here he lowered his voice and drew her aside—"I rely on you to make my work succeed at the concert. Manlius will conduct the band; but you must conduct Manlius. It is not enough to be a gentleman and a contrapuntist in order to conduct. You comprehend?"

"Yes, Monsieur, I understand perfectly, perfectly. I will do my best. I shall be inspired. How magnificent it is!"

"Allow me to congratulate you, sir," said one of the old gentlemen, advancing. "Myself and colleagues have been greatly struck by your work. I am empowered to say on their behalf that whatever difference of opinion there may be among us as to the discretion with which you have employed your powers, of the extraordinary nature of those powers there can no longer be a doubt; and we are thoroughly gratified at having chosen for performance a work which displays so much originality and talent as your fantasia."

"Ten years ago," said Jack, looking steadily at him, "I might have been glad to hear you say so. At present the time for compliments is past, unless you wish to congratulate me on the private interest that has gained my work a hearing. My talent and originality have been my chief obstacles here."

"Are you not a little hasty?" said the gentleman, disconcerted. "Success comes late in London; and you are still, if I may say so, a comparatively young man."

"I am not old enough to harp on being comparatively young. I am thirty-four years old; and if I had adopted any other profession than that of composer of music, I should have been earning a respectable livelihood by this time. As it is, I have never made a farthing by my compositions. I don't blame those who have stood between me and the public: their ignorance is their misfortune, and not their fault. But now that I have come to light by a chance in spite of their teeth, I am not in the humor to exchange pretty speeches with them. Understand, sir: I do not mean to rebuff you personally. But as for your colleagues, tell them that it does not become them to pretend to acknowledge spontaneously what I have just, after many hard years, forced them to admit. Look at those friends of yours shaking their heads over my score there. They have *heard* my music; but they do not know what to say until they *see* it. Would you like me to believe that they are admiring it?"

"I am confident that they cannot help doing so."

"They are showing one another why it ought not to have been written—hunting out my consecutive fifths and sevenths, and my false relations—looking for my first subject, my second subject, my working out; and the rest of the childishness that could be taught to a poodle. Don't they wish they may find them?"

The gentleman seemed at a loss how to continue the conversation. "I hope you are satisfied with the orchestra," he said after a pause.

"No, I am not," said Jack. "They are overcivilized. They are as much afraid of showing their individuality as if they were common gentlemen. You cannot handle a musical instrument with kid gloves on. However, they did better than I hoped. They are at least not coarse. That young woman is a genius."

"Ye-es. Almost a genius. She is young, of course. She has not the— I should call it the *gigan*tic power and energy of such a player, for instance, as—"

"Pshaw!" said Jack, interrupting him. "I, or anybody else, can get excited with the swing of a Chopin's polonaise, and thrash it out of the piano until the room shakes. But she! You talk of making a pianoforte sing—a child that can sing itself can do that. But she can make it speak. She has eloquence, the first and last quality of a great player, as it is of a great man. The finale of the fantasia is too coarse for her: it does violence to her nature. It was written to be played by a savage—like me."

"Oh, undoubtedly, undoubtedly! She is a remarkable player. I did not for a moment intend to convey—" Here Manlius rapped his desk; and Jack, with an unceremonious nod to his interlocutor, left the platform. As he passed the door leading to the public part of the hall, he heard the voice of the elder lady.

"My child, they seek to deceive you. This Monsieur Jacques, with whose music you are to make your debut here, is he famous in England? Not at all. My God! he is an unknown man."

"Be tranquil, Mother. He will not long be unknown."

Jack opened the door a little way; thrust his face through; and smiled pleasantly at the pianist. Her mother, seeing her start, looked round and saw him grimacing within a yard of her.

"Ah, Lord Jesus!" she exclaimed in German, recoiling from him. He chuckled, and abruptly shut himself out of her view as the opening unison of the *Coriolan* overture sounded from the orchestra. The old gentleman who had congratulated him had rejoined the others in the stalls.

"Well," said one of them, "is your man delighted with himself?"

"N-no, I cannot say that he is—or rather perhaps he is too much so. I am sorry to say that he appears to be rather morose—soured by his early difficulties, perhaps. He is certainly not an agreeable person to speak to."

"What did you expect?" said another gentleman coldly. "A man who degrades music to be the vehicle of his own coarse humor, and shows by his method of doing it an ignorant contempt for those laws by which the great composers established order in the chaos of sounds, is not likely to display a courteous disposition and refined nature in the ordinary business of life."

"I assure you, Professor," said a third, who had the score of the fantasia open on his knees, "this chap must know a devil of a lot. He plays old Harry with the sonata form: but he must do it on purpose, you know, really."

The gentleman addressed as Professor looked severely and incredulously at the other. "I really cannot listen to such things whilst they are playing Beethoven," he said. "I have protested against Mr. Jack and his like; and my protest has passed unheeded. I wash my hands of the consequences. The Antient Orpheus Society will yet acknowledge that I did well when I counseled it to renounce the devil and all his works." He turned away; sat down on a stall a little way off; and gave all his attention ostentatiously to *Coriolan*.

The pianist came presently and sat near him. The others quickly surrounded her; but she did not speak to them and showed by her attitude that she did not wish to be spoken to. Her mother, who did not care for *Coriolan* and wanted to go home, knitted and looked appealingly at her from time to time, not venturing to express her impatience before so many members of the Antient Orpheus Society. At last Manlius came down; and the whole party rose and went into the performers' room.

"How do you find our orchestra?" said Manlius to her as she took up her muff.

"It is magnificent," she replied. "So refined, so quiet, so convenable! It is like the English gentleman." Manlius smirked. Jack, who had reappeared on the outskirts of the group with his hat on—a desperately ill-used hat—added, "A Lithuanian or Hungarian orchestra could not play like that, eh?"

"No, truly," said the Polish lady, with a little shrug. "I do not think they could."

"You flatter us," said Manlius, bowing. Jack began to laugh. The Polish lady hastily made her adieux and went out into Piccadilly, where a cab was brought for her. Her mother got in; and she was about to follow when she heard Jack's voice again, at her elbow.

"May I send you some music?"

"If you will be so gracious, Monsieur."

"Good. What direction shall I give your driver?"

"F—f—you call it Feetzroysquerre?"

"Fitzroy Square," shouted Jack to the cabman. The hansom went off; and he, running recklessly through the mud to a passing Hammersmith omnibus, which was full inside, climbed to the roof, and was borne away in the rain.

LOVE AMONG THE ARTISTS (1881)

RICHARD WAGNER

≫≫≪≪

A Pilgrimage to Beethoven

≫≫ ━━ ≪≪

When Wagner was a starving young German in Paris, he lived like the
hero of his story, by writing galops and potpourris. But older musicians
aided him by letting him publish articles and stories in the *Gazette
Musicale*. This "Visit to Beethoven" (the original published title) was
serialized in that weekly in November and December 1840.

≫≫ ━━ ≪≪

Want-and-Care! Thou patron saint of the German musician—unless he happens to be musical director of a Court theater—Want-and-
Care, thine be the name first praised in these recollections from my
life! Yes, let me sing thee, staunch companion of my existence. Thou
hast been faithful and hast never left me, warding off the approaches
of fickleness and shading me from the burning rays of Good Fortune. Thou hast kept me in the shadows, free from the empty
vanities of this earth: thanks be to you for this constancy of affection. Yet were it possible, some day pray find another favorite, for
out of pure curiosity I should be glad to discover how life would
seem *without* thee. I beg thee in any case to plague our political
dreamers, the lunatics who would unify our Germany under one
ruler. Think of it, there would be but *one* Court theater, one solitary post of Kapellmeister! What then would my prospects be, what
could I hope for, when even now, with a quantity of German
royal theaters, my chances are few and dim. But I see that I blas-
pheme. Forgive, O patron saint, the criminal wish I have just uttered! Thou canst read in my heart and know that I am wholly
thine, even were there a thousand theaters and kings in Germany.
Amen!

I never undertake anything without first repeating this prayer of
mine—hence could not tell the story of my pilgrimage to Beethoven.

And in case this important document should be published only after my death, I feel I must say who I am. Otherwise much might remain obscure. Heed, then, listening world and literary executor!

The place of my birth is a medium-sized town in the center of Germany. I am by no means sure what nature intended me to be; I only remember that one evening I heard for the first time a symphony of Beethoven's, that it gave me a fever and I fell ill. When I recovered I had become a musician. This incident probably explains why, despite my later acquaintance with beautiful music by other composers, I have nonetheless always loved, honored, and worshiped Beethoven before all others. From that day forth I had no greater pleasure than to delve so deeply into his genius that at last I imagined myself a part of it. And as such—a very small fragment—I began to revere myself and to entertain elevated ideas, in short, to develop into what sensible people call an idiot. Still, my madness was very good natured and did no harm to mankind. The bread afforded me in these circumstances was extremely dry, the wine most watery. For with us, O listening world and literary executor, giving lessons brings only a bare subsistence wage!

Thus did I live for some time in my garret until it suddenly occurred to me that the man whose creations I revered above all else was still alive. I could not understand why I had never thought of this before. Perhaps it had never entered my mind that Beethoven could exist, could be eating bread and breathing air, like the rest of us. But this Beethoven was living in Vienna nevertheless, and he too was a poor German musician.

My peace of mind was now gone. All my thoughts led to only one wish—*to see Beethoven!* No Moslem has ever yearned more devoutly to visit the Prophet's grave than I to see the lodging where Beethoven dwelt.

But how to go about carrying out my plan? To Vienna is a long way, and I, poor devil, was earning barely enough to keep body and soul together. I must find some exceptional means of procuring the money needed for the journey. I took a few piano sonatas, which I had composed on the master's model, to a publisher. The man made it clear in a word or two that I was a fool with my sonatas. He advised me, if I ever wanted to turn an honest penny, to make some sort of name for myself by composing galops and potpourris. I shuddered; but my desire to see Beethoven got the upper hand. I composed galops and potpourris. All that time, however, I could not for shame cast a single glance on Beethoven's works, lest I should defile them.

Yet even this youthful sacrifice of my innocence did not bring me cash, for the publisher explained again that I must first earn some sort of name. I shuddered once more and fell into despair. That despair engendered some capital galops, and for these I actually touched coin. At last I believed I had put by enough to carry out my plan. But two years had passed, during which I constantly feared that Beethoven might die before I had conquered fame with my galops and potpourris. Thanks be to God, he survived the dazzlement of my name—worshipful Beethoven, forgive me this renown; 'twas acquired that I might see thee!

Joy! My goal was in sight. Who more blessed than I? I might shoulder my bundle and set off toward Beethoven. A holy awe gripped me as I crossed my threshold and turned my steps southward. Of course, I should have preferred a seat in the stagecoach, not because I feared the fatigue of hiking (what hardships would I not have borne on such a mission!) but because I should have reached Beethoven so much sooner. But I had done too little for my fame as galop composer to be able to pay coach fare. So I endured all the weariness and deemed myself lucky to be able to manage as I did. O my yearnings, my dreams! No homecoming lover, long separated from the beloved of his youth, could be happier than I.

And so I came to fair Bohemia, the land of harp players and street singers. In a small village I came upon a group of strolling musicians —a small orchestra comprising a bass, two violins, two horns, a clarinet, and a flute; besides whom there was a woman who played the harp and two others with good voices. They played dances and sang songs; people gave them money, then they moved on. On a lovely shady place off the highroad where they had camped, I met them again as they were eating. I joined them, told them I was also a wandering minstrel, and we soon became friends. As they played their dances, I shyly asked them whether they also played my galops. The darlings! They knew nothing about my works. How good this made me feel!

I then asked whether they knew any music other than dances. "Yes, of course," they answered, "but it's only for us, not for gentry." They unpacked their sheets—and I saw the great Beethoven septet. Amazed, I asked whether they played that too.

"Why not?" retorted the eldest. "Joseph has hurt his hand and still cannot play second violin, otherwise we'd give you a treat." Beside myself, I snatched up Joseph's violin, gave my word to do the best I could as substitute, and we began the septet.

What a delight! There, on a highway in Bohemia, under the open sky, the Beethoven septet—played by dance musicians, yet with a purity, a precision, a depth of feeling such as one seldom finds in the most accomplished virtuosos. Great Beethoven, we brought thee a worthy offering.

We had just reached the finale when on the road, which at that point made an upward bend toward the hills, appeared an elegant carriage that slowly and noiselessly drew near. It came to a stop in front of us. An extremely tall and extremely blond young man was reclining within. He listened rather attentively to our music, took a notebook out of his pocket, and made a few jottings. Then he let drop a gold piece and drove away with a few words of English to his servant; from which it dawned on me that he was an Englishman.

The incident upset us; luckily we had finished playing the septet. I embraced my friends and wanted to accompany them, but they apprised me that from this point on they were leaving the highroad and striking across the fields toward their native village. Had Beethoven himself not been the man awaiting me, I should surely have gone with them. As it was, we parted with affectionate farewells. Later it occurred to me that no one had picked up the Englishman's coin.

At the next inn that I entered to refresh my body, I found the Englishman seated at a well-laid table. He stared at me a good while and at last addressed me in passable German.

"Where are your colleagues?" he asked.

"Gone home," I replied.

"Bring out your violin," he went on, "and play something. Here's money."

This annoyed me. I explained that I did not play for money, and that besides I had no instrument. I told him briefly how I had come to be with those strollers.

"Those were good musicians," rejoined the Englishman, "and the Beethoven symphony was pretty good too."

His remark struck me, and I asked him whether he also made music.

"Yes," he answered. "Twice a week I play the flute, on Thursdays the French horn, and on Sundays I compose."

That was not bad. I goggled. In all my life I had never heard tell of English traveling musicians. I supposed they must be fairly successful to be able to go about in such a splendid equipage. I asked whether he was a professional.

I waited a long while for my answer; at last he drawled out the fact that he had a good deal of money. I now saw my mistake; I had offended him with my question. At a loss for something to say, I finished my simple meal in silence. But the Englishman, after another long stare, began again. "Do you know Beethoven?" he asked.

I replied that I had never been in Vienna but was at that very moment on my way there to carry out my strongest impulse, which was to visit the worshiped master.

"Where do you come from?" he asked.

"From L——" [1]

"That's not so far! I come from England and I too want to meet Beethoven. We shall both meet him. He is a very famous composer."

[1] Presumably Leipzig, Wagner's birthplace; a fact in keeping with the R. (for Richard) of the narrator's name.

What an amazing coincidence, thought I to myself. Great master! What opposites dost thou not draw to thyself! On foot and by coach they wend their way toward thee! My Englishman interested me, but I must confess I did not envy him his conveyance. It seemed to me that my pilgrimage on foot was more pious and holy, and that it must bring me greater blessings than to him his proud journey in state.

At that point the postilion blew his horn; the Englishman drove off, shouting to me that he would be seeing Beethoven first.

I had hardly walked a few hours on his track when I unexpectedly came upon him again. He was on the highway. One of the wheels of his carriage was broken, but he still sat inside with majestic calm, his footman up behind, even though the carriage was tilting over to one side. I learned that they were waiting for the postilion who was to bring a smith back from the nearest village. Since the valet spoke only English I decided to go myself to the village and speed the postilion and smith on their way. In fact I found the former in a tavern, where with the aid of brandy he was not concerning himself over much about the Englishman. Nevertheless I soon brought him and the smith back to the broken carriage; the damage was repaired, the Englishman promised that he would announce my arrival to Beethoven and drove off.

How great was my surprise to come upon him once again the following day! This time there was no broken wheel: he was quietly stopped in the middle of the road, reading a book. He seemed quite pleased to see me coming on my way toward him.

"I've already waited several hours," said he, "because it occurred to me that I was wrong not to invite you to drive with me to Beethoven's. Driving is rather better than walking. Come into the carriage."

I was astonished anew. For an instant I really hesitated whether I ought not to accept his offer. But I quickly remembered the vow I had made the day before as I saw the Englishman rolling off: I had vowed under any circumstances to carry out my pilgrimage on foot. I said this in so many words. It was the Englishman's turn to be amazed. He could not grasp the idea. He repeated his invitation, as well as the fact that he had waited several hours, despite the delay occasioned at his inn by the more thorough repairing of the broken wheel. I remained firm, and he drove off, wondering.

The truth is I felt a secret dislike for him, for I had a presentiment that he would yet bring me into serious trouble. Moreover, his veneration of Beethoven and his intention of visiting him struck me rather as the idle whim of a gentleman than as the deep inner necessity of an enthusiastic soul. Hence I preferred to let him go rather than to desecrate my pious yearning by sharing his company.

But as if my fate intended to prepare me for my future dangerous association with this gentleman, I met him once more on the evening of the same day. He was halted in front of an inn and, as it seemed, still waiting for me. He sat backward in his carriage and was looking down the street along which I came.

"Sir," he began, "I have again waited for you a considerable time. Will you drive with me to Beethoven's?"

This time my astonishment was mixed with secret terror. This uncommon stubbornness to serve me was inexplicable, except on the supposition that the Englishman, having noticed my growing dislike for him, was determined to encompass my destruction. With undisguised irritation I once more turned down his offer. Whereupon he loftily cried out, "Goddam! You do not care much for Beethoven. I shall be seeing him soon." And away he flew.

This time was truly the last that I encountered this islander on the long road to Vienna.

At last I trod the streets of Vienna: the end of my pilgrimage had been reached. With what feelings did I enter this Mecca of my faith! All the weariness of my long and hard journey was forgotten; I was at the goal, within the walls that enclosed Beethoven.

I was too deeply moved to be able to think of carrying out my purpose immediately. Of course, I inquired where Beethoven lived, but only in order to find lodgings in the neighborhood. Almost opposite the house in which the master lived there was a none too fashionable hostelry. I took a little room on the fifth floor and there prepared myself for the great event of my life—a visit to Beethoven.

After having rested for two days, fasted and prayed, but not cast another closer look upon Vienna, I mustered my courage, left my hostel, and marched straight across the way into the remarkable house. I was told that Beethoven was not at home. That suited me quite well, for it gave me more time to collect my wits. But when four times more during the day I was given the same reply, and with a certain increasing firmness of tone, I began to account it an unlucky day and gave up my visit in despair.

As I wandered back to the inn my Englishman greeted me from the second floor with a fair show of cordiality.

"Have you seen Beethoven?" he cried.

"Not yet; he was out," I replied, speculating on our paths crossing once again. The Englishman met me on the stairs and urged me with marked friendliness to enter his room. "My dear sir," said he, "I have seen you go into Beethoven's house five times today. I have myself been here for quite a while and have pitched camp in this wretched inn so as to be close to Beethoven. Take it from me, Beethoven is very hard to get a word with; he would seem to be a very capricious gentleman. At first I called on him six times a day and each time was turned away. Now I get up very early and I sit at my window until late evening in order to see when Beethoven goes out. But the gentleman seems *never* to go out."

"So you think that Beethoven was at home today as usual and had me turned away?" I cried, aghast.

"Naturally; you and I have been denied access. And I find it most disagreeable because I have not come to make Vienna's acquaintance but Beethoven's."

This was very distressing news to me. Nonetheless I tried my luck again the next day, but again in vain—the gates of heaven were shut against me.

My Englishman, who from his windows watched my fruitless attempts with the closest attention, had now reliably found out that Beethoven's rooms did not face the street. He was a nuisance but stubborn beyond belief. My patience, on the contrary, was nearly at

an end, for which I had better reason than he: a whole week had
gone by without my getting sight of my goal, and the price of my
galops hardly allowed me a long sojourn in Vienna. Little by little
I began to despair.

I told my sorrows to the innkeeper, who smiled and promised to
let me know the cause of my bad luck, if on my side I promised not
to tell the Englishman. Suspecting him to be my unlucky star, I made
the promise.

"You see," said my good host, "quite a few Englishmen come here
to see and meet Herr von Beethoven. This annoys Herr von Beethoven a good deal, and he has become so furious at the insistence of
these people that he has made it impossible for any stranger to come
near him. He is an odd gentleman anyhow, and one must forgive
him. But it all brings business to my inn—we're generally full of
Englishmen, and their difficulty in getting to see Herr Beethoven
makes them stay longer. But since you promise not to scare off my
clientele, I hope to find a way to get you through to Herr Beethoven." [2]

This was very edifying: I could not reach my goal—poor devil
that I was—because I was taken for an Englishman! My suspicion
was justified: the Englishman had been my undoing. At once I
thought of leaving the inn, since it seemed sure that everyone there
must be considered an Englishman by those across the street at Beethoven's. But the landlord's promise to find me an opportunity to
see and speak with Beethoven held me back. Meanwhile the Englishman, whom I now heartily loathed, had been practicing all manner
of intrigues and chicanery, without result.

Thus several fruitless days passed by during which the income
from my galops visibly shrank. At last mine host confided to me
that, if I would go to a certain beer garden I could not fail to see
Beethoven, for he went there daily at the same hour. At the same
time my adviser gave me an unmistakable description of the Master's personal appearance, so that I could not miss him. I came to

[2] The variant forms of Beethoven's name belong to the original.

life again and decided not to postpone my pleasure. I could not meet Beethoven when he left home because he used a back door: there was nothing for it but the beer garden.

But as bad luck would have it, I found him neither on that day nor on the next two. At last on the fourth day, as I bent my steps toward the fateful garden, I saw to my consternation that the Englishman was cautiously following me at a distance. The poor wretch, eternally posted at his window, had noticed that I went out every day at the same hour and, concluding that I must be on Beethoven's track, had made up his mind to turn this to his own advantage. He told me all this with the greatest aplomb and announced that he would follow me wherever I went. In vain did I try to put him off and make him believe I visited the beer garden for refreshment of a sort much too unfashionable for such as he. He remained unshakable, and I could only curse my fate. At last I tried rudeness, hoping to get rid of him by abuse. Far from letting it deter him, he gave me his softest smile. His *idée fixe* was to see Beethoven, and nothing else mattered.

And in truth that was the day on which I was at last to look upon the great Beethoven. Nothing can convey my excitement, and my rage too, as, seated by my fine fellow, I saw a man whose looks and bearing completely answered to the description my landlord had given me of the Master. The long blue overcoat, the tousled gray hair, the features and expression of face—all just in the likeness that my imagination had portrayed. There could be no mistake. I had known him at the first glance. He walked past us with quick short steps; awe and veneration held me enthralled.

The Englishman noticed all that went on within me. With eager eyes he watched the passer-by, who withdrew into the farthest corner of the as yet empty garden. He ordered wine and remained awhile, meditating. My beating heart told me, "It is he!" For a moment I forgot my neighbor and gazed with avid eyes and speechless emotion at the man whose genius had reigned over all my thoughts and feelings ever since I had learned how to feel and think. Involuntarily I began to murmur to myself and fell into a kind of monologue, which ended with the all-too-obvious words, *"Beethoven, it is thou, whom I now see?"*

Nothing escaped my appalling companion, who, bending toward me and holding his breath, had overheard my aside. I was shocked out of my ecstasy by the words, "Yes! That gentleman is Beethoven! Come, let's introduce ourselves at once!"

Vexed and alarmed, I held back the damnable Englishman by the elbow. "What are you doing?" I cried. "Do you want to expose us to ridicule—here in this place—with no regard for the proprieties!"

"Why," he replied, "it's a first-rate opportunity. We shan't easily find a better."

With that he took a kind of notebook from his pocket and was going to make a beeline for the man in the blue coat. Beside myself, I seized the lunatic's coattails and yelled at him, "Are you possessed?"

This scene had attracted the stranger's attention. He seemed painfully aware that he was the occasion of our uproar, and, hastily emptying his glass, he rose to go. The Englishman, observing this, wrenched himself free from my grasp so violently that one of his coattails was left in my hand, and hurled himself in Beethoven's path. The latter tried to avoid him, but the scoundrel stepped in front of him and, making him a bow in the latest English manner, addressed him as follows:

"I have the honor to present myself to the renowned composer and honored Sir Ludwig Beethoven."

That was enough. At his first words Beethoven had thrown a glance at me and, springing aside with lightning speed, had disappeared from the garden. The irrepressible Briton was on the point of pursuing the fugitive when I seized his remaining coattail in one fierce motion. Somewhat surprised, he stopped and shouted at me, "Goddam! That man is worthy of being English. He must be a great man. I'm going to lose no time in making his acquaintance."

I was petrified. This ghastly adventure had brought to naught my last hope of fulfilling my heart's desire. I could see that henceforth any attempt on my part to approach Beethoven in the ordinary way would be futile. In my impecunious state I had only one thing to decide—whether to go home at once, all my labor lost, or to make one last desperate try to achieve my object. The first alternative made me shudder to the bottom of my soul. Who could come so near the gates of blessedness and see them shut against him without feeling annihilated?

But before giving up salvation, I would take one more desperate step. But *what* step, what way should I take? For a long time I could think of nothing coherent. My mind was paralyzed; nothing arose in my imagination but the recollection of what I had lived through when I was hanging on to the dreadful Englishman's coattails. I had caught Beethoven's quick glance at my wretched self in this catastrophic position, and I knew what his look meant: he had taken me for an Englishman! How then undertake to dispel the Master's suspicion? Everything hung on my being able to let him know that I was a simple German soul, naturally very poor, but rich in supernatural enthusiasm.

So at last I decided to pour out my heart on paper—which I did. I wrote. I briefly recounted my life history, how I had become a musician, how I worshiped him and had come to want to know him in person, how I had devoted two years to making my name as a galop composer, how I had begun and ended my pilgrimage, the sorrows I had endured at the Englishman's hands, and what a cruel plight was mine at present. As I felt my heart grow lighter with the recital of my woes, the sense of relief gave my words a certain measure of familiarity. I inserted in my letter some quite frank and fairly strong reproaches against the Master for the unjust severity with which he was treating my poor self. And I closed the letter with a real burst of inspiration; I could see stars before my eyes as I wrote the address: "To Herr Ludwig van Beethoven." I then uttered a silent prayer and delivered the letter at Beethoven's house.

As I returned full of enthusiasm to my hostelry, why was I again plagued with the sight—Heaven defend me!—of the fearsome

Englishman! He had observed my latest move from his window and could read the joy of hope in my face. That was enough to put me once more in his power. In fact he met me on the stairs with the question, "What luck? When do we see Beethoven?"

"Never, never!" I exclaimed in despair. "You shall never see Beethoven in this life. Leave me alone, you appalling wretch, we have nothing in common!"

"On the contrary," he coolly retorted, "we have a great deal in common: what, sir, have you done with my coattail? Who gave you permission to lay violent hands upon it? Do you know that you are responsible for Beethoven's attitude toward me? How could he deem it respectable to consort with a gentleman wearing only one coattail?"

Beside myself at finding the blame retorted upon me, I cried, "You shall have your coattail back, and may you keep it as a shameful reminder of the way you insulted the great Beethoven and brought disaster on a poor musician! Farewell, and let us never see each other again!"

He tried to restrain me and quiet me down, assuring me that he had plenty of other coats in excellent condition, and begging me to tell him when Beethoven would receive us. But I would not be pacified and stormed upstairs to my garret. I locked myself in and waited for Beethoven's answer.

How can I describe what went on within me—and all about me —when the next hour actually brought me a scrap of music paper inscribed in a hasty hand with the words: "Forgive me, Herr R——, if I ask you not to call upon me until tomorrow morning. Today I have to finish and send off some music by the post. Tomorrow I shall expect you.—Beethoven."

I fell on my knees and first thanked heaven for this exceptional mercy; my eyes grew dim with scalding tears. Then my feelings broke out in wildest joy. I jumped up and danced about in my little room like a lunatic. I don't quite know what I danced, except that to my great shame I suddenly found that I was whistling one of my galops for it.[3] This depressing discovery brought me to my senses. Leaving the attic and the inn, I burst forth into the streets of Vienna, drunk with joy.

God forgive me! but my troubles had made me forget that I was in Vienna. How charmed I was by all the jolly ways of the dwellers in this imperial city. Being in high spirits, I found everything most spirited. The rather shallow pleasure-seeking of the Viennese seemed to me the true freshness of genuine life; their frivolous and not very fastidious sensuality I took for a native receptivity to the beautiful. I cast an eye at the five theater announcements for that day—Heavens! On one of them I read, "*Fidelio,* opera by Beethoven."

I had to go, no matter how this melted away the earnings from my galops. Just as I came in the overture began. It was the revised version of the opera that, be it said to the credit of the profound Viennese, had failed under its earlier title *Leonore.* I had never heard the opera in its rehandled form, so it can readily be imagined what delights I experienced as I listened to the new score for the first time. The role of Leonore was played by a very young girl, who despite her age seemed already wedded to Beethoven's genius. What fire, what poetry, what affecting depth in her portrayal of the amazing heroine! Her name was Wilhelmine Schröder,[4] and she has earned the high distinction of revealing this work of Beethoven's to the German public. Even that night I could see that the superficial Viennese were gripped by uncommon enthusiasm. For my part, I was in the seventh heaven. I was transfigured and worshiping the genius which had brought me, like Florestan, out of darkness and chains into freedom and light.[5]

That night I could not sleep. What I had gone through and what was in store for me the next day were too much and too overpowering for me to weave calmly into a dream. I lay awake, feeling hot

[3] In the original published version, the hero stops dancing when he hears a ghostly whistling of one of his own galops—a Hoffmannesque touch that Wagner removed eight years later.

[4] Later Mme. Schröder-Devrient (1804–1860).

[5] An allusion to the plot of *Fidelio;* see p. 246.

and cold in anticipation of my standing before Beethoven. Finally
the dawn broke, and I impatiently counted the hours until the
proper time for a morning call. At last it struck, and I set out. Here
was the greatest event of my life—the very thought overwhelmed
me.

But I had one more dreadful ordeal to go through. Leaning against
the doorpost of Beethoven's house, my evil spirit, the Englishman,
was waiting for me. The monster had bribed the whole world, including our landlord, who had read Beethoven's open note even
before me and had betrayed its contents to the Briton.

A cold sweat came over me at the sight of him. All my heavenly
bliss, all poetic exaltation deserted me: I was once again in his power.

"Come," began the villain, "let us call on Beethoven."

My first thought was to escape by a lie and pretend that I was not
on my way to Beethoven's at all. Only he left me no loophole by
telling me with the greatest candor how he had discovered my secret and how determined he was not to let me go until we had
both seen Beethoven. I then tried to dissuade him from his purpose
by fair words—in vain! I flew into a rage—in vain! Finally I hoped
to outwit him by my fleetness of foot. Like an arrow, I darted up the
steps and tore at the bell like a maniac. But before the door could be
opened, my gentleman was beside me, clutching at the tails of my
coat and saying, "Don't run away from me! I have a claim on your
coattails and shall hang on to them until we stand in Beethoven's
presence."

I swung around in a fury, trying to tear myself loose—yes, I was
being tempted to the point of resorting to violence against the bully-
ing son of Britannia—when the door opened. An old serving maid
appeared and looked on our curious stance with a dour expression.
It seemed as if she would fling the door to at once, but in my agony
I cried out my name and protested that I had been invited by Herr
Beethoven himself.

The old lady was hesitating, for the look of the Englishman
seemed to arouse her suspicions, when—as luck would have it—

Beethoven himself appeared at the door of his study. I seized my chance and stepped quickly in, wishing to address apologies to the Master. But in the same motion I yanked the Englishman in with me, for he still held my garment tight. He had made good his warning and only let me go when we both stood before Beethoven. I bowed and stammered out my name, and although, of course, he could not hear it, the Master seemed to know that I was the person who had written to him. He asked me to come into his room, and the Englishman, disregarding Beethoven's astonished glance, slipped in quickly after me.

Here was I in the holy of holies. But the ghastly embarrassment which the Briton was causing me robbed me of any capacity for enjoying my good fortune. Nor was Beethoven's outer appearance inherently such as to put one at ease. He wore some rather untidy indoor clothes, with a red woolen scarf wrapped around his middle. His long, bushy gray hair hung tousled over his brow, and his dour, forbidding expression did nothing to lessen my distress. We sat down at a table strewn with papers.

No one spoke. Everyone was ill at ease, and Beethoven clearly resented having to receive two instead of one. At last he began, rather harshly, "So you came from L——?" I was going to answer but he broke in and passed me a sheet of paper and a pencil. "Write it down, I can't hear."

I knew of Beethoven's deafness and had been prepared for it in my mind. Nevertheless it was like a stab through the heart when I heard his hoarse, deadened voice saying, "I can't hear." To live poor and joyless in this world, to know of no other intoxicant but the power of sound, and be forced to say, "I cannot hear!" That instant was to me a complete revelation of Beethoven's outer appearance, the deep furrows in his cheeks, the somber dejection of his features, the set defiance of his lips: *he could not hear!*

Confused and hardly knowing what I was about, I wrote down an apology, together with a brief account of the mishap by which I found myself in the Englishman's company. The latter sat all the while dumb, with satisfied contemplation of Beethoven, who, as soon as he had read my lines, turned rather sharply toward the intruder and asked him what he wanted.

"I have the honor—" began the Briton.

"I can't understand you," cried Beethoven without letting him finish. "I do not hear and do not much like to speak. Please to write down what you want with me."

The Englishman calmly took counsel with himself for a moment, then drew an elegant music case from his pocket and said to me, "That will do—please write, 'I beg Herr Beethoven to look over my composition, and when a passage is not to his liking, to be good enough to put a cross opposite.'"

I wrote out his request word for word, in the hope of getting rid of him at last. And so it turned out. When Beethoven had done reading, he smiled curiously, set down the Englishman's composition on the table, nodded curtly, and said, "I'll send it."

My gentleman was quite satisfied. He stood up, made an especially courtly bow, and took his leave. I breathed a deep breath—he was gone.

For the first time I really felt I was within the inner sanctum. Beethoven's own features perceptibly brightened; he looked at me quietly for a moment, then began.

"That Briton has been a thorn in your flesh? Take comfort in my plight: these traveling Englishmen have plagued me nearly out of my senses. One day they come to stare at a poor musician, and the next at a rare animal. It grieves me to have confused you with such a man. You wrote to me that you liked my works. I am glad, for these days I have very little hope that people will like my things."

This confidence removed all my embarrassment. I felt a thrill of joy at his simple words. I wrote down that I was certainly not the only man who felt enthusiastic about Beethoven's creations; that I wished for nothing better than to procure for, let us say, my native city the honor of his visit, so that he might convince himself of the influence his works produced on the entire public.

"I can readily believe," he rejoined, "that my compositions please people more in North Germany. The Viennese irritate me. They hear such poor stuff all the time that they cannot be serious about serious things."

I tried to contradict him by citing the performance of *Fidelio* the day before, saying the public had greeted it with the liveliest enthusiasm.

"H'm, h'm!" grumbled the Master. "*Fidelio,* yes! But I say the nitwits applaud it out of vanity, imagining that in revising it I was following their advice. Now they pay me back for my trouble and shout 'Bravo!' They're an easygoing lot and anything but learned. Still, I'd rather be with them than with cleverer people. Now tell me, did you like *Fidelio?*"

I gave an account of the impression made on me by the previous night's performance and remarked that the work had gained enormously by the additional numbers.

"Tedious labor!" returned Beethoven. "I am no opera composer. At least, I know of no opera house in the world for which I should care to write another opera. If I ever made an opera to please myself the public would stay away from it, because it would contain nothing like arias, duets, trios, and all the filler they stuff operas with today. What I should write, no singers would sing and no public would listen to. All they know and care about is glittering falsehoods, brilliant nonsense, and cloying emptiness. Whoever should make a true musical drama would be taken for a fool, and he certainly would be one if he did not keep such a work to himself but insisted on exhibiting it to these people."

"But how," I asked all aglow, "would one go about composing a work of that kind?"

"As Shakespeare did when he wrote his plays," replied Beethoven with passion. Then he went on, "Anyone willing to custom-tailor odd bits of things to show off young women with mediocre voices, so that they will get bravos and handclapping, had better become a Parisian dressmaker and give up dramatic composition. For my part, I was not made for such fooleries. I am well aware that clever people say I know my job as an instrumental composer but will never feel at home in vocal music. They are right, because to them vocal music means nothing but opera; and from feeling at home in that kind of nonsense, Heaven preserve me!"

At this point I ventured to ask whether anyone hearing his *Adelaide* [6] would dare deny him the most brilliant calling as a composer for voice.

"Well," he replied after a pause, "*Adelaide* and similar things are only trifles, after all, which serve the professional virtuosos appropriately enough to show off their best fireworks. But why shouldn't vocal music become, just like the instrumental, a great and serious genre; a genre treated with as much respect by the silly vocalists who perform it as I require from the orchestra for one of my symphonies? The human voice is a God-given fact—a far finer and nobler maker of sound than any instrument. Why can't it be used with the same freedom, to produce entirely new effects? The very nature of its peculiarities would require special treatment to insure its prominence, which in turn would lead to the most manifold combinations. Instruments are the primal organs of the natural creation; what they express can never be clearly defined and fixed: they reproduce the primitive feelings themselves, as they emerged from the chaos of the first Creation, when possibly no human being existed who could receive them into his heart.

"But the human voice is quite other. Its genius is to represent the heart and its exclusive individual sensibility. Its character is thereby limited, but it is clear and explicit. Now let these two elements be joined! Let the wild, infinite elemental feelings reproduced by the instruments be brought together with the clear, definite emotions of the human heart reproduced by the voice of man. The entrance of this second element will soothe and still the struggle of the elemental feelings and give them a definite forward course; while the human heart, by taking up these primordial passions, will be so immensely broadened and strengthened as to become capable of sensing with perfect clarity its earlier indefinite intimations of the

[6] Cantata for soprano and piano, Op. 46.

All-highest, thereby transforming them into godlike consciousness.[7]

Here Beethoven paused a moment as if exhausted. Then he went on with a little sigh, "Of course, in trying to solve this problem one will run into many an obstacle. In order to have songs there must be words. But who would be able to fashion in words the poetry needed as a basis of union for all the elements? The poem lags behind because words are too feeble for the task. Soon you shall see a new composition of mine which will remind you of what I have just told you. It is a symphony with choruses. Let me stress again how hard I found it to overcome the inadequacy of the poetical art for my purpose. I finally chose Schiller's beautiful "Ode to Joy." It, at any rate, is a noble and uplifting poem, though far from expressing what in this connection no verses in the world could say."

To this day, I can hardly believe my good fortune in having had Beethoven's own help in understanding his gigantic last symphony, which was at that time finished but not yet known to anyone. I uttered to him my fervent thanks for this rare privilege, and also conveyed my delighted surprise at the news that we might look forward to a new great work of his composition. Tears came to my eyes; I could have knelt at his feet.

Beethoven seemed to notice my agitation. He looked and smiled at me half sadly, half mockingly, and said, "When my new work is out and being discussed, you might stand up for me. Remember how I am: for the clever people will think me mad, or pretend to. But you can see, Herr R——, that I am not quite a lunatic yet, even though wretched enough to become one. People want me to write what *they* fancy to be the good and the beautiful. They do not seem to reflect that even a poor devil like me must have his own ideas and cannot compose otherwise than as I feel. And *their* beautiful notions, I can't feel them at all." Then he added ironically, "That's the cause of all my troubles."

With that he stood up and paced the room with short quick steps.

[7] The French version of this final clause gives it a clear and sensible meaning which is hard to find in the original German.

Moved to the depths of my heart as I was, I stood up too. I knew I was shaking. It was of course impossible to continue the conversation either by signs or by writing, and I was aware that the time had come when my visit might begin to seem burdensome to the Master. To write a word of heartfelt thanks and farewell struck me as too commonplace. All I did was to seize my hat, walk up to Beethoven, and let him read in my eyes what passed in my mind.

He seemed to understand. "You are leaving?" he asked. "Shall you stay in Vienna awhile?"

I wrote that my journey had been for the sole purpose of seeing him, and since he had honored me with so unusual a reception, I was overjoyed to feel my aim accomplished and would return home the next day.

Smiling, he replied, "You told me in your letter how you earned the money for the trip. You should stay in Vienna and write galops —that kind of goods is in great demand."

I explained that I was done with all that, knowing of no other cause worth such a sacrifice.

"Well, well," he said, "you never can tell. I might have done better, old fool that I am, to have written galops. The way I have gone, I'll always starve. Pleasant journey to you," he added. "Think of me and take heart from it in all your troubles."

My eyes brimming with tears, I was about to go when he called to me. "Hold on! We must settle the musical Englishman's hash. Let's see where to put those crosses!"

He seized the Briton's music case and skimmed through it with a smile. Then he carefully restored its contents, wrapped it in a piece of paper, took a thick scoring pen and drew a huge cross from one edge of the cover to the other. He then handed it to me with the words, "Please give the lucky man his masterpiece. He is an ass, and yet I envy him his long ears. Farewell, dear friend, and remember me kindly."

With this he dismissed me, and I stumbled my way out of his room and his house.

At the hotel I found the Englishman's servant packing his master's trunk in the carriage. His goal, too, had been reached, and I had to confess that he too had shown endurance. I hurried to my room and made ready to begin my homeward trek on the morrow. I had to laugh aloud as I glanced at the cross on the cover of the Englishman's music case. But it was a souvenir of Beethoven and I really grudged giving it to the besetting devil of my pilgrimage. I quickly made up my mind: I took off the wrapping, dug out my galops, and stuck them into this damning envelope. To the Englishman I sent his composition without a cover, but with a little note in which I said that Beethoven envied him, for he had really not known where he should put a cross.

As I was leaving the inn I saw my wretched fellow-traveler getting into his carriage. "Good-by," cried he, "you have done me a great service. It was good to make Beethoven's acquaintance. Will you come with me to Italy?"

"What are you going to do there?"

"I want to meet Signor Rossini, he is also a well-known composer."

"Good luck to you! I have met Beethoven, and that's quite enough for me."

We parted. I cast one more feeling glance at Beethoven's house and took my way northward, my heart uplifted and ennobled.

A GERMAN MUSICIAN IN PARIS (1840)

HECTOR BERLIOZ

➤➤➤ ◄◄◄

An Artist from the Grocer's

➤➤➤ ─── ◄◄◄

The setting of Berlioz's *Evenings with the Orchestra* is the pit of an opera house in which the narrator meets with his friends, the members of the orchestra. When a masterpiece is being played, all listen to the music; but when a dull or cheap work is performed, only a few instrumentists keep up the pretense of playing, so that the rest can talk and tell stories.

➤➤➤ ─── ◄◄◄

Third Evening: Performance of *Der Freischütz.*

No one in the orchestra speaks. Each musician is intent on his task, which he carries out zealously and lovingly. During the intermission one of them asks me if it is true that at the Paris Opera a real skeleton was introduced in the infernal scene. I reply in the affirmative and promise to relate the biography of the poor fellow the next day.

Fourth Evening: "A Debut in *Der Freischütz:* a Necrological Tale"; "Marescot, A Study in Plastic Surgery."

A very insipid Italian opera of the modern school is being performed. Hardly have the musicians arrived when the majority of them, putting aside their instruments, remind me of the promise I made yesterday. They form a circle around me. The trombones and the big drum are strenuously at work. The circumstances are in our favor; we have another hour or two of duets and unison choruses. I cannot decline to tell the desired story.

The conductor, who always pretends not to know that we carry on literary diversions, leans back a little, so as to listen more easily. The prima donna has shrieked so fearful a high D sharp that we thought she was in the middle of her confinement. The public stamps with joy; two huge bouquets alight on the stage. The diva bows and goes off. She is recalled, returns, bows a second time, and goes off again. Recalled once more, she hastens to reappear, bows anew, and since we cannot tell when this rigmarole will end, I begin.

"In 1822 I lived in the Latin Quarter, where I was supposed to be studying medicine. When performances of the *Freischütz* were being given at the Odéon, under the title of *Robin des bois,* which denoted the adaptation by M. Castil-Blaze,[1] I went nightly, in spite of my studies, to hear the disfigured masterpiece of Weber. I had by that time all but thrown my scalpel into the bushes. But one of my former fellow-students, Dubouchet, who has since risen to be one of the most sought-after doctors in Paris, often accompanied me to the theater, for he shared my musical fanaticism. At the sixth or seventh performance, a big red-haired booby who sat beside us in the stalls took it into his head to hiss Agatha's aria in the second act, alleging that it was Gothic music and that nothing in the entire opera was any good except the waltz and the hunters' chorus. As you may guess, he was hustled outside: that was our way of discussing matters in those days; and Dubouchet, readjusting his somewhat crumpled cravat, shouted to the crowd, "The incident should cause no surprise. I know the fellow—he is a grocer's assistant in the rue Saint-Jacques!" At which the parterre applauded wildly.

"Six months later, having done himself too well at his master's wedding breakfast, this poor devil of a grocer's assistant falls ill and has himself carted to the hospital of La Pitié; he is well cared for, dies, and is not buried—as may readily be surmised.

"Our young fellow, well cared for and duly dead, comes by chance under the eyes of Dubouchet, who recognizes him. The pitiless medical student of La Pitié, instead of shedding a tear over his vanquished enemy, hastens to purchase the corpse and says, as he hands it to the attendant of the operating room, "François, here is a subject for dry preparation; but see that you do it with care; he is an acquaintance of mine."

[1] See pp. 552 and 555–56.

"Fifteen years roll by (fifteen years! how long life seems when one does nothing with it!), the manager of the Opera entrusts me with the composition of the recitatives in the *Freischütz* [2] and the staging of the masterpiece, the costumes being naturally put in charge of Duponchel."

"Duponchel!" simultaneously exclaim five or six musicians. "Do you mean the celebrated inventor of the dais, the man who introduced the dais into opera as the principal element of success? The author of the dais in *La Juive,* in *La Reine de Chypre,* in *Le Prophète,* [3] the creator of the floating dais, the wonderful dais, the dais of daises?"

"The very same, gentlemen. And so, as Duponchel was once more in charge of the costumes, processions, and daises, I called on him to find out his plans for the properties in the infernal scene, wherein his dais, unfortunately, could have no place.

"'By the way,' I said, 'we need a skull for the evocation of Samiel, and skeletons for the apparitions; I hope you are not going to give us a pasteboard skull or skeletons of painted canvas, like those in *Don Giovanni.'*

"'My dear fellow, there is no other way of doing it; it is the regular procedure, the only way.'

"'What do you mean, the only procedure! Suppose I supply you with something genuine, natural—a real skull, a real man, made of bones, but without flesh on them, what will you say to that?'

"'Upon my word, I shall say that it is excellent, perfect. I shall find your device admirable.'

"'Well, then depend on me, you shall have it.'

"Whereupon I jump into a cab and drive in double quick time to the house of Dr. Vidal, another of my former operating-room comrades. He too has made a fortune; it is only physicians who make a living.

"'Have you a skeleton you can lend me?'

[2] The original opera calls for spoken dialogue between numbers, which is contrary to the fixed rule of the Paris Opera.

[3] Operas by Halévy (the first two) and Meyerbeer.

" 'No, but I have a fairly good head, which, I am told, once belonged to a German savant who died of poverty and grief; whatever you do, don't spoil it, I value it greatly.'

" 'Don't worry; I will be responsible for it.'

"I put the doctor's skull in my hat, and off I go.

"On the boulevard, fate, which delights in pranks of this kind, brings me face to face with Dubouchet, whom I had lost track of, and the sight of him inspires me with a brilliant idea.

" 'Hello, there!'

" 'How are you?'

" 'Very well, thanks; but never mind me, the question is, how is your music lover?'

" 'What music lover?'

" 'Why, the grocer's assistant, of course, the fellow we bundled out of the Odéon for having hissed Weber's music, the one who was so carefully "prepared" by François.'

" 'Ah, I get you. Why, he is in the best of health, thank you. He stands clean and neat in my consulting room, quite proud of being so artistically jointed and built up. Not a bone of him missing, he is a masterpiece. Only the head is damaged a little.'

" 'Well, then give him to me; he is a youth with a future. I want to introduce him into the Opera; there is a part for him in the next work.'

" 'What do you mean?'

" 'You'll see!'

" 'Oh, well, if it's a theatrical secret—and if you promise to explain later, I won't insist on knowing now. The music lover shall be delivered to you.'

"No time is lost in conveying the dead man to the Opera, though in a case far too short for him. I hail the general utility man.

" 'Here, Gattino!'

" 'Ay, ay, sir.'

" 'Open this case. You see that young man?'

" 'I do, sir.'

" 'He is to make his debut at the Opera tomorrow. Make him a nice little box in which he can be comfortable and stretch his legs.'

" 'Yes, sir.'

" 'As for his costume, take an iron rod and plant it in his back-bone, so that he may hold himself as straight as M. Petipa when meditating a pirouette.'

" 'Yes, sir.'

" 'You will next fasten four candles together, which you will place in his hands, lighted; he is a grocer, they will be familiar to him.'

" 'Yes, sir.'

" 'But as his head is not in the best of condition—you can see it has been a bit chipped—we must substitute this other one.'

" 'I follow you, sir.'

" 'It once belonged to a scientist—that doesn't matter—who died from starvation—no need for that to concern us. As to the other skull, that of the grocer, who died of indigestion, you will make a slight slit on its very top—don't be afraid, nothing will come out of it—so that it may receive the point of Gaspard's sword in the evocation scene.'

" 'Very good, sir.'

"My orders were carried out and from that time, at every performance of the *Freischütz,* just as Samiel exclaims, 'I am here!' a thunderclap is heard, a tree crashes to earth, and our grocer, who was once so hostile to Weber's music, appears amid the crimson glow of Bengal lights, enthusiastically brandishing his lighted torch.

"Who could have foreseen the dramatic vocation of the fellow? Who ever would have thought that he might some day make his debut precisely in that opera? He has a better head now, and more good sense: he no longer hisses— *Alas, poor Yorick!"*

"Well, now, that makes me sad," said Corsino simply. "For all his having been a grocer, this beginner, when all is said and done, was almost a human being. I don't like to play with death like this. If in his lifetime he hissed Weber's score, I know people who are far more guilty and whose remains have not been vilified with such cynical impiety. I too have lived in Paris, and in the Latin Quarter at that; and there I have seen at work one of those wretches who, taking advantage of the impunity allowed them by French law, practice infamous operations on musical works. There are people of all sorts in this Paris of ours. Some of them beg their bread at street corners. Others earn theirs by night, a lantern in one hand and a hook in the other; some comb out the gutters for their food; others tear posters and sell them to paper dealers; a little more useful are the men who kill and skin old horses at the Montfaucon. The fellow I am speaking of killed and skinned the works of celebrated composers.

"Marescot by name, his trade was to arrange all kinds of music for two flutes, or for one guitar, but especially for two flageolets, and then publish it. Since the music of the *Freischütz* did not belong to him (everyone knows that it 'belonged' to the translator and improver of the libretto, who had labored with such genius to make it worthy of figuring as *Robin des bois* at the Odéon), Marescot did not dare practice his trade on that. This broke his heart, for, as he would say, he had 'an idea' which, applied to a certain part of Weber's opera, would bring him in big money. I occasionally saw this practitioner, and somehow he had taken a liking to me. Our musical tendencies were nevertheless not the same, as you can imagine. As a result I almost let him suspect what I thought of him, and on one occasion so far forgot myself as very nearly to tell him my opinion of his musical abattoir. This embroiled us somewhat, and for six months I did not set foot in his workshop.

"Notwithstanding all his assaults on the great masters, his appearance was in general rather wretched and his clothing decidedly threadbare. One fine day, however, I met him stepping out briskly under the arcades of the Odéon in a brand-new frock coat and high boots, and wearing a white tie; I even think that on that day—so greatly had fortune transformed him—his hands were clean.

"'Heavens!' I exclaimed, absolutely dazzled at the sight of him. 'Have you had the misfortune to lose a rich American uncle, or to have become someone's collaborator in a new opera of Weber's, that I behold you so spruce, so furbished, so astounding?'

"'I,' he replied, 'a collaborator? What next? I need no collaborator;

I elaborate Weber's music without any help, and I am thriving very well by it. You don't believe me—well, let me tell you that I have at last realized my idea, and I was not mistaken when I told you that it was worth money, a very great deal of money, an immense amount of money. Listen. Schlesinger, the Berlin publisher, owns the *Freischütz* music in Germany; he was fool enough to buy the rights to it, the simpleton. True, he did not pay a high price, but so long as Schlesinger did not publish that Gothic music, it remained, here in France, the sole property of the author of *Robin des bois,* by virtue of the words and the improvements with which he had adorned it. So I could not touch it. But as soon as it was published in Berlin, it became public property here, no French publisher having been willing, as you can well believe, to pay the Prussian publisher for the reprint rights to such a work.

" 'I was now free to snap my fingers at the *French* author's rights, and to publish *my* piece without any words, in accordance with my great idea. I refer to Agatha's prayer in A flat, in the third act of *Robin des bois.* You remember that it is in three-four time, and the pace rather lulling. It is accompanied by syncopated horn parts that are very difficult and as stupid as can be. I thought to myself that by putting the song into six-eight time, marking it allegretto, and accompanying it intelligibly—that is, with the rhythm proper to that time, a quarter note followed by an eighth, the rhythm of drums in a quick march—it would make a very pretty piece, which would be bound to succeed. I therefore wrote out my piece that way, scored for flute and guitar, and published it, allowing Weber's name to stand on it. Now it has caught on so well that I am selling it, not by the hundreds, but by the thousands. The sales go up daily. It alone will bring me in more than the entire opera brought that blockhead of a Weber; more even than it brought M. Castil-Blaze, who is a clever fellow just the same. That's what it is to have ideas!'

"What do you say to that, gentlemen? I feel pretty sure that you will take me for a historian and hence not believe me. And yet I have told you an absolute fact. I may add that for a long time I kept a copy of Weber's prayer thus transfigured by the *idea* which made the *fortune* of M. Marescot, French publisher of music, professor of the flute and guitar, in business rue Saint-Jacques, at the corner of the rue des Mathurins, in Paris."

The opera is over; the musicians file out, looking back at Corsino with an air of mocking disbelief. Some even allow the vulgar word "legpull" to escape their lips.

I can vouch, however, for the authenticity of his story, for I knew Marescot. He has in fact a good many more achievements of the kind to his credit.

EVENINGS WITH THE ORCHESTRA (1852)

LEO TOLSTOY

➤➤➤ ◄◄◄

Natasha Sings for Her Lover

Nothing easier than to say in a conventional tone, "Till tomorrow." What was frightful was to go home, to see one's sisters, mother, father, to tell them everything and ask them for money so as to keep one's word of honor.

No one had gone to bed. The young people had had supper after returning from the theater, and stood around the piano. When Nicolas entered the room he felt himself enfolded in the poetical atmosphere of love which filled their house then, and which seemed—after Dolohov's proposal and the ball at Iogel's—to have gathered like a cloud before a storm over the heads of Sonia and Natasha. Both girls had on the blue dresses they had worn for the theater and they looked very pretty, as well as aware of being so. They were chatting and laughing near the piano. Vera and Shinshin were playing checkers in the drawing room. The Countess, while waiting for her husband and her son, was playing solitaire in company with an old gentlewoman who was living with them. Denisov, his eyes shining and his hair ruffled, was seated at the piano, one leg thrown back, and was touching the keys with his thick fingers, striking chords as he rolled his eyes and tried to find, with the aid of his slight and husky yet true voice, an accompaniment for the quatrain he had just composed in honor of "The Enchantress":

> Enchantress, oh, say whence the power flows
> Which in my heart awakens ecstasies;
> Oh, tell me whence is fed the fire that glows,
> And in my heart enkindles melodies.

Passion made his voice vibrate and he fixed his black eyes on

Natasha, who was upset but happy. "That's charming! It's just right!" she cried. "Now, one more stanza!"

"Everything here is just as before," thought Nicolas to himself.

"Ah, here he is!" cried Natasha.

"Is father at home?" he asked.

"How glad I am that you've come," said Natasha, not answering him. "We're having such a good time. Vasily Dmitrich is staying one more day just to please me."

"No, father's not home yet," said Sonia.

"Nicolas, come here, my dear," cried his mother from the other end of the room.

Nicolas went to kiss her hand and sat down without a word next to her, following with his eyes the fingers which laid out the cards for another game. The noise of laughter and voices reached them from the other side. "Come, now," Denisov was saying, "don't make me coax you. Sing me the barcarolle, now do!"

The Countess looked at her son who was still silent. "What is the matter?" she asked.

"Nothing," he replied as if weary of a repetitious question. "Is father coming home soon?"

"I expect so."

"Nothing here is different!" he kept thinking to himself. "They know nothing. . . . Oh, where can I hide my head!" And he returned to the piano where Sonia was beginning to play the introduction to the barcarolle. Natasha was about to sing and Denisov was looking at her with a consuming gaze.

Nicolas started to walk up and down. "What an idea to make her sing! What *can* she sing? What do they find so enjoyable about it all!"

Sonia struck a chord. "Oh God, oh God!" he was saying to himself. "I am a lost creature, a dishonored man. Yes. All I can do now is to blow my brains out. Why must they sing? Leave this place? But after all, why shouldn't they go on—it's all one to me." And Nicolas, somber and sullen, kept walking up and down and avoiding his sisters' eyes.

"Nicolas, what's the matter?" Sonia's glance seemed to be asking, for she had at once noticed his gloom. Natasha too, with her quick instinct, had been struck by her brother's mood, but her mind was so far from any idea of sadness, pain, or remorse, her gaiety was so exuberant, that (as so often happens in youth) she soon stopped wondering about him. "I'm having too good a time," she thought, "to spoil my fun by trying to share a worry not my own. And then, I'm probably wrong and he's as happy as I."

"Now, Sonia!" said she, springing into the middle of the room, where she imagined that the acoustics ought to be better. She lifted her head and let her arms hang at her sides, like a dancer, and seemed to be saying in answer to Denisov's passionate look: "This, this is the way I am!"

"What is she so pleased about?" thought Nicolas. "Why isn't she bored?"

Natasha took the first note, her chest filled and heaved, her eyes took on a deep expression. At that moment she was not thinking of anything or anybody. Her mouth, half open and smiling, was pouring forth sounds such as any throat can emit at any time, with exactly the same inflexions, and such as on a thousand occasions will leave us absolutely cold, but which make us shiver and weep with emotion on the thousand and first.

Natasha had seriously studied singing during the winter, chiefly on account of Denisov, whom her voice enraptured to the seventh heaven. She no longer sang like a child and one no longer heard the clumsy efforts of a pupil. But although of uncommon range, her voice—according to the connoisseurs—was still insufficiently trained. And yet in spite of their critique the connoisseurs involuntarily yielded to the pleasure which this selfsame voice afforded, even when it showed itself incapable of sustained breath or other virtuoso feats. Long after it had ceased to resound they would have asked nothing better than to hear it again. One could sense in it a sweet virginal purity, an unconsciousness of its power, and an unlabored velvety softness, which no one would have wanted to change in any way, for fear of breaking the spell.

"What, what is this?" thought Nicolas, wide-eyed in surprise at hearing her sing in this fashion. "What's happened to her? How she sings!" Forgetting himself, he waited for each successive note with feverish impatience, and for a time he knew nothing else in the world but the passage in three-four time of *"O mio crudele affetto."* [1] "What an absurd life is ours!" thought he. "Misfortunes, money, Dolohov, hatred, honor—none of that matters. Here is reality: Natasha, my little dove, let's see you reach the high note—she's done it! God be praised!" To reinforce the note he found himself singing it with her. "How nice! I hit it too!" And the vibration of his note awoke in his soul whatever was best and purest. Beside this superhuman, this divine sensation, what mattered his gambling loss and his pledged word? Foolishness! One could kill and rob and still be happy.

WAR AND PEACE (1869)

[1] "Oh, what cruel pain I feel." The various musical indications given in this passage are hard to reconcile with one another and make the identification of this barcarolle difficult, if indeed the reference is to an actual piece.

THOMAS LOVE PEACOCK

≫≫≫ ≪≪≪

Wine, Woman, and Song

≫≫ ──────────────────────────────── ≪≪

The father-in-law of George Meredith was a classical scholar, a gourmet, and a musician. His operatic and other musical reviews still make good reading, and his novels in dialogue form are interspersed with musical talk and musical events. The chapters that follow are from his last and maturest work.

≫≫ ──────────────────────────────── ≪≪

I

I love not him, who o'er the wine cup's flow
Talks but of war, and strife, and scenes of woe:
But him who can the Muses' gift employ,
To mingle love and song with festal joy.[1]

The dinner and dessert passed away. The ladies retired to the drawing room: the gentlemen discoursed over their wine. Mr. Mac-Borrowdale pronounced a eulogium on the port, which was cordially echoed by the divine in regard to the claret.

MR. FALCONER: Doctor, your tastes and sympathies are very much with the Greeks; but I doubt if you would have liked their wine. Condiments of sea water and turpentine must have given it an odd flavor; and mixing water with it, in the proportion of three to one, must have reduced the strength of merely fermented liquor to something like the smallest ale of Christophero Sly.

THE REV. DR. OPIMIAN: I must say I should not like to put either salt water or turpentine into this claret: they would not improve its bouquet; nor to dilute it with any portion of water: it has to my mind, as it is, just the strength it ought to have, and no more. But the Greek taste was so exquisite in all matters in which we can bring

───────────

[1] Peacock's translation from Anacreon.

84

it to the test, as to justify a strong presumption that in matters in which we cannot test it, it was equally correct. Salt water and turpentine do not suit our wine: it does not follow that theirs had not in it some basis of contrast, which may have made them pleasant in combination. And it was only a few of their wines that were so treated.

LORD CURRYFIN: Then it could not have been much like their drink of the present day. "My master cannot be right in his mind," said Lord Byron's man Fletcher, "or he would not have left Italy, where we had everything, to go to a country of savages; there is nothing to eat in Greece but tough billy goats, or to drink but spirits of turpentine."

THE REV. DR. OPIMIAN: There is an ambiguous present, which somewhat perplexes me, in an epigram of Rhianus: "Here is a vessel of half wine, half turpentine, and a singularly lean specimen of kid: the sender, Hippocrates, is worthy of all praise." [2] Perhaps this was a doctor's present to a patient. Alcaeus, Anacreon, and Nonnus could not have sung as they did under the inspiration of spirit of turpentine. We have from Athenaeus, and Pliny, and the old comedians, that the Greeks had a vast variety of wine, enough to suit every variety of taste. I infer the unknown from the known. We know little of their music. I have no doubt it was as excellent in its kind as their sculpture.

MR. MINIM: I can scarcely think that, sir. They seem to have had only the minor key, and to have known no more of counterpoint than they did of perspective.

THE REV. DR. OPIMIAN: Their system of painting did not require perspective. Their main subject was on one foreground. Buildings, rocks, trees, served simply to indicate, not to delineate, the scene.

MR. FALCONER: I must demur to their having only the minor key. The natural ascent of the voice is in the major key, and with their exquisite sensibility to sound they could not have missed the obvious expression of cheerfulness. With their three scales, diatonic, chromatic, and enharmonic, they must have exhausted every possible expression of feeling. Their scales were in true intervals; they had

[2] From the Palatine Anthology.

really major and minor tones; we have neither, but a confusion of both. They had both sharps and flats: we have neither, but a mere set of semitones, which serve for both. In their enharmonic scale the fineness of their ear perceived distinctions which are lost on the coarseness of ours.

MR. MINIM: With all that they never got beyond melody. They had no harmony, in our sense. They sang only in unisons and octaves.

MR. FALCONER: It is not clear that they did not sing in fifths. As to harmony in one sense, I will not go so far as to say with Ritson that the only use of the harmony is to spoil the melody; but I will say that to my taste a simple accompaniment, in strict subordination to the melody, is far more agreeable than that Niagara of sound under which it is now the fashion to bury it.

MR. MINIM: In that case, you would prefer a song with a simple pianoforte accompaniment to the same song on the Italian stage.

MR. FALCONER: A song sung with feeling and expression is good, however accompanied. Otherwise, the pianoforte is not much to my mind. All its intervals are false, and temperament is a poor substitute for natural intonation. Then its incapability of sustaining a note has led, as the only means of producing effect, to those infinitesimal subdivisions of sound, in which all sentiment and expression are twittered and frittered into nothingness.

THE REV. DR. OPIMIAN: I quite agree with you. The other day a band passed my gate playing "The Campbells are coming"; but instead of the fine old Scotch lilt, and the emphasis on "Oho! oho!" what they actually played was, "The Ca-a-a-a-ampbells are co-o-o-o-ming, Oh-o-ho-o-o! Oh-o-ho-o-o"; I thought to myself, There is the essence and quintessence of modern music. I like the old organ music such as it was, when there were no keys but C and F, and every note responded to a syllable. The effect of the prolonged and sustained sound must have been truly magnificent:

> Where, through the long-drawn aisle and fretted vault,
> The pealing anthem swelled the note of praise. . . .

Who cares to hear sacred music on a piano?

MR. MINIM: Yet I must say that there is a great charm in that brilliancy of execution which is an exclusively modern and very modern accomplishment.

LORD CURRYFIN, *who, having observed Mr. MacBorrowdale's determination not to be drawn into an argument, amused himself with asking his opinion on all subjects:* What is your opinion, Mr. MacBorrowdale?

MR. MACBORROWDALE: I hold to the opinion I have already expressed, that this is as good a glass of port as ever I tasted.

LORD CURRYFIN: I mean your opinion of modern music and musical instruments.

MR. MACBORROWDALE: The organ is very good for psalms, which I never sing, and the pianoforte for jigs, which I never dance. And if I were not to hear either of them from January to December, I should not complain of the privation.

LORD CURRYFIN: You are an utilitarian, Mr. MacBorrowdale. You are all for utility—public utility—and you see none in music.

MR. MACBORROWDALE: Nay, not exactly so. If devotion is good, if cheerfulness is good, and if music promotes each of them in proper time and place, music is useful. If I am as devout without the organ, and as cheerful without the piano, as I ever should be with them, that may be the defect of my head or my ear. I am not for forcing my tastes or no-tastes on other people. Let every man enjoy himself in his own way, while he does not annoy others. I would not deprive you of your enjoyment of a brilliant symphony, and I hope you would not deprive me of my enjoyment of a glass of old wine.

THE REV. DR. OPIMIAN:

Tres mihi convivæ prope dissentire videntur,
Poscentes vario multum diversa palato.[3]

MR. FALCONER: Nor our reverend friend of the pleasure of a classical quotation.

THE REV. DR. OPIMIAN: And the utility, too, sir: for I think I am indebted to one for the pleasure of your acquaintance.

[3] Three guests dissent most widely in their wishes:
With different taste they call for different dishes. [Peacock's note.]

MR. FALCONER: When you did me the honor to compare my house to the Palace of Circe. The gain was mine.

MR. PALLET: You admit, sir, that the Greeks had no knowledge of perspective.

THE REV. DR. OPIMIAN: Observing that they had no need of it. Their subject was a foreground like a relievo. Their background was a symbol, not a representation. "No knowledge" is perhaps too strong. They had it where it was essential. They drew a peristyle, as it appeared to the eye, as accurately as we can do. In short, they gave to each distinct object its own proper perspective, but to separate objects they did not give their relative perspective, for the reason I have given, that they did not need it.

MR. FALCONER: There is to me one great charm in their painting, as we may judge from the specimens in Pompeii, which, though not their greatest works, indicate their school. They never crowded their canvas with figures. They presented one, two, three, four, or at most five persons, preferring one and rarely exceeding three. These persons were never lost in the profusion of scenery, dress, and decoration. They had clearly defined outlines, and were agreeable objects from any part of the room in which they were placed.

MR. PALLET: They must have lost much in beauty of detail.

THE REV. DR. OPIMIAN: Therein is the essential difference of ancient and modern taste. Simple beauty—of idea in poetry, of sound in music, of figure in painting—was their great characteristic. Ours is detail in all these matters, overwhelming detail. We have not grand outlines for the imagination of the spectator or hearer to fill up: his imagination has no play of its own: it is overloaded with *minutiae* and kaleidoscopical colors.

LORD CURRYFIN: Detail has its own beauty. I have admired a Dutch picture of a butcher's shop, where all the charm was in detail.

THE REV. DR. OPIMIAN: I cannot admire anything of the kind. I must take pleasure in the thing represented before I can derive any from the representation.

MR. PALLET: I am afraid, sir, as our favorite studies all lead us to extreme opinions, you think the Greek painting was the better for not having perspective, and the Greek music for not having harmony.

THE REV. DR. OPIMIAN: I think they had as much perspective and as much harmony as was consistent with that simplicity which characterized their painting and music as much as their poetry.

LORD CURRYFIN: What is your opinion, Mr. MacBorrowdale?

MR. MACBORROWDALE: I think you may just buz that bottle before you.

LORD CURRYFIN: I mean your opinion of Greek perspective?

MR. MACBORROWDALE: Troth, I am of opinion that a bottle looks smaller at a distance than when it is close by, and I prefer it as a full-sized object in the foreground.

LORD CURRYFIN: I have often wondered that a gentleman so well qualified as you are to discuss all subjects should so carefully avoid discussing any.

MR. MACBORROWDALE: After dinner, my lord, after dinner. I work hard all the morning at serious things, sometimes till I get a headache, which, however, does not often trouble me. After dinner I like to crack my bottle and chirp and talk nonsense, and fit myself for the company of Jack of Dover.

LORD CURRYFIN: Jack of Dover! Who was he?

MR. MACBORROWDALE: He was a man who traveled in search of a greater fool than himself, and did not find him.[4]

THE REV. DR. OPIMIAN: He must have lived in odd times. In our days he would not have gone far without falling in with a teetotaler, or a decimal coinage man, or a school-for-all man, or a competitive examination man, who would not allow a drayman to lower a barrel into a cellar unless he could expound the mathematical principles by which he performed the operation.

MR. MACBORROWDALE: Nay, that is all pragmatical fooling. The fooling Jack looked for was jovial fooling, fooling to the top of his bent, excellent fooling, which, under the semblance of folly, was both

---

[4] *Jacke of Dover His Quest of Inquirie, or His Privy Search for the Veriest Foole in England.* London, 1604. Reprinted for the Percy Society, 1842. [Peacock's note.]

merry and wise. He did not look for mere unmixed folly, of which there never was a deficiency. The fool he looked for was one which it takes a wise man to make—a Shakespearean fool.

THE REV. DR. OPIMIAN: In that sense he might travel far, and return, as he did in his own day, without having found the fool he looked for.

MR. MACBORROWDALE: A teetotaler! Well! He is the true Heautontimorumenos, the self-punisher, with a jug of toast-and-water for his Christmas wassail. So far his folly is merely pitiable, but his intolerance makes it offensive. He cannot enjoy his own tipple unless he can deprive me of mine. A fox that has lost his tail. There is no tyrant like a thorough-paced reformer. I drink to his own reformation.

MR. GRYLL: He is like Bababec's faquir, who sat in a chair full of nails, *pour avoir de la considération*. But the faquir did not want others to do the same. He wanted all the consideration for himself, and kept all the nails for himself. If these meddlers would do the like by their toast-and-water, nobody would begrudge it them.

THE REV. DR. OPIMIAN: Now, sir, if the man who has fooled the greatest number of persons to the top of their bent were to be adjudged the fittest companion for Jack of Dover, you would find him in a distinguished meddler with everything who has been for half a century the merry-andrew of a vast arena, which he calls moral and political science, but which has in it a dash of everything that has ever occupied human thought.

LORD CURRYFIN: I know whom you mean; but he is a great man in his way, and has done much good.

THE REV. DR. OPIMIAN: He has helped to introduce much change; whether for good or for ill remains to be seen. I forgot he was your lordship's friend. I apologize, and drink to his health.

LORD CURRYFIN: Oh, pray, do not apologize to me! I would not have my friendships, tastes, pursuits, and predilections interfere in the slightest degree with the fullest liberty of speech on all persons and things. There are many who think with you that he is a moral and political Jack of Dover. So be it. Time will bring him to his level.

MR. MACBORROWDALE: I will only say of the distinguished personage that Jack of Dover would not pair off with him. This is the
true universal science, the oracle of *La Dive Bouteille.*

MR. GRYLL: It is not exactly Greek music, Mr. Minim, that you
are giving us for our Aristophanic choruses.

MR. MINIM: No, sir; I have endeavored to give you a good selection, as appropriate as I can make it.

MR. PALLET: Neither am I giving you Greek painting for the
scenery. I have taken the liberty to introduce perspective.

THE REV. DR. OPIMIAN: Very rightly both, for Aristophanes in London.

MR. MINIM: Besides, sir, we must have such music as your young
ladies can sing.

THE REV. DR. OPIMIAN: Assuredly; and so far as we have yet heard
them rehearse, they sing it delightfully.

After a little more desultory conversation, they adjourned to the
drawing rooms.

II

> This, this is life, when pleasure drives out care.
> Short is the span of time we each may share.
> Today, while love, wine, song, the hours adorn,
> Today we live: none know the coming morn.[5]

LORD CURRYFIN's assiduities to Miss Gryll had discomposed Mr.
Falconer more than he chose to confess to himself. Lord Curryfin,
on entering the drawing rooms, went up immediately to the young
lady of the house; and Mr. Falconer, to the amazement of the reverend doctor, sat down in the outer drawing room on a sofa by the
side of Miss Ilex, with whom he entered into conversation.

In the inner drawing room some of the young ladies were engaged with music, and were entreated to continue their performance. Some of them were conversing or looking over new publica-
tions.

[5] Peacock's translation from the Palatine Anthology.

After a brilliant symphony, performed by one of the young visitors, in which runs and crossings of demisemiquavers in *tempo prestissimo* occupied the principal share, Mr. Falconer asked Miss Ilex how she liked it.

MISS ILEX: I admire it as a splendid piece of legerdemain; but it expresses nothing.

MR. FALCONER: It is well to know that such things can be done; and when we have reached the extreme complications of art, we may hope to return to Nature and simplicity.

MISS ILEX: Not that it is impossible to reconcile execution and expression. Rubini identified the redundancies of ornament with the overflowings of feeling, and the music of Donizetti furnished him most happily with the means of developing this power. I never felt so transported out of myself as when I heard him sing *Tu che al ciel spiegasti l' ali.*

MR. FALCONER: Do you place Donizetti above Mozart?

MISS ILEX: Oh, surely not. But for supplying expressive music to a singer like Rubini, I think Donizetti has no equal; at any rate no superior. For music that does not require, and does not even suit, such a singer, but which requires only to be correctly interpreted to be universally recognized as the absolute perfection of melody, harmony, and expression, I think Mozart has none. Beethoven perhaps: he composed only one opera, *Fidelio;* but what an opera that is! What an effect in the sudden change of the key, when Leonora throws herself between her husband and Pizarro: and again, in the change of the key with the change of the scene, when we pass from the prison to the hall of the palace! What pathos in the songs of affection, what grandeur in the songs of triumph, what wonderful combinations in the accompaniments, where a perpetual stream of counter-melody creeps along in the bass, yet in perfect harmony with the melody above!

MR. FALCONER: What say you to Haydn?

MISS ILEX: Haydn has not written operas, and my principal experience is derived from the Italian theater. But his music is essentially dramatic. It is a full stream of perfect harmony in subjection to exquisite melody; and in simple ballad strains, that go direct to the heart, he is almost supreme and alone. Think of that air with which every one is familiar, "My mother bids me bind my hair": the graceful flow of the first part, the touching effect of the semitones in the second; with true intonation and true expression, the less such an air is accompanied the better.

MR. FALCONER: There is a beauty and an appeal to the heart in ballads which will never lose its effect except on those with whom the pretense of fashion overpowers the feeling of Nature.[6]

MISS ILEX: It is strange, however, what influence that pretense has, in overpowering all natural feelings, not in music alone.

"Is it not curious," thought the doctor, "that there is only one old woman in the room, and that my young friend should have selected her for the object of his especial attention?"

But a few simple notes struck on the ear of his young friend, who rose from the sofa and approached the singer. The doctor took his place to cut off his retreat.

Miss Gryll, who, though a proficient in all music, was particularly partial to ballads, had just begun to sing one.

THE DAPPLED PALFREY [7]

"My traitorous uncle has wooed for himself:
Her father has sold her for land and for pelf:
My steed, for whose equal the world they might search,
In mockery they borrow to bear her to church.

"Oh! there is one path through the forest so green,
Where thou and I only, my palfrey, have been:
We traversed it oft, when I rode to her bower
To tell my love tale through the rift of the tower.

"Thou know'st not my words, but thy instinct is good:
By the road to the church lies the path through the wood:
Thy instinct is good, and her love is as true:
Thou wilt see thy way homeward, dear palfrey, adieu."

[6] Braham [the singer] said something like this to a Parliamentary Committee on Theaters, in 1832. [Peacock's note.]

[7] Founded on *Le Vair Palefroi*: among the *Fabliaux* published by Barbazan. [Peacock's note.]

They feasted full late and full early they rose,
And churchward they rode more than half in a doze:
The steed in an instant broke off from the throng,
And pierced the green path, which he bounded along.

In vain was pursuit, though some followed pell-mell:
Through bramble and thicket they floundered and fell.
On the backs of their coursers some dozed as before,
And missed not the bride till they reached the church door.

The knight from his keep on the forest-bound gazed:
The drawbridge was down, the portcullis was raised:
And true to his hope came the palfrey amain,
With his only loved lady, who checked not the rein.

The drawbridge went up: the portcullis went down:
The chaplain was ready with bell, book, and gown:
The wreck of the bride-train arrived at the gate,
The bride showed the ring, and they muttered "Too late!"

"Not too late for a feast, though too late for a fray;
What's done can't be undone: make peace while you may":
So spake the young knight, and the old ones complied;
And quaffed a deep health to the bridegroom and bride.

Mr. Falconer had listened to the ballad with evident pleasure. He turned to resume his place on the sofa, but, finding it preoccupied by the doctor, he put on a look of disappointment which seemed to the doctor exceedingly comic.

"Surely," thought the doctor, "he is not in love with the old maid."

Miss Gryll gave up her place to a young lady, who in her turn sang a ballad of a different character.

LOVE AND AGE

I played with you 'mid cowslips blowing,
When I was six and you were four;
When garlands weaving, flower-balls throwing,
Were pleasures soon to please no more.
Through groves and meads, o'er grass and heather,
With little playmates, to and fro,

We wandered hand in hand together;
But that was sixty years ago.

You grew a lovely roseate maiden,
And still our early love was strong;
Still with no care our days were laden,
They glided joyously along;
And I did love you very dearly,
How dearly words want power to show;
I thought your heart was touched as nearly;
But that was fifty years ago.

Then other lovers came around you,
Your beauty grew from year to year.
And many a splendid circle found you
The center of its glittering sphere.
I saw you then, first vows forsaking,
On rank and wealth your hand bestow;
Oh, then I thought my heart was breaking,
But that was forty years ago.

And I lived on, to wed another;
No cause she gave me to repine;
And when I heard you were a mother,
I did not wish the children mine.
My own young flock, in fair progression
Made up a pleasant Christmas row:
My joy in them was past expression,
But that was thirty years ago.

You grew a matron plump and comely,
You dwelt in fashion's brightest blaze;
My earthly lot was far more homely;
But I too had my festal days.
No merrier eyes have ever glistened
Around the hearthstone's wintry glow,
Than when my youngest child was christened,
But that was twenty years ago.

Time passed. My eldest girl was married,
And I am now a grandsire gray;
One pet of four years old I've carried
Among the wild-flowered meads to play.

In our old fields of childish pleasure,
Where now, as then, the cowslips blow,
She fills her basket's ample measure,
And that is not ten years ago.

But though first love's impassioned blindness
Has passed away in colder light,
I still have thought of you with kindness,
And shall do, till our last good night.
The ever-rolling silent hours
Will bring a time we shall not know,
When our young days of gathering flowers
Will be an hundred years ago.

MISS ILEX: That is a melancholy song. But of how many first loves is it the true tale! And how many are far less happy!

THE REV. DR. OPIMIAN: It is simple, and well sung, with a distinctness of articulation not often heard.

MISS ILEX: That young lady's voice is a perfect contralto. It is singularly beautiful, and I applaud her for keeping within her natural compass, and not destroying her voice by forcing it upwards, as too many do.

THE REV. DR. OPIMIAN: Forcing, forcing seems to be the rule of life. A young lady who forces her voice into *altissimo,* and a young gentleman who forces his mind into a receptacle for a chaos of crudities, are pretty much on a par. Both do ill, where, if they were contented with attainments within the limits of natural taste and natural capacity, they might both do well. As to the poor young men, many of them become mere crammed fowls, with the same result as Hermogenes, who, after astonishing the world with his attainments at seventeen, came to a sudden end at the age of twenty-five, and spent the rest of a long life in hopeless imbecility.

MISS ILEX: The poor young men can scarcely help themselves. They are not held qualified for a profession unless they have overloaded their understanding with things of no use in it; incongruous things too, which could never be combined into the pursuits of natural taste.

THE REV. DR. OPIMIAN: Very true. Brindley would not have passed as a canal-maker, nor Edward Williams [8] as a bridge-builder. I saw the other day some examination papers which would have infallibly excluded Marlborough from the army and Nelson from the navy. I doubt if Haydn would have passed as a composer before a committee of lords like one of his pupils, who insisted on demonstrating to him that he was continually sinning against the rules of counterpoint; on which Haydn said to him, "I thought I was to teach you, but it seems you are to teach me, and I do not want a preceptor," and thereon he wished his lordship a good morning.

GRYLL GRANGE (1861)

[8] Builder of Pontypridd, in Wales, which takes its name from the remarkable one-arch bridge over the Taff (1755).

ROBERT SCHUMANN

》》》 《《《

A Meeting of the House of David

I

Toward the end of the year 1833 there were to be found in Leipzig a number of mostly younger musicians, who foregathered of an evening, casually, first of all for conviviality and companionship, but also and not less for the exchange of thoughts upon a subject which to them was like food and drink—the art of music. One cannot say that the conditions of music then obtaining in Germany were particularly encouraging. On the stage Rossini was king, at the piano Herz and Hunten ruled almost exclusively. And yet only a few years had passed since Beethoven, C. M. von Weber, and Franz Schubert had lived among us. To be sure Mendelssohn's star was rising, and wonderful things were being reported of a Pole named Chopin. But it was only later that these two produced lasting effects.

One day the notion occurred to our young hotheads, why not cease to look on idly, and instead pitch in so that things may improve; pitch in, so that the poetry of our art may come again into honor.

Thus did the first portions of a new journal of music [1] come into being. But the joy of a firm union of young energies was not vouchsafed for long. Death took its toll upon one of the best-beloved members, Ludwig Schunke. A few others at various times left Leipzig. The enterprise was for a while on the point of dissolution when one of the group—indeed the whimsiest of the brotherhood, a musician who had so far dreamed his life away at the key-

[1] The famous *Neue Zeitschrift für Musik,* which lasted from 1834 to the Second World War.

board rather than dealt with books—made up his mind to take over the editorship of the journal. He kept it for ten years, that is, until 1844.[2] The result was a series of essays, from which the following [is] taken. Most of the views expressed in them are still his views today. What he feared and hoped as he wrote about the several aspects of art has been proved true by the passage of time.

But another society must be mentioned here, a society which was more than secret, since it existed solely in the mind of its founder—the society of the House of David.[3] It appeared to set forth, not unsuitably, the different aspects of the philosophy of art, and to reveal the contradictory characters of artists. Of these last Florestan and Eusebius were the most strongly marked, while Master Raro served as mediator between them. This company of the House of David runs like a red thread through the pages of the periodical, connecting "truth and poetry" in humorous fashion. Later, these good companions, whose appearance had not displeased the early readers of the journal, disappeared entirely from its pages. From the moment when a "Peri" led them away to a remote sphere, no one has seen any literary work from their hands.[4]

May these collected pages, mirroring as they do an exciting period, also help remind my contemporaries of many events now almost washed away by the flowing stream of time.

II[5]

Eusebius just walked in quietly through the door. You know that ironic smile on his pale face which he makes so teasing. I was sitting with Florestan at the keyboard. Florestan, as you know, is one of those rare musicians who, as it were, anticipate, forestall, what-

[2] This was Schumann himself.

[3] So named in honor of the Psalmist, and with his wars against the Philistines in mind.

[4] An allusion to Schumann's score *Paradise and the Peri* (1843).

[5] This essay, the first important recognition of Chopin as composer, appeared in 1831.

ever is new, unusual, and forward-looking. Today, however, he was
headed for a surprise. With the words, "Hats off, gentlemen, a new
genius!" Eusebius put down a piece of music on the stand. We were
not to look at the title. I leafed absent-mindedly through the notes
—a secret enjoyment of soundless music which has something magical about it. I feel, moreover, that every composer has his own peculiar note pattern for the eye: Beethoven looks different on paper
from Mozart, something like the difference between Jean-Paul's
prose [6] and Goethe's. Here in this new work it seemed as if strange
eyes were staring wonderingly at me—flowerlike eyes, eyes of basi-
lisks, of peacocks, of maidens. In places the pattern grew clearer: I
thought I discerned Mozart's *"La ci darem la mano"* [7] intertwined
with a hundred chords. Leporello seemed to wink at me as Don Juan
flew past in his white cloak.

"Now play it," urged Florestan. Eusebius complied, while we
listened, huddling in a window seat. Eusebius played like one possessed and exhibited before the mind's eye an endless number of
the most living figures of life. It was as if the enthusiasm of the
moment had stretched the power of his fingers beyond the common
limits. To be sure, the performer's reward consisted in nothing
more—our heavenly smiles excepted—than in the remark that these
variations must be something by Beethoven or Franz Schubert, supposing these composers to have been virtuosos of the keyboard.
Whereupon he read out from the title page only this:

> *"'La ci darem la mano,'* varied for Pianoforte
> by Frederic Chopin, Work No. 2."

We both exclaimed, "Number Two!" Our faces shone with uncommon astonishment and little could be distinguished among our
random exclamations: "I should say that *is* certainly something!
—Chopin! I've never heard the name.—Who can he be?—A genius,
anyhow!—Whose is the laughter, Zerlina's or Leporello's?"

There ensued a scene which I shan't attempt to describe. Ele-

---

[6] Jean-Paul Richter (1763–1825); see pp. 492–93.

[7] "Hand in hand, we'll go": Don Juan's wooing song to Zerlina in the first
act of Mozart's *Don Giovanni*.

vated by wine, by Chopin, and by discussion, we sallied forth to Master Raro, who laughed uproariously and showed no curiosity about Work Number Two.

"I know you and your newfangled enthusiasms," said he. "Now just bring around your Chopin to my place"—which we promised to do the next day. Eusebius soon said good night, while I remained a while longer with Master Raro. Florestan, who for some time had had no lodging, tramped through the moonlit streets to my house.

About midnight I found him in my room, lying on the sofa, his eyes closed. "Chopin's variations," he muttered as in a dream, "go round and round my head. Certainly," he continued, "the whole piece is at once dramatic and thoroughly Chopinesque. The introduction, however self-contained—can't you just recall Leporello's leaping about in thirds?—seems to me least suited to the whole. But the theme—though why did he write it in B flat?—and the variations, and the finale, and the adagio—those are something: genius oozes from every bar. Of course, my dear Julius, most of the talking is done by Don Juan, Zerlina, Leporello, and Masetto: Zerlina's answer in the theme is full of her loving heart; the first variation should perhaps be called elegant and coquettish—in it the Spanish grandee jests delightfully with the peasant lass. The love-making becomes obvious in the second variation, which is much more familiar, comical, and teasing, exactly as when two lovers nudge each other and giggle together. But how changed is the mood of the third! It conveys pure moonlight and magic spells. Masetto stands off at a distance and swears rather audibly, which, however, does not trouble Don Juan in the least."

"But what about the fourth variation, what do you think of it?"

"Well, Eusebius played it quite cleanly—does it not spring saucy and bold and go straight to the man, although the adagio—it seems to me natural that Chopin should repeat the first part—is in B flat minor, which is most suitable as a moral warning to Don Juan regarding his true intention. It is surely evil and also beautiful that Leporello eavesdrops from behind a bush, laughing and mocking, and that oboes and clarinets magically beckon as they sing out, and that the budding B flat major aptly depicts the first kiss of love. But all this is as nothing compared to the last section—have you a little more wine, Julius?—for that is the whole Mozart finale—champagne corks popping, flasks and glasses tinkling together, and Leporello's voice in between; then the tenacious, vehement spirits and the escaping Don—after which comes the close, which by its beautiful calm truly concludes."

Only in Switzerland, wound up Florestan, had he ever received an impression comparable to this closing scene—when on a beautiful day (he said) the evening sun climbs higher and higher, to the very summit of the mountains and finally the last ray disappears. Then comes a moment such that one thinks one sees the white giants of the Alps closing their eyelids. One can only feel that one has seen a celestial vision. "Now wake up, Julius, wake up to other dreams, and sleep!"

"Dearest Florestan," I replied, "these personal impressions are doubtless to be praised, however subjective they may be. And little as Chopin needs to let his genius overhear programs of this sort, yet I bow my head to that genius, to his endeavor, and to his mastery."

At which point we fell asleep.

COLLECTED ESSAYS (1854)

CHARLES DICKENS

➤➤➤ ⋘⋘⋘

Parting Serenade at Todgers's

"Never, my dear Miss Pecksniffs," said Mrs. Todgers, when they retired to rest on the last night of their stay; "never have I seen an establishment so perfectly broken-hearted as mine is at this moment
of time. I don't believe the gentlemen will be the gentlemen they
were, or anything like it—no, not for weeks to come. You have a
great deal to answer for; both of you."

They modestly disclaimed any wilful agency in this disastrous
state of things, and regretted it very much.

"Your pious Pa, too!" said Mrs. Todgers. "There's a loss! My
dear Miss Pecksniffs, your Pa is a perfect missionary of peace and
love."

Entertaining an uncertainty as to the particular kind of love supposed to be comprised in Mr. Pecksniff's mission, the young ladies
received the compliment rather coldly.

"If I dared," said Mrs. Todgers, perceiving this, "to violate a
confidence which has been reposed in me, and to tell you why I
must beg of you to leave the little door between your room and
mine open tonight, I think you would be interested. But I mustn't
do it, for I promised Mr. Jinkins faithfully that I would be as silent
as the tomb."

"Dear Mrs. Todgers! What can you mean?"

"Why then, my sweet Miss Pecksniffs," said the lady of the house;
"my own loves, if you will allow me the privilege of taking that freedom on the eve of our separation, Mr. Jinkins and the gentlemen
have made up a little musical party among themselves, and *do* intend in the dead of this night to perform a serenade upon the stairs
outside the door. I could have wished, I own," said Mrs. Todgers,

with her usual foresight, "that it had been fixed to take place an hour or two earlier; because, when gentlemen sit up late, they drink, and when they drink, they're not so musical perhaps, as when they don't. But this is the arrangement, and I know you will be gratified, my dear Miss Pecksniffs, by such a mark of their attention."

The young ladies were at first so much excited by the news, that they vowed they couldn't think of going to bed, until the serenade was over. But half an hour of cool waiting so altered their opinion that they not only went to bed, but fell asleep; and were moreover not ecstatically charmed to be awakened some time afterwards by certain dulcet strains breaking in upon the silent watches of the night.

It was very affecting, very. Nothing more dismal could have been desired by the most fastidious taste. The gentleman of a vocal turn was head mute, or chief mourner; Jinkins took the bass; and the rest took anything they could get. The youngest gentleman blew his melancholy into a flute. He didn't blow much out of it, but that was all the better. If the two Miss Pecksniffs and Mrs. Todgers had perished by spontaneous combustion, and the serenade had been in honour of their ashes, it would have been impossible to surpass the unutterable despair expressed in that one chorus, "Go where glory waits thee!" It was a requiem, a dirge, a moan, a howl, a wail, a lament; an abstract of everything that is sorrowful and hideous in sound. The flute of the youngest gentleman was wild and fitful. It came and went in gusts, like the wind. For a long time together he seemed to have left off, and when it was quite settled by Mrs. Todgers and the young ladies, that, overcome by his feelings, he had retired in tears, he unexpectedly turned up again at the very top of the tune, gasping for breath. He was a tremendous performer. There was no knowing where to have him; and exactly when you thought he was doing nothing at all, then he was doing the very thing that ought to astonish you most.

There were several of these concerted pieces; perhaps two or three too many, though that, as Mrs. Todgers said, was a fault on the right side. But even then, even at that solemn moment, when the thrilling sounds may be presumed to have penetrated into the very depths of his nature, if he had any depths, Jinkins couldn't leave the youngest gentleman alone. He asked him distinctly, before the second song began—as a personal favor too, mark the villain in that—not to play. Yes; he said so; not to play. The breathing of the youngest gentleman was heard through the keyhole of the door. He *didn't* play. What vent was a flute for the passions swelling up within his breast? A trombone would have been a world too mild.

The serenade approached its close. Its crowning interest was at hand. The gentleman of a literary turn had written a song on the departure of the ladies, and adapted it to an old tune. They all joined, except the youngest gentleman in company, who, for the reasons aforesaid, maintained a fearful silence. The song (which was of a classical nature) invoked the oracle of Apollo, and demanded to know what would become of Todgers's when CHARITY and MERCY were banished from its walls. The oracle delivered no opinion particularly worth remembering, according to the not infrequent practice of oracles from the earliest ages down to the present time. In the absence of enlightenment on that subject, the strain deserted it, and went on to show that the Miss Pecksniffs were nearly related to Rule Britannia, and that if Great Britain hadn't been an island there could have been no Miss Pecksniffs. And being now on a nautical tack, it closed with this verse:

> All hail to the vessel of Pecksniff the sire!
> And favouring breezes to fan;
> While Tritons flock round it, and proudly admire
> The architect, artist, and man!

As they presented this beautiful picture to the imagination, the gentlemen gradually withdrew to bed to give the music the effect of distance; and so it died away, and Todgers's was left to its repose.

MARTIN CHUZZLEWIT (1843)

FRANZ SCHUBERT

➤➤➤ ◄◄◄

Allegory on the Composer's Life
My Dream

Apart from a few poems, this self-analytic tale is the only literary work
from Schubert's pen.

I was one of many brothers and sisters. We had a good father and
mother. My love for them all was deep. One day my father took us
to a joyous banquet, where my brothers grew very merry; but I was
sad. My father then came to me and bade me taste the delicious
meats. But I could not, whereat my father in his anger banished me
from his sight. I turned on my heel, and with my heart filled with
infinite love for those who rejected it, I wandered off into a far country.

For years I was torn between great love and great sorrow. Then
came the news of my mother's death. I hastened back to see her, and
my father, softened by grief, did not oppose my return. I saw her lying dead. Tears welled from my eyes. I saw her lying there, looking just as she used to, a part of the dear past in which she would have
had us remain and share a common life.

Mourning, we followed her to the grave and saw the coffin slowly
sink. Henceforth I stayed at home as before. Then one day my father took me once more into his pleasure garden. He asked if I
liked it. But the garden looked repulsive to me, and I dared not
reply. Whereupon he asked me a second time, more impatiently,
if I liked the garden. In fear and trembling I said no.

At this my father struck me, and I fled. For the second time I turned
away, and my heart being filled with infinite love for those who
rejected it, I wandered once more into remote climes. Through many

long years I sang my song. But when I wanted to sing of love it turned to sorrow, and when I wanted to sing of sorrow it was transmuted into love.

Thus was I divided between love and sorrow.

And once I was told of a pure maiden who had just died. And around her tomb was a circle formed, within which numerous youths and old men revolved as though in a realm of endless bliss. They spoke softly lest they wake the maiden. Heavenly thoughts seemed to gush ceaselessly out of the maiden's tomb, like burning sparks, and they fell in a soft, noiseless shower on the young men. I longed to walk there too, but people said one could enter the circle only by a miracle. I went forward all the same, slowly and devoutly, eyes lowered upon the gravestone, and before I knew it I was within the circle, whence arose the sweetest melody. Then I felt, compressed as it were into an instant, the full measure of eternal bliss. I saw my father, loving and reconciled. He folded me in his arms and wept. And even more did I.

DIARY (1822)

HONORE DE BALZAC

≫»«≪

Dinner with Gambara

≫»——————————————————————————————«≪

Among the melodramatic tales which Balzac called "Philosophic Studies" and used as vehicles for his views, "Gambara" had the privilege of being first serialized in the *Gazette Musicale,* beginning in July 1837. The following condensation preserves the plot but omits several chapters that "analyze" music both real and imaginary. The action begins in 1831.

≫»——————————————————————————————«≪

I

Having expected to find one of those grotesque characters so often depicted by the German storytellers and put on the stage by librettists, Count Andrea found instead a man whose manner was simple and reserved, and whose bearing and behavior were not only free of any eccentricity but had a touch of nobility. Anything but ostentatious, his clothing yet was more becoming than his extreme poverty seemed to allow, while his linen argued the tender attentions of one who watched over all the details of his existence.

The Count raised moist eyes to Marianna, who did not blush, but gave him a half-smile wherein lay perhaps a trace of pride at the silent respect just paid her. Count Andrea was too much in love not to scan closely any sign of amiability, and he believed himself loved in return when he detected that he had been so well understood. Hence he now concerned himself with winning over the husband rather than the wife, and he trained all his batteries on poor Gambara, who, suspecting nothing, was absent-mindedly swallowing the *bocconi* of mine host, Signor Giardini. Count Andrea opened the conversation with a commonplace, but from the outset noticed that he was dealing with an intellect that, however blind it might seem on one given point, was remarkably competent on all others; the Count saw that he must not so much humor the whims of this astute fellow as try to understand his ideas.

The guests—hungry folk whose wit was sharpened by the spectacle of a meal, good or bad—revealed the most patent hostility toward poor Gambara and were only waiting for the end of the first course to give free rein to their pleasantries. A refugee whose steady ogling betrayed some ambitious projects as regards Marianna, and who apparently thought to enhance his merit in her eyes by casting ridicule on her husband, opened fire in a manner designed to acquaint the Count, as newcomer, with the traditions of the company.

"It's been quite a while," said he with a smile at Marianna, "since we've heard anything about the opera *Mohammed*. Could it be that engrossed by domesticity, seduced by the charms of a pot-roast existence, Paolo Gambara is neglecting his super-human talent, letting his imagination grow tepid, and allowing his genius to cool?"

Gambara knew all those present, and he felt himself inhabiting a sphere so far above them that he made no effort to repel their attacks. He did not answer.

"It is not given to everybody," the journalist went on, "to possess the intelligence requisite for understanding the musical productions of our good friend, and this fact doubtless accounts also for the non-performance of our divine maestro's works before the hospitable Parisians."

"And yet," said a composer of parlor songs, who so far had opened his mouth only to engulf whatever was being passed, "I know people of talent who do not disdain Parisian taste. I have some slight reputation in the musical world," he added with a modest air, "based on my vaudeville turns and drawing-room dances; but this will not keep me from shortly having a solemn mass performed. I composed it for the anniversary of Beethoven's death, and I am confident I shall be better understood in Paris than anywhere else. Will you," said he, turning to Andrea, "do me the honor of attending?"

"I thank you," said the Count. "I feel I am not equipped with the organs necessary for appreciating French melody. But were you the one to be commemorated and were Beethoven writing the mass, I should certainly attend."

This raillery put an end to the prodding of those who wanted to start Gambara on his obsession so as to entertain the newcomer. The Count was quite loath to make the noble and touching madness of the artist a show for vulgar wise men. He kept on chatting unaffectedly with Gambara, the while Signor Giardini's nose popped in and out between the speakers' replies. Each time that Gambara uttered some well-bred witticism or some paradoxical insight, the cook thrust in his head, threw a look of pity toward the musician, one of intelligence toward the Count, and whispered in the latter's ear, "E matto"—mad! But there came a time when the chef had to interrupt his judicious remarks in order to superintend the second course, which he deemed paramount.

During this brief absence Gambara leaned closer to Andrea's ear and said sotto voce, "Our good Giardini is putting our lives in jeopardy today with a dish of his own invention. I urge you to go warily, though his wife lent a hand to its preparation. The poor chap is bent on culinary innovations, the last of which was his undoing. He had to leave Rome without a passport, though he never mentions this. He had bought a well-known restaurant and was retained to cater for the reception of a newly made cardinal. Giardini thought this was his chance to attract attention to himself and he certainly did: that same night saw him accused of having tried to poison the whole papal conclave. He fled, left Rome, left Italy, without even packing. That was the last blow and now—" Gambara placed his finger in the center of his brow and shook his head. "For the rest," he added, "the fellow is very good-natured. My wife tells me we are much obliged to him."

Giardini appeared, carrying with great care a dish which he placed in the middle of the table, then took his seat modestly near Andrea, who was served first. As soon as he had tasted the confection, the Count felt an impassable barrier between the first and second mouthful. He was quite embarrassed; he did not want to disappoint the chef, who was watching him closely. For if a French chef cares not at all about the reception of a dish that has been paid for, an Italian must not be supposed to be so easily satisfied, and sometimes praise itself is not enough. To gain time, Count Andrea warmly commended Giardini and, slipping a gold piece to him under the table, bade him bring a few bottles of champagne, letting him take the credit for this largesse.

When the chef reappeared, all the plates were empty and the praises of the masterly host were ringing in the room. The champagne soon heated the Italians' heads, and the conversation, which had so far been restrained by the presence of a stranger, leaped over the bounds of suspicious reserve and flowed into the open field of political and artistic theorizing. Andrea, who knew no other intoxication than that of love and poetry, soon became the center of attention and adroitly led the discussion to musical matters.

"Please tell me," said he to the composer of dance tunes, "how the Napoleon of parlor songs condescends to undo Palestrina, Pergolese, and Mozart—those poor mortals who are going to give up the ghost in the face of your overwhelming *Mass for the Dead?*"

"Sir," replied the composer, "a musician is always embarrassed for an answer when his true retort calls for the cooperation of a hundred able performers. Mozart, Haydn, and Beethoven themselves are nothing without an orchestra."

"Nothing!" exclaimed the Count. "Yet everyone knows that the immortal author of *Don Giovanni* and the *Requiem* is named Mozart, whereas I am so unlucky as not to know the name of the fertile inventor of the *contredanses* which are so popular in the drawing rooms."

"Music exists independently of performance," said a conductor, who despite his deafness had caught a few words of the wrangle. "By simply opening the score of Beethoven's C Minor Symphony, a musician is at once transported into the realm of the imagination on the golden wings of the theme in G (which the horns soon take up in E). He beholds a new world, lighted up from time to time by dazzling sprays of sunshine, or darkened by the clouds of melancholy, or graced by divine song."

"Beethoven has been surpassed by the moderns," said the song writer with scorn.

"He is not even understood, how can he be surpassed?" asked the Count.

At this point Gambara took a large draught of champagne, matching his libation with a half-smile of approval.

"Beethoven," went on the Count, "has enlarged the scope of instrumental music, and nobody has yet followed in his footsteps."

Gambara protested with a movement of his head.

"His works are especially remarkable by the simplicity of their outline and the way in which this is adhered to. In most composers the instrumentation goes wild and the orchestral effects are designed merely to produce a momentary effect; they do not invariably sustain the architecture of the piece by their regular ordering. But in Beethoven the effects are, as it were, plotted in advance. They are like the disposition of regiments in a plan of battle. This corresponds exactly to the ways of a genius in another genre: in the magnificent historical novels of Walter Scott a character who may seem most extraneous to the action appears at a given moment, for reasons woven into the texture of the plot, and participates in the denouement."

"*E vero*—'tis true," said Gambara, who seemed to regain common sense in inverse ratio to sobriety.

Wishing to carry the test still farther, Andrea suppressed for a moment his real sympathies and began to attack the European reputation of Rossini. He put the Italian school on trial, as is done nightly in a hundred theaters—a trial invariably favorable to the school. It was quite a task. His first words gave rise around him to disapproving murmurs, but neither repeated interruptions, nor frowns, nor outcries, nor looks of pitying scorn stopped this fanatical devotee of Beethoven.

"Just compare," said he, "the sublime productions of the composer I speak of with what is conventionally called the Italian school—

what paucity of ideas, what laxity of style! Those standardized turns, banal cadences, inescapable *fioriture* thrown in haphazard, regard-less of the situation, that monotonous crescendo which Rossini has made fashionable and which now occurs in every piece—in short, these twitterings that make of music a kind of chatter, a cackle with flavor added—all this can sustain interest only in proportion to the singer's virtuosity. The Italian school has lost sight of the high mis-sion of art. Instead of drawing the crowd up to itself, it goes down to their level; it has won applause by appealing to vulgar tastes, which are always in the majority. That is street-corner charlatanism. As for Rossini's operas, which typify this sort of music—not to speak of his followers and imitators—they seem to me only fit to go with the antics of Punch and Judy, and to attract the gaping attention of idlers and vagrants. Why, I'd rather have *French* music! I needn't say more. Long live German music!—when it has melody," he added under his breath.

This harangue summed up the argument Andrea had been main-taining for some time, displaying in its metaphysics the assurance of a somnambulist on a rooftop. Gambara was impressed by so much subtlety, which he followed without losing the thread. He spoke up as soon as the other appeared to have finished. This revived attention among the listeners, some of whom were disposed to leave.

"You are pretty hard on the Italian school," said Gambara with a vivacity heightened by wine, "not that I care very much. Thanks be to God, I have nothing to do with those rather threadbare and more or less melodic tricks. But a man of the world should show a little gratitude to that classic land from which Germany and France drew their first precepts. While the works of Carissimi, Cavalli, Scarlatti, and Rossi were current throughout Italy, the violinists of the Paris Opera enjoyed the singular privilege of playing with their gloves on. Lulli, who extended the sway of harmony and was the first to classify dissonances, came to France and found only two men—a cook and a stone mason—who had enough voice and mu-sicianship to perform his music. He made a tenor of the one and metamorphosed the other into a baritone. At that time—if we except Johann Sebastian Bach—Germany had no idea of music. But, my dear sir," added Gambara in the modest tones of a man who apprehends disdain or ill will, "even though young, you must know all this from study or you would not speak with such assurance."

These last words made some of the company smile—those who had understood nothing of the distinctions drawn by Andrea. Giardini, who was sure the Count had uttered words at random, nudged him slightly for having perpetrated a joke of which he himself wanted to be co-author.

"There is, of course," went on Gambara, "some truth in what you have said. But take care! Your denunciation of Italian sensuality seems to espouse German idealism, which is as dangerous a heresy. If men endowed with senses and imagination, such as yourself, abandon one side only to join its opposite—if you cannot remain neutral—we shall forever incur the sarcasm of those who deny progress and who compare man's powers to a cloth that would not be long enough to cover Signor Giardini's table: to pull at one end would expose the other."

Giardini leaped out of his chair as if stung, but a second thought restored his restaurateur's dignity. He raised his eyes to heaven and once more prodded the Count, who began to think his host was madder than Gambara. The latter's grave and religious manner of speaking about art captivated the Milanese gentleman in the highest degree. Between these two forms of madness, one noble and the other vulgar, and each contemptuous of the other, to the great amusement of the crowd, the Count saw himself at one moment as if torn between sublimity and burlesque—the two facets of all human creations. Mentally snapping the chain of unbelievable accidents that had brought him to this smoky dive, he believed himself a prey to hallucinations and began to look upon Gambara and Giardini as on a pair of abstractions.

Meanwhile the orchestra conductor had discharged a last sally in reply to Gambara, and the guests were leaving amid uproarious laughter. Giardini ran off to make the coffee, which he intended to serve only to the elite of the banqueters. His wife was clearing the table. The Count, seated near the stove, between Marianna and Gambara, was precisely in the situation which the proverbial fool thought so desirable—sensualism on the left and idealism on the right. As for Gambara, he was meeting for the first time a man who did not laugh in his face. He therefore soon dropped generalities from his conversation and began to speak of himself, his life, his works, and the musical regeneration whose messiah he believed himself to be.

"Pray listen, you who so far have refrained from mocking me: I should like to tell you my life—not indeed to show off my constancy, whose source is outside myself, but in order to assert the greater glory of Him who has given me that strength. You seem to be a pious and good man. If you cannot believe me, at least you will pity me. Compassion is of man, faith is of God.

Count Andrea, with a blush, brought back under his chair a wandering foot that had been close to Marianna's, and, dwelling in thought upon her, listened to Gambara.

II

"I was born in Cremona," said the musician, "the son of an instrument maker who was a good enough performer but an even better composer. I was thus enabled when quite young to learn the laws of musical architecture in its double aspect of material and spiritual expression. As an inquisitive child I made observations which later had significance for my mature mind. The French drove my father and me from our house. We were ruined by the war. So that from the age of ten I was a wanderer, like all those who have carried in their heads new ideas about art, science, or politics. Such people, whether by fate or by their own intellectual bent, which is at odds with the conventions that circumscribe the bourgeois, are providentially driven to those places best fitted for their instruction. My passion for music led me from one theater to another through the length and breadth of Italy—living frugally, as the climate permits. At times I played bass in the orchestra; at other times I was among the chorus on the stage, or again under the stage with the mechanics. Thus did I study music in all its effects, testing the power of voice and instrument, searching out their differences and noting their combinations, hearing with the score and applying my father's teachings. I often went from place to place, mending instruments. It was a meager life in a land where the sun always shines, where art is to be seen on every hand, but where there is never any money for the artist. It has been so ever since Rome lost, all but in name, the headship of Christendom. Sometimes welcomed, and sometimes hounded for my poverty, my heart never gave up: I could hear voices within that foretold fame.

"Music seemed to me in its infancy, and I am of that opinion still. All our records of the musical world before the seventeenth century proved to my mind that the ancients had only melody. They knew nothing of harmony and its tremendous resources. Now music is both a science and an art. Its roots plunge into physics and mathematics, and this makes it a science. Physics is part of its being, since sound is a modification of the air, and air has components which find in us corresponding elements that answer, that vibrate sympathetically, and that are capable of enhanced significance by the application of thought. The particles perceived by our ears when they have been set in motion by the musician match ideas within us according to our capacities.

"I believe that the nature of sound is akin to that of light. Sound is light in another form, for both proceed by means of vibrations, which on reaching man are transformed by his nervous centers into thoughts. Like painting, music makes use of bodies endowed with the power of exhibiting this or that aspect of a basic substance in such a way as to produce patterns. In music the instruments play the role of the colors used by the painter. Inasmuch as any sound from a vibrating body is invariably linked with a major third and perfect fifth as overtones; and as it causes grains of dust on a taut parchment to form geometric patterns that are always alike in proportion to the different volumes of the emitted sound—regular patterns when one plays a common chord, irregular when one plays dissonances—I say that music is an art woven into the very heart of Nature. Though the physical laws of sound are but little known, the mathematical are much clearer.[1] Ever since the time when the numerical relations were first studied, harmony has been developed. To it we owe Haydn, Mozart, Beethoven, and Rossini—great geniuses who have produced a more perfect music than their predecessors, in spite of the fact that these were geniuses too. The old masters could sing but lacked the teachings of science to supplement those of art—a noble union, which enables moving melody and powerful harmony to be at one.

"Now if the mathematical laws of harmony have given us these four great musicians, what might we not accomplish if we discovered the physical laws in virtue of which—mark this well—we bring together in proportions as yet unknown the ethereal substance in the air and thereby not only produce music but also perceive the phenomena of light, vegetation, and life itself! Don't you see! Those laws would equip the composer with new powers by making possible instruments far superior to those we have, and perhaps result in a grander harmony than that which governs our present music.[2] If each modified sound corresponds to a given power, the union of all these powers must follow a genuine rule. Composers have so far worked with a substance they did not understand.

"Why do the woodwinds and the brass sound so unlike—say, the bassoon and the French horn—even though they work alike upon the gases of the air? Their unlikeness must result from some different mode of decomposing these gases, or from some manipulation of the basic elements which differs in each, so that they are restored to the air in modified form, according to principles we do not yet know. If we knew these principles, both science and art would benefit: what extends the realm of science helps art.

[1] Balzac is writing some thirty years before Helmholtz's conclusions about the physics of sound. Hence a good deal of the foregoing is wrongly or inadequately stated.

[2] Can this ether instrument be deemed an anticipation of the Theremin?

"Well, of these needful discoveries I have had intimations, and I have completed them. So far," said Gambara with increasing animation, "man has observed effects rather than causes! If causes were once understood, music would become the greatest of the arts. Why? Because it is the art that delves deepest into the soul. Painting shows you only what you see; poetry tells you only what the poet said. Music goes far beyond both: it shapes your thought and wakens your dormant memories. Imagine the thousand souls of an audience as a melody springs from the throat of Pasta,[3] whose performance exactly reproduces Rossini's intention when he wrote. Well, Rossini's phrase conveys, and develops in each soul, a thousand different poems. One sees the figure of a beloved long sought after; another sees some riverbank which he has trod, the sparkling waters and weeping willows, and the vague hopes that danced in those leafy nests. The woman over there recalls the many pangs of one hour's torturing jealousy; this one thinks of the unsatisfied longings of her heart: the glowing colors of her dream about the ideal being to which she gives herself paint for her the delights akin to those of the Woman Nursing an Illusion in the old Roman mosaic. A third foresees the realization that very night of some desire and plunges in thought into the flood of voluptuous sensations which already assault her breast in waves of fire. Music, and music only, has the power of making us draw upon the life within. The other arts give us but well-defined sensations of pleasure.

"But I digress. Those were my first notions. They were vague enough, I daresay, for an inventor always begins with but a dim dawning of new ideas. I carried them about with me in my knapsack, and they helped me to eat in cheerfulness my dry crust, moistened usually at a public fountain. I worked, composed melodies, played them on some instrument or other, and kept on my travels.

"Finally, when I was twenty-two, I came to Venice. There for the first time I found peace of mind. I had a tolerable life. I made the acquaintance of an old Venetian to whom my ideas appealed,

[3] Giuditta Pasta, famous singer of Italian roles (1798–1865).

who encouraged me in my researches, and who had me employed at
the Fenice theater. Living was cheap, my rent small. I lodged in
that famous Capello Palace whence emerged one evening the great
Bianca who became Grand Duchess of Tuscany. I imagined that
some day I too would emerge from obscurity and become famous.
I spent my evenings at the theater and my days at work. But I
struck disaster. The performance of an opera of which I had composed the score was a fiasco. My music for *The Martyrs* [4] proved
unintelligible. Give the Italians some Beethoven, and they lose
their bearings. None of them had the patience to stand the preparation of effects, consisting of the development of different motives,
played by separate instruments, which were then united in a grand
ensemble. I had counted on the success of *The Martyrs,* for we devotees of the diaphanous goddess Hope have a way of being too
sanguine.

"When a man thinks he is destined to accomplish great things
he finds it hard to keep his projects dark. A bushel with a light
under it usually has chinks through which a glimmer can be seen.
In the house where I lodged lived the family of Marianna, and the
hope of winning her hand—for she had smiled upon me—added to
my energies. After my fiasco I fell into a deep melancholy; I knew
full well into what abyss I had fallen. I could foresee a life of
wretched poverty and of struggles in which love would be stifled.
But Marianna acted like Genius itself: she overleaped all difficulties.
I shan't describe that early morsel of happiness which sweetened
my misfortunes. Frightened at my failure, I deemed Italy too un-
comprehending, too sunk in the slumbers of routine and singsong,
to accept the innovations I had in mind. I therefore turned to Germany. While traveling there, going first through Hungary, I heark-
ened to the thousand voices of Nature and tried to translate these
sublime harmonies by means of instruments that I constructed or
altered to that end. This was very costly and soon swallowed up all
our savings. And yet it was our golden time. Germany appreciated
my work, and I have never known anything finer than that period

[4] Ostensibly based on Chateaubriand's historical fiction (1809).

of my life. My tumultuous feelings as Marianna's companion defy analogy; her beauty at that time took on a celestial glow and power. Need I say it? I was blissful. During those moments of weakness I more than once let my passion speak the language of earthly harmonies and composed several melodies of the kind that are so popular in your circle, which are like nothing so much as constructions in Euclid.

"As soon as I was successful I found innumerable obstacles put in my path by my colleagues—all of them envious or stupid. I had heard France spoken of as the country where innovations were well received. I decided to go; my wife found the means, and we arrived in Paris. So far, no one had laughed at me to my very face, but in this dreadful city I had to endure this new kind of torture, to which poverty soon added its harassing cares. We were reduced to lodging in these dismal quarters, where for some months past we have been living solely on Marianna's earnings as seamstress to the wretched prostitutes who haunt this street. Marianna assures me that she has found among these women so much generosity and considerateness which I attribute to the ascendancy of her virtue—such purity that vice itself is bound to respect it."

"Don't give up hope," said Andrea. "It may be that you have come to the end of your trials. Until my efforts joined to yours have brought your works to public notice, you must allow a compatriot, and an artist too, to offer you an advance on the infallible returns of your next score."

"Whatever concerns our practical affairs is in my wife's hands," replied Gambara. "She will decide what we may accept without blushing from a gentleman such as you appear to be. For my part, it has been a long time since I have indulged in extended confidences, and I must beg your leave to withdraw. A melody beckons, comes and goes before me, dancing, naked and shivering, like a damsel who begs her love to return the clothes he has hidden from her. Farewell. I must go and clothe my mistress. My wife will keep you company."

He fled like a man who felt remorse at having wasted precious time, and Marianna in some embarrassment made as if to go with him. Andrea did not dare to hold her back. Giardini came to their joint assistance. "You heard your husband, Signora, ask you to settle some business affairs with my lord the Count."

Marianna sat down again but did not raise her eyes to Andrea, who hesitated to begin.

"Won't the confidence shown me by Signor Gambara," said Andrea, in a voice betraying emotion, "not be matched by his wife's? Won't the beautiful Marianna also tell me the story of her life?"

"My life," answered Marianna, "is the life of the ivy plant. As for the history of my heart, you must suppose me lacking in both modesty and pride if you can ask me to relate it after what you have just heard."

"Whom else can I ask?" exclaimed the Count, whose passion was depriving him of his wits.

"Ask yourself," retorted Marianna. "Either you have already understood me or you never will understand. Just ask yourself."

"I am willing to try—if you will listen. And this hand of yours that I have taken in mine must stay quietly there for as long as my narrative is correct."

"I am listening," said Marianna.

"A woman's life begins with her first love," declared Andrea. "Our dear Marianna began to live only from the day when she first beheld Paolo Gambara. She needed a great passion on which to ponder, and even more a worthy kind of weakness to prop up and protect. The admirable womanly nature which is Marianna's is possibly more inclined toward motherhood than toward love. You sigh? Perhaps I have touched on an unhealed wound in your heart. It was for you a fine part to assume when so young, that of guardian spirit to a great and ill-guided intellect. You said to yourself, 'Paolo will be my genius, I shall be his reason; together we shall form the quasi-divine being called angel—a sublime creature that enjoys and understands, in whom wisdom does not stifle love.'

"In the first glow of youth you could hear those 'thousand voices of Nature' which your poet wanted to reproduce. Enthusiasm held

you when Paolo displayed before you his riches of poetic vision as
he sought to give them form in the exalted but limited speech of
music. You worshiped him while his exalted frenzy carried him far
from you, for you believed that some day all these diverted energies
would be restored to love. You did not suspect the tyrannical and
jealous sway that Thought exerts on the intellect that has once become enamored of it. Before knowing you, Gambara had given himself to that exacting and vindictive mistress with whom you have
vainly been contending for him ever since. For one single instant
you had a glimpse of happiness. When he fell from the heights
where his spirit endlessly soars, Paolo was surprised to find reality
so sweet, and you may have thought that his madness would dissolve in the arms of love. But the dazzling vision by which you
were suddenly transported into the midst of passion shared rendered still more arid and dreary the lonesome path which was
yours.

"In the story your husband has just told us, as in the striking contrast between your countenance and his, I can read the secret
anxiety of your whole life, the painful truths of this ill-matched pair-
ing, of which you have assumed all the hardships. Even though
your conduct has always been heroic, and even though your courage
has not flagged once in the discharge of your taxing duties, it may
still be that in the silence of your solitary nights the heart in your
heaving breast did murmur in protest. Your most crushing burden was your husband's very magnanimity: had he been less noble,
less pure-minded, you might have been able to abandon him; but his
virtues sustained your own. As between your heroism and his, you
might wonder who would give in first. You pursued your own
great task exactly as Paolo pursued his visionary goal. Had you
been upheld and guided solely by love of duty, possibly victory would
have come easier. All you had to do was to deaden your heart within
you and translate your life into the world of abstractions. Religion
would have taken care of the rest. You would have lived by an
idea, like the holy women who extinguish the promptings of nature at the foot of the altar. But the personal attractions of your

Paolo, his elevation of mind, the precious and moving tokens of his tender regard, perpetually denied you the refuge of an ideal world to which virtue invited you. His reality enhanced within you inclinations that kept reviving a strength that was perpetually being drained by struggles with the ghost of love. You had not yet been attacked by doubt! The slightest gleam of hope drew you toward the sweet mirage like the will-o'-the-wisp. But at last the disappointments of many years have made you lose patience: patience would long since have deserted an angel. And today the mirage so faithfully pursued is known for a shadow, not a real body. For a madness which is so close to genius must be incurable in this world.

"Struck by this thought, you have been reflecting on your youth —sacrificed if not wholly lost, and you have come to the bitter recognition that Nature gave you a father when you sought a husband. You have asked yourself whether you have not overdone the duties of the spouse in belonging exclusively to a man who belongs exclusively to science—Marianna, don't take your hand away. What I say is true. You have cast your eyes about you, but you were unfortunately in Paris, and not in Italy where people know best how to love—"

"It is I who must finish the story," cried Marianna. "I would rather say those things myself. I will be frank with you, for I feel I am speaking to my best friend. Yes, it was in Paris that I experienced all that you have so clearly set forth. But when I saw you I was saved, for I had never before met the kind of love I had dreamed about since childhood. My condition and my lodgings necessarily kept me from meeting persons such as you. A few young men whose own position denied them the right to insult me became all the more odious by their levity as regards my position: some mocked my husband for a ridiculous old fool; others tried to ingratiate themselves with him so as to betray him. All of them spoke to me of leaving him; none understood the cult which I have vowed to maintain for that soul, which is remote from us because it is close to heaven. He is the friend, the brother whom I will ever serve, and you are the only one who has grasped what it is that binds me to

him. Tell me that you understand, and that you feel for my
Paolo an interest wholly sincere and without ulterior motive—"

"I accept your good opinion," interrupted Andrea, "but do not
probe further and force me to contradict you. I love you, Marianna,
as one loves in that blessed country which gave us birth. I love you
with all my soul and all my strength, but before laying my love
at your feet I want to be worthy of yours. I shall make one last
attempt to restore to you the man you have loved since your youth.
And while we await victory or defeat, you must accept without
shame the comforts I want to provide for you both. Tomorrow we
shall go together and find him a new place to live. Have you enough
regard for me to let me join you in your role of guardian?"

Marianna was astonished at his generosity. She gave her hand
to the Count, who left quickly, hoping to escape the civilities of
Signor Giardini and his wife.

Two chapters analyze Gambara's own opera Mohammed *and Meyerbeer's* Robert le Diable. *Gambara's extravagant talk and recourse to drink
prove to Marianna and the Count that Gambara is indeed "incurable."*

III

Six years later, in January 1837, quite a few of the musicians who
had had the misfortune of damaging their stringed or wind instruments would carry them to a dreadful and disgusting tenement in the
rue Froidmanteau, where an old Italian named Gambara dwelt
under the eaves. For five years now he had been abandoned by
his wife and left to himself. Many a mishap had befallen him. An
instrument built by him and named "Panharmonicon" had, instead of making his fortune as he hoped, been sold by order to pay
his debts, together with other belongings and a great weight of
music paper. The day after the forced sale his scores were used at
the Central Market to wrap up fruit, butter, and fish. Thus had
the three great operas to which the old man referred, but which his
companion, a former Neapolitan cook now turned junk dealer,

would call a mass of absurdities, been scattered throughout Paris
and been devoured by the suppliers of the grocery trade. No matter; Gambara's landlord had got his arrears of rent and the marshal
received his fee.

According to the secondhand dealer who bought up the leftovers
of the best banquets in town and served them to the whores of the
rue Froidmanteau, Signora Gambara had gone to Italy with a great
Milanese nobleman and no one had any idea what had become of
her. Perhaps fifteen years of penury had led her to encompass the
ruin of her nobleman through reckless spending; at any rate they
adored each other, and the Neapolitan cook had never seen the
like of such a passion.

One evening toward the end of that same January, as Giardini
and one of the prostitutes who had come to his shop for her dinner were chatting about the heavenly Marianna, so beautiful and
chaste and devoted, and yet in the end *just like all the others,* the
Giardinis and the girl saw in the street a bone-thin woman of blackened, dusty mien and nervous, palsied figure, who was scanning the
house numbers.

"Ecco la Marianna!" said Giardini in Italian.

*Gambara takes her back and to eke out their livelihood they play and beg
on the streets at night.*

About nine o'clock one evening [some months later] the beautiful Italian princess Massimilla di Varese took pity on the wretched
pair as she put forty francs into their almsbox. She questioned them
on recognizing from the woman's thanks that she must be a Venetian. Prince Emilio asked them the story of their misfortune and
Marianna told it, without complaining of either fate or man.

"Madame," concluded Gambara, who was sober that day, "we
are victims of our superior gifts. My music is beautiful, but when
music appeals to the mind instead of the senses, it needs an audience composed entirely of geniuses, for they alone have the faculty of
reconceiving it. My misfortune comes from having heeded the concerts that angels give and from supposing that men could under-

stand. The same happens to women when love assumes for them the aspect of the divine: men cease to understand."

That last sentence alone was worth the forty francs that the Princess had given; so she drew from her purse another gold coin and said that she would write to Count Andrea Marcosini.

"Please do not write, Madame," said Marianna, "and may God keep you ever beautiful!"

"Shall we take them on?" inquired the Princess of her husband. "For this man has remained faithful to the IDEAL which we have killed."

GAMBARA (1837–1839)

IVAN TURGENEV

-»» ««-

The Rough Diamond

"Of course, of course, I have no right to be in a bad humor, but as my luck would have it I ran into a 'rough diamond'; I spoke to him and I feel that these rough diamonds, these braggarts, will be the death of me."

"What rough diamond?" asked Litvinov.

"You know: that stout man whom one sees hereabouts and who imagines that he is a composer of genius. 'No doubt,' says he, 'I am a nonentity because I have never studied the art, but I may say, all comparisons aside, that I have more ideas and melodic gift than Meyerbeer.'

"In the first place, I felt like telling him, why the devil haven't you studied? And in the second place, leaving out Meyerbeer, there is twenty times the amount of musical ideas in one of those modest flute players of the least important among German orchestras than in all these self-appointed rough diamonds. Only, the flutist keeps his ideas to himself and does not go pestering the land of Mozart and Haydn with them; whereas our Russian braggart declares himself a genius as soon as he has composed the slightest waltz or parlor song, his thumbs in his waistcoat and a superior smile on his lips. It's the same thing in painting and in everything. Oh, those rough diamonds! I'm fed up with rough diamonds!"

Potugin took off his hat and fanned himself with his handkerchief. "Russia's fine arts," he went on, "Russia's industry! I know Russia's boastfulness and Russia's incapacity, but God forgive me, I've never met her fine arts. Our good little mother country, Orthodox Russia, could sink into Hades without changing or upsetting a button of the world's arrangements. Even the samovar, and sandals of birch bark, and the knout—our most important products—have not been invented by us. Our older inventions come from the Orient, the newer ones come from the West, and we continue to discourse on the originality of our national art and industry! A few young men have even discovered a Russian science—a Russian arithmetic. With us, two and two make four as they do everywhere else, but (it appears) more *gallantly!*"

SMOKE (1867)

CARL-MARIA VON WEBER

※※ ※※

The Wandering Minstrel

Throughout his life Weber planned and wrote fragments of a novel which he called *Tonkünstlerleben*. It was to contain autobiography, criticism, parody, and preachment, in addition to the common ingredients of novels. Below is an outline of the work, based on two of the plans Weber left.

Chapter One. I go on my travels. My reasons therefor. Reception in X's house.

Chapter Two. The town musician. Debate over methods of teaching. Views of other musicians. Quite exhausted by evening at home, he writes to his friend who has been away for some time and is now in Paris. The letter is about his disgust at giving concerts, etc.

Chapter Three. The concert. He gets to know casually a very charming girl, who also wants to travel. That evening the concert hall is empty: performing dogs have just arrived in town. Some of the musicians themselves are at the rival show because they receive twenty-four crowns more. The thought of Emily helps him to play well.

Chapter Four. Arrival in a large city. Feeling lonely and forlorn among strangers. Acquaintance with Diehl. The door slams, someone rushes down the steps upon him, gathers himself for a spring and embraces him warmly, thanking his luck to have fallen on such a one as Felix. "But, my dear sir, are you mad or do you take me for a fool? Who are you?"

"I? As far as I'm concerned, I am nobody at all, but may I ask who you are?"

"I"—sighing—"am also nothing in particular, though people are in the habit of calling men like me 'artists.' I also perform feats, such as bringing a publisher to the point of paying, and the like. If it please you, let's begin now the second year of our acquaintance."

Chapter Seven. Opera excerpts. Masked ball. A. taken for a Prince who loves Emily, saves her, confuses her with another girl.

Chapter Eight. Sleepless night.

Chapter Nine. A. spends a couple of disagreeable days in the most passionate state of mind. Can't even compose; grows a little calmer, looks by chance upon his fancy dress and puts on the coat. Searching mechanically through the pockets, finds the poem from the Devil to Emily and starts to set it to music. The poet helps—conversation about the purport of the song.

Chapter Ten. Some time passes without his seeing Emily again. She has become ill from fright. Diehl tells him that the person he has been getting to know is the pseudo Emily; that the Prince on making the discovery grew enraged and vilified his henchman.

Chapter Eleven. Makes several acquaintances in a new circle. Meets a traveling Declaimer-to-Music. X. accompanies him. Mad insights of the declaimer, a true vagabond. [Felix] is bidden to give lessons to the daughter of a very amiable old gentleman among those present.

Chapter Twelve. Diehl discloses the plan of a musical house of correction. (Marginal note: Three epigrams and the translation of the song *"Non far la smorfiosa."*) [1]

Chapter Thirteen. Goes into the house, finds the room empty, sits down at piano, improvises. The daughter of the house enters unnoticed, stands behind him, and calls out at the end. Startled out of his wits, he turns around and sees Emily. Transports on both sides. Father and mother finally come in, and a wonderful evening of music ensues, rich in warm feeling. Emily puts before him the works of her favorite composer, whom she prefers and venerates above all others: they are his own productions, which he has published under another name. He plays them magnificently, enthusiastically, Emily is enchanted, and he can hardly keep from revealing that he is the author. He sees the Prince on the Esplanade—

---

[1] "Don't act so affected."

a handsome man. Believes himself stared at by him. Upon Imagination and Credulity.

Chapter Fourteen. Goes daily to the house, improvises. Makes frequent use of favorite turns of phrase, by which Emily recognizes him as her composer. Fresh access of joy and amazement at his modesty. Remarks upon certain characteristics of each composer.

Chapter Fifteen. Comes home one day to find an invitation from the Prince. A pleasant circle. The Prince greets him warmly. Distrust on his part. Handsome words from the Prince on the treatment of artists.

Chapter Sixteen. Is drawn to the Prince against his will. Divides his time between him and Emily. Grows daily more intimate with her, though he has not yet dared to speak of the [kidnaping] scene at the masked ball. But he still wears the lilac favor on his breast. By chance Emily sees it on him, recognizes him as her savior, and is overcome with love. Declaration, etc. Protracted love scene.

Chapter Seventeen. Father and mother take notice and are glad. All they ask is that he give up the uncertain life of the artist and follow the career of a civil servant. His indecision. Assaulted by all the others, even by Diehl, who enumerates every disadvantage. Receives an unexpected offer from the Prince to remain as his companion.

Chapter Eighteen. He discloses this to Emily, and as she presses him to accept he tells her the story of the masked ball. Not even this can sway the parents. Vanity of women, even the best, in full luster. Decision to accept.

Chapter Nineteen. New connections. Court life. Reversed relations between Felix and the artists. Strange judgments of the latter upon him as amateur.

Chapter Twenty. The more his dependence on Emily grows (for she seems to be one soul and one mind with him in artistic matters), the more their views on life diverge. She, full of snares and half-truths, seeks indulgently to deceive herself; he, altogether candid and courageously straightforward. Odd, uncomfortable feelings arising between them.

Chapter Nineteen (b).[2] The Prince keeps his distance. Dario, of Italian extraction, is cold and arid—a mathematician contemptuous of music, an atheist under the mask of great sincerity, which at times puts on a devilish smoothness and dexterity. Like the rattlesnake, he attracts Felix to himself; Felix defends him against Diehl, who cannot suffer him at all.

Chapter Twenty (b). Uncomfortable feeling grows in Felix. He feels out of his element. Unfortunate, capricious moods—now unguardedly mad, now sunk in blackest melancholy. Quite incapable of work. It is at this period that the dream comes.

Chapter Twenty-One. Conspiratorial relations, meanwhile, between Emily and the Prince. The weak mother favors these; the father, a cheerful worldling, does not notice enough, takes it too lightly. Finally Felix decides to give up this "career" and everything with it, and to devote himself once more to art. In conclusion: The artist's Last Will and Testament.

A MUSICAL ARTIST'S LIFE (1809–1820)

[2] Alternative chapter from the second version of the outline.

ANN RADCLIFFE

>»-«<

Murder to Music

It was usual in the Gothic novel to introduce the distant strains of a violin, played by ghostly fingers, whenever villainy or death was at hand. Mrs. Radcliffe, the last of the school, combines music and crime in a manner sufficiently plausible to have won the praise of both Walter Scott and Balzac. This very chapter is their choice, though the plot it hatches is the common one designed to prevent the marriage of an unpedigreed girl to the Marchesa's son, the handsome Vivaldi.

> Along the roofs sounds the low peal of death,
> And conscience trembles to the boding note;
> She views his dim form floating o'er the aisles,
> She hears mysterious murmurs in the air,
> And voices, strange and potent, hint the crime
> That dwells in thought, within her secret soul.

The Marchesa repaired, according to her appointment, to the church of San Nicolo, and, ordering her servants to remain with the carriage at a side door, entered the choir, attended only by her woman.

When vespers had concluded, she lingered until nearly every person had quitted the choir, and then walked through the solitary aisles to the north cloister. Her heart was as heavy as her step; for when is it that peace and evil passions dwell together? As she slowly paced the cloisters, she perceived a monk passing between the pillars, who, as he approached, lifted his cowl, and she knew him to be Schedoni.

He instantly observed the agitation of her spirits, and that her purpose was not yet determined, according to his hope. But though his mind became clouded, his countenance remained unaltered; it was grave and thoughtful. The sternness of his vulture eye was, however, somewhat softened, and its lids were contracted by subtilty.

The Marchesa bade her woman walk apart, while she conferred with her confessor.

"This unhappy boy," said she, when the attendant was at some distance, "how much suffering does his folly inflict upon his family! My good Father, I have need of all your advice and consolation. My mind is perpetually haunted by a sense of my misfortune; it has no respite; awake or in my dreams, this ungrateful son alike pursues me! The only relief my heart receives is when conversing with you —my only counselor, my only disinterested friend."

The confessor bowed. "The Marchese is, no doubt, equally afflicted with yourself," said he, "but he is, notwithstanding, much more competent to advise you on this delicate subject than I am."

"The Marchese has prejudices, Father, as you well know; he is a sensible man, but he is sometimes mistaken, and he is incorrigible in error. He has the faults of a mind that is merely well disposed; he is destitute of the discernment and the energy that would make it great. If it is necessary to adopt a conduct that departs in the smallest degree from those common rules of morality which he has cherished, without examining them, from his infancy, he is shocked and shrinks from action. He cannot discriminate the circumstances that render the same action virtuous or vicious. How then, Father, are we to suppose that he would approve the bold action we meditate?"

"Most true!" said the artful Schedoni, with an air of admiration.

"We therefore must not consult him," continued the Marchesa, "lest he should now, as formerly, advance and maintain objections to which we cannot yield. What passes in conversation with you, Father, is sacred, it goes no further."

"Sacred as a confession!" said Schedoni, crossing himself.

"I know not," resumed the Marchesa, and hesitated; "I know not," she repeated in a yet lower tone of voice, "how this girl may be disposed of; and this it is which distracts my mind."

"I marvel much at that," said Schedoni. "With opinions so singularly just, with a mind so accurate yet so bold as you have displayed, is it possible you can hesitate as to what is to be done! You, my daughter, will not prove yourself one of those ineffectual declaimers who can think vigorously but cannot act so! One way only remains for you to pursue, in the present instance; it is the same which your superior sagacity pointed out and taught me to approve. Is it necessary for me to persuade *her* by whom I am convinced! There is only one way."

"And on that I have been long meditating," replied the Marchesa, "and, shall I own my weakness? I cannot yet decide."

"My daughter! can it be possible that you should want courage to soar above the vulgar prejudice in action, though not in opinion?" said Schedoni, who, perceiving that his assistance was necessary to fix her fluctuating mind, gradually began to steal forth from the prudent reserve in which he had taken shelter. "If this person was condemned by the law," he continued, "you would pronounce the sentence to be just; yet you dare not. I am humbled while I repeat it, you dare not dispense justice yourself."

The Marchesa, after some hesitation, said, "I have not the shield of the law to protect me, Father; and the boldest virtue may pause when it reaches the utmost verge of safety."

"Never!" replied the confessor warmly; "virtue never trembles; it is her glory, and sublimest attribute, to be superior to danger; to despise it. The best principle is not virtue till it reaches this elevation."

A philosopher might, perhaps, have been surprised to hear two persons seriously defining the limits of virtue at the very moment in which they meditated the most atrocious crime; a man of the world would have considered it to be mere hypocrisy; a supposition which might have disclosed his general knowledge of manners, but would certainly have betrayed his ignorance of the human heart.

The Marchesa was for some time silent and thoughtful, and then repeated deliberately, "I have not the shield of the law to protect me."

"But you have the shield of the church," replied Schedoni; "you should not only have protection, but absolution."

"Absolution! Does virtue—justice—require absolution, Father?"

"When I mentioned absolution for the action which you perceive to be so just and necessary," replied Schedoni, "I accommodated my speech to vulgar prejudice, and to vulgar weakness. And, forgive me, that since you, my daughter, descended from the loftiness of your spirit to regret the shield of the law, I endeavored to console you by offering a shield to conscience. But enough of this; let us return to argument. This girl is put out of the way of committing more mischief, of injuring the peace and dignity of a distinguished family; she is sent to an eternal sleep before her time—where is the crime, where is the evil of this? On the contrary, you perceive, and you have convinced me, that it is only strict justice, only self-defense."

The Marchesa was attentive, and the confessor added, "She is not immortal; and the few years more that might have been allotted her she deserves to forfeit, since she would have employed them in cankering the honor of an illustrious house."

"Speak low, Father," said the Marchesa, though he spoke almost in a whisper; "the cloister appears solitary, yet some person may lurk behind those pillars. Advise me how this business may be managed; I am ignorant of the particular means."

"There is some hazard in the accomplishment of it, I grant," replied Schedoni; "I know not whom you may confide in. The men who make a trade of blood—"

"Hush!" said the Marchesa, looking round through the twilight. "A step!"

"It is the friar's, yonder, who crosses to the choir," replied Schedoni.

They were watchful for a few moments, and then he resumed the subject. "Mercenaries ought not to be trusted—"

"Yet who but mercenaries—" interrupted the Marchesa, and instantly checked herself. But the question thus implied did not escape the confessor.

"Pardon my astonishment," said he, "at the inconsistency or, what shall I venture to call it? of your opinions! After the acuteness you have displayed on some points, is it possible you can doubt, that principle may both prompt and perform the deed? Why should we hesitate to do what we judge to be right?"

"Ah, Reverend Father," said the Marchesa with emotion, "but where shall we find another like yourself—another who not only can perceive with justness but will act with energy?"

Schedoni was silent.

"Such a friend is above all estimation; but where shall we seek him?"

"Daughter!" said the monk emphatically, "my zeal for your family is also above all calculation."

"Good Father!" replied the Marchesa, comprehending his full meaning, "I know not how to thank you."

"Silence is sometimes eloquence," said Schedoni significantly.

The Marchesa mused; for her conscience also was eloquent. She tried to overcome its voice, but it would be heard; and sometimes such starts of horrible conviction came over her mind that she felt as one who, awaking from a dream, opens his eyes only to measure the depth of the precipice on which he totters. In such moments she was astonished that she had paused for a moment on a subject so terrible as that of murder. The sophistry of the confessor, together with the inconsistencies which he had betrayed, and which had not escaped the notice of the Marchesa even at the time they were uttered, though she had been unconscious of her own, then became more strongly apparent, and she almost determined to suffer the poor Ellena to live. But returning passion, like a wave that has recoiled from the shore, afterward came with re-collected energy and swept from her feeble mind the barriers which reason and conscience had begun to rear.

"This confidence with which you have thought proper to honor me," said Schedoni at length and paused; "this affair so momentous—"

"Ay, this affair," interrupted the Marchesa in a hurried manner, "but when, and where, good Father? Being once convinced, I am anxious to have it settled."

"That must be as occasion offers," replied the monk thoughtfully. "On the shore of the Adriatic, in the province of Apulia, not far from Manfredonia, is a house that might suit the purpose. It is a lonely dwelling on the beach, and concealed from travelers, among the forests, which spread for many miles along the coast."

"And the people?" said the Marchesa.

"Ay, daughter, or why travel so far as Apulia? It is inhabited by one poor man, who sustains a miserable existence by fishing. I know him, and could unfold the reasons of his solitary life; but no matter, it is sufficient that *I know him*."

"And would trust him, Father?"

"Ay, lady, with the life of this girl—though scarcely with my own."

"How! If he is such a villain he may not be trusted! Think further. But now you objected to a mercenary, yet this man is one."

"Daughter, he may be trusted when it is in such a case; he is safe and sure. I have reasons to know him."

"Name your reasons, Father."

The confessor was silent, and his countenance assumed a very peculiar character; it was more terrible than usual, and overspread with a dark, cadaverous hue of mingled anger and guilt. The Marchesa started involuntarily as, passing by a window, the evening gleam that fell there discovered it; and for the first time she wished that she had not committed herself so wholly in his power. But the die was now cast; it was too late to be prudent, and she again demanded his reasons.

"No matter," said Schedoni in a stifled voice, "she dies!"

"By his hands?" asked the Marchesa with strong emotion. "Think once more, Father."

They were both again silent and thoughtful. The Marchesa at length said, "Father, I rely upon your integrity and prudence"; and she laid a very flattering emphasis upon the word integrity. "But I conjure you to let this work be finished quickly; suspense is to me the purgatory of this world; and not to trust the accomplishment of it to a second person." She paused and then added, "I would not willingly owe so vast a debt of obligation to any other than yourself."

"Your request, daughter, that I would not confide this business to a second person," said Schedoni with displeasure, "cannot be accorded to. Can you suppose that I myself—"

"Can I doubt that principle may both prompt and perform the deed?" interrupted the Marchesa with quickness, and anticipating his meaning; while she retorted upon him his former words. "Why should we hesitate to do what we judge to be right?"

The silence of Schedoni alone indicated his displeasure, which the Marchesa immediately understood.

"Consider, good Father," she added significantly, "how painful it must be to me to owe so infinite an obligation to a stranger or to any other person than so highly valued a friend as yourself."

Schedoni, while he detected her meaning and persuaded himself that he despised the flattery with which she so thinly veiled it, unconsciously suffered his self-love to be soothed by the compliment. He bowed his head, in signal of consent to her wish.

"Avoid violence if that be possible," she added, immediately comprehending him, "but let her die quickly! The punishment is due to the crime."

The Marchesa happened, as she said this, to cast her eyes upon the inscription over a confessional, where appeared, in black letters, these awful words: *"God hears thee!"* It appeared an awful warning. Her countenance changed; it had struck upon her heart. Schedoni was too much engaged by his own thoughts to observe or understand her silence. She soon recovered herself; and, considering that this was a common inscription for confessionals, disregarded what she had at first considered as a peculiar admonition; yet some moments elapsed before she could renew the subject.

"You were speaking of a place, Father," resumed the Marchesa. "You mentioned a—"

"Ay," muttered the confessor, still musing. "In a chamber of that house there is—"

"What noise is that?" said the Marchesa, interrupting him. They listened. A few low and querulous notes of the organ sounded at a distance and stopped again.

"What mournful music is that!" said the Marchesa in a faltering voice; "it was touched by a fearful hand! Vespers were over long ago!"

"Daughter," said Schedoni somewhat sternly, "you said you had a man's courage; alas! you have a woman's heart."

"Excuse me, Father; I know not why I feel this agitation, but I will command it. That chamber?"

"In that chamber," resumed the confessor, "is a secret door, constructed long ago."

"And for what purpose constructed?" said the fearful Marchesa.

"Pardon me, daughter; 'tis sufficient that it is there; we will make a good use of it. Through that door, in the night, when she sleeps—"

"I comprehend you," said the Marchesa, "I comprehend you. But why—you have your reasons, no doubt—but why the necessity of a secret door in a house which you say is so lonely, inhabited only by one person."

"A passage leads to the sea," continued Schedoni without replying to the question. "There, on the shore, when darkness covers it; there, plunged amid the waves, no stain shall hint of—"

"Hark!" interrupted the Marchesa, starting, "that note again!"

The organ sounded faintly from the choir and paused as before. In the next moment a low chanting of voices was heard mingling with the rising peal, in a strain particularly melancholy and solemn.

"Who is dead?" said the Marchesa, changing countenance. "It is a requiem!"

"Peace be with the departed!" exclaimed Schedoni and crossed himself. "Peace rest with his soul!"

"Hark to that chant!" said the Marchesa in a trembling voice. "It is a first requiem; the soul has but just quitted the body!"

They listened in silence. The Marchesa was much affected; her breathings were short and interrupted, and she even shed a few tears, but they were those of despair rather than of sorrow. "The body is now cold," said she to herself, "which but an hour ago was warm and animated! Those fine senses are closed in death! And to this condition would I reduce a being like myself! Oh, wretched,

wretched mother! to what has the folly of a son reduced thee!"

She turned from the confessor and walked alone in the cloister. Her agitation increased; she wept without restraint, for her veil and the evening gloom concealed her, and her sighs were lost amid the music of the choir.

Schedoni was scarcely less disturbed; but his were emotions of apprehension and contempt. "Behold, what is woman!" said he. "The slave of her passions, the dupe of her senses! When pride and revenge speak in her breast, she defies obstacles and laughs at crimes! Assail but her senses—let music, for instance, touch some feeble chord of her heart, and echo to her fancy, and lo! all her perceptions change; she shrinks from the act she had but an instant before believed meritorious, yields to some new emotions and sinks—the victim of a sound! O weak and contemptible being!"

The Marchesa, at least, seemed to justify his observations. The desperate passions, which had resisted every remonstrance of reason and humanity, were vanquished only by other passions; and her senses touched by the mournful melody of music, and her superstitious fears awakened by the occurrence of a requiem for the dead, at the very moment when she was planning murder, she yielded, for a while, to the united influence of pity and terror. Her agitation did not subside; but she returned to the confessor.

"We will converse on this business at some future time," said she. "At present my spirits are disordered. Good night, Father. Remember me in your orisons."

"Peace be with you, lady!" said the confessor, bowing gravely. "You shall not be forgotten. Be resolute, and command yourself."

The Marchesa beckoned her woman to approach, when, drawing her veil closer, and leaning upon the attendant's arm, she left the cloister. Schedoni remained for a moment on the spot, looking after her, till her figure was lost in the gloom of the long perspective; he then, with thoughtful steps, quitted the cloister by another door. He was disappointed, but he did not despair.

THE ITALIAN: OR, THE CONFESSIONAL OF THE BLACK PENITENTS (1797)

THOMAS HARDY

❦

Christmas at Mellstock

Though Hardy liked a few pieces from the concert repertory—
Mendelssohn, Wagner, Tchaikovsky—he was predominantly rural in
his musical tastes. As a youth he had been a passionate dancer, and
he always retained his love of homemade music, whether sacred or
profane.

I

The Assembled Choir

William Dewy—otherwise grandfather William—was now about
seventy; yet an ardent vitality still preserved a warm and roughened
bloom upon his face, which reminded gardeners of the sunny side
of a ripe ribstone-pippin; though a narrow strip of forehead, that
was protected from the weather by lying above the line of his hat
brim, seemed to belong to some town man, so gentlemanly was its
whiteness. His was a humorous and gentle nature, not unmixed with
a frequent melancholy; and he had a firm religious faith. But to
his neighbors he had no character in particular. If they saw him pass
by their windows when they had been bottling off old mead, or
when they had just been called long-headed men who might do anything in the world if they chose, they thought concerning him, "Ah,
there's that good-hearted man—open as a child!" If they saw him just
after losing a shilling or half a crown, or accidentally letting fall a
piece of crockery, they thought, "There's that poor weak-minded man
Dewy again! Ah, he'll never do much in the world either!" If he

passed when fortune neither smiled nor frowned on them, they merely thought him old William Dewy.

"Ah, so's—here you be!—Ah, Michael and Joseph and John—and you too, Leaf! a merry Christmas all! We shall have a rare logwood fire directly, Reub, if it d'go, by the toughness of the job I had in cleaving 'em." As he spoke he threw down an armful of logs, which fell in the chimney corner with a rumble, and looked at them with something of the admiring enmity he would have bestowed on living people who had been very obstinate in holding their own. "Come in, grandfather James."

Old James (grandfather on the maternal side) had simply called as a visitor. He lived in a cottage by himself, and many people considered him a miser: some, rather slovenly in his habits. He now came forward from behind grandfather William, and his stooping figure formed a well-illuminated picture as he passed toward the fireplace. Being by trade a mason, he wore a long linen apron reaching almost to his toes, corduroy breeches and gaiters, which, together with his boots, graduated in tints of whitish-brown by constant friction against lime and stone. He also wore a very stiff fustian coat, having folds at the elbows and shoulders as unvarying in their arrangement as those in a pair of bellows: the ridges and the projecting parts of the coat collectively exhibiting a shade different from that of the hollows, which were lined with small ditch-like accumulations of stone and mortar dust. The extremely large side pockets, sheltered beneath wide flaps, bulged out convexly whether empty or full; and as he was often engaged to work at buildings far away—his breakfasts and dinners being eaten in a strange chimney corner, by a garden wall, on a heap of stones, or walking along the road—he carried in these pockets a small tin canister of butter, a small canister of sugar, a small canister of tea, a paper of salt, and a paper of pepper; the bread, cheese, and meat, forming the substance of his meals, hung up behind him in his basket among the hammers and chisels. If a passer-by looked hard at him when he was drawing forth any of these—"My larders," he said, with a pinched smile.

"Better try over number seventy-eight before we start, I suppose?" said William, pointing to a heap of old Christmas carol books on a side table.

"Wi' all my heart," said the choir generally.

"Number seventy-eight was always a teaser—always. I can mind him ever since I was growing up a hard boy-chap."

"But he's a good tune, and worth a mint o' practice," said Michael.

"He is; though I've been mad enough wi' that tune at times to seize en and tear en all to linnet. Ay, he's a splendid carrel—there's no denying that."

"The first line is well enough," said Mr. Spinks; "but when you come to 'O, thou man,' you make a mess o't."

"We'll have another go into en, and see what we can make of the martel. Half an hour's hammering at en will conquer the toughness of en; I'll warn it."

" 'Od rabbit it all!" said Mr. Penny, interrupting with a flash of his spectacles, and at the same time clawing at something in the depths of a large side pocket. "If so be I hadn't been as scatterbrained and thirtingill as a chiel, I should have called at the schoolhouse wi' a boot as I cam up-along. Whatever is coming to me I really can't estimate at all!"

"The brain hev its weaknesses," murmured Mr. Spinks, waving his head ominously.

"Well, I must call with en the first thing tomorrow. And I'll empt my pocket o' this last too, if you don't mind, Mrs. Dewy." He drew forth a last and placed it on a table at his elbow. The eyes of three or four followed it.

"Well," said the shoemaker, seeming to perceive that the sum total of interest the object had excited was greater than he had anticipated, and warranted the last's being taken up again and exhibited, "now, whose foot do ye suppose this last was made for? It was made for Geoffrey Day's father, over at Yalbury Wood. Ah, many's the pair o' boots he've had off the last! Well, when 'a died, I used the last for Geoffrey, and have ever since, though a little doctoring was wanted to make it do. Yes, a very quaint humorous last it is now, 'a b'lieve," he continued, turning it over caressingly. "Now, you notice that there"—pointing to a lump of leather bradded to the toe—"that's a very bad bunion that he've had ever since 'a was a boy. Now, this remarkable large piece"—pointing to a patch nailed to the side—"shows an accident he received by the tread of a horse, that squashed his foot a'most to a pomace. The horseshoe cam full-butt on this point, you see. And so I've just been over to Geoffrey's, to know if he wanted his bunion altered, or made bigger in the new pair I'm making."

During the latter part of this speech Mr. Penny's left hand wandered toward the cider-cup, as if the hand had no connection with the person speaking; and bringing his sentence to an abrupt close, all but the extreme margin of the bootmaker's face was eclipsed by the circular brim of the vessel.

"However, I was going to say," continued Penny, putting down the cup, "I ought to have called at the school"—here he went groping again in the depths of his pocket—"to leave this without fail, though I suppose the first thing tomorrow will do."

He now drew forth and placed upon the table a boot—small, light, and prettily shaped—upon the heel of which he had been operating. "The new schoolmistress's!"

"Ay, no less; Miss Fancy Day: as nate a little figure of fun as ever I see, and just husband-high."

"Never Geoffrey's daughter Fancy?" said Bowman, as all glances present converged like wheel-spokes upon the boot in the center of them.

"Yes, sure," resumed Mr. Penny, regarding the boot as if that alone were his auditor; "'tis she that's come here schoolmistress. You knowed his daughter was in training?"

"Strange, isn't it, for her to be here Christmas night, Master Penny?"

"Yes; but here she is, 'a b'lieve."

"I know how she d'come here—so I do!" chirruped one of the children.

"Why?" Dick inquired, with subtle interest.

"Parson Maybold was afraid he couldn't manage us all tomorrow at the dinner, and he talked o' getting her jist to come over and help him hand about the plates, and see we didn't make beasts of ourselves; and that's what she's come for!"

"And that's the boot, then," continued its mender imaginatively, "that she'll walk to church in tomorrow morning. I don't care to mend boots I don't make; but there's no knowing what it may lead to, and her father always comes to me."

There, between the cider-mug and the candle, stood this interesting receptacle of the little unknown's foot; and a very pretty boot it was. A character, in fact—the flexible bend at the instep, the rounded localities of the small nestling toes, scratches from careless scampers now forgotten—all, as repeated in the telltale leather, evidencing a nature and a bias. Dick surveyed it with a delicate feeling that he had no right to do so without having first asked the owner of the foot's permission.

"Now, naibors, though no common eye can see it," the shoemaker went on, "a man in the trade can see the likeness between this boot and that last, although that is so deformed as hardly to be called one of God's creatures, and this is one of as pretty a pair as you'd get for ten-and-sixpence in Casterbridge. To you, nothing; but 'tis father's foot and daughter's foot to me, as plain as houses."

"I don't doubt there's a likeness, Master Penny—a mild likeness— a far-remote likeness, still, a likeness, as far as that goes," said Spinks. "But I haven't imagination enough to see it, perhaps."

Mr. Penny adjusted his spectacles. "Now, I'll tell you what happened to me once on this very point. You used to know Johnson the dairyman, William?"

"Ay, sure; that I did."

"Well, 'twasn't opposite his house, but a little lower down—by his pigsty, in front o' Parkmaze Pool. I was a-walking down the lane, and, lo and behold, there was a man just brought out o' the Pool, dead; he had been bathing, and gone in flop over his head. Men looked at en; women looked at en; children looked at en: nobody knowed en. He was covered in a cloth; but I catched sight of his foot, just showing out as they carried en along. 'I don't care what name that man went by,' I said in my bold way, 'but he's John Woodward's brother; I can swear to the family foot.' At that very moment up comes John Woodward, weeping and crying, 'I've lost my brother! I've lost my brother!' "

"Only to think of that!" said Mrs. Dewy.

" 'Tis well enough to know this foot and that foot," said Mr. Spinks. " 'Tis something, in fact, as far as that goes. I know little, 'tis true—I say no more; but show *me* a man's foot, and I'll tell you that man's heart."

"You must be a cleverer feller, then, than mankind in jineral," said the tranter.

"Well, that's nothing for me to speak of," returned Mr. Spinks solemnly. "A man acquires. Maybe I've read a leaf or two in my time. I don't wish to say anything large, mind you; but nevertheless, maybe I have."

"Yes, I know," said Michael soothingly, "and all the parish knows, that ye've read something of everything almost. Learning's a worthy thing, and ye've got it, Master Spinks."

"I make no boast, though I may have read and thought a little; and I know—it may be from much perusing, but I make no boast— that by the time a man's head is finished, 'tis almost time for him to creep underground. I am over forty-five."

Mr. Spinks emitted a look to signify that if his head was not finished, nobody's head ever could be.

"Talk of knowing people by their feet!" said Reuben. "Rot me, my sonnies, then, if I can tell what a man is from all his members put together, oftentimes."

"But still, look is a good deal," observed grandfather William absently, moving and balancing his head till the tip of grandfather James's nose was exactly in a right line with William's eye and the mouth of a miniature cavern he was discerning in the fire. "By the way," he continued in a fresher voice, and looking up, "that young crater, the schoolmistress, must be sung to tonight wi' the rest? If her ear is as fine as her face, we shall have enough to do to be up-sides with her."

"What about her face?" said young Dewy.

"Well, as to that," Mr. Spinks replied, " 'tis a face you can hardly gainsay. A very good face—and a pink face, as far as that goes. Still, only a face, when all is said and done."

"Come, come, Elias Spinks, say she's a pretty maid and have done wi' her," said the tranter, again preparing to visit the cider barrel.

II

Going the Rounds

Shortly after ten o'clock the singing-boys arrived at the tranter's house, which was invariably the place of meeting, and preparations were made for the start. The older men and musicians wore thick coats, with stiff perpendicular collars, and colored handkerchiefs wound round and round the neck till the end came to hand, over all which they just showed their ears and noses, like people looking over a wall. The remainder, stalwart ruddy men and boys, were mainly dressed in snow-white smock-frocks, embroidered upon the shoulders and breasts, in ornamental forms of hearts, diamonds, and zigzags. The cider-mug was emptied for the ninth time, the music books were arranged, and the pieces finally decided upon. The boys in the meantime put the old horn lanterns in order, cut candles into short lengths to fit the lanterns; and a thin fleece of snow having fallen since the early part of the evening, those who had no leggings went to the stable and wound wisps of hay round their ankles to keep the insidious flakes from the interior of their boots.

Mellstock was a parish of considerable acreage, the hamlets com-posing it lying at a much greater distance from each other than is ordinarily the case. Hence several hours were consumed in play-ing and singing within hearing of every family, even if but a single air were bestowed on each. There was East Mellstock, the main village; half a mile from this were the church and the vicarage, called West Mellstock, and originally the most thickly populated portion. A mile northeast lay the hamlet of Lewgate, where the tranter lived; and at other points knots of cottages, besides solitary farmsteads and dairies.

Old William Dewy, with the violoncello, played the bass; his grandson Dick the treble violin; and Reuben and Michael Mail the tenor and second violins respectively. The singers consisted of four men and seven boys, upon whom devolved the task of carrying and attending to the lanterns, and holding the books open for the players. Directly music was the theme, old William ever and instinctively came to the front.

"Now mind, naibors," he said as they all went out one by one at the door, he himself holding it ajar and regarding them with a critical face as they passed, like a shepherd counting out his sheep. "You two counter-boys, keep your ears open to Michael's fingering, and don't ye go straying into the treble part along o' Dick and his set, as ye did last year; and mind this especially when we be in 'Arise, and hail.' Billy Chimlen, don't you sing quite so raving mad as you fain would; and, all o' ye, whatever ye do, keep from making a great scuffle on the ground when we go in at people's gates; but go quietly, so as to strik' up all of a sudden, like spirits."

"Farmer Ledlow's first?"

"Farmer Ledlow's first; the rest as usual."

"And, Voss," said the tranter terminatively, "you keep house here till about half-past two; then heat the metheglin and cider in the warmer you'll find turned up upon the copper; and bring it wi' the victuals to church porch, as th'st know."

Just before the clock struck twelve they lighted the lanterns and started. The moon, in her third quarter, had risen since the snow-storm; but the dense accumulation of snow-cloud weakened her power to a faint twilight, which was rather pervasive of the landscape than traceable to the sky. The breeze had gone down, and the rustle of their feet, and tones of their speech, echoed with an alert rebound from every post, boundary stone, and ancient wall they passed, even where the distance of the echo's origin was less than a few yards. Beyond their own slight noises nothing was to be heard, save the occasional howl of foxes in the direction of Yalbury Wood, or the brush of a rabbit among the grass now and then, as it scampered out of their way.

Most of the outlying homesteads and hamlets had been visited by about two o'clock; they then passed across the Home Plantation toward the main village. Pursuing no recognized track, great care was necessary in walking lest their faces should come in contact with the low-hanging boughs of the old trees, which in many spots formed dense overgrowths of interlaced branches.

"Times have changed from the times they used to be," said Mail, regarding nobody-can-tell-what interesting old panoramas with an inward eye, and letting his outward glance rest on the ground, because it was as convenient a position as any. "People don't care much about us now! I've been thinking, we must be almost the last left in the county of the old string players. Barrel organs, and they next door to 'em that you blow wi' your foot, have come in terribly of late years."

"Ah!" said Bowman, shaking his head; and old William, on seeing him, did the same thing.

"More's the pity," replied another. "Time was—long and merry ago now!—when not one of the varmits was to be heard of; but it served some of the choirs right. They should have stuck to strings as we did, and keep out clar'nets, and done away with serpents. If you'd thrive in musical religion, stick to strings, says I."

"Strings are well enough, as far as that goes," said Mr. Spinks.

"There's worse things than serpents," said Mr. Penny. "Old things pass away, 'tis true; but a serpent was a good old note: a deep rich note was the serpent."

"Clar'nets, however, be bad at all times," said Michael Mail. "One Christmas—years agone now, years—I went the rounds wi' the Dibbeach choir. 'Twas a hard frosty night, and the keys of all the clar'nets froze—ah, they did freeze!—so that 'twas like drawing a cork every time a key was opened; the players o' 'em had to go into a hedger and ditcher's chimley corner, and thaw their clar'nets every now and then. An icicle o' spet hung down from the end of every man's clar'net a span long; and as to fingers—well, there, if ye'll believe me, we had no fingers at all, to our knowledge."

"I can well bring back to my mind," said Mr. Penny, "what I said to poor Joseph Ryme (who took the tribble part in High-Story Church for two-and-forty year) when they thought of having clar'nets there. 'Joseph,' I said, says I, 'depend upon't, if so be you have them tooting clar'nets you'll spoil the whole set-out. Clar'nets were not made for the service of Providence; you can see it by looking at 'em,' I said. And what cam o't? Why, my dear souls, the parson set up a barrel organ on his own account within two years o' the time I spoke, and the old choir went to nothing."

"As far as look is concerned," said the tranter, "I don't for my part see that a fiddle is much nearer heaven than a clar'net. 'Tis farther off. There's always a rakish, scampish countenance about a fiddle that seems to say the Wicked One had a hand in making o'en; while angels be supposed to play clar'nets in heaven, or som'at like 'em, if ye may believe picters."

"Robert Penny, you were in the right," broke in the eldest Dewy. "They should ha' stuck to strings. Your brass man, is brass—well and good; your reed man, is reed—well and good; your percussion man, is percussion—good again. But I don't care who hears me say it, nothing will speak to your heart wi' the sweetness of the man of strings!"

"Strings forever!" said little Jimmy.

"Strings alone would have held their ground against all the new-comers in creation." ("True, true!" said Bowman.) "But clar'nets was death." ("Death they was!" said Mr. Penny.) "And harmoni-ums," William continued in a louder voice, and getting excited by these signs of approval, "harmoniums and barrel organs" ("Ah!" and groans from Spinks) "be miserable—what shall I call 'em—miserable—"

"Sinners," suggested Jimmy, who made large strides like the men and did not lag behind like the other little boys.

"Miserable machines for such a divine thing as music!"

"Right, William, and so they be!" said the choir with earnest unanimity.

By this time they were crossing to a wicket in the direction of the school, which, standing on a slight eminence on the opposite side of a cross lane, now rose in unvarying and dark flatness against the sky. The instruments were retuned, and all the band entered the enclosure, enjoined by old William to keep upon the grass.

"Number seventy-eight," he softly gave out as they formed round in a semicircle, the boys opening the lanterns to get a clearer light, and directing their rays on the books.

Then passed forth into the quiet night an ancient and well-worn hymn, embodying Christianity in words peculiarly befitting the simple and honest hearts of the quaint characters who sang them so earnestly.

> Remember Adam's fall,
>   O thou man:
> Remember Adam's fall
>   From Heaven to Hell.
> Remember Adam's fall;
> How he hath condemn'd all
> In Hell perpetual
>   Therefore to dwell.
>
> Remember God's goodnesse,
>   O thou man:
> Remember God's goodnesse,
>   His promise made.
> Remember God's goodnesse;
> He sent His Son sinlesse
> Our ails for to redress,
>   Our hearts to aid.
>
> In Bethlehem He was born,
>   O thou man:
> In Bethlehem He was born,

For mankind's sake.
In Bethlehem He was born,
Christmas Day i' the morn:
Our Saviour did not scorn
    Our faults to take.

Give thanks to God alway,
    O thou man:
Give thanks to God alway
    With heart-felt joy.
Give thanks to God alway
On this our joyful day:
Let all men sing and say,
    Holy, Holy!

Having concluded the last note, they listened for a minute or two,
but found that no sound issued from the schoolhouse.

UNDER THE GREENWOOD TREE (1872)

Criticism

ROMAIN ROLLAND

❯❯❯ ❮❮❮

Making the Rounds

Rolland's novel in many volumes, *Jean-Christophe,* deals chiefly with the experiences of a young German musician in Paris at the turn of the century—1900 to 1910.

Of his own accord, Théophile Goujart came a few days later to seek out Christophe in his garret. He seemed not at all upset at finding him in such poor surroundings. He was on the contrary, most charming, and said to him, "I thought you might enjoy hearing a little music from time to time, and since I have press tickets for everything, I've come to pick you up."

Christophe was delighted. He was touched by the kind thought and returned effusive thanks. Goujart seemed quite different from what he had been the first night. In tête-à-tête he put on no side; he was easygoing, almost shy, and eager to learn. Only in front of others did he automatically resume his superior airs and dogmatic tone. To be sure, his eagerness to learn had a practical motive. He showed no curiosity about anything except the current scene, but he wanted to know what Christophe thought of a score just received, of which he himself could scarcely give an account since he was barely able to read notes.

They went together to a symphony concert. The entrance was common to the hall and to a cabaret. By a tortuous corridor one reached a windowless auditorium where the atmosphere was stifling. The seats were narrow and too close together. Part of the audience

158 CRITICISM

was standing, blocking the exits—French lack of comfort through-out.

A man who seemed to be cankered by incurable boredom was conducting at top speed one of the Beethoven symphonies, as if he could hardly wait to get it over with. From the neighboring music hall the strains of the cabaret show's bumps and grinds came and mingled with the funeral march of the *Eroica*. The concert audience kept straggling in, settling down, and staring at one another. As soon as they had stopped coming, they began leaving. Christophe was exerting all his powers of concentration to follow the work through the distractions of this county fair. By dint of strenuous effort he was even beginning to enjoy parts of it—for the orchestra was competent and Christophe had long been deprived of symphonic music—when Goujart seized his arm and, in the middle of a movement, said to him, "Time for us to go. We're due at another concert."

Christophe frowned but did not answer. He followed his guide, who took him halfway across Paris and brought him to another hall, redolent of the stable. There, on other days of the week, they gave pantomimes and cheap plays. For music in Paris is like those penniless workmen who go halves on a single room—when one gets out of bed, the other comes from his work into the warmed sheets. In this hall as in the other, no fresh air, of course. Since the days of the Sun King Louis XIV, the French have deemed it unhealthful, and the sanitary code of theaters, as formerly that of Versailles, is that the air should be kept unbreathable.

A noble-looking, white-haired man was unleashing with the gestures of a lion tamer an act from a Wagnerian opera. The poor beast—that is to say, the act—resembled those menagerie animals who are petrified by the footlights and who must be whipped if they are to remember that they were once wild beasts. Some large female Philistines and a gaggle of little geese were witnessing this show with a smile on their lips. After the wild beast had roared and the tamer had bowed, and both had been rewarded by the spectators' making a rumpus, Goujart attempted to take Christophe with him to a third concert. But this time Christophe clamped both hands on the arms of his seat and declared he would not budge. He was sick and tired of rushing from place to place to catch a morsel of opera here and some crumbs of symphony there. In vain did Goujart try to explain that music criticism in Paris was a trade in which it was more important to see than to listen. Christophe retorted that music was not made to be taken on the run, between cabs, that it required a more collected mood. This hash of concerts gave him nausea; he wanted only one at a time.

He was in fact astonished at this proliferation of music. Like most Germans, he believed that in France the art occupied but a secondary place. He expected that it would be served to him in very small portions, though exquisite. As it was, he had his choice, to begin with, of no less than fifteen concerts in one week. There was at least one each evening and sometimes two or three—at the same hour and in opposite quarters of town. As for Sunday, there were always four, all at the same hour. Christophe marveled at this greediness and gaped at the size of the programs. He had thought hitherto that his compatriots enjoyed a monopoly of these debauches of sound, which had so often disgusted him in Germany. Now he saw that the Parisians could easily match them in this form of guzzling: two symphonies, one concerto, one or two overtures, one act from opera —all indiscriminately mixed: German, Russian, Scandinavian, French; champagne, beer, ginger ale and wine, the public gulped them down at a sitting without turning a hair. Christophe wondered that these French lightweights had such strong stomachs. But he had missed the point. They needed no stomachs, for they were sieves; nothing stayed with them.

Christophe was not long in noticing that this vast amount of music boiled down in fact to very little. At every concert he found again the same names and the same pieces. These copious programs revolved in one narrow circle: virtually nothing before Beethoven; almost nothing after Wagner. And in between, what gaps! It seemed as if music were equivalent to five or six celebrated Germans, three or four Frenchmen and (ever since the Franco-Russian alliance) half a dozen Muscovite numbers. Nothing from the older French composers. Nothing from the great Italians. Nothing from the German titans of the seventeenth and eighteenth centuries. Nothing from contemporary German music—with the sole exception of Richard Strauss who, being shrewder than the rest, came each year to impose his new works on the Paris public. No Belgian music, no Czechish, and what was most astounding, no French music by contemporaries.

Yet of the French school everybody spoke in mysterious terms, as of a thing that was revolutionizing the world. Christophe kept watching for a chance to hear this music, for his inquiring mind was broad and unprejudiced; he was consumed with a desire to hear something new and to admire the works of genius. But despite his efforts he did not manage to hear the modern French, for he did not include under that head some three or four little pieces, of fine texture but coldly and carefully complicated, which had hardly held his attention.

JEAN-CHRISTOPHE IN PARIS (1908)

G. K. CHESTERTON

→→→ ←←←

Music with Meals

A newspaper comment on something I recently wrote has given me a momentary illusion of having really got hold of what is the matter with modernity. For that serpent is as slippery as an eel, that demon is as elusive as an elf. But for the moment I thought I had him—or at least a perfect specimen of him. I wrote recently to the effect that music at meals interferes with conversation. And certain people at once began to discuss whether music at meals interferes with digestion. And in that one detail I seemed to have caught the very devil himself by the tail.

Those who read my article know that I never even mentioned digestion. I never even thought of it. It never crosses my mind while I am eating meals. It certainly never crosses my mind when I am listening to music. Least of all did it ever cross my mind while I was writing that particular article. And the idea that it should cross anybody's mind, not to say occupy anybody's mind, in connection with the other controversy seems to me a compendium of all the dullness, baseness, vulgarity, and fear that make up so much of the practical philosophy of this enlightened age. What I complained of was not that music interfered with animal assimilation, but that it interfered with human speech, with the talk of taverns like the Tabard or the Mermaid, with the talk of Dr. Johnson or Charles Lamb, with the *Noctes Ambrosianae* or the Four Men of Sussex; with all the ancient Christian custom of men arguing each other's heads off and shouting each other down for the glory of reason and the truth. Those great talkers no more thought about their digestion at dinner than the heroes of the Iliad or the Song of Roland felt their own pulses and took their own temperatures in the thick of the battle. It is true that I did not confine myself to complaining of meals being spoiled by music. I also complained of music being spoiled by meals. I was so impertinent as to suggest that if we want to listen to good music we should listen to it, and honor it with our undivided attention. A fine musician might surely resent a man treating fine music as a mere background to his lunch. But a fine musician might well murder a man who treated fine music as an aid to his digestion.

But what interests me is this swift, unconscious substitution of the subject of digestion, which I had never mentioned, for the subject of human intercourse, which I had. It has hidden in it somewhere a sort of secret of our social and spiritual abnormality. It is a sort of silent signal of all that has gone wrong with our brains and tempers and memories and hearts—and also, doubtless, digestions. It is so significant that it is worth while to attempt to resolve it into the elements that make it the monstrous and ominous thing it is. Before this evil and elusive creature escapes me once more, I will attempt to dissect it and make a sort of diagram of its deformities.

First, there is that stink of stale and sham science which is one of the curses of our times. The stupidest or the wickedest action is supposed to become reasonable or respectable, not by having found a reason in scientific fact, but merely by having found any sort of excuse in scientific language. This highly grotesque and rather gross topic is supposed to take on a sort of solemnity because it is physiological. Some people even talk about proteids, vitamins—but let us draw a veil over the whole horrid scene. It is enough to note that one element in the hideous compound is a love of talking about the body as a scientific thing—that is, talking about it as if it were a serious thing.

Next, there is a morbidity and a monstrous solitude. Each man is alone with his digestion as with a familiar demon. He is not to allow either the wine or the music to melt his soul into any sociable spirit of the company. Wine is bad for his digestion and music is good for his digestion. He therefore abstains from the one and absorbs the other in the same inhuman isolation. Diogenes retired into a tub and St. Jerome into a cave; but this hermit uses his own inside as his cavern—every man is his own cask, and it is not even a wine cask.

Third, there is materialism or the very muddiest sort of atheism. It has the obscure assumption that everything begins with the digestion, and not with the divine reason; that we must always start at the material end if we wish to work from the origins of things. In their hapless topsy-turvy philosophy, digestion is the creator and divinity the creature. They have at the back of their minds, in short, the idea that there is really nothing at the back of their minds except the brute thing called the body. To them, therefore, there is nothing comic or incongruous about saying that a violin solo should be a servant of the body or of the brute; for there is no other god for it to serve.

There also hides in the heart of this philosopher the thing we call hypochondria and a paralyzing panic. I have said that it serves the body; but many men in many ages have served their bodies. I doubt if any men in any ages were ever so much afraid of their bodies. We might represent in some symbolic drama a man running down the street pursued by his own body. It is inadequate to say of this sort of thing that it is atheism; it would be nearer the truth to say it is devil-worship. But they are not even the red devils of passion and enjoyment. They are really only the blue devils of fear.

Then there is what there always is in such philosophy, the setting of the cart to draw the horse. They do not see that digestion exists for health, and health exists for life, and life exists for the love of music or beautiful things. They reverse the process and say that the love of music is good for the process of digestion. What the process of digestion is ultimately good for they have really no idea. I think it was a great medieval philosopher who said that all evil comes from enjoying what we ought to use and using what we ought to enjoy. A great many modern philosophers never do anything else. Thus they will sacrifice what they admit to be happiness to what they claim to be progress; though it could have no rational meaning except progress to greater happiness. Or they will subordinate goodness to efficiency; though the very name of good implies an end, and the very name of efficiency implies only a means to an end. Progress and efficiency by their very titles are only tools. Goodness and happiness by their very titles are a fruition; the fruits that are to be produced by the tools. Yet how often the fruits are treated as fancies of sentimentalism and only the tools as facts of sense. It is as if a starving man were to give away the turnip in order to eat the spade; or as if men said that there need not be any fish, so long as there were plenty of fishing rods. There is all that queer inversion of values in talking about music as an aid not only to dinner, but even to the digestion of dinner.

There is more generally a flat, unlifted, unlaughing spirit, that can accept this topsy-turvydom without even seeing that it is topsy-turvy. It does not even rise high enough to be cynical. It does not utter its materialistic maxim even as a pessimist's paradox. It does not see the joke of saying that the Passion Music can assist a gentleman to absorb a veal cutlet, or that a mass of Palestrina might counteract the effects of toasted cheese. What is said on this subject is said quite seriously. That seriousness is perhaps the most frivolous thing in the whole of this frivolous society. It is a spirit that cannot even rouse itself enough to laugh.

In short, it is the magic of that one trivial phrase, about music and digestion, that it calls up suddenly in the mind the image of a certain sort of man, sitting at a table in a grand restaurant, and wearing a serious and somewhat sullen expression. He is manifestly a man of considerable wealth; and beyond that he can only be described by a series of negatives. He has no traditions, and therefore knows nothing of the great traditional talking that has enriched our literature with the nights and feasts of the gods. He has no real friends, and therefore his interests are turned inwards, but more to the state of his body than of his soul. He has no religion, and therefore it comes natural to him to think that everything springs from a material source. He has no philosophy, and therefore does not know the difference between the means and the end. And, above all, there is buried deep in him a profound and stubborn repugnance to the trouble of following anybody else's argument; so that if somebody elaborately explains to him that it is often a mistake to combine two pleasures, because pleasures, like pains, can act as counterirritants to each other, he receives only the vague impression that somebody is saying that music is bad for his digestion.

GENERALLY SPEAKING (1929)

ROBERT BURTON

❊

The Secret Power of Musick

Many and sundry are the means which philosophers and physicians have prescribed to exhilarate a sorrowful heart, to divert those fixed and intent cares and meditations, which in this malady so much offend; but, in my judgement, none so present, none so powerfull, none so apposite, as a cup of strong drink, mirth, musick, and merry company. . . . Musick is a roaring-meg against melancholy, to rear and revive the languishing soul; *affecting not only the ears, but the very arteries, the vital and animal spirits, it erects the mind and makes it nimble.* This it will effect in the most dull, severe, and sorrowfull souls, expell grief with mirth; *and, if there bee any cloudes, dust, or dreggs of cares yet lurking in our thoughts, most powerfully it wipes them all away,* and that which is more, it will perform all this in an instant—*chear up the countenance, expell austerity, bring in hilarity, informe our manners, mitigate anger.* Many other properties Cassiodorus reckons up of this our divine musick, not only to expell the greatest griefs, but it *doth extenuate fears and furies, appease cruelty, abateth heaviness; and, to such as are watchfull, it causeth quiet rest; it takes away spleen and hatred,* bee it instrumentall, vocall, with strings, winde; it cures all irksomness and heaviness of the soul. Labouring men that sing to their work, can tell as much; and so can souldiers when they go to fight, whom terror of death cannot so much affright, as the sound of trumpet, drum, fife, and such like musick, animates. *It makes a childe quiet,* the nurses song; and many times the sound of a trumpet on a sudden, bells ringing, a carremans whistle, a boy singing some ballad tune early in the street, alters, revives, recreates a restless patient that cannot sleep in the night, etc. In a word, it is so powerfull a thing that it ravisheth the soul, *regina sensuum,*[1] the queen of the senses, by sweet pleasure (which is an happy cure); and corporall tunes pacifie our incorporeall soul: *sine ore loquens, dominatum in animam exercet,* and carries it beyond it self, helps, elevates, extends it. Scaliger gives a reason of these effects, *because the spirits about the heart take in that trembling and dancing air into the body, are moved together, and stirred up with it,* or else the minde, as some suppose, harmonically composed, is roused up at the tunes of musick. And 'tis not onely men that are so affected, but almost all other creatures. You know the tale of Hercules, Gallus, Orpheus, and Amphion (*felices animas* Ovid cals them) that could *saxa movere sono testudinis,* etc. make stocks and stones, as well as beasts, and other animals, dance after their pipes: the dog and hare, wolf and lamb, as Philostratus describes it in his images, stood all gaping upon Orpheus; and trees, pulled up by the roots, came to hear him.

Arion made fish follow him, which, as common experience evinceth,[2] are much affected with musick. All singing birds are much pleased with it, especially nightingales, if we may beleeve Calcagninus; and bees amongst the rest, though they be flying away, when they hear any tingling sound, will tarry behinde. *Harts, hindes, horses, dogs, bears, are exceedingly delighted with it.* Elephants, Agrippa addes, and in Lydia in the midst of a lake there be certain floating ilands, (if ye will beleeve it) that, after musick, will dance.

But to leave all declamatory speeches in praise of divine musick, I will confine my self to my proper subject: besides that excellent power it hath to expell many other diseases, it is a soveraigne remedy against despair and melancholy, and will drive away the divel himself. Canus, a Rhodian fidler in Philostratus, when Apollonius was inquisitive to know what he could do with his pipe, told him, *that he would make a melancholy man merry, and him that was merry much merrier than before, a lover more inamoured,*

---

[1] This phrase and others in this passage are translated by Burton in the words immediately preceding or following the Latin.

[2] Carew of Anthony in his Description of Cornwall saith of whales that they will come and shew themselves dancing at the sound of a trumpet. [Burton's note.]

a religious man more devout. Ismenias the Theban, Chiron the Centaure, is said to have cured this and many other diseases by musick alone: as now they do those, saith Bodine, that are troubled with S. Vitus Bedlam dance. Timotheus the musician compelled Alexander to skip up and down, and leave his dinner (like the tale of the frier and the boy); whom Austin [3] so much commends for it. Who hath not heard how Davids harmony drove away the evill spirits from king Saul? (I Sam. 16) and Elisha, when he was much troubled by importunate kings, called for a minstrel; *and, when he played, the hand of the Lord came upon him* (II Kings 3). Censorinus reportes how Asclepiades the physician helped many frantike persons by this means, *phreneticorum mentes morbo turbatas.*—Jason Pratensis hath many examples, how Clinias and Empedocles cured some desperately melancholy, and some mad, by this our musick; which because it hath such excellent vertues, belike, Homer brings in Phemius playing, and the Muses singing at the banquet of the gods. Aristotle, Plato,[4] highly approve it, and so do all politicians. The Greekes, Romanes, have graced musick, and made it one of the liberall sciences, though it be now become mercenary. All civill common-wealths allow it: Cneius Manlius (as Livius relates) brought first out of Asia to Rome singing wenches, players, jesters, and all kinde of musick to their feasts. Your princes, emperours, and persons of any quality, maintain it in their courts: no mirth without musick. Sir Thomas Moore, in his absolute Utopian common-wealth, allowes musick as an appendix to every meal, and that throughout, to all sorts. Epictetus cals *mensam mutam praesepe,* a table without musick a manger; for *the concent of musicians at a banquet is a carbuncle set in gold; and as the signet of an emerald well trimmed with gold, so is the melody of musick in a pleasant banquet.* Lewes the eleventh, when he invited Edward the fourth to come to Paris, told him, that, as a principall part of his entertainment, he should hear sweet voices of children, Ionicke and Lydian tunes, exquisite musick, he should have a ......, and

[3] St. Augustine, *City of God,* Bk. XVII, chap. 14.

[4] Respectively: *Politics,* Bk. VIII, chap. 5; *Laws,* II.

the Cardinal of Burbon to be his confessor; which he used as a most plausible argument, as to a sensuall man indeed it is. Lucian is not ashamed to confess that he took infinite delight in singing, dancing, musick, womens company, and such like pleasures; *and if thou* (saith he) *didst but hear them play and dance, I know thou wouldst be so well pleased with the object, that thou wouldst dance for company thy self: without doubt thou wilt bee taken with it:* So Scaliger ingenuously confesseth, *I am beyond all measure affected with musick; I do most willingly behold them dance; I am mightily detained and allured with that grace and comeliness of fair women; I am well pleased to bee idle amongst them.* And what young man is not? As it is acceptable and conducing to most, so especially to a melancholy man; provided alwaies, his disease proceed not originally from it, that he bee not some light *inamorato,* some idle phantastick, who capers in conceit all the day long, and thinks of nothing else, but how to make jigs, sonnets, madrigals, in commendation of his mistress. In such cases, musick is most pernicious, as a spur to a free horse will make him run himself blinde, or break his wind; for musick enchants, as Menander holds; it will make such melancholy persons mad; and the sound of those jigs and horn-pipes will not bee removed out of the ears a week after. Plato, for this reason, forbids musick and wine to all young men, because they are most part amorous *ne ignis addatur igni,* lest one fire increase another. Many men are melancholy by hearing musick; but it is a pleasing melancholy that it causeth; and therefore, to such as are discontent, in wo, fear, sorrow, or dejected, it is a most present remedy: it expells cares, alters their grieved minds, and easeth in an instant. Otherwise, saith Plutarch, *musica magis dementat quam vinum;* musick makes some men mad as a tygre; like Astolphos horn in Ariosto, or Mercuries golden wand in Homer, that made some wake, others sleep, it hath divers effects: and Theophrastus right well prophesied, that diseases were either procured by musick, or mitigated.

ANATOMY OF MELANCHOLY (1621)

CONSTANT LAMBERT

-»» «-

The Spirit of Jazz

Constant Lambert is considered by many to have written the best book on modern music, brief extracts from which appear in these pages. But his main musical activity has been as composer and conductor, particularly in his connection with the Sadlers Wells opera and ballet companies. Mr. Lambert was born in 1905 and died in 1951.

Jazz is naturally dependent for its progress on the progress of the sophisticated material used as a basis for its rhythmic virtuosity. The sudden postwar efflorescence of jazz was due largely to the adoption as raw material of the harmonic richness and orchestral subtlety of the Debussy-Delius period of highbrow music. Orchestral color of course is not a thing that can really be appreciated in itself; it is largely dependent for its color on the underlying harmonies. The harmonic background drawn from the Impressionist school opened up a new world of sound to the jazz composer, and although the more grotesque orchestral timbres, the brute complaints of the saxophone, the vicious spurts from the muted brass, may seem to belie the rich sentimentality of their background, they are only thorns protecting a fleshy cactus—a sauce piquante poured over a nice juicy steak.

Jazz, or to be pedantically accurate, "ragtime," from having a purely functional value—a mere accompaniment to the tapping of toe and heel, the quick linking of bodies and the slow unburdening of minds—has suddenly achieved the status of a "school," a potent influence that can meet the highbrow composer on his own terms. Though popularly regarded as being a barbaric art, it is to its sophistication that jazz owes its real force. It is the first dance music to bridge the gap between highbrow and lowbrow successfully. The

170

valse has received august patronage from Beethoven onward, it is true, but the valses of the nineteenth-century composers are either definite examples of unbending or definite examples of sophistication—sometimes both. Chabrier's *Fête Polonaise* has an harmonic and orchestral elaboration far beyond anything imagined by the popular valse writers of his time, but the modern highbrow composer who writes a foxtrot can hardly hope to go one better than Duke Ellington, if indeed he can be considered as being in the same class at all. In the nineteenth century the split between the classical and popular came between a follower of Liszt, let us say, and a follower of Gungl. Today the split occurs between a composer like Kurt Weill and a composer like Jarnach—both of them pupils of Busoni.

The same rapprochement between highbrow and lowbrow—both meeting in an emotional *terrain vague*—can be seen in literature. Though Byron wrote a poem about the valse there is little in common between his poems and the popular songs of the period; Rossetti kept his limericks and his sonnets severely apart; and though Dowson frequented the breezy music halls of his day there is no touch of Dolly Gray about Cynara. In the poetry of T. S. Eliot, however—particularly in "Sweeney Agonistes"—we find the romantic pessimism of the nineteenth century expressed in the music-hall technique of the twentieth-century lyric writer, not ironically but quite genuinely. "This is the way the world ends, this is the way the world ends, this is the way the world ends, not with a bang but a whimper" echoes not only the jingle of the jazz song but its sentiment. Whimpering has indeed become recognized as one of the higher pleasures.

MUSIC HO! (1934)

SIDNEY LANIER

→» «←

Music Is Infinite

Flutist, composer, and poet, author of the Centennial Cantata of 1876,
Lanier was a born and trained musician who has left a volume of excellent essays on music. The following is from a manuscript fragment
first printed in his collected works.

All shades in an American audience; from those who cry give us
a tune, something quick and devilish, to those who find in music a
religion of the emotions and a comfort and triumph in the darkest
hour of the soul. Composers must not be characterized. We must not
take Beethoven and Mozart and stick a pin through each one like
so many bugs and butterflies in a glass case, and say this one Beethoven belongs to the class of the big beetles (Coleoptera gigans)
and Mozart to the class of the butterflies (——!). If we do, the composers will become as dry and dusty as an entomologist's collection.

In the same way we must not assign too definite *ideas* to musical
compositions: this means longing etc., this means etc., etc. (Bayard
Taylor's experience with Wagner's music: one of the party said it
meant moonlight, another sea, another so and so, etc., etc.: on the
other hand, that burlesque orchestra piece where the sun was represented rising over Pike County, Arkansas, (piccolo and drum) etc.)
Cf. Thos. Hood's *Musical Party*. Music is vague: purposely so. This
is no objection. If it is, the Bible must fall. The Bible furnishes a
text for every creed. The Mormon allows you to have twenty wives,
and furnishes you good authority from the Bible, while the old
George Raff and his Harmonists (and the Catholic Priest) allow
you no wife, and give you good authority from the Bible: the slave
holder draws his warrant from the Bible, the abolitionist draws
his warrant from the Bible: the Unitarian proves from the Bible

that there is but one person in the Godhead, the Trinitarian that there are three. Arnold reads the plain and lucid statements of St. Matthew and Paul and arrives at Rationalism, while from the more mystical writings of St. John a thousand mystagogues construct a thousand forms of belief. This is because the Bible is so great; and it is purely because music is so great that it yields aid and comfort to so many theories.

NOTES AND FRAGMENTS (Undated)

FERRUCCIO BUSONI[1]

➤➤➤ ◄◄◄

The Unity of Music

It is time to recognize that all the manifestations of music constitute a *unity*. It is time to say farewell to the subdividing of music based on its purpose, its forms, or the means it employs—as is still done today. It is time to be persuaded that the sole differences consist in its *contents* and *quality*.

By *purpose* I have in mind the three fields of opera, church, and concert music; by *form,* such things as lyric, dance, fugue, or sonata; by *means employed,* the use of the human voice or of instruments, and, among these, the orchestra, the quartet, the piano, and their multiple combinations.

Music, in whatever shape and place and however paired, remains music and nothing else. It may enter into and become part of a given genre, but only through the imagination, by means of a title or motto, or of a text, or by reason of the situation in which it is placed. But there is no such thing as music that bears the indelible imprint of *church music* and is recognizable as such. I am convinced that no one hearing a fragment of Mozart's *Requiem* or Beethoven's *Missa Solemnis* can detect and define it as ecclesiastical unless he knows the text or title.

The Gregorian chant, which is univocal and bare, entirely devoid of harmony, is strictly bound up in our imagination with the idea of the church, and we hear it as church music in the same way as the style of Palestrina. Yet the love songs of Palestrina's time are identically similar to an offertory—the text and the occasion alone differentiate the two. When Pope Gregory set the rules for the liturgy, there was no other style of music, and we are bound to ad-

[1] See head note p. 443.

174

mit that a romance of that time was not very different from that which today we think we distinguish as originating in music of the church.

Our sensibility responds in just the same way to "operatic music" insofar as—by a slavish habit—a given attitude has been as if naturalized there, and now *seems* operatic because we have learned to know it at the theater. Yet the operatic attitude proper is but a formula in which music has the smallest part. Usually what it amounts to is a sort of give and take that the opera-makers closely ape one from the other; also a concession to the singing and often a device to make up for the lack of a more elevated expression, or else to fashion some clever passage work.

In "concert music"—beginning with Haydn, and wherever it exists as a living art—we continually find theatrical reminiscences, especially in Beethoven's minor mood: long stretches in his allegro movements follow the pace and expression of *opera buffa*. Such a remark in no way lessens the value of the music. Art is the interpretation of life, and the theater is such in ever-greater measure than the other arts. For which reason it is natural that living music should bear an affinity with the music of the theater.

SKETCH FOR A PREFACE TO *DR. FAUSTUS* (1921)

JULES RENARD
AND MAURICE RAVEL

➤➤ ⫷⫷

Music and Nature

➤➤ ——————————————————————————————— ⫷⫷

Jules Renard (1864–1910) was a novelist and playwright of the naturalistic school who specialized in the minute recording of human and
animal life.

➤➤ ——————————————————————————————— ⫷⫷

January 12. M. Ravel, the composer of *Histoires Naturelles,*[1] swarthy,
rich, and subtle, insists that I go tonight to hear his melodies.

I tell him how ignorant I am of music, and ask what he has
added to the *Histoires.*

"My aim is not to add anything," he says, "but to interpret."

"What does that mean?"

"Why, to say in music what you say in words when you look at
a tree, for example. I think and feel in sounds, and I should like to
think and feel the same things as you. One kind of music is instinc-
tive, made of feelings—that is my kind. Of course one must first
learn the craft. Then there is the intellectual kind—d'Indy's music.[2]
Tonight there will be hardly anybody there who is not a d'Indy.
They reject feeling, which they refuse to go into. My mode of thought
is the opposite, but they find my work interesting since they are
willing to play it. It is a trial of considerable importance to me. But
of one thing I am sure: the performer is absolutely first-rate."

RENARD'S *JOURNAL* (1907)

[1] A volume of sketches published by Renard in 1896, illustrated by Toulouse-
Lautrec in 1899.
[2] Vincent d'Indy (1851–1931); see p. 284.

THOMAS DE QUINCEY

>>> <<<

How Music Imitates

The first elementary idea of a Greek tragedy is to be sought in a serious Italian opera. The Greek dialogue is represented by the recitative, and the tumultuous lyrical parts assigned chiefly, though not exclusively, to the chorus on the Greek stage, are represented by the impassioned airs, duos, trios, choruses, etc., on the Italian. And here, at the very outset, occurs a question which lies at the threshold of a Fine Art—that is, of *any* Fine Art: for had the views of Addison upon the Italian opera had the least foundation in truth, there could have been no room or opening for any mode of imitation except such as belongs to a *mechanic* art.

The reason for at all connecting Addison with this case is, that *he* chiefly was the person occupied in assailing the Italian opera; and this hostility arose, probably, in his want of sensibility to good (that is, to Italian) music. But whatever might be his motive for the hostility, the single argument by which he supported it was this— that a hero ought not to sing upon the stage, because no hero known to history ever summoned a garrison in a song, or charged a battery in a semichorus. In this argument lies an ignorance of the very first principle concerned in *every* Fine Art. In all alike, more or less directly, the object is to reproduce in the mind some great effect, through the agency of *idem in alio.* The *idem,* the same impression, is to be restored; but *in alio,* in a different material—by means of some different instrument. For instance, on the Roman stage there was an art, now entirely lost, of narrating, and in part of dramatically representing, an impassioned tale, by means of dancing, of musical accompaniment in the orchestra, and of elaborate pantomime in the performer. *Saltavit Hypermnestram,* he danced (that is, he represented by dancing and pantomime the story of) Hypermnestra. Now, suppose a man to object, that young ladies, when saving their youthful husbands at midnight from assassination, could not be capable of waltzing or quadrilling, how wide is this of the whole problem! This is still seeking for the *mechanic* imitation, some imitation founded in the very fact; whereas the object is to seek the imitation in the sameness of the impression drawn from a different, or even from an impossible fact. If a man, taking a hint from the Roman "Saltatio" (*saltavit Andromachen*),[1] should say that he would "whistle Waterloo," that is, by whistling connected with pantomime, would express the passion and the charges of Waterloo, it would be monstrous to refuse him his postulate on the pretense that "people did not whistle at Waterloo." Precisely so: neither are most people made of marble, but of a material as different as can well be imagined, viz., of elastic flesh, with warm blood coursing along its tubes; and yet, for all that, a sculptor will draw tears from you, by exhibiting, in pure statuary marble, on a sepulchral monument, two young children with their little heads on a pillow, sleeping in each other's arms; whereas, if he had presented them in waxwork, which yet is far more like to flesh, you would have felt little more pathos in the scene than if they had been shown baked in gilt gingerbread. He has expressed the *idem,* the identical thing expressed in the real children; the sleep that masks death, the rest, the peace, the purity, the innocence; but *in alio,* in a substance the most different; rigid, non-elastic, and as unlike to flesh, if tried by touch, or eye, or by experience of life, as can well be imagined. So of the whistling. It is the very worst objection in the world to say, that the strife of Waterloo did not reveal itself through whistling: undoubtedly it did not; but that is the very ground of the man's art. He will reproduce the fury and the movement as to the only point which concerns you, viz., the effect upon your own sympathies, through a language that seems without any relation to it: he will set before you what *was* at Waterloo through that which was *not* at Waterloo. Whereas any direct factual imitation, resting upon painted figures drest up in regimentals,

[1] He (the actor) danced (the role of) Andromache.

and worked by watchwork through the whole movements of the battle, would have been no art whatsoever in the sense of a Fine Art, but a base *mechanic* mimicry.

This principle of the *idem in alio,* so widely diffused through all the higher revelations of art, it is peculiarly requisite to bear in mind when looking at Grecian tragedy, because no form of human composition employs it in so much complexity.

THE *ANTIGONE* OF SOPHOCLES (1846)

MARTIN LUTHER

⇛⇚

In Praise of Music

Luther played both the flute and the guitar, sang and composed hymns, as well as indited thoughts and essays on his favorite art.

Music is one of the greatest gifts that God has given us: it is divine and therefore Satan is its enemy. For with its aid many dire temptations are overcome; the devil does not stay where music is.

Music is among the highest of the arts: its sounds bring the words of a text to life. It puts to flight all sad thoughts, as we see happened to Saul.[1]

Many of our courtiers would boast of saving our overlord the three thousand florins a year that he spends on music; but they squander in other ways three times as much. Music must be supported by the king and the princes, for the maintenance of the arts is their duty no less than the maintenance of the laws. Private citizens, however much they may love art, cannot afford to support it. Duke George, landgrave of Hesse, and John Frederic, elector of Saxony, have had a full complement of musicians, vocal and instrumental; and now the Duke of Bavaria, the Emperor Ferdinand, and the Emperor Charles are doing the same.[2]

After a concert in his own house, December 17, 1538

If God gives us such boons in this life, which is but a vale of trials and tears, what will it be like hereafter!

Singing is a noble art and a good exercise. It has nothing to do with worldly affairs, with the strife of the market place and the rivalries

---

[1] Allusion to I Samuel 16:23.
[2] Ferdinand, Charles V's brother, colleague and successor to the Empire.

of the court. The singer fears no evil; he forgets all worry and is happy. . . .

I have always been very fond of music. I would not change my little knowledge of music for a great deal. Whoever is proficient in this art is a good man, fit for all other things. Hence it is absolutely necessary to have it taught in the schools. A schoolmaster must know how to sing or I shan't tolerate him. Nor must one ordain young fellows into the priesthood unless they have learned and practiced the art during their schooling.

In fact, I want all the arts, but especially music, dedicated to the service of Him who has created and given them to us. The Christian religion is a religion of joyousness, for God has through his Son made our hearts joyful. Anyone who truly believes this cannot help saying it and singing it with gladness. . . . Anyone who won't say it and sing it shows that he doesn't really believe it.

To a harpist:

Friend, play me an air, as David did. Indeed, I think that if the Psalmist were to return among us, he would be surprised to find how many have skill in his art.

How is it that we have so many and such excellent examples of secular music, while our sacred music is frigid and dull? [To illustrate his meaning he sang, first, one or two German folksongs, and then one or two of the commonest hymns.] As for those who despise music, the dreamers and the mystics, I despise them. I shall ask the prince, out of all this money we have, to establish a good band.

To Ludwig Senfl,[3] Court musician of Bavaria, asking for a musical setting:

My love of music has made me overcome any fear I might have of being rebuffed by you on your seeing at the bottom of this request a name which is doubtless odious to you. The same devotion and faith in music makes me hope at the same time that correspondence with me will not involve you in trouble or vexations. The

[3] (? –1555); composer of a famous imitative piece, *"Kling-Klang."*

Grand Turk himself could not make the request of a letter on this subject a matter of discredit to you. Except for theology, there is no art that can be placed in comparison with music.

TABLE TALK AND *LETTERS* (1530–1541)

P. E. VERNON

The Ear Is Not Enough

At the time of writing, the author was research fellow in both psychology and sacred music at Cambridge University.

Music is generally regarded as essentially something that is heard, and though, admittedly, various factors may occasionally affect appreciation, yet these are thought of as irrelevant and having little bearing on the music itself. I wish to show how many and how important are such factors, music without them being an impossibility. Only when they are taken into account and their musical significance is considered does it become possible to point the way to an adequate theory as to the nature of aesthetic appreciation.

I have been investigating the subject of the appreciation of music and its psychology at Cambridge, using ordinary discussions, questions, introspections, and observations, certain psychological tests, and also two experimental concerts at which members of the audiences (each numbering about fifty people of all degrees of musicianship) tried to write down what they had actually thought about and felt while listening. Previous investigators in this sphere seem to have depended almost entirely on gramophone music, and often appear only to have played bad music to more or less unmusical people; neither the title nor the composer of the music were told to the subjects of such experiments, and an extremely artificial and abnormal situation resulted. To demonstrate this effect my first concert was as normal as possible, ordinary chamber music, such as a Mozart trio, sixteenth-century and Brahms songs, Bach and contemporary pianoforte music, being performed under usual concert conditions by members of the Cambridge University Musical

Club. At a second concert the conditions were abnormal, the performers being behind a curtain and the program announced only in
outline, e.g., violin suite, two songs, etc. It consisted of music almost wholly unknown to the audience, especially chosen to throw
light on certain points.

Now it would obviously be difficult to write out very complete
introspections while listening, hence the following method was developed and proved to be fairly satisfactory, not disturbing appreciation of the music unduly. The introspective records (which were
treated confidentially) were on the whole quite good and clear. After
each item of music the audience were asked to indicate, individually,
how much they had attended to, thought about, or felt certain general categories or headings by giving each 0, 1, 2, or 3 marks according to its relative importance for them in that item. These
headings were given in printed directions and explained in a pre-
liminary talk. The audience were required to use only those which
seemed to them necessary to summarize all their thoughts and feelings while listening—for example: anything irrelevant to the music
—visual images (mental pictures); bodily movements and rhythmic
responses; thoughts as to the identity of the music, composers, performers; interest in other technical aspects of the music; the goodness or badness of the music; feelings aroused; aesthetic appeal.

During the rest of each interval (five to ten minutes), or, if it did
not distract them, during the music, they amplified their marks
by describing as fully as possible any details of their experiences.

The audience were quite serious and interested throughout; at
the first concert only 18 per cent complained at all of the situation;
at the second 47 per cent, including all the most musical, admitted
to being somewhat distracted, but the majority rather enjoyed being free from performers' mannerisms and the noise of applause.
The main difficulty in working out the results was that no two people mean the same thing by aesthetic appeal or value, nor do they
estimate their wandering of attention and the like by the same
standards. But both the marks, the remarks, and the data obtained
by other methods supplemented one another, and it was possible to

obtain a good deal of evidence by noting what characteristics were prominent in the more musical subjects of the investigation, what in the less musical. Certain questions with regard to their musical education and other factors were answered at the time, and my personal knowledge of more than three-quarters of them was of the greatest use.

The first and most obvious non-musical factor is wandering of attention from the music to various associations (recollections of previous performances, and so on) and often to quite irrelevant affairs. To many this free play of the imagination is a source of considerable pleasure, and some people, with but little knowledge of or interest in music, are definitely stimulated to think about extraneous matters by having music going on when not attending. (Tolstoy and Stendhal were presumably of this type.) Analogous is the use of music to help factory workers engaged on monotonous and rhythmic jobs; sailors and savages also often work much better when they sing.

At the concerts the marks for this first category varied with the length of the items, and with their lack of emotional and intellectual interest. I found quite definitely that the more musical, on the average, attend better than the unmusical, for the musician develops a musical sentiment or conscience which debars him from enjoying such lapses, and helps him to concentrate.

The more representational the music the more easily are associations aroused, so that many listeners like to weave emotional dramas into what they hear; any work that attains much popularity is inevitably supplied with a program, whether the composer intended it or no. In about one-third of the audience either the emotional flux aroused by the music or its physical characteristics may lead on into sporadic visual images, while up to 10 per cent may enjoy the music because it evokes a continuous kind of dream which they watch as if at a theater. This phenomenon of visualization only appears in people with a low degree of mental control, and so increases in frequency with fatigue; it requires a passive, almost hypnotic, state without any critical or objective attitude toward the music. The visual

imagery of savages and primitive peoples is very vivid, so that this is
probably one of the main effects of music on them; hence the magical
powers ascribed to music in the many legends like that of Orpheus.
That music is not capable of suggesting specific scenes has often been
proved. However, there is some consistency in its effect. For example, in a polka from Casella's *Puppazetti,*[1] played as a pianoforte
duet, about one-fifth of the audience saw either wooden or foreign
soldiers, or a war dance of Red Indian or African natives, and the
like (thus combining symbolically the martial, rhythmic, and strange
characteristics of the music). Though visualization is not absent
in some people in the most abstract music, yet, together with emotional interpretations, it is naturally most common in songs, opera,
and avowed program music. The more musical, however, often say
that when listening to music such as *L'Après-midi d'un Faune* they
may at first visualize scenes or incidents; when they get to know it
better they forget the program and listen to it more abstractly. Some
never make use of such associations or interpretations at all. I find
that the more musical also have, on the average, a considerable
preference for orchestral and chamber music concerts over choral
concerts and operas, and show little appreciation of any vocal music.
When they do listen to songs they pay but little attention to the
words; in fact, at the second concert it was demonstrated that an
audience of average musical level takes remarkably little notice of
the text, for to a song by Campion [2] the following words were sung:

> Now that the sun hath sunk and risen,
> And she the world hath all forgiven,
> Though youth is wanting far and nigh,
> Yet from the embers falls the sky.

> Do not like others when the time
> Seeking their passion from the rime,
> Though without e'er full straightly given
> Fast with a step too slow for heaven.

[1] Alfredo Casella (born 1883), Italian pianist, composer, and critic. The
Puppazetti is an orchestral suite (1917).

[2] Thomas Campion (1567–1620), English poet, composer, and theorist about
both arts.

Actually only 6 per cent noticed that these words were nonsense; 16 per cent found them uninteresting, or in some way suspected that they were unusual, or thought them badly enunciated (as a matter of fact they were sung very clearly, but this is a natural psychological reaction to nonsense words); 15 per cent thought they had attended to the words but noticed nothing wrong; and the remaining 63 per cent took no notice of the sense of the words at all.

Now though the abstract type of listeners combine in condemning the representational effects of music, yet too much technical interest may be equally distracting from full appreciation. Thinking about the cleverness of the composer, or of oneself for elucidating his cleverness, may easily become an end in itself, presumably gratifying some self-assertive or constructive instinct; but such pleasure is hardly aesthetic. Yet the attitude is to a large extent inevitable, even when (as in the second experimental concert) an attempt is made to eliminate it by dispensing with programs, in the hope that the music may be appreciated solely for itself. Although the audience were particularly requested not to regard the concert as a guessing competition, all but the most unmusical 12 per cent speculated as to the composers, their period, the performers, etc., in most of the items; the more musical half got about two-fifths of their guesses right, the less musical about one-quarter. The latter made fewer technical allusions, but criticized the performers more than the musical. The first item was a violin suite consisting of four movements, none of them originally written for the violin, by Purcell, Berlioz (Fugue on Brander's song from *Faust*), Rameau, and Mozart. Only about the most musical 20 per cent noticed any heterogeneity of styles, and not more than a third of these suspected it to be a hoax. Incidentally this shows that the supposed necessity for coherence and continuity in a sonata or suite, and the objection to music being transcribed, have little weight for the great majority of listeners. In another item, a Purcell "Ground in Gamut," only 16 per cent (again the most musical) noticed the ground bass; most of the rest, not knowing what it was about, were rather bored. Finally an original improvisation in the modern style was played,

introducing the tune of "God Save the King"; only one person noticed this theme, two guessed that it was an improvisation, while
most of the others ascribed it to some such composer as Debussy,
Stravinsky, Scriabin, or Goossens.

It appears, therefore, that abnormal conditions merely distort
technical interest and make it more prominent; they are, in fact,
most unsound. We inevitably interpret what we hear in the light of
our past musical or non-musical experience; we build up special
knowledge and means of perception so as to put ourselves into the
appropriate period and style of the composer or of the title of the
piece. We try to appreciate Beethoven's music not as a poor edition of Bach's, nor a funeral march as a gigue, but each for its own
qualities. Completely abstract (that is, purely auditory) music is
unattainable; and as music was primarily connected with words or
other non-musical meaning, so-called absolute music being a later
specialization, the representational attitude is almost equally un-
avoidable. Most musicians attach some significance to words such
as *allegro* and *scherzo,* or even more suggestive ones such as
agitato, maestoso, and *perdendosi,* so that they have no right to
condemn fancy titles, analytic programs, and the like; all help in
the comprehension of the composer's intention. Nor is music generally of itself abstract or program, but is largely what different listeners make of it. One person on hearing, say, a Handel gigue may
visualize people dancing round a maypole; another will concentrate solely on the composer's technical devices. All that one can
safely assert is that, among musicians with most experience, on the
one hand the emotions tend to be controlled, integrated, and to
lose their concrete reference, and on the other hand technical interests tend to be regarded as means to an end, to be used for getting
the most out of music; but that, for fullest appreciation, they should
become largely automatic and subconscious.

We must now return to visualization. In certain cases it assumes
more musical forms. For instance, at the second concert many of the
audience mentally saw the performers behind the screen; naturally
this must be an almost constant element among a large number of

people who listen in to broadcast music. The innumerable portraits in the *Radio Times* probably help in this process, and increase the so-called human element. Visual or other non-auditory means are also used in the actual perception and recall of music by most of the ordinary listeners, and even by about 10 per cent or more trained musicians. Some visualize the notes that are being played on the score or on the instruments, or else their names, or the name of the key; others respond to music not in terms of sound but by a sub-conscious tendency to hum it. Many also hear or think of music muscularly. They raise their heads or contract some other muscle when the music rises, or they perceive it in terms of their hands at the pianoforte or other instruments. Thus several of my audience noticed that their fingers tried to follow those of the pianists, others felt that they wanted to dance, especially in strongly rhythmic music. In slow movements any audience obviously sinks down with relaxed muscles; but it seems that, for most people, full perception of music requires that the body should be in good muscular tone and well braced; standards of taste are often lowered when one is reclining in a comfortable chair; possibly this is partly responsible for the high level of the tastes of a Promenade concert audience, many of whom have to stand up and are correspondingly capable of appreciating "strong" music. Rhythm is an aspect of music that is more of a bodily than an auditory nature; over three-quarters of my audience acknowledged making considerable or moderate bodily responses to it, though often only feeling tendencies to move their legs, hands, etc., rather than actually swaying them to and fro. Again, the more musical seem to respond less overtly, more mentally or implicitly. We see, therefore, that much that is non-auditory may be quite efficient and helpful in appreciation, and far from being non-musical.

A phenomenon rather similar to visualization of scenes is "colored hearing," or synaesthesia, out of about a hundred people with whom I dealt there were half a dozen genuine cases. As an example, one man, when he hears the chord of A major, sees the color green and then remembers that green is A, so that he has absolute pitch through color. For him the colors are essentially tonal, so that those corresponding to related keys are similar. They are only seen when a piece is characteristically in one key; in this case the notes of the music were seen mentally superimposed on a background of the prevailing key color. Many other people have associations: for example, the trumpet reminding them of scarlet, the flute of blue, etc.; but real synaesthetic colors seem to be inextricably bound up with the actual perception and recollection of the notes. Synaesthetic persons always regard their colors as quite natural, and, until they inquire into the matter, imagine that everyone is like themselves in this respect, while actually no two synaesthetics are likely to agree in their color schemes. Scriabin was a synaesthetic who very strongly associated odors as well as colors with music.

About half a dozen more subjects saw moving or stationary patterns when listening to music; such phenomena may appear ridiculous or incredible, yet of musicians with absolute pitch (say 30 to 40 per cent) the majority often have precisely analogous associations of keys, not with colors but with various emotional characteristics. They often state, for example, that the overture to *Die Meistersinger* could be in no other key but C major, and that E major is typical of such music as Mendelssohn so often wrote, and, as a corollary, that the overture to *Tannhäuser* is weakened by being largely written in E. Naturally such opinions may seem quite illogical to those who do not generalize in this way, which presumably results from associating this key, so often used by Mendelssohn, with one's emotional attitude toward him and his works, and then projecting this attitude, often unconsciously, on to the works of other composers in the same key. But again, even those without absolute pitch may associate specific chords or progressions with the style of, say, Vaughan Williams, or Franck, so that in general these are not, I think, non-musical phenomena. There is no essential difference between colored hearing, seeing patterns, giving keys special characteristics, and mere generalizations about the style of well-known composers. Like the translation of heard music into terms of sight or muscles, they are merely modes of thinking, analogous to different languages; they are found at all musical levels, and there is no reason why everyone should not have individual peculiarities of this type without finding them to be irrelevant or distracting from the highest appreciation.

So far we have been considering some of the apparently non-musical responses or effects produced by music. We may now pass on to nonmusical influences or stimuli that affect music.

The first of these are visual sensations; a few people listen with their eyes closed, but the great majority receive and react to a very large number of visual impressions while they are supposed to be listening. But this does not mean that all this side of their mental activity is wasted from a musical point of view. The amateur musician may attain to a fuller perception and appreciation of music by following the score, thus aiding hearing with vision; or by watching performers he may keep his attention more closely on the music and may follow the inner parts by seeing the appropriate instruments playing. Again, there is the important factor of intuition, a kind of subconscious perception by one member of a group of the bodily expressions of the thoughts and feelings of the rest, and hence an automatic realization of the "atmosphere" or significance of these aggregate thoughts and feelings. A performer or a lecturer does not necessarily take conscious note of the stillness or fidgeting of his audience, but always knows by intuition if he is holding them or no. And on the listener's side, if a soloist, or a conductor and orchestra, are working up to a furious climax, or playing a very rhythmic piece, the audience tends to follow them and intuit their mental and bodily state by becoming similarly moved. Watching the performers also helps by intuition in the apprehension of their personalities which they express in the music, and so of their contribution to the total experience, for most people would allow, for example, that a Beethoven sonata played by Busoni was a far more valuable experience than the same sonata played note-perfectly by an average pianist. Any intuition or attitude in one member of the performers or audience is reciprocally reinforced by all the rest if they are sympathetically inclined toward one another and similarly interested in the music. Hence it is (as Brent-Smith points out) that Kreisler cannot attempt to play good music at an ordinary "celebrity" concert, since he realizes that the audience are not in sympathy with him toward it. Several of my subjects find that they can only obtain full musical enjoyment if they are among sympathetic companions. Again, few would not admit that pleasant or suitable surroundings, even if not specifically attended to, enhance their appreciation. Thus an organ recital in a cathedral is aesthetically more valuable than the same recital in an ugly concert hall, though the latter may be acoustically superior.

However, among the musically more advanced the whole process of musical perception is so integrated that surroundings, performers, score, etc., are often regarded as distracting, and are seldom considered in deciding whether to go to concerts. They are often able to listen "ideally," that is, to value the music they hear largely by their own ideas as to how it should be played rather than by how it actually is played.

Personality and the like are only too apt to become objects of interest *per se;* a Pachmann, for example, is more often distracting and nonmusical than relevant and helpful to appreciation, in that he tends to overbalance the music. I find an interesting division between people who like singers because their personality "gets across" and the more musical people who, conversely, dislike most singers, especially female ones, because they are trying to "make an effect."

This brings us at once to the role of gregarious factors in musical appreciation. Frank Howes has dealt with them very fully in his "Borderland of Music and Psychology," but has, I think, as regards musical people, considerably overemphasized them. His thesis is, roughly, that aesthetic appreciation is impossible without the gregarious satisfaction obtained by listening to music together with a large number of other people who are similarly moved; the amount of applause is determined not by the depth of feeling or the intensity of pleasure experienced, but by the homogeneity of feeling evoked in the whole audience. He regards applause as a necessity, since

the audience feels, often subconsciously, after sitting still and listening for a long time, that it must do something, hence it is psycho-
logically unjustifiable to discourage applause between the movements of a symphony or quartet. He also states, in support of this,
that true musical enjoyment can never be obtained in solitude from
the gramophone or broadcast music, or from playing the pianoforte
to oneself. Now it must be acknowledged that the gregarious or fel-
lowship feeling of seeing and hearing a large orchestra, or applauding in unison with a huge audience, are highly pleasurable to most
people of the more or less unmusical type. But I find that as a rule
the more musical people prefer string quartets and chamber music
to orchestral music; they also object to being carried away, as a large
group of people so often is, or to descending with the group to a
lower level in the scale of civilization and self-control. Similarly,
the desire to applaud, especially between movements, obviously becomes controlled and tends to disappear in really musical audiences,
so that almost the only reasons why we do applaud, it seems to me,
are convention, politeness to the performers, or the hope of getting
an encore. Most of my audience, at the second concert, were glad to
be relieved from it, and in general at Cambridge chamber music
concerts it seldom lasts more than twenty seconds as compared with
the one or two minutes that are so familiar at Promenade concerts
and the like. In fact, one theory of aesthetics that contains a good
deal of truth states that the essential features of the aesthetic experience are a complete equilibrium and harmony whereby there is no
tendency to action at all; after it one should be as ready to do any
action as willingly as any other, since all one's instincts and impulses
have been satisfied, and it is only insofar as the experience is incomplete that there is a disposition toward any one action such as
applause. Again, a large proportion of musical people seem to prefer to listen to broadcast or gramophone music when it is sufficiently
well reproduced, and they like to play the pianoforte to themselves
so as to escape these gregarious factors. However, people vary considerably in the strength of their gregarious and social tendencies,
and for some this gregarious satisfaction is an essential element

in their musical appreciation, and not necessarily to be condemned.

Many other non-auditory stimuli obviously affect musical appreciation, e.g., one's general comfort, recent emotional experiences, one's relative familiarity with different instruments, and various outside interests; the connection between mathematics or science and the higher appreciation of music is very marked. Hence the formalist's assumption that the artistic faculty is quite unconnected with ordinary life cannot be upheld. Temperament, personal and racial prejudices are of great importance; Parry, in his *Art of Music*, gives several examples of the influence of environment on music. The connection is, however, obscured by the factor of compensation, as, for instance, when very submissive people seem to like very vigorous music, or very aggressive ones like sentimental stuff. The unpopularity of German music among English audiences during the war is an illustration of the effect of non-musical prejudices, though here again the more musical were less influenced in their opinions. Similarly, I attempted to show the influence of a composer's name in my second concert by having played a nocturne by Field. Most of the audience were unable to guess the composer, or knew it already, but, as I had hoped, the remaining 18 per cent thought it was by Chopin, and their remarks indicate all their usual prejudices for, or usually against, Chopin, e.g., "the Victorian drawing-room atmosphere" (the piece really having been composed in about 1814).

We largely adopt our tastes from the musical minority whose opinions we respect, and reject those of the unmusical majority. But this subjective nature of musical standards is a commonplace of musical criticism which I need not emphasize.

The conclusions of the discussion may now be pointed out. As a psychologist I have no intention of entering into the controversy as to the ethics of various factors, emotion, intellect, etc., in music. I have merely tried to show that a great many apparently non-musical factors always occur in the appreciation of various people to various degrees, depending on their individual mental and temperamental peculiarities and musical training, and that they may almost all of them help in the perception of music or add to the enjoyment or value obtained. On examining the part played by such factors at the lowest and highest musical levels and in the poorest and fullest appreciation, it seems that some of them tend to disappear or to become subconscious or controlled and integrated; so that it is only attention to any one aspect (be it intellectual, emotional, gregarious, or anything else), to the detriment of or distraction from the whole, that is really non-musical. The average marks given to different categories by individual members and by the whole of my audiences demonstrate the truth; the average marks for aesthetic appeal or value of different items did not run parallel either with the marks for intellectual interest nor with those for emotion, but were almost exactly parallel with the sum of these two headings. From another approach, namely, genetic studies or case histories of several of my subjects, one finds that people usually seem to possess initially either, (a) a mainly objective, critical, or analytic attitude toward music, or, (b) a mainly subjective and emotional one. As their musical experience has developed each attitude has become more tinged with the other till they fuse in the fullest appreciation. Each person should be able to synthesize all his various dispositions, tendencies, instincts, impulses, etc., as many elements as possible being included. Thus we are justified in concluding that aesthetic appreciation, which we are now led up to via our examination of non-musical effects and influences, consists not so much in an absolute and definite experience that only a few highly cultured people attain to, but in this ideal organization and synthesis.

MUSICAL TIMES (1929)

SIR THOMAS BROWNE

→»» «««

Music and the Deity

It is my temper, and I like it the better, to affect all harmony; and sure there is musick even in the beauty, and the silent note which *Cupid* strikes, far sweeter than the sound of an instrument. For there is a musick where ever there is a harmony, order or proportion; and thus far we may maintain the musick of the Sphears: for those well-ordered motions, and regular paces, though they give no sound unto the ear, yet to the understanding they strike a note most full of harmony. Whosoever is harmonically composed, delights in harmony; which makes me much distrust the symmetry of those heads which declaim against all Church-Musick. For my self, not only from my obedience, but my particular Genius, I do embrace it: for even that vulgar and Tavern-Musick, which makes one man merry, another mad, strikes in me a deep fit of devotion, and a profound contemplation of the first Composer. There is something in it of Divinity more than the ear discovers: it is an Hieroglyphical and shadowed lesson of the whole World, and creatures of God; such a melody to the ear, as the whole World well understood, would afford the understanding. In brief, it is a sensible fit of that harmony, which intellectually sounds in the ears of God. I will not say with *Plato,* the soul is an harmony, but harmonical, and hath its nearest sympathy unto Musick: thus some whose temper of body agrees, and humours the constitution of their souls, are born Poets, though indeed all are naturally inclined unto Rhythme. This made *Tacitus* in the very first line of his Story, fall upon a verse, and *Cicero* the worst of Poets, but declaiming for a Poet, falls in the very first sentence upon a perfect Hexameter. I feel not in me those sordid and unchristian desires of my profession; I do not secretly

implore and wish for Plagues, rejoyce at Famines, revolve Ephem-
erides and Almanacks, in expectation of malignant Aspects, fatal
Conjunctions, and Eclipses: I rejoyce not at unwholesome Springs,
nor unseasonable Winters; my Prayer goes with the Husbandman's;
I desire every thing in its proper season, that neither men nor the times
be put out of temper.

RELIGIO MEDICI (1642)

PHILIP HESELTINE

※ ※

The Idea of a Song

Known as a composer under the pseudonym Peter Warlock, Heseltine
(1894–1930) managed in his short life to endow English music with some
magnificent songs, to write two scholarly works, and to edit a lively periodical, *The Sackbut,* to which the following was the Foreword.

Among the Chippewa Indians of North America, we are told,
"there is no musical notation; a picture of the idea of a song is
drawn on a bark strip, from which another person who has never
heard it can sing it accurately."

This, like so much in the art of so-called primitive races, puts us
all to shame. We cannot draw a picture of the idea of a piece of music
from which another person who has never heard the music can get an
accurate impression of what it is about. Yet if musical criticism has
any purpose in it, that purpose is surely to convey, by words perhaps rather than by pictures, "the idea of a song" to others who
have never heard it.

Our chief enemy is Time. We can hold the score of a symphony
in our hand complete and whole and all at once: but to hold the music
signified by that score, the idea of the song, in the mind in a like
completeness and wholeness is a very different and vastly more difficult proposition. When listening to music we are subject to all the
limitations that time imposes: but when we reflect upon what we
have heard, when we try to sum it all up, to distill its quintessence,
we have to pit ourselves against time in an effort to transcend its
restrictions on the mind.

To see a piece of music whole, like a picture, to grasp the rhythm
and design not merely of particular sections but of the entire work
—and, as the result of this process, to be able to comprehend and

share with its composer the complex synthesis of mental and emotional states the work expresses—such is the task of the writer on music.

This being admitted, it becomes painfully apparent that when we speak or write about music—and here the professional critic is in much the same case as the man who tries to record the impressions of his first concert—we embark upon a well-nigh impossible task.

Music, for us, begins where words end: how then should we adequately translate music into words? Only the simplest music yields to our attempts to draw a satisfactory verbal picture of the idea underlying it. We have lost the art of the old magicians who could compass the universe in a pentacle.

Music, one may say, is the outward and audible signification of inward and spiritual realities: implying, it would seem, that there is something else behind or beyond the music itself, that is not the music. And yet, some will reply, are we justified in assuming the separateness of the two things? Is it not, in a sense, the expression that makes the thought, the symbol that makes the reality, that *is* —as far as we can ever know it—the reality?

The fact is that when we come to the fundamental question of what music really is, we are all—composers, critics, and public alike —very much in the dark. Music's a rum go. Composers cannot really tell you how or why they write this or that kind of music, and professional critics are inclined to avoid the simpler and profounder problems of the art, taking refuge in technicalities which the ordinary music lover—who is always more interested in music's relation to life than in its relation to other music—finds more bewildering than the most abstruse specimen of actual composition. Thus the simplest and most natural questions of the non-musician are apt to prove the most embarrassing to the theorist or the critic who has so long taken these elementary problems for granted as already solved, that he has no answer but gibberish or evasion. The plain man is kept perpetually in the position of the child who is "not old enough" for the intelligence he demands. Nevertheless the general public has frequently welcomed and understood the man of original creative genius long before his fellow-composers and critics have ceased chattering their protests against his drunken and disorderly conduct.

[Hence] it is to be hoped that something may be done to break down the barrier of unnecessary modesty which so frequently prevents the non-professional music lover from contributing to discussions on musical subjects, by showing him that music is not the esoteric mystery that many of its professors and pseudo-critical jargon-mongers would have him believe, and that the only honorable ideal of the musical critic is so to educate and enlighten his public that he himself, as a professional institution, will in the end become unnecessary.

FOREWORD TO *THE SACKBUT* (1920)

MUSIC AND DRAMA

JEAN-JACQUES ROUSSEAU

꠸꠸ ꠸꠸

The Paris Opera in 1760

A musician all his life, Rousseau not only composed and copied music, but contributed voluminously to its theory. In his influential novel, *The New Héloïse,* he inserted the following bit of satire in the form of a letter addressed by the hero, Saint-Preux, to his country cousin, Mme. d'Orbe.

Imagine a crate about fifteen feet long and proportionately wide: that is the stage. On each side are placed a row of screens on which the setting of the acts to be played are crudely painted. The backdrop is a big curtain, similarly daubed and almost always torn, which may represent caverns on earth or holes in the sky, depending on the perspective. Everyone who walks across the stage behind this curtain produces a sort of tremor in it which is rather attractive. The sky is represented by some bluish rags that hang from rods or ropes like laundry on a line. The sun, which is occasionally to be seen, is a torch inside a lantern. The chariot for the gods and goddesses is made of two-by-fours hung like a swing within a frame, the god sitting on a transverse board in front of which is bunched some tinted cloth—the cloud appropriate to the god's magnificence. Near the bottom of the machine stand two or three stinking candles, which, while the illuminated personage waves and shrieks in his little swing, smoke him up to his heart's content —incense worthy of the god.

Since chariots form the most important part of the opera's equipment, you can from these infer the rest. The troubled sea consists of long structures of blue cloth or cardboard mounted on parallel rods and turned by urchins. Thunder is a heavy cart drawn across the beams—by no means the least touching instrument of this delightful band. Lightning is achieved by throwing handfuls of resinous pitch on a lighted torch; but a real bolt calls for a fuse and rocket.

The stage is provided with little square trapdoors which on being opened signify that demons are coming up from the cellar. Should they need to rise into the air, they are cleverly replaced by straw demons of brown buckram, or sometimes by actual chimney sweeps who majestically vanish into the aforementioned blue rags. But what is really tragic is when the ropes jam or break, for then the infernal spirits or immortal gods fall and break their legs and are sometimes killed. To all this you must add the monsters used to lend excitement to certain scenes (such as dragons, lizards, tortoises, crocodiles, or large toads), which, by perambulating the stage in a menacing way, permit us to witness the Temptations of Saint Anthony. Each of these characters is animated by a lout of a Savoyard who actually hasn't sense enough to act the dumb beast.

But what you cannot imagine is the frightful cries, the prolonged bellowings, which fill the theater during the performance. You see actresses virtually in convulsions as they rend from their lungs the most violent ululations; both fists clenched against the breast, the head thrown back, cheeks aflame, veins bursting, and diaphragm heaving. It is impossible to say which is the more unpleasantly assailed, the eye or the ear; these motions cause as much pain to those who look as the singing to those who listen, but what is still more astonishing is that the howls and cries are almost the only thing applauded by the audience. From the handclapping you might suppose a company of deaf-mutes in a frenzy of delight at catching here and there a few piercing sounds, and eager to encourage their repetition. For my part, I am convinced that people applaud a prima donna as they do the feats of the strong man at a fair. The sensations are painfully disagreeable, hard to endure, but one is so glad when it is all over that one cannot help rejoicing. Remember, besides, that this style of singing at the Opera is used to express the tenderest, most courtly thoughts of Quinault; [1] think of the Muses, the Graces, the Cherubs—Venus herself—uttering their souls with such delicacy, and you can judge!

THE NEW HELOISE (1761)

[1] Librettist of Lulli's operas (1635–1688); see p. 273.

ROGER NORTH

≫≫ ≪≪

Semi-Operas

Attorney General under James II, historian, and biographer, Roger North (1653–1734) also left sizable manuscripts about music, which until the middle of the last century were known only through extracts in Dr. Burney's *History*.

It had bin strange if the gentlemen of the theaters had sate still all this while, seeing as they say a pudding creep, that is, a violent inclination in the towne to follow musick, and they not serve themselves of it. Therefore Mr. Betterton who was the chief ingineer of the stage, contrived a sort of plays, which were called Operas, but had been more properly styled Semi-Operas, for they consisted of half musick, and half drama. The chief of these were *Circe*,[1] *The Fayery Queen*,[2] *Dioclesian*,[3] and *King Arthur*;[4] which later was composed by Purcell, and is unhappyly lost. These were followed at first, but by an error of mixing two capitall entertainments, could not stand long. For some that would come to the play hated the musick, and others that were very desirous of the musick, would not bear the interruption that so much rehearsal gave; so that it is best to have either by it self intire.

MEMOIRS OF MUSICK (1728)

[1] By Charles Davenant, music by Banister (1676).
[2] Adapted from *Midsummer Night's Dream*, music by Purcell (1692).
[3] Adapted from Beaumont and Fletcher's *Prophetess*, music by Purcell (1690).
[4] Text by Dryden (1691). The score as we have it lacks five of the original numbers.

EDMUND GURNEY

⇝ ⇜

The Fallacy of Music-Drama

A Cambridge psychologist who died prematurely, soon after finishing
the essay here excerpted, Gurney has left two solid achievements—*The
Power of Sound* (1880) and, in collaboration with Frederic Myers,
Phantasms of the Living (1886).

Most students of the *Oper und Drama* [1] must have admired, as in a
dream, the earnest minuteness with which every sort of conscious
reference, theoretic and practical, is read into the past history of Opera
and its public; the only point of view omitted being that which recognizes in the genus opera-goer, through all its varieties, a whole-
sale indifference to theory, and a quite unpractical habit of enjoying
what it may and enduring what it must. So on contemporary questions, one may encounter in the writings of Wagner and his school
page after page of quite delightful reading, as long as one can abstract one's self from all thought of Music and Language as one has
actually experienced them. "Melodies" which last a whole evening;
"infinite form"; union of Poetry and Music, "each at his highest,"
while yet both emanating from a single inventive source—or if from
two, at any rate from a dramatist with music sufficiently on his brain
to be able to accept Wagner's dictum that the sole test of worthy
dramatic writing is suitability to be sung throughout, and from a
musician in whom literary sensibilities are so dominant as to render
him barren of notes, until fertilized by the minutest verbal details
of the poem where his *melos* is "implicit"; a consequent mutual in-
terdependence of words and notes extending to the "finest ramifications" of the phrases; the sufficiency of alliteration, if unintermittent,
to keep "feeling on a four hours' stretch of poetical excitement"; the

[1] Wagner's polemical and theoretical work in two volumes (1850).

deliverance of Music from the burden of time and the materially based laws of rhythmic stimulation, which have held it in such timid awe; the abandonment of the difficult search—difficult even to the facile Haydn, and to Beethoven matter for raving and stamping—after those rare combinations of sound which shall arrest and fascinate the attention, and which are unnecessary now that every variety of human emotion turns out to be expressible in sound-material at a moment's notice by a vague sort of poetic inspiration, and can be turned on and off as easily as the horns or the big drum—it all seems so comfortable for all concerned, till one remembers that the greatest melodies in the world, though years may have gone to their making, vary in length between a few seconds and a few minutes; that form is as essentially finite in time as in space; that even taken in its loosest and most ambiguous sense, and with the aid of devices and modes of amplification which are out of the question in opera, a musical form could not well be made to cover half an hour—while, in its more vital and definite sense, a few score of bars are the limit of the stretch in the direction of infinity which it will stand without either (1) going back on its own phrases, or (2) changing to something else, or (3) falling to pieces; that no considerable musician, with the possible exception of Wagner himself, has ever shown himself so much as a tenth-rate poet, and that not one in a hundred of even *his* most conscientious alliterations has any relation to feeling at all; that while by far the greater part of first-class dramatic poetry is eminently unsuited, an immense amount of less noticeable verse is eminently suited, for dramatic musical setting; that notes and words, being things absolutely disparate, can artistically concur only by both doing their independent duty from their independent resources, and so "ramifying" into phrases of independent significance and independently coherent growth; that in Music the spiritual power is so rooted in the temporal, that definite and unchangeable relations of time-length, felt as such, belong to the inmost nerve and fiber of musical vitality; that Music will artistically express human emotion only on the one condition that she shall first artistically impress human ears; and that there is no royal road to that impressiveness by which a composer can shirk the pursuit of definite (and therefore extremely finite) forms in the dim region of rhythmically directed impulse, or the fashioning forth from the shapeless material, often by slow degrees, of that which he may first have divined only in shadowy outline. And here every clause shears off a glory from the brilliant Wagnerian fantasy, and substitutes a piece of dry truth. Every clause, too, if fully traced out, would become only truer and drier, and might demand the reader's attention to abstract-looking terms like "key," and "tonality," and even to more distinct technicalities like "modulation" and "diminished sevenths"; in place of the familiar words and concrete images and vivid glimpses of life and nature with which the critic of visual art can light up his page. Not that there would be any difficulty in proving to the most casual reader that in mechanically whistling "Tommy, Make Room for Your Uncle" he has been exhibiting the essential meaning of tonality and modulation as truly as if he had written a symphony; or that the amused surprise of the chorale-like parody of the same melody in a recent London burlesque was ample guarantee for the general susceptibility to the artistic use of diminished sevenths. But it will be enough here to refer as a basis to two cardinal distinctions; of which one marks off Music as an art from other arts, and the other defines the two great elements of which Music itself consists. Music, then, as, first and foremost, a presentative and not (like Poetry, Painting, and Sculpture) a representative art; its distinctive function being unceasingly to present us, and uniquely to impress us, with things peculiar to itself, and unable to draw their impressive quality from any extraneous source, and in that sense always "absolute," to whatever further connections they may lend themselves. And its elements are abstract form and abstract color, i.e., form and color which occur nowhere outside it.

There is something so stale in the very look of these distinctions that I almost blush once again to write them down; yet the full point of them, which was never so important as now, is almost habitually missed. Everybody knows, indeed, that the melodic and harmonic

combinations of Music cannot portray particular scenes and people
in the same way that the forms of Painting can; everybody recognizes, too, that a tune is an *arrangement* of notes, and something different from the particular sort of tone color or *timbre* of the particular instrument on which the notes are rendered. But press these
axioms a little further, or expand them into truths only just less
elementary, and what sort of recognition do they get? Do not nineteen out of every twenty concert-books practically deny that in Music
at its highest no less than its lowest, the freedom from obligation
to portray or represent extends just as much to *emotions* as to
scenes and people, and that the most distinctive impressions made
by Music are emotional after a sort as little definable by a list of
the passions as the sound-forms themselves by the lines of geometry?
Again, does not the fashionable habit of just giving the passing
glance of a single hearing to highly wrought works absolutely set
at naught the fact that from every point of view the form, which may
have cost nothing, and which almost invariably takes some acquaintance fully to reveal itself, is quite beyond comparison more important than the color, which may have cost hundreds of pounds
and which reveals itself in a moment?

   "But has not Wagner," it will be said, "produced such vital strains?"
Of course he has: if he had not, we should not be talking about him.
They are what give him a lasting place among the great—were
they more abundant in relation to his whole production, one might
say among the greatest—of the musical hierarchy; but unfortunately
they are just exactly *not* what his theories support or account for,
and just exactly *not* what is representative of his influence on others.
No one, after marveling at the opening tune of *Tannhäuser* or
the opening act of the *Meistersinger,* goes home and writes a twin
to it; but it is only too easy to take the hint that bits of impressive
or attractive motive are things as important to *ménager* as they are
hard to make; and that the public will enter no protest if the gaps
between them are filled up with the declamatory odds and ends
provided something on the stage be more or less occupying their a

tention, and the accompanying crashes and currents of orchestral noise be sufficiently full and varied.

Here, then, in the dazzling wealth of the modern orchestra, lay the great temptation; and Wagnerism in modern Music means, before all things, succumbing to it. Not, of course, that in an Opera the orchestra need be pedantically restricted to its highest mission, that of revealing, or helping the voices to reveal, really noble form. The form may be far from melodically inventive, may even run very much to mere figure-passages or chromatic scales on a rudimentary basis of brass and drum, and yet, as long as it is rhythmically coherent, may produce really successful and exciting scene-painting; as notably in the ride which opens, and the fire-charm which closes, the last act of the *Walküre*. But such scenes, necessarily few and far between, are not in the least representative of the verbal parts of the opera; and it is in these latter that Wagner's orchestral opportunities, flanked by his theory of "spreading his melody boldly," lead perpetually to such disastrous results. Professing to cast off Beethoven's shackles, i.e., the conditions of key and time by which alone successions of sound can be made organic, he "throws himself fearlessly into the sea of music"; and, sinking, finds himself naturally in the variegated home of invertebrate strains, things with no shape to be squeezed out of, no rhythmic ribs to be broken, tossed hither and thither, as hard to grasp as jellyfish, as nerveless as strings of seaweed. And to realize what this entails on the hearer, we have to translate these shapeless shapes, just like any other sound-forms, into terms of motion—of something which we do not just look at, but have in a way to live; they mean *our* enforced flurry, *our* active impotence. But their creator is wise in his generation. Give the public from a couple to a score of firm bars they can seize and feel reliance in, and keep their eyes employed; and on those terms their ears will be quite content to stray about without landmark or clue, arrested a moment by the trumpets, looking vainly for direction to the voices, bustled on again by the fiddles (to whom, as to the rest of the orchestra, the chase is the best fun in the world), any way and every way, for the next quarter of an hour; or, if they are in danger of turning restive amid these "passages that lead no-where," these keyless flounderings on the ever-shifting quicksands of diminished sevenths, let one of the established motives crop up now and again for their support, and the faithful creatures will welcome it as an undeserved gratuity.

But *are* they quite so content? We seem to have got a long way from Rousseau; but what would he have said? He stated very distinctly his opinion of Rameau's recitatives, *"que tout le monde admire en bâillant"*: how would he have regarded the "noble declamation" of the modern *melos?* Brave words, and still confronted, after the lapse of a century, with the same humble fact. Successions of sound which have no melodic cogency, which as they proceed impress the ear with no sense that their notes ought to have, or to have had, this direction or duration rather than that or the other, not only have no possible element of nobility but are all exactly on a par. The unshaped, the fortuitious, the abortive, as such, admits neither development nor degree; and it would specially have interested Rousseau to remark that an enormous proportion of the notes sung by Wotan and his companions, and standing not in musical subordination to some interesting orchestral motive but on their own declamatory legs, might just as well have been written by Rameau as by Wagner. Still, I think that on the whole he would have admitted a considerable improvement. Not only are Wagner's dramas, however crude in conception and lame in language, yet often redeemed in parts by well-imagined scenic effect; but none of his representative works are wanting in splendid musical features. The second act of *Lohengrin* itself has, between the part which is strongly repulsive and the part which is feebly attractive, about a score of bars of that ineffable kind which makes one doubt whether music should be called a spinal or a cutaneous affection. But, clearly, if the scores are ever to become thousands, the first point is that the somewhat blind combination of faith, hope, and charity which supports the public through the formless tracts should not be mistaken for an *artistic* exercise; and that each inarticulate member of that public should learn explicitly to distinguish mere

sensuous thrills and transient surprises of the ear from the true abid-
ing objects of his and every musician's ideal world. Some natural
tolerance of ungraspable sound may be admitted: there are doubtless persons who easily resign themselves to regard its presence as a
vaguely emotional background to the passing scene, getting sub-
dued or emphatic, bright or gloomy at appropriate places, like the
gestures of the actors or the clouds that figure so largely in the
Wagnerian stage effects. But the average opera-goer, the "naïve lay-
man" for whom Wagner expressly professes to write, is far more
distinctly "musical" than this; and, while accepting as the normal
operatic dispensation an immense amount of sound that has no
significance for him, still lives musically only for the passages of
tangible form—genuine specimens of what I have elsewhere called
the "Ideal Motion." And by this I do not mean merely bits that
are rhythmically and tonally coherent; for Wagner's phrase-building,
even where not incoherent or violently strained, is often singularly
uninventive; witness (to take a single instance which can be suggested without music type) the shamelessly frequent piling up of a
sham crisis, by the mere repetition of a tuneless fragment on suc-
cessively higher steps of the scale. Still less do I mean mere bits of
leitmotiv, real or spurious, which may dodge in and out of the
petty hubbub of the *Rheingold,* or drift despairingly amid the tur-
moil of the second and third acts of the *Götterdämmerung,* too
helpless themselves to help even a drowning ear. I mean passages
of genuine musical invention that can be welcomed and clung to;
passages in which the ear's path seems new indeed, but preordained;
whose mastery the ear owns in the process, not of being dragged
about at their mercy, but of itself mastering them. And these, for
all the treating them as belonging to "one large melody," and concealing their transience by the avoidance of frank full closes, are
often just as truly titbits as if they were embedded in *recitativo secco,*
just as much the plums of Wagner's as of Verdi's confectionery.
Music of the most individual and haunting kind it would indeed be
absurd to demand throughout a long operatic scene. But there are
many grades from the order of excellence which insures vivid and

loving remembrance to that which merely insures pleased and active recognition on acquaintance; and sufficient individuality to
satisfy the latter test is surely the least we can accept in the majority
of the musical sentences of any scene that aspires to the dignity
of healthy popular art.

"But how splendid the plums can be when we get them!" Yes,
indeed; that is what so greatly complicates the Wagner question. . . .

And here we have really merged into the assertion and vindica-
tion of our second cardinal point—Music's constant and characteristic independence, alike at its highest and lowest, of ideas and emotions known and namable outside itself. The reason why Wagner
has been safely able to ignore this elementary fact in musical psychology is this—that the clear perception of it demands something
quite alien both to the actual impressions of the art, and to the
habits of mind of most of those impressed, namely, a moment or
two of deliberate analysis. For want of this, those whose very intuition of musical beauty exemplifies the fact are often the first to
deny and resent it. "You talk about beautiful music not expressing things," one of them will urge; "why to me the bits of music I
most care about express things beyond all words, whole worlds of
emotion, and infinity and eternity into the bargain." Quite so; that
is accurate; that is a way they have; and it is just what is *not* (however much compatible with) the expression of this or that particular emotion—i.e., of that which is proved *not* to be beyond all words
by being accurately definable *in* words, as gaiety, dejection, yearning, triumph. And whoever remembers the places where he gets
this ineffable feeling will find on looking that while it is only *occasionally* connected with the sense of Music which has no need or
power of fusion with Poetry and Drama; and can ignore the all-
essential work of divining and fashioning forth the cogent way for
notes to go, to which the makers of modern Music devoted their
whole energy, and which, so far from excluding any more definable
sort of expression, will alone lift such expression out of the me-

chanical into the aesthetic region.[2] And I would fain pause for a moment on the wanton injustice that is done to Opera itself by not recognizing that even here, in the very sphere where Music is summoned to take on the depiction of definable passions to the utmost of her power, the vague but powerful expression of these is but a fraction of what she has done and is ready to do for word and scene; that the emotional element in her, which is her own, and therefore unnamable, is not on that account condemned to an isolated existence; that the ethical suggestion may become so fragmentary, or the tinge of special sentiment so faint, as practically to vanish in the atmosphere of purely musical delight, and yet that that delight will glorify and transfigure and seem part of the inmost essence of any at all artistic elements in that to which it is wedded. In that transfiguration, what is serious takes on sublimity, and what is ludicrous gets edged with loveliness; nay, even hackneyed things will become haunting, and commonplace things possessing. It would be an immense gain if composers would only put to various specimens of music commonly called "expressive" the simple test of asking how far, if heard in detachment, each would inevitably suggest some particular namable idea or sentiment and no other; and would thus learn explicitly to recognize how extremely loose and general are the conditions of external reference within which Music, *if true to itself,* may still be most genuinely dramatic in the sense of enormously intensifying dramatic effect. To those who had thus consciously confuted for themselves the central principle emphasized in almost every page of the *Oper und Drama* we might readily concede the advantage of possessing, in word and

[2] As Music stands so singularly apart among human interests, so the various things that can be said about it always seem to me in a special degree connected among themselves, and incapable of being supplied from analogy. The result is that an omission (and in a paper of this length very much, of course, has to be omitted) may suggest a flaw. To guard myself against this, and still more against a possible charge of one-sidedness and dogmatism, I may perhaps be allowed to refer especially to the chapters on Color, Expression, Opera, and Criticism, in the *Power of Sound.* [Gurney's note.]

scene, a definite starting point, *raison d'être,* and control, for their inventive stream; without having always to fear the chartered libertinism so characteristic of modern "dramatic" writing. And truly a theory which would exclude from the stage such music as half the solos in *The Beggar's Opera* and half the concerted pieces in *Fidelio,* as *"Batti batti"* and the minuet in *Don Giovanni,* as the prize song in the *Meistersinger* and the shadow song in *Dinorah,* as the pilgrims' hymn in *Tannhäuser* and the gypsy chorus in *Preciosa* [3] —inventions whose power to impress the hearer may be proved in any popular concert room to lie just in expressing themselves, but which borrow from their stage concomitants almost as much romance as they lend—is negatively as great an outrage on this joint art of opera as the positive one which "unites" Poetry and Music by dogging bald words with intervals flung out of a bag.

Here, then, in the false theory of expression, lay the second great trap. The prosaic fallacy that the essence of Music is vague namable expressiveness, instead of definite unnamable impressiveness, is only carried out by making the expressiveness itself mechanical and independent of any impressiveness whatever. And the root fallacy was the more dangerous to Wagner, in that just as color was the practical, so this is the theoretical, mode of excusing and concealing the fitfulness of his enormous musical gift.

WAGNER AND WAGNERISM (1883)

---

[3] *Dinorah* is Meyerbeer's *Pardon de Ploërmel* (1859); *Preciosa,* a play for which Weber wrote music (1821).

STENDHAL

⇒⇒⇒ ⇐⇐⇐

Banish the Libretto

Please note that I speak throughout of the music, not of the words, which I never know. I always recast for myself the words of an opera. I catch the poet's situation and take from him a single word, just one, to designate the sentiment. For example, I find in Mustafa [1] a man who is bored with his greatness and his mistress, and yet is a prince not without vanity. The full complement of words might well spoil this notion for me. Too bad! No doubt it would have been better had Voltaire or Beaumarchais written the libretto. It would then be as delightful as the music. One could read it without the least disenchantment. But since Voltaires are scarce, it is fortunate that the charming art which concerns us can manage so well without the aid of a great poet. Only one must not be so rash as to read the libretto. At Vicenza I noticed that people perused it the first night in order to get an idea of the action. At each successive number one read the first verse, which names the passion or the nuance of the sentiment depicted by the music. Never during the next forty performances did it occur to anyone to open that little book covered with gold paper.

In Venice, Mme. B——, who also feared the disagreeable effect of the libretto, would not allow it in her box even on the first night. Someone summarized the plot for her very briefly, and then by means of numbers gave her in four or five words the subject of each air, duet, or ensemble—for example, jealousy of Ser Taddeo, passionate declaration of Lindor, coquetting of Isabella with the Bey. [1] This résumé was followed by the first verse of the air or duet. I saw that

---

[1] In Rossini's *L'Italiana in Algeri* (1813).

215

everyone found this idea most convenient, and that is the way they should edit librettos for amateurs who—really I don't know how to avoid sounding conceited—for amateurs who love music as they love it in Venice.

LIFE OF ROSSINI (1824)

CLAUDIO MONTEVERDI

-》》 《《-

The Passionate Style

Reflection shows the principal emotions of mankind to be three: anger, equanimity, and supplication or humility. This truth is corroborated by what the great philosophers say, as well as by the character of the human voice with its high, low, and middle pitch. It is further manifested clearly in the art of sound through its three-fold expressions—passionate, soft, and calm. But though I have carefully searched the works of earlier composers, I have not been able to find any examples of the passionate style—only of the calm and soft. Yet Plato speaks of the agitated style in the third book of his *Republic* when he describes "that kind of harmony which fittingly imitates the voice and accents of a brave man going into battle."

Now I am aware that contrasts are what stir our souls, and that such stirring is the aim of all good music. As Boethius puts it: "Music was given us either to purify or to degrade our conduct." Accordingly, I set about by study and effort to rediscover this style of expression, and finding that all the best philosophers declare that a Pyrrhic, that is to say, a rapid, tempo should be used for all warlike or agitated dances, and on the contrary a slow tempo for the opposite situations, I pondered the repeated quarter note, which seemed to me to correspond to a spondee when performed by an instrument. And when I reduced this note to sixteenths, and matched these one-to-one with a speech connoting anger and disdain, I could hear in this simple example the likeness of the effect I was seeking —and this even though the voice could not keep pace with the speed of the instrument.

In order to test the device still further, I had recourse to the divine Tasso, as being the poet who expresses most aptly and most naturally in words the passions he wishes to describe. I turned to the account he gives of the combat between Tancred and Clorinda [1] and there I found as subject for my music the two contrary passions of battle and prayer on the point of death.

In the year 1624 I offered my work [2] for a hearing by the noblest citizens of Venice at the house of the Honorable Gerolamo Mozzenigo, knight and notable of the Venetian Republic, who is my special patron and protector. I was heard, much applauded, and praised.

My principles having met with success in the imitation of anger, I pursued my investigations by further diligent study and produced divers compositions, both sacred music and chamber works, which were so successful in point of style that other composers praised them not only in words but also in their writings, by imitating my technique in their own works, to my great honor and joy.

PREFACE TO *MADRIGALS OF WAR AND LOVE* (1638)

---

[1] In the twelfth canto of *Jerusalem Delivered*.

[2] The famous *Combattimento,* in which among other innovations are to be found effective tremolos and pizzicati.

THOMAS LOVE PEACOCK

-»» «««-

Mangled Operas and the Star System

Between 1815 and 1835, Peacock was known among London men of
letters as a critic of plays and operas no less than as an essayist and book
reviewer attached to several magazines. The occasion of the long review
essay from which the following is taken was the appearance of the fourth,
enlarged edition of Lord Mount Edgcumbe's *Musical Reminiscences*.
The noble lord, second earl of the name, was an amateur composer who
lived between 1764 and 1839, and whose reminiscences span the years
1773–1834.

The object proposed by the Italian Opera is to present the musical
drama in the most perfect possible form. To this end there must be,
in the first place, a good drama: an interesting story, intelligibly
told in good poetry, and affording ample scope for strong and
diversified expression: good music, adapting the sound to the sense,
and expressing all the changes and trains of feeling that belong to
the ideas and images of the drama: good performers—persons of
good figures and features—picturesque in action, and expressive in
countenance—with voices of fine tone and great power, having true
intonation, scientific execution, and above all, or rather as the crown
of all, expression—expression—expression: the one all-pervading and
paramount quality, without which dramatic music is but as a tinkling
cymbal: elegant and appropriate dresses—beautiful scenery—a chorus,
each of whom should seem as if he knew that he had some business
of his own in the scene, and not as if he were a mere unit among
thirty or forty automata, all going like clockwork by the vibrations
of the conductor's pendulum: a full orchestra of accomplished musicians, with a good leader—and especially without a conductor
keeping up, in the very center of observation, a gesticulation and a
tapage that make him at once the most conspicuous and most noisy

personage in the assembly, distracting attention from the sights and sounds that ought exclusively to occupy it—an affliction to the eye, and a most pestilent nuisance to the ear. But, with all this, there should be (as there used to be) an audience regulating its costume and its conduct by the common conventional courtesies of evening society; not with men wearing hats among well-dressed women, and rubbing dirty boots against white petticoats; nor with an influx of late-comers, squeezing themselves between the crowded benches, and sitting down in the laps of their precursors, as we have both seen and suffered. We are aware that some advocates for universal liberty think that the morning liberty of the streets should be carried into all evening assemblies; but, looking back to the Athenians, we cannot consider that cleanliness and courtesy are incompatible with the progress of freedom and intelligence.

Now, by following out the principal points which we have enumerated a little in detail, we shall see what we have had, and what we have wanted—what we are likely to have, and what we are likely to continue to want—for the bringing together of the constituent portions of a perfect musical drama. Lord Mount Edgcumbe touches all these points. We shall content ourselves, on the present occasion, with citing a few of his observations, and expressing our own opinions in a subsequent commentary:

The opera in England, for the period of ten years after the departure of Catalani,[1] will afford much less room for observation than any of the preceding, as far as the singers are concerned; for, with one or two exceptions, there were not any of whom I feel inclined to say much, because there is not much to be said in their praise. But so great a change has taken place in the character of the dramas, in the style of the music, and in its performance, that I cannot help enlarging a little on that subject before I proceed farther.

One of the most material alterations is, that the grand distinction between serious and comic operas is nearly at an end, the separation of the

---

[1] Angelica Catalani (1780–1849), one of the most accomplished sopranos of the nineteenth century. She left England in 1813 after seven years during which she was the most tyrannical and most highly paid of prima donnas.

singers for their performance entirely so. Not only do the same sing in both, but a new species of drama has arisen, a kind of mongrel between them, called *semi-seria,* which bears the same analogy to the other two that that nondescript the melodrama does to the legitimate tragedy and comedy of the English stage. . . .

He adds:

The consequence of this is that all the new dramas written for Rossini's music are most execrably bad, and contain scarcely one line that can be called poetry, or even one of common sense.

This sweeping condemnation is by no means merited. Some of Rossini's libretti are detestable enough; but there is much good dramatic poetry in some of them, *Tancredi* and *Semiramide* [2] especially. It is true that in these dramas the Italian poet had only to condense the essence of Voltaire's tragedies, but the task is well executed. The libretto of Donizetti's *Anna Bolena* [3] is an excellent dramatic poem.

It is seldom that we are enabled to judge fairly either of an Italian libretto, or of the music of an opera as a whole. For example, in 1832 Mr. Monck Mason professed to bring forward Pacini's *Gli Arabi nelle Gallie.* [4] He first cut it into halves, and put the second half aside, or into the fire. He then cut away the beginning and substituted that of Rossini's *Zelmira.* [5] He then tacked a strange air, we forget from whence, to the middle, by way of an end, and thus presented to the public both author and composer literally without head or tail. The critics discovered that the drama was nonsense, and that much of the music was stolen; and Pacini and his poet bore the blame which belonged to the manager. This mode of murdering reputations ought to subject the offender to an action for damages. "I was induced, unfortunately," says Lord Mount Edgcumbe, "to go one night to see *Gli Arabi nelle Gallie,* a very poor opera by

[2] 1813 and 1823 respectively.
[3] I.e., Anne Boleyn, 1830.
[4] *The Arabs in Gaul,* 1827.
[5] 1821.

Pacini." What he saw was poor enough, but it was not Pacini's opera. In the same season Bellini's *La Straniera*,[6] which has much beautiful melody, and an interesting and intelligible story, founded on the Vicomte d'Arlincourt's *L'Etrangère*,[7] was presented in such a chaotic fashion that the intentions of both poet and composer remained an unfathomable mystery.

These liberties are taken more or less with the works of all masters, from the greatest to the least. Mozart himself does not escape them. Interpolation indeed he does escape. The audiences of the King's Theatre are justly strict in this one point only, that they will not permit the sewing on of an extraneous purple shred to any of his great and sacred textures. But garbled and mutilated his works are abominably, to fit the Procrustean bed of an inadequate company, or to quadrate with the manager's notions of the bad taste of the public. A striking instance of this is in the invariable performance of *Il Don Giovanni* without its concluding sestetto. Don Juan's first introduction to a modern English audience was in a pantomime (at Drury Lane we believe), which ended with the infernal regions, a shower of fire, and a dance of devils.[8] Mozart's opera has, properly, no such conclusion. Flames arise—a subterranean chorus is heard— Don Juan sinks into the abyss—the ground closes above him— Leporello remains on the stage: a strongly marked modulation leads from the key of D minor into that of G major, with a change from common time andante to triple time allegro assai; and the other characters, ignorant of the catastrophe, rush in to seek their revenge:

> *Ah! dov' è il perfido,*
> *Dov' è l'indegno?* [9]

Leporello explains the adventure, and after a general exclamation, a solemn pause, and an exceedingly sweet larghetto movement, in

[6] *The Foreign Woman,* 1829.

[7] Victor Prévost, Vicomte d'Arlincourt (1789–1856) wrote a number of semi-successful works, foreshadowing the preciosity of the Decadents.

[8] This seems to have been "traditional" since the second Viennese production of 1791.

[9] "Ah, where is the faithless, the worthless Don . . ."

which the dramatis personae dispose of themselves, *"Or che tutti, o mio tesoro,"* the opera is wound up by a fugue in D major—*"Questo è il fin di chi fa mal":* [10] one of the very finest things in dramatic music, and the most appropriate possible termination of the subject; and yet is this most noble composition, this most fitting and genuine conclusion, sacrificed to a dance of devils flashing torches of rosin, for no earthly reason but that so ended the Drury Lane pantomime.

Le Nozze di Figaro and *Il Flauto Magico* [11] both require a better and more numerous company than is ever assembled in this country. If we have in the former an Almaviva, a Figaro, a Contessa, and a Susanna, it is the usual extent of our good fortune. We have seldom an endurable Cherubino; Marcellina is generally a nonentity: Barbarina always so; Bartolo, Basilio, and Antonio take their chance, which is seldom good for any of them, and never for all; and Don Curzio is for the most part abrogated.

Il Don Giovanni and *Le Nozze di Figaro* are both specimens of excellently written libretti, separating most effectively the action and passion from the ratiocination of the originals; but we have seen the latter especially performed in such a manner, that if we had known nothing of it but from the representation, we should have found it incomprehensible; and this sort of experiment on things which we know well should make us cautious of pronouncing summary judgment on things of which we know nothing but from the showing of the King's Theatre.

Il Flauto Magico is a well-written libretto, but the subject is too mystical to be interesting, or even generally intelligible; and this is a great drawback on its theatrical popularity, which has never approached that of the *Giovanni* and *Figaro,* though the music exhausts all the fascinations of both melody and harmony, and may be unhesitatingly cited as the absolute perfection of both. It requires more good singers than either of the others, and it requires them the

[10] "Now that all have gone, my darling . . . ," and "Such is the end of all evil doers. . . ."

[11] *The Marriage of Figaro* and *The Magic Flute.*

more imperatively, as it depends more exclusively on the music. It requires seventeen voices besides the chorus. The music which is assigned to the three nymphs and the other genii is almost supernaturally beautiful: for this alone there should be six good voices, and there are, without these, six principal and five secondary parts. We may therefore despair of ever hearing this opera performed as it ought to be.

The works of Italian composers do not require, in any instance that we remember, so many performers. Those of the most modern composer of any name—Bellini—are singularly restricted in their principal parts. He seems to endeavor to defend himself against the caprices and jealousies of the performers by giving them nothing to quarrel about. A prima soprano, a primo tenore, a primo basso, and the ordinary components of a chorus, can perform his *Pirata*.[12] There can be no dispute here about pre-eminence, but the general effect is necessarily meager. But the progress of self-conceit among singers has made this result inevitable. A prima soprano is now to be found everywhere, and a seconda nowhere; and though many who assume to be first are scarcely fit to be second, they will not be content with what they are fit for, but will be first or nothing. There appears to be this great difference between a German and an Italian company—that the Germans will cooperate to the production of general effect, and the Italians will look to nothing but their own individual display. We have seen, in a German opera, the same person taking a principal part one night, and singing in the chorus the next. We have seen the same with the French; but with the Italians this never occurs. A German author and composer may therefore give fair scope to their subject; but the Italians must sacrifice everything to their company, and all in vain, except for the first production—for to the whims and inefficiency of every new company the unfortunate opera must be refitted and garbled. Bellini's is the true plan for his own reputation. A soprano, a tenor, a bass, and a chorus there must be in every company, and they can have nothing to quarrel for; but the musical drama must be ruined if this

[12] 1827.

were to become the rule of its construction. And the scheme, after all, is not always successful: for in 1830 the prima donna transposed the middle and end of *Il Pirata,* in order that she might finish it herself instead of the tenor.

"Ma femme, et cinq ou six poupets," will not make a company in the opinion of any one but Catalani's husband.[13] No one, indeed, who has seen and heard Catalani, or Pasta, or Malibran, or Giulietta Grisi, would willingly dispense with one such prima donna; but the single star should not be worshiped exclusively to the sacrifice of the general effect. She can be but a component, however important, part of it; and if the general effect fails, the star will fall.

But with us, though the star cannot shine if the general effect be bad, no general effect, however otherwise excellent, will produce attraction without a star. In 1832, though the star of the French opera of *Robert le Diable* (Madame Cinti) [14] was but one of the fourth magnitude, yet with her eclipse the opera fell. The manager has collected stars, but not a company: there is a soprano too much, and a contralto too little—a tenor wanting, and a basso to spare: they patch up a performance as they may—altering, garbling, omitting, interpolating—and the result is a bad concert instead of a good opera. A good opera is a whole, as much in the music as in the poetry, and cannot be dislocated and disfigured by omissions and interpolations, without destruction to its general effect.

Lord Mount Edgcumbe justly observes that

a mean economy prevails in all the inferior departments, with regard to secondary singers, the chorus, and orchestra: the scenery, decorations, and wardrobe are in every respect unworthy of the largest theater in the country.

But the enormous expense of the principal singers and dancers would not alone render this mean economy necessary, if it were not

[13] A soldier and gambler in the French diplomatic service, named Valabrègue. His remark was: "My wife and five or six dolls (*poupées*)—that's all you need [for an opera]."

[14] Laure Cinthie Damoreau (1801–1863), French soprano who sang under the name of Cinti.

for the enormous rent exacted for the house. By a rough calculation which we made the other day, it appeared to us that the Italian Opera has been carried on in England for about a century and a quarter, at an average net loss of £5,000 a year; but of late years the Opera has yielded what would have been a liberal profit to the proprietors of the theater, if it had been carried on by the proprietors, and not by a lessee, saddled with a disproportionate rent.

Lord Mount Edgcumbe reprobates the novel introduction of a conductor into the orchestra, not playing himself but beating time with a noisy baton. Assuredly our Italian opera conductor verifies the remark of Dr. Burney: [15]

> Rousseau says, that the more time is beaten the less it is kept; and it is certain that when the measure is broken, the fury of the musical general, or director, increasing with the disorder and confusion of his troops, he becomes more violent, and his strokes and gesticulations more ridiculous in proportion to their disorder.

Lord Mount Edgcumbe makes some observations on the change which has taken place in the appearance and conduct of the audience of the King's Theatre, which we fully agree with him is a change altogether for the worse. We confess we have a prejudice in favor of sitting at our ease among well-mannered company, and we have been elbowed and annoyed out of all endurance of the pit at the Opera. Amongst the principal causes of this change is the profuse admission of orders; and on what ground these are given we saw the other day some curious evidence in a case in the Court of Requests. One of the former managers of the Opera had set up a paper called the *Theatrical Critic,* which did not succeed, and had left off in debt to the editor two guineas, for which important amount he was summoned; and it appeared that, in postponing the payment, he had told the editor a box was always at his service. After this we need not wonder at the heterogeneous composition of the audience in the pit. Assuredly those who pay have a right to complain, if they find all the places preoccupied by those who do not. They do not complain, however, but they exercise another right

[15] See p. 331.

more fatal to the management, and more just to its misconduct—
the right of staying away. In short, as Lord Mount Edgcumbe justly
observes:

The whole system is radically bad; and nothing can restore the Opera
in this country to its former respectable and agreeable footing, or the
performances to that excellence which a public paying so dearly has a right
to expect, but a total reformation, an entire change of proprietors, of
managers, of all parties connected with the theater, I had almost said,
hampered and embarrassed as it is, of the theater itself.

We should be sorry to change the theater, because it is the finest
vehicle for sound in Europe; but we wish to see it thoroughly re-
formed in all the points to which we have adverted, and in another
very important matter—that of its exits and its entrances. It was
not intended for a crowd, but it is now often crowded, legitimately
or artificially; and the occurrence of a fire on a crowded night would
ensure the destruction of the audience. It is surrounded, or rather
built in, by shops and taverns, and even the alarm of fire in any
one of these would occasion incalculable mischief.

But it is vain to anticipate any reform of this theater while it is
in the hands of the assignees of a bankrupt estate, who think only of
exacting the utmost possible rent within the year—(a double rent,
in short: first, a fair return on the capital; and, second, a most un-
fair and unjustifiable tax on the monopoly of the license)—from
an impresario who is only an annual tenant, who can, therefore,
make no prospective arrangements—who is always taken unpro-
vided at the beginning of the season—who thinks of nothing but
how to make both ends meet at the end of it—who trusts to his
skill in the "detection of a star" to redeem himself by a temporary
attraction in the course of it—and who, if he can fill the theater by
a fiddler or a dancer, is content to let the opera take its chance.

COLLECTED ESSAYS (1835)

BEAUMARCHAIS

❯❯❯ ❮❮❮

A New Kind of Opera

During his high-spirited career, the author of the Figaro comedies tried his hand at many things, including the fomenting of American Independence. Reforming opera was no doubt a more difficult enterprise, whence the need for a diplomatic preparation of the public, as shown below.

Ast ego barbarus sum [1]

To the Opera Subscribers who would like to like Opera

Not the art of singing, not that of modulation, nor the combining of sounds—not music in itself—is my present theme. My theme is the action of poetry on music and the reaction of music on dramatic poetry in works where the two arts are conjoined. I want to analyze not so much a new opera as a new means of making opera interesting.

To predispose you to listen to me with some favor, let me say, dear contemporaries, that I know of no century in which I should prefer to have been born, no nation to which I would rather belong. Apart from the charms of French society, I find that for the last thirty or forty years there has been among us a lively sense of enterprise—a general desire to enlarge thought by intelligent research and to increase the happiness of all by the use of reason.

The last century is often cited as an age of great literature. But what is literature among man's many useful endeavors? A noble exercise of the mind. Our century will be instanced as one of deep science and philosophy, rich in discoveries, full of energy and rea

[1] But then I'm a barbarian.

son. The mind of the nation seems to be in a happy kind of crisis: a bright light over all things makes each one feel that everything could be better. People are concerned, agitated, resourceful; they innovate and reform; and from the profound science of government to the frivolous art of making melodies; from the heights of genius upon which we behold Voltaire and Buffon, down to the easy and lucrative trade of criticizing that which one cannot do, I see throughout all classes of society a desire for accomplishment and right opinion, for the extension of one's ideas, knowledge, pleasures, and the increase of one's contributions to the common good. Thus it is that everything grows, prospers, and improves. Let us, if possible, see if we can improve a great type of entertainment.

The mind needs relaxation. After the compulsory strain of business one must follow one's hobby—this one hunts, the other drinks; this one gambles, another intrigues. For my part, lacking as I do all these diversions, I have fashioned a modest opera. To forestall argument, I will readily agree that of all literary frivolities the most frivolous is to write a poem of this kind. I agree also that if the author of such a work were going to complain of the little esteem he gains by it, he would be ridiculously unhappy and unhappily ridiculous—the silliest man among all his enemies.

But whence this contempt for the poem of an opera? When all is said and done, the making is not so easy as it seems. Can it be that the French nation is fonder of songs than of music and prefers vaudeville and its epigrams to music and its madrigals? Someone has said that the French really like ditties but only pretend (from vanity) to like music. I would not press the point for fear of confirming it. I would incline rather to believe that our indifference to operatic poems is due to the fact that in opera the poor jointing of the constituent arts creates confusion in the mind as to their respective ranks, and as to the pleasure to be expected from each.

Their true ranking, it seems to me, is as follows: first, the plot or invention of the subject which sustains the interest; then the beauty of the poem, including narrative skill; next the charm of music, which is but a new expressiveness added to the charms of verse;

finally, the ornament of the dance, whose gaiety or loveliness relieves certain static situations.

Yet by a reversal peculiar to opera, it would seem that the play counts as nothing but a vulgar excuse for displaying every other merit. The accessories have usurped the first place, while the fundamental subject has become a trifling accessory. It is a mere canvas on which everybody else embroiders. How has this come about? Why is it that the most zealous followers of opera (myself among them) are always bored at a performance? This is the ancient problem which I shall now try to explain in my own way.

I start from the conviction that the public cannot err. Led by pleasure, it will follow wherever pleasure is to be found. If one kind of satisfaction eludes the spectator, he turns to something else. Bored at the opera because he cannot hear the words, he recoups himself with music. But this art, deprived of the dramatic interest which the poem might give, merely tickles the ear and must soon yield to the dance, which, moreover, holds the eye. As regards this undermining of true theatrical art, obviously, the spectator is right and the spectacle wrong.

Boileau once wrote to Racine: "There will never be such a thing as a good opera, for music cannot tell a story." In his day he was right. He might even have added: "Music cannot carry on a dialogue." No one suspected then that this development was possible. Again, in a letter of that great man who thought of everything and wrote of everything—I mean Voltaire—one reads these remarkable words: "The opera is but a social meeting place where one goes on certain days, without quite knowing why. It is a house where everybody goes, even though one cares nothing for the host and finds him utterly dull." Before Voltaire, La Bruyère had said: "Clearly, opera is a sketch for a grand spectacle; I can form a notion of it; but I cannot tell how such perfect music and such regal expense have so perfectly and regally bored me."

Speaking for myself, who am sensitive to the pleasure of good music and who delight in many a piece at the keyboard, I find the same piece burdensome when it is restored to the operatic setting from which it came. And I think I know why. There is too much music in dramatic music. To adopt the crude maxim of the justly celebrated Chevalier Gluck, our opera *puzza di musica:* it stinks of music. I conclude that music in an opera should be like poetry— only another means of embellishing speech and one which must not be used to excess.

Our dramatic poets long ago noticed that the splendor of words and the poetical lavishness which are proper to the ode were too exalted for the stage. They knew that in order to hold attention they must tone down this poetic bedazzlement and bring verse closer to nature. A play requires the simple and native truth. This reform accomplished in drama remains to be carried out in music.

But here the vain musician, lacking taste or genius, may want to lord it over the poet or make of his music an independent work. The play had then better look out for itself. The spectator sees only incoherence, divided interest, disconnected effects, and want of unity. For two purposes cannot produce a single result and must necessarily spoil the show. Therefore, just as a French author says to his translator, "Since you are Italian, turn this into Italian, but without adding extraneous matter," so I, as dramatic poet, will say to my collaborator, "Since you are a musician, translate this poem into music, but do not, like Pindar, wander off into irrelevancy and sing of Castor and Pollux apropos of an athletic victory: they have nothing to do with the case."

I cannot repeat often enough that musical excess is the vice of our grand opera. Music is what makes it so slow. As soon as the actor sings, the action stops—that is, if he sings merely to sing—and when the action stops the spectators' minds wander. "But," you will say, "what else can the poor actor do but sing? It is his only idiom." "True, but he should try to make us forget it." The composer's art ought to accomplish precisely this. Let the subject be sung for the same reason that it is couched in verse—as an ornament. I want an added charm, not a cause for distraction. I who have faithfully cherished music, at all times and places, find myself saying to it with an ungracious shove of the shoulder, 'Out of my way, Music!

Why repeat yourself so much? Why so slow? Instead of lively narration, you give us twice-told tales. Instead of depicting passion, you
cling to empty words!" [2] What is the upshot? While the poet makes
every effort to save words and tighten his style, the musician contrariwise dilutes his, doles out syllables, dissolves them in repeats,
saps their strength, and kills their meaning. The one pulls this way,
the other that. In between I yawn and leave the hall.

To bring me back, and pleasure with me, let us try to re-establish
the several arts of opera in their natural order. Does not the very
word "opera" signify their union? Carrying forward the efforts made
by Chevalier Gluck in his *Iphigénie* and *Alceste,* let us add a few remarks on librettos and their employment.

In the first place, an opera must be neither a tragedy nor a comedy,
though it has connections with each and may embrace both. I should
therefore not choose a wholly tragical subject. The tone would be so
austere that entertainments would seem dropped incongruously from
on high. Let us equally avoid a pure comedy plot. Passion and
grandiose moments are alike incompatible with it, and hence the
corresponding music would be too lacking in nobility. I rather think
that for an opera historical subjects are less successful than imaginary
ones. Must we then treat the impossible wonders of fairyland, which
strike us as shocking or absurd? Experience has shown that the in-
tervention of the gods and the unraveling of the plot by magical
means invariably leave us cold. Now, mythological subjects usually
exhibit these defects, and in my system I can only afford to ration music if I am lavish with dramatic excitement. Again, since
the slow pace of musical discourse forbids amplification in words,
the interest must be concentrated on the groupings, the masses,
which must be strong and clear. Situations are paramount in the
theater, but they are indispensable in lyric drama, for sheer movement has to replace the other kind of eloquence.

I infer from all this that one should strike a happy medium be-

[2] Beaumarchais quotes these five lines from his Preface to *The Barber of
Seville* (1775).

tween legendary and historical drama. I also think that civilized manners are too regular for the theater. Oriental manners, being less orderly and familiar, leave the imagination freer and seem best suited to opera. Wherever despotism reigns, contrasts are marked —slavery is close to power, love next to ferocity. The passions of the great rage unchecked. One may behold in a single person the most abysmal ignorance and the most unlimited power, an unworthy cowardice and a contemptuous pride of place. In such climes, I see the abuse of power trifling with the lives of men and the modesty of women. Rebellion and tyranny go hand in hand, for the despot makes everyone tremble, and he trembles himself, simultaneously. This chaos is very much to the point. It spurs the poet's imagination and disturbs his mind so as to produce *strangenesses*—to use Montaigne's expression. These, in short, are the circumstances most favorable to opera; they allow every kind of atmosphere, just as the seraglio permits every kind of situation. Within them, one can be by turns lively, solemn, gay, playful, menacing, or jocose. The very religions of the Orient have something wondrous about them which compels attention and promotes suspense.

And now suppose it possible to crown the whole with a great philosophical idea—indeed make the subject arise from the idea— then the resulting entertainment would not be idle. All right-thinking men would in fact be grateful for such an opera. Though partisanship might set the dogs of ignorance and envy howling, the public would still recognize that a work of this sort was not to be despised. The response might even encourage men of greater genius to repeat the attempt and offer to the greatest nation in the world a new genre for their delectation.

Whatever others may do, such has been my aim. *Tarare* is the title of my opera, but it is not the subject. The subject is that of the following maxim, which is at once severe and comforting:

> Man! Thy merit on the earth,
> Does not depend upon thy birth:
> It springs from character alone,

Now music, the invincible obstacle to character portrayal, forbade my making known my dramatis personae in their remote setting, essential though this knowledge is for any enjoyment. I therefore devised a new kind of prologue, in which is presented all that has to be known about the persons of the drama and its plot. The spectator thus begins *in medias res,* without effort, and in possession of the facts: the prologue is my exposition. Made up of aerial beings, shades and spirits, it constitutes the miraculous part of the poem. Operatic tradition suggested this device, of which I saw no reason to deprive the genre: magical wonders are excellent when used in moderation.

After I had finished my poem I came across an Arabian tale which resembles it and which reminded me that long ago I had heard it read to me in the country. The reader of this preface can look up Volume III of *The Genii*[3] and discover what I owe to the Arabian, as well as note how the confused memory of a striking thing can work in the memory and fertilize the mind without one's being aware of it.

But what belongs far more to another hand is the beautiful music of my friend Salieri.[4] This great composer, who is the glory of the Gluckist school, possesses the style of the master together with a natural sense of taste, of judgment, of drama and, what is more, a wealth of ideas. To comply with my views he has had the courage to give up a quantity of musical splendors; they adorned his score but made the play too long and retarded *the action.* Surely the vigor, the speed, the proud and energetic tone of the work will indemnify him for his many sacrifices. And his score will refute the likely objection that my poem lacks lyricism: it was never our aim to be lyrical, but only to make music dramatic. "My dear friend," I would say to Salieri, "the trouble with opera is that it is effeminate in word and thought, out of subservience to music. Let us dare to raise the art to the level of sinewy verse and powerful situations, then we may recapture those vaunted effects attained in the drama of the ancient

[3] I.e., the Arabian Nights.
[4] Antonio Salieri (1750–1825).

Greeks." Our conversations would, I believe, have made an excellent Poetics for the makers of opera, for M. Salieri is a born poet and I am something of a musician. Without this concurrence I doubt whether success would have been possible.

During rehearsals our work aimed at reducing the recitative to the level of speech without destroying musical harmony, and I must praise the singers for their efforts in this direction. Short of speaking altogether, no musician could have done better, and the spoken voice would have deprived the work of the orchestral reinforcement which our able composer employed whenever appropriate.

Two other precepts, both very short, comprised the rest of my doctrine for the rehearsals. To our most willing actors I said, "Enunciate clearly"; and to the best orchestra in the world I said, "Control your ardor. Rightly understood and applied, this counsel will make us deserving of attention." For I had discovered another secret worth imparting. I found that the reason people cannot hear at the Opera is that they have lost the habit of listening. No doubt boredom is the ultimate cause, yet I have noticed that in several modern works, which are full of good things, certain passages absolutely compel the public to hear. Accordingly, whether I deserve it or not, I beg the fullest attention for the première of *Tarare*. If I do not deserve it, let the public avenge itself afterward with the most infernal noise.[5]

PREFACE TO *TARARE* (1787)

[5] Precisely what happened at the dress rehearsal. But the first night was successful and the opera enjoyed a run of several months.

FRIEDRICH NIETZSCHE

※ ※

The Greatness of Wagner [1]

On that dismal cloudy day of May 1872, when the foundation stone had been laid on the heights of Bayreuth amid torrents of rain, and Wagner was driving back to the town with a small party of us, he was exceptionally silent, and there was that indescribable look in his eye as of one who has turned his gaze deeply inwards. That day happened to be the first of his sixtieth year, and his whole past now appeared as but a long preparation for this great moment. What went through Wagner's mind on that day, how he became what he is, and what he is yet to be—we who are nearest to him can imagine up to a certain point: we can follow him in his self-examination. But to understand his great achievement we must try to see through his eyes, and then, having understood, we can vouch for that achievement's fruitfulness.

. . . It is typical that a modern man gifted with exceptional talents should as a child and youth so seldom be blessed with ingenuousness and simple originality that he is hardly able to have these qualities at all. As a matter of fact, men of rare talent, such as Goethe and Wagner, more often achieve ingenuousness in manhood than during their tender years of childhood and youth. This is especially true of the artist, who, being born with a more than usual capacity for imitating, falls a prey to the morbid multiplicity of modern life as to an infectious childhood disease. As a child he will more nearly resemble an old man. The amazingly sincere picture of a representative of youth that Wagner gives us in the Siegfried of the *Nibelungen Ring* could only have been conceived by a grown man,

[1] See head note p. 312.

and by one who had found his youth but late in life. Wagner's maturity, like his adolescence, came late and he is, in this respect at least, the very reverse of the precocious type.

. . . The characters an artist creates are not himself, but the series of creations to whom it is clear that he is deeply attached must somehow reveal something of his nature. If you recall Rienzi, the Flying Dutchman and Senta, Tannhäuser and Elizabeth, Lohengrin and Elsa, Tristan and Marke, Hans Sachs, Wotan and Brunhilde —all these characters are linked together by a hidden current of strong moral feeling, which as it flows through them becomes ever purer and clearer. Here we respectfully and diffidently come into the presence of the innermost secret of Wagner's soul and its development. In what other artist do we find this same quality to the same degree? Schiller's characters, from the Robbers to Wallenstein and William Tell, do indeed pursue an ennobling course, and also reveal something of their author's progression; but in Wagner the plane is higher and the scope much greater. I find, for example, in the *Ring of the Nibelungen,* when Brunhilde is awakened by Siegfried, a passage of the most moral music that I have ever heard. Wagner attains here to such a height of saintly feeling that our mind unconsciously seeks a likeness among the glistening peaks of ice and snow in the Alps—so pure, inaccessible, solitary and chaste, yet so bathed in love beams, does Nature show herself in these forms that clouds and tempests—and even the sublime itself—seem to lie below.

Now looking down from such a height upon Tannhäuser and the Flying Dutchman, one begins to understand how Wagner as a human being developed, how restlessly and darkly he began; how he stormed to satisfy his lusts, to seize power, and taste those raptures of delight from which he often fled in disgust; how he wanted to throw off discipline, to forget, negate, and renounce everything; hurling himself like a flood, now into this valley, now into that, leaving no remote or hidden corners uncovered.

In the night of these half-subterranean convulsions a star appeared and glowed high above him with a sad brilliancy: as soon as he recognized it, he named it Fidelity, unselfish faith. But why did this star strike him as the brightest and purest of all? What special meaning did the word "fidelity" carry for him as a conscious being? The bare fact is that it has etched itself upon all his thoughts, all his deeds. His works contain an almost complete series of the finest and most beautiful examples of fidelity: that of brother to sister, of friend to friend, of servant to master; of Elizabeth to Tannhäuser, of Senta to the Dutchman, of Elsa to Lohengrin, of Isolde, Kurvenal, and Marke to Tristan, of Brunhilde to the most mystic vows of Wotan—and these are but a few. It is Wagner's most personal and characteristic experience, which he reveres like a religious mystery. He names it Fidelity and never tires of imparting it to hundreds of different characters, of endowing it with his sublimest thought, so overflowing is his gratitude. In a word, it spells his awareness that the two sides of his nature have remained faithful each to each, that the creative, ingenuous, and brilliant elements arising out of free and unselfish love have kept pace with the dark, the intractable, and the tyrannical side.

Examined in detail and without prejudice, Wagner's life may be said—to borrow an expression of Schopenhauer's—to consist largely of comedy, indeed of burlesque. What the feelings must have been that accompanied his awareness of living, for long stretches of time, a paradoxically undignified life, how they must have acted upon an artist, who more than anyone else, perhaps, breathed freely only in elevated spheres—all this only a philosopher can imagine. In the midst of such confusion, which should be described in detail in order to inspire the amount of pity, awe, and admiration that it deserves, Wagner developed a talent for acquiring knowledge, which even in a German—a son of the nation most bent upon learning—was really extraordinary. Moreover, this talent was threatened by another danger, more overwhelming than that of leading an existence without apparent rule or discipline, carried hither and thither by distracting illusions: from a tyro testing his strength, Wagner became a thorough master of music and the theater, as well as an inventive technician in the realm of the practical prerequisites of his art. No one can any longer deny him the glory of having given us the supreme models for the large-scale execution of lofty conceptions.

But Wagner came to be something more than this, and in order to this accomplishment he had to reach the highest degree of culture by sheer study. How wonderfully he achieved this end! It is a delight to follow his progress. All was grist to his mill; the materials drawn from all sides became a part of him, and the larger and heavier the resulting structure became, the stouter was the arch of the organizing thought that sustained it.

And yet access to the arts and sciences has seldom been more difficult for any man than for Wagner; he often had to break his way through to reach them. The restorer of primitive drama, the discoverer of the place of art in the true human society, and poetic interpreter of ancient philosophies, the thinker, the historian, the critic and aesthetician, the master of language, the mythologist and the myth-maker, the man, in short, who first closed the circle around these wonderful and beautiful products of an eternal spirit in a single *Ring,* and who engraved upon this solid piece of work the runic characters of his thought—what a wealth of knowledge Wagner had to store up and master, in order to be and to do all this! And at the same time this mass of material was just as powerless to arrest the motion of his will as a single detail—however attractive—was to divert his purpose from its goal.

Wagner concentrated upon all of life, past and present, the light of an intelligence strong enough to take in the most remote regions within its scope. That is why he is a simplifier of the universe. The simplification of the universe is possible only to him whose eye has been able to master the vastness and wildness of an apparent chaos, and to relate and unite things which before had lain helplessly apart. Wagner did this by discovering a connection between two objects that seemed to dwell apart as though in separate spheres—that between music and life, and likewise that between music and drama. Not that he invented nor was the first to create this relationship: they have always existed; they lie, as it were, at everybody's feet. But as is so often true of a great problem, this was like a precious stone which thousands kick underfoot before one man finally picks it up. Wagner asked himself why an art such as music should have become so very important a feature of modern life.

One need not think meanly of life in order to suspect a riddle behind this question. On the contrary, it is only when the great forces of existence are accounted for, and the living energies regarded as striving toward conscious freedom and independence of thought, that music appears as a riddle of the present. Surely one must admit that music could hardly have been born in our own day. What then is the meaning of its presence among us? An accident? A single great artist might certainly be an accident, but the appearance of a whole group of artists, such as the history of modern music shows—a group only once before equaled on earth, that is to say in the time of the Greeks—a fact so striking as this leads one to think that perhaps necessity rather than accident is at the root of the phenomenon. The meaning of this necessity is the riddle Wagner answers.

For he was the first to recognize an evil as widespread as civilization itself: language is everywhere diseased, and the curse of this dread disease weighs heavily upon the whole of man's development. Language having more and more abandoned its true function—the expression of strong feelings, which it was once able to convey in all their simplicity; and having been forced to strain after the virtually impossible achievement of communicating the reverse of feeling—that is to say thought—its strength has become so exhausted by this excessive enlargement of its duties during the relatively short span of modern civilization that it is no longer able to perform the function which alone justifies its existence, namely, helping those who suffer to communicate about the sorrows of existence. Man can no longer make his misery known to others by means of language, hence cannot really express himself any longer.

. . . If now the music of our German masters burst upon mankind when it was sick to this degree, what is the real meaning of this music? Only this: genuine feeling—the enemy of all convention, of artificial estrangements and misunderstandings between man and man. This music signifies a return to Nature, and at the same time a purification and refashioning of Nature. For the need of such a return took shape in the souls of the most loving of men; and *through their art, Nature transformed into love made its voice heard.*

Let us regard this as *one* of Wagner's answers to the question, "What does music mean in our time?" He has a second. The relation between music and life is not merely that which exists between one kind of language and another; it is also the relation between the perfect world of sound and that of sight. Regarded merely as a spectacle, and compared with other and earlier forms, modern life is characterized by an indescribable barrenness and enfeeblement, despite the unspeakable garishness that rejoices the superficial observer. If one looks a little closer at the impression made on oneself by this vehement and kaleidoscopic play of colors, does not the brilliant, blazing whole seem to consist of the shimmer and sparkle of innumerable little stones borrowed from former civilizations? Is not everything one sees merely a compound of clumsy bombast, apish gesticulations, arrogant superficiality? a ragged suit of motley for the naked and the shivering? a deceptive dance of joy enjoined upon an invalid? airs of overbearing pride put on by one who is sick unto death? And moving all about with such speed and confusion that they are thereby disguised and hidden: sordid impotence, devouring dissension, solicitous ennui, dishonest misery! The appearance of humanity these days is mere appearance, and nothing more: in what he now puts forth, man has himself become invisible. He is masked off, blotted out.

In fact, the remnants of the creative faculty in art, still surviving in such countries as France and Italy, are all concentrated upon this one task of concealing. Wherever the demands of form are still made, in society, conversation, literary style, or the relations among

states, men have unconsciously come to believe that they are adequately met by a kind of agreeable simulation, quite the opposite of
genuine form conceived as a necessary relation among the parts of
a figure—a relation which has nothing to do with the "agreeable"
or the "disagreeable," since it is necessary and not optional. . . .
How far this simulation is agreeable at times, and why it pleases
everybody to see modern man doing his best to dissemble, everyone can judge in the exact degree to which he himself happens to
be modern. "Only galley slaves can recognize one another," says
Tasso, "and if we make a mistake of identity, it is only out of courtesy, and with the hope that others in turn will mistake us."

Now, in this world of forms and intentional misunderstandings,
what purpose is served by the occurrence of beings overflowing with
music? With noble candor and impersonal passion they pursue their
course to a grand and unrestrained rhythm; they glow with the
mighty and peaceful fire of music, which breaks forth into the light
of day from their inexhaustible depths—and all this to what end? To
the end of helping music express the longing that it feels for the
company of its natural ally, gymnastics, through which it takes on
its necessary *form* in the order of visible phenomena. In its search
and longing for this ally, music becomes the arbiter of the whole
visible world and of the world of deceptive, topical phenomena. And
this is Wagner's second answer to the question, "What is the meaning of music in our times?" "Help me," he cries to all who have ears
to hear, "help me to discover that culture of which my music, being
the rediscovered language of genuine feeling, seems to foretell the
existence. Remember that the soul of music now seeks a body, and
that with your aid it wants to become visible in movement, deeds,
institutions, and customs!"

THOUGHTS OUT OF SEASON (1876)

HECTOR BERLIOZ

⇛ ⇚

The Limits of Music

All his life as theorist and composer, Berlioz fought against the musical literalism inherited from the eighteenth century, while seeking at the same time to define the true relation of music, drama, and words.

I

Let us begin by discussing *imitation* in music, not in the technical sense which refers to fugue and the fugal style, but in the sense of producing certain noises which describe or depict by musical means objects whose existence we are aware of only through our eyes. This notable element of art, which not a single great composer of any school has neglected to use, whether or not his attempts were successful, and which admittedly has seduced more than one into ridiculous and deplorable errors, has seldom been treated with any fullness or examined with judgment. I shall therefore try to throw some light on the darker side of its theory, while seeking the criterion by which to determine when its application ceases to be art and falls into absurdity after exhibiting the silly and the grotesque.

M. Joseph Carpani, the excellent Italian critic to whom we owe, among other things, a volume of letters on the life and works of Haydn,[1] will help us in our search. His views on the matter seem those of a man gifted with musical good sense and a proper feeling about the true limits of the art of music. Yet he appears to me not to have sufficiently brought out the main features of the subject. Hence the present attempt to fill in the gaps left by his discussion, which I mean to follow step by step.

[1] *Le Haydine* (Milan, 1812), by Giuseppe Carpani (1763–1825).

In one of his letters about the famous oratorio *The Creation*,[2] in which Haydn makes frequent use of the descriptive style, M. Carpani remarks that long before Haydn composers had been making use of the imitative means open to the musician; of these the critic distinguishes two kinds—the physical and the emotional. The first he calls direct, the second indirect.

By direct imitation [says M. Carpani], I mean the imitation of sounds as they occur in the throats of animals, or as they are made by the air vibrating in different ways around solid bodies. The air soughs through foliage, bellows in caverns, murmurs along uneven places, etc., all of which it is proper for music to imitate, even though it be not its highest prerogative. Such imitations are difficult and deserve credit. It is said that a Greek was once asked to go and hear a man whistle like a nightingale. "Not I," replied the Greek, "I have heard the actual bird." The reply has been wrongly lauded. "My dear logician," I should have said to him, "it is precisely because the song is not made by a bird that it is worth hearing and admiring. If some one told you to look at a battle painted by Giulio Romano and you replied, 'I have seen a real battle,' what sense would there be in the rejoinder? It is exactly because you have witnessed real battles that you must find pleasure in seeing art reproduce the likeness with a little colored earth."

Here M. Carpani seems to me to go seriously astray by borrowing an argument from a comparison with painting. That art may not indeed have any other object than to reproduce with fidelity, to give a beautiful imitation of Nature; whereas music is in most cases an art *sui generis*. It is sufficient unto itself, and possesses the power to charm without having recourse to any kind of imitation. Painting, moreover, cannot encroach on the domain of music; but music can by its own means act upon the imagination in such a way as to engender sensations analogous to those produced by graphic art. This point, however, belongs to the second part of our subject, that which M. Carpani calls indirect or emotional imitation. As to the first, the direct or physical imitation of the sounds and noises of Nature, here is what I would say about it, and what our author fails to bring out:

[2] (1798).

If we are to accept imitation among musical devices without detracting from music's independent power or nobleness, the first condition is that imitation shall virtually never be an *end* but only a *means;* that it shall never be considered (except very rarely) the main musical idea, but only the complement of that idea, joined to the main idea in a logical and natural manner.

The second condition to making imitation acceptable is that it shall concern something worthy of holding the listener's attention, and that it shall not (at least in serious works) be used to render sounds, motions, or objects that belong outside the sphere which art cannot desert without self-degradation.

The third condition is that the imitation, without aping reality as by an exact substitution of Nature for art, shall nonetheless be close enough for the composer's intent to avoid misconception in the minds of an attentive audience.

The fourth and last condition is that this physical imitation shall never occur in the very spot where *emotional* imitation (expressiveness) is called for, and thus encroach with descriptive futilities when the drama is proceeding apace and passion alone deserves a voice.

To illustrate and support the foregoing distinctions, I shall take examples from the great masters of music and poetry (for in this matter music and poetry have a common stake), and I shall begin with Beethoven. It might seem as if the "Storm" in the Pastoral Symphony were a magnificent exception to our first rule, which allows imitation only as a means and not as an end. For this symphonic movement is wholly given over to the reproduction of the divers noises heard during a violent storm which breaks suddenly over some village festivities. First a few drops of rain, then the rising wind, the thunder grumbling dully in the distance, the birds seeking shelter; finally the approaching gale, the boughs that split, men and animals scattering with cries of dismay, the shattering bolts of lightning, the floodgates of heaven opening, the elements let loose —chaos.

And yet this sublime depiction, which outstrips anything that had ever been attempted in the genre, actually falls within the category of *contrasts* and *dramatic effects,* which are required by the scope of the work. For it is preceded and followed by gentle and smiling scenes to which it acts as a foil. That this is so may be tested by imagining this storm transplanted into another composition in which its presence would not be motivated: it would unquestionably lose a great deal of its effectiveness. Hence this piece of imitation is strictly speaking a means of achieving contrast, devised and managed with the incalculable power of genius.

In *Fidelio,* on the other hand, a work by the same composer, we find another piece of musical imitation of very different purport from the one just reviewed. It occurs in the famous duet at the grave: the jailer and Fidelio dig the place where Florestan is to be buried. Half-way through their toil the pair unearth a large rock and roll it with difficulty to one side. At that point the double basses of the orchestra play a strange and very brief figure—not to be confused with the ostinato phrase of the basses which runs through the whole piece —by which it is said Beethoven wished to imitate *the dull sound of the rolling stone.*

Now this imitation, being in no way necessary either to the drama or to the effectiveness of the music, is really an end in itself for the composer: he imitates in order to imitate—and at once he falls into error, for there is in such imitation no poetry, no drama, no truth. It is a sad piece of childishness, which one is equally grieved and surprised to have to complain of in a great master. The same could be said of Handel, if it be true—as is commonly said—that in his oratorio *Israel in Egypt* he tried to reproduce the flight of locusts, and this to the point of shaping accordingly the rhythmic figure of the vocal parts. Surely that is a regrettable imitation of a subject even more regrettable—unworthy of music in general and of the noble and elevated style of the oratorio.

Haydn, on the contrary, in his essentially descriptive works *The Creation* and *The Seasons,* does not seem to have lowered his style appreciably when, in order to follow the poem, he applied imitation to such agreeable noises as the warbling of turtledoves—an imitation that is, moreover, quite exact.

This brings us back to Beethoven and the Pastoral. There has been frequent criticism of the song of the three birds toward the end of the "Scene by the Brook." As regards the suitability of this imitation, it seems obvious enough. Most of the quiet voices of the waters, earth, and sky naturally find a place here and contribute easily to the serene magnificence of the landscape, but they are not all equally capable of faithful rendering. Beethoven wanted to make the quail, the cuckoo, and the nightingale heard in his orchestra. Now, the first two are unmistakable from the very outset, whereas it is clear that no listener would ever recognize the nightingale in its pretended imitation without being told. The reason is that the fixed sounds of the quail and cuckoo are available in our scale and our instruments, but the voice of the nightingale, sometimes plaintive, sometimes brilliant, and ever irregular, is not imitable. It is odd that this fact of observation has escaped the many composers who have similarly tried and failed to ape the elusive vocalizations of the warbler of dusk.

One may mention other imitations which reason does not exactly reprove but which have been so long in the public domain that they have become vulgar; so that the musician who uses them must show rare tact or strong inspiration to ennoble them or give them the appearance of freshness. In one of the duets of *William Tell*, for example, under Arnold's words "I seek the field of glory," there is a prolonged rhythmic pedal point for trumpets. Its effect seems to me commonplace, or at any rate open to criticism of a kind that a man of judgment such as M. Rossini should not make himself liable to. On the other hand, in Gluck's *Armide* the clamor of war with which the composer accompanies Dunois' exclamation "Our general summons you!" makes the most phlegmatic listener thrill with enthusiasm; it will remain, regardless of the revolutions of taste, as one of the most dazzling strokes of genius.

When, finally, physical imitation is used as a means, there is a pitfall into which some of the greatest poets have fallen, and to which I shall draw the attention of musicians. When Talma, playing Orestes, used to hiss the *s*'s as he exclaimed, *"Pour qui sont ces serpents qui sifflent sur vos têtes?"* [3] far from being terrifying he always made me want to laugh. For it seemed to me clear, then as now, that this solicitude of Orestes to imitate the hissing of serpents when his soul is filled with terror, his heart with despair, and his head with ghostly visions, was directly opposed to any idea we may form of what is dramatically natural and likely. Obviously Orestes is not *describing* the Furies; he imagines that he is actually seeing them. He hails them, pleads with them, defies them; and one must be a very docile spectator not to find comic a piece of imitation ascribed to such a sufferer at such a juncture.

As against this, Virgil's many imitative passages strike me as most felicitous, for he has taken care to put them in the narratives made by his characters or in the descriptions for which the poet himself is responsible, e.g., *"Ruit alto a culmine Troia; Nox atra cava circumvolat umbra; Quadrupedante putrem sonitu quatit ungula campum,"* etc.[4]

II

The kind of imitation that M. Carpani calls *emotional* is designed to arouse in us by means of sound the notion of the several passions of the heart, and to awaken solely through the sense of hearing the impressions that human beings experience only through the other senses. Such is the goal of *expression, depiction,* or *musical metaphors.* As regards expressive power, I doubt whether the arts of drawing and even of poetry can equal music. It is only the infatuation of a certain celebrated composer's followers, joined to their total lack of musical feeling and education, that has enabled them to defend their idol on the ground that all musical accents were interchangeable, whence it followed that the composer of *Otello* [5]

[3] "For whom these snakes that hiss atop your heads?"—from Racine's *Andromaque,* Act IV, scene 5.

[4] From the *Aeneid.*

[5] Rossini (1816).

was not guilty of nonsense or absurdity, since no music could be *true*. He himself refuted them in masterly fashion by his score of *William Tell*.[6] But it would be tedious to dwell on the point.

Musical *depiction,* as I shall show in a moment, is not quite the same thing as a musical *metaphor* and does not seem to me to be nearly so genuine a possibility. The famous naturalist Lacépède,[7] who among his scientific colleagues passed for a very fine composer, says somewhere that "since music has only sounds at its disposal, it can act only through sound. Hence in order to produce the signs of our perceptions these signs must themselves be sounds." But how can one express musically things that make no sound whatever, such as the denseness of a forest, the coolness of a meadow, the progress of the moon? Lacépède answers, "By retracing the feelings these things inspire in us." And our Italian critic finds this sort of imitation worthy, admirable, enchanting. He deems it the musical sublime. I am far from sharing that opinion, and I incline rather to think him mistaken—deceived, like many other writers, by a play on words or, if you prefer, by the lack of precision noticeable in the terms that define the subject.

Is there, for example, any single, fixed manner in which we are affected by the sight of a forest, a meadow, or the moon in the sky? Assuredly not. The woods whose shade and coolness will draw a reminiscent sigh from the happy lover will make the jealous or jilted man gnash his teeth, and will fill his heart with gall at the thought of his happy rival. Meanwhile the hunter will approach it full of eagerness and expansive joy, whereas the maiden will look upon it with secret fears. Now music will easily express blissful love, jealousy, carefree gaiety, anxious modesty, violent threats, suffering and fear, but whether these feelings have been caused by the sight of a forest or anything else, music is forever incapable of telling us. And the pretension to extend the prerogatives of musical expression beyond these already spacious limits strikes me as

---

[6] Rossini (1829).

[7] Count Bernard de Lacépède (1756–1825), known chiefly as a botanist, wrote operas as well as a widely read treatise, *The Poetics of Music* (1785).

wholly untenable. Hence there are hardly any composers of real merit who have wasted their time in pursuit of such an illusion. Their business was quite other, and their achievement far superior to these so-called imitations. If some few have occasionally given up music in favor of something which, after all, is neither music nor painting—and thus given up substance for shadow—I am inclined to think that art as a whole has not lost much thereby, and that in their case substance and shadow equally lacked merit.

Handel, it is true, tried in one of his works to depict a natural phenomenon which has nothing to do with sound or even with silent rhythm, and which affects no one, I should imagine, in any determinate manner—the phenomenon of falling snow. I find it quite impossible to understand how he hoped to get a grip on such a subject once he had made up his mind to imitate it in music.

I shall be told, perhaps, that there exist admirable examples of musical depiction which must be taken account of, if only as exceptions. But on looking closer it becomes clear that these poetical beauties in no way overstep the vast circle, within which our art is circumscribed by its very nature. For these imitations are not in fact offered us as pictures of objects but only as images or analogues. They help to reawaken comparable sensations by means which music undoubtedly possesses. Yet even so, before the original of these images can be recognized, it is strictly required that the hearer be notified of the composer's intent by some indirect means, and that the point of the comparison be patent. Thus Rossini is thought to have depicted in *William Tell* the movement of men rowing. In point of fact all he has done is to mark in the orchestra a *rinforzando* accented at regular intervals—an *image* of the rhythmic straining of the oarsmen, whose arrival has been announced by the other characters.

Again, Weber is credited with having painted the moonlight in the accompaniment to Agatha's aria in the second act of *Der Freischütz;* this is because the calm, veiled, and melancholy coloring of the harmonies and the chiaroscuro of the instrumental timbre form a faithful metaphor or *image* of the pale light of the moon, and, moreover, admirably express the dreaminess of lovers beneath the moon, whose assistance Agatha just then invokes.

Of certain other compositions one may say that they represent a broad expanse or infinity itself, because the composer has been able to suggest to the ear, through the breadth of his melodies, the grandeur and clarity of the harmony and the majesty of the rhythm —all of these being set off by contrary effects—impressions analogous to those a climber might feel on the summit of a mountain when beholding in space the splendid panorama suddenly unrolled *before his eyes*. And here, too, the truth of the *image* will appear only if the listener has taken the pains to inform himself ahead of time about the subject treated by the musician.

It is evident that the possibility of *arousing emotions by images,* that only words sung or spoken can identify, is very far from sustaining the ambitious and vain design of positively denoting by musical means objects that are inaudible or rhythmless.

There is to be sure another kind of *image* that fastens on the words of vocal music, but it succeeds only in shackling expression at large by dwelling on accessory details regardless of meaning. This sort of image is almost invariably childish or petty. How many asininities of this sort could be pointed out in the works of more or less renowned composers! Some cannot come to the word "Heaven" without leaping to a high note: another would think it a disgrace not to speak of Hell in the lowest vocal register. One makes the dawn rise and another makes the night fall. Nothing is so unbearable as this mania for continually playing on words—a mania which, it must be said, is gradually being cured. For to judge from J. J. Rousseau's assault upon his contemporaries, it was never more prevalent nor more acute than among the French musicians of the last century.

III

It is already more than twenty years since I first analyzed [8] in some detail Gluck's system of dramatic composition and the exposition of it which he gives in the dedicatory epistle prefixed to his Italian score of *Alceste*. Perhaps I may be allowed to recur to it and to add a few fresh observations on the subject.

"When I undertook," says Gluck, "to write music for the opera *Alceste,* I made it my aim to avoid all the abuses which the ill-considered vanity of the singers and the weak compliance of composers had brought into Italian opera, and which had made of the most beautiful and pompous of all spectacles the most boring and ridiculous. I sought to bring back music to its true function, that of seconding poetry by strengthening the expression of the feelings and the purport of the situations without interrupting action or paralyzing it through superfluous ornaments. I felt that music should add to poetry what is added to correct draftsmanship by lively color and the adroit use of light and shade, which help to give figures life without distorting their true contours.

"I carefully avoided interrupting an actor in the heat of speech merely so that he could wait for the end of a refrain. Nor did I make him hold a convenient vowel in the midst of his remarks on the pretext of exhibiting at length the agility of his voice or of giving him a chance to breathe before the orchestra provided him with a cadence. I did not hurry over the second part of an aria, passionate and significant though it might be, that I might finish the piece despite the continuation of the sense, and so help the singer to show off his ability to vary an air indefinitely. In short, I tried to prevent those abuses which reason and common sense have long since rebelled against.

"I conceived the idea that the overture should prepare the spec-

[8] That is, in 1834. This third part of the present composite essay was written some twenty-five years later than the first two sections.

tators for the character of the action about to be shown them, and should indicate its subject: that the several instruments should be called into play only in proportion to the intensity of the mood or passion depicted, and that there should not be too great a discrepancy in dialogue between the recitatives and the arias. Throughout, the meaning should not be broken up, nor the forward movement or excitement of a scene checked without reason. Again, I conceived that my task was to attain a beautiful simplicity rather than to show off intricacy at the expense of clarity. I set no value on the discovery of novelty unless it was suggested by the situation or linked in some way with expressiveness. Finally, there was no rule that I did not feel I should readily sacrifice for the sake of the right effect."

This credo seems to me in the main worthy of all praise for its straightforwardness and good sense. Its underlying principles, however absurdly and monstrously perverted of late years, rest upon judicious arguments and a true feeling for dramatic music. Apart from the few reservations to which we shall turn in a moment, these principles are of such excellence that the majority of great composers of all nations have for the most part followed them. But it may be asked whether in promulgating this theory, which the slightest feeling for art in his day—or indeed ordinary common sense —would have shown to be called for, Gluck did not carry its application too far? This seems a conclusion hard to avoid after one has impartially studied Gluck's own works. For he himself did not rigorously apply his principles throughout. Thus in the Italian version of *Alceste* there are recitatives accompanied by a figured bass, very likely for chords on the cembalo (clavichord), as was the custom in Italian theaters at the time. The result is that there is a *very marked discrepancy* between recitative and aria.

Again, several of the arias are preceded by a long instrumental solo; hence the singer must keep silent *until the end of the refrain*. Moreover, Gluck makes frequent use of a form of air which his theory of dramatic music should exclude. I mean the *aria da capo*,

of which each section is sung twice, without any reason assigned
for the repeat, but rather as if the public had shouted "Encore!" Such
is Alceste's air:

> Never did I cherish life
> But as showing thee my love;
> Oh, a thousand deaths befall me,
> If they but prolong thy days!

Why, when the melody has come to a cadence on the dominant,
should the song start all over again without any change in the vocal
or orchestral part: "Never did I cherish life, etc."? Surely the dramatic sense is spoiled by such a repetition, and if anyone should
have avoided this offense against plausibility and naturalness it is
Gluck. Yet he commits the fault in nearly every one of his works.
The composers who followed him have proved much stricter than
he in this regard, and no comparable example is to be found in modern music.

As for his saying that music in a lyric drama has no other end but
to add to poetry what color adds to drawing, I think he is guilty of
a fundamental error. The musician's task in an opera, it seems to
me, is of far greater importance. His work includes both drawing
and color; and to carry on Gluck's simile, the words are the *subject*
of the painting, hardly anything more. Expression is by no means
the sole aim of dramatic music; it would be foolish and pedantic
to disdain the purely sensual pleasure that we find in certain aspects of melody, harmony, rhythm, or instrumentation, independently
of their relation to the depicting of sentiments and passions in a
drama.

And even if one should want to deprive the hearer of these
pleasures, and not let him refresh his attentiveness by withdrawing it for a moment from the main object, there would still be
numerous occasions when the composer must alone sustain the interest of the lyric drama. In dances, for example, in pantomimes and
marches, and in all the pieces where instrumental music is the only
fare, what, given the absence of words, becomes of the poet's su-
premacy? There, surely, music must contain both drawing and color.

If one excepts a few of those brilliant sonatas for orchestra in which the genius of Rossini disported itself so gracefully, it is a fact that up to thirty years ago most of the instrumental compilations which the Italians honored with the name of overtures were grotesque absurdities—and how much more absurd a hundred years since. Gluck himself, under the influence of bad example, and being, as one must admit, not so great a musician, strictly so called, as he was a composer of scene music, permitted himself to put forth that incredible inanity, the *Orpheus* overture. He did better for *Alceste* and still better for *Iphigénie en Aulide.* His theory of expressive overtures gave the momentum that led to the creation of symphonic masterpieces which, despite the failure and the oblivion that overtook the operas they were written to introduce, have remained standing, like superb gateways to fallen temples.

Yet here again, by overdoing a sound idea, Gluck fell into error; not this time by limiting the power of music, but by ascribing to music a power it will never possess. For he says that the overture must indicate the *subject* of the drama. Musical expressiveness cannot go so far. It may well enough render joy, sadness, gravity, playfulness; it will show a striking difference between the joy of a pastoral people and that of a warlike nation, between the grief of a queen and the sorrow of a village girl, between calm, serious meditation and the ardent reveries which precede the bursting forth of the passions. Or again, by using the characteristic musical styles of different peoples, it will be able to distinguish the serenade of an Abruzzi brigand from that of a Tyrolese or Scottish huntsman, the evening march of religious pilgrims mystically inclined from that of a troop of cattlemen coming home from the fair. Music will be able to contrast extreme brutality, vulgarity, and the grotesque with angelic purity, nobility, and innocence. But if it wishes to go beyond this immense circle, music will have to have recourse to speech, whether sung, recited, or read. Thus the overture to *Alceste* will foretell scenes of desolation and tenderness, but it will never impart either the object of this tenderness nor the cause of this desolation.

It will never inform the spectator that Alceste's husband is a king of Thessaly whom the gods have condemned to death unless he can find someone who will sacrifice himself in his place. Yet that is the true *subject* of the play. Some readers may possibly be astonished to find the writer of the present essay vindicating such principles, since some persons believe, or affect to believe, that his opinion on the expressive power of music goes as far beyond the truth as theirs falls short of it. They have accordingly ascribed to him in all generosity their whole share of foolishness—be it said in passing, with no hard feelings.

The third proposition of Gluck's whose fitness I shall take the liberty of questioning is that in which he professes to attach no importance to "the discovery of new effects." Composers had already blackened a good deal of score paper by the time Gluck wrote, and any musical discovery whatever, though it were but indirectly connected with dramatic expression, was not to be despised.

For the rest, I believe that no one could successfully attack their cogency, even including the last assertion, which proclaims Gluck's indifference to the rules, and which many professors will find a blasphemous impiety. Though Gluck was not, I repeat, equal as a musician, strictly so called, with some of those who came after him, he was certainly enough of a musician to have the right of answering his critics as Beethoven once did: "Who forbids this harmony?" "Why, Fux, Albrechtsberger, and a dozen other theorists." "Well, I allow it." Such superb assurance better becomes the musician than the poet; he has better grounds for believing in the acceptability of his neologisms, for his language is not of a conventional sort.

We now know what Gluck's theory about dramatic music was. Without question, his *Alceste* is one of the most magnificent applications of it he ever made. One would have to be a great writer, a poet with a soul on fire, worthily to describe such a masterpiece of grace touched with grief, such a model of antique beauty, so striking an exemplar of musical philosophy united to so much sensibility and elevation. And would the greatest of poets, after all, be equal to the task? Music like this is indescribable; it must be heard and felt. What can one say of those who do not feel it, or feel it dully? They are unfortunate, and surely to be pitied.

ON IMITATION IN MUSIC (1837)
THE *ALCESTIS* OF EURIPIDES (1862)

CAMILLE SAINT-SAENS

⋙ ⋘

The Composer as Psychologist

Nothing is more difficult than to speak about music. The attempt is very arduous for musicians themselves and nearly impossible for others. The strongest, subtlest minds can lose their bearings. Recently a "prince of critics," tempted by the allurements of the Wagner question, addressed his luminous mind to it and was soaring on powerful pinions, was spiraling upward to the heights—the while I admired his daring yet confident flight across the azure sky—when suddenly, like ancient Icarus, he sank heavily to the ground by declaring that musical drama "may exploit the realm of philosophy but cannot enter into psychology." I rubbed my eyes, only to read further that music is an art that has no insight into the soul and cannot enter into its inmost recesses. Its hold on human passions is "strictly limited to the grand passions in their fullest and healthiest manifestations."

I must be permitted to differ with the illustrious and justly admired writer just quoted. It will perhaps be conceded that I have some claims to understanding the hidden resources of an art in the midst of which I have lived, since childhood, like a fish in water.[1] Well, I have invariably found this art by nature unable to convey purely abstract ideas—and what else is the domain of philosophy if not abstract ideas?—whereas, on the contrary, music is all-powerful when it comes to expressing the several degrees of passion, the infinite nuances of feeling. Insight into the soul, the exploration of its inmost recesses, is precisely its most congenial task, the scene of its triumphant success. Music takes up where speech leaves off, it

[1] Saint-Saëns was a child prodigy on the piano, who gave his first public concert at the age of ten.

utters the ineffable, makes us discover in ourselves depths we had not suspected, conveys impressions and states of being that no words can render. That is, incidentally, why dramatic music has so often been able to get along with mediocre words—to say no worse of them; for at times music is the original Logos; it is music that creates the whole; words take second place or become actually needless.

With his ingenious system of leitmotives (ugly word!) Richard Wagner has extended still farther the reach of musical expressiveness by making clear the secret thoughts of his characters beneath and beyond the words they speak. This device had been forecast and sketched out before him, but few paid attention to it before the appearance of the works in which it was fully developed. Take a very simple example, chosen from among a thousand: Tristan asks, "Where are we?" Isolde replies, "Near the goal," but the music is that which previously accompanied the words "Head destined for death," which she whispered while gazing at Tristan. The listener understands at once what "goal" she has in mind. Now tell me, is that philosophy or is it psychology?

Unfortunately, like all delicate and complex agencies, this particular one is frail; it acts on the spectator only if he can distinctly hear the words and if he possesses a first-rate musical memory. Still, that is not my main point and the reader will kindly excuse this digression.

So long as commentators stick to describing the beauties contained in Wagner's works there is nothing—apart from a tendency to partiality and hyperbole, which is not surprising—that one can object to. But as soon as they come to the heart of the question, as soon as they try to explain how music drama differs from lyric drama and either from opera; as soon as they tell us why music drama must of necessity be symbolic and mythical, how it must be "thought musically" and must reside not in the voices but in the orchestra, how impossible it is to employ for music drama the same kind of music as for opera; as soon as they define the "essence of the leitmotiv" and so on ad infinitum—in short, as soon as they seek to indoctrinate us about all these beautiful things, a thick fog overspreads the discourse, strange words crop up, and incoherent sentences multiply like genii out of a bottle: to put it politely, what is said defies human understanding. Nor am I thinking back to the fabulous and short-lived *Revue Wagnérienne*,[2] which announced one fine day to its stupefied readers that henceforth it would be written in intelligible prose. The wisest and coolest writers of today have not escaped the contagion.

Being myself endowed by nature with a stock of naïveté that the passing years have not exhausted, I have repeatedly tried to understand. I said to myself, "Light is not wanting, hence it is my sight which is at fault." I blamed my native stupidity and made genuine efforts to catch the meaning of those learned dissertations; so much so that on one occasion, finding these same impenetrable arguments over the signature of a critic who is usually crystal clear, I wrote to him asking whether he could not favor my deficient eyes with a little more light. He was gracious enough to publish my letter with his reply below—a reply that answered nothing, threw no light, and left things as they were. Since then I have given up the struggle and have started to look rather for the causes of this amazing phenomenon.

No doubt there is more than one cause. Possibly the original theory itself, from which the whole discussion springs, is somewhat lacking in clarity. "When I reread my theoretical works," Richard Wagner once said to Villot,[3] "I can no longer understand them." It is therefore hardly surprising that others should experience difficulties.

We are told that it is a new idea, or rather one revived from the ancient Greeks—like the noble *Jeu de l'Oie* [4]—to want to make a perfect whole of music, drama, pantomime, and scenic display. I am sorry, but this is not true. The idea has ever been the basis of opera for as long as opera has existed. The way of going about it may

[2] Edited by Edouard Dujardin from 1885 to 1888 and numbering among its contributors most of the French Symbolist poets and Naturalistic novelists.

[3] Frédéric Villot (1809–1875), patron and bibliographer of the arts.

[4] A game on the principle of Parcheesi.

have been faulty, to be sure, but the intention was there; and the way of going about it was not invariably so faulty as some would like to think. When Mlle. Falcon sang in the *Huguenots,* when Mme. Malibran played in *Otello,* when Mme. Viardot appeared in *Le Prophète,*[5] the public's emotions were roused to the highest pitch. People were horror-stricken at the blood-strewn scenes of the Saint Bartholomew; they shuddered at the fate of Desdemona; or thrilled with Fides, the mother finding her son as a Prophet surrounded by the pomp of the Church when she had thought him dead. The spectator was thoroughly satisfied.

Now Richard Wagner has in his turn put the stamp of his own personality on his art. His system has achieved a new, close, and powerful union of the several arts comprised in lyric drama. Very good. But is this system definitive, is it The Truth? No, it is not, because it cannot be: no system can be definitive. If it were possible, art would then have reached perfection, which we know to be out of the reach of man. If it were possible, subsequent art would only be a hodgepodge of imitations whose being such would make them as worthless as they would be superfluous. The different elements of lyric drama will always tend toward perfect equilibrium without ever finding it, no matter what the attempts at solving the problem.

Formerly, people willingly forgot the drama in order to listen to the voices, and if the orchestra took it upon itself to be too engrossing there was complaint that it distracted attention.

Nowadays, the public heeds the orchestra, trying to follow the myriad interwoven lines and the iridescent play of tone-color. In so doing they forget to hear and see what is said or done upon the stage. The new system almost completely annihilates the art of singing, and boasts of this. Thus the sole *living* instrument, *the* instrument par excellence, is no longer entrusted with the rendering of melodic phrases. Other instruments, made by our hands in feeble imitation of the human voice, sing in its place. Is this not a handicap?

[5] Rossini's *Otello* (1816), Meyerbeer's *Huguenots* (1836) and *Prophète* (1849).

Never mind, let us go on. The new art, by its complexity, imposes on the performer, and even on the listener, a considerable strain, an effort that is sometimes superhuman. Again, the special sensuous delights that result from the unheard-of employment of harmonic and orchestral combinations give rise to a nervous excitement, an extravagant exaltation, which go beyond the legitimate aims of art. The brain is overtaxed to the point of becoming unsettled. I am not criticizing, I am only describing: the ocean may drown you and the lightning kill, but they are no less sublime for that.

Go one step further. It seems contrary to good sense to put the drama in the orchestra when it obviously belongs on the stage. Yet I freely admit that in the present instance all argument leaves me indifferent. Genius has its reasons which Reason knows nothing of. But I think the facts sufficiently prove that the new art has defects like everything else in the world. It is by no means the perfect, definitive art, after which one can safely pull up the ladder. The ladder is always there, and, as Victor Hugo says, the top rung is ever unoccupied.

⫸ ⫷

By now,[6] the demand that lyric drama be based on legend has been given up. Else it would be necessary to condemn the most celebrated Russian operas, and that wouldn't do. But "method" is still invoked, and at once the discussion becomes snarled, for one method seems to be approved at the expense of others, which creates not a few perplexities.

At this point I shall have to argue somewhat on my own behalf, in connection with my *Henry VIII*,[7] which has been said not to follow "the right method." My intention is not, of course, to defend my music as such, nor to protest the judgments it has brought forth; that is not done. But I may be permitted to speak of the drama and of the manner in which the music is adapted to it. I am told that the work is superficial in every part, lacking in depth, a mere façade; that the minds of the characters are never exhibited;

---

[6] Some dozen years later than the preceding section.
[7] Produced in Paris in 1883.

that the king, who is all sweetness and light at first, turns suddenly to ferocity without pretext or preparation, and so on and so forth. I am referred to *Boris Godunov* and told, "There is historical drama of the right sort for music."

I have seen this famous *Boris* and heard it with the liveliest interest. I noticed impressive as well as delightful pieces in it, and others that were less so. I noticed in one scene an insignificant little monk who in the next scene suddenly became tsar; I saw a whole act filled with processions, bell-ringing, popular songs, and dazzling costumes. In another was a nurse in charge of some little children, to whom she told fairy tales. Then there was a love duet for which nothing had prepared us and which led to no sequel; also some incomprehensible festivities at night, played in total darkness, and, finally, some funereal scenes in which M. Chaliapin was magnificent. In all this, I cannot help it if I failed to find the inner life, the psychology, the preparation and the motivation of which my critics deplore the absence in *Henry VIII*.

"To Henry nothing is sacred," says the book at the outset, "friendship, love, pledged word, or human law—he tramples all as passion moves him." When a little later the smiling king offers holy water to the ambassador whom he is receiving, the orchestra takes up as he speaks the music of that earlier scene and thus casts light into the interior of his mind. Such is the way in which the work has from beginning to end been "superficially" composed.

Of course, I should add that no effort has been made to indoctrinate the public by means of disquisitions upon these details. There has been no singling out of the "theme of treachery," the "theme of cruelty," the "theme of duplicity," the theme of such-and-such, and the theme of what-you-will. Lacking this fashionable aid, my critics can be excused for having missed the point.

Not a word, we are told, not a scene lets us see the workings of Henry's mind. Come, now! What about the big scene with its horrible piling up of one piece of hypocrisy on another? Is there in all this no passion at work? What more do the Russian librettos offer? Or subjects taken from legend?

To sum up: myth or legend affords one advantage to lyric drama and one only—the miraculous. For the rest myth rather entails a disadvantage. How can characters who never existed, or in whose existence no one any longer believes, excite interest by themselves? They do not prop up the music and poetry, as is erroneously thought; it is the music and the poetry that prop them up and give them life. Who would endure the interminable harangues of the woeful Wotan without the superb music that goes with them? Would Orpheus weeping the loss of Eurydice move us as deeply if Gluck had not from the first few notes gripped our hearts? And without Mozart's music what should we think of the puppets in *The Magic Flute?*

Let us then allow musicians to choose their opera librettos—no less than the form of their operas—in accordance with their temperaments. How many young talents are wasted today because they feel obligated to follow the word of command! The truth is that all great artists, and the illustrious Richard more than any other, paid not the slightest attention to criticism. Like the miller in the fable, they followed their own bent and they were right.

PORTRAITS ET SOUVENIRS (1903)
ECOLE BUISSONNIERE (1913)

W. J. TURNER

➤➤ ≪≪

Bury the Program

By vocation a poet, Turner (1889–1946) was professionally a music critic for the *New Statesman* and other periodicals. He gave permanent form to some of his ideas in his biographies of Mozart, Beethoven, Wagner, and Berlioz, from the last of which the following is taken.

I ask any musician who reads these pages to consider the following facts. I would not venture to assert that my instinct for music was secondary to my instinct for words, yet what talent I have is entirely literary. But I do not need any program—and never did need a program—to understand Berlioz's *Symphonie fantastique,* my pleasure in hearing it being purely musical and precisely of the same nature as my pleasure in hearing any one of Beethoven's quartets. Further, I find the greatest difficulty in even reading the "programs" or literary explanations of pieces of music, and am never helped or in any way enlightened as to the music by them.[1]

I carry this so far that I have never even read and rarely understood the texts of the majority of operas I have heard. For me music always speaks adequately without any words, and I judge it (rightly or wrongly) without reference to words. Even in the case of a modern opera like *Wozzeck* [2] I have never read Büchner's play, and on the sole occasion on which I heard *Wozzeck* I did not understand one word in a hundred of the German text. But this did not prevent me from enjoying Berg's music or from having very definite opinions about it. In short, I am of the opinion that the whole ancient controversy about program music was the result of a misconception and

---

[1] One reason for this may be my literary sense, for all these texts and "programs" bore or irritate me by their (for me) unreadableness. [Turner's note.]

[2] *Wozzeck,* an opera by Alban Berg. [Turner's note.]

is a controversy about an illusion. The text of an opera, the words of a song, the program of a symphony or tone poem, or whatever name in the future may be given to any musical composition is of *no importance or significance whatever*. I know this will be going too far for the majority of musicians; nevertheless I am convinced that it is true, literally and strictly true.

In order, however, to help make my meaning clearer, I will offer an analogy. If a painter like Cézanne were to make two pictures, two "still lifes," one a picture of an apple and one a picture of a pear; and suppose in the catalogue by a mistake "The Pear" was numbered as "The Apple," and vice versa. Now the fact that one picture had as its subject an apple and the other a pear would have no bearing on the pictorial or artistic merit of the paintings. In fact, when looking at them you wouldn't bother about the subjects "apple" or "pear" at all. But if you looked at the catalogue and saw the apple picture labeled as "The Pear," you would be worried at once. Why "The Pear"? you would ask. And unless you noticed that the pear picture was labeled "The Apple" and so surmised immediately that it was a simple mistake in cataloguing, you would be so fretted by this incongruity that you would no longer be able to look at the picture as a picture, a work of pictorial art, at all.

Now this is what happens with program music and opera. Those whose innate sense of music is weak fasten on the label and cannot hear the music for seeing the label. Take the label off, bury it, and let them forget it utterly (if they can); and only then will they be able to listen to the music and hear what it is. But even then they may hear nothing at all, just as anyone whose pictorial sense is weak is incapable of seeing a picture but sees only a likeness to something. If the likeness to the label is for him invisible he declares it to be a bad picture, but he really doesn't know what a picture *is*, good or bad. So those who say Berlioz's music is not music are simply saying they can't see its likeness to the label. To them I say, tear off the label, forget all about it, and listen again. If they have ears they will find it is music, pure music. Indeed, what else can it be, being merely a succession of sounds? The merit of this succession of sounds, its virtue, must be judged, can only be judged, by listening to it and ignoring all words, labels, descriptions, analyses, and explanations.

Now, I am perfectly aware that a deeper question is involved here, namely, the relation of the artist to his nominal subject. But people in general are not discussing this problem when they are discussing "program" music, abstract or representative art, or "pure" poetry; and I do not propose to discuss it either, for this is not the place for it. I will only say that in any case what is primarily important is the *relationship* between the artist and his subject. One can no more estimate the value of the *subject in itself* in a work of art than one can estimate the relative value of a sparrow or an eagle, a vegetable or a man, in the love of God. It is the love that gives value, and I do not propose, I repeat, to attempt to explain why God loves a sparrow or why Berlioz loves Harriet Smithson and composes a *Symphonie fantastique* rather than a string quartet. The value of the *Symphonie fantastique*—as of the C Sharp Minor Quartet (Beethoven's Opus 131)—depends equally upon what Berlioz and Beethoven respectively *give* in their work. If Van Gogh chooses to paint a sunflower and Rembrandt an old woman, the virtue of their pictures depends entirely upon Van Gogh and on Rembrandt, and not upon the sunflower or the woman—which have both been the subjects of many lifeless and valueless but recognizable paintings. And if any humanist says there is more life in an old woman than in a sunflower, I reply, "How do you know?" It may be so, but to choose an old woman rather than a sunflower as a subject of a picture does not ensure a better picture.

I therefore dismiss all this loose talk of "pure" music in the abstract as leading nowhere. We can only judge music as music, and its value is entirely independent of its program or label. If anyone says to me that Beethoven's Pastoral Symphony is inferior to his Second Symphony because the former has a "program" and the latter has none, I simply do not understand him; his words seem to me to have no more meaning than if he were to say that the Sixth Symphony was inferior to the Second because six is an inferior number to two, or vice versa.

BERLIOZ, THE MAN AND HIS WORK (1934)

CHARLES GOUNOD

≫≫ ≪≪

Palestrina

This music—severe, ascetic, horizontal, and calm, like the boundary of the ocean; monotonous by dint of serenity; anti-sensual and yet so intense in its contemplativeness that it sometimes attains to the ecstatic—made at first a strange, almost disagreeable impression upon me. Was it because of the very style of these works, which was entirely new to me? Was it the particular sonority of these special voices which my ear heard for the first time? Or was it the strong attack, strong to the point of roughness, emphatic like hammer strokes, which gives such high relief to the performance by stressing the entrances of each voice into the rich, close-spun web of the polyphony? I could not say. The fact remains that this impression, bizarre though it was, did not repel me. I went back for more, and then more, and in the end could not do without it.

There are works which must be seen or heard in the spot for which they were designed. The Sistine Chapel is one of these exceptional places—a unique monument. The colossal genius who decorated its ceiling and altar walls with his incomparable visions of Genesis and Judgment Day, the artist who painted the Prophets as if he were their equal, will never again find his peer, any more than will Homer or Phidias. Men of that caliber do not return a second time. They are summations: they embrace a universe, they exhaust it and finish it off. They have spoken, and after them none dare repeat. But Palestrina's music seems like a sung translation of Michelangelo's great poem, and I am inclined to think that the two masters throw light one upon the other for the common understanding. The beholder teaches the hearer and vice versa; and to such a degree that after a time one begins to wonder whether the Sistine Chapel, considered as paint and music, is not the product of one and the same inspiration. Music and painting interpenetrate in perfect and sublime unity, so that it seems the double utterance of a single thought, the double voice of a single hymn. What one hears is like the echo of what one sees.

There are indeed so many analogies between Michelangelo's work and that of Palestrina, such a family likeness, that it is hard not to infer an identical set of qualities—I almost said, of virtues—in these two extraordinary intellects. In both we find the same simplicity, the same humility in the use of materials, the same absence of concern with effect, the same disdain for what might appeal. One feels that the physical skill, the handling, is no longer of any moment, and that only the soul, with its gaze unshakably bent upon the higher spheres, is intent on imparting through forms at once submissive and wholly mastered the full sublimity of its contemplation. Even the general uniformity of shading that characterizes this music and these paintings contributes to the impression of a voluntary rejection of all shades. The art of these two men is as it were a sacrament, in which the tangible symbol is little more than a veil cast over the living reality of the divine. And that is why neither the one nor the other of these two great masters makes an immediate appeal. In all things we are caught first by the outer brilliancy of surface. Here, nothing of the kind: one must penetrate beyond the visible and the tangible.

On hearing a work by Palestrina, one feels something like the effect produced by reading one of Bossuet's great pages. One finds nothing striking along the way; but by the end one has been carried to the heights. Faithful and docile servant of the thought, the word has neither arrested nor diverted the reader for its own sake, and thus you have scaled the peak without shock or error, led by a mysterious guide who has hidden his own traces and kept his secret.

It is this absence of visible devices, of worldly artifices, of vain sophistication, which makes the really great works altogether inimitable. In order to reach their level nothing less is required than the mind **that** conceived them and the bliss that inspired them.

MEMOIRS (1896)

ROMAIN ROLLAND

⇉≫ ≪⇇

Johann Sebastian Bach

He could hear the thunders of Johann Sebastian Bach's oceanic soul: the winds and storms, the gusts and scudding clouds, the peoples intoxicated with joy, fury, or pain; he could hear Christ, the Prince of Peace, soaring above them, his heart full of pity; the cities awakened by the watchman's cry, rushing with joyful clamor toward the divine Bridegroom, whose steps shake the world; he could hear the roaring fountainhead of thoughts, passions, and musical forms; of heroic life, Shakespearean hallucinations, and Savonarola-like prophecies; of visions—pastoral, epic, or apocalyptic—that were contained within the narrow frame of the small-statured cantor from Thuringia, with his bright eyes and double chin, his upturning brows and wrinkled lids. He could readily see him—somber, jovial, a trifle ridiculous; at once Gothic and rococo, quick to anger, stubborn, serene, gripped by a passion for life and a nostalgia for death. He could see him in the schoolroom, acting the pedant with genius amid blowsy and lousy boys who were gross and beggarly besides, whose screechy voices jarred, with whom he occasionally fought like a carter, and one of whom once beat him black and blue. He could see him at home among his twenty-one children, thirteen of whom died before him and one of whom was born an idiot. The others, good musicians, would play for him. Illnesses, burials, sordid quarrels, want of money, unrecognized genius—and above it all his music and his faith, liberation and light, the glimpse of long-awaited and finally captured Bliss, which was God and God's burning Word, almost consuming, horrifying, destroying him. . . . Oh, Power! Power! Blessed thunderbolt of Power!

JEAN-CHRISTOPHE IN PARIS (1908)

VOLTAIRE

※ ※

Lulli and Rameau

Hitherto French music—or at least French vocal music—has not satisfied the taste of any other nation. It could hardly do so, because French prosody differs from that of all other European languages: we always stress the last syllable, whereas everybody else leans on the penultimate or, like the Italians, on the syllable before. Our tongue is the only one that ends words with mute *e*'s, which are not pronounced in ordinary utterance but must be sounded in singing, and are so sounded with complete uniformity—*gloir-uh, victoir-uh, barbari-uh, furi-uh*. That is enough to make our airs and recitatives unbearable to anyone not accustomed to them.

Then again the climate denies to our voices the lightness afforded to the Italian. We have never acquired the habit, long in use at the papal and other Italian courts, of depriving men of their virility in order to endow them with voices more beautiful than women's. All this, added to the slow pace of our songs, which is in sharp contrast with our national vivacity, will always make French music the property of the French alone.

Yet, in spite of these causes, foreigners who have resided in France a long time will agree that our musicians have composed masterpieces by suiting melodies to our speech, and that this musical declamation is often admirably expressive. But it seems so only to accustomed ears, and it requires perfect execution. We need actors: in Italy singers are enough.

Our instrumental music has somewhat suffered from this same monotony and sluggishness which is objected to vocal works; but not a few of our symphonies, and especially our dance tunes and ballets, have won greater approval among foreign nations. They are often played as additions to many Italian operas. Indeed, scarcely any other kind is to be heard at the court of a king who maintains the best opera house in Europe, and who among many unusual talents has cultivated music especially.[1]

Jean-Baptiste Lulli, who was born in Florence in 1633 and was brought to France in his fourteenth year, as yet knowing only the violin, was the true father of music in France. He accommodated his art to the genius of the language. This was his only hope of success, though it should be noted that at the time Italian music had not yet abandoned the gravity and noble simplicity that we still find admirable in Lulli's recitatives. Nothing can be closer to these than the famous motet *"Sunt breves mundi rosae,"* [2] which used to be sung all over Italy in the seventeenth century.

It is important to remark that in such purely declamatory music as this, which is like the melopoeia of the ancients, it is chiefly the natural beauty of the words that produces the beauty of the song. One can declaim with art only what deserves to be said. This was quite misunderstood in the time of Lulli and Quinault. The other poets were jealous of Quinault but not of the musician. Hence Boileau attacked him for

> . . . his cold immoral platitude
> Which even warmed by Lulli still is lewd.

But the tender passions that Quinault expressed so well were a faithful account of the human heart rather than any lewdness. Quinault's diction gave warmth to Lulli's music a good deal more than the other way round. Quinault was in fact much Lulli's superior, for one reads him still, whereas Lulli's recitative can no longer be sung. In their day it was believed that the poet owed his reputation to Lulli, but time sets everything in its place. Quinault had a share in the rewards given by Louis XIV to the notables of his reign, but only a slight share—all the great gifts went to Lulli.

It took these two men and some actors to make of a few great

---

[1] Frederick the Great of Prussia.
[2] "The roses of this world last but a day."

scenes from *Atys, Armide,* and *Roland* a spectacle of a kind that neither antiquity nor any contemporary people ever possessed. As for the separate arias, large and small, they were not in keeping with the perfection of those great scenes. These airs were in the style of our noels, or akin to the Venetian barcarolles. No one in those days asked for anything better. The feebler these melodies were, the more easily they stayed in the memory. But the recitatives were so superb that not even Rameau could equal them. "I need singers," he would say, "and Lulli wants actors." Rameau has cast a spell upon our ears, Lulli cast his spell upon the listener's soul. It was one of the happy advantages of the age of Louis XIV that Lulli found a Quinault.

After Lulli, all other musicians, such as Colasse, Campra, Destouches, and the rest, simply imitated him until Rameau came, when, by the depth of his harmony, he surpassed them and made of music a new art.

THE AGE OF LOUIS XIV (1752–56)

RICHARD WAGNER

※ ※

Beethoven's Day

If we wish to form a picture of a day in the life of our sacred genius, we can do no better than to derive it from one of his own marvelous compositions. But we must not deceive ourselves. We must hark back to what was said earlier, when referring the genesis of music as an art to the phenomenon of dreaming, and use simple analogy— not identify one thing with another. To illustrate such a typical day from Beethoven's inner life, I will choose the great C-Sharp-Minor Quartet, and what can hardly be done while listening to it—for then we are forced to forgo all mechanical comparisons and give ourselves entirely to the direct revelation of another world—we can in a measure achieve by simply calling up this tone poem in our memory. Yet, even so, the reader's fancy must add the living details of the picture to the bare outline I here offer.

The long, opening adagio, surely the saddest utterance ever made in notes, I should call the awakening on the dawn of a day which "in its whole long course shall not fulfill a single wish, not one." [1] It is at the same time a penitential prayer, a communing with God out of a firm belief in the Eternal Good. The mind's eye then perceives the consoling vision (allegro ⁶⁄₈), which it alone can descry, wherein the longing becomes a sweet and playful though plaintive daydream. The image of the dream takes waking form as the loveliest of memories. Then, with the short transitional passage (allegro moderato), it is as if the master, recalling his art, were settling down to practice its magic. Its power he summons afresh (andante ²⁄₄) in order to conjure up one graceful figure, the blessed embodi-

[1] From Goethe's *Faust*.

ment of native innocence, and he finds unending rapture in that figure's ceaseless, unheard-of transformations under the prismatic lights which his immortal genius casts upon it.

Then we seem to see him, profoundly happy by virtue of his own effort, direct his glowing vision upon the outer world (presto $\frac{2}{2}$). Once more nature stands before him as in the Pastoral Symphony, radiant with his inner joy. It is as if he heard the native accents of the apparitions that dance before him in a rhythm now gay, now gross. He looks on life and seems to ponder (brief adagio $\frac{3}{4}$) how to fashion the tune for life itself to dance to—a short but gloomy spell of brooding, as if the master were sunk in the lowest depths of his dream. One look has shown him the essence of the world: he wakes anew and strikes the strings to sound a dance the like of which the world had never before heard (allegro finale). It is the whole world dancing: frenzied joy, the cry of pain, the transports of love, the acme of bliss, fury, riot, agony, infatuation, suffering. The lightning flickers and thunder growls, and above it the stupendous Performer who rules and moves it all, who leads it masterfully from whirl-wind to cataract, to the edge of the abyss, smiles to himself, for to him the magic is child's play. And now night beckons; his day is done.

BEETHOVEN, A CENTENARY ESSAY (1870)

CLAUDE DEBUSSY

※ ※

The Conductor

The Société des Grandes Auditions de France did not give me admittance to its performance of *Parsifal,* which was recently given at the Nouveau-Théâtre under the direction of M. Alfred Cortot.[1] M. Cortot is the French musician who has profited most from the customary pantomime of the German conductors. He has the same lock of hair as Nikisch [2] (who, by the way, is a Hungarian), and this lock proves to be in the highest degree arresting because of its agitation in conformity with each nuance. See how it droops, weary and sad, in the softer passages, a barrier to all communication between M. Cortot and the orchestra. Then see it rear itself proudly for the music's martial strains. At such moments M. Cortot lunges at the orchestra, pointing his stick menacingly, like the *banderilleros* when they mean to irritate a bull. But the players are as cool as Eskimos—they've been through much worse than this. Then, like Weingartner,[3] the conductor leans affectionately toward the first violins, whispering intimate secrets into their ears. Next he turns upon the trombones and galvanizes them with a gesture which seems to say, "Come on, boys, put some punch into it! See if you can't manage to be trombones out of this world!"—and the obedient trombones conscientiously start swallowing down their tubes.

It is only fair to add that M. Cortot knows his Wagner to the last detail and that he is a thorough musician. He is young and his love of music is disinterested. These are reasons enough not to hold it against him that his gestures are less useful than ornamental.

M. CROCHE, ANTI-DILETTANTE (1911)

[1] Born 1877; better known as pianist.
[2] Arthur Nikisch (1855–1922), onetime leader of the Boston Symphony.
[3] Felix Weingartner (1863–1942), Austrian conductor of international repute.

SAMUEL BUTLER

-»» «««-

Handel

Handel fulfilled Butler's ideal of the good man and great artist. Handelian chords are quoted in *Erewhon,* Butler took composition lessons from Handel's biographer, William Rockstro (1823–1895), and he fashioned the words and music of Handel-like cantatas that combine pastiche and parody.

I

As a boy, from twelve years old or so, I always worshiped Handel. Beethoven was a *terra incognita* to me till I went up to Cambridge; I knew and liked a few of his waltzes but did not so much as know that he had written any sonatas or symphonies. At Cambridge Sykes tried to teach me Beethoven but I disliked his music and would go away as soon as Sykes began with any of his sonatas. After a long while I began to like some of the slow movements and then some entire sonatas, several of which I could play once fairly well without notes. I used also to play Bach, and Mendelssohn's "Songs without Words," and thought them lovely, but I always liked Handel best. Little by little, however, I was talked over into placing Bach and Beethoven on a par as the greatest, and I said I did not know which was the best man. I cannot tell now whether I really liked Beethoven or found myself carried away by the strength of the Beethoven current which surrounded me; at any rate I spent a great deal of time on him, for some ten or a dozen years.

One night, when I was about thirty, I was at an evening party at Mrs. Longden's and met an old West End clergyman of the name of

Smalley (Rector, I think, of Bayswater). I said I did not know which was the greatest—Handel, Bach, or Beethoven.

He said, "I am surprised at that; I should have thought you would have known."

"Which," said I, "is the greatest?"

"Handel."

I knew he was right and have never wavered since. I suppose I was really of this opinion already, but it was not till I got a little touch from outside that I knew it. From that moment Beethoven began to go back, and now I feel towards him much as I did when I first heard his work, except, of course, that I see a *gnosis* in him of which as a young man I knew nothing. But I do not greatly care about *gnosis,* I want *agape;* and Beethoven's *agape* is not the healthy robust tenderness of Handel, it is a sickly maudlin thing in comparison. Anyhow I do not like him. I like Mozart and Haydn better, but not so much better as I should like to like them.

Handel and Domenico Scarlatti were contemporaries almost to a year, both as regards birth and death. They knew each other very well in Italy, and Scarlatti never mentioned Handel's name without crossing himself, but I have not heard that Handel crossed himself at the mention of Scarlatti's name. I know very little of Scarlatti's music and have not even that little well enough in my head to write about it; I retain only a residuary impression that it is often very charming and links Haydn with Bach; moreover, that it is distinctly un-Handelian.

Handel must have known and comprehended Scarlatti's tendencies perfectly well: his rejection, therefore, of the principles that lead to them must have been deliberate. Scarlatti leads to Haydn, Haydn to Mozart, and hence, through Beethoven, to modern music. That Handel foresaw this I do not doubt, nor yet that he felt, as I do myself, that modern music means something, I know not what, which is not what I mean by music. It is playing another game and has set itself aims which, no doubt, are excellent but which are not mine.

Of course I know that this may be all wrong: I know how very limited and superficial my own acquaintance with music is. Still I have a strong feeling as though from John Dunstable, or whoever it may have been, to Handel the tide of music was rising, intermittently no doubt, but still rising, and that since Handel's time it has been falling. Or, rather, perhaps I should say that music bifurcated with Handel and Bach—Handel dying musically as well as physically childless, while Bach was as prolific in respect of musical disciples as he was in that of children.

What, then, was it, supposing I am right at all, that Handel distrusted in the principles of Scarlatti as deduced from those of Bach? I imagine that he distrusted chiefly the abuse of the appoggiatura, the abuse of the unlimited power of modulation, which equal temperament placed at the musician's disposition, and departure from well-marked rhythm, beat, or measured tread. At any rate I believe the music I like best myself to be sparing of the appoggiatura, to keep pretty close to tonic and dominant and to have a well-marked beat, measure, and rhythm.

Handel was a greater man than Homer (I mean the author of the *Iliad*); but the very people who are most angry with me for (as they incorrectly suppose) sneering at Homer are generally the ones who never miss an opportunity of cheapening and belittling Handel, and, which is very painful to myself, they say I was laughing at him in *Narcissus*.[1] Perhaps—but surely one can laugh at a person and adore him at the same time.

II

If you tie Handel's hands by debarring him from the rendering of human emotion, and if you set Bach's free by giving him no human emotion to render—if, in fact, you rob Handel of his opportunities and Bach of his difficulties—the two men can fight after a fashion, but Handel will even so come off victorious. Otherwise it is absurd to let Bach compete at all. Nevertheless the cultured vulgar

[1] A Handelian cantata, words and music by Samuel Butler and H. F. Jones (1888).

have at all times preferred gymnastics and display to reticence and the healthy, graceful, normal movements of a man of birth and education, and Bach is esteemed a more profound musician than Handel in virtue of his frequent and more involved complexity of construction. In reality Handel was profound enough to eschew such wildernesses of counterpoint as Bach instinctively resorted to, but he knew also that public opinion would be sure to place Bach on a level with himself, if not above him, and this probably made him look askance at Bach. At any rate he twice went to Germany without being at any pains to meet him, and once, if not twice, refused Bach's invitation.

Rockstro says that Handel keeps much more closely to the old Palestrina rules of counterpoint than Bach does, and that when Handel takes a license it is a good bold one taken rarely, whereas Bach is niggling away with small licenses from first to last.

⋙ ⋘

People say the generous British public supported Handel. It did nothing of the kind. On the contrary, for some thirty years it did its best to ruin him, twice drove him to bankruptcy, badgered him till in 1737 he had a paralytic seizure which was as near as might be the death of him, and, if he had died then, we should have no *Israel,* nor *Messiah,* nor *Samson,* nor any of his greatest oratorios. The British public only relented when he had become old and presently blind. Handel, by the way, is a rare instance of a man doing his greatest work subsequently to an attack of paralysis. What kept Handel up was not the public but the court. It was the pensions given him by George I and George II that enabled him to carry on at all. So that, in point of fact, it is to these two very prosaic kings that we owe the finest musical poems the world knows anything about.

⋙ ⋘

Rockstro told me that Sir Michael Costa,[2] after his severe paralytic stroke, had to conduct at some great performance—I cannot be sure, but I think he said a Birmingham Festival—at any rate he came in looking very white and feeble and sat down in front of the

[2] Impresario and orchestra conductor in England (1808–1884).

orchestra to conduct a morning rehearsal. Madame Patey was there, went up to the poor old gentleman and kissed his forehead.

It is a curious thing about this great singer that not only should she have been (as she has always seemed to me) strikingly like Handel in the face, and not only should she have been such an incomparable renderer of Handel's music—I cannot think that I shall ever again hear anyone who seemed to have the spirit of Handel's music so thoroughly penetrating his or her whole being—but that she should have been struck with paralysis at, so far as I can remember, the same age that Handel was. Handel was struck in 1737 when he was fifty-three years old, but happily recovered. I forget Madame Patey's exact age, but it was somewhere about this.

—»» ««-

It cost me a great deal to make Ernest [in *The Way of All Flesh*] play Beethoven and Mendelssohn; I did it simply *ad captandum*. As a matter of fact he played only the music of Handel and of the early Italian and old English composers—but Handel most of all.

—»» ««-

It takes as great a composer as Handel—or rather it would take as great a composer if he could be found—to be able to be as easily and triumphantly commonplace as Handel often is, just as it takes —or rather would take—as great a composer as Handel to write another Hallelujah chorus. It is only the man who can do the latter who can do the former as Handel has done it. Handel is so great and so simple that no one but a professional musician is unable to understand him.

—»» ««-

After all, Dr. Morell [3] suited Handel exactly well—far better than Tennyson would have done. I don't believe even Handel could have set Tennyson to music comfortably. What a mercy it is that he did not live in Handel's time! Even though Handel had set him ever so well he would have spoiled the music, and this Dr. Morell does not in the least do.

—»» ««-

[3] Thomas Morell (1701–1784), English theologian and lexicographer who wrote the text of Handel's *Judas Maccabeus*.

Handel and Shakespeare have left us the best that any have left us; yet, in spite of this, how much of their lives was wasted. Fancy Handel expending himself upon the Moabites and Ammonites, or even the Jews themselves, year after year, as he did in the fullness of his power; and fancy what we might have had from Shakespeare if he had gossiped to us about himself and his times and the people he met in London and at Stratford-on-Avon instead of writing some of what he did write. Nevertheless we have the men, seen through their work notwithstanding their subjects, who stand and live to us. It is the figure of Handel as a man, and of Shakespeare as a man, which we value even more than their work. I feel the presence of Handel behind every note of his music. Neither was self-conscious in production, but when the thing has come out Shakespeare looks at it and wonders, whereas Handel takes it as a matter of course.

—»» ««—

Handel left no school because he was a protest. There were men in his time, whose music he perfectly well knew, who are far more modern than Handel. He was opposed to the musically radical tendencies of his age and, as a musician, was a decided conservative in all essential respects—though ready, of course, to go any length in any direction if he had a fancy at the moment for doing so.

NOTE-BOOKS (c. 1890)

VINCENT D'INDY

➤➤➤ ⬦⬦⬦

César Franck Is Inspired

Pupil of Franck, composer, and co-founder of the famous Paris music school, the Schola Cantorum, d'Indy was the master's chief confidant and solicitous biographer.

"Father Franck" was one of those who—like many others—need stimulants in order to find ideas, but it was not by artificial means that he tried to spur his inspiration: he had recourse to music itself.

How many a time have we not seen him in a scrimmage with his piano, pounding out in a jerky yet constant fortissimo the overture to *Meistersinger,* or some other piece by Beethoven, Bach, or Schumann! After a shorter or a longer time, the deafening racket would dwindle into a murmur, then nothing—the master had found his idea.

All his life, whenever he could, Franck used this method of enticing inspiration by means of musical noise. One day, in the course of composing one of his last works, a pupil came upon him during one of these struggles with some piano piece which he was remorselessly butchering. The pupil expressed surprise at the choice of such music, to which the old master rejoined, "Oh that's only for a workout; when I want to find something really good, I play over my *Beatitudes*; [1] in the long run that's what serves me best."

CESAR FRANCK (1912)

[1] The composer's own piano arrangement of his oratorio for soloists, chorus, and orchestra (1879).

BERNARD SHAW

⇒≫ ≪⇐

Sir George Grove and Beethoven

To Sir George I must have been a positively obnoxious person, not in the least because I was on the extreme left in politics and other matters, but because I openly declared that the finale of Schubert's Symphony in C could have been done at half the length and with twice the effect by Rossini. But I knew Beethoven's symphonies from the opening bar of the First to the final chord of the Ninth, and yet made new discoveries about them at every fresh performance. And I am convinced that "G" regarded this as evidence of a fundamental rectitude in me which would bear any quantity of superficial aberrations. Which is quite my own opinion too.

It may be asked why I have just permitted myself to write of so eminent a man as Sir George Grove by his initial. That question would not have been asked thirty years ago, when "G," the rhapsodist who wrote the Crystal Palace programs, was one of the best-ridiculed men in London. At that time the average programists would unblushingly write, "Here the composer, by one of those licenses which are, perhaps, permissible under exceptional circumstances to men of genius, but which cannot be too carefully avoided by students desirous of forming a legitimate style, has abruptly introduced the dominant seventh of the key of C major into the key of A flat, in order to recover, by forced modulation, the key relationship proper to the second subject of a movement in F: an awkward device which he might have spared himself by simply introducing his second subject in its true key of C." "G," who was "no musician," cultivated this style in vain. His most conscientious attempts at it never brought him any nearer than "The lovely melody then passes, by a transition of remarkable beauty, into the key of C major, in

285

which it seems to go straight up to heaven." Naturally the average Englishman was profoundly impressed by the inscrutable learning of the first style (which I could teach to a poodle in two hours), and thought "G's" obvious sentimentality idiotic. It did not occur to the average Englishman that perhaps Beethoven's symphonies were an affair of sentiment and nothing else. This, of course, was the whole secret of them. Beethoven was the first man who used music with absolute integrity as the expression of his own emotional life. Others had shown how it could be done—had done it themselves as a curiosity of their art in rare, self-indulgent, *unprofessional* moments—but Beethoven made this, and nothing else, his business. Stupendous as the resultant difference was between his music and any other ever heard in the world before his time, the distinction is not clearly apprehended to this day, because there was nothing new in the musical expression of emotion: every progression in Bach is sanctified by emotion; and Mozart's subtlety, delicacy, and exquisite tender touch and noble feeling were the despair of all the musical world. But Bach's theme was not himself, but his religion; and Mozart was always the dramatist and storyteller, making the men and women of his imagination speak, and dramatizing even the instruments in his orchestra, so that you know their very sex the moment their voices reach you. Haydn really came nearer to Beethoven, for he is neither the praiser of God nor the dramatist, but, always within the limits of good manners and of his primary function as a purveyor of formal decorative music, a man of moods. This is how he created the symphony and put it ready-made into Beethoven's hand. The revolutionary giant at once seized it, and, throwing supernatural religion, conventional good manners, dramatic fiction, and all external standards and objects into the lumber room, took his own humanity as the material of his music, and expressed it all without compromise, from his roughest jocularity to his holiest aspiration after that purely human reign of intense life—of *Freude*—when

> *Alle Menschen werden Brüder*
> *Wo dein sanfter Flügel weilt.*[1]

[1]   All men shall brothers be
        Where thy gentle pinion hovers.

In thus fearlessly expressing himself, he has, by his common humanity, expressed us as well, and shown us how beautifully, how strongly, how trustworthily we can build with our own real selves. This is what is proved by the immense superiority of the Beethoven symphony to any oratorio or opera.

In this light all Beethoven's work becomes clear and simple; and the old nonsense about his obscurity and eccentricity and stage sublimity and so on explains itself as pure misunderstanding. His criticisms, too, become quite consistent and inevitable: for instance, one is no longer tempted to resent his declaration that Mozart wrote nothing worth considering but parts of *Die Zauberflöte* (those parts, perhaps, in which the beat of *"dein sanfter Flügel"* is heard), and to retort upon him by silly comparisons of his tunes with *"Non piu andrai"* and *"Deh vieni alla finestra."* The man who wrote the Eighth Symphony has a right to rebuke the man who put his raptures of elation, tenderness, and nobility into the mouths of a drunken libertine, a silly peasant girl, and a conventional fine lady, instead of confessing them to himself, glorying in them, and uttering them without motley as the universal inheritance.

I must not make "G" responsible for my own opinions; but I leave it to his old readers whether his huge success as a program writer was not due to the perfect simplicity with which he seized and followed up this clue to the intention of Beethoven's symphonies. He seeks always for the mood, and is not only delighted at every step by the result of his search, but escapes quite easily and unconsciously from the boggling and blundering of the men who are always wondering why Beethoven did not do what any professor would have done. He is always joyous, always successful, always busy and interesting, never tedious even when he is superfluous (not that the adepts ever found him so), and always as pleased as Punch when he is not too deeply touched. Sometimes, of course, I do not agree with him. Where he detects anger in the Eighth Symphony, I find nothing but boundless, thundering elation. In his right insistence on the jocular element in the symphonies, I think he is occasionally led by his personal sense that octave skips on the bassoon and drum are funny to conclude too hastily that Beethoven was always joking when he used them. And I will fight with him to the death on the trio of the Eighth Symphony, maintaining passionately against him and against all creation that those cello arpeggios which steal on tiptoe round the theme so as not to disturb its beauty are only "fidgety" when they are played "à la Mendelssohn," and that they are perfectly tender and inevitable when they are played "à la Wagner." The passage on this point in Wagner's essay on Conducting is really not half strong enough; and when "G" puts it down to "personal bias" and Wagner's "poor opinion of Mendelssohn," it is almost as if someone had accounted in the same way for Beethoven's opinion of Mozart. Wagner was almost as fond of Mendelssohn's music as "G" is; but he had suffered unbearably, as we all have, from the tradition established by Mendelssohn's conducting of Beethoven's symphonies. Mendelssohn's music is all *nervous music:* his allegros, expressing only excitement and impetuosity without any ground, have fire and motion without substance. Therefore the conductor must, above all things, *keep them going;* if he breaks their lambent flight to dwell on any moment of them, he is lost. With Beethoven the longer you dwell on any moment the more you will find in it. Provided only you do not sacrifice his splendid energetic rhythm and masterly self-possessed emphasis to a maudlin preoccupation with his feeling, you cannot possibly play him too sentimentally; for Beethoven is no reserved gentleman, but a man proclaiming the realities of life. Consequently, when for generations they played Beethoven's allegros exactly as it is necessary to play the overture to *Ruy Blas,* or stone him to death—a practice which went on until Wagner's righteous ragings stopped it—our performances of the symphonies simply spoiled the tempers of those who really understood them. For the sake of redeeming that lovely trio from "fidgetiness," "G" must let us face this fact even at the cost of admitting that Wagner was right where Mendelssohn was wrong.

PEN PORTRAITS AND REVIEWS (1896)

FRANZ LISZT

>>> <<<

Chopin a National Poet

Prolific in all things, Liszt wrote much upon music and at one time
planned a series of volumes on his great contemporaries. The volume on
Chopin was the only one completed and published, originally in French.

Since nowadays the native folksongs of all countries are eagerly—
and quite rightly—being noted down and collected, it would seem
to us of even greater interest to give some attention to the characteristics of those artists who are especially inspired by the genius of
the nation to which they belong. So far only a few can be found
whose chief works do not emerge from either of the two great
divisions of Italian and German music. But it is likely that given
the tremendous expansion which our art seems destined to attain—
thus making our age a glorious era akin to that of the cinquecento in
painting—composers will arise whose works will be marked by an
originality due to the differences of climate, race, and national temperament. In music, presumably, as in the other arts, it will be possible to recognize the influence of native soil upon the greatest masters, and to discern in their works the influence of the popular mind.
It will appear therein more fully, more poetically, and more worthy
of study than in the crude and sketchy, or incorrect and clumsy, efforts of popular music itself.

Chopin will have to be classed among the first musicians who have
thus individualized in their own work the poetical feeling of a
whole nation—and not simply because he borrowed the rhythms of
polonaises, mazurkas, and cracowiennes, nor because he gave those
names to many of his works. Had he merely multiplied those patterns, reproducing the same outline and the same reminiscences of

a single experience, it would have soon become a tedious kind of imitation, and would only have been the proliferation of a monotonous form. It is on the contrary because he used these forms in order to express ways of feeling which are more usual in his country than elsewhere, that his name will remain as that of an essentially Polish tone poet; and also because these feelings may be found in all the forms that he employed. His preludes, études, scherzos, concertos, and especially his nocturnes—the short works as well as the largest—all exhibit the same sensibility in varying degrees of explicitness. It occurs modified and transformed in a hundred ways, yet always one and the same.

Pre-eminently a subjective composer, Chopin has given to all his creations the same life, and it is his own life which animates all his works. They are bound together in a unity which determines at once their beauties and their defects: both are the consequence of a single order of emotion, of an exclusive way of feeling—which indeed is essential if a poet is to cause the hearts of all his compatriots to beat as one.

F. CHOPIN (1852)

EUGENE DELACROIX

⇛ ⇚

Mozart and Modernism

Between the years 1853 and 1856, Delacroix's *Journal* dwells repeatedly on the theme embodied in the caption above, so that a little essay can be made by piecing together the entries made in the diary after each soirée that Delacroix attended.

Delightful music at Princess Marcelline's.[1] My recollection of the Mozart "Fantasia"—a somber piece which occasionally reaches the terrible, and whose title is lighter than the character of the music suggests. Then a Beethoven sonata, well known but admirable. This unquestionably gave me pleasure, particularly through the sad regions of the imagination. That man is always sad. Mozart is modern too, that is, he is not afraid to touch on the melancholy side of things, but, like the men of his time—French gaiety, the being compelled to deal only with attractive things and to banish from art and conversation whatever is gloomy and serves to recall our human condition—Mozart combines just enough of this touch of pleasurable sadness with the easy cheerfulness and elegance of a mind lucky enough to take in what is agreeable.

I argued with their good friend R——, who dislikes Cimarosa, who "sees nothing in him," as he says with a certain self-satisfied air. How different is Chopin! Just see, I said to them, how much he is a man of his own time, how he makes use of the advances that others have contributed to his art, how he loves Mozart without being like him. His friend Kiatkowski often used to chide him for the echoes of Italian music in his works, suggestions of Bellini and other moderns. That does not bother me much. What charm! And novelty besides!

[1] Princess Czartoriska.

In the evening, listening to the Mozart trio for viola, piano, and clarinet, I responded with delight to certain passages. The rest seemed to me monotonous. If I say that such works afford but a few pleasurable moments, I do not mean that it is the fault of the work. As regards Mozart, I am sure the fault was mine. In the first place, certain forms have become dated; they have been rehashed and ruined by all the later-comers, and this is enough to spoil the freshness of the work. It is in fact a matter for surprise that other parts have kept their charm for so long a time—time rushes by so fast in the matter of fashion and fine art, and after so much good and bad music patterned on this enchanting model.

Another reason why a creation by Mozart is less remarkable for that abrupt novelty which we find today in Beethoven and Weber is that *they* belong to our time. And then again, they lack the perfection of their predecessor. It is exactly the same effect as that produced by a sketch as compared with a finished monument, by a ruin or an incomplete structure as compared with the final form. Mozart outtops them all by his accomplished form.

⇛ ⇚

The Spectator speaks of what it calls "the greatest geniuses," [2] such as Pindar, Homer, the Bible, Shakespeare, etc., whose works are a confusion of things sublime and unpolished. Then it mentions those in which it discerns greater art, such as Plato, Virgil, and others. A mighty question! . . . What would be the use of a fine style and polish applied to crude or common ideas? Perhaps the men of the first rank are like those prodigals to whom much is forgiven because of their occasional good deeds. It's the old story of the sketch and the finished work, of the monument which exhibits only the main structural features until the completion and coordination of all the parts enable it to convey the sense of fixed limits. These necessarily lessen its effect on the imagination, which prefers vagueness, expands readily, and embraces great matters on a slight hint.

Even so, in the sketch for the monument as compared with its finished state, the imagination can hardly conceive things too un-

[2] This is Addison's *Spectator*, No. 160.

like the ultimate form, whereas in the works of genius in Pindar's manner are found monstrosities side by side with the grand and the beautiful. Corneille is full of such discrepancies, and so is Shakespeare. But Mozart is not so, nor are Racine, Virgil, and Ariosto. The mind feels pleasure throughout. . . .

If geniuses like Homer and Shakespeare present such disagreeable features, what shall we say of the imitators of this genre, the careless and abandoned? The *Spectator* scolds them quite justly, for nothing is more detestable: of all conceivable forms of imitation it is the worst and most foolish. Nor have I said that *original genius* is the warrant for the *Spectator*'s admiration of the Homers and Shakespeares. That subject calls for another discussion and a comparison with the Mozarts and the Ariostos, who seem to me nowise lacking in originality, for all the symmetry of their works.

I should add that the perfected works of a Racine or a Mozart do not at first make as deep an impression as those of geniuses who are less correct or more negligent. The salient parts of these last seem all the more striking because other parts nearby are more neutral, or downright bad.

In gazing at that beautiful tree (the oak at Antin) whose proportions are so fine, my ideas find fresh confirmation. If I stand far enough away to see all its parts at once, it seems of average size. But if I step underneath it, my impression is altogether different. Seeing only the trunk, which I can almost touch, and the rise of those mighty boughs stretching over my head like the arms of a forest giant, I am astonished by the scale of the parts; in short, I find it enormous and almost frightening by its size.

Could disproportion be a prerequisite to admiring? If, on the one hand, Mozart, Cimarosa, and Racine are less than striking because of the wonderful proportions of their works, may not Shakespeare, Michelangelo, and Beethoven move us by reason of the opposite cause? I am inclined to think so.

-»» «««-

Concert by the Saint-Cecilia Society. I really listened only to the *Eroica* symphony. I found the first movement splendid. The andante [3]

[3] The funeral march, actually an adagio.

is perhaps Beethoven's most tragic and sublime composition, but only halfway through. Then came Cherubini's "Consecration March," which I heard with pleasure. As for *Preciosa* [4] whether it was the heat or the brioche I had eaten beforehand, at any rate my immortal soul was paralyzed and I slept all the way through.

While listening to the first work I was thinking of the devices by which musicians try to establish unity in their compositions. The recurrence of motives is what they generally seem to consider the most effective way, but it is also the one which is most accessible to mediocre talent. Though this recurrence is in some cases very satisfying to the mind and the ear, when overdone it seems like a second-rate device, or indeed a mere trick. Is our memory so inadequate that it is impossible to establish relations among the several parts of a piece without relentlessly driving the main idea into our minds by continual repetition? A letter, a poem, or a piece of prose can show a deductive order, a unity which derives from the development of the ideas one from the other, and not from the repetition of the sentence which may be the chief point of the composition. In this regard musicians resemble the preachers who reiterate ad nauseam, in every connection, the text of their sermon.

I can think right now of several airs by Mozart whose logic and coherence are admirable yet free of repetitions: the aria *"Quì l'odio non facunda,"* [5] the chorus of priests in *The Magic Flute,* the trio and quintet in *Don Giovanni,* etc. These last are good-sized pieces, which only increases their worth. In his symphonies, of course, he sometimes repeats his main theme to the point of satiation. Perhaps he is following an established custom. The art of music seems to be more subject than the rest to the pedantic habits of the trade, which may give pleasure to people who are exclusively musicians but which always bore the hearer who is not versed in the technicalities of the craft, such as re-entries in learned fugues, etc.

However agreeable at times, as I just said, repetitions do not give

[4] Opera by Weber. Here, probably, only the overture is meant.
[5] Italian version of *"In diesen heil'gen Hallen,"* from the second act of *The Magic Flute.*

the feeling of unity so much as of weariness. Unity must come naturally out of the right elements, which is a secret of genius. The mind is so imperfect, so fugitive, that the man most sensitive to art will nonetheless invariably feel a kind of unease in the presence of a masterpiece, a hindrance to complete enjoyment, which is not to be dispelled by the lesser devices for creating a fictitious unity: repetition in music or the concentration of effects in painting. These are petty and trivial ingenuities, which the common run of artists seize upon and apply in that same spirit. . . .

Masterpieces would never grow old if they were wholly pervaded by true feeling. The language of passion and the impulses of the heart are ever the same. What inescapably marks with age—and may at times obscure—the greatest beauties is these "effective" devices which anyone can master. They are in vogue at the time the work was composed; they seem to be necessary ornaments for the idea. Fashion approves them, and they are generally responsible for the success of the work. Those artists who by a rare feat have done without these accessories are understood late in life and with great difficulty—or else by subsequent generations for whom the charm of the fashionable ornaments no longer exists.

There seems to be an ordained *mold,* into which everybody casts his thoughts, good or bad, and the most gifted, most original minds show the marks of it. What music can possibly withstand, after the passage of years, the taint of out-of-dateness imparted by the cadences and embroidery which made it popular when new? . . . We should deplore the sad condition into which certain inventions of original talents fall. The new sonorities and harmonies of Beethoven have already become the legacy, indeed the spoils, of the rawest beginner.

The public in its stupidity is now deserting Rossini for Gluck, just as it formerly deserted Gluck for Rossini. A ditty of the year 1500 is suddenly exalted above all that Cimarosa has written. Grant that the stupid herd must absolutely change from fad to fad for the good reason that it possesses no taste or discernment about anything whatever. But that men of the craft, that artists—or nearly—who are called "superior minds," should weakly tend themselves to all these vagaries passes understanding.

>>> <<<

I thought yesterday while going to Saint-Sulpice [6] of writing something on the regular progression of the arts: they keep refining and refining. The source of my ideas was the impression made upon me by hearing at the Princess's the compositions of Mozart that Gounod played through for us. This evening at the Countess d'Haussonville my impression was confirmed by hearing Mme. Viardot [7] sing the aria from *The Marriage of Figaro*. Bertin [8] was telling me that he thought this kind of music far too delicate and too subtly expressive ever to appeal to the public. But that is not what one ought to say, for in times like ours the public comes to love detail for itself, as a result of hearing works that have taught it to refine on everything. In our time, on the contrary, one must not paint in broad strokes if one is aiming at the public; indeed, breadth would only reach some few extremely rare minds who rise above the common requirements and who still feed on beautiful things of the best periods—in short, those who love the kind of beauty that is also simplicity.

Let us therefore paint in broad strokes. In primitive times works of art are not otherwise. The upshot of my thought is the need of belonging to one's own time. Voltaire in his *Huron* [9] makes the hero say that "Greek tragedies are good only for the Greeks," and he is right. It is absurd to go against the current and attempt archaism. Racine seems overrefined when compared with Corneille, and how much farther the moderns have gone along that path! Walter Scott and Rousseau, among the first, have delved and delved into vague impressions and feelings of melancholy which the ancients hardly suspected. And the moderns do not merely depict feelings, they also describe external facts, they take everything apart.

[6] Paris church where Delacroix was painting murals (1855–1861).

[7] Pauline García-Viardot; see pp. 261 and 373n.

[8] Childhood friend of Delacroix, newspaper owner, painter, and patron of the arts.

[9] A novel entitled *L'Ingénu* whose hero is a Huron (1767).

In music, the perfecting of the instruments or the invention of new ones tempts composers to go farther into certain sorts of imitation. The time will come when the real noise of the wind, the sea, or a waterfall will be physically imitated. . . . In the theater, it is imperative to improve scenery and costumes, and it is clear that this is not altogether in bad taste. Everything must be refined upon: all the senses must be satisfied, and there will in time be performances of symphonies accompanied by beautiful pictures, to complete the impression.

It is said that Zeuxis or some other painter of antiquity was showing a painting representing a great warrior or the horrors of war and had trumpeters play behind the picture to encourage the admiring spectators. It soon won't be possible to do a battle in paint without burning a little powder nearby, to edify the feelings thoroughly, or indeed to arouse them.

Already some twenty years ago, on the stage of the Opera, the scenery and props were made real in order to enhance the lifelikeness; for instance in the operas *La Juive* and *Gustave III*.[10] In the former one could see real statues and other accessories, which are usually painted in. In *Gustave,* there were real rocks—imitations, to be sure, but cut out of solid blocks. Thus from love of illusion no illusion was left.

I dined at Princess Marcelline's: duets for piano and bass by Mozart and Beethoven. . . . What a life mine is! I was thinking of this while listening to this superb music, especially Mozart's, which suggests the calm of an orderly epoch. I have come to the time of life when the tumult of passion no longer intrudes upon the delightful emotions aroused by objects of beauty. I have no knowledge of the paper work and drudgery that form the occupation of most men. Instead of thinking about business, I think only of Rubens or Mozart: my chief concern for a week at a time is a melody or a picture. . . .

JOURNAL (1853–1856)

[10] By Halévy and Auber respectively (1835 and 1833), both librettos by Scribe.

JOSEPH MAZZINI

➤➤ ◄◄

Meyerbeer's Achievement

The Italian liberator was another of the nineteenth-century publicists who wrote about everything, convinced as they were that the world must be made anew. The following is taken from an essay that appeared in an Italian journal in 1836.

One cannot be too thoroughly persuaded of the fact that if music is to flourish anew, it must be *spiritualized;* that if it is to rearise and exert power, it must be reconsecrated to a mission; that if we are not to see it sink into the useless and eccentric, we must join that mission to the general mission of the arts in our epoch, and seek in the epoch the true character of the art; in other words, we must make music *social* and identify it with the progressive movement of humanity. And we should be persuaded, too, that our business to-day is not to perpetuate or make over an *Italian school,* but rather *from Italy* to lay the foundations of a *European* school of music.

Now a European school of music can only be one which will take account of all the musical elements developed by the previous partial schools, and without suppressing any of them will harmonize and direct them toward a single end. When, therefore, I say that we must emancipate ourselves today from the Rossini school, I have in mind only the *exclusive* spirit of that school—the exclusive pre-dominance of melody and the exclusive attention to individuality which animates it, which makes it fragmentary, uneven, incoherent, and which limits it to materialism, that plague of any art, doctrine, or enterprise. Again I have in mind the divorce which that school has brought about between music and the march of society; the degradation which reduces art to the pastime of a small minority; the frivolous and venal habits with which it has tainted the sanctity of art. I do not propose an emancipation from individuality itself, which must ever remain the starting point of any music, and the lack of which in German music deprives it of half its energy.

Other improvements, of a technical sort, will also be required in a time of science: on these and others I shall not dwell. But choosing at random from the many that naturally suggest themselves to all who do not follow present-day musical drama with their ears alone, I may ask why accompanied recitative—once a principal part of opera and now so rare, perhaps because more difficult to sing than is generally supposed—should not assume in the music of the future a far greater importance and realize the full measure of its inherent power. Why should a mode of musical development capable (as Tartini's examples show) of the highest dramatic effect play so small a part in our musical drama? By this type of recitative the listener can be carried along at the composer's will through infinite gradations of feeling quite beyond the reach of the aria, and thus explore a particular sentiment or passion to the very depths, revealing the slightest movements of the heart without violating its secrets; it is a device which can anatomize inner conflicts, whereas the aria can only with difficulty express anything but their result. Recitative, moreover, does not distract the listener's attention from the meaning of the music to the mechanism of its execution, and thereby leaves its power over the soul undivided. Must such a mode of expression remain forever relegated to one corner of the drama instead of being enlarged and perfected—even at the expense of the often needless cavatina and inevitable *da capo?*

One might also get rid of the monotony engendered by the vulgar and tedious cadences, which we have come to regard as fated from eternity. Likewise, the arbitrary ornaments, the embellishments and additions that singers indulge in should be prohibited—at least until singers become a little more philosophical than they are now. Though war has been waged against these irrelevancies, they still occur often enough to break in upon true feeling, which they transform into a heartless and misplaced admiration. What a saving of time spent in these futilities could be effected and applied to the enhancement of the historical basis and aesthetic working out of the drama itself!

I know that most spectators already consider our operas too long, and it cannot be otherwise as long as the work lacks all spiritual intention. I speak for a time when public and drama will have reciprocally improved each other; for a time when the dramas of the divine Schiller, being felt and understood, will be produced without profane rehandlings, without the indignity of mutilation, and will be listened to in a reverent mood; for a time when musical drama will be offered to a people neither materialist, nor idle, nor frivolous, but, on the contrary, regenerated by the consciousness of a Truth which must be won by struggle and which yields the highest moral teachings. I speak for a time in which music will have added to its own power all the powers combined in a dramatic spectacle.

I know that for the artist to educate his public is slower work, and harder for us, than for Nature to fashion a genius as initiator of an epoch; but I know also that just for this reason the work of education should begin. The genius will do the rest.

And the power of genius itself will be multiplied a thousand fold when Poetry, today the servant, will once again be as she should, the sister of Music, and will harmonize with her as does the particular instance to the general statement, the number to the algebraic formula. In that epoch poets will write lyric dramas, not make verses or worse than verses. Poets and musicians, instead of degrading and tormenting themselves in their joint work, will faithfully devote themselves to their task as to a sacred office, calling one upon the other and uniting their inspiration as well as the powers of music and of poetry in a common social purpose. Then, then, genius will be magnified by the awareness of the goal and the greatness of the means, by faith in an immortality which none today dare hope for. It will rise to heights yet unattempted, and will draw from art secrets still unsuspected. Its Raphael-like melodies and unbroken harmonies will adumbrate that infinity to which our souls aspire, and of which we have a thousand intimations in woman, in the starry heavens, in beauty and greatness, in love and piety, in the memory of the dead and our hope of seeing them hereafter.

Genius will resolve the problems and conflicts which for a thousand years have agitated mankind—the struggle of good and evil, mind and matter, Heaven and Hell, the struggle symbolized by Meyerbeer, with touches worthy of Michelangelo, in an opera which will long repay study by artists—*Robert le Diable*.[1] For the mission that music must serve is to raise cold and casual belief to the height of enthusiastic faith in the potency of SACRIFICE, which is true virtue.

And genius will reward sacrifice, will aid and comfort the spirit which trusts itself to its guidance by leading it, from circle to circle, through the musical expression of all the passions, in a rising scale of sublime harmonies, in which every instrument will represent a feeling, every melody a true deed, every chord an assuagement of the soul; by which the soul will be raised above the mire of sensation and the tumult of the instincts to the angelic heavens beheld in vision by Weber, Mozart, and Beethoven—the heaven of pure rest, of moral serenity, wherein the soul is revigorated by love, where virtue is not faltering but secure, where martyrdom becomes immortal life, where maternal tears are transmuted into gems with which God adorns the brow of their sons, and where the sigh of the beloved becomes the kiss of holy and eternal love.

Neither to me who write these words, nor to our generation, born in a time destined only to foresee this genius and the art reborn through him, will that heaven be opened. We have the bitterness, not the solace of the Ideal. But to have had a glimpse of what will be for those who come after is enough to make it a duty that we should work toward the goal with all the means and talents at our command.

Perhaps if genius sufficed, instead of presentiment and distant hope, we might have the reality; that is, if reconstituting music required only genius and not the indefatigable, super-human energy to fight the desperate fight against prejudice, against the tyranny of commercial managers and the mob of careerists and the indiffer-

[1] First performed in Paris in 1831, five years before Mazzini wrote.

ence of the age, then we might perhaps find one among the living who, if he would, could become founder of an Italian-European school, and hence be the reformer—as he is the leader—of those who fight under the banner of the purely Italian school of Rossini. I refer to Donizetti, the only one whose eminently progressive talents show tendencies toward renovation, the only one, it seems to me, in whom one can have any hope today when one is thoroughly nauseated by the vulgar tribe of musical imitators who swarm over our Italian soil.[2]

Whether by Donizetti or by others, the reform of music must and will take place. Whenever a school or movement or epoch is exhausted, whenever a course has been run through and there is nothing to do but run through it again in the same footsteps, reform is imminent, inevitable, certain; for humanity cannot go backward. Let our young composers, then, prepare, dedicate themselves, as to a religious rite, to the inauguration of the new musical school. This is their time of knightly vigil, so let them remember how those who were about to receive knighthood prepared themselves by silence, solitude, and meditation upon the duties they were to assume, for the fulfillment of the mission to which they were dedicated the day after, in the generous hope of a new dawn.

Let our young artists enlarge their minds by the study of our national songs, of history and the mysteries of poetry and Nature, so as to enlarge their scope and take in wider horizons than those of academic textbooks and the ancient rules of art. Music is the fragrance of the universe, and to capture it for his works the artist must, by loving and faithful study of the harmonies that float on earth and in heaven, identify himself with the mind of the universe.

---

[2] Bellini, whose premature death we all deplore, was not, it seems to me, a progressive mind; nor would he, had he lived, ever have gone beyond the limits which his music now occupies. The most beautiful of his inspirations are to be found in *Pirata* and *Norma*. The duets *"Tu sciagurato"* and *"Tu m'apristi,"* which are so rarely sung in Italy, together with the last act of *Norma,* so like Raphael in form and conception, sum up all there is to Bellini. [Mazzini's note.] For the operas and composers mentioned in this article, see notes on pp. 224, 261, and 576.

Let them also study the masterpieces of music, the works of genius not of a single country, time, or school, but of all of these; and study not merely to dissect according to the dry and frigid methods of the professors, but rather to make their own the creative and unifying spirit which lives and moves in these works; and again, not to imitate it in narrow and servile fashion, but to emulate it as free men eager to link the new work to the great tradition.

→≫ ≪←

Since the foregoing article was written,[3] an immense step has been taken in advance. The problem, which may be said to have been musically stated by Meyerbeer in *Robert the Devil,* is not solved in the *Huguenots;* but its solution is at least suggested. That opera stands alone, a beacon to indicate to future composers the course through which Music may be directed toward a high social aim.

In his conception of *Robert the Devil,* the author has symbolized in Alice and Bertram the principles of Good and Evil, and the struggle between them for mastery over the human soul; but Robert himself is little more than passive in their hands, and throughout the course of the opera their forces appear equally balanced. The antagonistic principles oppose each other, something after the manner in which the Homeric gods fight *for* and *against,* rather than *through,* the individuals whose interests they defend or attack; the moral effect of the representation of the contest within a human breast is lost, and the final triumph of the good principle assumes the appearance of an accident or fatality, in which we rather contemplate a *fact* than confess a Providence. Moreover, the image of duty presented to us by the human agent is somewhat cold and rigid; faith triumphs over superstition, but it is faith unwarmed by enthusiasm, unsanctified by suffering.

In the *Huguenots,* on the contrary, while the interest of the struggle is increased by its revelation through human suffering and pas-

---

[3] This supplement, dated 1867, does not occur in the National Edition of Mazzini's works, but only in the four-volume English selection from the writings. It is therefore given in the English of the translator of that edition, who presumably was the only one to see the Italian original.

sion, the sense of a guiding Providence pervades the whole work. The sublime inspiration of faith and duty is the soul of the magnificent chorale with which the opera opens, and which throughout the piece re-echoes from time to time upon our hearts, holy as the chant of angels, yet stern and solemn as a passing bell; it finds its human expression in the austere, insistent, severe yet loving musical individuality of Marcel, in whom the rugged invincible earnestness of the *believer* ever rises above and dominates alike the lightest and most brilliant, or gloomiest and most bigoted, scenes of the Catholic world by which he is surrounded; so that his very presence on the stage arouses in the heart of the spectator the sense of a providential influence at work to bring about the triumph of good through human suffering, sacrifice, and love.

Nor is it only in the ruling conception that informs this opera that Meyerbeer has surpassed his predecessors and his own previous works. The hand of the master is revealed in the exquisite blending of the Italian and German elements of melody and harmony, which the music of the future is destined to combine. In *Robert,* the two elements are each represented by turns; rarely do we find them conjoined; but in the *Huguenots* they are inseparably united and fused into an harmonious whole. In a period of transition like our own, we may not expect the high priest of the music of the future to appear amongst us; but Meyerbeer is the precursor spirit sent to announce his coming.

While he has sketched for us the outlines of the musical drama of the future, and created musical individualities which remind one of the personages of Shakespeare, Meyerbeer has inherited from Weber, to whom he owes much, the power of reproducing in music the characteristics of local scenery and manners—witness the truly Breton *Pardon de Ploërmel,* the vision of Paris in the Middle Ages represented to us by the scene in the Pré aux Clercs at curfew time in the *Huguenots,* etc. etc. Moreover, he has, as I said, *moralized* the musical drama by making it the echo of our world and its eternal problem. He is no disciple of the atheistic school of *l'art pour l'art;* he is the prophet of the music to come, of that music whose high and holy mission will place it but one step below religion itself.

I lack time and space to do justice to Meyerbeer; nor can I do more than allude to the *Etoile du Nord,* the *Prophète,* and the *Africaine,* each of which is worthy of a separate essay; but the little I have said may, I hope, suffice to convince the musical reader of the necessity of an earnest and diligent study of the works of this great master.

Of German descent, though born in Italian Istria, one might almost fancy this combination of the two elements in his own person, significant, symbolic, and prophetic. The figure of Giacomo Meyerbeer appears before us as the first link between the two worlds, the complete union of which will constitute the highest music of the future.

THE PHILOSOPHY OF MUSIC (1836; 1867)

HEINRICH HEINE

-»»-«-

The Paris of Berlioz and Liszt

From 1830 until his death in 1856, Heine kept German periodicals supplied with Parisian news of all kinds. The need to entertain his readers
often led him to exaggerate or to make "good stories" out of scant materials. In this extract, the "facts" about his friend Berlioz are, to say the
least, fanciful.

Now, what is music? This question occupied me for hours before I
fell asleep last night. Music is a strange thing. I would almost say it
is a miracle. For it stands halfway between thought and phenomenon,
between spirit and matter, a sort of nebulous mediator, like and unlike each of the things it mediates—spirit that requires manifestation
in time, and matter that can do without space.

We do not know what music is. But what good music is we know
well enough; and even better, we know what music is bad. For of
the latter our ears receive a larger quantity. Musical criticism must
accordingly base itself on experience, not on *a priori* judgments; it
must classify musical compositions only by their similarities, and
take as standard only the impression that they create upon the majority.

Nothing is more futile than theorizing about music. No doubt
there are laws, mathematically strict laws, but these laws are not
music; they are only its conditions—just as the art of drawing and
the theory of colors, or even the brush and palette, are not painting,
but only its necessary means. The essence of music is revelation; it
does not admit of exact reckoning, and the true criticism of music
remains an empirical art.

Apart from Meyerbeer, the Parisian Académie Royale de Musique [1] boasts few composers of whom it would be worth the trouble to speak at length. Nonetheless the French Opera is most flourishing or, to speak more precisely, its box office greatly flourishes day by day. This state of prosperity began some six years ago with the directorship of the famous Dr. Véron, whose principles have since been adopted, with the same success, by the new director, M. Duponchel. I say "principles" because Dr. Véron did in fact have principles, born of meditation upon the world of art and science; and just as in his capacity as druggist he invented an admirably musical expectorant, so as an opera director he discovered a cure for music.[2]

Having noticed that a show at Franconi's gave him more pleasure than the best opera, he became convinced that the greater part of the public received the same impression; that most people went to the Opera out of habit, and enjoyed themselves there only when the beauty of the scenery, the dances, and the costumes gripped their attention so strongly that they could quite overlook—or overhear— the fateful, inescapable music. The great man thereupon had the stroke of genius by which he decided to satisfy the people's lust for spectacle so completely that the music scarcely annoyed them at all; and so well indeed that they could enjoy at the Opera the very same delights they found at Franconi's.

From these considerations you will have grasped the significance of French Grand Opera at the present time. It has made its peace with the enemies of music; and the well-to-do bourgeoisie crowds the Académie de Musique just as it does the Tuileries.[3] Meanwhile the best society has quitted the field. The true aristocracy, the elite distinguished by rank, birth, breeding, fashion, and leisure, has fled to the Italian opera, that musical oasis where the great nightingales of music forever trill, while round about the level sands stretch away, a Sahara of music.

Still, a few good concerts spring up now and again amid this

[1] The Paris Opera.
[2] Véron's fortune came from a patent medicine.
[3] Where Louis-Philippe held court.

waste and afford to the friends of music uncommon relief. This winter the Sundays at the Conservatoire were of this kind; again, a few private soirées in the rue de Bondy,[4] and especially the concerts of Berlioz and Liszt.

These last named are indeed the two most remarkable phenomena in the contemporary musical world; I say the most remarkable, not the most beautiful or the most rejoicing. From Berlioz we shall soon have an opera. Its subject is an episode from the life of Benvenuto Cellini, the casting of the "Perseus." Something extraordinary is expected, for this composer has already accomplished the extraordinary; his inclination is toward the fantastic, not so much linked with soul as with sentiment. He has a close affinity with Callot, Gozzi, and Hoffmann. Even his outward appearance suggests this. It's a pity that he has had his monstrous, antediluvian head of hair cut off; it used to bristle upon his brow like a forest upon a craggy cliff. That was how he looked when I saw him for the first time six years ago, and thus he will remain in my memory. It was at the Conservatoire, where a great symphony of his was being played—a bizarre night-piece, lighted up only at times in a sentimental way by the flitting about of a woman's dress, or else by the sulphurous gleam of irony.[5]

The best part of it is a Witches' Sabbath in which the Devil reads the mass and the liturgy is parodied with the most horrifying, bloodiest grotesqueries. It is a farce which gaily releases in us all the hidden snakes that we carry in our hearts. My neighbor in the next seat, a talkative young man, showed me the composer, who stood at the far end of the hall, in a corner of the orchestra, playing the kettledrums—for the drum is his instrument. "Do you see," said my neighbor, "a plump Englishwoman in one of the forward boxes? That is Miss Smithson. For three years M. Berlioz has been madly in love with her, and it is to this passion that we owe the symphony we shall hear today." And indeed there sat, in a forward

---

[4] In the hall of the Ambigu-Comique theater, otherwise devoted to melodrama.

[5] The *Symphonie fantastique,* Op. 4 (1830).

box, the famous actress from Covent Garden. Berlioz looked unswervingly in her direction, and whenever her glance met his, he beat upon his drum like a man in a fury. Miss Smithson has since become Mme. Berlioz and her husband has since let his hair be cut. As I heard his symphony again this winter at the Conservatoire, he sat once more behind the drums in the orchestra, the plump Englishwoman sat once more in a forward box, her glances once more met his—but he no longer struck the drums so furiously.

Liszt bears the closest relation to Berlioz and is the best performer of his works. I need not speak to you of his talent: his fame is European. He is without doubt the artist who finds in Paris the most unreserved enthusiasm, as well as the keenest opposition. It is significant that no one speaks of him with indifference. A man who lacks positive stature cannot in this world arouse either favorable or antagonistic passions. It takes fire to enkindle men, whether to hate or to love. What speaks most for Liszt is the respect with which even his enemies recognize his personal merits. He is a man of unruly but noble character, unself-seeking and without falseness.

Most noteworthy are his intellectual tendencies. He has a bent toward philosophizing. Even more than in his art, he is interested in the speculations of the several schools that attempt to solve the great all-embracing problems of heaven and earth. For quite a while he glowed with enthusiasm for the Saint-Simonian ideal; later he was wrapped up in the spiritualist, or, rather, the vaporistic ideas of Ballanche; now he is fervent about the Catholic republicanism of Lamennais, who has put the Jacobin's cap upon the cross. God only knows in what spiritual stall Liszt will next find his hobby horse. But his untiring search for divine light and leading remains praiseworthy; it testifies to his sense of holiness and religion.

That so restless a head, driven hither and thither by all the demands and doctrines of the day, a heart that feels the need to care for all the ills of humanity, and to stick his nose into every pot in which God cooks up the future, makes Franz Liszt anything but a peaceful pianist for settled citizens and complacent bourgeois—that goes without saying. When he sits at the piano and, having repeatedly pushed his hair back over his brow, begins to improvise, then he often rages all too madly upon the ivory keys and lets loose a deluge of heaven-storming ideas, with here and there a few sweet flowers to shed fragrance upon the whole. One feels both blessedness and anxiety, but rather more anxiety.

I freely confess that, much as I love Liszt, his music does not affect me agreeably. This is all the more so that I am a Sunday child and can also see ghosts where other people only hear them—that is to say, as you know, in each note struck by the master's hand, in each corresponding melodic phrase, in short, music is visible to my inner eye. . . .

It was in the concert for the benefit of the unfortunate Italians [6] that I last heard Liszt play this past winter. I forget what he played but I would swear it was variations upon themes from the Apocalypse. At first I could scarcely make them out, those four mystical beasts; I only heard their voices, especially the roaring of the lion and the croaking of the eagle. But the ox with a book in its mouth was very plain to see. What he played best was the Valley of Jehoshaphat. There were lists as in a tournament, and like spectators around the huge space were crowded the resurrected peoples, coffin-pale and trembling. First came Satan galloping in the lists, black-besaddled on a milk-white charger; and, riding slowly behind, Death on her pale horse. Last came Christ in golden armor, on a black steed. With his holy lance he first thrust Satan down, then Death—and the beholders rejoiced loudly. Stormy applause greeted Liszt's valiant playing. He left the piano exhausted, bowed to the ladies, and upon the lips of the beauties there was that melancholy-sweet smile.

It would be wrong of me to miss this occasion to mention another pianist who next to Liszt is most honored. I refer to Chopin, whose accomplishment is great not solely as a virtuoso of brilliant technical mastery but also as a composer. He is a man of the first rank, the darling of the elite which seeks in music the highest spiritual pleasure. Chopin's fame is aristocratic, it is perfumed with the approval of good society, it is as distinguished as his person.

[6] Exiles after unsuccessful uprisings.

. . . Yes, one must grant Chopin genius in the fullest sense of the word; he is not simply a technician, he is a poet and can express for us the poetry that lives in his soul; he is a poet in sound, and nothing is quite like the delights he lavishes on us when he sits at the keyboard and improvises. At such times he is neither Pole, Frenchman, nor German; he betrays a far higher origin, and seems to come from the land of Mozart, Raphael, and Goethe: his true native shores seem to be the dreamland of poetry.

LETTERS ON THE FRENCH STAGE (1837)

FRIEDRICH NIETZSCHE

➤➤➤ ⫷⫷⫷

Wagner as Actor

➤➤ ————————————————————————————— ⫷⫷

Contrary to common belief, Nietzsche felt and wrote down his chief
strictures against Wagner's mind and work before publishing his initial
eulogy (see p. 236). But in that first essay, being a very young enthusiast,
he palliated his doubts with hopes and arguments. Later on, he did not
so much "turn" against Wagner as reveal in violent language the substance of his first objections.

➤➤ ————————————————————————————— ⫷⫷

My objections to Wagner's music are physiological—why disguise
them as usual behind aesthetic formulas? Aesthetics is nothing else
than applied physiology. I base myself upon fact—indeed it is my
"small, real fact" [1] when I say that I breathe with difficulty as soon
as Wagner's music begins to act upon me. I say that my *foot* gets
annoyed and rebels against the music; my foot wants rhythm, dancing, marching. The rhythm of Wagner's *"Kaisermarsch"* keeps even
the young emperor [2] from marching in time with it. My foot asks of
music, above all, the pleasure of *good* pacing, stepping, dancing,
capering.

And then is not my stomach in revolt as well? my heart and the
circulation of my blood? It seems as if my bowels were saddened
too, and my throat made hoarse by imperceptible degrees: in order
to listen to Wagner I need medicated lozenges. And so I ask myself
the question: What, in the last analysis, does *my body as a whole*
require of music? For there is no such thing as the soul. Well, I
think my body needs lift, lightening, it needs all the animal func-
tions accelerated by light, bold, heedless, and proud rhythms; so that
our leaden life, our cast-iron existence, should lose its gravity under

[1] An allusion to Stendhal on novel writing: *de petits faits vrais*.
[2] William II, aged twenty-nine at his accession in 1888.

the influence of golden melodies, delicate, fluent as oil. My melancholy wants to find surcease in the crannies and abysses of *perfection*.

But Wagner makes one ail! What matters to me the theater? Of what value to me the cramps of its "moral" ecstasies which satisfy the crowd—and do not belong to the crowd? What do I care about the grimaces of the comedian? It is easy to see that my nature is essentially anti-theatrical. In the depths of my being I feel for the theater—*the art for the masses par excellence*—the infinite contempt that today every true artist feels. Mention *success* in the theater, and my regard hits bottom; *lack* of success, I prick up my ears and begin to pay attention.

Wagner, on the contrary—side by side with the Wagner who wrote the most solitary music there is—was essentially a comedian and man of the theater. He was the most enthusiastic mime-lover there has ever been, *even as a musician*. I may add in passing that if Wagner's theory declared the drama to be the goal and music only a means, his *practice* throughout has invariably been: "Attitudes are the goal; drama just as much as music is but a means." Music serves him to accentuate, to reinforce, to *in*ternalize the outward dramatic gesture of the comedian. Wagnerian drama is only a pretext for a number of interesting attitudes.

For beside all his other instincts, Wagner had the commanding instincts of a great actor—always and everywhere; and as I have said, he had these instincts as musician too. I managed to demonstrate this once to a fanatical Wagnerian with complete clarity—clarity and Wagnerism! I need say no more. But I had reason then for adding: "Why not be a little more honest with yourself? We're not in Bayreuth!" In Bayreuth one can be honest only in the mass; as an individual, one is a liar—a liar to oneself. One leaves oneself at home by going to Bayreuth; one gives up the right to choose and speak out; gives up one's taste and even one's courage, in other words, one's normal strength for facing God and men.

No one can bring to the theater the finest feeling for art, least of all the artist who works for the theater. There is no solitude there, and all perfection requires an absence of witnesses. At the theater one becomes people, woman, Pharisee, voter, founding-patron, nit-wit—Wagnerite. In the theater the most individual mind succumbs to the leveling spell of the mass. In the theater the neighbor is king, and one becomes a neighbor.

NIETZSCHE CONTRA WAGNER (1877-1888)

STENDHAL

⋙ ⋘

Rossini's "Barber of Seville"

The only works by Stendhal to achieve any circulation during his own life were his writings on Haydn and Mozart and especially his *Life of Rossini.* The conversational style, which deserts logic in favor of "jottings," is a part of Stendhal's method and should not deceive or discourage the unaccustomed reader.

If one ever wants to become intimately acquainted—for pleasure or out of mere curiosity—with Rossini's style, it is in *The Barber of Seville* that one must study it. For the composer's chief characteristic is undoubtedly writ large over that opera. It is this: Rossini, who is so adept at finales, ensembles, and duets, is feeble and pretty-pretty in the airs which should depict passion with simplicity. The *canto spianato* [1] is his downfall.

The Romans think that if Cimarosa [2] had composed the music of *The Barber,* it would have been a little less lively but more comic and infinitely more expressive. I wonder. Have you ever been a soldier? Have you trotted all over the globe? Has it happened to you to find suddenly once again at the waters of Baden a charming mistress whom you had worshiped ten years before at Dresden or Bayreuth? [3] The first moment of recognition is delightful, but the third or fourth day, you begin to feel too much delight, too much adoration, too much sweetness. The boundless devotion of this good dear German girl makes you regret, even if you will not admit it to yourself, the capricious piquancy of a haughty Italian who is both

---

[1] Song in smooth style.

[2] Opera composer (1749–1801) who died after imprisonment for his part in the attempted liberation of Italy from Bonaparte's troops.

[3] Stendhal is not knowingly prophetic. Bayreuth was then a sleepy little town where, in his army days, he may have spent some time.

beautiful and mad·—exactly the same impression that has just been made upon me by the admirable music of [Cimarosa's] *Matrimonio segreto,*[4] which has been revived in Paris for Mlle. de Meri.

The first day, on leaving the theater, I could see Rossini only as a pygmy. I remember saying to myself, "One must not be too quick about passing judgment; I am under the spell." Yesterday (August 19, 1823), on leaving the fourth performance of the *Matrimonio,* I had a glimpse of the towering monument which is Rossini's glory. The absence of dissonance makes itself cruelly felt in the second act of the *Matrimonio.* I find despair and misery expressed there with a flavor of rose water. We have progressed as regards misery since 1793.[5] The great quartet of the first act—

What sorrowful silence!

seems long. In a word, Cimarosa has more ideas than Rossini, and indeed better ideas, but Rossini has the better style.

A dilettante to whom I submitted this chapter on the *Barber* so that he could correct the errors of fact into which I so often fall— like the astrologer into a well, from looking at the heavens—said to me, "Is that what you mean to give as an analysis of an opera? Why, it's just whipped cream. I can't stand those frothy sentences! Come, get down to work seriously. Open the score; I'll play you the principal arias, and you will make a tight and reasoned analysis."

It is obvious in the chorus of serenaders which opens the *Barber* that Rossini is competing with Paisiello.[6] It is all sweetness and grace but there is no simplicity. Count Almaviva is weak and common; he is a French lover of the 1770s. By contrast, Rossini's full fire bursts out in the chorus—

A thousand thanks, my lord!

and this vivacity rises quickly to real verve and brilliance, which is

[4] *The Secret Marriage* (1792).
[5] Allusion to the Terror and Napoleonic wars.
[6] Composer of over a hundred operas (1741–1816), rival of Cimarosa and Napoleon's favorite musician.

not always true of Rossini. Here his soul seems to have been brought to incandescence by the very force of his wit. The Count withdraws as he hears Figaro coming, and as he goes he remarks—

> Yes, the dawn is hardly here,
> But love is—if not modesty.

How like an Italian! A lover, says the Count, permits himself everything. Everyone should feel that love is an excuse that covers everything in the eyes of those not concerned. But in northern climes, on the contrary, love is timid and fearful even before the unconcerned.

Figaro's cavatina—

> Make way for the steward!

as sung by Pellegrini, is and will long remain the masterpiece of French music. What fire, lightness, and wit in the line—

> By a barber of quality!

What expressiveness in—

> With the little wench . . .
> With the gentleman. . . .

This pleased the Parisians, though it could easily have been hissed because of the risqué meaning of the words.

The balcony scene of *The Barber* is divine for music; it is pure grace and tender naïveté. But Rossini slights it in order to reach the superb buffoonery of the duet—

> At the thought of clinking coin!

The first measures express to perfection the omnipotence of gold in the eyes of Figaro. Whereas the Count's exhortation—

> Come! let's see that clinking coin!

is that of a young nobleman who is not so much in love that he can't in passing make fun of Figaro's plebeian greed for money. I have spoken elsewhere of the marvelous rapidity of—

> Today there comes a regiment—
> Yes, but the colonel is my friend.

This passage seems to me Rossini's masterpiece in that particular

genre, which makes it the high point of musical art. I only regret
a touch of vulgarity in—

What an excellent invention!

That duet is what will kill French grand opera. No heavier enemy,
you will admit, could fall under a lighter assailant. It availed nothing
that French opera used to bore people of taste in the time of La
Bruyère,[7] a mere hundred and fifty years ago. That kind of opera
has survived sixty different ministries. To kill it, there had to appear
a genuine French music. The greatest criminals in the affair, after
Rossini, are MM. Massimino, Choron, and Castil-Blaze.[8]

Now let me brave again the charge of paradox. The air upon
Calumny seems to me only an extract from Mozart, made by an
extremely clever man who is himself capable of composing excellently
well. The air is too long for dramatic effect; yet it makes an admirable
contrast with the lightness of all the preceding songs. It was wonderfully sung at La Scala in Milan by M. Levasseur, who was much
applauded. In Paris he sings too timidly and gives the impression of
being afraid to make a mistake. Voltaire used to say that in order to
succeed in the arts, the theater especially, one must be possessed by
a demon.

MM. Meyerbeer, Morlacchi, Pacini, Mercadante, Mosca, Mayer,
Spontini, and others who are contemporary with Rossini are glad
enough doubtless to copy Mozart; but they have never yet found in
the scores of the great man an air like that upon Calumny. Without
pretending to make Rossini the equal of Raphael, I may say that it
is thus Raphael used to copy Michelangelo in the beautiful fresco of
Isaiah, in the church of St. Augustine, near the Piazza Navone in
Rome.

Not on purpose, but just because of the susceptibility to feeling
which makes for genius in the arts, Rossini has depicted in his music

[7] French satirist (1645–1696) who scorned Lulli's operas as absurdities.

[8] Respectively, voice teacher and composer; choral conductor; and adapter
of operas in Paris.

the women who loved him and whom, perhaps, he loved a little bit in return. Without knowing it, he took as arbiters of the melodies which he wrote at three in the morning the ladies with whom he had just passed the evening, and in whose eyes any tender or timid sentiment would have looked like the silliness of a college boy. Rossini owed his incredible success with women to a self-possession and disinterestedness out of the common. *The Barber* and several of the operas he has written since make me apprehend the effect of such success upon his art. Does he not owe his good fortune in love to the absence of any sense of distinction among women? I am inclined to fear that his luck with the Roman ladies has made him insensible to feminine grace. In *The Barber,* as soon as he has to be gentle he becomes elegant and affected, he never drops the temperate style. He is like Fontenelle the philosopher speaking of love.[9] This way of life is all very well in day-to-day affairs, but it will not do for real fame. I find a great deal more energy and abandon in Rossini's earliest works.

I should willingly conclude that if Rossini had been born with fifty thousand francs' income, like his colleague M. Meyerbeer, his genius would have fixed him in *opera buffa*. But he had to live. He knew that Mlle. Colbran, who sings only *opera seria,* was all-powerful in Naples; so, in the rest of Italy, is the police, which is as ridiculous in small things as it is impotent in great. It is the basic ideas of that same police, invented forty years ago by Leopold, Grand Duke of Tuscany, that have deprived Italy of that beautiful genre of native literature, the *commedia dell'arte,* or comedy played impromptu, which Goldoni thought he was displacing by his flat dialogue.

Here I can no longer set forth my meaning, even between the lines. I must appeal to the travelers who have spent a winter in Rome, or who know, for example, the stories about the elevation of the popes Pius VI and Pius VII. Those are the people which it is feared the words of an opera libretto will corrupt. Good Lord! Raise four more

---

[9] Fontenelle (1657–1757) acknowledged that there were three things he had never understood—women, gambling, and music. One recalls his remark: "Sonata, what do you want with me?"

companies of police, hang the twenty crookedest judges each year, and you'll be doing rather more for good morals. Putting aside theft, bribery-at-law, and other trifles of that sort, just think of what the morals must be in a country where all the employees of the state are celibate and live under such a climate with such opportunities! Why, two centuries of Napoleon's despotism would not succeed in establishing in Rome the decent and pure habits of a small English town—of Norwich or Nottingham.

But to return to *The Barber*—a long distance it may seem. Not so long as you suppose: a source of limpid water, full of taste and salubrity, springs from the foot of a mountain. Do you know how it came to be in the heart of the rock? Until we are given the demonstration of the *how*, I shall maintain that every condition of the mountains, the form of its valleys, the slope of its woods—everything has contributed to produce this delicious spring, at which the hunter slakes his thirst and recovers strength as by a miracle. All the governments of Europe establish conservatories; several princes really love music and sacrifice their budget to it; but do they manage to produce beings like Rossini and Davide, that is to say, great composers and great singers? No. There must consequently be some circumstance which is unknown but necessary in the life of beauteous Italy and Germany. It is less cold in the rue Le Peletier [10] than in Dresden or Darmstadt. Why then are the people rue Le Peletier more barbaric? Why does the orchestra of Dresden or Reggio perform divinely a crescendo of Rossini's which is found impossible in Paris?

I hear that in Vienna, where they had the bliss to hear simultaneously Davide, Mme. Fodor, and Lablache (1823), they always repeat the end of the trio—

Quiet, quiet, gently, gently . . .

I have the highest respect for the musical taste of the Viennese. They have had the honor of forming Haydn and Mozart. Metastasio,[11] who lived among them for forty years, carried the taste for art into high

[10] Site of the Paris opera house.
[11] Librettist, poet, and musician (1698–1782).

society. Finally the great lords, the richest in Europe, do not disdain being opera directors.

I certainly hope that if this book of mine still exists in 1840, it will be infallibly thrown into the fire. Just see what is done today with the essays on political theory written in 1789. Everything I have just been saying for an hour will seem feeble and commonplace in the salon of Merilde, that pretty young girl, aged ten, who so loves Rossini but prefers Cimarosa. The revolution that is beginning in music will totally eclipse the good old French taste. What a pity! . . . In fact, what seems obscure and risky in this book will be feeble and commonplace by 1833. The party committed to the good old things has only one recourse, and that is to drive out the Italians or mate them with Frenchwomen. Superb voices that did not know how to sing would soon destroy music.

Before I finish I should say a word about the peculiarities of Rossini's style; that seems to be a necessity connected with my subject. To speak of paintings in a book, to praise pictures, is an appalling task; but pictures at least leave a distinct impression, even on fools. What then must writing about music be like! Into what queer and absurd nonsense will not one fall! The reader may guess he won't have to go far to find examples.

Good music is only our *emotion*. It would seem that music gives us pleasure by compelling our imagination to feed for the moment on illusions of a certain kind. These illusions are not calm and sublime like those of sculpture, nor tender and dreamy like those of Correggio's paintings.

The first characteristic of Rossini's music is speed—a speed which removes from the soul all the somber emotions that are so powerfully evoked within us by the slow strains of Mozart. I find also in Rossini a cool freshness, which, measure by measure, makes us smile with delight. Any score seems heavy and tedious after one of Rossini's. If Mozart were a newcomer today, that is the judgment we should pass upon his music. We would have to hear him for two weeks on end before we could find pleasure in his work; he would be hissed the first night. If Mozart has survived Rossini's fame, if we often prefer him to Rossini, it is because he has the aid of our old admiration and the memory of the past pleasures he has afforded us. In general, it is people strong enough to resist ridicule who greatly prefer Mozart. The vulgar connoisseurs speak of him as vulgar men of letters speak of Fénelon. They praise him but would be in despair if suspected of writing like him.

Though Rossini's music is never heavy, it palls quite soon. The most distinguished judges in Italy who have heard his works for a dozen years want something new. What will the consensus be twenty years hence, when *The Barber of Seville* will be as old as the *Matrimonio segreto* or *Don Giovanni?* Rossini is rarely sad; but what is music without a touch of pensive sadness in it? "I am never merry when I hear sweet music" is said (in *The Merchant of Venice*) by the modern poet who best knows the secrets of the human heart—the author of *Cymbeline* and *Othello.*

Still, in our expeditious century, Rossini has one advantage: he can dispense with attentiveness.

In a drama where music seeks to express the shade or degree of the feeling indicated by the words, one must pay attention in order to be moved, which is to say, in order to find pleasure. There is an even more exacting requirement: one must have a heart in order to be moved. In a score by Rossini, on the contrary, each air or duet is usually but a brilliant concert piece—especially so in the operas written at Naples for Mlle. Colbran. And with these only the slightest degree of attention will procure pleasure; most of the time there is no need whatever to possess what people of feeling call heart.

I am aware that I must justify so provocative an assertion. Kindly open your piano and remind yourself of the first scene of the *Matrimonio segreto,* where Carolina enjoys the blissful presence of her lover. She makes a sweet remark on the happiness they could share—

If love could but run smooth . . .

These extremely simple words have given rise to one of the most beautiful musical phrases ever penned. Now Rosine, in *The Barber of Seville,* discovers that her lover is faithful after she has thought him a monster of ingratitude and baseness—a man who was selling her to Count Almaviva. In this instant of transport, the most heavenly that can be conceived, our thankless Rosine manages only to sing us some *fioriture,* which apparently suited the graceful voice of the first Rosine, Mme. Giorgi. These *fioriture,* fit for a pleasant concert, are sublime for nobody, but Rossini wanted to make them entertaining —and succeeded. He is without excuse. The happiness of the scene in question is far too great to be mere joyousness. Such is the principal fault of Rossini's second manner; he composes his scores by writing ornaments of the kind his singers were in the habit of adding ad lib to the songs of other masters. What used to be a more or less agreeable accessory, he often makes into the main dish.

Rossini, like all the other masters, writes operas in the confident belief that his two acts will be separated by an hour and a half of ballet or interlude. In France, where genuineness is hardly what is uppermost in the pursuit of pleasure, people would think themselves lukewarm about Rossini if they did not listen to him steadily for three hours on end. This musical glut, presented with so much wit to the European audience that has the least patience and the best dancers, is unbearable when *Don Giovanni* is being given, or any other *passionate* work of the kind. No one can hear the four acts of *The Marriage of Figaro* without a headache and a feeling of mortal lassitude. One thinks to forgo music for at least a week. But one feels entirely different after hearing uninterruptedly the two acts of *Tancred* or *Elisabeth:* Rossini's music, which at all points condescends to be nothing more than a concert piece, does very well under the theatrical habits of Paris, and emerges triumphant from the test. In all possible senses of the term, his is music ideally designed for the French, yet by working upon us daily it helps to make us worthy of more passionate accents.

LIFE OF ROSSINI (1824)

HUGO WOLF

✲✲✲ ✲✲✲

The Russian School

"Everything in moderation." This touted maxim of the wise proves true in art no less than throughout ordinary life. It applies equally to the excessive partaking of pigs' knuckles (as Mörike's poem "Everything in Moderation" points out) as to an excessive partaking of music, as Anton Rubinstein's [1] piano recitals in no little measure demonstrate. We certainly do not belong to the apostles of moderation. Abstinence, self-laceration, and mortification of the flesh are things we have never preached. We are not musical Trappists. But listening to a whole evening of Russia's hopeful music of the future would put even the most nihilistic patriots of the Czar's empire out of humor. "Out of tune" is the right word.[2] I would just as soon be turned by magic into an old woodwind as go through another such evening. I was so out of tune that even the most harmless triad could not allay my distrust for "The Power of Music."

Now the Poles, wherever and however they come face to face with the Russians, always get the worst of it in the end; but this time it went badly for the Russians, in spite of their numerical superiority. Yes indeed! Chopin played them a nasty trick. Eleven études by Chopin opened the manual affray at the last Rubinstein evening. It was a hot fight—eleven études: yet there were no broken bones. Melodious strains fell upon the ear; the ghosts of exotic flowers danced now their dithyrambic and wild, now their sweetly languishing rounds, to rhythms both emphatic and original. Music such as this may narcotize, but it will cause no aches and pains.

[1] (1830–1894).

[2] The author plays on the word *verstimmt*.

How different the Russians! And first of all the wild Balakirev.[3] What a glutton for notes! He gobbles everything down to the hair and hide! There's a Jacobin for you! Poor abused and slandered Berlioz! How innocent you are compared to this body-snatcher Balakirev. Not content with murdering music, this bloodthirsty villain also mocks at her corpse and jokes over the thousand wounds which in his fits of frenzy (composer's whims) he inflicts upon her. Fortunate Russia that produces such men of progress.

Only Tchaikovsky, among all these Cuis, Liadovs, Rimsky-Korsakovs,[4] and so forth, stands out as an honorable exception. Tchaikovsky really strives to create not merely Russian national music, but music first and foremost. His "Song without Words," his waltzes and romances, are charming inventions and finished compositions. His "Scherzo à la Russe" is also to my taste, even though the Russian-national element in that work overlays with a rough hand the lines of beauty, to the point of making them unrecognizable.

The most favorable impression, after that made by Chopin's études, came unquestionably from the compositions of Michael Glinka.[5] Glinka is the classicist as opposed to the new hyper-Romanticist direction of the modern Russian school. His operas, *A Life for the Czar* and *Ruslan and Ludmilla* [6] are also known in Germany and admired there. His piano pieces are melodious, delicately felt, and not without ingenious touches. The evening concluded with compositions by the two brothers Rubinstein.[7] The celebrated virtuoso revealed no especial talent in his choice of works to perform on this occasion. He could have done himself a better turn. Waltzes and Album Leaves by Nicholas Rubinstein constitute a fixture in the Rubinstein programs—and are known accordingly.

With this performance Anton Rubinstein has put a good piece

[3] Mili Balakirev (1836–1910).

[4] César Cui (1835–1918); Liadov (1855–1914); Nicholas Rimsky-Korsakov (1844–1908).

[5] Michael Glinka (1803–1857).

[6] 1836 and 1842 respectively.

[7] Anton and his brother Nicholas (1835–1881).

of work behind him. To have carried through an undertaking of this magnitude is something unique in the annals of concert-giving. It deserves to be called a superhuman feat if one thinks of *what* the thing involves. *How* it was done is of course a question of genius. Now Rubinstein managed like a genius the task that he set himself. And in another respect he supplied an example which showed the humane and generous quality of his convictions in the finest light. For apart from the proverbial largesse of Franz Liszt, hardly any instance compares with this, of giving seven piano recitals gratis for the benefit of indigent musicians and music lovers. This noble trait in Rubinstein's character is no less an ornament to the man than his genius is to the artist. And as the great public presents the laurel wreath to the celebrated man, so will the small community of Bösendorfer Hall dedicate in heartfelt gratitude a modest leaf of evergreen in faithful memory of true humanity.

COLLECTED CRITIQUES (1886)

SOME PREMIERES

IGNAZ MOSCHELES

➤➤➤ ◄◄◄

Johann Strauss in London

"Almack's" was a fashionable place of resort established by a Scotsman named Macall. It was later renamed Willis's Rooms, and young Thomas Hardy used to dance quadrilles there before the days of romps and galops.

By a recent and sudden change in taste, however, we saw the rise to popularity of Johann Strauss. Where he fiddles, all dance—dance they must. In the concerts which he gives with his small orchestra, people dance as they sit; at Almack's, the most fashionable of all subscription ballrooms, aristocratic little feet tap in time with his tunes. And we too, the other night, had the good fortune to dance to his playing. Old married people as we are, we felt as if young again. He himself dances, body and soul, while he plays—not with his feet but with his violin, which keeps bobbing up and down while the whole man marks the accent of every bar. He is a good-natured Viennese, none of your sophisticated worldlings, but lively and always cheerful—a pleasant change from the many melancholy specimens we have had.

JOURNAL (1838)

JOHN HILL HEWITT

※ ※

Fiasco in the White House

Anton Philip Heinrich (1781–1861), conductor, composer, violinist, and pianist, deserves to be remembered as the first man to play a Beethoven symphony in America—some time in the second decade of the nineteenth century, and in Kentucky at that. His efforts, though unavailing and ill rewarded, nevertheless defined a direction.

The eccentric Anthony Philip Heinrich, generally known as "Father Heinrich," visited Washington while I resided in that city, with a grand musical work of his, illustrative of the greatness and glory of this republic, the splendor of its institutions and the indomitable bravery of its army and navy. This work Heinrich wished to publish by subscription. He had many names on his list; but, as he wished to dedicate it to the President of the United States, and also to obtain the signatures of the Cabinet and other high officials, he thought it best to call personally and solicit their patronage.

He brought with him a number of letters of introduction, among them one to myself from my brother, a music-publisher in New York. I received the old gentleman with all the courtesy due to his brilliant musical talents; and, as I was the first he had called upon, I tendered him the hospitalities of my house—"potluck" and a comfortable bed; promising to go the rounds with him on the following morning and introduce him to President Tyler (whose daughter, Alice, was a pupil of mine) and such other influential men as I was acquainted with.

Poor Heinrich! I shall never forget him. He imagined that he was going to set the world on fire with his "Dawning of Music in America"; but alas! it met with the same fate as his "Castle in the Moon" and "Yankee Doodliad."

Two or three hours of patient hearing did I give to the most complicated harmony I ever heard, even in my musical dreams. Wild and unearthly passages, the pianoforte absolutely groaning under them, and "the old man eloquent," with much self-satisfaction, arose from the tired instrument and with a look of triumph asked me if I had ever heard music like that before. I certainly had not.

At a proper hour we visited the President's mansion and after some ceremony and much grumbling on the part of the *polite* usher, were shown into the presence of Mr. Tyler, who received us with his usual urbanity. I introduced Mr. Heinrich as a professor of exalted talent and a man of extraordinary genius. The President, after learning the object of our visit, which he was glad to learn was not to solicit an office, readily consented to the dedication and commended the undertaking. Heinrich was elated to the skies and immediately proposed to play the grand conception, in order that the Chief Magistrate of this great nation might have an idea of its merits.

"Certainly, sir," said Mr. Tyler; "I will be greatly pleased to hear it. We will go into the parlor, where there is a piano, and I will have Alice and the ladies present, so that we may have the benefit of their opinion; for, to confess the truth, gentlemen, I am but a poor judge of music."

He then rang the bell for the waiter, and we were shown into the parlor, and invited to take some refreshments at the sideboard. The ladies soon joined us, and in a short space of time we were all seated, ready to hear Father Heinrich's composition; I, for the second time, to be *gratified*. The composer labored hard to give full effect to his weird production; his bald pate bobbed from side to side and shone like a bubble on the surface of a calm lake. At times his shoulders would be raised to the line of his ears, and his knees went up to the keyboard, while the perspiration rolled in large drops down his wrinkled cheeks.

The ladies stared at the maniac musician, as they, doubtless, thought him, and the President scratched his head, as if wondering whether wicked spirits were not rioting in the cavern of mysterious sounds and rebelling against the laws of acoustics. The composer labored on, occasionally explaining some incomprehensible passage, representing, as he said, the breaking up of the frozen river Niagara, the *thaw* of the ice, and the dash of the mass over the mighty falls. *Peace* and *plenty* were represented by soft strains of pastoral music, while the thunder of our naval war-dogs and the rattle of our army musketry told of our prowess on sea and land.

The inspired composer had got about halfway through his wonderful production when Mr. Tyler restlessly arose from his chair and, placing his hand gently on Heinrich's shoulder, said, "That may all be very fine, sir, but can't you play us a good old Virginia reel?"

Had a thunderbolt fallen at the feet of the musician, he could not have been more astounded. He arose from the piano, rolled up his manuscript, and, taking his hat and cane, bolted toward the door, exclaiming, "No, sir; I never plays dance music!"

I joined him in the vestibule, having left Mr. Tyler and family enjoying a hearty laugh at the "maniac musician's" expense.

As we proceeded along Pennsylvania Avenue, Heinrich grasped my arm convulsively and exclaimed, *"Mein Got in himmel!* de peeples vot made Yohn Tyler Bresident ought to be hung! He knows no more apout music than an oyshter!"

He returned to New York by the next train, and I never heard any more of the "Dawning of Music in America."

Mr. Heinrich died quite poor in New York. He was, in his earlier days, a very wealthy and influential banker in the city of Hamburg. His fondness for music, however, drew him away from the less refined but more profitable operations in the money market.

SHADOWS ON THE WALL (1877)

CHARLES BURNEY

※※

The First Handel Festival

The friend of Dr. Johnson and the father of the author of *Evelina*, Dr. Charles Burney was the founder of musicology in England. His *History* and his *Travels* are still read for pleasure and instruction. The present description of the first Handel commemoration was written for the Royal Family.

PREFACE

A public and national tribute of gratitude to deceased mortals, whose labours and talents have benefitted, or innocently amused, mankind, has, at all times, been one of the earliest marks of civilization in every country emerged from ignorance and barbarism. And there seems no more rational solution of the mysteries of ancient Greek mythology, than to imagine that men, whose virtue and abilities surpassed the common standard of human excellence, had excited that degree of veneration in posterior times, which gave rise to their deification and apotheosis.

Such a gigantic idea of commemoration as the present, for the completion of which it was necessary that so many minds should be concentrated, must have been long fostering ere it took a practicable form, and was matured into reality. But from the conception of this plan to its full growth, there was such a concurrence of favourable circumstances as the records of no art or science can parallel: the Royal Patronage with which it was honoured; the high rank, unanimity, and active zeal of the directors; the leisure, as well as ardour and skill of the conductor; the disinterested docility of individuals; and liberal contributions of the public; all conspired to render this event memorable, and worthy of a place, not only in the annals of Music, but of mankind.

And indeed it was hardly possible for a Musical Historian not to imagine that an enterprize honoured with the patronage and presence of their Majesties; planned and personally directed by noblemen and gentlemen of the first rank; attended by the most numerous and polite audience that was ever assembled on a similar occasion, in any country; among whom, not only the King, Queen, Royal Family, nobility, and great officers of state appeared, but the archbishops, bishops, and other dignified clergy, with the heads of the law, would form an aera in Music, as honourable to the art and to national gratitude, as to the great artist himself who has given occasion to the Festival.

Handel, whose genius and abilities have lately been so nobly commemorated, though not a native of England, spent the greatest part of his life in the service of its inhabitants: improving our taste, delighting us in the church, the theatre, and the chamber; and introducing among us so many species of musical excellence, that, during more than half a century, while sentiment, not fashion, guided our applause, we neither wanted nor wished for any other standard. He arrived among us at a barbarous period for almost every kind of music, except that of the church. But, besides his oratorio choruses, which are so well intitled to immortality, his organ-pieces, and manner of playing, are still such models of perfection as no master in Europe has surpassed; and his operas were composed in a style so new and excellent, that no Music has since, with all its refinements of melody and symmetry of air, in performance, had such effects on the audience.

Indeed his works were so long the models of perfection in this country, that they may be said to have formed our national taste. For though many in the capital have been partial, of late years, to the compositions of Italy, Germany, and France; yet the nation at large has rather tolerated than adopted these novelties.

The English, a manly, military race, were instantly captivated by the grave, bold, and nervous style of Handel, which is congenial with their manners and sentiments. And though the productions of men of great genius and abilities have, since his time, had a transient

share of attention and favour; yet, whenever any of the works of
Handel are revived by a performer of superior talents, they are always heard with a degree of general satisfaction and delight, which
other compositions seldom obtain. Indeed, the exquisite manner in
which his productions are executed at the concert established for the
preservation and performance of old masters, stimulates a desire in
all who hear them to have a more general acquaintance with his
works. And it was, perhaps, at the late performance in Westminster
Abbey, that the compositions of this great master were first supplied
with a band, capable of displaying all the wonderful powers of his
harmony.

I

Early in the morning, the weather being very favourable, persons
of all ranks quitted their carriages with impatience and apprehension,
lest they should not obtain seats, and presented themselves at the
several doors of Westminster Abbey, which were advertised to be
opened at Nine o'clock; but the door-keepers not having taken their
posts, and the Orchestra not being wholly finished, or, perhaps, the
rest of the Abbey quite ready for the reception of the audience, till
near Ten o'clock; such a croud of ladies and gentlemen were assembled together as became very formidable and terrific to each
other, particularly the female part of the expectants; for some of
these being in full dress, and every instant more and more incommoded and alarmed, by the violence of those who pressed forward, in order to get near the door, screamed; others fainted; and
all were dismayed and apprehensive of fatal consequences: as many
of the most violent, among the gentlemen, threatened to break open
the doors; a measure, which if adopted, would, probably, have cost
many of the most feeble and helpless their lives; as they must, infallibly, have been thrown down, and trampled on, by the robust
and impatient part of the croud.

It was a considerable time after a small door at the west end was
opened, before this press abated: as tickets could not be examined,

and cheques given in return, fast enough, to diminish the candidates for admission, or their impatience.

However, except dishevelled hair, and torn garments, no real mischief seems to have happened. In less than an hour after the doors were opened, the whole area and galleries of the Abbey seemed too full for the admission of more company; and a considerable time before the performance began, the doors were all shut to every one but their Majesties, and their suite, who arrived soon after Twelve; and on entering the box, prepared for their reception, pleasure and astonishment, at the sight of the company and disposition of the Orchestra and Performers, were painted so strongly in their countenances, as to be visible to all their delighted subjects present. Eagerness and expectation for the *premier coup d'archet* were now wound up to the highest pitch of impatience; when a silence, the most profound and solemn, was gently interrupted by the processional symphony of the

CORONATION ANTHEM

And from the time that the first sound of this celebrated, and well-known composition, was heard, to the final close, every hearer seemed afraid of breathing, lest it should obstruct the stream of harmony in its passage to the ear.

From the progress which practical Music has made in this country, since Handel's time, it might, perhaps, be safely pronounced, that this Anthem was never so well performed, under his own direction. As I heard it myself at the Coronation of his present Majesty, when a numerous band was assembled under the direction of the late Doctor Boyce, I can, at least, venture to say that, in recollection, the performance then will bear no comparison with that now, in the same place, in honour of the composer.[1]

[1] There was, doubtless, the greatest propriety in saluting their Majesties, at their entrance, with the *Coronation Anthem;* and yet, I could not help wishing, that this performance, so different from all others, had opened with some piece in which every voice and every instrument might have been heard at the same instant; as such an effect might then have been produced, as can never be obtained by gradation: the difference between *nothing* and *something* being greater, than between any two degrees of excellence. Indeed, the most sudden

OVERTURE IN ESTHER

The first movement of this grave and majestic Overture has always astonished me, by the simplicity of its modulation; which, though almost rigorously confined to the diatonic intervals, and harmony of the key, is never monotonous in its effects. And the first bar of the melody, though so often repeated by the two violins, is so grateful and pleasing, as to be always welcome to the ear.

All the movements of this admirable Overture first appeared in Handel's *Trios,* as did many of those he introduced afterwards in his Organ Concertos. This overture, almost ever since it was composed, has been so constantly played at Saint Paul's, at the Feast of the Sons of the Clergy, that it now seems in a peculiar manner dedicated to the service of the Church.

THE DETTINGEN TE DEUM

This splendid production has been so frequently performed at Saint Paul's and elsewhere, that nothing could be added to its celebrity by my feeble praise. I shall only observe, that as it was composed for a military triumph, the fourteen trumpets, two pair of common kettle-drums, two pair of double drums from the Tower, and a pair of double-base drums, made expressly for this Commemoration, were introduced with great propriety; indeed, these last drums, except the destruction, had all the effect of the most powerful artillery.

There is some reason to suspect that Handel, in setting his grand *Te Deum* for the peace of Utrecht, as well as this, confined the meaning of the word *cry* to a sorrowful sense: as both the movements to the words—

"To thee all angels cry *aloud,"*

are not only in a minor-key, but slow, and plaintive. It contrasts well, however, with the preceding and subsequent movements. Indeed,

and *surprising* effect of this stupendous band, was, perhaps, produced by simultaneous tuning: as all the stringed-instruments performed this task, *à double corde,* and these strings being all *open,* their force was more than equal to that of two stopt-strings, upon two different instruments. [Burney's note.]

the latter glows with all the fire and vehemence of Handel's genius for polyphonic combinations and contrivances.

The grave and solemn praise of the *Apostles, Prophets,* and *Martyrs,* measured by the constant majestic motion of the base, is well symbolized.

> *"Thou sittest at the right hand of God,"* etc.,

is expressed in a strain that is remarkably pleasing, and which, in spite of forty years, still retains all the bloom and freshness of novelty: and

> *"We therefore pray thee help thy servants, who thou hast redeemed with thy precious blood,"*

is admirable, in fugue, modulation, and counterpoint, *à Capella;* as is the next movement, to the three verses:

> *"Make them to be numbered"*—
> *"O Lord save thy people"*—and
> *"Govern them and lift them up for ever,"*

with the additional merit of a happy verbal expression.

> *"Day by day we magnify thee,"*

is grand and well accented, though some of the trumpet passages are a little *viellis.* The art of fugue, both in that, and the next verse:

> *"And we worship thy name ever world without end,"*

is treated with Handel's usual clearness and felicity.

As he was sure of a great and varied band, when he composed this *Te Deum,* he has made as judicious a use of the several instruments of his Orchestra, as a painter could do of the colours on his palette: now exhibiting them in their full lustre, singly; then augmenting or diminishing their force, by light and shade, and often by combination with others, making them subservient to different purposes of expression and effect.

> *"Vouchsafe, O Lord, to keep us this day without sin,"*

is set to an exquisite strain, in which the modulation is no less surprising, learned, and curious, than pathetic and pleasing.

The last movement:

"O Lord, in thee have I trusted," etc.,

is what the Italians would allow to be *ben tirato.* Indeed, it is an excellent display of Handel's resources in discovering and availing himself of the most latent advantages which every simple as well as artificial subject affords him. The symphony of this Chorus, which is chiefly constructed upon a *ground-base,* beginning by two trumpets, that are afterwards joined by the other instruments, is stately and interesting, though in the measure of a common minuet. The long solo part, after the symphony, for a contralto voice, with soft and sparing accompaniments, renders the subsequent sudden burst of all the voices and instruments the more striking. And the latter part, in fugue, with an alternate use of the ground-base, seems to wind up this magnificent production by

"Untwisting all the chains that tie
The hidden soul of harmony."

II

OVERTURE IN SAUL

The first movement of this admirable composition, so different from the common style of Overture, which Lulli had established, and to which all the composers in Europe, for more than fifty years, implicitly conformed, is extremely pleasing; and when it was first heard, must have surprised, by the grace and novelty of its conduct and passages.

Though the rest of this Overture was superseded, in favour of the *Dead March,* yet it is but justice to the author to say, that the second movement, with solo parts for the principal hautbois and violin, is so *chantant,* as perpetually to remind the hearer of a vocal duet, richly accompanied. The fugue, indeed with solo parts for the organ, was, perhaps, very judiciosly omitted; as the passages have been long in such favour with the imitators of Handel as to be rendered trite and vulgar. The *Minuet* will, however, always preserve its grace and dignity; being one of the few final movements of an Overture, which neither age, nor fashion, can deform.

THE DEAD MARCH IN SAUL

This most happy and affecting movement, which has retained its favour near half a century, and which is so simple, solemn, and sorrowful, that it can never be heard, even upon a single instrument, without exciting melancholy sensations, received here all the dignity and grandeur which it could possibly derive from the various tones of the most powerful, as well as best disciplined, band, that was ever assembled.

PART OF THE ANTHEM

WHICH WAS PERFORMED IN WESTMINSTER ABBEY AT THE FUNERAL OF HER SACRED MAJESTY QUEEN CAROLINE, 1737

"When the ear heard her, then it blessed her; and when the eye saw her, it gave witness of her." Job 29:11.

This elegant, mild, and sorrowing strain, after all the riotous clangor of jubilation in the *Te Deum,* and powerful percussion of drums, and tuneful blasts of trumpets and sacbuts, in the *Dead March,* was soothing and comforting to the ear. Contrast is the great source of our musical pleasure; for however delighted we may be with *quick, slow, loud, or soft,* for a certain time, variety is so necessary to stimulate attention, that the performance which is in want of the one, is never sure of the other. This charming movement is still so new, that it would do honour to the taste, as well as knowledge in harmony, of any composer now living. Handel had a versatile genius; and, if he had continued to write for the Opera, instead of the Church, there was no elegance or refinement which Hasse, Vinci, Pergolesi, and their successors, ever attained, that was out of his reach.

"She delivered the poor that cried, the fatherless, and him that

had none to help him"—Job 29:12. *"Kindness, meekness, and comfort were in her tongue"*—Eccles. 36:23. *"If there was any virtue,
and if there was any praise, she thought on those things"*—Phil. 4:8.

The trebles singing alone, and only accompanied in unison, by
treble instruments, at the words—*"kindness, meekness, and comfort
were in her tongue,"* had an admirable effect, in point of contrast,
with the full harmony of the rest of this charming Chorus. Indeed,
this *Naenia* contains all the requisites of good Music, in plain counterpoint: as good harmony, melody, rhythm, accent, and expression.
The beauties of this strain are of every age and country; no change
of fashion can efface them, or prevent their being felt by persons of
sensibility.

"Their bodies are buried in peace"—Eccles. 44:14.

This admirable fragment of solemn and sorrowful harmony, in
the Church style, almost wholly without instruments, is an excellent
introduction to the less plaintive strain which follows:

"But their name liveth evermore"—Ibid.

which is one of the most singular and agreeable Choruses I know,
and was performed with an accuracy, power, and spirit, which neither
that, nor, perhaps, any Music of the kind ever received before. Each
of the three movements from the *Funeral Anthem,* seemed to excite
such lively sensations of grief, as reminded all present of the ravages
which death had made among their particular families and friends,
and moved many even to tears.

GLORIA PATRI. From the Jubilate, 1713.
"Glory be to the Father," etc.

This Chorus, from the *Jubilate,* which Handel set at the same time
as the grand *Te Deum,* for the peace at Utrecht, and the only *Jubilate*
he ever composed, being in his grandest and most magnificent style,
received every possible advantage in the performance, from a correct
and powerful band, and the most mute and eager attention in the
audience.

III

ANTHEM. Composed about the Year 1719.

AIR AND CHORUS

O sing unto the Lord a new song; O sing unto the Lord all the whole earth." Ps. 96:1.

Madame Mara's voice and manner of singing in this plain and solemn air, so admirably accompanied on the hautbois by Fisher, had a sudden effect on myself, which I never before experienced, even from her performance of more pathetic Music. I have long admired her voice, and abilities in various styles of singing; but never imagined tenderness the peculiar characteristic of her performance: however, here, though she had but a few simple notes to deliver, they made me shiver, and I found it extremely difficult to avoid bursting into tears on hearing them. Indeed, she had not only the power of conveying to the remotest corner of this immense building, the softest and most artificial inflexions of her sweet and brilliant voice, but articulated every syllable of the words with such neatness, precision, and purity, that it was rendered as audible, and intelligible, as it could possibly have been, in a small theatre, by meer declamation.

CHORUS

"Declare his honour unto the Heathen, and his wonders unto all people—For the Lord is great, and cannot worthily be praised." Ps. 96:3, 4.

This Chorus is in a truly grand style, and produced great effects though there are only three vocal parts. The subject is reversed, at the latter end, in a most ingenious manner.

"He is more to be feared than all gods"—Ps. 96:3, 4.

Here the modulation is sublime, and truly ecclesiastic.

"The waves of the sea rage horribly; but yet the Lord who dwells on high is mightier"—Ps. 93:5.

Handel, in the accompaniments of this boisterous air, has tried, not unsuccessfully, to express the turbulence of a tempestuous sea; the style of this kind of Music is not meant to be amiable; but it contrasts well with other movements, and this has a spirit, and even roughness, peculiar to our author.

DUET

"O worship the Lord in the beauty of holiness." Ps. 96:9.

The solemnity of this movement may, perhaps, seem as much too languid to the admirers of the preceding air, as that may be too turbulent for the nerves of those who are partial to this. The truth is, that both verge a little on the extreme; but a composer, of such extensive powers of invention as Handel, dares every thing, for the sake of variety: and this Duet is much in the admired style of Steffani.

CHORUS

"Let all the whole earth stand in awe of him." Ibid. *"Let the heavens rejoice, and let the earth be glad; let the sea make a noise and all that therein is."* Ibid., 11.

In the last movement of this Chorus, when all the instruments are busied, such a commotion is raised, as constitutes one of Handel's most formidable hurricanes.

CHORUS IN ISRAEL IN EGYPT

"The Lord shall reign for ever and ever." Exod. 15:18.

This most admirable composition which is written *a due cori,* begins by the tenors and counter-tenors, in unison, accompanied only by a ground-base.

RECITATIVE

"For the horse of Pharaoh with his chariots," etc. Exod. 15.

Mr. Norris pronounced this and the following Recitative with the true energy of an Englishman, who perfectly comprehended and articulated the words.

CHORUS

"The Lord shall reign for ever and ever."

The return to this short strain of Chorus, after each fragment of Recitative, has a fine effect.

RECITATIVE

"And Miriam the prophetess, the sister of Aaron, took a timbrel in her hand: and all the women went out after her with timbrels and with dances." Exod. 15:19.

CHORUS

"Sing ye to the Lord, for he hath triumphed gloriously.[2] *The Lord shall reign for ever and ever. The horse and his rider he hath thrown into the sea."* Exod. 15:21.

The effects of this composition are at once pleasing, grand, and sublime! The aggregate of voices and instruments had here its full effect. And such is the excellence of this production, that if Handel had composed no other piece, this alone would have rendered his name immortal, among true lovers and judges of harmony.[3]

Upon the whole, the success of this day's performance may, with the utmost truth, be pronounced entire; as its effects surpassed the most sanguine expectations of the greatest enthusiasts for the honour of Handel, the glory of the profession, and prosperity of this grand enterprise. And, indeed, he must have been not only a fastidious, but

[2] Handel's uncertainty in whatever concerned the accent and pronunciation of our language appears very remarkably in his manner of setting this last Chorus; where he accents the words, *"For he hath triumphed gloriously,"* thus: *"Fŏr hĕ hăth trĭŭmphed gloriously."* But in the year 1738, when he composed the Oratorio of *Israel in Egypt,* our language was not very familiar to him; and he had then but little experience in setting it to Music. [Burney's note.]

[3] The art with which Handel, in the midst of all the fire of imagination and ebullition of genius, introduces a sober, *chanting* kind of *counter-subject,* while the other is carried on with uninterrupted spirit, is marvellous! [Burney's note.]

a very ignorant and insensible hearer, who did not receive new and exquisite pleasure from the composition and execution of the pieces which were this day performed.

But, in justice to the audience, it may be said, that though the frequency of hearing good Music in this capital, of late years, has so far blunted the edge of curiosity and appetite, that the best Operas and Concerts are accompanied with a buz and murmur of conversation, equal to that of a tumultuous croud, or the din of high 'Change; yet now, such a stillness reigned, as, perhaps, never happened before in so large an assembly. The midnight hour was never founded in more perfect tranquillity, than every note of these compositions. I have long been watching the operations of good Music on the sensibility of mankind; but never remember, in any part of Europe, where I attended Musical exhibitions, in the Church, Theatre, or Chamber, to have observed so much curiosity excited, attention bestowed, or satisfaction glow in the countenances of those present, as on this occasion. The effects, indeed, upon many were such as modern times have never before experienced. The *Choral power* of harmonical combinations affected some to tears, and fainting; while others were melted and enrapt, by the exquisite sweetness of *single sounds*. I had little leisure to contemplate the countenances of those around me; but, when I happened to turn my eyes from the performers, I saw nothing but tears of extacy, and looks of wonder and delight. Nothing, however, discovered the admirable discipline of the band, and unwearied and determined attention of the audience, so much as the *pauses,* which are so frequent in Handel's Music: for these were so unanimously calculated, and measured, that no platoon, or single cannon, was ever fired with more exact precision or unity of effect, than that with which the whole phalanx of this multitudinous band resumed its work, after all the sudden, and usually, unlimited cessations of sound, commonly called *pauses,* which, in general, catch loquacity in the fact; but now, at all these unexpected moments, the silence was found as awful and entire, as if none but the tombs of departed mortals had been present.

COMMEMORATION OF HANDEL (1785)

VARIOUS HANDS

>>> <<<

Beethoven's "Third" and "Fifth"

Announcement of the first public playing of the Eroica:

A grand Sinfonie in D Sharp Minor by Herr Ludwig von Beethoven and dedicated to His Highness Prince von Lobkowitz will be played on Sunday, April 7, 1805, at the Theatre an der Wien. The composer will have the pleasure of conducting it himself.

The Vienna correspondent of the "Allgemeine musikalische Zeitung":

I have heard a new sinfonie by Beethoven in E flat (erroneously announced as being in D sharp major) [1] under the composer's own direction. It was performed by a quite complete orchestra, but even this time I found no reason to change my earlier opinion. [2] Truly this new work of Beethoven's contains some grand and daring ideas, as one might expect from the powerful genius of the composer, and shows great expressive strength as well. But the sinfonie would be all the better—it lasts a whole hour—if Beethoven could reconcile himself to make some cuts in it and to bring into the score more light, clarity, and unity—virtues that were never absent from the Sinfonies in G Minor and C Minor of Mozart, those in C and D of Beethoven, and those in E Flat and D of Eberl. [3] Here in place of the andante there is a funeral march in C minor, which is developed fugally, but this fugue is completely lost and confused in the way it is handled.

[1] *Sic:* these several discrepancies of key are a telling part of the story. The Eroica is in E flat, the Fifth in C minor.

[2] At a private performance with incomplete instrumental forces, in December 1804.

[3] Anton Eberl (1766–1807), pianist and composer, friend of Mozart's.

Even after several hearings it eludes the most sustained attention, so that the unprepared connoisseur is really shocked. As a result this sinfonie was anything but enjoyed by the greater part of the audience.

Two and a half years later:

This reviewer remains, in spite of all that has been written on this work, of his original opinion, namely, that this symphony undoubtedly contains many beautiful and sublime things, but that these elements are mixed with many harsh things and longueurs, and that it will be able to acquire the purity of form of a work of art only by a thorough revision.

About the same time, a Berlin reviewer:

The symphony is full of originality; it is abundant and even excessive in its harmony, but also full of bizarre ideas. . . . On the whole, this symphony by no means made an impression comparable to that made by Mozart's and Haydn's. The applause of those who know went to the performers, for their skillful overcoming of great difficulties for about three-quarters of an hour.

※》》《《

After Beethoven's concert of December 1808, intended by him as a farewell to the Viennese, and containing for the first time the Symphony in C Minor, No. 5, the composer wrote to his publishers:

To begin with, the musicians had lost their place and made a mistake in the simplest passage imaginable. So I stopped them sharply and cried out loud, "Begin again!" It had never happened to them, and the public signified its satisfaction thereat.

The correspondent of the "Allgemeine musikalische Zeitung":

The first movement in C minor is a fiery allegro, a little obscure, noble in feeling and in working out, firmly and evenly developed. It is a worthy piece, which will afford real pleasure even to those who are attached to the older way of composing large symphonies. The andante is very original and attractive, composed as it is of the most heterogeneous ideas—gentle reverie and warlike fierceness. Its handling from beginning to end is *sui generis*. Under its appearance of arbitrariness it is possible to find in this remarkable piece much thought, a firm grasp of the whole, and a very careful elaboration. As for the ensuing scherzando (which is hardly playable by a large orchestra), we must confess ourselves unable to enjoy it, owing to its far too insistent whims. But humor in art—if I may be permitted the comparison—is not just like fine cooking, however elaborate it may be one must try and try again in order to ascertain what might prove pleasing. The finale is a tempestuous explosion, born of a powerful fancy, and such as one would hardly find in any other symphony.

E. T. A. Hoffmann, the following year:

Beethoven's instrumental music opens to us the realm of the vast and the mighty. Burning shafts of light pierce the gloom of that empire, where we discern giant shadows rising and falling, entwining themselves more and more closely about us, destroying everything within us and not merely the pain of an infinite desire. All pleasure springing forth in joyful notes sinks and disappears, yet it is in this distress of consuming love, joy, and oppression—as if our heart would burst in a single great chord uniting all our passions—that we continue to live and find ourselves made into enchanted seers.

Nothing could be simpler than the motif on which the master bases his whole allegro, but it will be noticed with amazement how he has arranged all the secondary motives, all the episodes, so that by means of their rhythmic connection with the first, they enhance the character of the entire movement. Of all this the first motif was only the bare hint. All the phrases are short; they consist of only two or three measures and are usually divided among themselves by the constant opposition of the strings and wind instruments. One might suppose this would produce nothing but a broken-up, incoherent effect; on the contrary, it is just that disposition of the whole, just that succession of short phrases and single chords, which raises to the highest pitch our feeling of unspeakably ardent desire.

Beethoven has kept to the ordinary sequence of movements in his symphony, but they seem fantastically linked together and the whole work resounds like a rhapsody of genius. Yet the mind of any sensitive listener will undoubtedly be struck deeply, intimately, by one *single* and lasting impression—that of desire, infinite, unappeasable—stretching to the very last chord. Even after the end, he will be unable to escape from that marvelous realm of spirit in which pain and pleasure envelop him in the guise of musical energies.

Twenty years later, F.-J. Fétis [4] writes of the Paris première:

Such a creation as the finale is above and beyond music. It is no longer flutes, horns, violins, and basses that one hears, it is the world which totters, the universe. . . . Unfortunately Beethoven never knows when to stop. Nearly all his most beautiful movements keep on beyond the bounds of their necessary development and spoil the impression they create by passages of more or less bizarre workmanship. That is because in spite of the immense capacity of his genius Beethoven lacks that good taste which was the mark of Haydn's and Mozart's work. If these two great artists had found the sublime idea of the march I have just spoken of, and the admirable way of linking it with the preceding scherzo, they would carefully have avoided falling into the extravagance which follows and which quickly cools the listener's enthusiasm for Beethoven's symphony.

The next month, also in Paris, young Berlioz:

Lesueur [5] consented to let me take him to the Conservatoire for one of the performances of the Symphony in C Minor. He wanted to listen to it conscientiously and without distractions of any kind, and so took a seat among strangers in the last row of a first-tier box, sending me elsewhere. When the symphony was over, I came down from

[4] See p. 562.
[5] Composer of operas and oratorios, famous teacher of Berlioz, Gounod, etc.

the upper tier in order to find out what Lesueur had felt and what
he thought of this extraordinary work. I met him in one of the corri-
dors. He was very red in the face and taking long strides.

"Well, master?" said I.

"Whew! I'm going out, I want some air, it's incredible, it's marvelous! It moved me so, it disturbed me and upset me so much that, on
leaving the box and trying to put on my hat, I thought I should never
find my head again. Leave me to myself. Come tomorrow."

I was exultant. The next day I was promptly at his house. The conversation turned at once to the masterpiece that had so deeply affected
us both. Lesueur allowed me to speak a little while, nodding with
a somewhat constrained air at my admiring exclamations. But it was
easy to see that I had no longer before me the same man as yesterday,
and that the subject was now painful to him. I kept on nevertheless
until Lesueur, from whom I had once again extorted an admission of
the deep emotion he had felt on hearing the symphony, shook his
head with a strange smile and said, "All the same, one ought not to
write music like that."

To which I replied, "Never fear, my dear master, there won't be
much written *like that*."

Poor human nature, poor dear master! His remark, so often echoed
by other men in similar circumstances, is a compound of stubbornness, regret, terror before the unknown, jealousy, and an implicit
admission of impotence. For to say "one ought not to write music
like that" when one has experienced its power and recognized its
beauty is to declare that one will not compose in that manner because
one feels that one could not even if one would.

LOUIS SPOHR

※≫ ≪※

First Baton in London

Spohr's fame as the composer of a *Faust* opera and many symphonies
has greatly dimmed since the last century (though his name is embalmed
in a verse of *The Mikado*). But his *Autobiography* is still full of interest,
if only for its revelation of the author as a true and energetic artist.
His span is 1784–1859 and the time of this narrative is the early spring
of 1820.

The time for my trip to London had now come. Since I had agreed
to buy for my wife in London a new Erard [1] harp with the improved
"double action" mechanism, we left her old instrument in Herr
Vogel's care. The Vogel family were delighted with this plan, for
now they were sure of seeing us again on our return journey.

Having arrived in Calais, I went at once to the packetboat office
to secure our berths. Then I took a walk to the port to see the ship on
which we were to sail in the afternoon. But as I saw that even inside
the harbor the sea was very rough and ran so high outside that the
waves broke high over the pier, I lost all heart for the journey and
hurried back to the shipping office in order to exchange our reservations for others on the following day.

In the afternoon, while taking a tour of the city with my wife, I
took good care not to bring her within sight of the sea, so that, dreading the passage as she did already, she might not see the raging waters.
The thought of having to cross at so stormy a time of year with my
delicate and nervous wife kept me from resting throughout the night,
and as soon as dawn broke I hurried again to the harbor to see whether
the storm had abated. It seemed to me that it had; I therefore hurried

[1] Famous firm of inventors and manufacturers of pianos and harps, established in both Paris and London.

Dorette on board and advised her to lie down at once in the cabin. A good-natured German who shipped as seaman on this English packet promised me to look after her and bring her whatever she might require. This allowed me to go up on deck, where in the open air I hoped to be able to withstand seasickness.

Meanwhile preparations had been made for casting off, and the vessel was being towed with long ropes close upon the left side of the pier by some sixty to eighty men. Hardly had we reached the end of the pier when we were caught up by a colossal wave and in a twinkling hurled to the other side of the harbor; we nearly hit the point of the right-hand jetty. At once the waves broke over the deck so that the ports and hatches and cabin doors had to be made fast. I alone of all the passengers remained on deck and sat on a bench near the main mast, around which stood various high coils of cable. Here I hoped to be protected from the flood that swept the deck. But soon the waves broke so high that in order to avoid being entirely swamped I had to climb up on the bench. I had not done this many times before seasickness overcame me and I found my strength ebbing. Nor was it long before I was wet through to the skin, in spite of my thick overcoat. This made my earlier discomfort even more unbearable. On top of this I was seized by violent cramps, especially after my stomach had nothing more to yield, and I hardly thought I would survive.

Fortunately the trip was uncommonly rapid—thanks to the storm. Nevertheless the three hours it lasted seemed to me an eternity. At last we arrived in Dover, but here a new misfortune awaited us; it proved impossible to make the harbor owing to the ebb tide, and the passengers had to disembark in the offing. As soon as we had anchored, boats were lowered and the passengers summoned to trans-ship. I now saw my fellow sufferers rise pale and shaky, like ghosts from the grave, and it was evident that they had not fared better down below than I had up on deck.

At length my poor wife also appeared, supported by the kind sailor, and seeming to suffer greatly. Just as I was about to hurry toward her, a young and beautiful girl, whom I had already noticed when we came on board, but who then had not deigned to look at me, suddenly threw her arms around my neck and without speaking a word held me close. I easily guessed the motive of this extraordinary behavior. The poor frightened creature had seen the way in which the first passengers had been expedited into the boats, which tossed high upon the still raging waves and then sank into an abyss, and again rose as high as the deck of our vessel—at which moment the sailors would throw in another passenger or piece of luggage. This procedure had so frightened the girl that she left the arm of her duenna and fastened on to me, who doubtless looked to her like the sturdiest man among the passengers. There was no time for explanations; I carried her into the boat, then hurried back to my wife to do the same for her. No sooner had I managed this as well than the still anxious beauty clung to me again, to Dorette's considerable surprise. But the dangers of the trip did not permit any remarks. After landing, the girl scarcely touched terra firma before she broke loose from me without a word of thanks, rejoined her companion, and walked away. That she was some young lady of quality accompanied by her governess can be readily inferred from this truly English behavior.

Having changed my dripping clothes at the inn, and quelled our reawakened appetites at the table d'hôte, and generally restored our strength for travel, we took our seats in the coach for London. We made most of the trip by night, and when we and our baggage were set down the next morning in London, I found myself in a real predicament. In spite of all my attempts I could find no one at the coach office or outside to whom I could make myself understood. I spoke not a word of English and no one there understood either German or French. I had no other recourse but to roam the streets and, while my wife watched the baggage, to hunt up an interpreter.

But it was still early morning and I met only people of the lower classes from whom I could not expect knowledge of a foreign tongue. There came at last a well-dressed man whom I addressed first in German, then as he shook his head, in French, telling him my plight. But he shrugged and walked away. A second person, however, who had witnessed the scene, approached me and asked in excellent French what it was I wanted. He was a courier on hire, and at my request he immediately hailed a cab for us to drive over to Mr. Ries,[2] whose address I fortunately remembered. We were now taken to the lodgings that had been reserved for us, where we could at last rest after the strain of the crossing and the night journey.

The next morning I was to be presented by Mr. Ries at the meeting of directors of the Philharmonic Society. I therefore took especial care about my toilette, and put on for this purpose one of the prize pieces in my wardrobe—a bright red waistcoat made of Turkish shawl material. On the Continent it was the latest fashion. But I had hardly appeared in the street when I found myself the target of public notice. The adult passers-by contented themselves with an amazed stare and went on their way, but the dear little urchins were loud in their comments, which I unfortunately missed, for I could not conceive what displeased them so. They gradually formed a procession in my wake, which became more and more vocal and unruly. A passer-by spoke to me and doubtless explained the cause, but his English was of no use to me.

Fortunately, Ries's house was not far from mine and I soon arrived. His wife, a charming young Englishwoman who spoke fluent French, gave me the clue to my adventure. George III had but recently died and national mourning had been decreed. By custom no one was to appear in public except in black. The rest of my costume, to be sure, was entirely black and therefore proper, but that unlucky red waistcoat only shone the more brilliantly by contrast. Mme. Ries told me that I could certainly thank my imposing stature and earnest expression for saving me from physical insults at the hands of the street urchins, namely, pelting with mud. To avoid all further offense, Ries drove with me first to my rooms and I exchanged my red waistcoat for a black one.

After I had been kindly welcomed by the directors of the Philharmonic, some of whom spoke German and others French, we discussed the program of my first concert. I was requested to play two

[2] Ferdinand Ries (1784-1838), Beethoven's pupil, an active member of the London Philharmonic, and famed as piano virtuoso and composer. See p. 546.

solos and to lead the orchestra from the first-violin desk. I replied
that I was ready to do the former, but must beg that I be allowed to
lead at a later concert, for my solos would appear to less advantage
if I was obliged to perform in two capacities on the same evening.
Obvious as this was to those of the directors who were soloists, it gave
rise to a long and lively argument before the point, which was contrary to custom, could be admitted.

Still greater offense was caused by my request to present at this
first concert only compositions of my own. The Philharmonic Society had made it a rule—designed to exclude the usual virtuoso's
worthless, empty concertos—to permit no such pieces to be played
except Mozart's and Beethoven's piano concertos, and to choose,
themselves, what soloists were to perform. When Ries had assured
them in English—hence, to me unintelligibly—that in Germany my
violin concertos would be put side by side with the works excepted
from their prohibition, my point was finally conceded. I therefore
appeared on the first Philharmonic program with my *Scena cantante* [3]
and, in the second half, with my Solo-quartet in E Major, and met
with general applause. It gave me special pleasure as a composer that
the directors now all shared Mr. Ries's opinion. And as a violinist
I was made happy by the fact that old Viotti,[4] who had always been
my model and who was to have been my teacher in youth, heard me
and told me many things in praise of my playing.

Having successfully weathered my first appearance in London, I
devoted the next day to delivering my letters of recommendation.
For me who knew not a word of English this was a grueling task and
I often got into difficulties. No one had told me that in London one
must knock at the street door, the gentlemen being supposed to announce themselves by loud, rapid, and reiterated knocks. I followed
rather the German custom of modestly ringing the bell, which in
London is only for tradesmen having business with the kitchen.
Therefore I could not understand why the servants who opened to

[3] The full title of this, Spohr's eighth violin concerto, is: *Scene in Vocal Style
and in Dramatic Mood*.
[4] Founder of the modern school of violin playing (1753–1824).

me stared in surprise and could hardly believe that I wanted to be announced to their masters.

Moreover, since the persons I visited occasionally knew as little German or French as their servants, there ensued some embarrassing moments. An amusing one occurred at Rothschild's, to whom I brought a letter of introduction from his brother in Frankfort and a letter of credit from Speyer. When Rothschild had taken and read my two letters, he said in a condescending tone, "I see here"—pointing to *The Times*—"that you've managed your business pretty well. Now I know nothing about music. My music is this"—striking his change pocket. "They hearken to it on the Exchange." And he laughed loudly at his own joke. Then, calling a clerk, without even asking me to sit down, he gave him the letter of credit and said, "Pay the gentleman his money." He gave me a nod and the audience was at an end. But as I reached the door he called out to me, "Perhaps some day you'll come and dine with me at my country place!" A few days later Mme. Rothschild did write to ask me to dinner, but I did not go although she repeated her invitation. Nevertheless my letter of introduction was not wholly useless, for when I gave my benefit concert he took a whole box.

At Mr. Ries's house I had also met M. Erard, the head of the London branch of Erard, frères, and together with my wife visited their showrooms to look at the improved harps. But we could not immediately make up our minds to choose one, because Dorette wanted first to try out which size of instrument suited her best, and whether she would get used to the new mechanism. M. Erard put an end to this hesitation by offering to lend her a harp of her choice for the duration of our stay in London. If it did not suit, she could exchange or return it. She accepted with thanks and began at once to practice; but at first could make no headway. The new harp, though of the smallest size, was nonetheless a good deal larger and more tightly strung than her own, and therefore required far more strength to play. It was also difficult for her to become accustomed to the new double action after having been used to the single from childhood. She soon discovered that it would take her several months before she could play in public on this harp. I decided accordingly to let her appear only once, at my benefit concert, to which it would give an added attraction.[5]

Meanwhile my turn had come to direct one of the Philharmonic concerts, and I managed to create no less a sensation than I had with my violin playing. It was still the custom at that time, when symphonies and overtures were played, for the pianist to have the score before him, not in order to conduct, but to read along and join in at will—which, when it was heard, produced a deplorable effect. The real conductor was the first violin, who gave the tempi and who, when the orchestra began to falter, gave the beat with his bow. Now an orchestra of the size of the Philharmonic, with its members sitting so far one from another, could hardly play exactly together under such conducting, and in spite of the excellence of the individual players the ensemble was a good deal poorer than one is accustomed to in Germany. I had therefore resolved that when my turn came to direct I would try to remedy the situation.

Fortunately, on the day when I was to direct, Mr. Ries was at the piano and he readily agreed to give up the score to me and to hold aloof from the proceedings. I took my stand at a special desk in front of the orchestra, drew my baton from my pocket, and gave the signal to begin. Quite shocked at this innovation, some of the directors wanted to protest, but as I begged them to grant me at least one trial, they calmed down. I knew thoroughly the symphonies and overtures which we rehearsed, having often played them in Germany.[6] I therefore could not only give the tempi in decisive fashion but also give the wind and brass the cues for all their entrances. This imparted a confidence they had never had before. I also took the liberty, whenever the execution was not satisfactory, to stop and offer polite but earnest comments on the performance, Ries translating my remarks to the gentlemen of the orchestra.

[5] Mme. Spohr finally gave up the harp as unhealthful, and performed only as piano accompanist to her husband.

[6] One of them was Spohr's new Symphony in D Minor, No. 2. The date was April 10, 1820.

Stimulated by all this to an uncommon degree of attention, and led with complete certainty by the *visible* beat, everyone played with a fire and precision such as no one had ever heard before. The result surprised and inspired the orchestra, and at the end of the first movement they expressed aloud their collective approval of the new manner of conducting, and thereby overruled all further opposition on the part of the directors.

In the vocal pieces, which I also took over at Mr. Ries's request, and especially in the recitatives, giving the beat with the baton (after I had explained the meaning of my movements) was completely successful, and the singers reiterated their satisfaction at the precision with which the orchestra now accompanied them.

The success of the evening was even greater than I had hoped. To be sure, at the beginning the audience was startled by the novelty and laid their heads together to whisper. But after the music had begun and the orchestra played the well-known symphony with unusual power and precision, the listeners gave their general approbation by their long sustained applause at the end of the first movement. The triumph of the baton was decisive, and no one was ever seen again at the piano during the performance of symphonies and overtures.

AUTOBIOGRAPHY (1861)

GIUSEPPE VERDI AND LOUIS ENGEL

※》》 《《

"La Traviata" in Venice

Intimate with many of the great composers of his century, Louis Engel
showed himself in his criticism and reminiscences at once an intelligent
and an amiable man. He was Shaw's predecessor on the London *World*.

In 1851, at the Fenice at Venice, Verdi produced *Rigoletto,* which
created one of those furores which carry the name of a composer with
electric power to the top of the column of glory. He himself had great
hopes for his score, but he was afraid for the famous air, *"La donna
è mobile."* [1] Being very easily retained, it might from the rehearsal get
into the streets and be sung all over the town before the first performance, and he would then appear to have copied instead of having
created the work. In order to prevent this possibility he did not let
the tenor have his air. At last Mirate [Merelli?],[2] fancying that
Verdi had not written it, pressed him, and Verdi always said, "Time
enough—you shall have it." And at last, at the general rehearsal, he
brought it. The air and the quartet above mentioned and the whole
opera were soon the property of the whole world.

In Paris a most amusing quarrel began between two papers—one,
La France Musicale, which praised every note of Verdi to the sky,
unreservedly, stupidly, with open partiality, so as even to make him
enemies through this puffing injustice; the other, the *Gazette
Musicale,* which with nearly equal violence and injustice attacked
him, so much so, that they said there was not a melody, not a *morceau
d'ensemble* in *Rigoletto,* which nevertheless contained some of the
most popular airs the world has known, and the most admirable
quartet. The *hinc illae lachrymae* was that both papers were owned

[1] "Woman is fickle."
[2] Opera manager.

by publishers. *La France* by the publisher of Verdi's works, the *Gazette* by the publisher of Meyerbeer's works. Their fighting only advertised the opera immensely and thereby increased its fame.

Not two years after this eventful performance Verdi produced (in the first week of the year 1853) *Il Trovatore*. To say that *Il Trovatore* conquered the world is not saying too much, because there is scarcely a village in Europe or America where those instruments of torture against which fortunately an Act of Parliament does protect us [Englishmen], the barrel organs, don't grind the *Miserere* or "*Il Balen*" or some piece of that score.[3] Let those who pretend that the first necessity for a successful opera is a good libretto read the idiotic exposé of this *Trovatore,* the first idea of which comes from an extremely interesting Spanish sketch of the same name, by a gifted youth only seventeen years old. Antonio García Gutíerez is the author of a book so excellent that one cannot imagine how it was possible for Piave to convert it into such rubbish, which, nevertheless, inspired Verdi with that treasure of sparkling melodies his score is studded with.

Paris, London, Rome, St. Petersburg, brought it out with the greatest artists the lyric stage has known. It is one of the most remarkable events of musical publication that this opera, which in single airs, in arrangements for all kinds of instruments, bands, quadrilles, waltzes, etc., yielded untold sums, brought not one penny of English money to its composer. No copyright! Just as it happens to us all in America.

While the *Trovatore* was being rehearsed at Rome, Verdi had nearly finished another opera, *La Traviata,* which was performed at Venice in March 1855. The *Traviata* is certainly his most melodious, most original, least exaggerated work; it possesses at the same time the greatest of his qualities and the fewest of his faults. Yet *La Traviata* made a complete fiasco. Here again, *embonpoint* rendered the situation ridiculous. Mlle. Donatelli, an immensely stout woman, yet a good singer, played the "Traviata." When in the last act the doctor came to see the poor consumptive, she, falling on the floor in

[3] See p. 462 for the situation forty years earlier. "*Il balen*"—"the lightning of her glance," aria from *Il Trovatore.*

a fit, raised such a cloud of dust that the doctor became invisible, and the Venetians roared outright. Moreover, the tenor was so hoarse that he could barely be heard, and the baritone, imagining that his was only a secondary part, took no trouble with it, and the work was sacrificed.

→» «←

The next morning and again two days later, Verdi wrote as follows:

To Emanuele Muzio [4]   Venice, March 7, 1853
   Dear Emanuel: *La Traviata,* last night, a fiasco. The fault? Was it mine or the singers? Time will tell!

To Vincenzo Luccardi [5]
   Dearest Luccardi: I did not write to you after the première of *Traviata;* I write to you after the second night. It is a fiasco, a decided fiasco! I don't know who is to blame. Better not to speak of it. I shan't tell you anything about the music, and you will permit me to tell you just as much about the way it was sung.

To Giulio Ricordi [6]
   Dear Ricordi: I am sorry to have to send you bad news, but I cannot conceal the fact: *La Traviata* was a fiasco. Don't try to fathom the reason why; that's the way it is. Farewell, farewell!

LOUIS ENGEL, *FROM MOZART TO MARIO* (1886)
VERDI, *LETTERS* (1853)

[4] Friend, pupil, and defender of Verdi.
[5] Verdi's scene designer and friend.
[6] Verdi's publisher; see p. 576.

VLADIMIR STASSOV

"*Boris Godunov*"

To the Editor of "Novoye Vremya":

Our operas resemble chickens that can't defend themselves against a powerful cook. At any day and hour of his choice some Terenti or Pakhom has the right to catch the most talented Russian opera by the wings, chop off its legs or tail, cut its throat and cook a fricassee of his own invention. When Moussorgsky's *Boris* was being considered, I remember hearing some profound connoisseurs saying with an important mien and with their customary aplomb that the entire fifth act was quite superfluous, that it simply had to be cut off, or, at least, that it should be transposed, and played before the fourth act. O God, it was just like being in the kitchen! . . . Poor Glinka paid bitterly all his life for the famous "experience" of those who surrounded him. "Count Vielgorsky," says Glinka in his *Memoirs,* "made merciless cuts in *Ruslan* (after its first performances) and often in its best parts, saying with a self-satisfied air, 'Am I not a master at making *coupures!*'" This self-satisfied air and merciless barbarity continue to this day. . . . The other day all Petersburg saw with amazement that the entire fifth act of *Boris* had been discarded, and this without consulting or notifying anybody. One goes to hear an opera as it has been conceived and created by its author, and not as some manager thinks it should be! It may be objected, "Yes, but we have the author's consent!" While you hold the author in your claws, he'll consent to anything. He can't defend himself or protest, and when his entire opera may be removed from the calendar he has no alternative but to consent. Not everyone has the fortitude of a Beethoven or a Schubert, not everyone is big enough to withdraw his work rather than have it mutilated. . . .

OCTOBER 27, 1876

LAFCADIO HEARN

※ ※

Bizet's "L'Arlésienne"

One of the greatest of recent theatrical successes in Paris is the lyrical drama entitled *L'Arlésienne*—the joint creation of Alphonse Daudet and of his lamented friend Bizet, the author of *Carmen*. As the work will doubtless be widely appreciated in this country, our readers may be interested in the history of the composition—a history at once romantic and pathetic, and curiously illustrative of the fickleness of public favor. Several foreign journals have narrated the story, but none so prettily as *Le XIXe Siècle* in its issue of May 6.

The history of *L'Arlésienne* carries us back thirteen years to the period of depression immediately following the tremendous shock of the Franco-Prussian war, and the convulsions of the Commune. The world of artists and writers had suffered severely in those great struggles; some of the most celebrated names in the French literature of the century found place upon the endless roll-call of the dead; many a mighty painter and sculptor had been swept away by the wind of battles, and the surviving members of the grand companionship of art and belles-lettres mostly found themselves ruined. Among these were Alphonse Daudet, the novelist; and César Bizet (who always signed himself Georges), the musician—both already illustrious. Bizet at the age of *eleven years* had taken the solfeggio prize at the Conservatory; had in his nineteenth year won the great prize of Rome; and had subsequently given to the theater two audaciously original and exquisite compositions, *Les Pêcheurs de Perles* and *La Jolie Fille de Perth*. Daudet had published a number of dainty and delightful little things, *Les Amoureuses, Le Petit Chose* (said to be partly autobiographical), the uniquely humorous *Tartarin de Tarascon,* and the *Lettres de mon Moulin*—charming sketches which have found translators in almost all European countries. It was in the latter work that first appeared the story entitled *L'Arlésienne*—the story of a young Provençal who dies for love.

Both the novelist and the musician, whose last pecuniary resources had been wrested from them by the hard necessities of the war, began to look about them anxiously for a chance to repair their losses by good work. Both had families to care for, and the situation was desperate. Publishers refused to risk their capital in any undertaking; the newspapers, seriously affected in their finances, could not or would not pay a respectable price for fiction; and the bookstores had little patronage to encourage them. Only one way to success seemed still open—the theater; and Daudet proposed to his friend Bizet an opera based on the story of *L'Arlésienne*. Bizet readily acceded; and produced in a short time one of the most delicately beautiful musical creations ever composed—full of passionate Southern melody, of strangely delightful variations upon quaint Provençal themes.

Everything seemed propitious. Great critics believed the music would enthuse Paris. Admirable actresses had been found for the leading parts—many of whom have since become famous. The directors were hopeful; the support of the press seemed assured. . . . *L'Arlésienne* was performed for the first time at the Vaudeville Théâtre, on October 1, 1872.

It was a momentous evening for both Daudet and his friend; the first had everything to gain, the latter much to lose. As the French journalist who describes the events of that evening remarks, nothing is so utterly a failure as the failure of a theatrical piece. There is often some hope for an unpopular book; if it contains aught of real talent, it may work its way slowly but steadily into public notice; it may be suddenly resurrected from dusty oblivion by some timely sensation, some great social excitement about the very theme upon which it treats. But the theatrical failure is apparently irremediable, and the petty whim, malice, or mere indifference of critics, or of audiences, may bring about such a failure. Even literary giants have been driven from the stage forever, and masterpieces hopelessly damned by nothing more than popular ill humor. To Daudet a failure meant the closure of all theatrical doors against him for long years, and the destruction of a hundred projects—among which was a drama in preparation founded on the theme which afterwards was to form the plot of that admirable novel, *Fromont Jeune et Risler Aîné.*

There was a large audience, but a strange one—an assembly made somber of aspect by the multitude of mourning robes—an assembly wearied to nervousness by the long strain of the war, saddened by memories of death, anticipating in a visit to the theater rather the consolation of social distraction than the pleasure of studying a rare and charming art. The music was admirably performed, but no one seemed to hear it; the text was faultlessly declaimed, yet no one appeared to listen. People with programs upon their knees were discussing politics in whispers; others, who had met as if by chance, thought and spoke only of their bereavements. The vast gloom of the war seemed to fill all the theater; and the ghosts of a thousand haunting sorrows drew away the gaze of the spectators from the stage. The audience seemed to have forgotten the mock drama, and to remember only the terribly real drama in which all had taken part; they stared without seeing, as in dream; they felt no passing emotion; they uttered no applause. *L'Arlésienne* was concluded in a great buzz of indifference; and its close was marked only by a moment of icy silence, as though all present had suddenly awoke to the knowledge of the fact that a lyrical drama had just been performed of which they had not heard a word.

Daudet went home in despair, destroyed the manuscript of his unfinished play, and after a while bravely sat down to write the novels which were destined to make his fortune. It was slow work but sure success. Bizet wrote *Carmen;* but the public waited for his death to admire it.

. . . Thirteen years passed by; and Daudet's name had become familiar to the whole civilized world. Fame smiled upon him, and wealth; translations of his novels appeared simultaneously in England, Germany, Spain, Italy, Russia, and America; his *Sapho* reached a sale of eighty thousand copies within a few months of its appearance. Bizet was long dead; but his marvelous music had conquered indifference, had mastered criticism, had compelled the enthusiasm of a thousand audiences. And suddenly the fickle and forgetful public, moved by some strange souvenir, remembered *L'Arlésienne* while remembering Bizet. So it happened that on the fifth of May, 1885, a great concourse of people found themselves in the Odéon, madly applauding the music they had refused to hear thirteen years before, weeping at the spectacle that had left them unmoved in 1872. There were new decorations, new costumes, and other actors; but the words and the music were the same, and *L'Arlésienne* was a triumph! . . . Daudet, sitting alone, watched the tumultuous pleasure of the crowd but never smiled; doubtless he saw beside him the shadow of the dead musician, the beloved friend, gazing as one that seeks to speak in vain, yearning for the utterance denied to those who dwell forever in the Place of Silence.

EDITORIAL (New Orleans, 1885)

EDUARD HANSLICK

➤➤➤ ◄◄◄

Brahms' Second Symphony

Long the butt of the Wagnerians, Hanslick (1825–1904) has only recently been re-appraised with fairness. Though he recanted his early "modernism" somewhat unpleasantly, he is a good representative of the neo-classic school which accelerated Brahms' recognition.

The new work was a great, a universal success. Seldom has public enjoyment been so sincerely and warmly expressed. Brahms' First Symphony, which was presented a year ago, was a work for serious connoisseurs capable of following with a magnifying glass its minutest ramifications. This Second Symphony is like the sun shedding its warmth over connoisseurs and laymen alike. It belongs to all who yearn for good music, whether capable of grasping difficulties or not.

Among Brahms' works, the nearest to it in style and mood is the Sextet in B Flat, the most popular of his instrumental works—so popular, indeed, that the later, more complicated quartets have ridden on its popularity. The new symphony glows with a healthy freshness and clarity. It is easy to understand throughout, even though it offers much to listen to and ponder. Much in it is new, yet there is none of that unfortunate modern tendency to insist on novelty in the sense of the unprecedented. Nor are there coy glances at extraneous realms of art—no hidden or overt borrowings from poetry or painting. It is all purely musical in conception and form, and purely musical in effect. It affords incontrovertible proof that one can still write symphonies after Beethoven—not *everyone,* of course—in the old forms and on the old foundations.

Richard Wagner and his adherents deny not only the possibility of writing symphonies after Beethoven's, but also the *raison d'être* of pure instrumental music as such. The symphony is said to have become superfluous since its transplantation into opera by Wagner. The farthest concession is to admit the compatibility of modern musical philosophy with Liszt's *Symphonic Poems* in one movement, based on definite poetic programs. This idiotic, fatuous theory has been cooked up for the domestic requirements of the Wagner-Liszt ménage, and if any further refutation of it were needed, none could be more brilliant than the long succession of Brahms' instrumental works—particularly this Second Symphony.

Its chief characteristic can be best defined as cheerful serenity, at once gentle and manly. It is lively and serious, good natured and reflective by turns. The first movement opens with a tenderly overcast horn theme and resembles a serenade in mood, which becomes more pronounced in the scherzo and finale. This first movement, an allegro moderato in three-four time, envelops us as in a melodic wave on which we gaily sport, undisturbed by two lightly intruding Mendelssohnian reminiscences. After the reserved and melodious beauty of its last fifty measures, the movement is followed by a broad, singing adagio in B major. Here the thoughtful development of the themes strikes me as more meaningful than the themes proper; on which account it has less success with the public than the other three movements.

The charming scherzo with its delicate motives, in tempo a minuet, is twice interrupted by a presto in two-four time which brightens its surroundings like an evanescent spark. The finale is still more lively, yet cozy in its glowing good cheer. How unlike the stormy finales of the modern school! Mozartian blood flows in its veins.

This D major symphony is to the C minor rather an antithesis than a companion piece. Possibly the effect of the First Symphony on the public is like that of reading a work of erudition, full of deep philosophic ideas and hidden intimations. Brahms' tendency to cloak or stifle anything that might have the appearance of "effect" is evident in the C minor to an excessive degree. The listener cannot possibly take in all the motives and fragments of motives, which at times seem like flowerets hibernating beneath the snow and at other times resemble remote specks beyond the clouds. The Second Symphony has nothing to compare with the grandiose pathos of the finale in the First Symphony. But by way of compensation it surpasses the latter by a uniform shading and a sunny clarity that are not to be underestimated. Brahms has managed to control the imposing but dangerous skill by which he hides his ideas within the polyphonic texture or subjects them to contrapuntal crucifixion. If the thematic working out is less amazing, the themes themselves are fresher and more flowing, their development is more natural and perspicuous—hence more effective. I cannot say enough to express my delight at the fact that Brahms, having given such a forceful rendering of Faustian striving in his First Symphony, should have turned back to the blossoms of the earth in spring in his Second.

CONCERT REVIEWS (1878)

The Musical Life

GEORGE SAND

>>> <<<

Art and Revolution

>>> <<<

Moved like many other artists of her time by the teachings of Saint-Simon, George Sand wrote about socialism in both fictional and essay form. The friend addressed below was Michel de Bourges (1789–1853), an independent and very courageous thinker, who throughout the century led the fight for republicanism in France. At the time of this open letter he was George Sand's lover, which perhaps increases the merit of her resistance to his Spartan views.

>>> <<<

Friend, you rebuke me for "social unbelief"; you tell me that whatever exists outside the rules of Utility can never become either truly great or truly good. You say that my indifference is a crime and a bad example, and that I must overcome it or accept moral suicide—as it were cut off my right hand and lose the power to communicate with my fellow man. You are hard on me, but that is the way I like you. From you the call to Virtue deserves my admiration and respect.

You say again that any doctrine of non-participation is an excuse for cowardice or selfishness, because no human act can avoid being helpful or harmful to mankind. Whatever my ambition is, according to you, whether it is to be admired or to be loved, I must become serviceable—and with discrimination; I must serve thoughtfully, doctrinally, scientifically—that is to say, I must be a professional Friend of Man. I usually answer those who talk to me like this by being facetious or sophistical. But here it is different. I recognize your right to preach to me the Virtuous Word, to which I am indeed so resistant that I find it hard even to repeat it after you. For my trouble has been that others have always tried to baptize me into their creed with impure hands. . . . What has convinced and touched me is the simplicity and purity of all your words and deeds.

I do not know whether the day will ever come when men will be able to tell infallibly and with finality what is useful for Man. I am not going into details now about the system you have adopted, though the other day I was making fun of it. But if you put it to me so that I must reason it out (no small victory of your mind over mine), I will freely admit that the great law of equality and fair sharing, for all its present inapplicability in the eyes of those who fear it, and for all the uncertainty of its coming, looks to me, from my retired cell, as the first and only invariable law of ethics that I have ever been able steadily to conceive.

Yet what I feel bound to add, my dear Everard, is that your virtue does not seem to me required of everyone, but of a few only. What is required of all is honesty. Do you be virtuous and I'll try to be honest. . . . Let the governed be honest, temperate, straightforward—in short, let them be *moral beings,* and the governors will be able to build on them a stable edifice. . . . O Republic, dawn of justice and equality, divine Utopia, sun of a conceivable Eden of the future, hail! Shine in the sky and be desired on earth. If thy reign come here below sooner than seems probable, thou shalt find me ready to accept it and already clothed according to the laws of thy austerity!

Yes, I am yours, whatever the color of your flag, provided your cohorts be on the road to the Republic of the Future; in the name of Jesus, who has but one true apostle now on earth; in the name of Washington and Franklin, who did not go far enough and who have left us a task to do; in the name of Saint-Simon,[1] whose disciples are marching straight toward the sublime and terrible goal of the redistribution of wealth (God protect them!). Provided that good may prevail and that those who believe in it prove it good, I am a trooper in your ranks.

[1] Count Henri de Saint-Simon (1760–1825) social reformer on Christian and "technocratic" lines.

But on your side, friend, you might tell me what you are really after when you declaim against artists. Abuse them all you want, but respect Art. Vandal! I like your impudence—to want to put sackcloth and wooden shoes on Taglioni [2] and use the hands of Liszt to turn a wine press, you who dissolve in tears at the song of any warbler and cause riots in the theater to prevent Otello's choking Malibran! [3] Our austere citizen wants to banish artists as superfluous drones in the good society, but Monsieur loves vocal music and grants a reprieve to singers. I trust that painters will find among you a good fellow who knows about painting and will keep you from walling up the windows of the studios!

As for the poets, they are your first cousins; when you are trying to influence the crowd from the top of your soapbox, you dare not disdain the poets' forms of speech and the machinery of their eloquence. Go to the poets and learn metaphor and how to use it! Besides, the genius of the poet is an elastic substance, easy to handle. No conqueror has ever lacked a bard. Praising is a profession like any other, and when the poets say just what you wish, you may let them say what *they* wish. For all they want is to sing and make themselves heard. And yet, O venerable Dante, thy Muse, with its tones of ringing bronze, could surely never have been swayed to perjury.

But tell me again what you complain of in artists. The other day you blamed them for all the evils of society; you called them "dissolving elements"; you accused them of dispersing energy, of corrupting morals, of weakening the mainsprings of the will. Your denunciation did not quite come to an end, and your charges remained vague because I yielded to a foolish impulse and argued with you. I should have listened, and you might then have found better reasons. As it is, you really gave me nothing to think about, pleasant or unpleasant, and that was the first time this has ever happened between us.

[2] Famous ballerina (1804?–1884).
[3] Famous singer (1808–1836), daughter of Manuel García and sister of Pauline Viardot. *Otello* is Rossini's opera.

Is it art itself you are putting on trial? As if *it* cared what you and your friends and all the systems in the world thought about it! You're trying to snuff out a sunbeam. You can't mean that. If I had to refute you I should simply bring out the old commonplaces: flowers smell good; summer warmth is grateful; birds have feathers—and asses have much longer ears than horses.

If it isn't art you want to kill, then it can hardly be artists either, for as long as mortals believe in Jesus there must be priests, and no power on earth will keep a man from taking in his heart a vow of humility, pity, and chastity. So there must be some accidental misunderstanding here, between the sons of the new republic of Rome and those of the old Babylon. What caused it? I am in the dark. The other day one of your friends, which is to say one of ours, a true republican, declared with some seriousness that I deserved death. The devil take me if I know what he meant by it, but I am nonetheless pleased. I glory in it for all I am worth, and since that time I never fail to tell all my friends in confidence that I am a literary and political figure of the first importance, one able to disturb the leaders of his own party by his superior intellect and influence on society. This surprises my friends a little but they are kind enough to share my satisfaction.

Now let us examine the case against my colleagues in art. Not that I want to defend them; I should be afraid of being let off as innocent and thus miss the honors of martyrdom. . . . But as regards the others—what have they done, the poor dears? Apart from Lord Byron and myself, there is not one capable of encompassing the death even of a fly. Of course, I readily confess that we all deserve the name of Sophists. The new teaching has spread everywhere, as far as the legs of the ballet at the Opera. Berlioz has even made it into a fantastic symphony. Unfortunately for the ancient wisdom, when you will hear Berlioz's March to Execution, you will feel a certain tremor in your nervous system, untamed lion though you may be; and it is possible that you will start to roar exactly as when you are trying to save Desdemona from Otello. It will be hard on me as your companion, for I have a reputation to maintain as a sober subscriber to the Conservatoire concerts. So the least you can do is to confess that this new music is rather better than that which we used to have in Sparta under Lycurgus. . . .

You're going to say that I am not being serious. I *am* serious. Berlioz is a great composer, a man of genius, a true artist. And since his name comes apropos, let me say I am delighted to have the chance of telling you that he is a real artist, for I see you have no notion of it. When we argued the other day you mentioned several pseudo-artists and railed at them. There was a leather man, a dealer in furs, a peer of the realm, an apothecary. There were others (more famous, according to you) of whom I had never heard. I can see that you take shadows for real men, stockbrokers for true artists, and our garrets for pleasure domes.

Now Berlioz *is* an artist. He is poor, proud, and courageous. Maybe he is scoundrel enough to think to himself that all the peoples of the universe are not as important as a chromatic scale used in the right place—just as I happen to prefer a white hyacinth to the crown jewels. But bear in mind that a man can hold such crazy ideas and yet not be the enemy of the human race. You are all for blue laws, as Berlioz is for sixteenth notes and I am for flower gardens—each to his taste.

When the time comes to build the Great City of the Mind, you may be sure everyone will help build it according to his powers: Berlioz with pick and shovel, I with my golden toothpick, the rest with their two arms and their will. But the New Jerusalem will, I trust, have days of rest and joy, and it will be permitted to some to go back to their pianos, and to others to cultivate their gardens—each innocently following his capacities and tastes.

What are you yourself guilty of, pray tell, when you contemplate the heavens at midnight, poeticizing to the rest of us about the galaxy? What if I should interrupt you in your sublimities with the stupid and brutal question, "What use is it? Why waste your brain cells on conjecture? Will it feed and clothe anybody?" You would answer that it feeds noble emotions and renews mystical enthusiasm in those who painfully toil for the good of mankind. It helps them to hope, to dream of the Deity, and to rise courageously above the petty miseries of human affairs by fixing their thoughts on the future Utopia. What made you what you are, Everard, if not the habit of dreaming at night? What gave you the strength to continue so long amid trouble and thankless toil, if not the religious enthusiasm of the artist? And it is you, the most candid, lovable, and unworldly among men of genius, who wage war on the singing priests of your own God! You are Saul and you want to kill David because he plays the harp so well that in listening to him you are transported.

LETTERS FROM A TRAVELER (1835)

SERGEI PROKOFIEV

※

Statement to the Soviet

Because the condition of my health deprives me of the opportunity to attend and to participate in the general meeting of composers, I wish to express in this letter, which I ask you to read at the meeting, my thought concerning the decision of the Central Committee of the Party of February 10, 1948.

The decision of the Central Committee of February 10, 1948, has separated the rotten threads from the healthy ones in the creative work of composers. No matter how painful it is for many composers, myself included, I agree to the resolution of the Central Committee, which establishes the condition for making the whole organism of Soviet music healthy. The resolution is especially valuable because it exposes a formalistic direction foreign to the Soviet people, a direction leading to the impoverishment and downfall of music, and with great clarity shows us the goals which we must reach for the best interests of the Soviet people.

I shall talk of myself. Elements of formalism were already peculiar to my music fifteen or twenty years ago.

The contagion appeared evidently from contact with a number of Western friends. After the exposure by *Pravda* of formalistic mistakes in the Shostakovich opera, I thought a great deal about the creative manner of my music and came to the conclusion that such a direction was incorrect. As a result, there followed a search for clear and more expressive language. In a number of my following works, *Alexander Nevsky, Zdravitza, Romeo and Juliet,* the Fourth Symphony, I attempted to liberate my work from the element of formalism, and I consider I have succeeded to a certain extent. The existence of formalism in several of my compositions is probably explained by a certain complacency and by insufficiently clear recognition that it is totally unwanted by our people. However, after the resolution which has shaken to the depths our whole society of composers it became apparent exactly what specific music is needed by our people, and the ways of curing the formalistic ailment have become clear.

I have never doubted the importance of melody. I like melody very much, and I consider it the most important element in music, and I labor many years on the improvement of its quality in my compositions. The most difficult task for a composer is to find a melody comprehensible even to the uninitiated audience. Here he is confronted with many dangers. He can fall into trivial or mundane paths, or into rewriting that which has already been composed. For this reason, the composing of more complicated melodies is considerably easier. It sometimes happens that the composer works over his melody and corrects it for so long that, without noticing it, he makes it extremely complicated and loses its simplicity. In the process of work, I fell into this trap.

When composing, there must be special vigilance that the melody remain simple but, at the same time, does not become cheap, sweet, or imitative. This is easier to say than to achieve. And all my efforts will be directed to making these words more than a mere formula, enabling me to apply them in my future works.

I am also guilty of atonality, which is often related to formalism, although I must confess with happiness that I began to yearn for tonal music long ago. Then I felt that the construction of musical composition "in tone" is construction of the building on a solid base, but construction "without tone" is construction on the sand. Besides, the greater range of opportunity in tonal and distonal music than in atonal and chromatic music is especially well demonstrated by that impasse in which Schönberg and his followers find themselves. In some of my compositions of recent years individual atonal moments can be found. Without feeling any special sympathy for this device, I still use it, particularly for contrast, and to accent tonal passages. In the future I hope to overcome this device.

In my operatic creations I am often reproached when using a recitative rather than a singing line. I like the stage as such very much. I consider that a man having come to the opera has a right to demand impressions not only for the ear but also for the eye. (Otherwise he would not have gone to an opera but to a concert.) But movement on the stage can be better adapted to recitative, whereas singing to a certain degree demands immobility on the stage. I remember how painful it was to look at the stage during some Wagnerian operas, when for the duration of a whole act of about an hour in length not a single person moved. This very fear of immobility has prevented my concentration on singing for a long time. In connection with the resolution, I meticulously considered this question and came to the conclusion that in each opera libretto there exist passages absolutely demanding recitative, and passages absolutely demanding singing. But there are also certain passages, and these passages require an enormous place, sometimes as much as half of the whole opera, which the composer may interpret according to his own wish, either by recitative or by aria. Let us take, for example, Tatyana's letter from *Eugene Onegin;* it would have been very easy to write a large part in recitative, but Tchaikovsky has used his musical language in the direction of singing and has presented the whole letter as a great aria, which has the advantage that it is performed with some simultaneous action on the stage. In this manner it gives food not only for the ear but also for the eye. It is in this direction that I wish to place my work on my new opera on a contemporary Soviet subject, *The Story of a Real Man* by Polevoy.

I was greatly pleased by the instruction in the resolution on the desirability of polyphony, especially in choir and ensemble singing. This is a really interesting problem for a composer, and a real pleasure for the listener. In the above-mentioned opera I intend to introduce trios, duets, and counterpoint development of choir, for which I make use of the extremely interesting notes of northern Russian folksongs. The clear melodies and as much as possible simple harmonic language, such are other elements which I will try to obtain in this opera.

In conclusion, I should like to express my gratitude to our Party for the clear decisions of the resolution, which help me to find a musical language comprehensible to our people, worthy of our people and of our great country.

ON SOVIET MUSIC: DOCUMENTS (1948)

HECTOR BERLIOZ

→≫ ≪←

An Interview with the Police

We had hardly finished paying our musicians, copyists, printers, instrument makers, masons, roofers, joiners, carpenters, upholsterers, ushers, and guards when the Prefect of Police, who had charged us the modest sum of 1238 francs for his men—at the Opera the charge is but 80 francs—summoned us urgently before him.

"What is it about?" I asked my colleague Strauss.[1] "Have you any idea?"

"Not the least."

"Perhaps M. Delessert is conscience-stricken at having made us pay so dear for his useless minions. Could he be thinking of a refund?

"Not likely!"

We come before the Prefect, who addresses me. "Sir! It grieves me to say that you have committed a very serious offense!"

"Pray, what is that?" I rejoined in astonishment.

"You have surreptitiously added to the program of your Festival Concert a selection calculated to arouse political passions of a sort the government wants to allay and indeed suppress. I refer to the chorus from *Charles VI,* which was not listed in the first announcements of the concert.[2] The Minister of Interior has cause to be gravely annoyed by the demonstrations which that chorus provoked, and I am entirely on his side in the matter."

[1] A French impresario unrelated to the Viennese Strausses.

[2] The chorus occurs in Act III, scene 2, of the opera by C. and G. Delavigne, music by Halévy, first performed on March 17, 1843. The provocative lines are: "Down with tyrants! Never, never in France will the English rule." The greater part of the audience at Berlioz' concert, several thousand strong, sang the words in unison with the performers, presumably in protest against the government's pro-English policy.

"Your Honor," I replied as coolly as I could, "your supposition is altogether wrong. It is indeed true that the selection from *Charles VI* did not appear on the very first announcements, but I learned that M. Halévy felt aggrieved at not being represented on an occasion when nearly all the great composers of our time were being played. I therefore consented to his publisher's suggestion and added the chorus, on account of its suitability for a large body of singers such as I had. That was the sole reason for the choice. Personally I have not the slightest sympathy with the outbursts of nationalism that may occur in 1844 about a scene that goes back to the days of Charles VI.[3] As for the 'surreptitious addition' of that scene to my program, the charge is so little founded that the incriminated piece has figured on all the placards in Paris for more than eight days. It was posted all during that time on the very walls of your Prefecture. Be good enough to entertain no doubt whatever of this fact and to disabuse the Minister of Interior accordingly."

M. Delessert, a trifle abashed, declared himself satisfied, and even excused himself for the unmerited rebuke he had inflicted upon me. But from that day forth a censorship of concert programs has been established. One may not now sing in public a parlor song by Bérat or by Mlle. Puget without an authorization from the Minister of Interior countersigned by a Police Commissioner.

MEMOIRS (1844)

[3] That is, the days of Agincourt (1415), when Henry V of England made himself king of France.

MOLIERE

⇢⇢⇢ ⇠⇠⇠

Patron and Professional

ACT I

The overture is played by a large number of instruments, and in the center of the stage the Music Student is seen seated at a table, composing a melody which M. Jourdain has ordered for a musical entertainment.

MUSIC TEACHER, *speaking to his musicians:* Come here, go into that room and rest while we wait for him to show up.

DANCING MASTER, *speaking to the dancers:* And you, too, over on this side.

MUSIC TEACHER, *to the Music Student:* Is it finished?

STUDENT: Yes.

MUSIC TEACHER: Let's see. . . . Yes, that's fine.

DANCING MASTER: Is it something new?

MUSIC TEACHER: Yes, it's a melody for a serenade which I've had him compose while we're waiting for our man to wake up.

DANCING MASTER: May I see what it's like?

MUSIC TEACHER: You'll hear it, with dialogue, when he comes down. He won't be long.

DANCING MASTER: Our duties, yours and mine, are nothing to sneeze at any more.

MUSIC TEACHER: You're right. We have found just the man for us. This Jourdain, with his notions of nobility and fashion, means a neat little income for both of us. I wish the world were full of people like him.

DANCING MASTER: Not altogether. For my part, I could wish that he knew a little more than he does about the things we do for him.

MUSIC TEACHER: It's true he knows little but he pays much, and right now that's what our two arts of music and dancing need more than anything else.

DANCING MASTER: Well, I must say that I feed pretty well on praise. Applause goes to my heart, and I insist that in all the arts it's torture to perform for fools and to receive nothing but stupid philistinism for the pains of creation. You cannot deny that it's more fun to work for people who have some appreciation of art, people who can see the fine points and know how to applaud them, and so make a man enjoy his work by flattering compliments. Yes indeed, the most agreeable reward is to have an intelligent audience recognize and like what we do; nothing better than enlightened praise! Nothing, in my opinion, repays us better for all our effort.

MUSIC TEACHER: Granted. I enjoy praise too. But incense isn't food. Pure praise never paid the rent. You have to mix it with something more solid, and the best manner of praising I know is to do it in the palm of my hand. You are, of course, absolutely right about Jourdain. His notions are shallow, he says the wrong thing about everything and applauds at the wrong time, but his money is a great corrective, in excellent taste, his approval makes a clinking noise, and as you can see for yourself, this ignorant businessman counts for more in our lives than the cultivated lord who introduced us here.

DANCING MASTER: There's something in what you say, but I think you put a little too much stress on money. Self-interest is so low a thing that a well-bred man must not betray a passion for it.

MUSIC TEACHER: Still you readily take the cash when our good man hands it out.

DANCING MASTER: Of course. But I don't make it my sole blessedness. And I wish that he had good taste as well as cash.

MUSIC TEACHER: So would I. That's what you and I are trying to impart just as hard as we can. He gives us a chance to make ourselves known and he pays to have us produce what others will praise and enjoy—a fair exchange.

DANCING MASTER: Here he comes.

Enter Jourdain, in his dressing gown and nightcap, two valets, some musicians and dancers.

JOURDAIN: Well, gentlemen! What about it? Will you show me your little trifle?

DANCING MASTER: I *beg* your pardon, what little trifle?

JOURDAIN: You know: your prologue or dialogue of song and dance.

DANCING MASTER: Well, well!

MUSIC TEACHER: We're quite ready, M. Jourdain.

JOURDAIN: I kept you waiting a little, because I was being fitted out like people of quality, and my tailor had sent me silk stockings which I thought I never could pull on.

MUSIC TEACHER: We are here, M. Jourdain, to await your pleasure.

JOURDAIN: Well, don't either of you go until they bring me my suit so you can see me in it.

DANCING MASTER: Whatever you say.

JOURDAIN: You will see me properly attired from head to foot.

MUSIC TEACHER: We do not doubt it in the least, sir.

JOURDAIN: I had this Indian print made up. . . .

DANCING MASTER: It's lovely indeed.

JOURDAIN: My tailor told me that people of quality dress this way in the morning.

MUSIC TEACHER: It's most becoming.

JOURDAIN: Hey there! Valet! Both valets!

FIRST VALET: What is it, sir?

JOURDAIN: Nothing. I just wanted to see if you could hear me. *Turning to the two teachers:* What do you think of their liveries?

DANCING MASTER: Magnificent, magnificent.

JOURDAIN, *half opening his gown to show his red velvet breeches and green velvet vest:* I had this informal suit made for my morning devotions.

MUSIC TEACHER: It's very elegant, very.

JOURDAIN: Valet!

VALET: Yes, sir.

JOURDAIN: The other valet.

SECOND VALET: Yes, sir.

JOURDAIN: Hold my gown. *To the two artists*: How do you think I look?

DANCING MASTER: Very well, M. Jourdain; you couldn't look better.

JOURDAIN: Now about this little trifle of yours.

MUSIC TEACHER: First I'd like to play for you an air which he (*pointing to the music student*) has just composed for the serenade you have ordered. He is one of my students, and he is particularly talented at this sort of thing.

JOURDAIN: Good enough, but you shouldn't have a *student* compose the music I order. You yourself were by no means too talented to do it yourself.

MUSIC TEACHER: Oh, but you must not deceive yourself. Student in this case doesn't mean what student usually means. This scholar is of the kind that know as much as the great masters. What he has written is as beautiful as can be. Just listen!

JOURDAIN: Give me my gown, so I can listen better. Wait! I think I'd hear better without it. No! Bring it back and put it on. It will be more suitable.

GIRL MUSICIAN, *singing:*

> Day and night, I languish and pine from distress
> Since your eyes, O Iris! have pierced me of late;
> But if someone who loves you these rigors oppress,
> Pray what would you do to a person you hate?

JOURDAIN: A depressing sort of song. It puts me to sleep. Can't you liven it up here and there?

MUSIC TEACHER: But, sir, the music must fit the words.

JOURDAIN: Not long ago I learned a very pretty one. Let's see—how did it go?

DANCING MASTER: I'm sure I don't know.

JOURDAIN: It had sheep in it—

DANCING MASTER: Sheep?

JOURDAIN: Yes. I have it! *He sings:*

> I thought Jenny a dear,
> I thought Jenny as sweet

> As the lambs that do bleat.
> But she's proven, I fear,
> Her heartless deceit:
> She's more cruel to me
> Than a tigress could be!

There! Isn't it pretty?

MUSIC TEACHER: Oh, very pretty.

DANCING MASTER: And you sing it so well!

JOURDAIN: Never had a music lesson in my life.

MUSIC TEACHER: You should study music, M. Jourdain; you've taken up dancing and there's a very close connection between the two—

DANCING MASTER: They broaden the mind for the appreciation of beauty.

JOURDAIN: Do society people study music?

MUSIC TEACHER: It goes without saying.

JOURDAIN: Then I will. But I don't know how I'll find time, because, besides the fencing teacher, I've also hired a master of philosophy who is to start with me this morning.

MUSIC TEACHER: Philosophy is something, no doubt, M. Jourdain, but music, music!

DANCING MASTER: Music and dancing . . . music and dancing, that's all you need to know!

MUSIC TEACHER: There is nothing so useful to the State as music.

DANCING MASTER: And nothing is so necessary to man as dancing.

MUSIC TEACHER: Without music a State cannot survive.

DANCING MASTER: Without dancing man cannot act.

MUSIC TEACHER: All the political upheavals, all one sees in the world, occur only from a failure to learn music.

DANCING MASTER: All the miseries of man, all the disasters recorded in history—the mistakes of statesmen, the blunders of great generals—all came to pass only from not knowing how to dance.

JOURDAIN: How so?

MUSIC TEACHER: Well, doesn't war result from discord among men?

JOURDAIN: True.

MUSIC TEACHER: Then if all men learned music, would this not remove discord, and bring about concord, or universal peace?

JOURDAIN: You are right.

DANCING MASTER: When a man commits a fault, either in the conduct of his affairs, or in the governing of a state, or in the commanding of an army, does not one say, "That was the wrong step to take"?

JOURDAIN: Yes, that's what people say.

DANCING MASTER: Now, can taking the wrong step result from anything except ignorance of dancing?

JOURDAIN: True! You are both absolutely right.

DANCING MASTER: We only meant to show you the virtue and usefulness of music and dancing.

JOURDAIN: I quite understand.

MUSIC TEACHER: Would you now care to see our productions?

JOURDAIN: Yes.

MUSIC TEACHER: You will remember, mine is just a little attempt I once made to show how many different feelings music can express.

JOURDAIN: Very good.

MUSIC TEACHER, *to the musicians:* Come forward. *To Jourdain:* You must imagine them dressed as shepherds—

JOURDAIN: Why always shepherds? That's all one sees everywhere one goes.

MUSIC TEACHER: It's indispensable when you want to make people talk through the medium of music. Verisimilitude calls for shepherds. They have sung and piped from time immemorial, whereas it's hardly likely that princes or merchants should converse to music or express their sentiments in song. Shepherds play on pipes, you know, and sing to themselves when they're alone.

JOURDAIN: Never mind, never mind, let's get on. *Here follows a pastoral trio executed by one female and two male voices.* Finished? Is that the end?

MUSIC TEACHER: Yes.

JOURDAIN: Not badly put together; there were one or two very good lines.

DANCING MASTER: And now may I present my attempt to bring together the most varied steps and the most graceful movements of which dancing is capable?

JOURDAIN: Is it still shepherds?

DANCING MASTER: Whatever you fancy. *To dancers:* Let's begin. *Here follows a ballet.*

ACT II

JOURDAIN: Very clever, I must say. Those people certainly know how to get about.

MUSIC TEACHER: And when we combine the dancing with the music, you will find the effect still finer. This ballet we have fashioned for you will strike you as something really delightful.

JOURDAIN: It's for this afternoon, don't forget. The person for whom all this is intended will do me the honor of coming here to dine this evening.

DANCING MASTER: Everything is ready, M. Jourdain.

MUSIC TEACHER: But I might add that even this is not nearly enough! A man like you, who is interested in magnificence and who has a bent toward the beautiful, ought to give musicales every Wednesday —or every Thursday.

JOURDAIN: Is that what society people do?

MUSIC TEACHER: Why, of course.

JOURDAIN: Then I will too. Is it nice?

MUSIC TEACHER: Unquestionably. You'll need at least three voices— soprano, contralto, and bass, accompanied by a bass viol, a theorbo, and a clavichord to play the continuo, and two violins for the refrains.

JOURDAIN: And a marine trumpet.[1] That's my favorite instrument, it's so smooth.

MUSIC TEACHER: You had better leave it to us.

JOURDAIN: Anyhow, don't forget to send me some men this afternoon to sing while we're at table.

MUSIC TEACHER: Rest assured that you will have everything you need.

---

[1] Not a brass instrument, as might be supposed, but a single-stringed "nun's violin," the prototype of all bowed instruments.

JOURDAIN: Above all, let the ballet be grand.

MUSIC TEACHER: You will be satisfied, I promise you. Among other things, they will dance some minuets—you'll see—

JOURDAIN: Ah! The minuet's my dance. I want you to see me do it. Come, dancing master!

DANCING MASTER: Your hat, sir, if you please. *Jourdain reaches for his valet's hat and puts it over his own nightcap. The teacher takes his hands and sings a minuet:* La, la, la, la, la, la . . . try to keep in step. La, la, la, la, la, your right foot!—La, la, la . . . don't move your shoulders so much, la, la, la . . . your arms look as though amputated, la, la, la . . . your head up! Turn the toes out, straighten up the whole body!

JOURDAIN: Oh!

MUSIC TEACHER: That couldn't have been better.

JOURDAIN: By the way, show me how to bow to a Marquise. I'll have to know how this afternoon.

DANCING MASTER: The proper bow to make to a Marquise?

JOURDAIN: Yes, a Marquise named Dorimène.

DANCING MASTER: Give me your hand.

JOURDAIN: No, just do it and I'll remember.

DANCING MASTER: Very well. If you wish to bow with the utmost respect, you must first make a backward bow, then walk toward her with three bows forward, and at the third go down about the level of her knees.

JOURDAIN: Show me a little. *The dancing master makes three bows.* Right.

Enter Valet.

VALET: Sir, the fencing master is here.

JOURDAIN: Tell him to come in for my lesson. I want you two to watch me.

Enter Fencing Master, followed by valet holding two foils. The Master puts one in Jourdain's hand.

FENCING MASTER: Now, sir, first we bow. Your body straight. Lean just a little on the left thigh. Your legs not so far apart. Your feet on a line. Your wrist opposite your hip. The tip of the foil level with your shoulder. The arm not quite so extended. The left hand at the height of the eye. The left shoulder less hunched. The head straight and the glance assured. Now, advance! Keep the body steady. Now, a thrust in quart . . . and follow through. One, two. . . . Steady! Once again, full strength. Jump back! When you thrust, M. Jourdain, thrust with the foil, and flatten out the body! One, two . . . now thrust in tierce and follow through. Forward . . . body firm . . . forward . . . thrust from where you are. One, two, take position again. Once more . . . leap back . . . en garde, M. Jourdain, en garde! *The Fencing Master lunges at him two or three times, all the while shouting, "En garde, en garde."*

JOURDAIN: Oh!

MUSIC TEACHER: You are marvelous, M. Jourdain.

FENCING MASTER: As I told you before, the whole secret of fencing lies in two things—giving and not receiving—and, as I demonstrated to you the other day, it is impossible that you should receive if you know how to turn your enemy's foil away from the line of your body; and this, in turn, depends altogether upon a little movement of the wrist, either inward or outward.

JOURDAIN: So that, according to you, one is sure to kill his man, and not be killed, even though one has no heart for the business?

FENCING MASTER: Precisely. Didn't you watch the demonstration?

JOURDAIN: I did.

FENCING MASTER: And hence the high regard in which we fencers must be held in the State. The art of fencing is thereby shown superior to all the useless arts, such as dancing or music or—

DANCING MASTER: Just a moment, master swordsman. Kindly speak of dancing with more respect.

MUSIC TEACHER: And remember the proper way to treat the excellence of music.

FENCING MASTER: Well, I must say you are an amusing pair to pretend to compare your arts to mine.

MUSIC TEACHER: My, what self-complacency!

DANCING MASTER: A regular baboon with his chest protector!

FENCING MASTER: Why, you little jumping jack, I'll teach you how to dance! *To Music Teacher:* As for you, musicaster, I'll soon show you how to sing.

DANCING MASTER: Ironmonger, I can beat you at your trade.

JOURDAIN, *to the Dancing Master:* You must be mad to quarrel with a man who knows tierce from quarte and kills a man according to demonstration.

DANCING MASTER: A fig for his demonstrations, and his tierces and his quartes!

JOURDAIN: Gently I tell you.

FENCING MASTER, *to the Dancing Master:* What was that, you whippersnapper?

JOURDAIN: Here! Here! Master Fencer!

DANCING MASTER: What was that, old cart horse?

JOURDAIN: Dancing Master, please!

FENCING MASTER: If I ever get my hands on you—

JOURDAIN: Not so loud!

DANCING MASTER: If my hands find their way—

JOURDAIN: Easy, easy.

FENCING MASTER: I'll give you a polishing—

JOURDAIN: For pity's sake!

DANCING MASTER: When you get from me the drubbing that—

JOURDAIN: I *beg* of you!

MUSIC TEACHER: Please, M. Jourdain, allow us to teach him manners.

JOURDAIN: Good God! Why don't you stop!

Enter Teacher of Philosophy.

JOURDAIN: Welcome, welcome, Philosopher. You are just in time with your philosophy. Come and pacify these three.

TEACHER OF PHILOSOPHY: What is the matter here, gentlemen?

JOURDAIN: They have had words over the respective merits of their professions and have nearly come to blows.

TEACHER OF PHILOSOPHY: But gentlemen!—Is this a proper way to behave? Have you not read Seneca's "Treatise on Anger"? Is there anything lower or more shameful than a passion which makes of man a ferocious beast? And should not reason always govern our actions?

DANCING MASTER: How do you mean? He comes here and starts calling us names, expressing contempt for my art, which is dancing, and for his, which is music—

TEACHER OF PHILOSOPHY: The wise man is above all the names that anyone may call him. And the best answer to make to insults is patient moderation.

FENCING MASTER: But they both had the audacity to compare their professions to mine!

TEACHER OF PHILOSOPHY: Why should that raise your bile? It is unbecoming in man to quarrel about fame and position. The sole distinction between one man and the next is wisdom and virtue.

DANCING MASTER: Still, I maintain that the art of dancing is one which cannot be esteemed too highly.

MUSIC TEACHER: And I that music is an art that has been venerated through the ages.

FENCING MASTER: While I keep telling them that fencing is the greatest and most indispensable of the arts.

TEACHER OF PHILOSOPHY: And what of philosophy, gentlemen? I must say I find all three of you somewhat impertinent to speak in front of me with such arrogance, and to brazenly give the name of arts and sciences to things not even worthy of the name of skill and which really belong under the common name of trades—that of cutthroat, fiddler, and acrobat.

FENCING MASTER: Out with you, pseudo-philosopher!

MUSIC TEACHER: Out, you heavy-handed highbrow!

DANCING MASTER: Out, you vulgar blockhead!

TEACHER OF PHILOSOPHY: What! Bumpkins that you are! *The Philosopher rushes upon them, but all three pummel him in unison.*

JOURDAIN: My dear Philosopher!

TEACHER OF PHILOSOPHY: Loathsome, impudent louts!

JOURDAIN: My dear Philosopher!

FENCING MASTER: Scurvy animal!

JOURDAIN: Gentlemen, please!

DANCING MASTER: Academic ass!

JOURDAIN: Gentlemen!

TEACHER OF PHILOSOPHY: Scoundrels!

JOURDAIN: My dear Philosopher!

MUSIC TEACHER: The devil take the meddler!

JOURDAIN: Gentlemen!

TEACHER OF PHILOSOPHY: Rascals, traitors, rogues, convicts!

JOURDAIN: My dear Philosopher! Gentlemen! My dear Philosopher! Gentlemen! My dear Philosopher! *Exeunt all four, struggling.* Oh, well! Fight to your hearts' content. *I'm* not going to spoil this dressing gown to keep the peace among you. I'd be a fool to interfere and get a knock on the head for my pains.

LE BOURGEOIS GENTILHOMME (1670)

P. T. BARNUM

-»» «««-

The Jenny Lind Enterprise

The figures supplied in great detail by Barnum show that Jenny Lind
gave a hundred concerts in twenty cities during the season 1850–1851, and
earned $175,000; Barnum, half a million.

And now I come to speak of an undertaking which my worst enemy
will admit was bold in its conception, complete in its development,
and astounding in its success. It was an enterprise never before or
since equaled in managerial annals. As I recall it now, I almost
tremble at the seeming temerity of the attempt. That I am proud of
it I freely confess. It placed me before the world in a new light; it
gained me many warm friends in new circles; it was in itself a fortune to me—I risked much but I made more.

It was in October 1849 that I conceived the idea of bringing Jenny
Lind to this country. I had never heard her sing, inasmuch as she
arrived in London a few weeks after I left that city with General
Tom Thumb. Her reputation, however, was sufficient for me. I
usually jump at conclusions, and almost invariably find that my
first impressions are correct. It struck me, when I first thought of
this speculation, that if properly managed it must prove immensely
profitable, provided I could engage the "Swedish Nightingale" on
any terms within the range of reason. As it was a great undertaking,
I considered the matter seriously for several days, and all my "cipher-
ings" and calculations gave but one result—immense success.

Reflecting that very much would depend upon the manner in
which she should be brought before the public, I saw that my task
would be an exceedingly arduous one. It was possible, I knew, that
circumstances might occur which would make the enterprise disastrous. "The public" is a very strange animal, and although a good

knowledge of human nature will generally lead a caterer of amusements to hit the people, they are fickle, and ofttimes perverse. A slight
misstep in the management of a public entertainment frequently
wrecks the most promising enterprise. But I had marked the "divine
Jenny" as a sure card, and to secure the prize I began to cast about
for a competent agent.

I found in Mr. John Hall Wilton, an Englishman who had visited
this country with the Sax-Horn Players, the best man whom I knew
for that purpose. A few minutes sufficed to make the arrangement
with him, by which I was to pay but little more than his expenses
if he failed in his mission, but by which also he was to be paid a
large sum if he succeeded in bringing Jenny Lind to our shores,
on any terms within a liberal schedule which I set forth to him in
writing:

New York, *November* 6, 1849

Mr. J. Hall Wilton:

Sir:—In reply to your proposal to attempt a negotiation with Mlle.
Jenny Lind to visit the United States professionally, I propose to enter into
an arrangement with her to the following effect: I will engage to pay all
her expenses from Europe, provide for and pay for one principal tenor
and one pianist, their salaries not exceeding together one hundred and fifty
dollars per night; to support for her a carriage, two servants, and a friend
to accompany her and superintend her finances. I will furthermore pay
all and every expense appertaining to her appearance before the public,
and give her half of the gross receipts arising from concerts or operas. I
will engage to travel with her personally and attend to the arrangements,
provided she will undertake to give not less than eighty nor more than
one hundred and fifty concerts, or nights' performances.

Phineas T. Barnum

I was at my Museum in Philadelphia when Wilton arrived in
New York, February 19, 1850. He immediately telegraphed to me,
in the cipher we had agreed upon, that he had signed an engagement
with Jenny Lind, by which she was to commence her concerts in
America in the following September. I was somewhat startled by
this sudden announcement; and feeling that the time to elapse before her arrival was so long that it would be policy to keep the en-

gagement private for a few months, I immediately telegraphed him not to mention it to any person, and that I would meet him the next day in New York.

When we reflect how thoroughly Jenny Lind, her musical powers, her character, and wonderful successes, were subsequently known by all classes in this country as well as throughout the civilized world, it is difficult to realize that, at the time this engagement was made, she was comparatively unknown on this side the water. We can hardly credit the fact that millions of persons in America had never heard of her, that other millions had merely read her name, but had no distinct idea of who or what she was. Only a small portion of the public was really aware of her great musical triumphs in the Old World, and this portion was confined almost entirely to musical people, travelers who had visited the Old World, and the conductors of the press.

The next morning I started for New York. On arriving at Princeton we met the New York cars, and, purchasing the morning papers, I was surprised to find in them a full account of my engagement with Jenny Lind. However, this premature announcement could not be recalled, and I put the best face on the matter. Anxious to learn how this communication would strike the public mind, I informed the conductor, whom I well knew, that I had made an engagement with Jenny Lind, and that she would surely visit this country in the following August.

"Jenny Lind! Is she a dancer?" asked the conductor.

I informed him who and what she was, but his question had chilled me as if his words were ice. Really, thought I, if this is all that a man in the capacity of a railroad conductor between Philadelphia and New York knows of the greatest songstress in the world, I am not sure that six months will be too long a time for me to occupy in enlightening the public in regard to her merits.

I had an interview with Wilton and learned from him that, in accordance with the agreement, it would be requisite for me to place the entire amount stipulated, $187,500, in the hands of the London bankers. I at once resolved to ratify the agreement, and immediately sent the necessary documents to Miss Lind and Messrs. Benedict and Belletti.

I then began to prepare the public mind, through the newspapers, for the reception of the great songstress. How effectually this was done is still within the remembrance of the American public. As a sample of the manner in which I accomplished my purpose, I present the following extract from my first letter, which appeared in the New York papers of February 22, 1850:

> Perhaps I may not make any money by this enterprise; but I assure you that if I knew I should not make a farthing profit, I would ratify the engagement, so anxious am I that the United States should be visited by a lady whose vocal powers have never been approached by any other human being, and whose character is charity, simplicity, and goodness personified.
>
> Miss Lind has great anxiety to visit America. She speaks of this country and its institutions in the highest terms of praise. In her engagement with me (which includes Havana), she expressly reserves the right to give charitable concerts whenever she thinks proper.
>
> Since her debut in England, she has given to the poor from her own private purse more than the whole amount which I have engaged to pay her, and the proceeds of concerts for charitable purposes in Great Britain, where she has sung gratuitously, have realized more than ten times that amount.

The people soon began to talk about Jenny Lind, and I was particularly anxious to obtain a good portrait of her. Fortunately a fine opportunity occurred. One day, while I was sitting in the office of the Museum, a foreigner approached me with a small package under his arm. He informed me in broken English that he was a Swede, and said he was an artist, who had just arrived from Stockholm, where Jenny Lind had kindly given him a number of sittings, and he now had with him the portrait of her which he had painted upon copper. He unwrapped the package and showed me a beautiful picture of the Swedish Nightingale, enclosed in an elegant gilt frame, about fourteen by twenty inches. It was just the thing I wanted; the price was fifty dollars, and I purchased it at once. Upon showing it to an artist friend the same day, he quietly assured me that it was a cheap lithograph pasted on a tin back, neatly varnished, and made to appear like a fine oil painting. The intrinsic value of the picture did not exceed thirty-seven and one-half cents!

≫≫ ≪≪

On Wednesday morning, August 21, 1850, Jenny Lind and Messrs. Benedict and Belletti set sail from Liverpool in the steamship *Atlantic,* in which I had long before engaged the necessary accommodations, and on board of which I had shipped a piano for their use. They were accompanied by my agent, Mr. Wilton, and also by Miss Ahmansen and Mr. Max Hjortzberg, cousins of Miss Lind, the latter being her secretary; also by her two servants, and the valet of Messrs. Benedict and Belletti.

It was expected that the steamer would arrive on Sunday, September 1, but, determined to meet the songstress on her arrival whenever it might be, I went to Staten Island on Saturday, and slept at the hospitable residence of my friend, Dr. A. Sidney Doane, who was at that time the Health Officer of the Port of New York. A few minutes before twelve o'clock, on Sunday morning, the *Atlantic* hove in sight, and immediately afterwards, through the kindness of my friend Doane, I was on board the ship and had taken Jenny Lind by the hand.

After a few moments' conversation she asked me when and where I had heard her sing.

"I never had the pleasure of seeing you before in my life," I replied.

"How is it possible that you dared risk so much money on a person whom you never heard sing?" she asked in surprise.

"I risked it on your reputation, which in musical matters I would much rather trust than my own judgment," I replied.

I may as well state that although I relied prominently upon Jenny Lind's reputation as a great musical *artiste,* I took largely into my estimate of her success with all classes of the American public her character for extraordinary benevolence and generosity. Without this peculiarity in her disposition, I never would have dared make the engagement which I did, as I felt sure that there were multitudes of individuals in America who would be prompted to attend her concerts by this feeling alone.

Thousands of persons covered the shipping and piers, and other thousands had congregated on the wharf at Canal Street to see her. The wildest enthusiasm prevailed as the steamer approached the dock. So great was the rush on a sloop near the steamer's berth that one man, in his zeal to obtain a good view, accidentally tumbled overboard, amid the shouts of those near him. Miss Lind witnessed this incident and was much alarmed. He was, however, soon rescued, after taking to himself a cold duck instead of securing a view of the Nightingale. A bower of green trees, decorated with beautiful flags, was discovered on the wharf, together with two triumphal arches, on one of which was inscribed, "Welcome, Jenny Lind!" The second was surmounted by the American eagle and bore the inscription, "Welcome to America!" These decorations were not produced by magic, and I do not know that I can reasonably find fault with those who suspected I had a hand in their erection. My private carriage was in waiting, and Jenny Lind was escorted to it by Captain West. The rest of the musical party entered the carriage, and, mounting the box at the driver's side, I directed him to the Irving House.[1] I took that seat as a legitimate advertisement, and my presence on the outside of the carriage aided those who filled the windows and sidewalks along the whole route in coming to the conclusion that Jenny Lind had arrived.

A reference to the journals of that day will show that never before had there been such enthusiasm in the City of New York, or indeed in America. Within ten minutes after our arrival at the Irving House, not less than twenty thousand persons had congregated around the entrance in Broadway, nor was the number diminished before nine o'clock in the evening. At her request I dined with her that afternoon, and when, according to European custom, she prepared to pledge me in a glass of wine, she was somewhat surprised at my saying, "Miss Lind, I do not think you can ask any other favor on earth which I would not gladly grant; but I am a teetotaler, and must beg to be permitted to drink your health and happiness in a glass of cold water."

[1] At Broadway and Chambers Street.

At twelve o'clock that night she was serenaded by the New York Musical Fund Society, numbering, on that occasion, two hundred musicians. They were escorted to the Irving House by about three hundred firemen, in their red shirts, bearing torches. There was a far greater throng in the streets than there was even during the day. The calls for Jenny Lind were so vehement that I led her through a window to the balcony. The loud cheers from the crowds lasted for several minutes, before the serenade was permitted to proceed again.

I have given the merest sketch of but a portion of the incidents of Jenny Lind's first day in America. For weeks afterwards the excitement was unabated. Her rooms were thronged by visitors, including the magnates of the land in both Church and State. The carriages of the wealthiest citizens could be seen in front of her hotel at nearly all hours of the day, and it was with some difficulty that I prevented the "fashionables" from monopolizing her altogether, and thus, as I believed, sadly marring my interests by cutting her off from the warm sympathies she had awakened among the masses. Presents of all sorts were showered upon her. Milliners, mantua-makers, and shop-keepers vied with each other in calling her attention to their wares, of which they sent her many valuable specimens, delighted if, in return, they could receive her autograph acknowledgment. Songs, quadrilles, and polkas were dedicated to her, and poets sung in her praise. We had Jenny Lind gloves, Jenny Lind bonnets, Jenny Lind riding hats, Jenny Lind shawls, mantillas, robes, chairs, sofas, pianos —in fact everything was Jenny Lind. Her movements were constantly watched, and the moment her carriage appeared at the door it was surrounded by multitudes, eager to catch a glimpse of the Swedish Nightingale.

Before her arrival I had offered two hundred dollars for a prize ode, "Greeting to America," to be sung by Jenny Lind at her first concert. Several hundred "poems" were sent in from all parts of the United States and the Canadas. The duties of the Prize Committee, in reading these effusions and making choice of the one most worthy the prize, were truly arduous. The "offerings," with perhaps a dozen exceptions, were the merest doggerel trash. The prize was awarded to Bayard Taylor for the following ode:

GREETING TO AMERICA

WORDS BY BAYARD TAYLOR—MUSIC BY JULIUS BENEDICT

I greet with a full heart the Land of the West,
 Whose Banner of Stars o'er a world is unrolled;
Whose empire o'ershadows Atlantic's wide breast,
 And opens to sunset its gateway of gold!
The land of the mountain, the land of the lake,
 And rivers that roll in magnificent tide—
Where the souls of the mighty from slumber awake,
 And hallow the soil for whose freedom they died!

Thou Cradle of Empire! though wide be the foam
 That severs the land of my fathers and thee,
I hear, from thy bosom, the welcome of home,
 For Song has a home in the hearts of the Free!
And long as thy waters shall gleam in the sun,
 And long as thy heroes remember their scars,
Be the hands of thy children united as one,
 And Peace shed her light on thy Banner of Stars! [2]

This award, although it gave general satisfaction, yet was met with disfavor by several disappointed poets, who, notwithstanding the decision of the committee, persisted in believing and declaring their own productions to be the best. This state of feeling was doubtless, in part, the cause which led to the publication, about this time, of a witty pamphlet entitled "Barnum's Parnassus; being Confidential Disclosures of the Prize Committee on the Jenny Lind Song."

Various extracts from this brochure were copied in the papers daily, and my agents scattered the work as widely as possible, thus efficiently aiding and advertising my enterprise and serving to keep up the public excitement.

---

[2] It is said that the poet's three stanzas were cut down to two, in order to make it easier for the singer to learn the words in short order.

Jenny Lind's first concert was fixed to come off at Castle Garden,[3] on Wednesday evening, September 11, and most of the tickets were sold at auction on the Saturday and Monday previous to the concert. John N. Genin, the hatter, laid the foundation of his fortune by purchasing the first ticket at two hundred and twenty-five dollars. It has been extensively reported that Mr. Genin and I are brothers-in-law but our only relations are those of business and friendship. The proprietors of the Garden saw fit to make the usual charge of one shilling to all persons who entered the premises, yet three thousand people were present at the auction. One thousand tickets were sold on the first day for an aggregate sum of $10,141.

On the Tuesday after her arrival I informed Miss Lind that I wished to make a slight alteration in our agreement. "What is it?" she asked in surprise.

"I am convinced," I replied, "that our enterprise will be much more successful than either of us anticipated. I wish, therefore, to stipulate that you shall receive not only a thousand dollars for each concert, besides all the expenses, as heretofore agreed on, but after taking fifty-five hundred per night for expenses and my services, the balance shall be equally divided between us."

Jenny looked at me with astonishment. She could not comprehend my proposition. After I had repeated it, and she fully understood its import, she cordially grasped me by the hand and exclaimed, "Mr. Barnum, you are a gentleman of honor: you are generous; it is just as Mr. Bates told me; I will sing for you as long as you please; I will sing for you in America—in Europe—anywhere!"

On Tuesday September 10, I informed Miss Lind that, judging by present appearances, her portion of the proceeds of the first concert would amount to ten thousand dollars. She immediately resolved to devote every dollar of it to charity; and, sending for Mayor Woodhull, she acted under his and my advice in selecting the various institutions among which she wished the amount to be distributed.

My arrangements of the concert room were very complete. The great parterre and gallery of Castle Garden were divided by imaginary

---

[3] Off the tip of Manhattan island, on the site of an old fort.

lines into four compartments, each of which was designated by a lamp of a different color. The tickets were printed in colors corresponding with the location which the holders were to occupy, and one hundred ushers, with rosettes and bearing wands tipped with ribbons of the several hues, enabled every individual to find his or her seat without the slightest difficulty. These arrangements were duly advertised, and every particular was also printed upon each ticket. In order to prevent confusion, the doors were opened at five o'clock, while the concert did not commence until eight. The consequence was that although about five thousand persons were present at the first concert, their entrance was marked with as much order and quiet as was ever witnessed in the assembling of a congregation at church. These precautions were observed at all the concerts given throughout the country under my administration, and the good order which always prevailed was the subject of numberless encomiums from the public and the press.

The reception of Jenny Lind on her first appearance, in point of enthusiasm, was probably never before equaled in the world. As Mr. Benedict led her toward the footlights, the entire audience rose to their feet and welcomed her with three cheers, accompanied by the waving of thousands of hats and handkerchiefs. This was by far the largest audience to which Jenny Lind had ever sung. She was evidently much agitated, but the orchestra commenced, and before she had sung a dozen notes of *"Casta Diva,"* [4] she began to recover her self-possession, and long before the *scena* was concluded, she was as calm as if she were in her own drawing room. Toward the last portion of the cavatina, the audience were so completely carried away by their feelings that the remainder of the air was drowned in a perfect tempest of acclamation. Enthusiasm had been wrought to its highest pitch, but the musical powers of Jenny Lind exceeded all the brilliant anticipations which had been formed, and her triumph was complete. At the conclusion of the concert Jenny Lind was loudly called for, and was obliged to appear three times before the audience

[4] From Bellini's *Norma.* The concert began with the *Oberon* overture and an aria for Belletti from Rossini's *Mohammed II.*

could be satisfied. They then called vociferously for "Barnum," and I reluctantly responded to their demand.

On this first night Mr. Julius Benedict firmly established with the American people his European reputation as a most accomplished conductor and musical composer; while Signor Belletti inspired an admiration which grew warmer and deeper in the minds of the American people to the end of his career in this country.

It would seem as if the Jenny Lind mania had reached its culminating point before she appeared, and I confess that I feared the anticipations of the public were too high to be realized, and hence that there would be a reaction after the first concert; but I was happily disappointed. The transcendent musical genius of the Swedish Nightingale was superior to all that fancy could paint, and the furor did not attain its highest point until she had been heard. The people were in ecstasies; the powers of editorial acumen, types, and ink were inadequate to sound her praises. The Rubicon was passed. The successful issue of the Jenny Lind enterprise was established. I think there were a hundred men in New York, the day after her first concert, who would have willingly paid me two hundred thousand dollars for my contract. I received repeated offers for an eighth, a tenth, or a sixteenth equivalent to that price. But mine had been the risk, and I was determined mine should be the triumph. So elated was I with my success, in spite of all obstacles and false prophets, that I do not think half a million of dollars would have tempted me to relinquish the enterprise.

Upon settling the receipts of the first concert, they were found to be somewhat less than I anticipated. The sums bid at the auction sales, together with the tickets purchased at private sale, amounted to more than twenty thousand dollars. It proved, however, that several of the tickets, bid off at from twelve to twenty-five dollars each, were not called for. In some instances, probably the zeal of the bidders cooled down when they came out from the scene of excitement and once more breathed the fresh sea breeze which came sweeping up from the Narrows, while perhaps, in other instances, bids were made by parties who never intended to take the tickets. I can only say, once for all, that I was never privy to a false bid, and was so particular upon that point that I would not permit one of my employees to bid on, or purchase, a ticket at auction, though requested to do so for especial friends.

The amount of money received for tickets to the first concert was $17,864.05. As this made Miss Lind's portion too small to realize the ten thousand dollars which had been announced as devoted to charity, I proposed to divide equally with her the proceeds of the first two concerts, and not count them at all in our regular engagement. Accordingly, the second concert was given September 13, and the receipts, amounting to $14,203.03, were, like those of the first concert, equally divided. Our third concert, but which, as between ourselves, we called the first regular concert, was given Tuesday, September 17, 1850.

I could fill many volumes with printed extracts which are nearly all of a similar tenor to the following unbought, unsolicited editorial article, which appeared in the *New York Herald* of September 10, 1850 (the day before the first concert given by Miss Lind in the United States):

. . . Three years ago, more or less, we heard Jenny Lind on many occasions when she made the first great sensation in Europe by her début at the London Opera House. Then she was great in power—in art—in genius; now she is greater in all. We speak from experience and conviction. Then she astonished, and pleased, and fascinated the thousands of the British aristocracy; now she will fascinate, and please, and delight, and almost make mad with musical excitement the millions of the American democracy. Tomorrow night, this new sensation—this fresh movement—this excitement excelling all former excitements—will be called into existence, when she pours out the notes of *"Casta Diva,"* and exhibits her astonishing powers—her wonderful peculiarities, that seem more of heaven than of earth—more of a voice from eternity than from the lips of a human being.

We speak soberly—seriously—calmly. The public expectation has run very high for the last week—higher than at any former period of our past musical annals. But high as it has risen, the reality—the fact—the concert—the voice and power of Jenny Lind—will far surpass all past expectation. Jenny Lind is a wonder, and a prodigy in song—and no mistake.

As usual, however, the *Herald* very soon "took it all back" and roundly abused Miss Lind and persistently attacked her manager. As usual, too, the public paid no attention to the *Herald* and doubled their patronage of the Jenny Lind concerts.

After the first month the business became thoroughly systematized, and by the help of such agents as my faithful treasurer, L. C. Stewart, and the indefatigable Le Grand Smith, my personal labors were materially relieved; but from the first concert on the eleventh of September, 1850, until the ninety-third concert on the ninth of June, 1851, a space of nine months, I did not know a waking moment that was entirely free from anxiety.

I could not hope to be exempted from trouble and perplexity in managing an enterprise which depended altogether on popular favor, and which involved great consequences to myself; but I did not expect the numerous petty annoyances which beset me, especially in the early period of the concerts. Miss Lind did not dream, nor did any one else, of the unparalleled enthusiasm that would greet her; and the first immense assembly at Castle Garden somewhat prepared her, I suspect, to listen to evil advisers. "Do you not see, Miss Lind, that Mr. Barnum is coining money out of your genius?" said they; of course she saw it, but the high-minded Swede despised and spurned the advisers who recommended her to repudiate her contract with me and take the enterprise into her own hands. I, however, suffered much from the unreasonable interference of her lawyer, Mr. John Jay, and Jenny afterwards expressed to me her regret that she had for a moment listened to the vexatious exactions of her legal counselor.

→≫ ≪←

It is not my purpose to enter into full details of all of the Lind concerts, though I have given elsewhere a transcript from the account books of my treasurer, presenting a table of the place and exact receipts of each concert. This will gratify curiosity and at the same time indicate our route of travel. Meanwhile, I devote a few pages to interesting incidents connected with Miss Lind's visit to America.

Jenny Lind's character for benevolence became so generally known that her door was beset by persons asking charity, and she was in the receipt, while in the principal cities, of numerous letters, all on the same subject. Her secretary examined and responded favorably to some of them. He undertook at first to answer them all, but finally abandoned that course in despair. I knew of many instances in which she gave sums of money to applicants, varying in amount from twenty, fifty, five hundred, to a thousand dollars, and in one instance she gave five thousand dollars to a Swedish friend.

One night, while giving a concert in Boston, a girl approached the ticket-office, and, laying down three dollars for a ticket, remarked, "There goes half a month's earnings, but I am determined to hear Jenny Lind." Miss Lind's secretary heard the remark, and a few minutes afterwards coming into her room, he laughingly related the circumstance, "Would you know the girl again?" asked Jenny with an earnest look. Upon receiving an affirmative reply, she instantly placed a twenty-dollar gold piece in his hand and said, "Poor girl! give her that with my best compliments." He at once found the girl, who cried with joy when she received the gold-piece, and heard the kind words with which the gift was accompanied.

The night after Jenny's arrival in Boston a display of fireworks was given in her honor, in front of the Revere House, after which followed a beautiful torchlight procession by the Germans of that city.

On her return from Boston to New York, Jenny, her companion, and Messrs. Benedict and Belletti, stopped at Iranistan, my residence in Bridgeport, where they remained until the following day. The morning after her arrival she took my arm and proposed a promenade through the grounds. She seemed much pleased and said, "I am astonished that you should have left such a beautiful place for the sake of traveling through the country with me."

The same day she told me in a playful mood that she had heard a most extraordinary report. "I have heard that you and I are about to be married," said she; "now how could such an absurd report ever have originated?"

"Probably from the fact that we are 'engaged,' " I replied. She enjoyed a joke and laughed heartily.

"Do you know, Mr. Barnum," said she, 'that if you had not built Iranistan, I should never have come to America for you?"

I expressed my surprise and asked her to explain.

"I had received several applications to visit the United States," she continued, "but I did not much like the appearance of the applicants, nor did I relish the idea of crossing three thousand miles of ocean; so I declined them all. But the first letter which Mr. Wilton, your agent, addressed me, was written upon a sheet headed with a beautiful engraving of Iranistan. It attracted my attention. I said to myself, a gentleman who has been so successful in his business as to be able to build and reside in such a palace cannot be a mere 'adventurer.' So I wrote to your agent, and consented to an interview, which I should have declined, if I had not seen the picture of Iranistan!"

"That, then, fully pays me for building it," I replied; "for I intend and expect to make more by this musical enterprise than Iranistan cost me."

"I really hope so," she replied; "but you must not be too sanguine, you know; 'man proposes but God disposes.'"

Jenny Lind always desired to reach a place in which she was to sing, without having the time of her arrival known, thus avoiding the excitement of promiscuous crowds. As a manager, however, I knew that the interests of the enterprise depended in a great degree upon these excitements. Although it frequently seemed inconceivable to her how so many thousands should have discovered her secret and consequently gathered together to receive her, I was not so much astonished, inasmuch as my agent always had early telegraphic intelligence of the time of her anticipated arrival, and was not slow in communicating the information to the public.

Our orchestra in New York consisted of sixty. When we started on our southern tour, we took with us permanently as the orchestra, twelve of the best musicians we could select, and in New Orleans augmented the force to sixteen. We increased the number to thirty-five, forty or fifty, as the case might be, by choice of musicians residing where the concerts were given. On our return to New York from Havana, we enlarged the orchestra to one hundred performers.

The morning after our arrival in Washington, President Fillmore called, and left his card, Jenny being out. When she returned and found the token of his attention, she was in something of a flurry. "Come," said she, "we must call on the President immediately."

"Why so?" I inquired.

"Because he has called on me, and of course that is equivalent to a command for me to go to his house."

I assured her that she might make her mind at ease, for whatever might be the custom with crowned heads, our Presidents were not wont to "command" the movements of strangers, and that she would be quite in time if she returned his call the next day. She did so, and was charmed with the unaffected bearing of the President, and the warm kindnesses expressed by his amiable wife and daughter, and consented to spend the evening with them in conformity with their request. She was accompanied to the "White House" by Messrs. Benedict, Belletti, and myself, and several happy hours were spent in the private circle of the President's family.

Mr. Benedict, who engaged in a long quiet conversation with Mr. Fillmore, was highly pleased with the interview. A foreigner, accustomed to court etiquette, is generally surprised at the simplicity which characterizes the Chief Magistrate of this Union. In 1852 I called on the President with my friend the late Mr. Brettell, of London, who resided in St. James' Palace, and was quite a worshiper of the Queen, and an ardent admirer of all the dignities and ceremonies of royalty. He expected something of the kind in visiting the President of the United States, and was highly pleased with his disappointment.

Both concerts in Washington were attended by the President and his family, and every member of the Cabinet. I noticed, also, among the audience, Henry Clay, Benton, Foote, Cass, and General Scott, and nearly every member of Congress. On the following morning, Miss Lind was called upon by Mr. Webster, Mr. Clay, General Cass, and Colonel Benton, and all parties were evidently gratified. I had introduced Mr. Webster to her in Boston. Upon hearing one of her wild mountain songs in New York, and also in Washington, Mr.

Webster signified his approval by rising, drawing himself up to his full height, and making a profound bow. Jenny was delighted by this expression of praise from the great statesman. When I first introduced Miss Lind to Mr. Webster, at the Revere House, in Boston, she was greatly impressed with his manners and conversation, and after his departure, walked up and down the room in great excitement, exclaiming, "Ah! Mr. Barnum, that is a man; I have never before seen such a man!"

We visited the Capitol while both Houses were in session. Miss Lind took the arm of Hon. C. F. Cleveland, representative from Connecticut, and was by him escorted into various parts of the Capitol and the grounds, with all of which she was much pleased.

⇶ ⫷

With all her excellent and even extraordinarily good qualities, however, Jenny Lind was human, though the reputation she bore in Europe for her many charitable acts led me to believe, till I knew her, that she was nearly perfect. I think now that her natural impulses were more simple, childlike, pure and generous than those of almost any other person I ever met. But she had been petted, almost worshiped, so long, that it would have been strange indeed if her unbounded popularity had not in some degree affected her to her hurt, and it must not be thought extraordinary if she now and then exhibited some phase of human weakness.

Like most persons of uncommon talent, she had a strong will which, at times, she found ungovernable; but if she was ever betrayed into a display of ill temper she was sure to apologize and express her regret afterwards. Le Grand Smith, who was quite intimate with her, and who was my right-hand man during the entire Lind engagement, used sometimes to say to me, "Well, Mr. Barnum, you have managed wonderfully in always keeping Jenny's 'angel' side outside with the public."

More than one Englishman—I may instance Mr. Dolby, Mr. Dickens' agent during his last visit to America—expressed surprise at the confirmed impression of "perfection" entertained by the general

American public in regard to the Swedish Nightingale. These things are written with none but the kindest feelings toward the sweet songstress, and only to modify the too current ideas of superhuman excellence which cannot be characteristic of any mortal being.

As I have before intimated in giving details of my management of the enterprise, believing, as I did when I engaged her, in her "angelic" reputation, I am frank enough to confess that I considered her private character a valuable adjunct, even in a business point of view, to her renown as a singer. I admit that I took her charities into account as part of my "stock in trade." Whenever she sang for a public or private charity, she gave her voice, which was worth a thousand dollars to her every evening. At such times, I always insisted upon paying for the hall, orchestra, printing, and other expenses, because I felt able and willing to contribute my full share toward the worthy objects which prompted these benefits.

This narration would be incomplete if I did not add the following:

We were in Havana when I showed to Miss Lind a paper containing the conundrum on "for getting" and "for-giving," at which she laughed heartily, but immediately checked herself and said, "O! Mr. Barnum, this is not fair; you know that you really give more than I do from the proceeds of every one of these charity concerts."

And it is but just to her to say that she frequently remonstrated with me and declared that the actual expenses should be deducted and the thus lessened sum devoted to the charity for which the concert might be given; but I always laughingly told her that I must do my part, give my share, and that if it was purely a business operation, "bread cast upon the waters," it would return, perhaps, buttered; for the larger her reputation for liberality, the more liberal the public would surely be to us and to our enterprise.

I have no wish to conceal these facts; and I certainly have no desire to receive a larger meed of praise than my qualified generosity merits. Justice to myself and to my management, as well as to Miss Lind, seems to permit, if not to demand, this explanation.

RECOLLECTIONS (1869)

LEO TOLSTOY

※※ ※※

An Opera Is Rehearsed

When in the name of simplicity Tolstoy revolted against modern life and art, he turned first against the most complicated, conventional, and expensive of the arts—hence the most vulnerable: opera.

In every large town enormous buildings are erected for museums, academies, conservatoires, and dramatic schools, and for performances and concerts. Hundreds of thousands of workmen—carpenters, masons, painters, joiners, paper-hangers, tailors, hairdressers, jewelers, molders, typesetters—spend their whole lives in hard labor to satisfy the demands of art; so that hardly any other department of human activity, the military excepted, consumes so much energy as this.

Not only is enormous labor spent on this activity, but in it, as in war, the very lives of men are sacrificed. Hundreds of thousands of people devote their lives from childhood to learning to twirl their legs rapidly (dancers), or to touch notes and strings very rapidly (musicians), or to sketch with paint and represent what they see (artists), or to turn every phrase inside out and find a rhyme to every word. And these people, often very kind and clever and capable of all sorts of useful labor, grow savage over their specialized and stupefying occupations, and become one-sided and self-complacent specialists, dull to all the serious phenomena of life and skillful only at rapidly twisting their legs, their tongues, or their fingers.

But even this stunting of human life is not the worst. I remember being once at the rehearsal of one of the most ordinary of the new operas which are produced at all the opera houses of Europe and America.[1]

[1] This opera, if not imaginary, has not been identified by Tolstoy scholars, and the scene does not suggest any work described in the histories of the genre.

I arrived when the first act had already commenced. To reach the auditorium I had to pass through the stage entrance. By dark entrances and passages, past immense machines for changing the scenery and lighting the stage and the theater, I was led through the vaults of an enormous building; and there in the gloom and dust I saw workmen busily engaged. One of these men—pale, haggard, in a dirty blouse, with dirty, work-worn hands and cramped fingers, evidently tired and out of humor—went past me, angrily scolding another man. Ascending by a dark stair, I came out on the boards behind the scenes. Amid various poles and rings and scattered scenery, decorations, and curtains, stood and moved dozens, if not hundreds, of painted and dressed-up men in costumes fitting tight to their thighs and calves, and also women, who were, as usual, as nearly nude as might be. These were all singers, or members of the chorus, or ballet dancers, awaiting their turns. My guide led me across the stage and, by means of a bridge of boards, across the orchestra, in which perhaps a hundred musicians of all kinds, from kettledrum to flute and harp, were seated, to the dark pit stalls.

On an elevation, between two lamps with reflectors and in an armchair placed before a music stand, sat the director of the musical part, baton in hand, managing the orchestra and singers, and in general the production of the whole opera.

The performance had already commenced, and on the stage was being represented a procession of Indians who had brought home a bride. Besides men and women in costume, two other men in ordinary clothes bustled and ran about on the stage: one was the director of the dramatic part, and the other, who stepped about in soft shoes and ran from place to place with unusual agility, was the dancing master, whose salary per month exceeded what ten laborers earn in a year.

These three directors arranged the singing, the orchestra, and the procession. The procession, as usual, was enacted by men and women in couples with tinfoil halberds on their shoulders. They all came from one place and walked round and round again and then stopped. The procession took a long time to arrange: first the Indians with halberds came on too late, then too soon; then at the right time but crowded together at the exit; then they did not crowd but arranged themselves badly at the sides of the stage—and each time the whole performance was stopped and recommenced from the beginning. The procession is preceded by a recitative, delivered by a man dressed up like some variety of Turk, who, opening his mouth in a curious way, sings, "Home I bring the bri-i-ide." He sings, and waves his arm (which is of course bare) from under his mantle. The procession commences. But here the French horn, in the accompaniment of the recitative, does something wrong; and the director, with a shudder as if some catastrophe had occurred, raps with his stick on the stand. All is stopped, and the director, turning to the orchestra, attacks the French horn, scolding him in the rudest terms—as cabmen abuse one another—for taking the wrong note. And again the whole thing recommences. The Indians with their halberds again come on, treading softly in their extraordinary boots; again the singer sings, "Home I bring the bri-i-ide." But here the pairs get too close together. More raps with the stick, more scolding, and a recommencement. Again "Home I bring the bri-i-ide," and again the same gesticulation with the bare arm from under the mantle; and again the couples, treading softly with halberds on their shoulders, some with sad and serious faces, some talking and smiling, arrange themselves in a circle and begin to sing. All seems to be going well, but again the stick raps and the director in a distressed and angry voice begins to scold the men and women of the chorus. It appears that when singing they had omitted to raise their hands from time to time in sign of animation. "Are you all dead, or what? What oxen you are! Are you corpses, that you can't move?" Again they recommence, "Home I bring the bri-i-ide," and again, with sorrowful faces, the chorus women sing, first one and then another of them raising their hands. But two chorus girls speak to each other—again a more vehement rapping with the stick. "Have you come here to talk? Can't you gossip at home? You there in red breeches, come nearer. Look at me! Begin again!" Again "Home I bring the bri-i-ide." And so it goes on for one, two, three hours. The whole of such a rehearsal lasts six hours on end. Raps with the stick, repetitions, placings, corrections of the singers, of the orchestra, of the procession, of the dancers—all seasoned with angry scolding. I heard the words, "asses," "fools," "idiots," "swine," addressed to the musicians and singers at least forty times in the course of one hour. And the unhappy individual to whom the abuse is addressed—flautist, horn blower, or singer—physically and mentally demoralized, does not reply, and does what is demanded of him. Twenty times is repeated the one phrase, "Home I bring the bri-i-ide," and twenty times the striding about in yellow shoes with a halberd over the shoulder. The conductor knows that these people are so demoralized that they are no longer fit for anything but to blow trumpets and walk about with halberds and in yellow shoes, and that they are also so accustomed to dainty easy living that they will put up with anything rather than lose their luxurious life. He therefore gives free vent to his churlishness, especially as he has seen the same thing done in Paris and Vienna, and knows that this is the way the best conductors behave, and that it is a musical tradition of great artists to be so carried away by the great business of their art that they cannot pause to consider the feelings of other artists.

It would be difficult to find a more repulsive sight. I have seen one workman abuse another for not supporting the weight piled upon him when goods were being unloaded, or at haystacking, the village elder scold a peasant for not making the rick right, and the man submitted in silence. And however unpleasant it was to witness the scene, the unpleasantness was lessened by the consciousness that the business in hand was necessary and important and the fault for which the elder scolded the laborer was one which might spoil a necessary undertaking.

But what was being done here? For what, and for whom? Very likely the conductor was tired out, like the workman I passed in the vaults; it was even evident that he was; but who made him tire himself? And why was he tiring himself? The opera he was rehearsing was one of the most ordinary of operas for people who are accustomed to them, but also one of the most gigantic absurdities that could possibly be devised. An Indian king wants to marry; they bring him a bride; he disguises himself as a minstrel; the bride falls in love with the minstrel and is in despair, but afterward discovers that the minstrel is the king, and everyone is highly delighted.

That there never were nor could be such Indians, and that they were not only unlike Indians but that what they were doing was unlike anything on earth except other operas, was beyond all manner of doubt; that people do not converse in such a way as recitative, and do not place themselves at fixed distances, in a quartet, waving their arms to express their emotions; that nowhere except in theaters do people walk about in such a manner, in pairs, with tinfoil halberds and in slippers; that no one ever gets angry in such a way, or is affected in such a way, or laughs in such a way, or cries in such a way; and that no one on earth can be moved by such performances—all this is beyond the possibility of doubt.

Instinctively the question presents itself: For whom is this being done? Whom *can* it please? If there are occasionally good melodies in the opera, to which it is pleasant to listen, they could have been sung simply without these stupid costumes and all the processions and recitatives and hand-wavings.

The ballet, in which half-naked women make voluptuous movements, twisting themselves into various sensual wreathings, is simply a lewd performance.

So one is quite at a loss as to whom these things are done for. The man of culture is heartily sick of them, while to a real workingman they are utterly incomprehensible. If anyone can be pleased by these things (which is doubtful), it can only be some young footman or depraved artisan, who has contracted the spirit of the upper classes but is not yet satiated with their amusements, and wishes to show his breeding.

And all this nasty folly is prepared, not simply, nor with kindly merriment, but with anger and brutal cruelty.

It is said that it is all done for the sake of art and that art is a very important thing. But is it true that art is so important that such sacrifices should be made for its sake? This question is especially urgent because art, for the sake of which the labor of millions, the lives

of men, and above all love between man and man, are all being sacrificed—this very art is becoming something more and more vague and
uncertain to human perception.

For the production of every ballet, circus, opera, operetta, exhibition, picture, concert, or printed book, the intense and unwilling
labor of thousands and thousands of people is needed at what is often
harmful and humiliating work. It were well if artists made all they
require for themselves, but as it is, they all need the help of workmen,
not only to produce art but also for their own usually luxurious
maintenance. And one way or other they get it, either through pay-
ments from rich people, or through subsidies given by the government (in Russia, for instance, in grants of millions of rubles to
theaters, conservatoires, and academies). This money is collected
from the people, some of whom have to sell their only cow to pay the
tax, and who never get those aesthetic pleasures which art gives.

WHAT IS ART? (1898)

JAMES AGATE

※»«※

Coaching the Aspirant

The incomparable diarist of *Ego* was bred to music from the age of seven and was never very far from a piano, a concert hall, or a working musician. The following extract from his autobiography is one of the very few accounts in print of what must be a fairly common scene.

Came home and spent the afternoon in a three-cornered wrangle with K. and Leo, who, now that we have got the boy virtually onto the platform at the National Gallery, wants to shove him off with a program of elusive works which even the highbrows wouldn't stand for. Finally we reached a compromise. But not until I had taken the floor and Trafalgar Square'd K. as blisteringly as I could. Something like this:

"My dear Alexis: There is a quotation from Shakespeare which is so hackneyed that I shouldn't dare to use it in any of my articles. (*J. A. recites the lines from* Julius Caesar *about the tide in the affairs of men.*) Every English schoolboy knows these lines, but you, Alexis, being a Slav, may not know them. They bear directly on your engagement at the National Gallery, for this is the turn of your tide. You must not miss it, Alexis. Remember, you are not a great pianist making assault upon a London which is waiting for you; you are just an unknown pianist begging admission at the doors. (*Alexis grunts.*) Now you must realize that there may be some critics of importance at your concert. You are a virtuoso, and as such belong to what they call the 'virtuosic brood.' Some of them do accept pianism, it is true; but they only do so when it is a question of some rendering of, say, a theme of Tallis by members of the Dolmetsch family and performed on instruments not later than 1600. You might get the *Times* critic, who, when William Murdoch died last week, told us that he had far too much mind to be a solo pianist. And, by the way, he wasn't talking complete nonsense. Now, the National Gallery people have no interest whatever in you, either as virtuoso or musician. In so far as you exist at all, you are part of their scheme, which is to educate musical taste among the London masses. If you can help, all well and good. As Howard Ferguson hinted to you today, they want some early Beethoven; if you can fill the bill with that you will be a success with them.

"Now please listen carefully, my dear boy. I want you to understand clearly that it is not young Kligerman that they want; it is young Beethoven. And they don't want young Beethoven seen through the eyes of young Kligerman; they want young Beethoven seen through their eyes. In other words, as they want London's masses to see him. If you can give them this, good. It is the price you pay for getting your foot in the magic circle. But a dreadful trap awaits you. Perhaps Leo will tell you what he thinks of your early Beethoven. I make no bones about saying that I think it appalling, and I have listened to you playing early Beethoven for over an hour. Let me give you an analogy taken from the world of horses. In a racehorse, as perhaps you know, all that matters is how quickly the animal can get from one place to another; what he looks like during the process doesn't matter. But with a show harness horse what matters is the majesty, the rhythm, shall I say, the poetry of his motion; how long he takes in covering the ground is of very little account. Do you see this? Now do you understand the trap I speak of? You take your Beethoven at a terrific lick because it is in your blood to feel your Beethoven that way. Personally I think you are wrong, but I know you and therefore don't impute a wrong motive. But the musical critics, who don't know you, will assume that you are using Beethoven as a medium for showing off. And that will be the beginning, and, I fear, the end of Alexis Kligerman."

There was a silence, and then Leo, who likes to play Eusebius to my Florestan,[1] said quietly, "I think you ought to be told, Alexis, that if you are going in for the early Beethoven sonatas you ought to

[1] See p. 99.

accustom yourself to getting a bird's-eye view of each movement as a whole, just as if you were looking at some building from the air. I am afraid you still only consider a piece passage by passage; in that way there will never be any sense of continuity, you will be like those old actors who recited their parts without knowing or bothering to know what the others had said before or were going to say afterwards. . . . I think James is right about your playing too fast. I can understand that; it has something to do with your Slavonic temperament. But don't give way to it in early Beethoven. There was nothing Slavonic there; only German solidity, French elegance, and Italian lyricism exquisitely blended. When you begin your Opus 10, your *Pastorale,* your *Pathétique* . . . leave your Slav ego outside on the mat. Be Western. We are placid, unhysterical people in the West, you know; we don't tear a passion to tatters. Tradition must not be despised, either. If you can bear to hear James read to you how Kean played Othello, how Phelps played Prospero, or Irving Hamlet, then you must listen to people who can tell you how von Bülow, Rubinstein, Stavenhagen, and d'Albert played these early sonatas. Let your presto be a moderato; but let your adagio approach andante."

It must not be imagined that these orations were uninterrupted. It is only fair to give Kligerman's point of view, and this I reconstruct from his vigorous splutterings and expostulations. Had we given him time for a considered speech it would have gone something like this:

"That what you say is very well. But you suppose I shall make great success with methods which are so reactionary? What will people call me?—they will call me tame, with no life and no fire and no passion. You say 'von Bülow.' Good. But I am told he played like a volcano extinct. I—I am twenty-two. I am Siegfried, not Wotan. I do not believe that the critics want this, or that, or the other. I believe the critics want a sincerity, an enthusiasm, and I do not think they want the beaten track, a performance like everyone else. To me, my tempi in Beethoven are right. He was young when he wrote these sonatas: you think then one shall play them like an old man? No, no. Beethoven was virtuoso also: shall one then not play quick passages like virtuoso? In 'classic' Beethoven I do not believe: I believe only in Beethoven romantic, poetic. Is he not a prince, a prophet, a pioneer? . . . Is he not. . . ." By this time our good Alexis had become so excited that his face had become dead-white, his eyes shone like arc lamps, and he thumped my mantelpiece until I was afraid he would injure his wrist. Then the decanter came to our aid, and thus ended the "struggle for an artist's soul." In novels and on the screen this means whether some starving artist should degrade his soul by allowing some rich woman to seduce his body. But Leo and I are not concerned with any such twaddle. The point is: Can we detach this young man's mind from his fingers?

EGO 6 (1942)

HUGO WOLF

⟫⟪

When to Applaud

Why in the name of heaven and all its angels must the searching fire
of enthusiasm always come out through hands and feet? Why must
there be clapping and stamping? Does the public's hands and feet
constitute the movable lightning rod for the electrified soul? I ask
whether applauding is allowable under all circumstances, whether
it is a force of nature—or only a bad and stupid habit.

Yet I do not want to be understood as pleading against applause
universally. Let people continue to clap, but only when the work
itself in some measure calls for it, when it concludes brilliantly and
loud, when its character is festive, gay, warlike, or heroic. Would
anyone deny that the close of the *Coriolan* overture affects the soul
in a different way from the close of the *Egmont?* [1] The gradually
rising dawn of freedom over the grave of Egmont, which shines
there at the end like the rays of the sun over an oppressed people,
powerfully lifts up the listener's heart. He feels inspirited, elevated,
free. He desires to join in the common jubilation, he applauds, he
keeps shouting "Bravo!" We can all join in because we feel at one
with liberated peoples: applause is here in its proper place.

But after the frightful tragedy of Coriolan's annihilated ego, does
Beethoven's hero awaken no other impulse but the desire to escape
at once from so deep an impression? Does not the eye stare madly, as
if into a magic mirror in which the gigantic shadow of Coriolan
slowly disappears . . . ? I say that if when the last note has barely
ceased to resound you are again jolly and pleased, and you babble and
criticize and clap, then you have not looked into the magic mirror,
you have seen nothing, felt nothing, heard nothing, understood nothing—nothing, nothing: *not a thing!*

COLLECTED CRITIQUES (1885)

[1] Both overtures by Beethoven.

DENIS DIDEROT

⇉≫ ≪⇇

Rameau's Nephew

Based on fact, this famous dialogue between the French Encyclopedist
and the nephew of the composer Rameau was first made known through
Goethe's translation of a manuscript copy that had found its way to
Germany. The scene is a café in the Palais Royal.

After a moment's silence on both our parts, during which he paced
up and down whistling and singing, I spoke, in order to bring him
back to a discussion of his talent. I said:

MYSELF: What are you doing now?

HE: Nothing.

MYSELF: That must be very fatiguing.

HE: I was empty-headed enough to begin with, but I went to hear
the music of Duni [1] and our other young composers, and that finished me.

MYSELF: So you like this new genre?

HE: No doubt about it.

MYSELF: You manage to find beauty in these newfangled melodies?

HE: Do I manage! Ye gods! Don't doubt for a moment that I do!
What declamation! What truth of expression!

MYSELF: Every imitative art finds its model in Nature. What is the
musician's model when he fashions a melody?

HE: Let's begin with a more general question: What is a melody?

MYSELF: I confess that is beyond me. We are all alike, really, we
remember words, which we think we understand from the frequent
and even correct use we make of them. But our minds contain only
vague notions. When I utter the word "melody," I have no clearer

[1] Italian composer of comic operas (1709-1775).

424

idea than you and most of your colleagues when you say, "Reputation, blame, honor, vice, virtue, modesty, decency, shame, ridicule."

HE: A melody is a vocal or instrumental imitation using the sounds of a scale invented by art—or inspired by nature, as you prefer; it imitates either physical noises or the accents of passion. You can see that by changing a few words in this definition it would exactly fit painting, eloquence, sculpture, or poetry.

Now to come to your question: What is the musician's model? It is declamation if the model is alive and a thinking being; it is physical noise if the model is inanimate. Consider declamation as one line, and song as another, which twists snakelike about the former. The more the declamation, which is the prototype of song, is vivid and true, the more the song shaped upon it will intersect it at many points. The truer the melody, the more beautiful it will be—and that is what our younger musicians have so well understood.

I say nothing of meter, which is another condition of melody; I dwell on expressiveness. Nothing is more self-evident than the maxim I read somewhere: *"Musices seminarium accentus"*—"Accent is the source of melody." From this you can infer how difficult and how important it is to know how to handle recitative. There is no beautiful air from which one cannot make a beautiful recitative, and no beautiful recitative from which an able composer cannot make a beautiful air. I would not guarantee that a good reciter will sing well, but I should be surprised if a good singer did not know how to recite well. You must believe all I have been saying, for it's true.

MYSELF: I should like nothing better than to believe you, if I were not prevented by a small difficulty.

HE: The difficulty is?

MYSELF: Only this, that if the new music is sublime, it follows that the music of the divine Lulli, of Campra, of Destouches, of Mouret, and—be it said between us—of your dear uncle, must be a trifle dull.

HE, *coming close and answering in my ear:* I shouldn't like to be overheard, for there are hereabouts plenty of people who know me —but it *is* dull. Not that I worry myself much about the dear uncle—

if "dear" has to come into it. He is made of stone: he could see my tongue hanging out a foot long and he would not give me a glass of water. But try as he will—with the octave, the leading note—*tum-tum-ta-ta-tum, toot-toot-toot, tra-la-toot*—even though he makes a racket like the very devil, some people are beginning to catch on; they will no longer take banging for music—and certainly not *his* banging. The police should forbid any person, of whatever rank, to have Pergolese's *Stabat Mater* performed. That *Stabat* should have been burned by the public hangman.[2] Yes, these confounded *bouffons* with their *Serva Padrona* and their *Tracallo* have given us a stout kick in the butt. That's why Rebel and Francoeur [3] cry out to heaven. They say all is lost: "they are ruined; if these fair-ground musicians are allowed to keep on our national music is done for; the so-called Royal Academy—the Opera—might as well shut up shop." And there is some truth in it. The old fogies who have been going there every Friday for thirty or forty years no longer have a good time. They are bored, they yawn without knowing why. They ask themselves and can't answer. They should ask *me*. As things are going now, Duni's prophecy will come true, and I'm willing to give up living in four or five years if, after *The Painter in Love with His Model*, you find as much as an alley cat in our celebrated Opera house.

The good souls! They've already abandoned their symphonies to hear the Italian ones.[4] They thought they could accustom their ears to these new instrumental pieces without changing their taste as regards the vocal—as if symphonies were not in relation to songs (except for the greater freedom afforded by the range of instruments and the dexterity of the fingers) what songs are to declamation; as if the violin did not ape the singer, who in turn will become the ape of the violin when acrobatics will have replaced beauty. The first one who played Locatelli [5] was the apostle of the new music. Next! Next! We shall all become accustomed to the imitation of passionate

---

[2] I.e., so that the French might not be won over to the Italian music.

[3] Directors of the Opera orchestra in Paris.

[4] "Symphonies" here mean operatic overtures and interludes.

[5] Pietro Locatelli (1693–1764), famous violinist and composer, pupil of Corelli.

accents or of natural phenomena by means of voices and instruments
—which is the whole exent of music's purpose. D'you think we'll also
keep our taste for flights, dreams, glories, triumphs, and victories?
Not so you can notice it, Joe! Did anyone imagine that the public
could learn to weep or laugh at tragic or comic scenes when "musi-
cated," to respond to the tones of fury, hatred, and jealousy, the true
plaints of love, the irony and pleasantries of the Italian or French
theater, and that in spite of all this the public would continue to admire *Ragonde* or *Platée*.[6] You bet your life—go cut it with a knife!
That they could once learn how easily, softly, gently the Italian
tongue, with its natural harmony, flexible prosody, easy ellipses and
inversions, suited the art and motion of music, the turns of song and
the measured pace of sounds—and yet would overlook the fact that
French is stiff, heavy, pedantic, and monotonous? Well, well, well,
they persuaded themselves that after weeping with a mother bewail-
ing the loss of her son, and shuddering at the decree of a tyrant committing murder, they would not be bored with their fairyland, their
insipid mythology, their saccharine love songs, which show the poet's
bad taste no less than the sterility of the music matched thereto. The
good souls!

It could not and cannot be. The true, the good, and the beautiful
will prevail. Their rights may at first be challenged, but in the end
are acknowledged and people do yield their admiration. Inferior
things may be esteemed for a time, but the end is a great yawn. Go
ahead, gentlemen, yawn away, yawn to your heart's content, don't be
afraid! The power of nature and of the trinity that I worship will
never be overcome by the forces of darkness—the True which is the
father, engenders the Good, which is his son, whence comes the Beautiful, which is the Holy Ghost. Change is gradual. The foreign god
takes his place humbly next to the native idol, little by little asserts
itself, and one fine day elbows out his fellow—before you can say
Jack Robinson, there's the idol flat on its back.

MYSELF: There is some sense in almost everything you've said.

HE: Sense? I'm glad! The devil take me if I've been making any

[6] Operas by Mouret and Rameau respectively.

special effort. I speak as it comes. I'm like the opera musicians when my uncle came on the scene. If I'm on the point, well and good. It only shows that a man of the trade will always speak about it more sensibly than any Academy or all the Duhamels in the world.[7]

And now he paces up and down again, humming in his throat some arias from Duni's operas, occasionally raising arms and eyes to the skies: "It's beautiful, God, but it's beautiful! Why? How can a man sport a pair of ears and ask such a question?" He was getting into a passion and beginning to sing, his voice growing louder as his passion increased. Next he gesticulated, made faces and twisted his body, and I thought to myself, "There he goes—losing control and working himself up to a scene." True enough, he suddenly burst out very loud, "I am but a poor wretch. . . . My lord, my lord, I beg you to let me go! . . . O Earth, receive my gold and keep my treasure safe, my soul, my life, O Earth! . . . There is my little friend . . . *Aspettare e non venire . . . A Zerbina penserete . . . Sempre in contrasti con te si sta. . . .* " He jumbled together thirty different airs, French, Italian, comic, tragic—in every style. Now in a baritone voice he sank to the pit; then, straining in falsetto, he tore to shreds the upper notes of some air, imitating the while the stance, walk, and gestures of the several characters; being in succession furious, mollified, lordly, sneering. First a damsel weeps and he reproduces her kittenish ways; next he is a priest, a king, a tyrant; he threatens, commands, rages. Now he is a slave, he obeys, calms down, is heartbroken, complains, laughs; never overstepping the proper tone, speech, or manner called for by the part.

All the chess players in the café had left their boards and gathered around us. The windows of the place were occupied from outside by passers-by who had stopped on hearing the commotion. They guffawed fit to crack the ceiling. He notices nothing, he keeps on, in the grip of spiritual possession, an enthusiasm so close to madness that it seems doubtful whether he will recover. He may have to be put into a cab and taken to a padded cell, still singing fragments of Jomelli's

[7] An academic writer on trades he did not practice.

Lamentations.[8] He reproduces with incredible precision, fidelity, and warmth the most beautiful passages of each scene. That magnificent recitative in which Jeremiah describes the desolation of Jerusalem he drenches in tears which draw their like from every onlooker. His art was complete—delicacy of voice, expressive strength, true sorrow. He dwelt on the places where the musician had shown himself a master. If he left the vocal part, it was to take up the instrumental, which he abandoned suddenly to return to the voice, linking them so as to preserve the connection and unity of the whole, gripping our souls and keeping them suspended in the most singular state of being that I have ever experienced.

Did I admire him? Yes, I did admire. Was I moved to pity? I was moved. But a streak of derision was interwoven with these feelings and denatured them.

Yes, you too would have burst out laughing at the way in which he aped the different instruments. With swollen cheeks and a somber throaty sound, he would give us the horns and bassoons. For the oboes he assumed a shrill yet nasal voice, then speeded up the emission of sound to an incredible degree for the strings, for whose tones he found close analogues. He whistled piccolos and warbled traverse flutes, singing, shouting, waving about like one demented, being in himself dancer and ballerina, singer and prima donna, all of them together and the whole orchestra, the whole theater; then redividing himself into twenty separate roles, running, stopping, glowing at the eyes like one possessed, frothing at the mouth. . . .

HE: Our passions have to be strong. The tenderness of the musician and the poet must be extreme . . . the aria must be the peroration of the scene. We need exclamations, interjections, suspensions, interruptions, affirmations, and negations. We call out, invoke, clamor, groan, weep, and laugh openly. No more witticisms, epigrams, neat thoughts —they are too unlike Nature. And don't get it into your head that the old theatrical acting and declamation can give us a pattern to

[8] A setting of *Jeremiah*. Jomelli (1714–1774) was a forerunner of Gluck in operatic reform.

follow. Not likely! We want it more energetic, less mannered, more genuine. Simple speeches, the ordinary utterance of passion, will be all the more necessary that our French language is more monotonous, less accented. The animal cry or that of man in a passion will supply the accent. . . .

As he spoke, the crowd around us had withdrawn, whether from no longer being able to hear or from having lost interest in the subject; for in general man is like a child and prefers being amused to being instructed. The chess players had resumed their boards and we were alone in our corner. Seated on the bench, his head resting against the wall, his arms hanging and his eyes half closed, he said:

HE: I don't know what's the matter with me; when I came here I was feeling rested and in good form. Now I am exhausted, worn out, as if I had walked thirty miles. It came upon me suddenly.

MYSELF: Should you like something to drink?

HE: With pleasure. My throat feels rough, I am a little faint, and my chest hurts. This happens to me every day and I have no notion of the cause.

MYSELF: What shall you take?

HE: Whatever you say. I am not hard to please. Poverty has accustomed me to everything.

He drank two or three glasses of lemonade without noticing, and would have drowned himself like a spent swimmer had I not moved the bottle, which he sought distractedly, not knowing what he was about. I then said to him:

MYSELF: How is it that with such fineness of feeling, so much sensibility where musical beauty is concerned, you are so blind to the beauties of morality, so insensible to the charm of virtue?

HE: It must be that virtue requires a special sense that I lack, a fiber that has not been granted me. My fiber is loose, one can pluck it forever without its yielding a tone. Or else I have spent my life with good musicians and bad people, whence my ear has become very sharp and my heart quite deaf. And then there is heredity. My father's blood is the same as my uncle's; my blood is like my father's. The paternal molecule was hard and obtuse, and like a primordial germ it has affected all the rest.

MYSELF: Do you love your son?

HE: Do I love him? I am crazy about him.

MYSELF: And will you do nothing to thwart in him the effect of his accursed paternal molecule?

HE: I'll try, but (I think) in vain. If he is fated to become a good man, trying won't do any harm. But if the molecule decides that he shall be a ne'er-do-well like his father, the pains I might take to make him an honest man would be very dangerous. Before the molecule could recapture him and reproduce the state of perfect abjection which I have reached, it would take endless time. He would waste his best years. So at the moment I hold my hand, I simply observe him and let him come along. He is already greedy, cozening, rascally, lazy, and a liar: I am afraid he is a pedigreed beast.

MYSELF: And you will make him a musician so that the likeness can be complete?

HE: A musician! A musician! Sometimes I look at him and grind my teeth and say to myself, "If you ever learn a note, I really think I'll twist your neck."

MYSELF: But why so?

HE: It leads nowhere.

MYSELF: It leads everywhere.

HE: Yes, if you excel. But who can guarantee that his child will excel? It's ten thousand to one that he will be a wretched note scraper like me. Do you know that it would be easier to find a child able to govern a kingdom than a great violinist?

MYSELF: I think on the contrary that any likely talent, even if mediocre, can lead a man to fortune, provided the country has no morals and lives on luxury and debauch. I myself once heard the following conversation take place between a sort of patron and his would-be protégé. The latter had been recommended to the former as a useful and serviceable man:

"My dear sir, what can you do?"

"I am a fairly good mathematician."

"Good enough. But after you have taught mathematics for ten or twelve years by running the streets of Paris, you will have only three or four hundred francs a year."

"I have also studied law."

"If Puffendorf and Grotius came back to life they would starve in the gutter."

"I am well versed in geography and history."

"If there were any parents who really cared about their children's education, your fortune would be made. But such parents do not exist."

"I am a tolerable musician."

"Why didn't you say so at once? Just to show you what your gift is worth to you, let me say this: I have a daugher; come every day at seven-thirty and give her a lesson until nine. I shall pay you two hundred and fifty francs a year and give you all your meals at our house. The rest of the day is yours to dispose of for your profit."

HE: And what happened?

MYSELF: If the man had been clever he would have grown rich—which is all you seem to care about.

HE: No doubt. Gold, gold is everything; and everything, without gold, is nothing. Therefore, instead of having my son's head stuffed with grand maxims which he would have to forget under pain of being a pauper, this is what I do whenever I have a gold piece—not often, to be sure: I plant myself in front of him, draw the piece from my pocket, show it to him with admiring looks, raise my eyes to heaven, kiss the gold in front of him, and to show him still more forcibly the importance of the sacred coin I stammer out the names and point out with the finger all the things one can buy with it—a beautiful gown, a beautiful hat, a good cake; next I put the coin in my pocket, parade before him proudly, pull up my coattails, and strike my waistcoat where the money lies. Thus do I make him understand that it is from that coin I draw the self-assurance he beholds.

MYSELF: Nothing could be better. But what if some day, being deeply persuaded of the value of money, he should—

HE: I follow you! One must shut one's eyes to that. There is no principle of conduct wholly without drawbacks. At the worst, one goes through a bad half-hour, then all is over.

MYSELF: Yet in spite of your wise and courageous views, I continue to think it would be a good thing to make him a musician. I know of no better way to approach the rich, to serve their vices and to turn one's own to advantage.

HE: True. But I have projects even more certain of success. Ah, if I only had a daughter! But no man can do as he likes—he must take what he gets and do the best he can with it. For which purpose one must not, like most fathers, stupidly give children who are destined to live in Paris the education of ancient Sparta. One might as well plot their ruin. If the native training is bad, the fault lies with the manners and customs of my country, and not with me. Whoever be responsible, I want my child happy, or what amounts to the same thing, honored, rich, powerful. I know the easiest ways to accomplish this, and I mean to teach them to my son early in life. If you wise men blame me, the majority (and success itself) will absolve me. He will have gold—it's I who tell you so, I guarantee it—and if he has a great deal, he will lack nothing, not even your admiration and respect.

MYSELF: You might be wrong.

HE: If so, he can do without the latter, like many other people.

There was in all he said much that one thinks to oneself, and acts on, but that one never says. This was in fact the chief difference between my man and the rest of us. He admitted his vices, which are also ours: he was no hypocrite. Neither more nor less detestable than other men, he was franker than they, more logical, and thus often profound in his depravity. I was appalled to think of what his child would become under such a tutor. It was clear that if he was brought up on a system so exactly framed on our actual behavior, he would go far—unless he was prematurely cut off on the way.

HE: Never you fear! The important thing that a good father must do is not so much to give his child vices that will bring him wealth and foolish traits that will make him a favorite of the great—everybody does as much: not systematically like me, but by casual precept and example. No, what is more difficult is to teach him the golden art by which he can avert disgrace, shame, and the penalties of the law. These last are dissonances in the harmony of society, which one must know how to use, prepare, and resolve. Nothing is duller than a progression of common chords. One wants some contrast, which breaks up the clear white light and makes it iridescent.

MYSELF: Very good. Thanks. Your comparison brings me back from morals to music. I digressed in spite of myself, for to speak frankly, I like you much better as musician than as moralist.

HE: And yet I am only second-rate in music, whereas I am a superior moralist.

MYSELF: I rather doubt this; but even were it so, I am an honest man and your principles do not suit me.

HE: So much the worse for you. Oh, if I only had your talent!

MYSELF: Leave my talent alone; let's go back to yours.

HE: If I could express myself as you do! But my vocabulary is a damned mongrel—half literary and well bred, half guttersnipe.

MYSELF: Don't think I speak well. I can only tell the truth, and, as you know, that doesn't always go down.

HE: It's not for telling the truth that I envy you your gifts. Just the opposite—to tell lies. If I only knew how to throw together a book, how to turn a dedication, intoxicate some fool with praises, and make my way among women!

MYSELF: As for all that, you know much more about it than I do; I am not even fit to be your pupil.

HE: Oh, what abilities you are letting go to waste, not even suspecting what they're worth!

MYSELF: I reap whatever I sow, no more, no less.

HE: If that were true, you wouldn't be wearing these coarse clothes —linen coat, woolen stockings, thick-soled shoes, and superannuated wig.

MYSELF: Granted. One must be terribly clumsy if one isn't rich after sticking at nothing to acquire wealth. But there are people like me, you see, who don't consider wealth the most important thing in the world—queer people.

HE: Very queer. No one is born that way. It's an acquired idea; it's unnatural.

MYSELF: Unnatural for man?

HE: Just unnatural. Everything that lives, man included, seeks its well-being at the expense of whoever withholds it. I'm sure that if I let my little savage grow up without saying a word to him, he would of his own accord want to be richly dressed, magnificently fed, liked by men and loved by women, and concentrate on himself all the goods of life.

MYSELF: If your little savage were left to himself and to his native blindness, he would in time join the infant's reasoning to the grown man's passions—he would strangle his father and sleep with his mother.

HE: Which only proves the need of a good education. There's no argument. But what is a good education if it is not one that leads to all the enjoyments without trouble or danger?

MYSELF: I am almost with you there, but let's not go into it.

HE: Why not?

MYSELF: Because I think we are only superficially in agreement, and that if we look into the question of troubles and dangers, we shall no longer be at one.

HE: And what's the harm of that?

MYSELF: Let it go, I say. What I know on the subject I shan't be able to teach you. You will have an easier time teaching me what you know about music, of which I am ignorant. Dear Rameau, let us talk music; and tell me how it is that with your remarkable power for understanding, remembering, and rendering the most beautiful works of the great masters, with your contagious enthusiasm for them and for conveying them, you have never done anything that amounts to anything.

Instead of answering me, he started nodding with his head and, uplifting a finger heavenward, cried out, "My star! My star! When

Nature fashioned Leo,[9] Vinci,[10] Pergolese, Duni, she smiled on them. She put on a grave imposing mien when she made my dear uncle Rameau, who for a dozen years was called "the great Rameau," though soon nobody will have heard of him. But when she slapped together his nephew, she made a face, then another face, and still another." As he said these words he was making all sorts of faces, depicting contempt, disdain, irony; he seemed to be kneading a ball of dough within his fingers while grinning at the absurd shapes he was imparting to it.

This done, he made a gesture as if throwing the outlandish creation far from him. . . .

RAMEAU'S NEPHEW (1762; publ. 1823)

[9] Neapolitan opera composer (1694–1744).
[10] Of the same Neapolitan school (1690–1730).

MAX MARETZEK

※ ≪

Cabals and Cantatori

Rowdyism in the theater was still common as late as 1850. In New York, the Astor Place Theater was particularly the scene of riots. Those arising from the international rivalry between the visiting English actor Macready and the native Forrest are well known, but their operatic counterpart, here described, has been given less notice. The immediate cause was the refusal of the tenor Benedetti to sing following the defection of his compatriot Mme. Truffi. The manager, E. P. Fry (a former bookkeeper), imprudently substituted a French prima donna, Mme. Laborde, and the war was on. The date is 1848, and the narrator is an excellent Czech conductor (1821–1897), whose English has been preserved, though his punctuation has been amended.

Upon the Friday evening in question, three distinct parties were to be found in the Astor Place Opera House.

These were the personal friends of the manager, E. P. Fry; those who supported the refractory tenor, Benedetti; and the public.

The first of these came simply and purely for the purpose of hissing Benedetti and sustaining Mr. Fry in his attempt to control him. This was, it must be confessed, a very praiseworthy example of private friendship. The second of the three parties were the friends of the culprit. These appeared on this night with the purpose of doing precisely the contrary. This, you must grant, was at least to the full as praiseworthy. But the public also chose to be present en masse. A part of them undoubtedly came with the simple view of enjoying the row which was expected by all, a virtuous pleasure which is in general keenly appreciated by them. The remainder had, however, paid their money solely to have the satisfaction of giving a lesson to each of the belligerents.

Plans for the evening's campaign had been arranged beforehand by either of the two first parties.

Benedetti, who would be exposed to the primary outbreak of the popular indignation, artfully fomented by the friends of the management, was prepared with a lengthy speech. In it, he would touch upon every possible point of accusation against him. He would explain, modify, denounce, entreat, bully, and apologize—appealing to the well-known generosity and kindness of the public, while he announced his thorough good will, and asserted his at least as thorough good faith toward the management. In fact, it was a very commonplace, everyday sort of theatrical speech with which he had primed himself—a sort of oration which the public ought long since to have known by heart, but by which it is still content to be deceived on almost every occasion.

Thus read the program issued from the camp of the manager: Benedetti was by all means to be hissed off the stage. Then, when the confusion had reached its highest point, Mr. Fry was to appear before the audience. After a flattering reception, he was to address the audience and request as a personal favor their pardon of Benedetti. Was it not at once obvious that all who were present would say, "What a noble-hearted, fine, and generous fellow we now have for a manager!" After this, he would give utterance to a few modest remarks, composed expressly for this occasion, and then retire, followed by a sedulously prolonged and deafening cheering.

Now let us see what really chanced upon this evening.

The house was crammed from the top to the bottom. Every seat was taken. The avenues in the parquet [1] were thronged by those who had been attracted by the scandal. It was another proof that Art is by no means the principal thing to be cultivated by a management that would rejoice in attracting large audiences.

When the introduction was over, [2] Benedetti appeared. He was immediately greeted by a storm of hisses, which were as quickly broken in upon by thunderous acclamation. This at length stilled, and he began to sing. That man, however, who would have heard a note after the first bar must have had good ears. Screams, whistles,

[1] I.e., the aisles in the orchestra.

[2] The overture; the opera was Bellini's *Norma.*

clapping, hisses, trampling of feet, roaring, menacing outcries, and gesticulations of every kind filled the theater. You might have imagined that the inmates of some half a hundred madhouses had broken loose. To catch a note from the orchestra was as impossible as to listen to the singing. After a brief time, chaos having roared itself hoarse began to shape itself into some intelligible form, and a few cries of "Order! Order!" were occasionally heard.

"What order?" retorted the friends of the manager. "Off the stage with the rascal!"

"No! no! Go on, give us a tune," roared the public.

"Order! Order!"

"Off the stage with him! He wouldn't sing when we wanted him. He shan't sing now!"

"Apologize to Fry."

"Fry be damned! Apologize to Mme. Laborde."

"Never mind Laborde! Apologize to the public."

"The public doesn't want an apology."

"Give us a song!"

"Yes, yes! 'Yankee Doodle'!" shouted a part of the public.

"We don't want 'Yankee Doodle.' 'Carry him back to Old Virginny.'"

"Order! Order!"

For some time Benedetti stood all this very quietly. Occasionally he would open his mouth with the attempt to sing. It was perfectly hopeless, and his lips would close again almost as quickly as they had separated. At length he advanced a few steps and performed a curious pantomime expressive of his desire to speak. The public is at all times a curious animal. Its curiosity at present therefore restored order. But this order menaced Mr. Fry's program of proceedings with the destruction of its utility. He and those of his friends who were with him behind the scenes trembled lest by these means their own tactical arrangements might be turned by their astute enemy against themselves.

"Ladies and gentlemen!" said Benedetti. "I came here to sing—"

"So you did!"

"Why the deuce don't you then?"

"Give us 'Yankee Doodle'!" roared a voice from the gallery.

Benedetti gazed on the audience with an air of unabashed majesty as he mildly inquired, "Shall I sing or withdraw?"

"Sing!"

"Withdraw!"

"Yes!"

"No!"

"Yes! Yes!"

"No! No!" were the cries and screams that broke from every part of the theater, while from the gallery "Give us 'Yankee Doodle'!" was heard again.

"No! No!"

"Yes! Yes! Yes!"

Now whether this "Yes! Yes!" applied to singing or withdrawing, or the vocalization of "Yankee Doodle," it would be impossible to say, and Benedetti stood for a moment completely nonplused.

To correct his misappreciation of their desires, he therefore repeated the question: and drawing himself up in a graceful and expressive position was preparing to proceed with the rest of his previously prepared speech when the acuteness of one of Mme. Laborde's friends frustrated his intention. This was M. Nourrit, an old stager and old stage-manager who, seeing the turn matters were about to take, pulled the wire and gave the signal for dropping the curtain. Down it at once came, between the internally irate and externally most pacific tenor, cutting short any further colloquy between himself and the public.

With a brief compliment to Nourrit for his strategic skill, Mr. Fry settled his new pair of spectacles securely upon the bridge of his nose and rushed out to the footlights.

But what was his astonishment to find that the flattering reception indicated in his program was by no means accorded him. There must have been some unaccountable error committed by those to whom his arrangements had been entrusted. He gazed wildly around the house, but hisses, catcalls, and objurgations couched in the most derogatory terms were all that could be afforded him. In his horror, he would not have endured it as long as Benedetti had done but for the suggestions of some of the members of his orchestra. These, with a keen relish for his most unmistakable nervousness, encouraged him not to leave the battleground. At length, agitated and trembling, he was permitted to stammer out his speech, hissed by the friends of the tenor, applauded by his own, and laughed at by the public—after which the performance was allowed to go on.

Never, possibly, had Benedetti or Laborde sung better, and very certainly never was there a greater amount of merriment elicited by any farce than was then called forth by the lyrical tragedy of *Norma*. Nay! It would have seemed that on this evening scarcely an American was present who did not understand Italian. The slightest bearing upon the private affairs of the vocalists into which the words of the opera or the acting might be tortured was immediately taken up by the audience. Witty commentaries were passed from one to the other and received with unbounded merriment. In the scene in which Pollio speaks about Norma, in the finale to the first act when Norma reproaches Pollio, and in the duo when she tells him that "at length he is in her hands," the most ludicrous exclamations were heard from the gallery and immediately caught up by those who were in the parquet and boxes. But when in the last scene Pollio implored Norma to pardon him and the exclamation—

"Ah! troppo tardi ti ho conosciuto!" [3]

bursts from him, the merriment of the public could no longer be repressed, and the opera concluded amidst a general outburst of laughter from the public, the chorus, and the orchestra, in which even Fry's and Benedetti's personal friends were almost against their will obliged to join.

The former gentleman made money upon this evening, but it brought the Opera House into bad repute, while he himself incurred

[3]   "Ah, too late have I come to know thee!"

a large amount of personal discredit, even among his own friends. Bennett [4] also consecrated a certain amount of space in his columns daily to the abuse of the Opera. It may safely be affirmed that this was the only thing which induced the public to visit the establishment. Indeed, had our manager answered and attempted to refute the daily charges brought against him by the *Herald,* I entertained—and still entertain—not the slightest doubt but that he could have turned the excitement caused by these articles greatly to his own advantage. However he preferred to keep his wrath smoldering, and was wont to say, in answer to my hints upon the advisability of entering upon a more retaliatory course, "Never mind. Mr. Bennett shall pay the piper, and I will dance. I shall sue him for heavy damages."

CROTCHETS AND QUAVERS (1855)

[4] James Gordon Bennett, editor of the *New York Herald.*

BERNARD VAN DIEREN AND FERRUCCIO BUSONI

❊

What Gives Us Pause

Still insufficiently known as a composer, yet sure of a place in modern music, Bernard Van Dieren (1884–1936) has left a volume of essays that merit attention for their original thought and prose. The other person in the dialogue is Ferruccio Busoni (1866–1924), who was a composer, piano virtuoso, and writer on music. See pp. 174 and 583.

My own action once served to bring home to him the roots and the consequences of such misunderstandings. We were together visiting a South German town. Busoni had promised to show me some interesting buildings. In the course of our walk he entered a dark court and then mounted a wide, dimly lit stone staircase. I followed without question. We arrived at what unexpectedly proved a restaurant on the first floor. On the landing he turned round to say:

BUSONI: You are a queer fellow!

MYSELF: What makes you think so?

B.: You never asked where I was going. . . .

M.: Well, are we not "out for a walk" together?

B.: We are; in fact I took you here for a glass of wine.

M.: It did not look in the least like a place where that could be found: it looked to me more like a coiners' den, but I would naturally follow where you go.

B.: I suppose it does seem natural to you! I would have wanted to know what came next.

M.: Speak of reversed roles! I once felt you did something quite as odd.

B.: And when may that have been?

M.: You remember when you wanted us to hear Liszt's "Figaro," which you had just discovered. You asked me to turn the pages. The manuscript was illegible, and you played your own additions that were not marked on it. Not unnaturally, I soon lost my way. Yet by never a whisper or a nod did you tell me when to turn next.

B.: But I played the whole work to a finish!

M.: I admired that as much as I could while feeling so disgruntled. You must realize that you made me feel foolish. It was unkind. . . .

B.: But you said nothing.

M.: I should have had to interrupt you. No, on that occasion it was I who was expecting a word or a sign. And more reasonably, I think.

B.: And you didn't get it! Now I suppose that this time again you think it was for me to speak first?

M.: Not this time. There was nothing here like one page hiding all the following ones. I should soon enough discover where you were leading me. Very much as if I listened—without any impediment— to some of your music. I should not begin arguing before I had seen what you were getting at.

B.: Unfortunately that is what I find people nearly always do. So perhaps your way is best after all. What could not one do if listeners had the patience to reserve critical observations!

M.: Since we are here, let us go in and have the wine. *Seated with the bottle.* You were lamenting that much you could do is left un- done. You said people should refrain from mentally formulating their criticisms while you addressed them. That they should surrender for the moment, until they knew where you were leading them. Did I get it right?

B.: That is more or less what I had in mind.

M.: Did you refer to remembered disillusions? Or are you thinking of the future, and of works as yet unwritten?

B.: Of both, but chiefly of so much music I should like to write for which I do not yet trust myself. Perhaps I ought to say, for which I don't trust my public yet—unless I were to adapt my writing to their habits. I should love to set some of those wondrous speeches of Don Quixote. His address to the goatherds in the first book, for instance. There I feel I could achieve something of real worth.

M.: It seems an exceptionally suitable subject. It is a great pity that you hesitate.

B.: I should want to say so infinitely much that I hardly trust the power of music to convey all that presses itself on my imagination.

M.: It is strange that you should distrust your powers for the task —even counting the limitations of music. As strange as that you distrust my rational mentality when you think I behave in an unexpected way. Honestly, I think it is "queer" when you say there is something of mystery about me. In the incident I recalled, I showed my confidence in you, as I always should where music is concerned. And that, after all, is what you desire.

B.: What you say sounds flattering. I ought to be pleased. Perhaps most people speak too soon in daily affairs too, and spoil me for the appreciation of your silences.

M.: You would not want me to argue more, or sooner, music or no music?

B.: Mercy! Don't I know that you can beat anybody in debate? Besides, out of my own mouth you have already convinced me.

M.: Granted my debating prowess, why not take it as a compliment if I follow your lead without a word, or listen to your words or your music without itching to interrupt?

B.: Well, perhaps I was slow to see my mistake. Perhaps I did not like having to admit it. Anyhow, you were right. You usually are.

M.: Please! Don't make it too good! You only make me blush. Let us rather empty our glasses and drink to the Don Quixote speeches.

(They were, alas, never composed, and the more's the pity, for Busoni should have succeeded with their mixture of the fantastic, the burlesque, and mellow wisdom better than anyone.)

B.: Don't be too sanguine. You will have enough composer's miseries to come to the conclusion that sometimes it is better to leave cherished projects unexecuted.

M.: From choice or from need? Are you thinking of the jealous lover hiding his mistress, or of Berlioz abandoning a symphony after he had calculated the cost?

B.: Both, I am afraid. You ought to make yourself quite independent of composition for your existence. You should, like Rousseau, copy music, for instance.

м.: What on earth brings you to this? You know very well that he did not make anything like a living out of it. Besides, there were no trade unions in his way. I have tried, and found it difficult to enter that closely guarded domain.

в., *reproachfully:* You have been sending in a work for a competition! Did you imagine that any jury would give *you* a prize? Is it likely?

м.: Oh, that is what you were driving at all the time. Do reflect; I must at least make an honest attempt. You once got a prize yourself, you know.

в.: You don't suppose that I was one-tenth as much of a formed composer then as you are now? A single page of your music will frighten anyone who is ever acceptable as a member of a jury.

м.: But you cannot deny that you are on juries yourself? Wouldn't you give me a chance?

в.: I could not; I should recognize the first bar.

м.: Worse luck! We are turning in a vicious circle. I had hoped that some dishonesty on a jury might bring me a chance some day.

в.: It will! When it is too late! When you don't need it any more for your name. Even then, materially, it won't help you much. And don't forget that a sentimental jury will have other friends. You have nothing to expect from that, I repeat. No, you ought to make a living from something that has nothing to do with music. Then you could afford to write whatever pleased you.

м.: Ouch! Don't you know that I shall be looked upon as an amateur and an interloper, and shunned by all musicians?

в.: Publishers used to accept my works because of my fame as a pianist. But that fame stands in my way with the public.

м.: Because they think you ought to be *only* a pianist. What would they think of "only an amateur"? *You* despise amateurs.

в.: If you were taken for one, that would not make you one. Still, I admit the objection. I see no way out for you. I should like to give you an income for a number of years so that you could work with complete freedom. Only, honestly, I have been carefully calculating—I cannot manage it. People think I am a wealthy man: I am nothing of the sort. However much I should like to, I simply have not the money.

There are not many composers who would think of such assistance to a confrère, and if Busoni, in this case, was not in a position to do what his feeling prompted, it was because he always had most lavishly given away money, right and left, to pupils and struggling musicians, and sacrificed much of his time to teaching them [1] and performing their works.

If he ever complained of anything, it was that his example had not borne fruit, that younger men, when their successes had made them financially competent, were not in their turn ready to give of what they had acquired, to others less fortunate, whose work might enrich music if not themselves.

He could never understand selfishness, whether reasoning or unreasoning, and one could not point to a nobler trait in his character, or to one that showed better how loyal and truehearted an artist he was.

His duty, he felt, was to art, and in every sense.

DOWN AMONG THE DEAD MEN (1935)

---

[1] It will be remembered that he never accepted remuneration. [Van Dieren's note.]

APROPOS OF INSTRUMENTS

THOMAS HARDY

→»» «««

The Organ Blower's Complaint

This frame of mind naturally induced an amazing abstraction in the organist, never very vigilant at the best times. He would hear the cathedral clock strike one, and go the next minute to see what time it was. "I never seed such a man as Mr. Julian is," said the head blower. "He'll meet me anywhere out-of-doors, and never wink or nod. You'd hardly expect it. I don't find fault, but you'd hardly expect it, seeing how I play the same instrument as he do himself, and have done it for so many years longer than he. How I have indulged that man, too! If 'tis Pedals for two martel hours of practice I never complain; and he has plenty of vagaries. When 'tis hot summer weather there's nothing will do for him but Choir, Great and Swell together, till yer face is but a vapor; and on a frosty winter night he'll keep me there while he tweedles upon the Twelfth and Sixteenth till my arms be scrammed for want of motion. And never speak a word out-of-doors!"

THE HAND OF ETHELBERTA (1876)

ARTHUR SCHOPENHAUER

⟫⟩⟨⟪

The Russian Horn

The trenchant philosopher, who did much by his writings to give music intellectual dignity, was himself a good musician and a devotee of Italian opera.

Whoever is a whole man, a man par excellence, is no fraction of the human race, but a self-sufficient unit. Ordinary company may in this respect be likened to Russian-horn music. Each horn has only one note, and only by carefully edging in their parts can the instrumentists play a piece.[1] Now this monotone of a Russian horn is precisely what you get from most people's minds. How many of them actually look as if they had at no time more than one and the same thought—incapable of another! This explains why they are so dull, and also why they are so gregarious and always try to forgather in herds. The monotony of his own being makes the lone man intolerable to himself: *"Omnis stultitia laborat fastidio sui"* [2]—only when you bring a number of them together in a group do you obtain anything from them—just like the music from those horns.

On the contrary, a man of brains is like a virtuoso who can give a concert all by himself. Or he is like a piano, which is in itself a small orchestra. Such a man is a small world, and what the others produce by playing all together, he offers in the unity of one consciousness. Like the piano, he is not a part of the symphony but is naturally fitted to play solo. He plays in solitude, perhaps, or if with others, then only as principal, to others' accompaniment—like the

[1] The Russian bands often numbered as many as one hundred players. The instruments are straight conical tubes of varying length, with mouthpieces almost at right angles.

[2] Every kind of idiocy suffers its own disgust.

449

piano; or else he gives the true pitch, as in singing—like the piano.

Now those who like company can deduce the rule from this comparison, that deficiency of quality in those we meet must be made up for somehow by quantity. With one intelligent being, though he be the only one, it is possible to have all the social intercourse that may be desired; but when we are forced to deal with none but ordinary people, it is best to collect a crowd of them, so that by collaboration something may result, on the analogy of the horns. And may Heaven grant you patience for the job!

MAXIMS OF WORLDLY WISDOM (1850)

CHATEAUBRIAND

❧ ❧

Of Bells

The Genius of Christianity marks a date in the religious history of France after the Revolution. By reviewing in one work all the psychological, social, historic, and artistic merits of the Church, Chateaubriand initiated a revival of faith. Music necessarily concerned him at many points.

It seems from the outset a rather remarkable thing that a means could be found to awaken by one hammer stroke a single emotion at the same moment in a thousand different hearts, and so compel the winds and the clouds to carry the thoughts of man. Then, considered as harmony, bells undoubtedly possess a beauty of the first order—that which artists call *grandeur*. The sound of thunder is sublime solely because it has grandeur, magnitude. And thus it is with the winds and the sea, with volcanos, waterfalls, or the voice of a whole people.

With what pleasure would Pythagoras, who gladly heard the blacksmith's hammer, have listened to our bells on the eve of a religious ceremony! The soul may be melted by the strings of a lyre, but it is not fired with enthusiasm as when aroused by the thunderbolts of battle or by an imposing peal that proclaims in the realms above the glory of the Lord of Hosts.

And yet this is not the most wonderful characteristic of the sound of bells, which has so many secret links with our being. How often, in the silence of the night, has not a distant ringing of bells, a faint reverberation, as of a heart expiring in agony, struck and amazed the ear of the adulteress? How often have these echoes not reached even the atheist who, in his impious vigil, was perhaps daring to write that there is no God! The pen falls from his hand as he hears the dreadful knell of death which seems to be saying, "Is there indeed no God?" Oh, why did not such sounds disturb the sleep of our oppressors! Mysterious religion that by the sole magic of sounding bronze can change pleasures into torments, shake the atheist, and make the assassin drop his knife!

Softer feelings are also linked with the sound of bells. When at dawn in harvest time one hears together with the lark the soft tinklings that rise from our hamlets, one thinks the guardian angel of the crops is rousing the toilers by breathing into some Hebrew instrument the stories of Zipporah or Naomi. It seems to me that were I a poet, I should not disdain the "bell rung by ghosts" which hangs in the old chapel by the wood, nor that which out of a sacred fear resounds in our villages to avert lightning, nor again that which is heard at night in certain seaports to guide the helmsman through the reefs.

On feast days the carillon adds to the general gladness. But in calamity these same sounds become dreadful to hear. The hair upon the head still rises at the very thought of the days of flame and carnage accompanied by the clangor of the tocsin. Who of us can have lost the memory of the cries, howls, and screams, broken by intervals of silence during which scattered shots or some solitary lamenting voice could be heard, and above all the deep hum of the bell tolling the alarm, or the quiet strokes of the cathedral clock marking the spent hour?

Had bells been attached to any other monument but our churches, they never would have touched the moral sympathies of our hearts. It was God himself who commanded the angel of victory to fling into the ether the peals that proclaim our triumphs, and the angel of death to toll for the leave-taking of the soul He is summoning to Him. Thus does a Christian society communicate by a thousand secret voices with Divinity, and its roots lose themselves mysteriously at the source of all mystery.

Let then the bells call together the faithful; the voice of man is not pure enough to bring to the foot of the altar repentance, innocence, and sorrow.

THE GENIUS OF CHRISTIANITY (1802)

CHARLES DICKENS

※ ※

The Solitary Cello

He handed her down to a coach she had in waiting at the door; and if his landlady had not been deaf, she would have heard him muttering as he went back upstairs, when the coach had driven off, that we were creatures of habit, and it was a sorrowful habit to be an old bachelor.

The violoncello lying on the sofa between the two chairs, he took it up, without putting away the vacant chair, and sat droning on it, and slowly shaking his head at the vacant chair, for a long, long time. The expression he communicated to the instrument at first, though monstrously pathetic and bland, was nothing to the expression he communicated to his own face, and bestowed upon the empty chair: which was so sincere, that he was obliged to have recourse to Captain Cuttle's remedy more than once, and to rub his face with his sleeve. By degrees, however, the violoncello, in unison with his own frame of mind, glided melodiously into "The Harmonious Blacksmith," which he played over and over again, until his ruddy and serene face gleamed like true metal on the anvil of a veritable blacksmith. In fine, the violoncello and the empty chair were the companions of his bachelorhood until nearly midnight; and when he took his supper, the violoncello set up on end in the sofa corner, big with the latent harmony of a whole foundry full of harmonious blacksmiths, seemed to ogle the empty chair out of its crooked eyes, with unutterable intelligence.

DOMBEY AND SON (1846)

HECTOR BERLIOZ

->>> <<<-

The Flute

For quite a while this instrument remained in many ways most imperfect. But now, thanks to the skill of a few makers and to the
device generalized by Boehm from Gordon's invention, it plays as
true and as evenly as can be desired. All the woodwind instruments
will shortly achieve the same status. It is not hard to understand why
up to now their intonation was anything but irreproachable: the distance between the holes bored in the tube was determined by the span
of the player's fingers instead of by the rational division of the length
of the tube according to the laws of physics. Gordon first, and later
Boehm, proceeded to ascertain the points of subdivision of the vibrating body, and to bore the holes at those points regardless of the con-
venience, or even the feasibility, of playing the instrument. They
felt confident of being able somehow or other to make possible the
application of the fingers to each of these holes.

Once the instrument had been made "true" by this procedure, they
invented a mechanism of rings and keys which were so placed that
the performer's fingers could easily shut or open all the holes out of
the normal reach. By this means the old fingering was necessarily
changed and the performers had to study new exercises. But after
some little practice, the new instruments afforded them so many advantages in return for their effort that there is no doubt a few years
more of dissemination through example, and of persuasion by word of
mouth, will see the adoption of the new Gordon and Boehm woodwinds, to the entire exclusion of the old.

Within the last few years the compass of the flute has been extended by two half-steps in the bass and three in the treble, which
brings the whole range to three octaves. The sonority of the flute is

gentle in the medium register, rather piercing in the upper, and strongly characterized in the bass. The timbres of the medium and high notes have no very marked expression of their own. They can be used for melodies and accents of various kinds, but they are unable to rival the naïve gaiety of the oboe or the noble tenderness of the clarinet. Consequently it seems as if the flute were an instrument almost devoid of characteristic expression, which one may therefore introduce, any and everywhere, for the sake of the ease with which it can perform quick passages and sustain the high notes of the orchestra in completing high-register chords.

All this is in general quite true, yet if one studies the flute closely, one discovers that it possesses an expressiveness of its own, and an aptitude for rendering certain moods that no other instrument can compete with. If it is desired to impart to a sad melody an accent of desolation, though at the same time humble and resigned, the weak sounds of the medium range, in the keys of C minor and D minor especially, will unfailingly supply the necessary nuance. Only one master seems to me to have fully availed himself of this pale coloring: I mean Gluck. In listening to the air-pantomime in D minor which he wrote for the scene of the Elysian Fields in *Orpheus,* one perceives at a glance that only a flute should play the melody. An oboe would have sounded too childlike, and its voice would not have seemed sufficiently pure; the English horn is too grave; a clarinet would have done well enough no doubt, but some of the notes would have been too loud, and none of the softer notes could have been kept to the mild, veiled, self-effacing sonority of the F natural in the medium and the first B flat above the staff, which give so much melancholy to the flute in this key of D minor where they recur.

Finally, neither the violin, nor the viola, nor the cello, whether alone or in groups, was proper for the plaint, sublime to the highest degree, of a desperate and suffering shade. It required the very instrument that Gluck chose. And his melody is so conceived that the flute lends itself to all the anxious moments of this unending pain, still marked as it is by the passionate accents of earthly life. At first it is a scarcely audible voice, which seems afraid of being heard; then it moans quietly, rises to the pitch of repining, then to that of deep sorrow, as of a heart torn by incurable wounds, and falls back gradually into plaintiveness, the sweet moaning and murmuring of a soul resigned to grief—what a poet!

TREATISE ON ORCHESTRATION (1844)

JEREMY COLLIER

-»> «-

An Instrument for War and Peace

Jeremy Collier (1650–1726) was the Royalist bishop who tried to purge
English drama after the Restoration by writing his notorious *Short
View of the English Stage*. His essays on less polemical subjects were
widely read and his opinions disseminated, often, through quotation in
Addison's *Spectator*.

Indeed Musick, when rightly ordered, cannot be prefer'd too much.
For it re-creates and exalts the Mind at the same time. It composes the
Passions, affords a strong Pleasure, and excites a Nobleness of
Thought. But the manner of the Conveyance of Sounds, which is as
it were the Basis of Musick, is unintelligible. For what can be more
strange, than that the rubbing of a little *Hair* and *Cat-gut* together,
shou'd make such a mighty alteration in a Man that sits at a distance?

But this wonder of *Perception* is not peculiar to the *Ear:* For the
Operations of all the *Senses* are in some respect incomprehensible.
The sense of *Hearing,* as well as that of *Sight,* seems to be of a supe-
rior Order to the rest. It commands a satisfaction at a greater distance,
strikes a finer stroak and makes a single Object divide itself without
Lessening. For instance: A Man may see the light of a Candle, and
hear a Voice or Instrument, as well if there be ten in the Room as if
he was there alone. The stream of Sounds, though cut into several
Rivulets, comes as full to the Ear as if it had but one Channel to feed.
The *Tast* and *Touch* are, if one may say so, more narrow Spirited.

The Force of Musick is more wonderful than the Conveyance.
How strangely does it awaken the Mind! It infuses an unexpected
vigour, makes the impression agreeable and sprightly, and seems to
furnish a new Capacity as well as a new opportunity of Satisfac-

tion. Have you not observed a Captain at the Head of a Company, how much he is altered at the Beat of a Drum? What a vigorous Motion, what an erected Posture, what an enterprising Visage, all of a suddain? His blood charges in his veins, his Spirits jump like Gunpowder, and seem impatient to attack the Enemy.

And here it may not be improper to consider, whether there may not be some *Counter-sounds;* which may give the Mind as high a disgust, as the other can a pleasure. For the Purpose: I believe 'tis possible to invent an *Instrument* that shall have a quite contrary effect to those Martial ones now in use. An *Instrument* that shall sink the Spirits and shake the nerves, and curdle the blood, and inspire Despair, and Cowardice, and Consternation, at a surprising Rate. 'Tis probable the roaring of Lions, the warbling of Cats and Scritch-Owls, together with a mixture of the howling of Dogs, judiciously imitated and compounded, might go a great way in this Invention. Whether such Anti-Musick as this might not be of Service in a Camp, I shall leave to the Military Men to consider.

AN ESSAY OF MUSICK (1702)

FREDERIC HARRISON

-⇾⇾⟨⟨-

The Concert Hall

Trained as a historian but dedicated to the spread of Positivism and
general culture, Harrison spent his life writing articles, letters, and
reviews on a multitude of subjects.

One of the leading features of the reorganization of London, as I can
conceive it in the future, will be the formation of permanent centers
of musical culture. Music is the most social, the most affecting, the
purest of the arts; the one most deeply connected with the moral side
of civilization. It stands alone in the arts as hardly capable of being
distorted to minister to luxury, evil, or ostentation. One can hardly
imagine vicious music, or purse-proud music, or selfish music. It is
by its very nature social, emotional, and humanizing. Hence I hold
music to be the art which specially concerns all social reformers and
popular teachers. And, as we have pointed out to Mr. Ruskin and the
aesthetic pessimists, these latter ages cannot be called deficient in art,
since they have immensely magnified the most human of all the arts
of sense.

I am no musician, and do not pretend to say a word about music
as an art. But, as one who delights in music, and who has long sought
to bring out its social and civilizing mission, I have been very much
struck with the fact that music is dependent in a curious degree on
the material conditions of our civic life. Pictures, statues, poems, can
be sent about and multiplied in various forms ad infinitum. The
poorest home can contain a Shakespeare, a cast, or an engraving. A
great cathedral may impress the spirit of millions, even as they walk
to their business under its shadow. But music of a high kind, though
it knows no limitations of country, age, or material—though it is free
of time, space, and matter—does need trained powers of execution,

the combination of suitable hearers and performers, and above all, a place exactly corresponding to the kind of art performed.

Music is peculiarly dependent, both for its artistic and social value, on the material conditions of social organization. It needs three things: (1) highly trained executants; (2) a permanent and duly trained audience; (3) a *place* of performance, convenient to the audience, and suitable to the artistic conditions.

Now London easily gives us the first. But by its enormous inorganic bulk it makes the second condition very rare and difficult. And strangely enough, in spite of its wealth and energy, perhaps by reason of its wealth and energy, it does not give us the third. I have been from my youth a diligent attendant at many of our best series of concerts; and in days when I had more leisure, I made great sacrifices and underwent great trouble to do so. But the huge floating mobs of London, and the rage of "undertakers" to collect mobs, have almost driven me out and make me nearly hopeless. I have watched scores of times how all serious music and all serious artists have to educate their audience gradually by a long and conscientious work of cultivation. A great musician has, I hold, more to do to train his audience than to train his orchestra. No audience can become worthy to listen to great music fitly performed unless it is a permanent and painstaking audience; unless it labors honestly to understand the master and his interpreters. And it is just this permanence and this self-educating spirit that the floating mob of London chokes. Just as the audience is pulling itself together and becoming fit to be played to, the series of concerts becomes fashionable, or the season begins; the mob breaks in, and all goes wrong. How delightful the —— day concerts used to be till fine people took them up, and till the balls began. Who can listen to a chaconne whilst a bare-shouldered dowager and her three daughters are hurrying past one to the first dance! No, a permanent self-respecting, art-respecting audience must consist of quiet people, living within a moderate distance of each other and of the concert hall. And this we cannot have till London is grouped into smaller social units.

Besides, London with all its wealth and size does not give us suitable concert halls. They are all either too big, ill shaped for musical purposes, inconveniently placed, or repulsively like a schoolroom. I cannot call to mind one concert hall in London which does not sin in one or other of these four conditions. To ask us to listen to a great violin in company with three thousand others (some of them talking German, American, or Cockney; some of them hurrying out to a "crush") is mere torment. No, I will no longer go to hear the finest violin solo on earth with more than four or five hundred of my fellow-beings; and I should greatly prefer three hundred. To give what is facetiously called "a concert" in a colosseum which holds fifteen thousand people is an impertinence. Time was when I never missed an oratorio. But I have never heard one yet, in an arena which seems designed for a bullfight or a hippodrome. And much as I honor Mr. Manns, I cannot now spend a day in going to Sydenham in order to hear three pieces, the utmost that I care for at the same sitting. There is not one perfect concert hall in London. The —— and the —— are only fit for public meetings; the —— will do for a symphony, but it is too big for a solo or a quartet. The —— is pretty; but its proper purpose is a fancy ball. In the —— and the —— one can hear a quartet to advantage; but then they look like a classroom in a board-school, and the seats are as bad as a third-class box on the South-Eastern Railway. The ideal concert hall should hold five hundred persons comfortably; it should be within an easy walk of their homes; it should have ample passages, exits, cloakrooms, artists' and committee rooms, it should have pure air, cool temperature, no gas, no noise, and no suggestions either of Mohawk Minstrels or fried fish. Lastly, it should be beautiful: architecture, decoration, and fittings should be of an art worthy to invite us to the high art we meet to cultivate. London has no such concert hall; and it is a burning shame.

MEMORIES AND THOUGHTS (1898)

PRINCESS LIEVEN

→≫≪←

The Barrel Organ

In this unmusical country [1] there are dreadful barrel organs which go up and down the streets—there is one playing under my windows right now, which is so out of tune that it almost makes me weep and I find it nearly impossible to continue this letter to you. When I am forced to listen to discordant sounds, I cannot keep a single clear idea in my head. I feel a physical distress that immediately affects my mental faculties.

LETTER TO METTERNICH, JULY 11, 1820

[1] England.

B. H. HAGGIN

※※ ※※

Music on Records

We hear a piece of music as it comes to us through a player's mind; it sounds different as it comes through different minds; and I judge a performance by considering whether the character, the quality, the significance it imparts to the music is what my own understanding of the composer and the work leads me to believe correct. If I accept Stokowski's performance of the bacchanale from *Tannhäuser* it is because he gives the music the character I think a bacchanale by Wagner should have; if I reject Stokowski's performance of music from *Boris Godunov* it is because the fever and glitter and luxuriance that are eminently suitable to Wagner's bacchanale completely falsify the character and significance of the quietly profound music of Moussorgsky. Or if I object to what Heifetz does in a passage of the third movement of Franck's Violin Sonata, it is because the constant holding back then hurrying, and hurrying then holding back, contradict not only Franck's direction that the passage be played *molto dolce e tranquillo,* but the character and emotional significance which, it is clear from this direction, Franck wants the passage to have.

In the eyes of a record company anything it issues cannot be less than a masterpiece, and the man who performs it is not only a great artist but exactly the right great artist for the work. Actually the company is out to sell records, and the records that sell are the ones made by the currently celebrated players, and of these a very small number indeed are what can be called great artists—that is, men who are endowed not only with fleet fingers but with musical understanding and taste and integrity. Most people understand that an actor can have wonderful gifts of voice and movement and presence, and misuse them; they understand that a painter named Sargent could use a superb technical equipment to achieve slick effects; but they don't understand that an orchestral conductor can have phenomenal technical powers that enable him to produce miraculous sounds with an orchestra, and use these powers to produce miraculous sounds that falsify almost every composer and work he conducts.

Moreover, even a great artist is not equally great in everything he does. An actor plays one role better than another; a conductor does better with the music of one composer than with another. For the music, if it amounts to anything, is not a mere spinning of notes, but in each case a product of human imagination and feeling; and the conductor brings to these his own imagination and feeling, which may match better in one case than in another. But a record company that uses a performer only because of the selling power of his currently celebrated name is not concerned with what, if anything, he does well; and the result is instance after instance of poor matching of performer to music.

The Pro Arte Quartet, which earned its reputation with excellent performances of modern works, now records quartets and quintets of Mozart, for which it has neither the feeling nor even the necessary technical virtuosity. Again, there are conductors who do better than Koussevitzky with Beethoven's *Eroica* and Mozart's G Minor; whereas to hear Koussevitzky's performances of Debussy is to realize that one had never really heard the works before. Yet Koussevitzky records the *Eroica* and the G Minor, but not a note of Debussy; and Debussy's *Iberia* is recorded by Barbirolli, not because he is the right conductor for the work—which he very evidently is not—but because he is the conductor of the New York Philharmonic Symphony Orchestra, and without regard for the fact that he is a good conductor for the music of Haydn and Mozart.

MUSIC ON RECORDS (1938)

TOM S. WOTTON

-»»-««-

Notes on Drums

Tom S. Wotton will be remembered as the most thorough student of
Berlioz and the compiler of a *Dictionary of Foreign Musical Terms*
that is in equal degree accurate and inspired. But as this extract shows,
Wotton wrote on a variety of musical subjects and was the successful
author of a comedy praised by Bernard Shaw.

A drum seems to be a simple enough affair. Yet, as we shall see,
more confusion has arisen in connection with it than with any other
instrument of the orchestra. There are seven kinds specified in modern scores, and, roughly arranged in order of infrequency, they are
these:

1. Oriental drums.
2. Tabors.
3. Tenor drums (side drums without a snare).[1]
4. Tambourines.
5. Snare drums (side drums possessing a snare).
6. Bass drums.
7. Kettledrums.

ORIENTAL DRUMS

These include any drum which at present belongs to any country
outside Occidental civilization. The drums are of varied shape and
size, and the composer seldom deigns to specify them beyond giving
them a name which bears little or no resemblance to their native appellation.

In Ippolitov-Ivanov's *Scènes caucasiennes* we find *piccoli timpani*

---

[1] A snare consists of eight to ten strands of catgut (or its substitutes) which
are loosely strung across that head of the drum which is not beaten. The vibrations of the snare produce a characteristic rattling effect.

orientali marked in the score. Possibly the instruments are well known to Russian musicians, but there is no description given of them, despite the prominent part they play in No. 2 of the suite.

These drums, of which the Russian name is apparently *Timplipito,* may be described as a couple of ginger jars of different sizes, bound together by a strip of rawhide, which also serves to secure the two membranes. The pair are played with a couple of little drumsticks, and cannot be tuned, remaining at the pitch decreed by Providence and the vagaries of the drying hide. The choice of jars of appropriate size may ensure the notes being approximately a fifth apart.

The Tarbouka, from the Arabic *darâboukkeh,* is a species of drum used throughout Northern Africa, the Egyptian form being shaped like an inverted vase, with a membrane in place of the original bottom. The neck of the vase is tucked under the arm, and the skin struck by both hands, the left beating the edge, and the right, the center. In the orchestra a small drumstick is used, and the instrument is shaped like a flower pot, with a membrane on the larger end. In both cases the shell is of pottery. . . .

THE TENOR DRUM

The essential distinction between the tenor drum and the snare drum is the absence of a snare in the former. Nowadays it may be said to be larger than the snare drum, but this was not always so. Usually its shell is made of wood, in agreement with the textbooks, but, from the catalogues of the makers, this is not invariably so. Both it and the snare drum are "side drums," inasmuch as they are both slung on the left side, and beaten with a pair of drumsticks—occasionally somewhat heavier in the case of the tenor drum. Unfortunately, however, "side drum" is the ordinary English term for a snare drum, which at once makes for confusion. Why are musicians so careless in their nomenclature? A golfer would cease to be considered as such if he confused his clubs in similar fashion.

THE TAMBOURINE

The French for the tambourine is *Tambour de Basque* (with the occasional omission of the *de*)—an inappropriate one since, according to Jacquot (*Dictionnaire des instruments de musique*), the only drum used in the Basque Provinces is the tabor, a statement confirmed by a letter in the *Daily Telegraph* some years ago. I have given already an Italian and a German name, and the possible confusion that may arise from their use. *Tamburello* for the first, and *Schellentrommel* or *Baskische Trommel* for the second (all three terms to be found in scores), would avoid this.

The instrument is too well known to need any description, but it must be pointed out that the "jingles" (the little cymbals strung on wires in the hoop) are not always to be found. Lalo, in his *Le Roi d'Ys* (1888) specifies a tambourine without them, since such a one is used in Brittany, the scene of the opera.

THE SNARE DRUM [2]

Amongst the minor mysteries of life must be placed the fact that when average individuals are asked to describe a kettledrum they immediately move their hands to the left, while they endeavor, with varying success, to imitate the characteristic rattle of the snare drum. But I do not know whether the average English or German musician rises much above the level of the average individual when he dubs "any old drum" slung at the side as a "side drum," or a *"Kleine Trommel,"* as the case may be. The French are much more precise in their nomenclature. With them, a drum with a snare is called a *Caisse claire,* as opposed to the *Caisse sourde* (dull), an obsolescent name for the *Caisse roulante.* The ordinary term for a snare drum—*Tambour*—is employed specifically for the military side drum, which nowadays invariably has a snare.

Numerous "tricks" are possible on the snare drum, though few of them have penetrated into the realm of legitimate music. In *La Tragédie de Salomé,* Florent Schmitt directs his snare drum to play *sur le bois* (on the wood, i.e., on the ropehoop), and in *Catalonia,*

---

[2] The official name of the instrument is "side drum," and, as far as I am aware, no drummer would call a tenor drum by that name. I have used throughout the alternative of "snare drum" to avoid any possible confusion. [Wotton's note.]

Albéniz instructs his drummer to beat on the music desk—a process which some purists might insist was not playing the drum at all! Zandonai, in his *Primavera in Val di Sole,* for one passage directs the performer to play *vicino al metallo,* i.e., on the edge of the membrane near the metal shell, and in another, *sul metallo,* i.e., on the shell itself.

THE BASS DRUM

The correct English name for the *Grosse Caisse* (*Gran Cassa* or *Grosse Trommel*) is "bass drum," and has been for the past hundred and fifty years at least. It is somewhat necessary to stress the point, because some English authorities have given "long drum" and "double drum" as equivalent names for the instrument. A form of tenor drum has been called a "tambour long," and with reason, since its length (as with a tabor) greatly exceeded its diameter. Although I should be sorry to assert that a bass drum has never been made of the dimensions of a section of the Channel Tunnel, it obviously could not have been used for marching purposes, when the depth of the instrument is limited by the width of a man's chest. In any case, the bass drum was called so in 1787, as we know from an account for band-fitting sent in by the bandmaster of the Royal Artillery.

Like the tenor one, the bass drum can be tuned to some extent, and possibly an artistic drummer might have a different tension on the skins for depicting the dull sound of distant cannon and in a brilliant march, heavily instrumentated. Kastner mentions two apparently unsuccessful attempts to produce a bass drum tunable to definite notes. The only indication as to pitch is, as far as I am aware, in Verdi's *Requiem,* where, for the *"Dies Irae,"* the rope is directed to be "very taut in order that this syncopation may be short and very loud"—chords for full orchestra on the accented beats are followed by strokes on the unaccented ones for bass-drum solo. Verdi, by the way, though he may have abused the instrument at times, was one of the first to employ it for pianissimo rhythmical effects.

Strauss, Mahler, and others have revived the *Rute* (rod or birch) which seemingly was a constant appendage of the bass drum, when it was introduced into Europe by the Turkish Janissaries in the eighteenth century.[3]

KETTLEDRUMS

These instruments are dealt with so exhaustively in the treatises and dictionaries that there is little to remark here. In many modern works chromatic kettledrums, of which the tuning can be altered instantly, are specified. Experiments in this direction have been made for the past hundred years, but none of them have been entirely satisfactory. If animals could be persuaded to grow homogenous skins, chromatic drums might be a success. Unfortunately, until now they have evinced little interest in their future artistic life, and their skins stretch unevenly, with the result that a drum will possibly require more adjustment at one portion of its circumference than at another. And this can only be achieved by means of the six to ten screws of the ordinary model.

The kettledrums seem to have been regarded as too dignified for many tricks to be played on them. Snare drumsticks are used in *Petrouchka,*[4] first fortissimo in what is practically a roll on F sharp, and secondly mezzo forte on G and B flat alternately. In the score of the *Enigma Variations* [5] we find a similar effect in Number XIII. On the first performance a couple of half-crowns seem to have been used for the pianissimo roll. The directions being also given in German, the composer may have hesitated as to which German piece best corresponded to the musical value of a prewar half-crown; or perhaps he concluded that drumsticks were more likely to be found in an orchestra than coins of the realm.

MUSICAL TIMES (1930)

---

[3] Reintroduced—to be quite exact—since the Crusaders brought back from Palestine the bass and other drums. [Wotton's note.]

[4] By Igor Stravinsky (1911).

[5] By Edward Elgar (1899).

ANONYMOUS

→»→ ←«←

The Orchestra

It is mere folly to talk as the professors talk of a standard orchestra. There never has been a perfect orchestra; there is not a perfect orchestra yet; there is not likely to be a perfect orchestra for many years to come; and instead of regretting that we are moving away from the orchestra of Mozart's and Haydn's time, we should rejoice on that very account. Why two flutes should be right and three flutes shameful extravagance; why the double clarinet should be looked upon as an unauthorized interloper; why the tubas should be thought the inferiors of the trombones merely because they came in later—these and a hundred other things pass the comprehension of everyone who gives ten minutes of serious thought to the orchestra.

The truth is that instead of repelling all the new instruments, we should welcome them, welcome them as helping to make the orchestra a genuine instrument. It is time to be done with the art of faking, which is the only art explained in any book of instrumentation yet written; it is time to say that as there are plenty of players available and we are no longer living around the courts of petty three-square-mile princelets, we should have a complete orchestra. And a complete orchestra would include a complete flute group—a treble, alto, tenor, and bass flute; the complete oboe group that the best bands have at present . . . and so on right through the orchestra. One of the most important things would be to complete the string group. We want a true tenor, running down to the G beneath the tenor C; the violas would then play a true alto part in their best register. We want also the six-stringed double bass with frets, to avoid the present sudden disappearance of the bass part. When these things are done we shall be on the way to getting an orchestra worth writing for.

EDITORIAL, *THE MUSICIAN* (April 1900)

Fantasies and Confessions

W. F. APTHORP

>>> <<<

Sonata Form in Food

For many years W. F. Apthorp (1848–1913) supplied the notes for the
Boston Symphony programs, setting the genre of mixed anecdote, biography, reminiscence, and criticism. A good musician and facile writer,
he often ventured, as is seen below, into the even higher genre of musical
fiction.

"Stop monkeying with your chartreuse before you've finished your
coffee, like a brute beast that has no soul, and I will prove to you that
the regularly planned French dinner is in the sonata form—there can
be no doubt about it."

"Fire away," said the other, "I'm quite willing to be educated in
the higher gastronomy."

"Well, then! here it is," Guloston went on, lighting his cigar at one
of the candles on the table, "here it is. In the first place, you must
know that the French dinner of the old school, the good old school,
was divided into two parts, two *services,* as the technical name is.
The first began with the *relevés—*"

"I always thought the first began with the soup," put in Harmon,
"or oysters."

"Not a bit of it! There's where you make a fatal, an unpardonable
mistake!" cried Guloston, "an error that would knock my theory on
beam ends! The first *service* begins with the *relevés,* the *grosses
pièces chaudes;* then come the *entrées.* The second *service* begins with
the *rôts,* plain meat or game, with salad; these are followed by the
entremets, the vegetables and sweets. Now, both these two *services*
must be in equilibrium, they must counterbalance each other exactly;
there must be as many *rôts* in the second as there have been *relevés* in
the first, as many *entremets* as *entrées.* You understand that?"

"Yes, I see that," replied Harmon, "but I must say I'm a bit curious about the soup."

"Ah! my dear fellow," went on Guloston enthusiastically, "the soup and *hors d'oeuvres* belong properly to neither *service;* the soup is nothing more nor less than a free introduction to the whole dinner. As you musical sharps say, the free introduction—in slow tempo—is not a real factor of the form at all; it is only a preparation for what is to follow. As for the *hors d'oeuvres,* their very name shows that they are outside the circle of the form: they are nothing but free light skirmishing, and have no thematic importance. They follow the soup— or, if you take them in the sense of the Italian *antipasti,* as we do our oysters in this country, they come before the soup—and have no influence upon the form whatever. They should be eaten *freiphantasierend,* just tasted, a bit here and a bit there; not dwelling upon any particular flavor, but skipping daintily from one to another, like eating harlequin-ice. *Hors d'oeuvres,* in the French sense—that is, coming after the soup—might be compared to a free, premonitory transition passage leading over from the introduction to the main body of the movement. You understand so far, Harmon?"

"Yes, I understand so far: the soup, with the *hors d'oeuvres* or *antipasti,* is the free introduction. Now for the sonata form proper!"

"Now for the sonata form proper; exactly!" said Guloston, blowing a ring from his cigar. "The *relevés*—of which there ought to be two, one of fish and one of meat—are the first and second themes. The *entrées*—of which there should be at least four, if there have been two *relevés*—represent the free fantasia, the working-out in detail of those two leading ideas of fish and meat."

"Wonderful!" exclaimed Harmon, tossing the stump of his cigarette into the fire, and taking a sip of chartreuse unreproved, before rolling another. "Wonderful! But how about your working-out of the two principal themes? I see the meat part of it clearly enough; but how about the fish part? The fish once done with, it doesn't return again."

"There's where you are totally and barbarically wrong," Guloston replied; "the idea that fish belongs exclusively to the beginning of the first *service* is that of the British barbarian and of his only slightly more civilized American descendant. There may be, and really should be, an *entrée* of fish, as well as of meat; remember such things as Thackeray lobster, or picked crabs; take little *bouchées* of oysters or clams, or *écrevisses bordelaise.* Any small dish with a sauce and garnish is an *entrée,* and consequently belongs in the second part of the first *service*—in the working-out. You mustn't forget that the *relevés* are essentially *grosses pièces,* big dishes; they, too, have a sauce and garnish, but the little things of a similar kind are *entrées.* Well, with the *entrées* the first *service,* the first part and free fantasia, comes to an end."

"Then comes the Roman punch—with perhaps a cigarette, I suppose," suggested Harmon. "Where do you make room for that in your sonata form?"

"Aha! *tu y es!*" cried Guloston, delighted. "A pupil who asks intelligent questions is a pupil worth having! Of course, we have Roman punch, and equally of course, we have a cigarette with it. And, as you seem to suspect, it is no regular nor necessary part of the form; only a delightful adjunct. The Roman punch and cigarette form a free poetic episode, not connected with any of the leading themes; you find such episodes now and then in symphonic first movements, though perhaps not so often as in dinners. But we can easily find an example. Let me see; yes, take the passage for the muted violins with the tremolo on the violas in the overture to *Euryanthe:* that is the Roman punch with a cigarette. The parallel could not be more accurate!"

"Good for you, my boy!" cried Harmon; "you keep your head and heels like a true master! Who would have thought of such a parallel! Well, let's get on to our second *service,* to the third part of the movement—since the first *service* includes the first part and the working-out."

"Ah! here you must follow me carefully," answered Guloston, "and for that you had better fill up your glass of chartreuse once more and pass me the bottle. Here the parallel becomes less exact, I admit; but it holds good, all the same, if you don't insist upon every i being dotted and every t crossed, like a mere Philistine pedant. Let us first consider the *rôts,* of which, as you will remember, there must be as many as there were *relevés* in the first *service.* These *rôts* represent the return of the principal themes in the third part of the movement. I admit that there is no fish in them; also that there is still another difference between them and their corresponding *relevés:* the *relevés* were dishes with sauce and a garnish—of mushrooms, truffles, or some other vegetables—and this same idea of sauce and *garniture,* of a more or less vegetable nature, was further carried out in the *entrées;* whereas the *rôts* are plain roast meat or game, without sauce or garnish—unless you call the salad a garnish, and, if the salad is not of the vegetable kingdom, what on earth is it? But let that pass for a moment; we should never ride a simile, or parallel, between two different arts to death. If we do, we come to grief, and all the poetry of the thing is lost!

"Let us accept the two *rôts* as the second *service* representatives of the two *relevés* in the first; like the *relevés,* they are *pièces de résistance,* solid meat, no matter how delicate; they mean a return to business, just as the return of the first theme does at the beginning of the third part of a symphonic movement. They are followed by the *entremets*—vegetables and sweets—which are equal in number to the *entrées* of the first *service,* and so serve as a sort of ideal counterpoise to them. Now, what are these *entremets?* Evidently they are the coda, the second free fantasia, as Beethoven developed it in the *Eroica,* to counterbalance the first one.

"And note just here how the difference in material between the two *services*—there being a want of perfectly exact correspondence between the *relevés* and the *rôts,* between the *entrées* and the *entremets* —instead of destroying my parallel, makes it ideally stronger and more exact. What is, after all, the main and characteristic difference between the first and third parts of a symphonic movement? Principally a difference in tonality, in key. The first part quits the tonic after the first theme; the third part sticks to the tonic. Now, there is nothing to correspond to the idea of tonality in gastronomy; so our dinner has to mark the difference between its first and second serv-

ices in some other way. And it does this by means that are purely its own, purely gastronomic. The coherent idea that runs through the first *service* is the presentation and working-out of two forms of esculent material—animal and vegetable food—*together;* for the sauces and garnishes are made up largely of vegetable ingredients.

"The idea of the second *service,* on the other hand, is the presentation and working-out of the same, or similar, material—animal and vegetable food—*apart* and *separately;* the *rôts* being all animal, and the *entremets,* all vegetable. In music, symphonic development proceeds from the simpler to the more complex; in gastronomy, it proceeds from the complex to the simple—just the reverse, you see. This is the main difference, depending wholly upon the different media of the two arts. In each of the two, this progression has its own reason of being, based upon the nature of man's receptive power—through the ear in one case, through the gullet in the other. The ear is fatigued in a very different way from the palate; the—"

"Stop! for heaven's sake, stop!" cried Harmon. "Let's stick to art, and stop short of metaphysico-physiology! I understand you perfectly; you are right as right can be. Your dinner in sonata form has entered into my comprehension, and I knock under with the best grace in the world. You've proved your point to the satisfaction of anyone whose soul is large enough to take in the delights of the table and the glories of music! And damned be the musician who has no love for eating and drinking! But wait a bit; what do you do with the dessert in your symphonic scheme? It strikes me, now that I think of it, that the dessert would be the real coda of a dinner."

"Hm!" said Guloston, looking thoughtfully at the stump of his cigar, "dessert—fruit, ices, cheese, nuts, and all that sort of thing—is something over and above, *par dessus le marché;* very desirable and even necessary, if you will, but still, like the soup and *hors d'oeuvres,* lying outside the circle of the form. It has its symphonic equivalent, too, although, to find it, we may have to leave first movements of symphonies and turn to the overture—which is, after all, in the same general form.

"You must know overtures enough that end with a perfectly free *apothéose,* as the French say; with a free ending that has no thematic connection with what has gone before, and merely serves to round off the whole with a brilliant or soothing farewell. Take the overture to *Egmont;* that ends in this way. I know that this sort of thing is technically called a free coda; but you must admit that it has nothing in common with the sort of coda Beethoven developed, that second free fantasia to which I have compared the *entremets.* If symphonic first movements seldom end with a 'dessert,' it is simply because they are first movements, and something more is still to come; that is why we find the 'dessert coda' more frequently in overtures: they are musically complete in themselves. Oh! the dessert presents no real difficulty: it lies outside the circle of the form.

"And now, if you don't want any more chartreuse, I'll beat you a game or two at three-ball caroms."

FROM THE COURT LIBRARY OF UTOPIA (1898)

CHARLES LAMB

※※ ※※

A Chapter on Ears

Despite this essay and the humorous verses, "Thoughts on Several Eminent Composers," Lamb was not so tone deaf as he liked to make out. His sister Mary and other friends record his pleasure at more than the airs he mentions below.

I have no ear.

Mistake me not, reader—nor imagine that I am by nature destitute of those exterior twin appendages, hanging ornaments, and (architecturally speaking) handsome volutes to the human capital. Better my mother had never borne me. I am, I think, rather delicately than copiously provided with those conduits; and I feel no disposition to envy the mule for his plenty, or the mole for her exactness, in those ingenious labyrinthine inlets—those indispensable side-intelligencers.

Neither have I incurred, or done anything to incur, with Defoe, that hideous disfigurement, which constrained him to draw upon assurance—to feel "quite unabashed," and at ease upon that article. I was never, I thank my stars, in the pillory; nor, if I read them aright, is it within the compass of my destiny, that I ever should be.

When therefore I say that I have no ear, you will understand me to mean—*for music*. To say that this heart never melted at the concord of sweet sounds, would be a foul self-libel. "Water parted from the sea" never fails to move it strangely. So does "In infancy." But they were used to be sung at her harpsichord (the old-fashioned instrument in vogue in those days) by a gentlewoman—the gentlest, sure, that ever merited the appellation—the sweetest—why should I hesitate to name Mrs. S., once the blooming Fanny Weatheral of the Temple—who had power to thrill the soul of Elia, small imp as he was, even in his long coats; and to make him glow, tremble, and blush with a passion, that not faintly indicated the dayspring of that absorbing sentiment which was afterwards destined to overwhelm and subdue his nature quite for Alice W——n.

I even think that *sentimentally* I am disposed to harmony. But *organically* I am incapable of a tune. I have been practising "God save the King" all my life, whistling and humming of it over to myself in solitary corners; and am not yet arrived, they tell me, within many quavers of it. Yet hath the loyalty of Elia never been impeached.

I am not without suspicion, that I have an undeveloped faculty of music within me. For thrumming in my wild way, on my friend A.'s [1] piano, the other morning, while he was engaged in an adjoining parlour—on his return he was pleased to say, "he thought it could not be the maid!" On his first surprise at hearing the keys touched in somewhat an airy and masterful way, not dreaming of me, his suspicions had lighted on *Jenny*. But a grace, snatched from a superior refinement soon convinced him that some being—technically perhaps deficient, but higher informed from a principle common to all the fine arts—had swayed the keys to a mood which Jenny, with all her (less cultivated) enthusiasm, could never have elicited from them. I mention this as a proof of my friend's penetration, and not with any view of disparaging Jenny.

Scientifically I could never be made to understand (yet have I taken some pains) what a note in music is; or how one note should differ from another. Much less in voices can I distinguish a soprano from a tenor. Only sometimes the thorough-bass [2] I contrive to guess at, from its being supereminently harsh and disagreeable. I tremble, however, for my misapplication of the simplest terms of *that* which I disclaim. While I profess my ignorance, I scarce know what to *say* I am ignorant of. I hate, perhaps, by misnomers. *Sostenuto* and *adagio* stand in the like relation of obscurity to me; and *Sol, Fa, Mi, Re,* is as conjuring as *Baralipton.*

[1] William Ayrton (1777–1858) music critic for the *Morning Chronicle.*

[2] Lamb means the bass, and not the musical shorthand that he names, perhaps on purpose.

It is hard to stand alone in an age like this—(constituted to the quick and critical perception of all harmonious combinations, I verily believe, beyond all preceding ages, since Jubal stumbled upon the gamut) to remain, as it were, singly unimpressible to the magic influences of an art, which is said to have such an especial stroke at soothing, elevating, and refining the passions. Yet, rather than break the candid current of my confessions, I must avow to you, that I have received a great deal more pain than pleasure from this so cried-up faculty.

I am constitutionally susceptible of noises. A carpenter's hammer, in a warm summer noon, will fret me into more than midsummer madness. But those unconnected, unset sounds are nothing to the measured malice of music. The ear is passive to those single strokes; willingly enduring stripes while it hath no task to con. To music it cannot be passive. It will strive—mine at least will—spite of its inaptitude, to thrid the maze; like an unskilled eye painfully poring upon hieroglyphics.

I have sat through an Italian Opera, till, for sheer pain, and inexplicable anguish, I have rushed out into the noisiest places of the crowded streets, to solace myself with sounds, which I was not obliged to follow, and get rid of the distracting torment of endless, fruitless, barren attention! I take refuge in the unpretending assemblage of honest common-life sounds; and the purgatory of the Enraged Musician [3] becomes my paradise.

I have sat at an Oratorio (that profanation of the purposes of the cheerful play-house) watching the faces of the auditory in the pit (what a contrast to Hogarth's "Laughing Audience"!) immovable, or affecting some faint emotion—till (as some have said, that our occupations in the next world will be but a shadow of what delighted us in this) I have imagined myself in some cold Theatre in Hades, where some of the *forms* of the earthly one should be kept up, with none of the *enjoyment;* or like that

>—Party in a parlour
>All silent, and all DAMNED.

[3] See p. 592.

Above all, those insufferable concertos, and pieces of music, as they are called, do plague and embitter my apprehension.

Words are something; but to be exposed to an endless battery of mere sounds; to be long a dying; to lie stretched upon a rack of roses; to keep up languor by unintermitted effort; to pile honey upon sugar, and sugar upon honey, to an interminable tedious sweetness; to fill up sound with feeling, and strain ideas to keep pace with it; to gaze on empty frames, and be forced to make the pictures for yourself; to read a book, *all stops,* and be obliged to supply the verbal matter; to invent extempore tragedies to answer to the vague gestures of an inexplicable rambling mime—these are faint shadows of what I have undergone from a series of the ablest-executed pieces of this empty *instrumental music.*

I deny not, that in the opening of a concert, I have experienced something vastly lulling and agreeable: afterwards followeth the languor and the oppression. Like that disappointing book in Patmos; or, like the comings on of melancholy, described by Burton, doth music make her first insinuating approaches: "Most pleasant it is to such as are melancholy given to walk alone in some solitary grove, betwixt wood and water, by some brook side, and to meditate upon some delightsome and pleasant subject, which shall affect him most, *amabilis insania,* and *mentis gratissimus error.* A most incomparable delight to build castles in the air, to go smiling to themselves, acting an infinite variety of parts, which they suppose, and strongly imagine, they act, or that they see done.

"So delightsome these toys at first, they could spend whole days and nights without sleep, even whole years, in such contemplations, and fantastical meditations, which are like so many dreams, and will hardly be drawn from them—winding and unwinding themselves as so many clocks, and still pleasing their humours, until at the last the SCENE TURNS UPON A SUDDEN, and they being now habitated to such meditations and solitary places, can endure no company, can think of nothing but harsh and distasteful subjects.

"Fear, sorrow, suspicion, *subrusticus pudor,* discontent, cares, and weariness of life, surprise them on a sudden and they can think of nothing else; continually suspecting, no sooner are their eyes open, but this internal plague of melancholy seizeth on them, and terrifies their souls, representing some dismal object to their minds; which now, by no means, no labour, no persuasions, they can avoid, they cannot be rid of, they cannot resist."

Something like this "SCENE TURNING" I have experienced at the evening parties, at the house of my good Catholic friend Nov——,[4] who, by the aid of a capital organ, himself the most finished of players, converts his drawing-room into a chapel, his week days into Sundays, and these latter into minor heavens.[5]

When my friend commences upon one of those solemn anthems, which peradventure struck upon my heedless ear, rambling in the side aisles of the dim Abbey, some five-and-thirty years since, waking a new sense, and putting a soul of old religion into my young apprehension—(whether it be *that,* in which the Psalmist, weary of the persecutions of bad men, wisheth to himself dove's wings—or *that other,* which, with a like measure of sobriety and pathos, inquireth by what means the young man shall best cleanse his mind)—a holy calm pervadeth me. I am for the time

—rapt above earth,
And possess joys not promised at my birth.

But when this master of the spell, not content to have laid a soul prostrate, goes on, in his power, to inflict more bliss than lies in her capacity to receive—impatient to overcome her "earthly" with his "heavenly"—still pouring in, for protracted hours, fresh waves and fresh from the sea of sound, or from that inexhausted *German* ocean, above which, in triumphant progress, dolphin-seated, ride those Arions Haydn and Mozart, with their attendant Tritons, Bach, Beethoven, and a countless tribe, whom to attempt to reckon up would but plunge me again in the deeps—I stagger under the weight of harmony, reeling to and fro at my wits' end; clouds, as of frankincense,

[4] Vincent Novello (1781–1861) was also a composer and music publisher and the founder of the well-known family of musicians who bear his name.
[5]   I have been there, and still would go;
    'Tis like a little heaven below.—DR. WATTS. [Lamb's note.]

oppress me—priests, altars, censers, dazzle before me—the genius of *his* religion hath me in her toils—a shadowy triple tiara invests the brow of my friend, late so naked, so ingenuous—he is Pope—and by him sits, like as in the anomaly of dreams, a she-Pope too—tri-coroneted like himself!

I am converted, and yet a Protestant; at once *malleus hereticorum,* and myself grand heresiarch: or three heresies centre in my person: I am Marcion, Ebion, and Cerinthus—Gog and Magog—what not? —till the coming in of the friendly supper-tray dissipates the figment, and a draught of true Lutheran beer (in which chiefly my friend shows himself no bigot) at once reconciles me to the rationalities of a purer faith; and restores to me the genuine unterrifying aspects of my pleasant-countenanced host and hostess.

ESSAYS OF ELIA (1821)

GIOACCHINO ROSSINI

※》》 《《

The Prayer from "Moses"

"My immortality?" said Rossini; "do you know what will survive me? (*sais-tu ce qui restera après moi?*) The third act of *Tell,* the second act of *Otello,* and *The Barber of Seville* from one end to the other."

Strange to say, of the Prayer of Moses,[1] that piece magnificent in its simplicity, he only once spoke to me, but what he then said is well worth repeating. I asked him was he in love, or very hungry and miserable, when he wrote that inspired page; for hunger as well as love has the power of making people write with lofty inspiration.

"I will tell you," he said, and from his ironical smile I saw some fun was coming; "I had a little misfortune; I had known a Princess B—g—e, and she, one of the most passionate women living, and with a magnificent voice, kept me up all night with duos and talking, etc. A short time after this exhausting performance, I had to take a tisane which stood before me, while I wrote that prayer. When I was writing the chorus in G minor I suddenly dipped my pen into the medicine bottle instead of the ink; I made a blot, and when I dried it with sand (blotting paper was not invented then) it took the form of a natural, which instantly gave me the idea of the effect which the change from G minor to G major would make, and to this blot all the effect—if any—is due."

LOUIS ENGEL, *FROM MOZART TO MARIO* (1886)

---

[1] From Rossini's oratorio *Mosè in Egitto* (1818), later made into an opera.

LEIGH HUNT

Musical Memories

I

My grandfather, though intimate with Dr. Franklin, was secretly on
the British side of the question when the American war broke out. He
professed to be neutral, and to attend only to business; but his neu-
trality did not avail him. . . . My mother at that time was a brunette
with fine eyes, a tall, ladylike person, and hair blacker than is seen of
English growth. It was supposed that Anglo-Americans already began
to exhibit the influence of climate in their appearance. . . . My
mother had no accomplishments but the two best of all, a love of
nature and of books. Dr. Franklin offered to teach her the guitar;
but she was too bashful to become his pupil. She regretted this afterwards, partly, no doubt, for having lost so illustrious a master. Her
first child, who died, was named after him. I know not whether the
anecdote is new; but I have heard that when Dr. Franklin invented
the Harmonica,[1] he concealed it from his wife till the instrument was
fit to play; and then woke her with it one night, when she took it
for the music of angels.

. . . My mother, though fond of music, and a gentle singer in her
way, had missed the advantage of a musical education, partly from
her coming of a half-Quaker stock, partly (as I have said before)
from her having been too diffident to avail herself of the kindness of
Dr. Franklin, who offered to teach her the guitar.

The reigning English composer at that time was "Mr. Hook," [2]
as he was styled at the head of his songs. He . . . had a real, though
small vein of genius, which was none the better for its being called

[1] The "musical glasses" encased in a machine.
[2] James Hook (1746–1827).

486

upon to flow profusely for Ranelagh and Vauxhall. He was the composer of "The Lass of Richmond Hill" (an allusion to a *penchant* of George IV), and of another popular song more lately remembered, " 'Twas within a mile of Edinborough town." The songs of that day abounded in Strephons and Delias, and the music partook of the gentle inspiration. The association of early ideas with that kind of commonplace has given me more than a toleration for it. I find something even touching in the endeavors of an innocent set of ladies and gentlemen, my fathers and mothers, to identify themselves with shepherds and shepherdesses in the most impossible hats and crooks. . . . The feeling was true, though the expression was sophisticate and a fashion; and they who cannot see the feeling for the mode, do the very thing which they think they scorn; that is, sacrifice the greater consideration for the less.

But Hook was not the only, far less the most fashionable composer. There were (if not all personally, yet popularly contemporaneous) Mr. Lampe, Mr. Oswald, Dr. Boyce, Linley, Jackson, Shield, and Storace, with Paesiello, Sacchini,[3] and others at the King's Theatre, whose delightful airs wandered into the streets out of the English opera that borrowed them, and became confounded with English property. I have often, in the course of my life, heard "Whither, my love?" and "For tenderness formed" boasted of as specimens of English melody. For many years I took them for such myself, in common with the rest of our family, with whom they were great favorites. The first, which Stephen Storace adapted to some words in *The Haunted Tower* is the air of La Rachelina in Paesiello's opera *La Molinara*. The second, which was put by General Burgoyne to a song in his comedy of *The Heiress* (1786) is *"Io sono Lindoro"* in the same enchanting composer's *Barber of Seville*.[4] . . . Every burlesque or *buffo* song, of any pretension, was pretty sure to be Italian. When Edwin, Fawcett, and others were rattling away in the happy comic songs of O'Keeffe, with his triple rhymes and illustrative jargon, the

[3] The composers worth identifying are: William Boyce (1710–1779), Giovanni Paesiello (1741–1816), and Antonio Sacchini (1734–1786).

[4] c. 1780.

audience little suspected that they were listening to some of the finest animal spirits of the south—to Piccinni,[5] Paesiello, and Cimarosa.[6]

. . . I must own that I am heretic enough (if present fashion is orthodoxy) to believe that Arne [7] was a real musical genius, of a very pure, albeit not of the very first water. He has set, indeed, two songs of Shakespeare's (the Cuckoo song and "Where the bee sucks") in a spirit of perfect analogy to the words as well as the liveliest musical invention; and his air of "Water parted" in *Artaxerxes* winds about the feelings with an earnest and graceful tenderness of regret, worthy in the highest degree of the affecting beauty of the sentiment.

. . . The other day I found two songs of that period on Robinson's music-stall in Wardour Street, one by Mr. Hook entitled "Alone, by the light of the moon"; the other, a song with a French burden, called *"Dans votre lit,"* an innocent production notwithstanding its title. They were the only songs I recollect singing when a child, and I looked on them with the accumulated tenderness of sixty-three years of age. I do not remember to have set eyes on them in the interval. What a difference between the little smooth-faced boy at his mother's knee, encouraged to lift up his voice at the pianoforte, and the battered gray-headed senior, looking again for the first time on what he had sung at the distance of half a century! Life often seems a dream; but there are occasions when the sudden reappearance of early objects, by the intensity of their presence, not only renders the interval less present to the consciousness than a very dream, but makes the portion of life which preceded it seem to have been the most real of all things, and our only undreaming time.

II

It was very pleasant to see Lord Byron and Moore [8] together. They

[5] Niccolo Piccinni (1728–1800).

[6] See p. 315.

[7] Thomas Arne (1710–1778).

[8] Thomas Moore (1779–1852), Irish poet and wit, biographer of Byron, and arranger of the ballads of his native land.

harmonized admirably: though their knowledge of one another began in talking of a duel. . . . Moore's acquaintance with myself (as far as concerned correspondence by letter) originated in the mention of him in the "Feast of the Poets." [9] He subsequently wrote an opera called *The Blue Stocking*, [10] respecting which he sent me a letter at once deprecating and warranting objection to it. I was then editor of the *Examiner:* I did object to it, though with all acknowledgment of his genius.

Moore . . . sang and played with great taste on the pianoforte, as might be supposed from his musical compositions. His voice, which was a little hoarse in speaking (at least I used to think so), softened into a breath, like that of the flute, when singing.

—»» ««—

[At Pisa] our manner of life was this. Lord Byron, who used to sit up at night writing *Don Juan* (which he did under the influence of gin and water), rose late in the morning. He breakfasted; read; lounged about, singing an air, generally out of Rossini; then took a bath, and was dressed; and coming downstairs was heard, still singing, in the courtyard, out of which the garden ascended, by a few steps, at the back of the house. The servants, at the same time, brought out two or three chairs. My study, a little room in a corner, with an orange tree at the window, looked upon this courtyard. I was generally at my writing when he came down, and either acknowledged his presence by getting up and saying something from the window, or he called out, "Leontius!" (a name into which Shelley had pleasantly converted that of "Leigh Hunt") and came up to the window with some jest or other challenge to conversation.

—»» ««—

[In Genoa] one night I went to the opera, which was indifferent enough, but I understand it is a good deal better sometimes. The favorite composer here and all over Italy is Rossini, a truly national genius, full of the finest animal spirits, yet capable of the noblest gravity. My northern faculties were scandalized at seeing men in the pit

[9] Poem by Hunt (1811).
[10] *M.P., or The Blue Stocking* (1811).

with *fans!* Effeminacy is not always incompatible with courage, but it is a very dangerous step towards it; and I wondered what Doria would have said had he seen a captain of one of his galleys indulging his cheeks in this manner. Yet perhaps they did so in his own times.

It was about this time [11] that I projected a poem of a very different sort, which was to be called "A Day with the Reader."

I proposed to invite the reader to breakfast, dine, and sup with me, partly at home and partly at a country inn, in order to vary the circumstances. It was to be written both gravely and gaily, in an exalted or in a lowly strain, according to the topics of which it treated. The fragment of "Paganini" [12] was a part of the exordium—

> So play'd of late to every passing thought
> With finest change (might I but half as well
> So write!) The pale magician of the bow, etc.

I wished to write in the same manner because Paganini with his violin could move both the tears and the laughter of his audience, and (as I have described him doing in the verses) would now give you the notes of birds in the trees, and even hens feeding in a farmyard (which was a corner into which I meant to take my companion), and now melt you into grief and pity, or mystify you with witchcraft, or put you into a state of lofty triumph like a conqueror. That phrase of "smiting" the chords—

> He smote; and clinging to the serious chords
> With godlike ravishment, etc.—

was no classical commonplace; nor, in respect to impression on the mind, was it exaggeration to say that from a single chord he would fetch out

> The voice of quires, and weight
> Of the built organ.

Paganini, the first time I saw and heard him, and the first moment he struck a note, seemed literally to strike it; to give it a blow. The house was so crammed that, being among the squeezers in "standing

[11] 1835.   [12] 1844.

room" at the side of the pit, I happened to catch the first sight of his face through the arm akimbo of a man who was perched up before me, which made a kind of frame for it; and there, on the stage, in that frame, as through a perspective glass, were the face, bust, and raised hand of the wonderful musician, with his instrument at his chin, just going to commence, and looking exactly as I have described him—

> His hand,
> Loading the air with dumb expectancy,
> Suspended, ere it fell, a nation's breath.
> He smote; . . .

AUTOBIOGRAPHY (1828–1850)

JEAN-PAUL RICHTER

⫸⫷

The Value of a Deaf Left Ear

The author of this essay, who has enjoyed precisely this good fortune since childhood, will consider himself fully repaid if through it any readers of *The Fashionable World* [1]—who may for years have been one-eared as Kant was one-eyed, without knowing it—can be induced to shut off one and the other ear alternately so as to discover whether one of the pair possesses the talent which he—the author—boasts of in his left.

Apart from the water shrew which, as everyone knows, is able to shut off its ears under water with a sort of flap; and again, except for bats which have ear muffs, I know of nobody—least of all men—who possesses earlids comparable to eyelids. Nearly everyone does hear—and generally not the pleasantest things. But suppose a man, contrariwise, who is endowed with one-sided deafness: he finds it easy with *one* finger to bring about the double-sided boon for as long as may be required. There are four places in particular which the One-eared sees opening before him like four new worlds of joy—the music room, the theater, the drawing room, and the bed.

. . . In the music room, where one is invited to enjoy artists who are not so much the Tuneful as the Mistuned, the gift of one-sided deafness is possibly as valuable as a good yawn. According to Haller, one is deaf for as long as one yawns, and kind Nature therefore prescribes yawning as the best protection against the influence of boredom. But a one-sidedly deaf person achieves the same end far more courteously when, instead of putting his hand before his mouth, he holds it (under some slight pretext) before his good ear—as I do

[1] The journal in which the essay appeared.

This enables one to rest in a pose of attentiveness for as long as the noxious tones continue.

Goethe wished that the performers should be invisible to the audience, that one might not see their contortions. Now if someone can artfully add to this the virtue of inaudibility, all the benefits that may be derived from bad concerts will, I believe, have been brought together. From good concerts a man who can move his limbs can benefit still more with one-sided deafness, for whenever the shouts and other expressions of praise, like bad prose, wreck and ruin the poetry of tone, he can easily change his position, withdraw his good ear, and simply turn the dead one toward the barbaric clapping of hands.

MISCELLANEOUS ESSAYS (1806)

P. I. TCHAIKOVSKY

My Taste in Classics

Probably after my death it will not be uninteresting to know what were my musical predilections and prejudices, especially since I seldom gave opinions in verbal conversation.

Shall start gradually and shall speak to the point, touching upon musicians living at the same time with me and about their personalities.

Shall start with Beethoven, whom it is usual to praise unconditionally and whom it is commanded to worship as though he were a god. And so what is Beethoven to me?

I bow before the greatness of some of his works—but I do not *love* Beethoven. My attitude toward him reminds me of what I experienced in childhood toward the God Jehovah. I had toward Him (and even now my feelings have not changed) a feeling of wonder, but at the same time also of fear. He created Heaven and earth, He too created me—and still even though I bow before Him, there is no *love*. Christ, on the contrary, inspires truly and exclusively the feeling of *love*. Though He was *God,* He was at the same time man. He suffered like us. We *pity* Him, we love in Him His ideal *human* side, And if Beethoven occupies a place in my heart analogous to the God Jehovah, then Mozart I love as the musical Christ. Incidentally, he lived almost as long as Christ. I think that there is nothing sacrilegious in this comparison. Mozart was a being so angelic, so childlike, so pure; his music is so full of unapproachable, divine beauty, that if anyone could be named with Christ, then it is he.

Speaking of Beethoven, I come to Mozart. According to my deep conviction, Mozart is the highest, the culminating point that *beauty* has attained in the sphere of music. No one has made me weep, has made me tremble with rapture, from the consciousness of my nearness to *that something* which we call the *ideal,* as he has done.

Beethoven has also made me tremble. But rather from something like fear and the pangs of suffering.

I cannot *discourse* on music and shall not go into details. However, I shall mention two details: (1) In Beethoven I love the middle period, at times the first, but I fundamentally *detest* the last, especially the last quartets. Here there are *glimmers*—and nothing more. The rest is *chaos,* over which, surrounded by an impenetrable fog, hovers the spirit of this musical Jehovah. (2) In Mozart I love *everything,* for we love *everything* in a person whom we love truly. Above all *Don Juan,* for thanks to it I learned what *music* is. Until that time (until my seventeenth year) I did not know any music except Italian, semi-music, however charming. Of course, loving everything in Mozart, I shall not start asserting that every insignificant work of his is a *chef-d'oeuvre.* Yes! I know that none of his sonatas, for example, is a great work, and *still* I *love* every one of his sonatas because it is *his,* because this musical Christ imprinted it with his serene touch.

Concerning the forerunners of both, can say that I play Bach gladly, for to play a good fugue is entertaining, but I do not recognize in him (as some do) a great genius. Handel has for me an entirely fourth-rate significance and he is not even entertaining. Gluck, despite the relative poverty of his creation, is attractive to me. I *like* certain things of Haydn. But all these four Muses are amalgamated in Mozart. He who knows Mozart also knows what is good in these four, because being the greatest and most potent of all musical creators, he was not averse, even, to taking them under his wings and saving them from oblivion. They are rays lost in the sun of Mozart.

DIARIES (1886)

BENVENUTO CELLINI AND
MICHEL DE MONTAIGNE

→»» «««-

Music and My Father

Cellini

My father began to teach me to play the flute and to sing at sight, but although I was of a very tender age, when little children usually take pleasure in piping and similar amusements, I felt only the greatest dislike for it, and I sang and played only in order to obey him. At that time my father made the most wonderful organs of wooden pipes, and the finest and best harpsichords that were then to be seen, as well as the most beautiful and excellent viols, lutes, and harps. He was an engineer, and worked miracles in making many sorts of machines such as drawbridges, fulling mills, and so on. In carving ivory he was the first artist who worked really well. But after he had fallen in love with the woman who was to be my mother—perhaps it was piping that brought them together, for to it he gave much more time than he should have—he was asked by the musicians of the Court to join them in performing. Having thus indulged himself a while, he was so strongly urged by them that he became one of their band. But Lorenzo de' Medici and Piero his son, who wished him well and saw him give all his time to piping, and neglect his engineering and artistic work, had him dismissed from the post of musician.

. . . At that time (which was before my birth), these musicians were all distinguished artisans, workers in silk or wool, who belonged to the trades known as the Major Arts, which accounts for my father's not thinking music beneath him. His chief desire in the world as regards myself was that I should become a virtuoso on the flute; but the greatest displeasure in the world for me was when he brought the subject up and told me that if I wanted to apply myself I should become the best man in the world.

As I have said, my father was a great friend and devoted servant of the house of Medici, and when I was still of quite a tender age, he once had me carried pig-a-back to make me play the flute, and I played the treble with the palace musicians in front of the Senate [of Florence]; and I read my notes while one of the ushers held me on his shoulders throughout. Whereupon, Soderini, who was then *gonfalonier,* took much pleasure in making me prattle, gave me candy, and said to my father, "Master Giovanni, you must teach him your other two great arts, and not only music." To which my father replied, "I do not want him to follow any other art but that of performer on the flute and composer. For if God gives him life, I shall make him the greatest man in the world." To these words, one of the elder statesmen rejoined, "Ah, Master Giovanni, do as the *gonfalonier* says; why should the boy be nothing more than a good musician?"

AUTOBIOGRAPHY (1558)

➤➤➤ ⸲⸲⸲

Montaigne

Among other things [my father] had been advised to make me enjoy learning and duty by securing the consent of my will and of my desire, as well as to train my mind in full freedom and gentleness without constraint or rigor: I may say he did this with such superstitious regard that, since some hold that it disturbs the tender brains of children to awaken them suddenly in the morning and snatch them violently at one stroke out of their sleep (into which they sink far deeper than we), he had me awakened by the sound of an instrument and never was without an attendant to serve me thus.

ON THE REARING OF CHILDREN (1588)

JONATHAN SWIFT

➤➤➤ ⬅⬅⬅

A Cantata
With Comments by Other Hands

From Sir Walter Scott's biography

The Dean himself did not affect either to be a judge or admirer of music, yet he possessed the power of mimicking it in a wonderful degree. A person regretting at his table that he had not heard Mr. Rosingrave, then just returned from Italy, perform upon the organ; "you shall hear him now," said Swift, and immediately started off into a burlesque imitation of the chromatics of the musician. This exploit led to the Dean's composing the celebrated cantata burlesquing the doctrine of imitative sounds in poetry and music. It was set to music by Dr. John Ecclin.

From Dr. Beattie's "Program Notes"

Here we have motions imitated, which are the most inharmonious, and the least connected with human affections, as the trotting, ambling, and galloping of Pegasus; the words high and deep have high and deep notes set to them; a series of short notes of equal lengths are introduced, to imitate shivering and shaking; an irregular rant of quick sounds to express rumbling; a sudden rise of the voice from a low to a high pitch to denote flying above the sky, a ridiculous run of chromatic divisions on the words "Celia dies"; with other droll contrivances of a like nature. The satire of the piece is levelled, not at absurd imitation only, but also at some other musical improprieties, such as the idle repetition of the same words, the running of long extravagant divisions upon one syllable, and the setting of words to music that have no meaning. Swift, though deaf to the charms of music, was not blind to the absurdity of musicians.

Swift's cantata

In harmony would you excel,
Suit your words to your music well, music well, music well,
Suit your words to your music well,
Suit your words to your music well.

For Pegasus runs—runs—every race
By gal——loping high or le—vel pace,
Or ambling or sweet Canterbury
Or with a down, a high down derry.
No! no victory, victory he ever got
By jog—ling, jog—ling, jog—ling trot
No Muse harmonious entertains
Rough, roist'ring rustic roar—ing strains
Nor shall you twine——the crack—ling, crackling bays
By sneaking, snivelling roun—delays.

Trolloping, lolloping, galloping, trolloping
Lolloping, galloping, trollop;
Lolloping, trolloping, galloping, lolloping,
Trolloping, galloping, lollop.
Now creep——sweep, sweep the deep:
See, see, Ce—lia dies, dies, dies, dies, dies, dies, dies;
While true lovers' eyes
Weeping sleep, sleeping weep, weeping sleep
Bo peep, bo peep, bo peep, bo peep, bo—bo—peeeep.

Now slowly move your fiddlestick
Now tantan, tantan, tantan-tivi,
Now tantan, tantan, tantan-tivi quick—
Now trembling shiv'—ring, quiv'—ring, quak—ing
Set hoping, hoping, hoping hearts of lovers aching.
Fly, fly! above the sky, Ramb—ling, gamb—ling,
Ramb————ling, gamb—ling.

From George Faulkner, Swift's publisher

When Arne, the famous composer,[1] was last in Ireland, he made application to me for this cantata (which I could not then procure), to set it to music; perhaps he may do it now, and bring it on the stage; which, if he does, will run more than *The Beggar's Opera;* and therefore I would have you get it engraved in folio, with scores for bass, etc., which will make it sell very well.

SCOTT'S *WORKS OF SWIFT* (1814–24)

[1] Thomas Arne (1710–1778), composer of operas and oratorios, author of "Rule Britannia" and several famous melodies for Shakespeare lyrics.

RUDOLF KASSNER

⋙ ⋘

Musical Brows

A free-lance philosophical writer, Rudolf Kassner has written about music, intellectual history, and English poetry. He was born in 1873, long resided in Vienna, and was at one time a close friend of Rilke. He now lives in Switzerland.

I have tried to show at several points in my works on Physiognomy that the so-called "musical brow," which stretches from ear to ear in a beautiful curve highly arched toward the middle, is the peculiarity not so much of the creators of music as of the mere performers, that is, the great conductors or executants on violin or piano. In other words, the creative musicians possess a physiognomy of the Eye-type no less than of the Ear-type; they are Eye-men as well as Ear-men. I find, to be sure, an exception in Mozart's face, but it is due, as I think, to absolute genius, which in his case makes use of the creature as a tool or, indeed, as a plaything. Mozart, to put it paradoxically, could have had any face whatever. His uncontested genius appeared most truly incognito or cloaked in the manner of the gods when they tread the earth. Everything about him, including his death, is as it were mythic, just as everything about Beethoven is human and dramatic.

Nothing in the study of Musical Physiognomy strikes me as so fascinating, and at the same time fruitful, as a comparison of the three brows of Bach, Beethoven, and Richard Wagner. Bach's brow is immobile, towering, *plane*—like the tablets of the law or like one of his scores engraved with failing eyes—all in immediate contact with the Ear. It is as when a person high placed in government or business has a private wire through which to speak at will, without switchboards or intermediaries. Another comparison: I [once] . . . looked up and saw how the summit of a mountain, stony and eternally snow-clad, towered ever higher than the clouds by which I had believed it was hidden; I ceased wondering and merely closed my eyes, for they were filled with tears. Just so is Bach's brow compared to Beethoven's, over which storms pass with blasting bolts, but which does not invariably tower above the clouds, as is true of the image before us.

As for Richard Wagner's brow, it forms but one piece with his occiput. It begins at the root of the nose and and goes all the way back to the nape of the neck. Who, on looking at Bach's face, would ever think of his occiput? In Beethoven likewise it is of no importance. In Bach's world heaven and earth are two separate realms; in Beethoven's they are at strife with each other. Richard Wagner's world would be tottering, it would be pure agitation without the stage. Richard Wagner's world would go astray in the Infinite, were it not enabled to make continually fresh starts through the stage or the means of staging. That is how I interpret this brow which reaches from the root of the nose all the way back to the nape of the neck.

DER GRÖSSTE MENSCH (1946)

MODESTE MOUSSORGSKY

→→→ ←←←

My Life and Works [1]

Modeste (Piotr) Moussorgsky, Russian composer, born in 1839, the sixteenth of March, province of Pskov, county of Toropetz; son of an ancient Russian family. Under the direct influence of his nurse, he became familiar with Russian fairy tales. This acquaintance with the spirit of the folk life was the main impulse of musical improvisations before he had learned even the elementary rules of piano playing. His mother gave him his first piano lessons, and he made such progress that at the age of seven he played small pieces by Liszt, and at nine played a grand concerto by Field before a large audience in his parents' house. His father, who worshiped music, decided to develop the child's ability—and entrusted his further musical education to An[ton] Herke in Petersburg. The professor was so satisfied with his pupil that when he was twelve he had him play a "Concerto Rondo" by Herz at a private charity concert in the home of the Court Lady-of-Honor, Ryumina. The success and impression made by the young musician's performance was such that Professor Herke, ever a severe critic of his pupils, presented him with a copy of Beethoven's Sonata in A Flat. At thirteen young Moussorgsky entered the Cadet School of the Guards and was honored by the particularly kind attention of the late Emperor Nikolai. It was then that Moussorgsky composed a little piano piece and dedicated it to his comrades. This piece was published by his father with the help of An. Herke. This was the first work of the young (talented) musician to appear in print. In school he visited a great deal with the religious instructor, Father Krupsky, thanks to whom he acquired a profound knowledge

[1] Written for a dictionary of musicians, this note anticipates the completion of certain works.

of the very essence of ancient Greek and Catholic church music. At the age of seventeen he entered the Preobrazhensky regiment. In the regiment his comrade Vanlyarsky introduced Moussorgsky to the genius Dargomizhsky. In the home of Dargomizhsky, Moussorgsky became friendly with the prominent workers of musical art in Russia, C. Cui and M. Balakirev.[2] With the latter the young nineteen-year-old composer studied the whole history of the development of musical art—with examples, with severe systematic analysis of all the most important musical creations by the composers of European art in their historical sequence, this study proceeded during regular readings together of the musical works on two pianos. Balakirev brought Moussorgsky close to the family of one of the most important connoisseurs of arts in Russia, the well-known art critic Stassov,[3] and with the sister of the genius-creator of Russian music Glinka. On his part Cui introduced Moussorgsky to the famous Polish composer Moniuszko. Shortly thereafter the composer came close and became friendly with other such talented composers, such as the present well-known professor of the Petersburg conservatory, N. A. Rimsky-Korsakov. This closeness to a talented circle of musicians, regular discussions, and the establishment of firm contacts with a wide circle of Russian scholars and writers, such as Vladimir Lamansky, Turgenev, Kostomarov, Grigorovich, Kavelin, Pisemsky, Shevchenko [Dostoyevsky], and others, particularly stimulated the mental activity of the young composer and gave it a serious, strictly scientific direction. The result of this fortunate closeness was a whole series of musical compositions on Russian folk life, and the friendly companionship in the home of Shestakova with Professor V. Nikolsky caused the creation of the grand opera *Boris Godunov,* based on a subject by the great Pushkin. In the family circle of Privy Councilor Purgold, a great lover of art, and with the collaboration of his nieces A. and N. Purgold, serious and talented interpreters of music, *Boris Godunov* was performed for a large gathering, in the presence of the distinguished Petrov, Platonova, Kommissarzhevsky, and Associate Director Lukashevich. Directly thereupon it was decided to stage three

[2] See p. 325.   [3] See p. 360.

scenes of this opera, although this very opera not long before had been rejected by the theater directorate. With the participation of the distinguished artist D. Leonova, the opera, supported on the shoulders of the above-named artists, was staged, finally, in its entirety with stupendous success. The impression it made on the audience, the artists, and the orchestra was astonishing. The success of the opera was a complete triumph for its author. Following this opera there were planned, with the assistance of the critic Stassov, Professors Nikolsky and Kostomarov, two more operas simultaneously: *Khovanshchina* and *The Fair at Sorochintzi,* based on Gogol. As a relaxation from this work there were composed the *Album Series* on the exhibition of the works of the genius architect Hartmann, *Danse macabre* (5 scenes) on a text by the author's friend Count Golenishchev-Kutuzov, and several songs with text by Count Al[exei] Tolstoy. In 1879 the distinguished Russian dramatic singer Leonova invited Moussorgsky to undertake a grand artistic tour of Russia and Little Russia, the Crimea and along the Don and the Volga. This journey, taking three months, was a genuine triumphal procession for the two important Russian artists: the talented composer and the well-known singer. On tour the author conceived the idea of transposing into music one of the as yet untouched, from the musical point of view, creations of the great Goethe: Song of Mephistopheles, in Auerbach's Cellar, about the Flea.[4] As an impression of the tour through the Crimea, Moussorgsky published two caprices for piano: "Baidari" and "Gursuf"; then there was composed and played by the author himself at several concerts a large musical picture, "Storm on the Black Sea." He is bringing to completion both grand operas— *Khovanshchina* and *Fair at Sorochintzi,* which are on the press, as well as a large suite on themes of the Trans-Caspian region. Several of the most sharply original pictures for singing—"Savishna," "The Orphan Girl," "The Naughty Boy," "Gopak" (Shevchenko), struck the author's friend von Madeweiss, who handed them over for safekeeping to the Strasbourg library with explanatory letters on these pieces by the author.

[4] In *Faust;* but Moussorgsky's statement is contrary to fact.

Two scherzi: B flat major and C sharp minor; the former was performed by an orchestra under the direction of A. Rubinstein, which was the first opportunity the author had to hear his work played by an orchestra, *Impromptu, Prelude* and *Menuet monstre,* "Savishna," "Gopak," "Gathering Mushrooms" (Mey), "Jewish Song" for orchestra and chorus, *The Destruction of Sennacherib* (Byron), *Jesus Navinus* [Joshua] (on ancient Israelite themes, recorded by the author), "The Naughty Boy," "The Magpie" (Pushkin), *Intermezzo symphonique, Kinderscherz, La Fileuse,* "King Saul" (after an Israelite text), "Jewish Song," "The Nurse's Child's Song," *Album from Childhood,* "Forgotten" (from the Central Asiatic war), "Night—A Fantasy" (from Pushkin), "Yeremushka" (Nekrasov); the polemical pieces: "The Classicist," *Penny Paradise,* "The Seminarist"— prohibited and circulated in a mass of handwritten copies, published abroad.

Moussorgsky cannot be classed with any existing group of musicians, either by the character of his compositions or by his musical views. The formula of his artistic *profession de foi* may be explained by his view, as a composer, of the task of art: art is a means of communicating with people, not an aim in itself. This guiding principle has defined the whole of his creative activity. Proceeding from the conviction that human speech is strictly controlled by musical laws (Virchow, Gervinus [5]) he considers the task of musical art to be the reproduction in musical sounds not merely of the mood of the feeling, but chiefly of the mood of human speech. Acknowledging that in the realm of art only artist-reformers such as Palestrina, Bach, Gluck, Beethoven, Berlioz, and Liszt have created the laws of art, he considers these laws as not immutable but liable to change and progress, like the entire spiritual world of man.

Under the influence of such developed artistic views of the composer on the tasks and character of his creative work—was a whole . . . [The manuscript breaks off.]

AUTOBIOGRAPHIC NOTE (JUNE 1880)

[5] German physiologist and Shakespeare scholar, respectively.

BRILLAT-SAVARIN

⇶ ⇜

Sing for Your Life

Jurist, diplomat, and exile in the United States (where he left his name attached to sauces and restaurants), Jean-Anthelme Brillat-Savarin (1755–1826) was never suspected of being a gastronomist until the publication of his great work in 1825.

It was in the worst days of the Revolution, and I was on my way to Dôle, to see the local representative Prot and obtain from him a safe-conduct which might prevent my being imprisoned and doubtless subsequently guillotined.

On reaching Dôle, I found Representative Prot very much prejudiced against me. He looked at me ominously and I thought I was going to be arrested. But my fright was quite wasted, for after some explanations he seemed to me to be softening a little.

I am not one of those whom fear renders cruel, and I may say I think the man was not a bad fellow. But he was a man of very limited capacities and did not know what to do with all the power that had been entrusted to him: he was like a child wielding Hercules' club. An acquaintance of mine whose name I am happy to set down here, M. Amondru, had a great deal of trouble to persuade him to accept an invitation to a dinner which I was to attend as well. Prot finally gave in, though he greeted me in a manner that was far from reassuring to me.

I was received somewhat better by Mme. Prot, whom I then approached to pay my respects. My circumstances must have at least aroused her curiosity. Among the first words that she said, she asked me if I loved music. What unexpected luck! She was passionately fond of it, and as I am myself a pretty fair musician, from that moment on our hearts beat in unison.

We talked before supper and discussed everything thoroughly. She mentioned certain treatises on composition—I knew them all. She spoke of the most fashionable operas—I had them by heart. She named the best-known composers—I had met most of them. She could not stop talking, not having run into anyone for quite a while with whom to discuss this favorite subject of hers. Though she talked as an amateur, I heard afterward that she had taught singing.

After supper she sent for some of her music. She sang, I sang, we sang. I never applied myself more strenuously, nor did I ever enjoy it more. M. Prot had already remarked several times that he was leaving, but she took no notice, and we were sounding like a pair of bugles in the duet from *La Fausse Magie* [1]—

"Do you recall the festive time?"—

when he notified her that they were leaving.

We concluded perforce. But in taking leave Mme. Prot said to me, "Citizen, a man who cultivates the fine arts as you do cannot be a traitor to his country. I know you have asked some favor of my husband. You shall have it. I give you my word: it is a promise."

Hearing these comforting words, I kissed her hand with heartfelt warmth, and, sure enough, the next morning I received my safe-conduct, duly signed and magnificently sealed. The purpose of my journey had been fulfilled. I returned home with head erect; and, thanks to Harmony, genial daughter of Heaven, my ascension was postponed for a period of years.

PHYSIOLOGY OF TASTE (1825)

---

[1] An opera by Grétry (1741–1813), first produced in 1775.

Correspondence

JOHANN SEBASTIAN BACH

To Georg Erdmann, Russian envoy at Danzig

Leipzig, October 28, 1730

EXCELLENCY:

Your Excellency will excuse an old friend and faithful servant who takes the liberty of intruding upon you. It is now four years since Your Excellency has favored me with a reply to my letter. . . . You have known me and my doings since youth and up to the time of my chapel-mastership at Cöthen.[1] I found there a noble prince who knew music and loved it, and there I hoped to end my days. But it so happened that His Highness married a princess from Bernburg, and it seemed to me that my master's love of music was cooling off, his lady being quite muse-less. It pleased God that I should be called here as musical director and cantor of St. Thomas's School,[2] even though at first it seemed to me intolerable to descend to the rank of cantor after having been chapel-master. That is why for three months I held back my decision. But the post was so favorably recommended to me that finally, and chiefly because my sons appear to be inclined toward study, I dared, in the name of the Almighty, to go to Leipzig. I passed an audition and then moved to the new place where, by the grace of God, I am still.

But as I find that (1) the duties are by far not so agreeable as they were described to me originally; and (2) that quite a few of the bonuses attached to the post have been withdrawn; that (3) the cost of living is very high here; and (4) that the authorities are rather strangely hostile to music, that I have to live in a state of almost constant struggle; that envy prevails and vexations are numerous; I find myself, so help me God, compelled to seek my fortune elsewhere. If Your Excellency knows of any suitable position for an old faithful servant in your city, I should be deeply obliged for your help and recommendation in securing it. I in turn will not fail to live up to

[1] I.e., up to 1717.   [2] In 1723.

the promise implied by your gracious intercession. I will truly do my best in the discharge of duty.

My salary here is seven hundred thalers, and when there are more burials than usual, the added fees raise this proportionately higher. But whenever the air is a little more healthful, the loss is great. Last year the fees for common burials showed a deficit of a hundred thalers. With four hundred thalers I could support myself in Thuringia more comfortably than here with twice that amount, for the cost of living in Leipzig is exorbitant.

I should also give you some details about my family. I remarried after the death of my first wife in Cöthen. From my first marriage I still have three sons and one daughter, as you may remember from seeing them at Weimar.[3] From my second, one son and two daughters are alive. My eldest boy is studying law; the other two are in the top two classes; my eldest daughter is not yet married. The children of my second marriage are still quite little, the eldest being only six. All are born musicians, which enables us to have family concerts with voice and instruments, for my wife has a nice soprano voice and my eldest daughter also does pretty well.

I would be overstepping the bounds of courtesy if I bored you with further details. I therefore close and remain, ever respectfully,

Your Excellency's most devoted servant,
Joh. Seb. Bach

[3] Between 1707 and 1717.

LORD CHESTERFIELD

To his son

London, June 22, 1749

DEAR BOY,

. . . I approve of your going to Venice, as much as I disapprove of your going to Switzerland. I suppose that you are by this time arrived, and, in that supposition, I direct this letter there. But if you should find the heat too great, or the weather offensive at this time of the year, I would have you go immediately to Verona, and stay there till the great heats are over, before you return to Venice.

The time you will probably pass at Venice will allow you to make yourself master of that intricate and singular form of government, which few of our travelers know anything of. Read, ask, and see everything that is relative to it. There are likewise many valuable remains of the remotest antiquity, and many fine pieces of the *antico moderno;* all which deserve a different sort of attention from that which your countrymen commonly give them. They go to see them as they go to see the lions, and kings on horseback, at the Tower here; only to say that they have seen them. You will, I am sure, view them in another light; you will consider them as you would a poem, to which indeed they are akin. You will observe whether the sculptor has animated his stone, or the painter his canvas, into the just expression of those sentiments and passions which should characterize and mark their several figures. You will examine likewise whether, in their groups, there be an unity of action or proper relation; a truth of dress and manners. Sculpture and painting are very justly called liberal arts; a lively and strong imagination, together with a just observation, being absolutely necessary to excel in either; which, in my opinion, is by no means the case of music, though called a liberal art, and now in Italy placed even above the other two: a proof of the decline of that country. The Venetian school produced many great painters, such as Paul Veronese, Titian, Palma, etc., by whom you will see, as well in private houses as in churches, very fine pieces. . . . A taste of sculpture and painting is in my mind as becoming as a taste of fiddling and piping is unbecoming a man of fashion. The former is connected with history and poetry, the latter, with nothing that I know of but bad company.

MARIA THERESA, EMPRESS OF AUSTRIA,[1] AND COUNT DE MERCY-ARGENTEAU

>>>——<<<

The Imperial family trusted Gluck and used him as secret envoy whenever he traveled between Vienna and Paris. Sometimes he carried political news, sometimes intimate information from the young queen, Marie Antoinette, indicating that her hoped-for pregnancy was not yet a fact. This eighteenth-century simplicity was matched by the duplicity embodied in Mercy-Argenteau, for he was little more than a spy set by Maria Theresa on her daughter, who never suspected his role.

>>>——<<<

Count de Mercy to the Empress

Paris, April 19, 1774

Today our celebrated chapel-master Gluck gives the first performance of his opera, *Iphigénie en Aulide,* which Mme. la Dauphine [2] will attend. The music has been greatly applauded at the rehearsals, and it is expected to mark an epoch in the reformation of French harmony, for this last is, as you know, very insipid and monotonous.

Maria Theresa to the Count de Mercy

Vienna, November 15, 1774

Count de Mercy, I also want to tell you in secret of the plan I have in mind, to see the French opera *Iphigénie* produced here for the arrival of my son Ferdinand and his wife.[3] They are coming here next year. The performers—and I want rather good ones—would have to be here by the end of August, and I think I would detain them until the end of November. You would be doing me a kindness to find out quietly whether I can count on such persons, and whether

---

[1] Properly Maria Theresia, but English usage has prevailed.

[2] Marie Antoinette, daughter of Maria Theresa; the Dauphin being the future Louis XVI.

[3] Fourth son of Maria Theresa, Duke of Modena.

they would be satisfied with reasonable fees for their trip here (where I should see them taken care of) instead of making extravagant demands. But since I want this opera production to be a surprise to the Emperor, to my daughter, and to the public, it matters greatly to me that the business be prepared secretly, and although I think you could talk about it with Gluck, it would have to be done cautiously, because I do not want to trust too much his taciturnity.

Count de Mercy to the Empress

Paris, January 15, 1775

. . . The queen [4] came to the Opera in Paris on Friday the thirteenth. The people, heavily congregated along the line of her passage, gave extraordinary and most lively evidence of their love for their queen. The same was true of Her Majesty's entrance into the theater, which was filled to overflowing. The opera represented was *Iphigénie,* composed by Gluck. In the second act of that piece occurs a chorus, of which Achilles sings the first verse while turning to his suite—

"Now sing in honor of your queen!"

Instead of this, the actor, moving forward toward the parterre and boxes, said—

"We sing in honor of our queen,
The union which binds her to our lord,
Will make us happy evermore!"

This was taken up by the public with incredible enthusiasm; nothing could be heard but shouts and handclapping, and what has never before happened at the Opera, the audience made the singers repeat the chorus while the public joined in with cries of "Long live the Queen!" It stopped the play for nearly fifteen minutes, and the queen was so moved that she shed a few tears.

[4] Louis XV had died in May 1774, which made the Dauphin and Dauphine king and queen.

Count de Mercy to the Empress

Paris, January 19, 1775

Your Sacred Majesty, the two very gracious letters dated last November 15, which the Count de Fossières gave me, require a separate answer, together with a few remarks on the means of carrying out Your Majesty's intention as regards producing the French opera *Iphigénie* in Vienna.

The undeserved importance which the Paris public ascribes to its Opera is no doubt the reason why the government has given a very special character to it, and to whoever is connected with it, thus making it into a national institution, regular and permanent. It is according to this notion that by letters patent of Louis XIV the acting troupe of the Opera constitutes a Royal Academy of Music, and that among several privileges which are as extraordinary as they are absurd, the profession of opera singer is declared to be compatible with the rank of nobility, so that a nobleman born may practice this calling without losing his rights or title—a privilege, however, which extends only to the singing actors, and from which the dancing actors are excluded.[5]

All these actors are on fixed salaries, paid by the City of Paris, and are guaranteed a retirement pension equal to half their salary. In addition, these same persons belong also to the King's Music and receive the fees assigned to such a post. The result is that the actors of the Paris Opera, being doubly bound, in perpetuity, to the service of the Court and of the City of Paris, may not contract any other engagements of their talents, nor absent themselves save by express order or permission of the King.

The foregoing means nothing but difficulties; yet since all difficulties must yield to the wishes of Your Majesty, I have given all my mind to resolving them. And first I conferred with Chapel-Master Gluck, enjoining him in such a manner to keep the secret that I am assured he will not violate it. Since at no time can the Paris Opera remain unoccupied, I suggested to Gluck that he compose at once a

[5] These letters patent were issued to Lulli, March 29, 1672; they gave him a monopoly and made his fortune. See p. 273.

new work, so contrived that it should be playable by the weaker performers, and by the understudies who are provided (in cases of necessity) to replace the leading actors which are essential to the *Iphigénie*. This new work, which Gluck has already begun, will perhaps require him to stay here a few weeks longer than his permission allows, but Your Majesty will deign not to consider this improper, since it comes about solely with a view to an expedient for carrying out your intentions.

To reduce the difficulty as far as possible, Gluck has managed things so that five leading actors and twelve voices for the chorus will suffice to produce his opera *Iphigénie*. Hence only seventeen persons will need transportation to Vienna. The only way, however, will be by an express order from the King. There is no doubt that the monarch will deem it a pleasure to serve Your Majesty in the contemplated object, about which such arrangements will have been made that the Paris performances will not be interrupted.

As for the expenses connected with this project, the outlay will be all the greater that the actors' fees will depend entirely on Your Majesty's pleasure and munificence. For as explained above, it is not possible to enter into contracts with the aforesaid actors. When Your Majesty will please to order it, I shall lay before your eyes an estimate of the likely cost. I close with the comment that the public here will surely be greatly flattered at the thought that Your Majesty should want to see a show of which the French nation has always felt proud —more so, I suspect, than the thing itself deserves.

Maria Theresa to the Count de Mercy

Vienna, February 4, 1775

Count de Mercy, after the information you have given me about the circumstances of the actors of *Iphigénie* at the Paris Opera, I find that the idea of having them brought here would be as awkward as it would be expensive. We will therefore not say another word about it.

P.S.—except in case Gluck may be able to bring a couple with him and give us an idea of the show between June and October; but I do not want to spend any money on it, nor have too many additional persons on my hands.

Count de Mercy to the Empress

Paris, February 20, 1775

I shall let Gluck know Your Majesty's intentions as regards giving in Vienna a sketch of the French operas, but I believe it could be done without bringing from here any singing persons. They could easily be replaced by a few French actors from the traveling comic opera troupes; Gluck's cleverness could manage with them, and that would save expense, for the outlay would be great even if only a very few actors of the Paris Opera were to travel.

Maria Theresa to the Count de Mercy

March 4, 1775

Count de Mercy, I deem it proper to abandon the project of having Gluck engage a few French actors to come here.

THE MOZARTS

Leopold Mozart to his wife

Rome, April 14, 1770

. . . You have no doubt often heard of the famous *Miserere,* which is so highly treasured that the musicians of the Chapel are forbidden, under pain of excommunication, to take a single part out of the Chapel, to copy it, or give it to anyone. *We now have it:* Wolfgang wrote it down,[1] and we would have sent it to Salzburg, with this letter, were our presence not required to produce it; for the style contributes more than the composition itself.[2] Accordingly we shall bring it with us, and it being one of the secrets of Rome, we do not want it to fall into other hands, lest we should incur directly or indirectly the censure of the Church.[3]

. . . Wolfgang is well and sends a *contredanse.* He would like Herr Hofmann[4] to make up the steps to it, and in such a way that when the two solo violins play, only two persons should dance as principals, and then whenever the band joins in with all the instruments, the whole company can dance. What would be most beautiful would be for five couples to dance the piece—the first pair taking the first solo, the second next, and so on, for there are five solos and five tuttis.

Mzt

Wolfgang to his sister Maria Anna (Nannerl)

Rome, April 21, 1770

Cara sorella mia! I beg you to find me the arithmetic lessons; you know you wrote them out yourself for me, and now I have lost them. So I have quite forgotten what I knew about it. Please copy them out with other examples and send them to me.

[1] Wolfgang was then in his fourteenth year.
[2] But see p. 606.
[3] This last clause is written in Latin.
[4] Dancing master at the Salzburg Court.

Manzuoli is under contract with the Milanese to sing my opera.[5] With this in mind he sang me four or five arias in Florence, including a few which I had to compose in Milan because people have not heard a single thing of mine for the theater which would enable them to judge whether I was capable of writing an opera. . . . I am now at work on the air *"Se ardire, e speranza."*

The same to the same [6]

Rome, April 25, 1770

Cara sorella mia! . . . Please do what I asked you to do the last time I wrote and answer me about it. I have played in two concerts and tomorrow shall play in one more. . . . This letter done, I shall finish a symphony of mine which I have begun, the aria is finished, another symphony is with the copyist (who happens to be my father) because we do not want to give it out to be copied, for then it would be plagiarized. To all my friends give my greetings, kiss my mother's hand for me, since I am (tra-la-lira) the

Wolfgango in germania e amadeo Mozartt in italia

In Leopold's hand: I kiss you both.

Maria Anna Mozart to her husband Leopold

Augsburg, October 14, 1777

We left Munich on the 11th at noon and arrived safe in Augsburg at nine in the evening; the journey was done in nine hours with a hired coachman who moreover fed his horses for an hour.

[*Wolfgang continues:*] So we made no mistake about the date. We wrote in the morning and will be off again (I think) next Friday, that is, day after tomorrow. Now hear how mightily generous these good Augsburgers have been! Nowhere have I been so overwhelmed with marks of honor as here. My first visit was to the mayor, Longo-

---

[5] *Mitridate, Rè di Ponto* (1770), Mozart's first opera seria.
[6] The original is in Italian.

tabarro.[7] . . . He gave me no peace but I must go with him upstairs to his son-in-law . . . while my cousin had the honor of waiting, sitting on a stool in the vestibule. I had to take hold of myself most manfully, otherwise I should have—most politely—said something. Upstairs I had the honor of playing for about three quarters of an hour on a good clavichord by Stein in the presence of the stiff-bosomed son and the long-legged young wife and the stupid old lady.

. . . Although I had asked them not to say who I was, Herr von Langenmantel thoughtlessly blurted out to Herr Stein, "I have the honor of introducing to you a virtuoso on the clavier," and began to snicker. I at once protested, saying I was only an unworthy pupil of Herr Siegl of Munich, who had charged me with a thousand compliments to him. He nodded negatives with his head and finally: "Is it possible that I have the honor of seeing Herr Mozart before me?" "Oh, no," I replied, "my name is Trazom and I have a letter for you." . . . I began to play. He could hardly open the letter in his eagerness to find out; he read only the signature. "Oh," he shrieked, and embraced me. He kept crossing himself and making faces and was terribly pleased. I'll tell you later about all his claviers. He then took me to a coffeehouse. When I stepped in I thought I would fall down overcome by the stench and fumes of tobacco. But for God's sake I had to stand it for an hour and pretend to enjoy it all, though I felt as if I were in Turkey.

He then talked a great deal about a certain Graf, a composer, but who has only written flute concertos.[8] He said, "Now there is a man who is really remarkable"—and other such exaggerations. I was sweating with nervousness, head, hands, my whole body. . . . My host would not yield but took me to Graf on the spot. Graf is indeed a fine figure of a man. He had on a dressing gown such as I should not be ashamed to wear on the streets. His words are all mounted on stilts and he usually opens his mouth before he knows what one is going to say; and often it shuts again without having done anything.

[7] Mozart italianizes the name of Herr von Langenmantel.
[8] Friedrich Graf (1727–1795) was a flute virtuoso who also composed for other instruments and achieved considerable renown in his day.

After many compliments he performed a concerto for two flutes. I had to play the first violin part. . . . When it was over I praised him highly, for he really deserves it. The poor man must have taken great pains over it; he must have studied hard. At length they brought in a clavichord . . . quite good though full of dust. Herr Graf, who is music director here, stood there like a man who had always thought himself very unusual in his wanderings from key to key and who now finds that one can be still more unusual, and yet not offend the ear. In short, they were all astounded. . . . I am

Wolfgang Mozart

Wolfgang to his father

Paris, May 1, 1778

. . . At last the Duchesse de Chabot appeared and asked me very courteously to make the best of the clavier in the room because none of her own was in condition—would I try it? I said I'd gladly play something but that it was impossible just then, for I could hardly feel my own fingers for the cold. I asked her whether I might be taken at least to a room where there was a fire. "Why, yes, of course, you are right," [9] was all the answer I got. She then sat herself down and began to draw for a whole hour, in company with some gentlemen who sat around a large table, while I had the honor of waiting for that whole hour. The doors and windows were open and my whole body was frozen as well as my hands and feet. I began to have a headache. There was deep silence,[10] and I hardly knew what to do, what with the cold, headache, and boredom. I kept thinking, "If it weren't for Mr. Grimm,[11] I'd leave at once. Finally, to make a long story short, I played on that miserable wreck of a pianoforte. But what was more irritating was that Madame and all the gentlemen did not interrupt their drawing for a moment, but kept right on, so that I had to play to the chairs, table, and walls.

[9] French in the original.
[10] Latin in the original.
[11] Baron Friedrich Melchior Grimm (1723–1807), German literary correspondent in Paris.

. . . Give me the best clavier in Europe with listeners who understand nothing, or won't understand and won't feel with me what I am playing, and I shall lose all pleasure and interest. I told Grimm all about it afterward. . . . People pay plenty of compliments but there it ends. They appoint a day, I play, they shout, "Oh, it's prodigious, inconceivable, amazing!" [12]—then good-by. . . . Paris has greatly changed; the French are not nearly so polite as fifteen years ago. Their manners verge on boorishness and their condescension is abominable.

. . . As far as music is concerned I am among sheer brute beasts. How can it be otherwise? In all their actions, feelings, and passions they are just the same—there is no place in the world like Paris. You mustn't think I exaggerate when I speak of the music here in this way. Ask anyone you like except a born Frenchman, and if he is at all reliable he will tell you the same. But here I am and I must stick it out for your sake. . . .

Wolfgang Amadè Mozart

Wolfgang to his father

Paris, September 11, 1778

I have duly received your three letters of the 13th, 27th, and 31st of August, but I shall reply only to the last because it is the most important. As I read it . . . I trembled with joy, for I saw myself already in your arms. To be sure—you will admit it yourself—no great fortune awaits me there,[13] but when I think once more of kissing and hugging my dearest father and sister,[14] I know of no other good fortune. That is in fact the one thing I can say in excuse to the people here who keep shouting in my ears that I must stay. I tell them, "What do you mean? If I am satisfied, that should be enough." There is one place I can call home and be in peace and quiet with the best of fathers and sisters—I can do what I want, for apart from my duties

[12] French in the original.
[13] In Salzburg.
[14] Mozart's mother had been with him in Paris and had died there two months before.

I am my own master—can count on a regular income—can go off when I like—can travel every second year. What more could I want?

The only thing, I tell you frankly, that makes me disgusted with Salzburg is that one cannot go about freely with everybody there, and that the musicians are not held in higher consideration, and—that the Archbishop puts no faith in intelligent, well-traveled people. For I assure you that people who do not travel—at least people in the arts and sciences—are pretty sorry creatures, and I promise you that if the Archbishop does not allow me to travel every other year, I cannot accept the appointment. A man of ordinary talent will always be ordinary, whether he travels or not; but a man of superior talent (which I cannot deny myself to be without being impious) will go to pieces if he remains forever in the same place. . . .

I hope to have an answer soon so as to be able to leave soon. Your most obedient son

Wolfgang Amadè Mozart

Wolfgang to his father

Vienna, May 19, 1781

Mon très cher Père: I too do not know how to begin this letter, for I cannot get over my astonishment and shall never be able to as long as you continue to think and write as you do. I must tell you there is not a single remark in your letter in which I can recognize my father —a father indeed, but not the dearest and best of fathers who cares for his own and his children's honor—in short, not *my* father. The whole thing must have been a dream. You are awake now, and need no reply from me on your arguments in order to be more than convinced that—*now more than ever*—I cannot change my decision.[15]

Yet I must take up some of the points in which my honor and character are most cruelly attacked. You say it was not right that I should resign from Vienna. I believe rather that if one is so minded (though at the time I was not, else I would have done it the first time) the most sensible thing to do is to do it from a place where one is

[15] To leave the Archbishop's employ.

contented and has the brightest prospects. No doubt you won't approve of this in the presence of the Archbishop, but to me you cannot but approve it. You say the only way to save my honor is to reverse my decision. How can you contradict yourself so! You must have forgotten, when you wrote this, that if I went back on my resolve I should be the lowest of the low. All of Vienna knows that I have left the Archbishop—and knows why—knows it was because my honor was wounded—and what's more, that it was for the third time. And now I am to give public evidence of the contrary—I am to make myself out a sniveling cur and the Archbishop a noble prince? No man can bring about the former, I least of all, and only God the latter—if he chooses to let him see the light.

Then you say I am wanting in affection for you, and therefore ought now to show it for the first time. Can you really be saying that? That I will never sacrifice my pleasures for your sake. What kind of pleasures have I here? The pleasure of worrying and toiling to fill my purse! You seem to think that I wallow in bliss and amusements. How you deceive yourself! That is, for the time being! Right now I have only just enough for my needs. But the subscription for my six sonatas is under way and then I shall have some money. All goes well, too, with the opera,[16] and in Advent I am to give a concert; then things will get better and better, because the winter season here is quite good. If you call it *pleasure* to be rid of a prince who does not pay and hounds one to death, then it is true my pleasure is great.

. . . All I can say to you is that on your account—solely on your account—I am very sorry that I was driven so far—I wish that the Archbishop had behaved more sensibly—if only in order that I might devote my whole life to you. To please you, dear father, I would sacrifice my fortune, my health, and my life—but my honor, that is to me beyond reach and it must be so to you. . . . Had I not thought of you, I should not have waited for him to say for the third time "Clear out of here!" without taking him at his word. What am I saying: Waited! I, *I* should have said it, and not he. . . . Dearest and best of fathers, ask of me anything you want but not that—anything

[16] *The Abduction from the Seraglio.*

but that—the mere thought makes me tremble with rage. I kiss your hands a thousand times and hug my sister with all my heart. Ever your most obedient son

Wolfgang Amadè Mozart

Wolfgang to his father

Vienna, October 13, 1781

. . . Now as to the libretto of the opera.[17] You are quite right as regards Stephanie's work.[18] Still, the poetry is in keeping with the character of the dumb, rude, and wicked Osmin. I know perfectly well that the versification is not of the best, but it fitted in so well with the musical ideas that were already knocking about my head that it could not fail to please me, and I'm willing to bet that in performance nothing will be amiss. As for the poetry of the original piece, I really can't complain. Belmont's aria, "Oh, what anxiety!" could hardly be better for music. Except for the "Hui" and "Sorrow rests in my heart" (as if sorrow could rest!), the aria is not so bad, especially the first part.

Besides, I should say that in an opera the poetry must be the obedient daughter of music. Why do the Italian comic operas please everybody, in spite of their wretched words, even in Paris, where I saw their success? Because in them Music reigns supreme and one forgets the rest. All the more will an opera succeed when the plot is well worked out, the words expressly written for the music and not twisted around for some miserable rhyme (which God knows never contributes to the value of a show but rather detracts from it)—I mean words or stanzas that distort the composer's whole conception. Verse is no doubt indispensable to music, but rhyme—for the sake of rhyme—is a curse. The pedants who follow that system will always come to grief, and their music too. What is best is for a good composer who understands the stage and is able to make useful sugges-

[17] Still *The Abduction from the Seraglio.*
[18] Gottlieb Stephanie (1741–1800), opera director who arranged the text of the *Abduction.*

tions to join a clever poet—that true phoenix. Then you needn't worry about success, even with the ignorant. But poets remind me of trumpeters with their tricks to show off. If we composers were to stick so faithfully to our rules (which were good enough when no one knew better), why, we'd manufacture music almost as useless as their librettos! . . .

W. A. Mozart

CHRISTOPH WILLIBALD GLUCK

Even more than today, the eighteenth century managed its musical affairs in print, by direct polemic, of which the following is a fair sample. La Harpe (1739–1803) was a self-made man and a miscellaneous writer of severely academic views.

To M. de la Harpe

Paris, October 1777

Sir:

I find it impossible for me not to yield assent to the very judicious remarks that you have just published upon my operas in your *Literary Review* of the 5th instant. I have nothing, absolutely nothing, to offer in rejoinder.

Hitherto I had been naïve enough to believe that music was like the other arts in being allowed to take all the passions as its domain, and that it should not give the less pleasure when it expressed the ravings of a madman or the cries of one in pain than when it depicted the sighings of love.

> There are no monsters, no enormities
> Which art by showing may not cause to please [1]

I had thought this maxim true for Music as for Poetry. It had been my creed that if song was to be marked throughout with the coloring appropriate to the sentiments it was required to express, then it must be modified whenever these changed and take on as many different accents as they present different nuances. I believed, finally, that voices, instruments, and all possible sounds—even silence itself—must tend toward one goal, which is expression; and that the union between words and music must be so close that the poem should seem no less molded on the music than the music on the poem.

These were not my only errors. I thought I had noticed that the

[1] From Boileau's *Art Poétique,* Canto III, 1–2.

529

French language was but slightly accented, and did not, like the Italian, make use of quantity. I had, moreover, been struck by another difference between the singers of the two nations. The ones seemed to have softer, more flexible voices; but the others had greater strength and put more energy into their performance; whence I concluded that Italian melody would not suit the French. And in going over the scores of your older operas, I found enough real beauties—despite an excess of trills, cadences, and other faults of song writing—to persuade me that the French had a sufficient tradition of their own.

Such, sir, were my ideas when I read your strictures. At once your light dissipated my darkness. I was aghast to discover that you had learned more about the art of my choice in a few hours' reflection than I had been able to master in forty years of practice. Your words demonstrate that it is enough to be a man of letters in order to speak well of everything. I am now convinced that the music of the Italian Masters is music par excellence, is Music itself; that in order to charm, melody must be regular and four-square, and that even in moments of confusion in which the dramatic hero passes from one emotion to another, the composer must throughout repeat the identical melodic motive.

I agree with you that, of all my works, *Orpheus* is the only tolerable one. I sincerely beg pardon of the god of taste for having *deafened* my hearers by means of my subsequent works. The number of times these other operas have been played, and the applause which the public was good enough to accord them, do not blind me to the fact that they are in truth pitiable. I believe this so strenuously that I am about to revise them, and since I note that you are all for tender strains, I am planning to make the raging Achilles sing in a manner so pathetic and soothing that the audience will be dissolved in tears.

As regards *Armide,* I am certainly not going to keep the poem as it is. For as you judiciously remark, "The librettos of Quinault,[2] although full of beautiful passages, are not properly constructed for music; they are superb poems, but bad operas." At the risk of turning into very bad poems, they shall become beautiful operas in the man-

[2] See pp. 203 and 273.

ner you prescribe, and I would ask you to introduce me to some versifier who will take *Armide* apart and put it together again with two airs in each scene. He and I shall confer about the number and meter of the lines, and provided he gives me enough syllables, I shall leave the rest to him. On my side, I shall get to work on music so as to banish from it all the noisy instruments, such as the kettledrum and the trumpet. There shall be heard in my orchestra only oboes, flutes, French horns, and violins—these last with mutes, of course. My only task will be to fit the words to the airs, which will not be difficult since both will be ready-made according to measure.

As a result, the part of Armide will cease to be "a monotonous and wearisome screaming." She will be an enchantress, and I will see to it that she sings an air of such regularity and squareness—to say nothing of tenderness—that the most flighty belle in the audience will be able to hear it without the slightest feeling of annoyance.

If some pedant should come to me and say, "Please take care that Armide outraged does not express herself like Armide intoxicated with love," I shall retort, "I do not want to *frighten the ear* of M. de la Harpe; I do not want to *parody Nature*—rather would I embellish it; hence instead of making Armide *scream,* I shall make her lull you." He may insist and remind me that Sophocles did not scruple to show the Athenians an Oedipus with bloodstained eyes, and that the recitative or sung declamation of this beautiful tragedy must have exhibited the eloquent sorrows of this unfortunate king in the accents of acute suffering; but I shall tell my critic that M. de la Harpe "does not want to hear the cries of a man in pain."

Have I not, sir, truly caught the meaning of your teaching? I have shown your remarks to several of my friends, one of whom said to me in returning them, "You should be grateful. M. de la Harpe gives you excellent advice. He has written his musical credo; do the like for him. Read his poetical and critical works and note down whatever displeases you. Now some people maintain that criticism has no effect but to wound the artist whom it concerns; and to prove this they say that poets have never been so much criticized as now, and have never been worse. But ask the journalists about this and see whether they think anything more useful to the State than their reviews. Some, again, may object that it is not your business as a musician to judge of poetry, but no one can find this more surprising than to see a poet and man of letters dogmatize about music."

Thus my friend. His reasoning seemed to me very sound. But despite the gratitude I owe to you, sir, I feel that after all I cannot reciprocate as I should. I am too afraid of incurring the fate of the lecturer who, in Hannibal's presence, made a long speech on the art of war.

JOURNAL DE PARIS, OCT. 12, 1777

JOSEPH HAYDN

To Fräulein Leonore ——?, later Frau Lechner

Esterhazy, July 6, 1776

Mademoiselle!

You will not take it in bad part if I hand over to you a hodgepodge in place of what you requested:[1] to describe such things in orderly fashion takes time, which I have not got; hence I did not dare write direct to Mons. Zoller himself,[2] and I hereby beg forgiveness.

I send only a crude sketch, for neither pride nor fame causes me to comply with the request but only the extreme kindness and the persuasive satisfaction expressed by such a truly learned *National* Society about my earlier works.

I was born on the last day of March 1733[3] in the small market town of Rohrau in Lower Austria, near Bruck on the Leitha. My late father, a wheelwright by trade and a subject of Count Harrach's, was by nature a great lover of music. He played the harp without knowing a note, and I, as a boy of five, was able to sing correctly after him all his simple little pieces. This led my father to send me to a relative of ours, the school director at Hainburg, where I was to learn the rudiments of music, together with other youthful essentials. God Almighty, to whom alone I owe these immeasurable blessings, gave me especially in music so much facility, that already in my sixth year I could sing with confidence some few masses in the choir, as well as play a little on the violin and clavier.

In my seventh year the late Herr Kapellmeister von Reutter, who was traveling by chance through Hainburg, heard my still feeble yet pleasing voice. He took me at once with him in the Chapel house,

[1] For transmission to Ignaz de Lucca, who was compiling a Who's Who, *Das gelehrte Oesterreich.*

[2] Possibly the landscape painter Franz Carl Zoller (1748–1829), who had conveyed the request.

[3] It seems that Haydn, though an eyewitness, makes mistakes here: he was born in 1732.

where together with ordinary studies I learned under very good masters the arts of singing, clavier, and violin. I sang soprano both at St. Stephen's and at the Court until my eighteenth year, and was much applauded. When I finally lost my voice, I had to scurry about painfully, devoting myself to the instruction of the young for eight full years. *N.B.:* in this miserable breadwinning many a genius is ruined, having no time for study.

This experience was unfortunately mine. I should never have accomplished the slightest thing if I had not zealously kept composing at night. I wrote diligently, though I was not thoroughly trained, until I had the good fortune to study the genuine fundamentals of composition with the renowned Herr Porpora, who was at that time in Vienna.[4] Finally, on the recommendation of the late Herr von Fürnberg (who was especially good to me), I was appointed music director at Count von Morzin's, and thereafter Kapellmeister at the Prince's,[5] where I hope to live my days and die.

Among my works the following have had the best reception: the operas—*Le Pescatrice, L'incontro improviso,* which has been produced before her Imperial Majesty, *L'infedeltà delusa;* the oratorio *Il ritorno di Tobia,* performed in Vienna.

The *Stabat Mater,* about which I received from a good friend the written (but undeserved) praise of our great master Hasse.[6] As long as I live I shall keep that written word like precious gold, not for what is said in it, but as coming from so great a man.

In the chamber style I have had the good fortune to please almost all the nations of the earth except the people of Berlin—as is shown by the public prints and other writings that have reached me. My only wonder is that the otherwise reasonable Berliners seem to find no happy medium when criticizing my works. In one weekly sheet they raise me to the skies; in another they hurl me sixty fathoms deep

---

[4] Nicola Antonio Porpora (1686–1766), opera composer of the Neapolitan school.

[5] Prince Nikolaus Joseph Esterhazy.

[6] Johann Adolf Hasse (1699–1783); pupil of Alessandro Scarlatti and Porpora; composer of operas and sacred music; long musical director at Dresden.

into the sea; and all this without explaining why. I know very well why: it's because they are not in a position to perform this or that of my works properly; from self-esteem they do not take the trouble to penetrate them truly. And there are still other causes which with God's help I shall account for at the proper time.

Herr Kapellmeister von Dittersdorf [7] of Silesia wrote to me not long ago begging me to refute their harsh attitude. I answered that one swallow does not make a summer: it may be that soon enough their mouths will be stopped by impartial people, and they will change their tune from sheer boredom. In spite of all this they go to much trouble to procure all my works, as the Imperial Ambassador to Berlin, Baron van Swieten, [8] assured me when he was in Vienna this past winter.

Enough of this.

Dear Mademoiselle Leonore!

You will be good enough to submit the present letter to Mons. Zoller, for his sound judgment, adding my best compliments:

my greatest ambition consists only in being justly considered by all the world an honest man—which is what I am. Any tributes of praise I dedicate to Almighty God, to whom alone I am indebted for them:

and my sole wish is never to offend my neighbor or my gracious Prince—still less my infinitely merciful God.

For the rest I remain, Mademoiselle, with all respects,
Your sincere friend and obedient servant,
Josephus Haydn in his own hand

---

[7] Karl Ditters von Dittersdorf (1739-1799).
[8] Austrian diplomat (1734-1803) who translated for Haydn the text of *The Creation* and *The Seasons*.

THOMAS JEFFERSON

To an unknown correspondent

Williamsburg, Va., June 8, 1778

... If there is a gratification which I envy any people in this world, it is to your country its music. This is the favorite passion of my soul, and fortune has cast my lot in a country where it is in a state of deplorable barbarism. From the line of life in which we conjecture you to be, I have for some time lost the hope of seeing you here. Should the event prove so, I shall ask your assistance in procuring a substitute who may be a proficient in singing and on the harpsichord. I should be contented to receive such an one two or three years hence, when it is hoped he may come more safely [1] and find here a greater plenty of those useful things which commerce alone can furnish.

The bounds of an American fortune will not admit the indulgence of a domestic band of musicians, yet I have thought that a passion for music might be reconciled with that economy which we are obliged to observe. I retain among my domestic servants a gardener, a weaver, a cabinet-maker, and a stone-cutter, to which I would add a vigneron.[2] In a country where, like yours, music is cultivated and practiced by every class of men, I suppose there might be found persons of these trades who could perform on the French horn, clarinet or hautboy, and bassoon, so that one might have a band of two French horns, two clarinets and hautboys, and a bassoon, without enlarging their domestic expenses.

A certainty of employment for half a dozen years, and at the end of that time to find them, if they choose, a conveyance to their own country, might induce them to come here on reasonable wages. ... The necessary expenses, when informed of them, I can remit before they are wanting, to any port in France, with which country alone we have safe correspondence.

I am, sir, with much esteem, your humble servant,

Th. Jefferson

[1] France and the American colonies being then at war with England.

[2] A vine tender. After the name of each trade except the last, Jefferson writes its Italian equivalent, which suggests the nationality, or at least the residence of the recipient.

NAPOLEON

To Fouché, Minister of Police

Potsdam, October 25, 1806

I enclose my approval of the voucher for the expense of putting on the ballet *Ulysses' Return*. Get a report on the details of this work and go to the first performance to make sure there is nothing wrong in it—you understand what I mean. The subject incidentally strikes me as excellent. It was I who suggested it to Gardel.

N.[1]

To Cambacérès, Arch-Chancellor

Berlin, November 21, 1806

While the army does its best to honor the nation, the men of letters, it would seem, do their best to dishonor it. I read yesterday the wretched verses that were sung at the [Paris] Opera. Really, it is a mockery. Why do you allow such improvisations to be sung there— they are only fit for vaudeville. Convey my displeasure to M. de Luçay. It was the business of M. de Luçay and the Minister of the Interior to see to it that something decent be performed. To accomplish this, it must of course be commissioned three months in advance, and not played any sooner. I hear a complaint that we have no literature. It is the fault of the Minister of Interior. It is absurd to order an eclogue from a poet as if one were ordering a new dress. The Minister should have taken steps toward the preparation of hymns for December Second.[2] If he has not already done so for this year, tell him to start making his arrangements now for next year.

N.

---

[1] Napoleon's signature has been reproduced in facsimile in the center of each endpaper of this book.

[2] The anniversary of the Coronation.

To M. de Rémusat, First Chamberlain

Paris, March 2, 1810

There should be given on May 26, *The Death of Abel;* [3] on Easter Monday the ballet *Perseus and Andromeda;* [4] then *The Bayadères* [5] two weeks after *Sophocles,* [6] *Armida* [7] in midsummer, *The Danaïdes* [8] in the fall, and *The Sabine Women* [9] by the end of May. In general, my plan is to provide as many novelties as possible during the month of Easter, since there will be a large number of visitors in Paris for the festivities.

N.

[3] Opera by Rodolphe Kreutzer.
[4] By Gardel, music by Méhul.
[5] By Catel.
[6] By Fiocchi.
[7] By Gluck.
[8] By Salieri.
[9] Ballet by Milon, music by Berton.

LORD BYRON

To John Murray

Venice, February 20, 1818

. . . Tomorrow night I am going to see *Otello*, an opera from our *Othello*, and one of Rossini's best, it is said. It will be curious to see in Venice the Venetian story itself represented, besides to discover what they will make of Shakespeare in music.

To Samuel Rogers

Venice, March 3, 1818

. . . They have been crucifying *Othello* into an opera (*Otello*, by Rossini): the music good but lugubrious; but as for the words, all the real scenes with Iago cut out, and the greatest nonsense inserted; the handkerchief turned into a *billet-doux*, and the first singer would not *black* his face, for some exquisite reasons assigned in the preface. Scenery, dresses, and music very good.

To John Cam Hobhouse

Venice, May 17, 1819

There has been a splendid opera lately at San Benedetto, by Rossini, who came in person to play the harpsichord. The people followed him about, cut off his hair "for memory"; he was shouted, and sonnetted, and feasted, and immortalized much more than either of the Emperors. . . . Think of a people frantic for a fiddler, or at least an inspirer of fiddlers.

I doubt if they will do much in the liberty line.

LUDWIG VAN BEETHOVEN

To Therese von Malfatti

Here, honored Therese, you have what I promised you, and were it not for most serious impediments you would be receiving even more, if only to show you that I always perform more for my friends than I promise. I hope and trust that you are pleasantly occupied and are having an agreeable time, though not too agreeable, so that you may also think of us.

It would probably be asking too much of you, or presuming too far on my own value, if I imputed to you the sentiment, "People are not together only when side by side; even the absent one lives in us still." Who would think of ascribing such a thing to the sprightly T. who takes life as it comes?

Amid your occupations, don't forget the piano or, indeed, music in general. You have such a talent for it, why not cultivate it thoroughly? You who have such an instinct for all that is beautiful and good, why not put it to use, and thus come to discern in this high art the perfection which shines down even on such as we.

I live very quietly and alone. Though now and then lights might arouse me, since you all left I feel in me a void here which nothing can fill. Over this feeling even my hitherto faithful art has been powerless. Your piano is ordered and you will soon have it. What a difference you will find between the theme I improvised one evening and the way I recently wrote it down for you! Make this out for yourself, but don't drink punch to help you. How lucky you are to be in the country so early! I shan't be able to enjoy that happiness till the eighth. I rejoice like a child at the thought of wandering among woods, copses, trees, grass, rocks. No man loves the country more than I do; for woods, trees, and rocks echo the thing man yearns for.

Soon you will receive some new compositions of mine, whose difficulties will not cause you to complain very much. Have you read Goethe's *Wilhelm Meister* or Schlegel's translation of Shakespeare?

One has so much leisure in the country that you might like me to send you these to read.

By chance it happens that I have an acquaintance in your neighborhood, so perhaps you'll see me appear some morning early, spend half an hour with you, and be off again. You see that I plan to cause you the shortest period of boredom possible.

Remember me kindly to your father and mother, though I have as yet no right to claim this privilege—also to your cousin Mm.[1] Farewell, my honored T., I wish you all that is good and beautiful in life. Remember me with gladness, forget my mad deeds, and be assured that no one more than I can wish to know you happy and prospering, and this even though you have little concern for

Your most devoted servant and friend
Beethoven

N.B. It would be really nice of you to drop me a line saying how I can be of service to you.

To George Thomson in Edinburgh [2]

Vienna, July 17, 1810

Sir:

Here, sir, are the Scottish airs, the greater part of which I composed *con amore* as a token I wished to give of my esteem for the Scottish and English nations by cultivating their national songs. As regards the repeat in the songs I composed for two voices, you may omit them at will and have them sung *senza replica.* Since I did not know whether or not any of those airs had more than one stanza, I had to compose them in such a way that they could be repeated if need be. Hence you will have to adjust them—to leave the repeats in the airs for more than one stanza and omit them for the rest.

I should greatly like to have the words of these Scottish songs, so as to make use of them in Germany as soon as you have published them in Scotland. You could even send them to me at once; I would

---

[1] This is said to allude to the Baroness Magdalene Gudenus.

[2] The original is in French.

have them translated and then wait for the notice of publication in Scotland, I would ask you to write out the words under the notes—just the melody.

As for the three quintets [?] and three sonatas, I accept your offer and trust they will suit you. You can have the hundred and twenty pounds sterling or the two hundred and forty ducats paid in two installments and in specie—the first half when I shall deliver the three quintets, the second half on delivery of the three sonatas, or vice versa.

As regards the airs with English words, I shall make you a very low price, to show you how much I want to serve you. That is why I am asking only twenty pounds sterling or forty ducats in cash for these airs. I could not compose them for less without being out of pocket, for I am offered more here for a dozen airs on German words, which present no language difficulties, whereas I have to have the English ones translated and look up questions of pronunciation, all of which is always a burden to me.

And lastly, about the length of time after which I would be allowed to dispose of these works in Germany, I think that six months for the quintets and sonatas and three months for the airs would suffice, counting from the day when you will publish them in Scotland. I must ask you, however, to answer me on this point.

Be assured, sir, of the high esteem with which I have the honor to be, sir, your most obedient servant

Ludwig van Beethoven

P.S. I do not want to forget to let you know that I have just received the sum of one hundred and fifty ducats for fifty-three Scottish airs [3] at Fries' banking house.

Several of my symphonies are arranged as quartets or quintets; if these arrangements suited you, I would send them at once. . . .

---

[3] More of these were Irish than Scotch, but, as Thayer has remarked, "For Beethoven everything was Scotch."

To Bettina Brentano [4]

Vienna, August 11, 1810

Dearest Friend!

No finer spring than this one—I say that and feel it because I have made your acquaintance. You must have noticed that in society I am just like a fish out of water, who twists and turns helplessly until a well-wishing Galatea throws him back into the mighty ocean. Yes, I was gasping on dry land, dearest Bettina, you caught me at a time when bad humor possessed me quite. But at sight of you it disappeared, I saw at once that you belonged to another world than this absurd one, to which with the best will one cannot listen. I myself am a miserable wretch and yet complain of others!! Of course you forgive me out of the goodness of your heart, which one sees in your glance; and out of your understanding, which lies in your ears—at least your ears know how to flatter when they listen.

My ears, alas, alas, are a blank wall through which I cannot easily hold friendly communication with men. If it were not so!—possibly! —I should have confided more in you. Could I but interpret the deep understanding look in your eyes which moved me so that I shall never forget it. Dear Bettina, dearest girl!—Art! Who understands it? With whom can one converse about this great goddess——!

How I cherish the few days when we gossiped together, or rather, corresponded: I have kept all the little notes that contain your sweet, clever, darling answers. So I can at any rate thank my bad hearing for the fact that the best part of our fugitive talks was noted down. Since you went away I have spent depressing hours, hours of darkness, in which one can do nothing; after you had left I must have walked up and down the Schönbrunner Allee for a full three hours, but I met no angel who could take such a hold on me as you, angel— forgive me, dearest friend, this departure from the key; I must be allowed such skips in order to relieve my heart.

Now, you have written to Goethe about me, haven't you? Oh that

[4] Later Bettina von Arnim (1785–1859). As a young girl she earned, and returned, the passionate devotion of both Beethoven and Goethe.

I might stick my head in a sack where I would hear and see nothing of the world's goings-on, since you, dearest angel, will not join me. But I shall surely have a letter from you? I feed on hope—it feeds half the world—and has been my nearest neighbor all my life; otherwise, what would have become of me? I send you, written out in my own hand, *"Kennst du das Land,"* [5] in memory of the hour when I met you. I also send you the rest of what I have composed since I parted from you, dear darling heart!—

> *Herz, mein Herz, was soll das geben,*
> *Was bedränget dich so sehr;*
> *Welch ein fremdes, neues Leben*
> *Ich erkenne dich nicht mehr.* [6]

Yes, dearest friend, you must answer me, you must write and say what will happen to me now that my heart has become such a rebel. Write to your most faithful friend

Beethoven

To Louis Schlösser [7]

Vienna, May 6, 1823

Herewith, my dear Schlösser, a letter to Cherubini [8] and one to Schlesinger, the publisher.[9] The latter's address you must find out by asking here at Steiner's in Paternostergässerl. Just say that I am sending you there with a recommendation to Herr Haslinger.[10] Tell Cherubini all the kind things you can think of, tell him my most ardent wish is that we should soon have a new *opera* by him, and that, altogether, I respect him above all our contemporaries. I hope

[5] Mignon's song in Goethe's *Wilhelm Meister.*
[6] "Oh my heart, what is it that oppresses thee so?
What is this strange new feeling—I recognize thee not."
[7] Darmstadt Kapellmeister who was then in Vienna and on friendly terms with Beethoven.
[8] Italian composer, long resident in Paris, where he headed the Conservatoire from 1822 till his death in 1842.
[9] German music firm with offices in both Berlin and Paris.
[10] Tobias Haslinger, assistant, later head, of Steiner's, Beethoven's publisher.

he received my letter and I am really eager to have a few lines from him. Also ask Schlesinger whether he received and delivered my letter to Cherubini and why I have not received my author's copies of the Sonata in C Minor.[11] I do beg you to write to me at once from Paris on both matters, i.e., Cherubini and Schlesinger.[12] At the Paris post office, where letters are simply put in a letter box, one must especially not forget to add the postage, otherwise the letters are kept there and cannot be obtained except by writing to Paris for them.[13] Heaven grant you all good things, I shall always be happy to know what you are doing.

Your devoted

Beethoven

To Anton Schindler

May [?] 1824

Papageno, don't talk of what I said about Prussia.[14] It is of no importance—only something like Martin Luther's *Table Talk*. I likewise request my brother not to give the sign and say nothing about it, whether at the upper or lower end of the Selchwurstgasse.

. . . Inquire of that arch-scoundrel Diabelli when the French copy of the Sonata in C Minor [15] is to be printed, so that I can have proofs to correct. I have stipulated as well that there shall be four copies for myself, of which one is to be on fine paper for the *Cardinal*.[16] If he

[11] Opus 111.

[12] Beethoven had written to Cherubini on March 15 asking him to induce the King of France to subscribe to the publication of the *Missa Solemnis*.

[13] Postage stamps were not yet in use, though prepaid mailing was displacing the original system of charge-on-delivery.

[14] In retaliation for what Beethoven took to be ill usage by the Secretary of the Prussian Embassy. "Papageno" and the sentence at the end of the paragraph about Beethoven's brother are a double allusion to Mozart's *Magic Flute*.

[15] Opus 111. Beethoven had already revised his own text several times but wanted it back once more.

[16] Beethoven's pupil, Archduke Rudolph of Austria, became Cardinal-Archbishop of Olmütz in 1819.

acts in his usual stiff-necked way, I will sing to him personally the bass aria in his own ancestral hall so that the vault and the ditch shall both resound with it.[17]

Your most obedient servant
Beethoven

To King George IV of England [18]

[c. 1823]

In the year 1813, at the desire of a number of English gentlemen residing here, the undersigned took the liberty of sending to Your Majesty his work entitled *Wellington's Battle and Victory at Vittoria,* which at that time no one else possessed. Prince Razoumovsky, who was then ambassador here, undertook to forward the work to Your Majesty by courier.

For many years the undersigned nursed the sweet hope that Your Majesty would most graciously let him know that the work had been duly received; but to this date he has not been able to boast of this good fortune and has had to content himself with the brief message of his excellent pupil, Herr Ries,[19] who informed him that Your Majesty had most graciously condescended to hand over the aforesaid work to the music directors, Mr. Salomon and Mr. Smart,[20] with a view to having it publicly performed in Drury Lane Theatre. The English newspapers announced this and added, as did Herr Ries, that this work was received with extraordinary success in London and everywhere else.

Since it has been vexing to the undersigned that he should learn of all this only indirectly, Your Majesty will surely forgive him on ac-

[17] Diabelli adroitly replied that he would note down this "aria," publish it and pay for it—which pacified the composer.

[18] Rough draft, not given here in full. The letter was sent but not acknowledged.

[19] Ferdinand Ries (1784–1838); see pp. 352 ff.

[20] J. P. Salomon, a native of Bonn, settled in London, where he died in 1815, so highly esteemed as a musician that he was buried in Westminster Abbey. Mr. Smart (later Sir George) was a violinist, an organist, and a composer (1776–1867).

count of his sensitiveness, and graciously allow him to observe that he has spared neither time nor expense to present this work to Your Majesty in as worthy a way as possible, with a view to affording Your Majesty pleasure.

From the foregoing facts the undersigned concludes that matters may have been placed before Your Majesty in a wrong light, and as the present most submissive request gives him another opportunity to approach Your Majesty, he takes the liberty of forwarding to Your Majesty the enclosed engraved copy of the *Battle of Vittoria* in full score. It was already prepared for this very purpose in the year 1815, and has been held back for this long time solely owing to the uncertainty in which the undersigned felt about this whole matter.

Convinced of the great wisdom and grace with which Your Majesty has always shown esteem and favor to art and artists, the undersigned flatters himself that Your Majesty will take this into account and will feel disposed to grant his most humble request.[21]

[21] Presumably to subscribe to the publication of the *Missa Solemnis*.

THOMAS LOVELL BEDDOES

To Bryan Waller Procter

Milan, June 8, 1824

Dear Procter,

If I do not dream, this is the city of Sforza, and today I have seen a picture of his wife by Leonardo da Vinci. Paris, Lyons, Turin, and Novara, and beautiful Chambéry in its bed of vines, they have passed before me like the Drury Lane diorama, and I almost doubt whether I have been sitting in the second tier or on the top of the diligence. Paris is far preferable to London as a place of amusement, and the manner of the lower orders is strikingly superior to that of their island equals. I saw the opera; the ballet much better than ours, but the music was French; the house is not nearly so commodious or elegant as Drury Lane, and the painting and mechanism of their scenery is not so dexterous and brilliant. The Teatro della Scala in this city I have not yet seen; it is considered only inferior to the San Carlo at Naples. . . .

June 9. Since I began this letter I have been to the top of the cathedral, and in the pit of the Teatro della Scala. The former is the finest church externally which I have seen; but the interior of Westminster's old Abbey is triumphant over the marble simplicity of the Milanese's conclave. . . .

Now for Della Scala. It is a vast theatre—six tiers of boxes, all hung with silk, disposed like our window curtains, of a light blue or yellow color; the pit, I should think, almost twice as large as Covent Garden's. The opera was *Tancredi* [1]—Madame Sesta, the prima donna, old but generally preferred to Pasta; [2] the primo basso a most extraordinary singer, with tones more like those of an organ than any human creature. The scenery is not, in my opinion, equal to the best at our theatres. One of the drops was a sort of Flemish painting, the subject a village carnival, very well executed. Such a thing would be

[1] By Rossini (1813). Mme. Sesta eludes further identification.
[2] See note p. 118.

548

novel at C.G.[3] if it could be well, but it must be very well done. Now that silk is so cheap too I think they might be a little more lavish of draperies; but we are not managers yet. The ballet, *i baccanali aboliti* [4] incalculably superior to ours or the French in the exquisite grace of the grouping, the countless abundance of dancers, and the splendours and truth of costume and decoration. The house was about one-third full, and the people all talking, so that there was a buzz outbuzzing the Royal Exchange all night, except during *"di tanti palpiti."* [5]

And what else have I seen? A beautiful and far-famed insect; do not mistake, I mean neither the Emperor of Austria nor the King of Sardinia, but a much finer specimen of creation—the firefly. Their bright light is evanescent, and alternates with the darkness; as if the swift wheeling of the earth struck fire out of the black atmosphere. . . . Tonight at twelve I leave Milan and shall be at Florence on Saturday long before this letter tastes the atmosphere (*pardonnez*— I mean the smoke) of London.

There and here,

Yours truly T.L.B.

P.S. If you see Mrs. Shelley, ask her to remember me, and tell her that I am as anxious to change countries with her, as she can be. If I could be any use in bringing the portrait [6] etc., it would be a proud task, but most likely I only flash over Florence: entering on the flood of the stars, and departing with their ebb.

---

[3] Covent Garden opera house in London.
[4] Author and composer untraceable.
[5] "O agitated heart," contralto aria from *Tancredi*.
[6] Of Shelley, to be used in the posthumous edition of his poems.

THE MENDELSSOHNS

Abraham Mendelssohn-Bartholdy to his children

Paris, July 2, 1819

You, my dear Felix,[1] must say precisely what kind of music paper you want—ruled or not ruled, and if the former, you must tell me exactly how it is to be ruled. When I went into a shop the other day to buy some, I found I had no idea myself what I was trying to buy. Read over your letter before sending it, and ask yourself whether, supposing it sent to you, you could understand what it says and could do the errand required.

Salomon-Bartholdy to his brother-in-law Abraham

1821

I cannot wholly agree with you about not indicating positively to Felix the calling he must follow. It would not interfere with his talent for music, which everybody acknowledges. A professional musician— the idea sticks in my throat. It is no career, no life, nothing to aim at. A man is no farther off at the beginning than at the end, and knows it. In fact, you are usually better off at first than at last. Let the boy study in the regular way and then prepare himself for the Civil Service by studying law at the university. His art will remain his friend and companion. If I understand the way things are going at present, there is more than ever a demand for people who have gone through the university. Should you intend to put him in business, let him enter a counting house early.

Felix to his family

Weimar, November 6, 1821

Now listen, all of you. Today is Tuesday. On Sunday, the Sun of Weimar, Goethe, arrived. We went to church in the morning and

[1] The composer, then aged ten years and five months.

heard half of Handel's music to the Hundredth Psalm. The organ, though large, is feeble. The one at St. Mary's, small as it is, is much more powerful. The one here has fifty stops, forty-four notes, and one thirty-two-foot pipe.

After church I wrote you that little word dated the fourth, then went to the Elephant Hotel, where I made a sketch of Lucas Cranach's house. Two hours later Professor Zelter came [2] calling out, "Goethe's come; the old man is here!" We hurried down at once and went to Goethe's house. He was in the garden, just coming around a hedge. Isn't it odd, dear father, that's how it was with you! He is very affable, but I do not think any of his portraits look like him. He then went through his interesting collection of fossils, which has recently been arranged by his son, and he kept repeating, "H'm, h'm, I'm quite satisfied."

After that I walked in the garden with him and Professor Zelter for about half an hour. Then to dinner. He does not look like a man of seventy-three, more like fifty. After dinner, Miss Ulrike, Goethe's sister-in-law, asked him for a kiss, and I did too. Every morning I have a kiss from the author of *Faust* and *Werther,* and every afternoon two kisses from my good fatherly friend Goethe. Just think of it!

In the afternoon I played to Goethe for about two hours, Bach fugues and my own improvisations. In the evening they made up a table for whist, and Professor Zelter, who took a hand in the beginning, said, "Whist means—you're to shut up!" That's one of his clinchers for you.

Zelter at the private rehearsal of Felix's opera The Two Nephews
February 3, 1824 [3]

My dear boy, from this day forward you are no longer an apprentice but a journeyman in the brotherhood of musicians. I proclaim your emancipation in the name of Mozart, Haydn, and old father Bach.

[2] Felix's music teacher as well as an old friend of Goethe's.
[3] Felix's fifteenth birthday. The opera was his fourth. It is in three acts and its subtitle is "The Uncle from Boston."

Felix to his sister Fanny

Paris, May 9, 1825

Your last letter made me furious—rather! . . . You talk of prejudice and preconceived ideas, of my being morose and querulous, and of the "land of milk and honey" as you call this Paris. Please stop and think a moment: are you in Paris or am I? Now, then, isn't it likely that I know what's what better than you? Is it my habit to let my judgment of music be influenced by prepossessions? But suppose it were, is Rode [4] prejudiced when he says to me, "This place is a musical shambles"? Is Neukomm [5] prejudiced when he says, "This is no country for orchestras"? Is Herz [6] prejudiced when he says, "Here the only thing the public likes and understands is variations on popular tunes"? And are ten thousand others prejudiced who damn Paris? . . . Read the *Constitutionnel:* what do they give at the Italian opera except Rossini? Read the catalogues: what do they publish and sell except romances and potpourris? Come and hear *Alceste,* [7] come and hear *Robin des bois;* [8] hear the soirées (which, by the way, you've confused with the *salons:* soireés are concerts at which you pay, and salons are musical parties); hear the music in the Royal Chapel—*then* pass judgment and call me down, but not now when *you* are the one who is full of preconceptions and blind with prejudice!

Felix to his family

Heidelberg, September 20, 1827

"O Heidelberg, o wondrous town, where all the day the rain pours

[4] Pierre Rode (1774–1830) French prodigy on the violin and composer of études still in use.

[5] Sigismund von Neukomm (1778–1858), pupil of Haydn, pianist in Talleyrand's household, and composer—it is said—of one thousand works.

[6] Heinrich Herz (1806–1888), brilliant German pianist long established in Paris; ridiculed by Schumann. See p. 98.

[7] Gluck's opera.

[8] Weber's *Freischütz* in garbled form. See pp. 73 and 555–56.

down!" That's the sophisticated line, but what care I, a student, a rake-hell, if it rains or not. There are grapes, instrument-makers, newspapers, inns, Thibauts—no, I'm exaggerating—there is *one* Thibaut left, but he's worth six: what a man! [9]

. . . It is odd—the man does not know much about music, even his knowledge of musical history is rather limited, he judges mostly by instinct and I understand more than he does, and yet I have learned a great deal from him and am much indebted to him. For he revealed to me the merits of old Italian music and has kindled in me his own enthusiasm for it. His words are aglow with enthusiasm, in fact I must say his language is really flowery. I have just left him, and as I had told him a good deal about Sebastian Bach, and said that he still did not know the fountainhead and the principal—which are all to be found in Sebastian—he said as I left, "Farewell! We shall found our friendship on Luis de Vittoria [10] and Sebastian Bach, as do two lovers who pledge each other to look at the moon and so feel in that way that they are close together."

Felix to his parents

Cologne, October 2, 1827

[My friends found that they] must be in Berlin by the sixth . . . so that even though I had virtually promised Schelble [11] to go back via Frankfort and attend the performance at the St. Cecilia Society of a Handel oratorio which I did not know, I made up my mind to return with them, the weather being so bad that at Horchheim I could hardly go outdoors. I was about to start last evening when suddenly the clouds left the hills, the mist vanished, the moon rose shin-

[9] Anton Friedrich Thibaut (1772–1840), distinguished German jurist and patron of music, collector of ancient Italian scores and author of a treatise on purity in his favorite art.

[10] Tomás Luis de Victoria (1535?–1611) Spanish composer of sacred music, usually associated with the Roman school of Palestrina.

[11] Johann Nepomuk Schelble (1789–1837), close friend of Beethoven, founder and director of St. Cecilia concerts at Frankfort until his death.

ing, and news came that on the right bank of the Rhine, all the way from Horchheim to Ehrenbreitstein, the gathering of the grapes would begin day after tomorrow.

At that point Uncle put in a word.[12] He gave me a glowing account of the pleasures and wonders of the grape gathering, and said that two days after it is over he goes himself to Frankfort, where he means to attend the St. Cecilia performance. If I stayed to cheer him and Auntie he would see me back in Berlin. When I argued that I had to finish my piano score,[13] he brought me the most beautiful music paper and demonstrated what a good quiet place I had to work in. So—I gave up. I'm finishing my tedious chore at Horchheim and shall have it behind me when I get home. I shall hear the St. Cecilia concert, to which Schelble is sending out special invitations in my honor. I shall take part in the grape gathering—dear God, forgive me, it is all too beautiful!

---

[12] Joseph Mendelssohn, older brother of Felix's father.
[13] Of still another opera, *The Wedding of Camacho,* which had brought forth cabals and criticism.

CARL-MARIA VON WEBER

To Castil-Blaze [1]

Dresden, October 15, 1825

Sir,[2]

There was a time when I considered it one of the chief pleasures of my proposed stay in Paris to make the acquaintance of the writer of *Opera in France* [3]—a work to which I shall always accord the great esteem it deserves. I was convinced that I could only benefit from conversation with a writer so remarkable for just and elevated views, and I congratulated myself in anticipation of knowing him. I leave you to judge, sir, how deeply grieved I must be after all this (which I may well instance), to see my hopes dashed by your behavior toward me.

First you undertake to adapt my opera *Der Freischütz* to the French stage. Nothing could be more flattering to me nor better fitted to earn my sincere gratitude. But you do not deem it necessary to discuss anything with the composer, nor impart your ideas as to the changes that might be indispensable for your public. You obtain the score through an entirely illegitimate channel (however legitimate it may have seeemd to you), for my opera being neither engraved nor published, no chapel-master and no music seller had the right to sell it. At last the opera is produced and you continue to ignore me, to the point of pocketing for yourself all the composer's royalties.

I witness all this and I still await from day to day the honor of a letter from you. It strikes me as impossible that a man of your standing, who holds the views you do about art, can forget entirely what one artist and gentleman owes to another. And yet I now hear that you have just published the *Freischütz* score. Ah! my dear sir, what is to become of all that is sacred to honor? How *can* you, who have not even acquired the legal right?

[1] See pp. 73 and 78.
[2] The original is in French, evidently Weber's own.
[3] I.e., Castil-Blaze himself.

I address myself, sir, to no one but yourself, to your probity, to all the noble sentiments you have so often expressed in speaking of art and what is due to it. Allow me to hope that nothing more than a piece of understandable negligence has caused you to forget the existence of the man who composed *Der Freischütz,* and be assured that I shall retain as far as possible the genuine regards to which your talents entitle you and with which I have the honor to be,

Yours, etc.,
Carl-Maria von Weber

ROBERT SCHUMANN

To D. G. Otten, Music Director at Hamburg

Dresden, April 2, 1849

Honored Sir:

You must think very badly of me for having waited so long to answer your kind note. I have in fact thought both of you and of your letter quite often—and gratefully—but will now make no more excuses, except the old one of the musician's laziness about writing words. We all prefer to deal with notes.

I wrote the symphony [1] in December 1845, when I had scarcely got over my illness, and it seems to me that my music betrays as much. Only in the last movement did I begin to feel like myself again, and I really began to recover only after I had finished the whole work. Otherwise it reminds me of a dismal period; that you should nonetheless take a sympathetic interest shows that even such gloomy sounds can find a receptive ear. Everything you say certainly proves that you thoroughly understand the music, and the fact that the doleful bassoon which I took particular pleasure in placing in the adagio did not escape you pleased me best of all.

I have long heard of your energy in promoting good music, especially through your Concertverein. Anything really good gets to be known without articles in the newspapers. Invisible good-natured sprites convey the news by air. For about a year I too have derived much enjoyment from a similar concert society. I refresh myself there with Palestrina, Bach, and other things that one does not hear elsewhere.

Do you know Bach's *Passion According to St. John,* the so-called little one? I'm sure you do! Now, don't you think it is much bolder, more powerful and poetical than the one according to St. Matthew? To me the latter seems to have been written some five or six years earlier. I think it contains tedious parts and is inordinately long. But

[1] In C Major, Op. 61. Otten had performed it and written about the "melancholy bassoon" in the adagio.

the other—how compact and full of genius, especially the choruses—and what consummate art! If the world could only attain a solid grasp of such works as that! But no one writes about it. The musical journals make the attempt now and then, but give it up again, because critics lack the needful knowledge and true conviction. That's how it is and always will be. But something has to be reserved for the few, scattered artist spirits, and they have indeed Palestrina, Bach, Beethoven's last quartets, etc.

So I greet you with the cordial cry "Forward together!"—i.e., we will not cease to make known, as far as in us lies, all that we recognize to be great and true. It brings its own reward.

With best regards,

Yours sincerely,

R. Schumann

ANONYMOUS

To an unknown correspondent [*in French*]

Vienna, May 15, 1769

The Court of Parma had summoned Clouc,[1] the chapel-master at Vienna, to make the opera which is to be given here during the celebration of the wedding.[2] This last having been postponed for the reasons that you know, he asked permission to come home on business of his own. It was granted on condition that he return to Parma when he should be needed. He went back a few days since.

Last night a person very familiar with the Court of Parma, who greatly admires the government there, and feels an attachment for that country, told me that Clouc was saying that in Parma one lives only in poverty, fear, and constraint, that he would not want to live there himself owing to the general confusion, and that the government rules by force and despotism. I pretended that I could not believe this, and replied that all foreign visitors left Parma delighted with the Court, with the government, and for other reasons. But this person answered that he had not heard him speak in that way himself, but that the people who had reported the words had no interest in falsifying them; and that besides he is a boorish German, a horse who can't see anything but his music, and that this was the only reason he had found nothing good in Parma except the music of the Court. This in fact connects somehow with what I have heard elsewhere. I had been told that Clouc praised the music of the Court of Parma, and never was I told that he praised anything else.

The other day, Calsabigi, Clouc's friend,[3] while speaking of the election of the Pope, said that it was a good thing the wedding was

---

[1] I.e., Gluck, also spelled Kluck in the writings of the time—hence the Gallicized version above.

[2] Between the Austrian archduchess Maria Amelia and the infante Don Ferdinand of Parma.

[3] Raniero da Calzabigi (1714–1795) was the librettist of Gluck's *Orfeo, Alceste,* and *Paride ed Elena,* as well as a critic whose ideas upon drama (he admired Shakespeare) contributed to the reform of opera initiated by Gluck.

postponed, for he knew through his friend that nothing was ready in Parma, that everything was in confusion, and that there would not have been a place for the wedded couple to live in. To that I answered that Clouc must have seen only the Molli palace and never once the garden palace and that of Colorno, and the apartments opposite San Paolo. Incidentally, this same Calsabigi had told me that Clouc was coming back to Vienna for three months; that would suggest the wedding will not be held very soon. If these things are true, since they are likely, I should be very sorry that such bad music should have been sent for from Vienna. People here hold the Court of Parma in high esteem, but they are also very quick to gather bad impressions. This Calsabigi has invited me several times to dine with him; I shall go on purpose and try to pick a day when his friend will be there too.

JOHANN WOLFGANG VON GOETHE

To Carl Zelter [1] *in Berlin*

Weimar, November 9, 1829

I too have now heard Paganini, and immediately thereafter, the same evening, I had your letter, which gave me to believe that my estimate of these marvels was quite reasonable. I thought they gave something less than enjoyment—which with me is always intermediate between sensation and understanding; something was lacking— a base to this pillar of flame and cloud. . . . This time I felt the lack of the necessary foundation, for both my mind and my ear. I heard only something meteoric, and could give no further account of it to myself. Yet it is curious to hear people, women especially, talk about it. Without any hesitation they give utterance to what are in fact confessions.

[1] See p. 551.

NICOLO PAGANINI

When Paganini arrived in Paris in February 1831—his first visit—he found lithographs on display which depicted him as a convict in chains, as a murderer caught in the act, and other discreditable guises. He addressed his defense to the musicologist and critic who was also his friend, F.-J. Fétis (1784–1871).

To F.-J. Fétis, editor of the Revue Musicale

Paris [1831]

Sir:

The French public has shown me such kindness and has been so generous with its applause that I am forced to believe in the renown which, it is said, preceded me in your city. I am also led to hope that my concerts have not fallen too far below their reputation. But had I any doubts about my notoriety, it would be dispelled by the zeal which I see your artists have used in portraying me and placarding with my name the walls of your capital. Unfortunately, they have not stopped at mere portraits, for walking one day on the Boulevard des Italiens, I saw in an engraver's window a lithograph purporting to depict "Paganini in Prison."

Well, said I to myself, here are honest folk using for their profit a certain slander which has dogged me for fifteen years. While I gazed and laughed at this travesty which the artist had tricked out with full details drawn from his imagination, I noticed that a large circle of passers-by had collected around me and, while audibly comparing my features with those of the youth in the picture, were remarking how much I had changed since my prison term.

I then saw that the affair was being taken seriously by those you call, I believe, "rubbernecks," and I inferred that the forgery was indeed a good business venture. It occurred to me that since everyone must live, I might as well furnish a few more anecdotes to the portraitists who are good enough to use me in this fashion, and so enlarge their repertory. It is to this end, sir, that I beg you to publish the present letter in your *Revue Musicale*.

The gentlemen in question have depicted me in prison, but they do not know how I came there; as to which they know exactly as much as I, or as those who first circulated the tale. There are several versions, which could supply as many different subjects for art. It has been said, for example, that having surprised my rival with my mistress, I courageously slew him from behind, at the moment when he was least capable of self-defense. Others have maintained that my jealous fury wreaked itself on my mistress alone, but there is no agreement about the mode of my dispatching her. Some say a dagger, others affirm that I chose to enjoy her sufferings by administering poison. Each has followed his free fancy, and I would extend the same liberty to the lithographers.

At any rate, this is what befell me at Padua about fifteen years ago: I had given a concert there with considerable success. The next day I was seated at the table d'hôte among sixty others—no one had noticed my entrance—when someone expressed his enthusiasm about the effect I had produced on the audience the day before. His neighbor seconded this praise, adding that *"there was nothing surprising in Paganini's virtuosity. It is the result of his being eight years in prison with only his violin to mitigate his solitary confinement. He was convicted for the cowardly murder of one of my friends, who happened to be his rival in love."*

Everyone was indignant, as you may imagine, at the baseness of the crime. Whereupon I spoke up and, addressing myself to the person who was so familiar with my history, begged him to tell me in what place and year this adventure had occurred. Everyone's eye turned to me in astonishment at discovering the chief actor of the tragedy. The narrator was much put out. It was no longer his friend who had perished—it had merely been said—he had been told—or rather he had believed—but no doubt he had been misled—. Thus, my dear sir, does the reputation of an artist become the plaything of idle talk—the sport of people who are too lazy to imagine that a man can as readily study and practice of his own free will in his room as locked up in a cell.

In Vienna a still more ridiculous rumor arose to test the credulity of some enthusiasts. I had played there some variations entitled *Le Streghe* (*The Witches*). They had proved rather effective; so that a gentleman (who was described to me as pale, melancholy, and rapt of gaze) asserted that he found nothing amazing in my technique, for all through my playing of the variations he had distinctly seen the Devil near me, guiding my bow arm. The Devil's striking resemblance to myself sufficiently proved my ancestry. The Devil was dressed in red, bore horns, and carried his tail between his legs. You can conceive, sir, that after so minute an identification it was impossible to doubt the report, and many persons were persuaded that they had at last found the secret of what is called my *tours de force*.

My peace of mind was long at the mercy of these stories. I vainly tried to show their absurdity. I pointed out that since the age of fourteen I have never ceased to play before public audiences; that for sixteen years I was orchestra conductor and music director at Lucca; that accordingly if I had spent eight years in prison for killing rival or mistress, it must have been at an earlier time and hence that I must have had this mistress and rival at the age of seven.

In Vienna I called on my ambassador, who testified that he had known me for nearly twenty years as a man of standing and probity, and this did quell for a time the course of slander. But it can never be wholly stilled, and I was scarcely surprised to find it springing out again in Paris. What, sir, am I to do? I see nothing open to me but to resign myself and let malice do its worst. Perhaps, though, I should apprise you of yet another anecdote that has lent color to the libelous attacks made upon me.

This is it: a violinist named D——i, resident in Milan, became friendly with a pair of shady characters and was persuaded to join them in an attack on the curate of a neighboring village, who was reputed to keep a large sum in his house. Fortunately, one of the trio lost heart and denounced the plot to the police, who seized D——i and his accomplice just as they reached the curate's house. They were condemned to twenty years in irons. But General Menou, after he became Governor of Milan, set the musician free after two years. Incredible as it may seem, that is the canvas for the embroidery fashioned to discredit me. A violinist whose name ends in *i* must be Paganini. The plot became the murder of my mistress or rival, so that none but myself could plausibly have been in prison. Still, since I was supposed to develop my new technique there, the irons had to be dispensed with and my arms left free.

I repeat: since they wish it so, against all probability, I must yield. But I cling to one hope, which is that after my death Calumny will let go its prey, and that those who have so cruelly avenged themselves for the reality of my fame will leave my ashes in peace.

Yours, etc.,

Paganini

JOHANNES BRAHMS

This document is made all the more poignant by the likelihood that at the time of writing Brahms and Clara Schumann were lovers.

To Julius Otto Grimm [1]

Heidelberg, September 1856

My dear Julius,

What must you think of me for not answering? Don't be angry! Had you been bright and a little more —— and written to Frau Klara [Schumann], you wouldn't have had to wait.

Rather than make excuses and so on, I'll give you some particulars about those days.

I had spent Schumann's birthday with him—June 8—and found him remarkably changed, suddenly, compared with the previous time. Then Frau Klara came back from England, and just as she arrived so did worse news from Endenich.[2] A week before his death, on the Wednesday, we had a telegraphic dispatch. I barely read, it said roughly this: "If you wish to see your husband while he still lives, come at once. His appearance is frightful to behold."

We drove over. He had had an attack which the doctors thought would be fatal. I don't know the right name—angina pectoris? I went to him, saw him in fact in an attack, and so greatly agitated that I, and the doctors too, dissuaded Frau Schumann from going to him and urged her to make the return trip.

Schumann just lay, taking nothing but an occasional spoonful of wine and jelly. Frau Schumann's misery was so great all this while that on Saturday evening I *had* to suggest that she come back again and see him.

Now we give thanks to God that it happened so, for it is now absolutely indispensable for her peace of mind. She saw him again on

---

[1] Organist, conductor, teacher, musicologist, and composer (1827–1903). Brahms roomed with him in Leipzig and they were friends till death.

[2] In the asylum of which Schumann was confined.

Sunday, Monday, and early Tuesday. He died in the afternoon about four o'clock.[3]

I cannot ever again experience anything so touching as the reunion of Robert and Klara.

At first he lay a long time with closed eyes, and she kneeled in front of him, more quietly than one would have thought possible. But he recognized her and again on the following days. Once he desired clearly to embrace her and threw his arm around her.

Of course he was no longer able to speak; one could only make out single words (perhaps imagine them), but even that must have pleased her. He often refused the wine that was offered him, but took it eagerly from her finger, for so long at a time and so ravenously, that one was convinced he recognized the finger.

Tuesday noon Joachim [4] from Heidelberg, which held us up a while in Bonn, otherwise we would have arrived before his death, but we were half an hour too late. He died as easily as you read these words. We should have breathed more freely once he had been released but could hardly believe it.

His death was so gentle that it almost passed unnoticed. His body looked calm, as if all were for the best. It would have been impossible for a woman to stand it much longer.

They buried him Thursday afternoon. I carried the wreath before the coffin, with Joachim and Dietrich.[5] The members of a choral society were pall bearers. There was trumpeting and singing.

The town had prepared ahead of time a beautiful spot for the event and had it decorated with five plane trees. Madame Klara found another kind of consolation in the institution itself. It set at rest all the evil rumors which had come to her ears about things—for example through Bettina—.[6] I might and could write it all to you—somehow —but it wouldn't do. You can imagine for yourself on the strength of these bare facts, how sad, how beautiful, how moving this death was.

[3] July 29, 1856.
[4] Famous violinist (1831–1907).
[5] Pupil of Schumann's.
[6] Bettina von Arnim (see p. 543) thought Schumann's doctor inadequate.

We (J[oachim], Kl[ara], and I) have put in order the papers that Schumann left: and that includes all he ever wrote! One comes to love and honor the man more and more as one has these closer dealings with him.

I shall delve deeper and deeper into all this.

Farewell. Forgive the hurried scrawl: there is no peace here for a peaceful letter. We are now in Heidelberg, after a few weeks on Lake Vierwaldstätter.[7]

If you write to Frau Schumann and me, address us at Düsseldorf, to which we are returning very soon.

But still here for another week!

My next one will be longer and calmer. Regards to your dear wife. And don't be angry with me.

Affectionately yours,

J. Brahms

(Notwithstanding—I send heartfelt greetings to you and your wife. Kl. Sch.) [8]

P.S. Frau Klara is as well as can be expected, but not so well as one could wish. I forgot that you would ask about her.

---

[7] In Switzerland.
[8] Added by Clara Schumann in her own hand.

EDGAR ALLAN POE

To James Russell Lowell

" . . . I am profoundly excited by music, and by some poems—those of Tennyson especially—whom, with Keats, Shelley, Coleridge (occasionally), and a few others of like thought and expression, I regard as the *sole* poets. Music is the perfection of the soul, or idea, of Poetry. The *vagueness* of exultation aroused by a sweet air (which should be strictly indefinite and never too strongly suggestive) is precisely what we should aim at in poetry."

CHARLES BAUDELAIRE

To Richard Wagner

Paris, February 17, 1860

Dear Sir:

I have always imagined that however used to fame a great artist may be, he cannot be insensible to a sincere compliment, especially when that compliment is like a cry of gratitude; and finally that this cry could acquire a *singular* kind of value when it came from a Frenchman, which is to say from a man little disposed to be enthusiastic, and born, moreover, in a country where people hardly understand painting and poetry any better than they do music. First of all, I want to tell you that I owe you *the greatest musical pleasure I have ever experienced*. I have reached an age when one no longer makes it a pastime to write letters to celebrities, [1] and I should have hesitated a long time before writing to express my admiration for you, if I did not daily come across shameless and ridiculous articles in which every effort is made to libel your genius. You are not the first man, sir, about whom I have suffered and blushed for my country. At length indignation impelled me to give you an earnest of my gratitude; I said to myself, "I want to stand out from all those imbeciles."

The first time I went to the Italian Theatre in order to hear your works,[2] I was rather unfavorably disposed and indeed, I must admit, full of nasty prejudices; but I have an excuse: I have been so often duped; I have heard so much music by pretentious charlatans. But you conquered me at once. What I felt is beyond description, and if you will be kind enough not to laugh, I shall try to interpret it for you. At the outset it seemed to me that I knew this new music, and later, on thinking it over, I understood whence came this mirage; it seemed to me that this music was *mine,* and I recognized it in the

---

[1] Baudelaire was thirty-nine, but still obscure, or else unfavorably known for his *Fleurs du Mal* published three years earlier.

[2] Wagner had just given three concerts there, consisting chiefly of overtures and choral excerpts from his earlier operas. The *Tristan* prelude was the only recent work.

way that any man recognizes the things he is destined to love. To anybody but an intelligent man, this statement would be immensely ridiculous, especially when it comes from one who, like me, *does not know music,* and whose whole education consists in having heard (most pleasurably, to be sure) some few fine pieces by Weber and Beethoven.

Next, the thing that struck me most was the character of grandeur. It depicts what is grand and incites to grandeur. Throughout your works I found again the solemnity of the grand sounds of Nature in her grandest aspects, as well as the solemnity of the grand passions of man. One feels immediately carried away and dominated. One of the strangest pieces, which indeed gave me a new musical sensation, is the one intended to depict a religious ecstasy.[3] The effect produced by the Entrance of the Guests and the Wedding Fête [4] is tremendous. I felt in it all the majesty of a larger life than ours. Another thing: quite often I experienced a sensation of a rather bizarre nature, which was the pride and the joy of understanding, of letting myself be penetrated and invaded—a really sensual delight that resembles that of rising in the air or tossing upon the sea. And the music at the same time would now and then resound with the pride of life. Generally these profound harmonies seemed to me like those stimulants that quicken the pulse of the imagination. Finally, and I entreat you not to laugh, I also felt sensations which probably derive from my own turn of mind and my most frequent concerns. There is everywhere something rapt and enthralling, something aspiring to mount higher, something excessive and superlative. For example, if I may make analogies with painting, let me suppose I have before me a vast expanse of dark red. If this red stands for passion, I see it gradually passing through all the transitions of red and pink to the incandescent glow of a furnace. It would seem difficult, impossible even, to reach anything more glowing; and yet a last fuse comes and traces a whiter streak on the white of the background. This will signify, if you will, the supreme utterance of a soul at its highest paroxysm.

[3] Baudelaire means the overture to *Lohengrin.*
[4] From *Tannhäuser,* Act II, and *Lohengrin,* Act III, respectively.

I had begun to write a few meditations on the pieces from *Tann-häuser* and *Lohengrin* that we listened to; but I soon saw the impossibility of saying everything.[5]

Similarly, this letter could go on interminably. If you have been able to read it through, I thank you. It only remains for me to add a few words. From the day when I heard your music, I have said to myself endlessly, and especially at bad times, *"If I only could hear a little Wagner tonight!"* There are doubtless other men constituted like myself. After all, you must have been pleased with the public, whose instinct proved far superior to the false science of the journalists. Why not give us a few more concerts, adding some new pieces? You have given us a foretaste of new delights—have you the right to withhold the rest? Once again, sir, I thank you; you brought me back to myself and to what is great, in some unhappy moments.

Ch. Baudelaire

I do not set down my address because you might think I wanted something from you.

---

[5] Baudelaire did publish an article on Wagner and his music about a year later, reproducing verbatim some of the remarks in this letter.

ALEXANDER BORODIN

To his wife Catherine in Moscow

St. Petersburg, September 19, 1875

. . . News of my musical activity in Moscow has spread with the speed of lightning since my first day here: Stassov Vladimir, with the Shcherbachovs, flew to me the next day and, of course, didn't find me home. Close upon this I received a whole series of floods of words from Vladimir Vasilyevich [Stassov], who, by the way, hasn't yet heard my music and won't until Sunday. I must admit I never expected my Moscow products to create such a furore—Korsinka is in ecstasy, Modeste [1] too, Ludmila Ivanovna has invited the Petrovs to listen to the products. I am particularly astonished by their sympathy for the first chorus [in Act I of *Prince Igor*], which we tried out with voices and—without bragging, I can say—they found it extremely effective, bold, and cleverly handled theatrically speaking. Konchak has obviously made the impression I wanted; except for a few awkwardnesses, purely vocal ones (which will have to be corrected), he comes out quite well in the singing. Korsinka particularly likes him. He, as well as Modeste, terribly likes that wild oriental ballet, which I composed last of all in Moscow; remember? the lively one, in 6/8? Of course all, in chorus, say that I should write the remainder quickly, without putting it in the bottom drawer. . . . Cui has completed *Angelo* and has given it to the printer; the opera will be given sometime in December for Melnikov's *bénéfice*. Korsinka has composed thirty-six fugues and sixteen canons; Modeste has finished the first act of *Khovanshchina,* and has done some work on the other acts. That's all for you about music. . . .

[1] I.e., Moussorgsky.

EMMANUEL CHABRIER

To the publisher Costallat

[c. 1883]

"I now know *The Tempest* by heart; there are many good things in it, but Blau [1] is right to want some expanding of the love story, otherwise Papa Prospero would get to be a bore. As for *drama,* properly so called, where is it? Are they really dramatic, those conspiracies among old ward-heelers—Alonzo, Antonio, Gonzalvo, Stefano? And those two crapulous rakes, Caliban and Interpocula [2]—who cares a rap about their backtracking across that island?

So—the business will have to be spiced up on t'other side. But we have, first, the idyll between Ferdinand and Miranda—of the finest color; second, the whole nuptial atmosphere and the spirits of the air in Act IV; not to mention, thirdly, a good bit of buffoonery with all the topers. Is that enough to make an opera? We'll see. But the fellow's first scene, at sea, is a poser: it's exactly *The Flying Dutchman* overture, which, alas, is not by me. It's a terror to do over again. Tempests and shipwrecks—*brr!* And after Wagner and Beethoven—*double brrr!* We must wait!

[1] The librettist.
[2] "Between-cups," i.e., Shakespeare's **Trinculo.**

SYDNEY SMITH

November 6, 1842

My dear Lady Holland,[1]

I have not the heart, when an amiable lady says, "Come to *Semiramis* in my box," to decline; but I get bolder at a distance. *Semiramis* would be to me pure misery. I love music very little—I hate acting; I have the worst opinion of Semiramis herself, and the whole thing (I cannot help it) seems so childish and so foolish that I cannot abide it. Moreover, it would be rather out of etiquette for a Canon of St. Paul's to go to an opera, and where etiquette prevents me from doing things disagreeable to myself, I am a perfect martinet.

All these things considered, I am sure you will not be a Semiramis to me, but let me off.

Sydney Smith

---

[1] Charming and tyrannical leader of the famous Whig salon, Holland House. She was then a widow, the third Baron Holland having died in 1840. Sydney Smith's daughter, also Lady Holland, was the wife of the eminent physician Sir Henry Holland. *Semiramis:* Rossini's opera (1823).

GIUSEPPE VERDI

To Giuseppina Appiani [1]

Paris, August 22, 1847

I owe you a great many letters, but you'll forgive me when I tell you all I have had to do here. Quite another thing than London, the Opera here! Just imagine being all day between two poets, two managers, two publishers—they always come in pairs; getting a prima donna engaged; working up the subject of a libretto, etc., etc., I tell you it's enough to drive one mad— But I have no intention of going mad, and I defy the whole tribe of opera-mongers, all the Parisians, all the papers *pro* and *con,* as well as the comic squibs in the *Charivari* and *Entr'acte.* Speaking of *Entr'acte,* you will find there a very funny article about me. I think Emanuele Muzio [2] took it with him to Milan—get him to show it to you.

I shall be here until about November 20, and at the end of that month I shall be admiring the cupola of the Duomo.

My health is better than in London. I enjoy Paris less than London and I have in fact an extreme dislike for the boulevards (hush! let no one hear my heresy!).

You ask for some account of Donizetti, [3] and I shall give you the news as it is, however painful. I have not seen him yet, having been advised not to, but I assure you I very much want to see him and if opportunity offers without its being known by anyone, I shall certainly do so. His physique is in good shape, except that he always holds his head bent over his chest and his eyes closed; he eats and sleeps well and says hardly a word, or if he does it is quite indistinct. When someone approaches, he opens his eyes for a moment, and if he is told "shake hands," he does it. It seems this is a sign that his mind is not all gone; and yet a doctor who is also his very close friend was telling me that these acts are done from habit and that it would be

[1] Née Contessa Stripelli, friend and confidante of Verdi's early years.

[2] See p. 359.

[3] Composer of many operas. Born in 1797, his mind gave way in the mid-forties and he died in 1848.

better if he were lively and even violently mad. There might then be some hope; as he is now, only a miracle could help. But on the other hand he is still as he was six months ago, a year ago—no better, no worse. Such is Donizetti's actual condition now. It is dreadful, it is just too dreadful! If there is any cheerful news I shall write to you instantly.

To Giuseppe Mazzini

Paris, October 18, 1848

I am sending you the hymn, even if a little late, but I hope it will arrive on time. I have tried to make it as popular and easy as I could. Do with it what you like; burn it if you think it not worthy. If you publish it, have the poet change some of the words at the beginning of the first and second stanzas, in which it would be good to have phrases of five syllables, with different meanings each time, as in the other stanzas—"We swear it," "Sound the trumpets," etc., etc. And of course, end the verse with a slide. In the fourth line of stanza two, the question must be altered to a positive and the meaning stopped with the verse. I could have set it as it stands, but then the music would have been less easy, hence less popular, and we would have missed our aim.

May this hymn, amid the music of cannon, soon be sung on the plains of Lombardy!

To Tito Ricordi [4]

October 24, 1855

. . . I know you can say "I have the right to do this; the law allows it." I know, I know. But I had hoped you would never use that kind of nonsense against me—me who have so often performed more than I promised or was obliged to; me who am to such a large extent the source of your colossal fortune. . . . Now, the sole condition—I

---

[4] Head of the Milan publishing firm of the same name, lifelong friend of Verdi.

asked no money whatever—was to have my scores printed correctly and properly published, and the latest ones are perfect travesties. . . .

But who cares about an artist's reputation! I can't help remarking on a discouraging fact, which is that during my already long career I have always found managers, publishers, etc., etc. hard, unyielding, implacable, ready to appeal to the contract or the lawbook—honeyed words and harsh deeds. I've never been considered anything but an object, a tool, to be used as long as it produces. It is sad to say but true.

To Signor Filippi

Genoa, March 4, 1869

Dear Sir:

I cannot possibly be offended by your article in *Perseveranza* on *La Forza del Destino*. If you felt obliged, amid much praise to add a little blame, this was wholly within your rights and you did well so to write. You must know, in any case, that I never complain of attacks, any more than I send thanks (perhaps there I am wrong) for favorable reviews. I love my own independence in all things, and I respect it in others. I am particularly grateful to you for your reserved attitude during my stay in Milan. Since you were to write about my opera, it was best not to let yourself be influenced by a handshake or a visit paid or received. As regards your article, since you ask me about it, I am free to tell you that it did not, and could not, displease me.

I knew nothing of the incident between you and Ricordi, but it may be that Giulio, who, I believe, prefers Donna Leonora's aria to many other compositions, was a little put out to find it impugned as an imitation of Schubert. If it is indeed that, then I am as surprised as Giulio, for, musical ignoramus that I am, it's years since I have heard Schubert's "Ave Maria," and it would have been hard for me to copy it. Don't think that when I speak of my *extreme ignorance of music* I am pretending. It is the simple truth. In my house there is hardly any music to be seen; I have never stepped into a music library, nor gone to a publisher's to read a piece. I keep up with the best contemporary operas, not by study, but by hearing them occasionally at the theater. In all this, I have a purpose that you will easily guess. Hence I repeat to you that of all composers, past or present, I am the least erudite. Let us be clear about this—and I say again, I am not "putting on" anything—when I refer to *erudition* I do not mean musical *knowledge*. I should be lying if I pretended that in my youth I did not study long and hard. That is why I now have a hand strong enough to shape sound as I like, and sure enough to obtain, usually, the effects that I imagine. And when I write something contrary to the rules, that is because the strict rule does not give me what I want, and because I do not really believe that the rules hitherto in force are all good. The textbooks of counterpoint need revising.

What a long letter! And what's worse, much of it is useless! Forgive me, please, and accept my sincere greetings.

FRANZ SCHUBERT

Vienna, November 12, 1828

Dear Schober: [1]

I am ill. I have had nothing to eat or drink for eleven days now, and can only stagger feebly and uncertainly between armchair and bed. Rinna [2] is treating me. If I take food I cannot keep it down.

So please be good enough to help me out in this desperate state with something to read. I have read Cooper's *Last of the Mohicans, The Spy, The Pilot,* and *The Pioneers.* If by any chance you have anything else of his, do please leave it for me with Frau von Bogner at the coffeehouse. My brother, who is responsibility personified, will bring it over to me without fail. Or indeed anything else.

Your friend,

Schubert

---

[1] Franz von Schober, a well-born youth only a few months younger than Schubert, became his devoted friend, patron, and roommate.

[2] Ernst Rinna von Sarenbach, Court physician. Schubert died of typhus on the nineteenth.

Maxims and Good Stories

WISDOM AND FAITH

Music has always been interwoven with my life—so much so that I can hardly imagine the one without the other. I am not sure that this is altogether a good thing, but it is too late now to change. With the passing of time I have learned to wean myself away from certain musical influences, and especially not to think of music as a refuge in times of trouble. On the contrary, it is just at those times that I avoid it. I no longer want to hear music except when I am serene and, if possible, happy. But to coddle one's melancholy by feeding it with the accumulated sadness of the Nocturnes—none of that!

JULIAN GREEN, *Journal* (1938)

I felt that besides wanting to hear music, I wanted to know things about music. I likewise felt that there was much to learn from other people's musical experiences and study of music. In due course, I learnt to take nothing on trust, not even praise or blame emanating from the writers whom I considered soundest and most sensitive and thoughtful; for I encountered a bewildering discrepancy of views. Here were two authors who agreed in their appraisement of Beethoven and Wagner but disagreed in their appraisement of Berlioz; another two agreed on Beethoven, Wagner, and Berlioz, but disagreed on Liszt; others, agreeing on Beethoven, Wagner, Liszt, and Berlioz would disagree on Strauss or Hugo Wolf, and so on.

M. D. CALVOCORESSI, *Musical Taste* (1925)

In every period the alarm sounds: "Today we have no great musicians, poets, painters." This is due to the fact that traditionally one keeps looking at the sequence of geniuses, which appears like an avenue of trees seen in foreshortened perspective, much thicker than in reality. Between one genius and the next is an average distance of half a century. They represent in fact the results acquired along the way. Between one genius and the next the talents are at work; they represent the links joining the two end points.

Let it therefore be the task and care of the contemporaries to recognize and appreciate the worth of these men of talents who conserve and connect. The geniuses, whatever the contemporaries may say, stand solid and rear their heights in full view. But contemporaries see only what they believe in and what they wish to believe; and they may not believe in what they see and what they hear.

FERRUCCIO BUSONI, *Reflections* (1921)

. . . Nothing is more a fashion then musick; no not cloathes, or language, either of which is made a derision to after times. And so it is of all things that belong to the pleasures of sence. For allowing that there is somewhat preferable in right reason, as some cloathes may be more convenient, and language concise, and significant; yet there is a great deal indifferent, and so much, that the prejudice of custome will get the better of it. And the grand custome of all is to affect novelty, and to goe from one thing to another, and despise the former. And it is a poorness of spirit, and a low method of thinking, that inclines men to pronounce for the present, and allow nothing to times past. Cannot wee put ourselves in *loco* of former states, and judge *pro tunc?* Therefore as to all *bon gusto* [1] wee ought to yield to the authority of the proper time, and not determine comparatively where one side is all prejudice. It is a shallow monster that shall hold forth in favour of our fashions and relishes, and maintaine that no age shall come wherein they will not be despised and derided. And if on the other side, I may take upon me to be a fidling prophet, I may with as much reason declare that the time may come when some of the present celebrated musick will be as much in contempt as *John come kiss me now, now, now,* and perhaps with as much reason, as any is found for the contrary at present.

ROGER NORTH, *Memoirs of Musick* (1728)

[1] Good taste.

You want my opinion on the following questions: What I require of the modern opera house . . . and also, what I hope for and expect, as a composer, from opera managers. As to the first, I want the classical operas produced as if they were modern, and vice versa. And as the composer of *Wozzeck,* I naturally hope that this opera of mine will be produced—but I do not expect it.

ALBAN BERG, Interview (1928)

[Is there not] a rudimentary redundancy in grand opera as exemplified in simultaneously showing a sword on the stage, speaking about a sword in the book, singing about a sword, and introducing a prearranged labeled sword motive in the orchestral part? In 1960 this will, surely, long ago have proved simply too insulting to the imagination of the least-educated spectator-auditor.

SIR WALFORD DAVIES, The Pursuit of Music (1944)

It is a great error to say, "Such and such a composer is a good orchestrator; such and such a work is very well instrumented." For orchestration is one of the aspects *of the very soul of the work*. The work is thought orchestrally and from its very conception carries with it a certain orchestral coloring proper to it and to its author. Is it possible to separate Wagner's music from its actual orchestration? That would be tantamount to saying of a painting by a given master, "What an admirable drawing with colors!"

NIKOLAI RIMSKY-KORSAKOV, Principles of Orchestration (1891)

Mahler had a very delicate ear for all natural sounds and could not help paying attention to them. Thus the call of the cuckoo in his First Symphony is given a pert, gay part; likewise the cry of peacocks, hens, and roosters. . . . In his little working house, which he greatly liked, there were none the less quite frequent causes of disturbance: the birds bothered him with their song, in spite of scarecrows and random discharges of shot. And then there were barking dogs, barrel organs, and brass bands. . . . He writes: "We are ever surrounded on all sides by barbarism which it is beyond man's power to overcome. The majority have no notion of what it means to respect another man's privacy. I tend more and more to think that only the deaf and blind are fortunate, cut off as they are from this miserable world, and I can well imagine that a musician might voluntarily deprive himself of his hearing, as Democritus is said to have made himself blind."

NATALIE BAUER-LECHNER, *Recollections of Gustav Mahler* (1923)

An artist can easily enough slip from sheer love of art into hatred of mankind.

JEAN-PAUL RICHTER, Introduction to Hoffmann's *Tales* (1813)

A splendid brass band has just been playing a few pieces on the street, in the rain. It felt like velvet to one's inner being. O Pythagoras, if music thus transports us into the skies, it is because music is harmony, harmony perfection, perfection our dream, and our dream is heaven. This world of strife, bitterness, selfishness, ugliness, and misery makes us sigh involuntarily for eternal peace, for boundless adoration and love without end. It is not so much the infinite that we long for as the beautiful. It is not Being nor the confines of Being that hem us in; it is evil, within us and without. There is no need to be great if we can only be in harmony with the order of the universe.

H.-F. AMIEL, *Journal,* March 17, 1870

This is Eros as the ancients felt him—seductive, playful, malicious, demonic, invincible. To perform this you need a real witch: I know of no song quite like it—and it must be sung in the Italian way, *not* the German!

FRIEDRICH NIETZSCHE, marginal note to the "Habanera" in *Carmen* (1881)

If I were to begin life again, I would devote much time to music. All musical people seem to me happy; it is the most engrossing pursuit, almost the only innocent and unpunished passion.

SYDNEY SMITH (c. 1840)

If ever you become a musical critic, Gemel, . . . you've got to realize that music is only one thing in the world. That the painter is a better man than the person who looks at his painting only insofar as painting goes. That the bricklayer is *in point of bricklaying* vastly superior to Beethoven, me, or anybody else who can't lay one brick on top of another. You must never let your work as an artist override your humanity. It is not a crime for a man to know nothing about art and care less.

JAMES AGATE, *Gemel in London* (1934)

Whenever a new composer comes along, the unanimous opinion of sober judges is that he doesn't know how to write for the voice. If he is successful—after his third opera—the sober judges have nothing more to say. "Sound opinions" are nothing but clichés, parrot cries.

EMMANUEL CHABRIER, *Letters* (1885)

The Germans, who make doctrines out of everything, deal with music learnedly; the Italians, being voluptuous, seek in it lively though fleeting sensations; the French, more vain than perceptive, manage to speak of it wittily; and the English pay for it without meddling.

STENDHAL, "Raison, Folie" (n.d.)

There never was a more imbecile notion than the twentieth-century cult of Pure Music, for the simple reason that although in one sense all music must be program music, since it is concerned with human emotions, in another sense music, insofar as it *is* music, can never be anything but pure.

W. H. MELLERS, "The Textual Criticism of Music," (1939)

I have tried . . . to prove that the formation of scales and of the tissue of harmony is a product of artistic invention, and is in no way given by the natural structure or by the natural behavior of our hearing, as used to be generally maintained hitherto. . . . Just as peoples whose tastes are differently inclined fashion very different buildings out of identical stones, so in the history of music we see the identical peculiarities of the human ear serve as the basis of very different musical systems.

HERMANN VON HELMHOLTZ, *Theory of Sound* (1862)

I can discover from a poet's versification whether or not he has an ear for music. To instance poets of the present day: from Bowles's and Moore's, I should know that they had fine ears for music; from Southey's, Wordsworth's, and Byron's, that they had no ears for it.

SAMUEL ROGERS, *Table Talk* (1856)

If I were in Berlin I should rarely miss the performances of the Möser Quartet. Of all the instrumental genres, I have always been able to follow this one best. You listen to four sensible persons conversing, you profit from their discourse, and you get to know the peculiar properties of their several instruments.

JOHANN WOLFGANG VON GOETHE, *Letters* (1829)

Numbers in music do not govern but merely enlighten. The hearing is the only channel through which their force is impressed upon the innermost soul of the attentive listener. . . . Hence the true target of music is not the eye, nor yet the reason properly so called, but simply and solely the Hearing, which imparts to the soul and to the understanding whatever enjoyment it experiences.

JOHANN MATTHESON, *Das neu-eröffnete Orchestre* (1713)

All the worst things happen in the best works, and the worst music appears to be streaked all through with the most luscious bits.

BERNARD VAN DIEREN, *Down Among the Dead Men* (1935)

I have spoken frequently in Parliament, and not always without some applause; and therefore I can assure you, from my experience, that there is very little in it. The elegancy of the style, and the turn of the periods, make the chief impression upon the hearers. Give them but one or two round and harmonious periods in a speech, which they will retain and repeat, and they will go home as well satisfied, as people do from an opera, humming all the way one or two favorite tunes that have struck their ears and were easily caught. Most people have ears, but few have judgment; tickle those ears, and, depend upon it, you will catch their judgments, such as they are.

LORD CHESTERFIELD, *Letters* (1749)

If I have time, I shall rearrange some of my violin concertos and shorten them.[2] In Germany we rather like length, but after all it is better to be short and good.

WOLFGANG AMADEUS MOZART, *Letters* (1778)

[2] Five works composed in 1775.

The artist must yield himself to his own inspiration, and if he has a true talent, no one knows and feels better than he what suits him. I should compose with utter confidence a subject that set my blood going, even though it were condemned by all other artists as antimusical.

GIUSEPPE VERDI, *Letters* (1854)

As I looked at a portrait of Wagner, I wondered how a head which looks like that of a stingy landlord could ever have produced *Siegfried*.

JULIAN GREEN, *Journal* (1932)

Only this much is certain, that as no mother bears children to see them blown to rags or choked in poison gas, so no composer plans his works for the monstrous fate of falling into the conventional concert program, to hang there like a soldier's body on the barbed wire.

BERNARD VAN DIEREN, *Down Among the Dead Men* (1935)

Good music isn't nearly so bad as it sounds.

HARRY ZELZER, Chicago impresario

If an inhabitant of another planet should visit the earth, he would receive, on the whole, a truer notion of human life by attending an Italian opera than he would by reading Emerson's volumes. He would learn from the Italian opera that there were two sexes; and this, after all, is probably the fact with which the education of such a stranger ought to begin.

JOHN JAY CHAPMAN, *Emerson and Other Essays* (1909)

Emotion is specific, individual, and conscious; music goes deeper than this, to the energies which animate our psychic life, and out of these creates a pattern which has an existence, laws, and human significance of its own. It reproduces for us the most intimate essence, the tempo and the energy, of our spiritual being; our tranquillity and our restlessness, our animation and our discouragement, our vitality and our weakness—all, in fact, of the fine shades of dynamic variation of our inner life. It reproduces these far more directly and more specifically than is possible through any other medium of human communication.

ROGER SESSIONS, "The Composer and his Message" (1941)

Music is the imagination of love in *sound*. It is what man imagines of his life, and his life is love.

W. J. TURNER, *Orpheus, or The Music of the Future* (1926)

DERISION AND INVECTIVE

Hell is full of musical amateurs: music is the brandy of the damned.

BERNARD SHAW, *Man and Superman* (1903)

Those things that act through the ears are said to make a noise, discord, or harmony, and this last has caused men to lose their heads to such a degree that they have believed God himself is delighted with it.

BARUCH SPINOZA, *Ethics* (1677)

One who opened Jowett's version [of Plato] at random and lighted on the statement that the best guardian for a man's "virtue" is "philosophy tempered with music," might run away with the idea that, in order to avoid irregular relations with women, he had better play the violin in the intervals of studying metaphysics.

F. M. CORNFORD, *The Republic of Plato* (1941)

Amidst all the follies of the age, there never was a greater than the immoderate passion of the people for music. Though amusement and recreation are sometimes necessary, yet when carried to excess they become vicious. Now so far did the luxury of this kingdom extend at the time when this plate [1] was first published, which was in the year 1741, that Italians (as being supposed to be the greater proficients) were brought over at considerable expense; and the poorest and least skilled among them, who from a want of ability or a want of means, could not continue in their own country, soon discovering our folly, gathered here in flocks and took possession of the place. When here, they were encouraged, and their wretched abilities looked upon as supernatural; they introduced a new style of music, which suited well the growing levity of this nation. The noble and ele-

[1] "The Enraged Musician," described in the next paragraph.

vated was immediately transformed into the trifling and insignificant: and the solemn and majestic sounds of British harmony gave place to the tinkling frippery of Italian singsong.

To ridicule this immoderate passion of the age for music, Mr. Hogarth published this print; in it he represents an Italian professor of music, at his study, enraged to the greatest degree at the astounding noise the motley group collected beneath the window are making, which seem assembled in order to annoy and distress him. By the inscription on the house over the way, he is also supposed to live in the neighborhood of a pewterer, whose constant hammering is no trifling annoyance to him. Our artist seems in this plate to have let none of the material or customary noises of London streets escape him. In front are some children at their sports, one of whom is hallooing and beating of a drum; another dragging a tile upon the stones, while a third is winding a racket. On the right is a ballad singer bawling out "The Lady's Fall," with a squalling infant in her arms; on the left, a man grinding a cleaver, whose machine is standing on the foot of a dog, and sets him yelping.

ANONYMOUS NOTE in early nineteenth-
century reprint of Hogarth's Works

A certain skilful action of his fingers as he hummed some bars and beat time on the seat beside him seemed to denote the musician; and the extraordinary satisfaction he derived from humming something very slow and long, which had no recognizable tune, seemed to denote that he was a scientific one.

CHARLES DICKENS, Dombey and Son (1846)

The expression consisted in being very soft on the words *love, peace,* etc., and then bursting into roars of triumph on the words *hate, war,* and *glory.* To this pattern Mr. Braham [2] composed many

---

[2] John Braham (1774–1856), English tenor. An example might be his once famous showpiece, "The Death of Nelson."

of the songs written for him; and the public were enchanted with a style which enabled them to fancy that they enjoyed the highest style of the art, while it required only the vulgarest of their perceptions.

LEIGH HUNT, *Autobiography* (1850)

I shall never be able to say . . . : "What a chorus! What an orchestra! This theater ranks first in the whole world!" It sticks in my throat. Again and again I have heard people say one after another in Milan (especially when I was putting on *La Forza del Destino*): La Scala is the first theater in the world. In Naples: the San Carlo is the first theater in the world. In Venice it was: La Fenice is the first theater in the world. In Petersburg: the first theater in the world. In Vienna: the first theater in the world (and that I would say too). And in Paris: the Opera is the first theater in two or three worlds.

GIUSEPPE VERDI, *Letters* (1879)

Italian music, its orchestration: the oboes play with the flutes,[3] the clarinets with the oboes, the flutes with the violins, the bassoons with the lower strings, the second violins with the first, the viola with the bass. The voices are ad lib., the violins as in the score.

CARL-MARIA VON WEBER (1818)

It has been said that because today more people hear Beethoven in twenty-four hours (on the radio) than heard him in his whole lifetime, the people have music. Momentarily disregarding the question of the quality of the emanations from the radio, we can say: yes, and a citizen doubtless sees more policemen now in twenty-four hours than Beethoven saw in his whole lifetime. The people hear more music, and *ipso facto* they are more musical? The people have more law, and *ipso facto* they are more lawful?

[3] I.e., the same notes.

The analogue is not so absurd. . . . Hearing more music—ninety-nine per cent of which is not Beethoven but the equivalent of the radio vibrations of frankfurters—accomplishes just one thing: ennui in the eardrum.

HARRY PARTCH, *Genesis of a Music* (1949)

The first thing to do on arriving at a symphony concert is to express the wish that the orchestra will play Beethoven's Fifth. If your companion then says "Fifth what?" you are safe for the rest of the evening.

DONALD OGDEN STEWART, *Perfect Behavior* (1922)

To know whether you are enjoying a piece of music or not, you must see whether you find yourself looking at the advertisements of Pears' soap at the end of the program.

SAMUEL BUTLER, *Note-Books* (c. 1890)

What most people relish is hardly music; it is rather a drowsy revery relieved by nervous thrills.

GEORGE SANTAYANA, *Reason in Art* (1917)

It's Prussian blue—it fades!
Attributed to JOHANN SEBASTIAN BACH about the music of his son EMANUEL.

Weber wanted a drama with which to unite his noble, spiritual melody. Meyerbeer, on the other hand, wanted an irresistibly mongrel, historico-romantic, diabolico-religious, emotionally fickle, bigoted-voluptuous, frivolously sacred, mysterioso-shameless hodgepodge to serve as subject for an extraordinarily strange music, which, owing to the leathery texture of his musical mind, never quite came off.

RICHARD WAGNER, *Opera and Drama* (1850)

The essential lack in Wagner is after all a want of sanitary plumbing. No amount of sentiment or passion can wholly make up for this. One feels all the time that the connection with the main is fraudulent.

JOHN JAY CHAPMAN, *Letters* (1895)

Do you think me so devoid of taste that I would stand there in front of the orchestra, violin in hand, but like a listener, while the oboe plays the only melody in the entire work?

PABLO SARASATE TO EDOUARD LALO apropos of Brahms' Violin Concerto (1879)

There is a definite limit to the length of time a composer can go on writing in one dance rhythm. This limit is obviously reached by Ravel toward the end of *La Valse* and toward the beginning of *Bolero*.

CONSTANT LAMBERT, *Music Ho!* (1934)

Brahms' *Song of Triumph* came at the end of the concert—a Handelian impersonation, unfortunately rather tiresome, like all of Brahms' impersonations. The program notes of the Friends of Music speak of this *Song of Triumph* as a "powerful work." Sheer puffing! Why has the free-handed author of these notes not blared it forth that Bruckner's *Te Deum* is a powerful work? Why these delicate distinctions? Or does the epithet "powerful" apply only to the voluminosity of the score? Is the public being prepared for a more prolonged torture? These warning signals at performances of Brahms might be valued as boons to a suffering humanity, were it not that there is a still more effective means of avoiding discomfort—the reader understands me!

HUGO WOLF, concert review, Jan. 16, 1887

The case was aggravated when the fanatical Wagnerian was a professional composer: being incapable of imitating what belongs solely to genius, he would cling desperately to whatever lay within the reach—whether because it was false or artificial—of any simple mortal of ordinary intelligence; thinking thereby to appropriate the glittering treasure which showed through the intermittent darkness. As for the non-musicians, I myself have known more than one whose mouth filled with anathemas and who *tore their raiment* at the least unfavorable judgment aimed at the idol they deemed sacrosanct.

MANUEL DE FALLA, "Notes on Wagner" (1933)

Ah, it's a pretty trade we're in! I'm writing piano pieces for four hands. Why do I do it? you ask. How in hell should I know, my poor d'Estaleuse! It's stupidity, of course—my publisher won't even take them. One will be too long—never too short, you'll observe; the other too difficult—never too easy; and none of them *practical!*

EMMANUEL CHABRIER, *Letters* (1884)

Lord! will the time ever come when nobody asks us what we were up to in our divine compositions! Pick out the fifths and leave us in peace!

ROBERT SCHUMANN, concert review (1838)

The study of old music, both sacred and profane—yes. But it would be a good idea to remember that not all the old music is beautiful either.

GIUSEPPE VERDI, *Letters* (1871)

No one, I conclude, would wish to see literature dicoursed about in the same pinchbeck and affected style as are painting and music; yet this is what will happen if the prolific weed of sham admiration is permitted to attain its full growth—the well-nigh universal habit of literary lying and pretense of admiration for certain works of which in reality we know very little, and for which, if we knew more, we should perhaps care even less.

JAMES PAYN, *Some Private Views* (1881)

TARADIDDLE

Music makes for exuberance and hyperbole, and this is sometimes aped by those whose blood stays cool but who would like excitement too. The point of the extravagant examples that follow in illustration of this fact is not that they are foolish, but that they are the foolishness of sensible men—a source of amusement and a warning, alike unintended, but worthy of all gratitude.

The first publication in English to supply enlightenment about *The Ring* was written and published in Germany in 1879 by the Wagnerites Hans and Ernst von Wolzogen. The present extract does not include the remarkable description of the "brangling and brustling" effects, which was omitted from the second and later editions of the *Guide*.

The bird warns again and again, when Mime with his old praise of his education, with the dusky harmonies of the cooking motive, and with the coaxing-crawling motive, or even with the charming tune of Nature's life, tries to obtrude his poisonous brewage upon the dragon killer. . . .

But to what end all precaution? As Siegfried with scorn and menace refutes the Walhall theme which is held up against his impatience, there, in the second half of the scene, Wotan's motive of wrath rises more and more, and between its most urgent repetitions cites—in vain—the horrors of the fiery blaze.

. . . With the accords of the Walhall-march the proud passage of the godly power once more rises and then descends in several repetitions of the world's destruction, closely following each other. Her lay becomes dark and low: "Holda's apples" are cited in vain. Gloomily the Walhall-theme dies away, the Rhinegold slowly arises in Wotan's resigned mind.

Thereupon ceases this excitement and a new lively, pompous symphonic set begins.

For the last time we hear Siegfried's motive, but the wild rush of the Götterdämmerung motive overpowers it with the utmost force:

flames cover the picture of the old gods and the melody of salvation through love waves *dim.* under ethereal harp sounds, as the freed and blessed spirit of love of the whole world's tragedy ascends to the eternal regions of his heavenly home!

HANS AND ERNST VON WOLZOGEN,
Guide through Wagner's Ring (1882)

On Handel's Messiah in Boston

I walked in the bright paths of sound, and liked it best when the long continuance of a chorus had made the ear insensible to the music, made it as if there was none; then I was quite solitary and at ease in the melodious uproar. Once or twice in the solos, when well sung, I could play tricks, as I like to do, with my eyes—darken the whole house and brighten and transfigure the central singer, and enjoy the enchantment.

This wonderful piece of music . . .

RALPH WALDO EMERSON, *Journal,* December 25, 1843

We need not seek farther whom we must put down on the title page of the *Eroica*. We musicians dedicate and consecrate with heart and brain, with hand and lips, the *Eroica* symphony to the greatest hero that has seen the light of day since Beethoven. We dedicate it to Beethoven's twin, the Beethoven of German politics, the Prince Bismarck. Prince Bismarck, hail!

HANS VON BÜLOW, speech after the Berlin Philharmonic Concert
of March 28, 1892

On Beethoven's Fourth Piano Concerto

At the beginning the piano emerges gently from dreams; this is truly Beethoven improvising. Two romantic themes, renunciation and hope, are gradually developed. When, after an orchestral interlude, the piano is heard again solo, it is as if a butterfly rose ecstatically from its cocoon. There are no fortissimos here, and when the call to new adventures sounds, the butterfly sinks back, dreaming. The whole thing is wrapped in dark-red velvet; at times it is as if one were caressing it with one's hands.

EMIL LUDWIG, *Beethoven, Life of a Conqueror* (1943), translated by George Stewart McManus

Weber may not have been a great composer, but he was without doubt a great opera composer. . . . Weber never produced a prize bloom nor perfected a single species, but the luxuriance of his colors is supreme, and ranges from delicacy to exoticism.

DENNIS ARUNDELL in *The Heritage of Music* (1934)

On Sir Thomas Beecham

"A Dean of Dignity"

What a scene in the vast crowded hall where thousands sat thick upon their chairs, so close and mingled and motionless as the music held them that they looked like painted frescos. What a wonderful silence, the silence of that throng, whence no rustle nor cough nor murmur came to taint the beauty of the song nor mar the orchestra's luminous flow!

What a moment . . . when Sir Thomas Beecham, while the audience broke into applause, came smiling to his place, bowing to his public, bowing to his orchestra, a dean of dignity, a marvel of mien, a figure straight from the Prado, specially released by Velázquez for the occasion. What a man! What a master of music! Till you have seen him conduct you do not know what movement can be.

He stands there and spreads his arms as if he were about to take a deep, deep dive, stands poised on the edge of melody, and then plunges, and then all the currents of sound swirl him about, and all its broad waves bear him nobly on their spread; his arms toss with the foam of notes, his fingers flash like silvered bubbles, as he cleaves the vocal waters.

All the gestures that man has ever known seem to be his under the sway of the music at once gushing from his own baton and drunk by his own heart. The delicacies and reverences of the eighteenth century, the sabre cuts of a captain of Napoleon's cavalry charging across Europe, the pleadings of an advocate, the prayers of a saint, the very kiss of a lover—all these he conjures up and draws upon and delivers as messages to his orchestra.

Sometimes he puts aside his baton and conducts with his hands alone, throws himself back and flings some divine missile at his players on the orchestra's edge, pommels the rhythm into his violins, and then flutters again into gentleness, and his fingers flicker and flicker, flicker and interweave, till they seem to be but running oil.

His singers tore at our hearts as we listened, to his orchestra I bow an untutored head for the joy they gave it, but him himself, the great conductor I shall never forget, and would adjure all to see him and swim with him where the great operas flow into the eternal sea.

J. M. N. JEFFRIES, *Daily Mail* (London), October 31, 1927

On the centenary performance of Beethoven's Missa Solemnis

Whatever may be said this year about the greatest musician that the heavens ever inspired on this earth will be no match for the respectful hearing of his own voice, for the flights of a pure and ardent soul, which arose from a human crowd in tears and which, in the heavenly light of the stained glass two hundred feet above the ground, touched divinity.

Le Matin (Paris), March 18, 1927

On Corelli

In the portrait by Howard painted about 1700 he has large regular features, bright deep-set eyes, and a general expression of calm and nobility. When he played upon the violin, however, his eyes blazed and he threw himself into convulsions.

On Maugars

He has left no indication of his repertory, but it probably consisted of well-known airs on which he devised brilliant variations.

On Gesualdo

Related to the great aristocratic families of Italy, Gesualdo was of a violent nature. In 1590 he ordered the murder of his wife Marie d'Avalos and her lover Fabrizio Carafa; after which tragic event he composed six books of madrigals, married Eleonora d'Este, and devoted himself to music.

> HENRY PRUNIERES, *A New History of Music,*
> translated by Edward Lockspeiser (1941)

We live in an age of remarkable progress, in which all the arts are being daily perfected. Mechanics especially is advancing fast and will soon bring you relief as regards performing upon your instruments.

> THE FRENCH MINISTERS OF FINE ARTS,
> addressing the Faculty of the Conservatoire,
> January 3, 1896

Tonight I go to another musical party at Marshall's, the late M.P. for Yorkshire. Everybody is talking of Paganini and his violin. The man seems to be a miracle. The newspapers say that long streamy flakes of music fall from his string, interspersed with luminous points of sound which ascend the air and appear like stars. This eloquence is quite beyond me.

> T. B. MACAULAY to his sister, May 27, 1831

CLASSIC TALES

This past winter, wishing to complement the program of the Conservatoire (inadequately enough, owing to lack of time), I devoted several concerts to the performance of the piano duets, trios, and quintets of Beethoven. I was almost sure they would bore my audiences, but I was equally sure no one would dare to object. As things turned out, there were some lively expressions of enthusiasm by which it would have been easy to be taken in, and hence to believe the crowd overcome by the power of genius.

But at one of the last concerts a change in the order of the pieces played put an end to that illusion. Without notice we performed a trio by Pixis [1] in place of Beethoven's and vice versa. The Beethoven was found feeble, commonplace, positively boring, and M. Pixis was deemed impertinent to risk comparison before an audience which had come solely to admire the work of the great master. I am far from suggesting that it was wrong to applaud the Pixis trio; but he himself can only smile with pity at the bravos of a public incapable of distinguishing the styles of such different compositions.

FRANZ LISZT, *Gazette Musicale,* July 16, 1837

Byron, to his childhood friend, Elizabeth Pigot: "I don't know how it is, I sing a great deal better to your playing than to other people's."

Elizabeth Pigot: "That's because I play to your singing, while others make you sing to their playing."

THOMAS MOORE, *Notes for the Life of Byron* (c. 1820)

The two great masters of poetry and music, Goethe and Beethoven, were taking a walk along the path through the woods one day in order to be able to exchange world-shaking ideas without hindrance.

[1] French composer of songs and chamber music (1788–1874).

Wherever they went, the people on their path made way for them and saluted them with great respect. Goethe, annoyed by this continual interruption, said, "What a nuisance! I don't seem ever able to avoid this kind of thing." To which, with a calm smile, Beethoven answered, "Don't let it bother Your Excellency: the greetings are probably meant for me."

Traditional in Teplitz since 1812

A Frenchman in Munich asks Giuseppe dall'Abaco:[2] Have you been to Paris?

Abaco: Yes.

F.: Did you go to the concert of sacred music?

A.: Yes.

F.: What do you think of the attack with the bow, did you hear the first attack with the bow?

A.: Yes, I heard the first and the last.

F.: What did you say? The last? What does that mean?

A.: Why, just that—the first and the last—and I may say the last gave me even greater pleasure.

WOLFGANG AMADEUS MOZART,
retelling it from Raaf,[3] *Letters* (1778)

First Rival Composer, while clapping: "What do you think of his piece?"

Second Rival Composer: "I think it's glorified dinner music."

Third Rival Composer: "Dinner music! It not only dines but it whines!"

One evening in Moscow, in E. P. Pyeskovskaya's flat, Lenin was listening to a sonata by Beethoven being played by Isaiah Dobrowein,

[2] Italian musician at Bonn (1709–1805).
[3] Anton Raaf, famous tenor (1714–1797).

and said, "I know nothing which is greater than the *Appassionata;* I would like to listen to it every day. It is marvelous, superhuman music. I always think with pride—perhaps it is naïve of me—what marvelous things human beings can do!"

Then, screwing up his eyes and smiling, he added rather sadly, "But I can't listen to music too often. It affects your nerves, makes you want to say stupid, nice things, and stroke the heads of people who could create such beauty while living in this vile hell. And now you mustn't stroke anyone's head—you might get your hand bitten off. You have to hit them on the head, without any mercy, although our ideal is not to use force against anyone. H'm, h'm, our duty is infernally hard."

MAXIM GORKY, *Days with Lenin* (1924)

You have heard of Mozart's celebrated feat of giving a notation of Allegri's *Miserere*.[4] But here is a good instance of the partial interpretation of happenings. It was not done at a first hearing, but after careful preparation. He heard it six times, helped and prompted by his very capable father, and even then his notation was so full of mistakes that his father destroyed the tentative score after the Pope had explained to the Archduke that the singers relied on memory and tradition. There were, therefore, legitimate excuses for Mozart, but nonetheless we see that it is wise to be wary about reputed feats of technical prowess in music.

BERNARD VAN DIEREN, *A Conference* (1929)

"When in doubt, play what's written!"—Harold Bauer to a pupil struggling over a passage. But later in the same piece: "Ah, but the right notes won't help you there!"

[4] This famous work in four, five, and nine parts, was sung in St. Peter's at Rome during Holy Week. The full score was not available, so that when Mozart's father took the boy, aged fourteen, to Italy, he arranged to have the young prodigy note the work down during performance. See p. 520.

Rossini, strolling on the Paris boulevards, runs into the director of the Opera, who tells him that the composer's *William Tell* has just been chosen for revival. It will be put on next month. Rossini: "What? All of it?"

Young and handsome, Liszt was first introduced to English society at the salon of Lady Blessington. At the end of the musical evening he wished to know from a third party her opinion of him. "Why, only this, that it's a shame to put a fine man like you at the piano!"

Cheerful Philistine to the leader of a new string quartet still struggling for recognition: "Well, here's hoping your little organization will grow!"

James Agate, meeting a friend, a member of the B.B.C. orchestra: "Who conducted this afternoon?"

Alec Whittaker, First Oboe: "Sorry, James, I forgot to look."

ENVOY

From continually shifting key, music may get to such a persistently enharmonic condition as to be never at any moment in less than two keys at once, and hence IN NO KEY AT ALL!

What next? Why, this next!

W. F. APTHORP (1898)

Sources and Acknowledgments
Index

List of Sources and Acknowledgments

The page numbers following each work indicate the passages used or excerpted from in the text. Chapter or section references are given when a book exists in many editions, and letters dated in the text are marked as "under date."

The Editor thanks the owners and publishers of copyright materials for permission to reprint. The details of these obligations are given after the titles to which they apply.

Agate, James. *Ego 6* (London, 1944), pp. 35–37.

———. Whittaker story, in *Ego 7* (London, 1946), p. 42.

———. On Gemel, in *Ego 8* (London, 1947), p. 208.

> Courtesy of Crown Publishers Inc., and George G. Harrap & Co., Ltd.

Amiel, H.-F. *Fragments d'un Journal Intime,* ed. Bernard Bouvier (3 vols., Geneva, 1922). Vol. II: pp. 158–59.

Anonymous. Editorial on "The Orchestra," in *The Musician,* April 1900, p. 114.

Anonymous. Letter on "Clouc," in J. Tiersot, *Lettres de musiciens écrites en français,* etc. (2 vols., Turin, 1924). Vol. I: pp. 55–56.

Apthorp, W. F. *By the Way: Being a Collection of Short Essays on Music and Art . . . from the Program Books of the Boston Symphony Orchestra* (2 vols., Boston, 1898). Vol. II: pp. 162–73; Envoy, in Vol. I, p. 157.

Arundell, Dennis. "Weber," in *The Heritage of Music,* ed. H. J. Foss (London, 1934), pp. 133–34.

Bach, Johann Sebastian. *Gesammelte Briefe,* ed. Erich H. Müller von Asow (Regensburg, 1938), under date. Epigram on his son's music, in *Musical Quarterly,* Oct. 1950, p. 506.

Balzac, Honoré de. "Gambara," in *Oeuvres Complètes* (50 vols., Paris: Ollendorff, 1901). *Etudes Philosophiques,* Vol. III: pp. 347–70 and 412–17.

Barnum, P. T. *Struggles and Triumphs: or, Forty Years' Recollections . . . Written by Himself* (Hartford, 1869), chaps. XVII–XXI.

Baudelaire, Charles. Letter to Richard Wagner, in *Revue Musicale,* Nov. 1, 1922, pp. 2–4.

Bauer-Lechner, Natalie. *Erinnerungen an Gustav Mahler* (Leipzig, 1923), pp. 81 and 138–39.

Beaumarchais, P.-A. Caron de. *Oeuvres Complètes* (Paris, 1861), pp. 205–209.

Beddoes, Thomas Lovell. Letter to Procter, in *Works,* ed. H. W. Donner (London, 1935), under date.

> Courtesy of Mr. Donner.

Beethoven, Ludwig van. Letters, in *Sämtliche Briefe,* ed. A. C. Kalischer (5 vols., Berlin and Leipzig, 1908), under dates. On "Beethoven's Third and Fifth," see Prodhomme and Berlioz. On his conversation with Goethe, see Goethe.

Berg, Alban. Interview, in Willi Reich, *Alban Berg* (Vienna, 1937), p. 173.

Berlioz, Hector. "An Interview with the Police" and "Beethoven and Lesueur," in *Mémoires* (2 vols., Paris, 1926). Vol. II: pp. 171–73; Vol. I: pp. 112–13.

———. "An Artist from the Grocer's," in *Soirées de l'Orchestre* (Paris, 1852 ff.), Third and Fourth Evenings.

———. "The Limits of Music," in *Gazette Musicale,* Jan. 1 and 8, 1837, and in *A Travers Chants* (Paris, 1862 ff.), pp. 152–58 and 189.

Berlioz, Hector. "The Flute," in *Traité d'Orchestration* (2nd ed., Paris, 1856), pp. 151–53.

Blessington, Marguerite, Countess. On Liszt, in *Correspondance de Liszt et de la Comtesse d'Agoult* (Paris, 1933), p. 433.

Borodin, Alexander. See Moussorgsky.

Brahms, Johannes. *Briefwechsel mit J. O. Grimm,* ed. Richard Barth (Berlin, 1908), pp. 43–46.

Brillat-Savarin, Jean-Anthelme. *Physiologie du Goût ou Méditations de gastronomie transcendante* (Paris, 1847). Part II: chap. 23.

Browne, Sir Thomas. *Religio Medici,* in *The Works,* ed. Charles Sayle (3 vols., Edinburgh, 1927). Vol. I: Part II, Sec. 9, pp. 100–101.

Bülow, Hans von. On Bismarck, in *Hans von Bülows Leben in seinen Briefen dargestellt,* ed. Marie von Bülow (2nd ed., Leipzig, 1921), p. 548.

Burney, Charles. *An Account of the Musical Performances in Westminster Abbey . . . in Commemoration of Handel* (London, 1785). Part I: pp. i–iv; Part II: pp. 25–41.

Burton, Robert. *The Anatomy of Melancholy* (11th ed. corrected, 2 vols., London, 1813). Vol. I: Part 2, Sec. 2, Mem. 6, Subs. 3, pp. 449–53.

Busoni, Ferruccio. *Scritti e pensieri sulla Musica,* ed. L. Dallapiccola and G. M. Gatti (Florence, 1941). "The Unity of Music," pp. 70–71; the other fragment, pp. 62–63.

Butler, Samuel. *The Note-Books,* in *Works* (Shrewsbury ed., 20 vols., London, 1926). Vol. XX: pp. 107–12 and 209.

   Courtesy of E. P. Dutton & Co., Inc., the Executors of Samuel Butler, and Jonathan Cape, Ltd.

Byron, George Gordon, Lord. *Letters and Journals,* ed. R. E. Protheroe (6 vols., London, 1898–1904). Vol. IV: pp. 204 and 214.

———. *Correspondence,* ed. John Murray (2 vols., London, 1922). Vol. II: pp. 111–12.

Calvocoressi, M. D. *Musical Taste and How to Form It* (London, 1925), pp. 2–3.

Cellini, Benvenuto. *La Vita,* ed. Carlo Cordié (2 vols., Milan, 1944). Vol. I: Bk. I, chaps v–vi, pp. 11–13.

Chabrier, Emmanuel. "Lettres Inédites," in *Bulletin de la S.I.M.,* Jan.–Feb. 1909. On composing "The Tempest," p. 122; two others, p. 6.

Chapman, John Jay. *Emerson and Other Essays* (New York, 1909), p. 83.

———. *Letters,* ed. M. A. DeWolfe Howe (Boston, 1937), p. 102.

Chateaubriand, René de. *Le Génie du Christianisme,* ed. Guizot (2 vols., Paris, 1885). Vol. II: Part IV, Bk. I, chap. 1, pp. 151–53.

Chesterfield, Philip Dormer Stanhope, Fourth Earl of. *Letters,* ed. Bonamy Dobree (6 vols., London, 1932). Vol. IV: pp. 1360–61 and 1458.

Chesterton, G. K. "Music with Meals" ("On Misunderstanding"), in *Generally Speaking* (New York, 1929), pp. 103–109.

   Courtesy of Dorothy Edith Collins, Methuen & Co., Ltd., and A. P. Watt & Son.

Collier, Jeremy. *Essays upon Several Subjects* (5th ed., 2 vols. in one, London, 1702–1703). Vol. II: pp. 19–24.

Cornford, F. M. *The Republic of Plato* (Oxford, 1941), pp. v–vi.

Davies, Sir Walford. *The Pursuit of Music* (London, 1944), p. 390.

Debussy, Claude. *M. Croche, Anti-Dilettante* (Paris, 1921), pp. 135–37.

Delacroix, Eugène. "Mozart," in *Journal, 1853–1856,* ed. André Joubin (3 vols., Paris, 1932). Vol. II: pp. 24, 42, 71, 102, 124, 154 ff., 317–18, 438–39, 481.

De Quincey, Thomas. *Works* (2nd ed., 17 vols., Edinburgh, 1862–78). Vol. XIII: "The *Antigone* of Sophocles," pp. 208–11.

Dickens, Charles. "Serenade at Todgers's," in *Martin Chuzzlewit,* chap. XI.

————. "The Solitary Cello," in *Dombey and Son,* chap. LVIII.

————. On the scientific musician, *ibid.,* chap. XXXIII.

d'Indy, Vincent. *César Franck* (6th ed., Paris, 1912), pp. 76–77.

Emerson, Ralph Waldo. *Journals,* ed. E. W. Emerson and W. E. Forbes (10 vols., Boston, 1909–14). Vol. VI: p. 479.

Engel, Louis. *From Mozart to Mario* (2 vols., London, 1886). Vol. II: Rossini, p. 72; Verdi, pp. 134–38.

Falla, Manuel de. "Notas sobre Wagner en su Cincuentenario," in *Cruz y Raya* (Madrid), Sept. 1933, pp. 67–80.

Gluck, Christoph Willibald von. Letter to La Harpe, in J.-G. Prodhomme, *Ecrits de Musiciens* (Paris, 1912), pp. 414–19.

Goethe, Johann Wolfgang von. *Briefwechsel zwischen Goethe und Zelter,* ed. Max Hecker (3 vols., Leipzig, n.d.), under date; on Möser Quartet, *ibid.* Beethoven anecdote, from various sources, *e.g.,* August Frankl, "Schiller, Beethoven, und Goethe in Karlsbad" (Carlsbad, 1862), pp. 9–10 and 16.

Gorky, Maxim. *Days with Lenin* (New York: International Publishers, 1932), p. 52.

Gounod, Charles. *Mémoires d'un Artiste* (Paris, 1896), pp. 99–104.

Green, Julian. *Journal* (3 vols., Paris, 1938–46). Vol. I: on Wagner, p. 111; Vol. II: on music, p. 188.

Gurney, Edmund. "Wagner and Wagnerism," in *Nineteenth Century,* March 1883, pp. 434–52.

Haggin, B. H. *Music on Records* (New York, 1938), pp. viii–xi.
    Courtesy of the Oxford University Press, Inc.
    Copyright 1938 by the Oxford University Press, Inc.

Hanslick, Eduard. *Concerte, Componisten und Virtuosen: 1870–1885* (Berlin, 1886), pp. 224–27.

Hardy, Thomas. *Under the Greenwood Tree* (London, 1872, 1912), chaps. III and IV.

————. *The Hand of Ethelberta* (London, 1876, 1912), chap. XLIV continued.
    Courtesy of The Macmillan Company.

Harrison, Frederic. "The Concert Hall" ("Music in Great Cities"), in *Memories and Thoughts* (New York, 1906), pp. 299–302.
Courtesy of The Macmillan Company.

Haydn, Joseph. Letter, in Willi Kahl, *Selbstbiographien deutscher Musiker des XVIIIten Jahrhunderts* (Cologne, 1948), pp. 83–86.

Hearn, Lafcadio. "L'Arlésienne," in *Editorials,* ed. C. W. Hutson (Boston, 1926), pp. 306–11.

Heine, Heinrich. *Gesammelte Werke,* ed. Gustav Karpeles (9 vols., Berlin, 1887). Vol. VII: "Letters on the French Stage," Nos. 9 and 10, pp. 132 and 145–53.

Helmholtz, Hermann von. *Die Lehre von Tonempfindungen* (6th ed., Brunswick, 1913), pp. 587–88.

Heseltine, Philip. Editor's Foreword, in *The Sackbut* (London), May 1920, pp. 7–9.

Hewitt, John Hill. *Shadows on the Wall, or Glimpses of the Past* (Baltimore, 1877), pp. 82–85.

Hogarth, William. "The Enraged Musician," in *Marriage à la Mode and Other Engravings* (New York: Lear, 1947), no pl. number.

Hoffman, E. T. A. [W]. *Gesammelte Schriften* (12 vols. in six, Berlin, 1844–45). Vol. VII: pp. 91–108; comment by Jean-Paul Richter, p. 6.

Hunt, Leigh. *Autobiography,* ed. Thornton Hunt (London, 1860). "Musical Memories," pp. 21–22, 41–45, 323–24, 355; on "expression," p. 124.

Jefferson, Thomas. Letter, in *The Writings,* ed. Paul Leicester Ford (10 vols., New York, 1893). Vol. II: pp. 158–60.

Jeffries, J. M. N. [J. M. N. J.]. "A Dean of Dignity," in *Daily Mail* (London), Oct. 31, 1927, p. 9.
Courtesy of Mr. Jeffries and the *Daily Mail*.

Kassner, Rudolf. *Der grösste Mensch: Auswahl aus den Schriften* (Amandus ed. Oesterreichische Vereinigung, Vienna, 1946), pp. 93–94.

Lamb, Charles. "A Chapter on Ears," in *Works*, ed. E. V. Lucas (7 vols., New York, 1903–1905). Vol. II: *Essays of Elia*, pp. 38–41.

Lambert, Constant. *Music Ho! A Study of Music in Decline* (London, 1934), pp. 206–207; on Ravel, pp. 197–98.
Courtesy of Charles Scribner's Sons and Faber and Faber, Limited.

Lanier, Sidney. *Centennial Edition of the Works* (10 vols., Baltimore, 1945). Vol. II: *Essays on Music*, ed. P. F. Baum, pp. 333–34.
Courtesy of The Johns Hopkins Press.

Lieven, Princess Dorothea. *Private Letters to Prince Metternich*, trans. Peter Quennell and Dilys Powell (New York, 1938), pp. 49–50.

Liszt, Franz. *F. Chopin* (Paris, 1852), pp. 146–48.

———. Pixis story, in *Gazette Musicale*, July 16, 1837, p. 341. See also Blessington.

Ludwig, Emil. *Beethoven, Life of a Conqueror*, trans. by George Stewart McManus (New York, 1943), p. 185.

Luther, Martin. *Gedanken über die Musik*, ed. F. A. Beck (Berlin, 1825), pp. 17, 18–23.

Macaulay, T. B. From *Life and Letters*, by G. O. Trevelyan (2 vols., London, 1876), under date.

Maretzek, Max. *Crotchets and Quavers: or, Revelations of an Opera Manager in America* (New York, 1855), pp. 41–47.

Maria Theresa. *Correspondance secrète entre Marie-Thérèse et le Comte de Mercy-Argenteau, avec les lettres de Marie-Antoinette*, ed. A. Arneth and A. Geffroy (2nd ed., 3 vols., Paris, 1875), under dates.

Mattheson, Johann. *Das neu-eröffnete Orchestre* (3 vols. in two, Hamburg, 1713–21). Vol. I: pp. 126–27.

Mazzini, Giuseppe. "Filosofia della Musica," in *Scritti, Editi ed Inediti* (Edizione Nazionale, 94 vols., Imola, 1906–43). Vol. 8: *Letteratura;* Vol. II: pp. 121–65.

———. Additional note of 1867, in *The Life and Works of Joseph Mazzini* (6 vols., London, 1864–70). Vol. IV: pp. 52–55.

Mellers, W. H. "The Textual Criticism of Music," in *Scrutiny*, March 1939, p. 480.

Mendelssohn-Bartholdy, Felix. Letters to and by, in *Die Familie Mendelssohn: 1729–1847*, ed. S. Hensel (7th ed., 2 vols., Berlin, 1891). Vol. I: pp. 93, 106–107, 147–48, 159, and 161–62.

Mercy-Argenteau, Count de. See Maria Theresa.

Molière (J.-B. Poquelin). *Le Bourgeois Gentilhomme*, in *Oeuvres* (2 vols., Paris: Didot, 1862). Vol. II: Acts I and II, pp. 338 ff.

Montaigne, Michel Eyquem de. *Essais*, ed. J.-V. Leclerc (4 vols., Paris, 1925). Vol. I: Bk. I, chap. xxv, p. 186.

Monteverdi, Claudio. Preface to *Madrigali guerrieri e amorosi*, in Domenico De Paoli, *Claudio Monteverdi* (Milan, 1945), pp. 247–49.

Moore, Thomas. "Notes for the Life of Byron," in *Prose and Verse*, ed. R. H. Shepherd (London, 1878), p. 420.

Moscheles, Ignaz. *Aus Moscheles Leben*, ed. by his wife (2 vols., Leipzig, n.d. [1873]). Vol. II: p. 28.

Moussorgsky, Modeste. "Autobiographic Note," in *The Musorgsky Reader: A Life . . . in Letters and Documents*, ed. and trans. by Jay Leyda and Sergei Bertensson (New

York, 1947), pp. 416–20.

Also in *The Musorgsky Reader:*

Borodin, Alexander. Letter to his wife, pp. 305–306.

Stassov, Vladimir. On *Boris Godunov,* p. 349.

Courtesy of W. W. Norton & Company, Inc.

Copyright 1947 by W. W. Norton & Company, Inc.

Mozart, W. A. *Briefwechsel,* ed. Hedwig and E. H. Mueller von Asow (Lindau im Bodensee, 1949); 2 vols. published, through the year 1778; under dates.

———. *Briefe,* ed. Ludwig Nohl (Salzburg, 1865), under dates and p. 161.

Napoleon I. Letters, in J. Tiersot, *Lettres de musiciens écrites en français,* etc. (2 vols., Turin, 1924). Vol. I: pp. 532–33.

Nietzsche, Friedrich. *Gesammelte Werke,* ed. "Musarion" (23 vols., Munich, 1922). Vol. VII: *Thoughts out of Season,* No. IV, Secs. 1, 2, 3, and 5; Vol. XVII: *Nietzsche contra Wagner,* Sec. 2. The note on the "Habanera," from *Friedrich Nietzsches Randglossen zu Bizets "Carmen,"* ed. Hugo Daffner (Deutsche Musikbuecherei, I; Regensburg, n.d.), p. 27.

North, Roger. *Memoirs of Musick,* ed. Edward F. Rimbault (London, 1846), pp. 115–17; on musical fashions, pp. 91–92.

Paganini, Nicoló. Letter, in F.-J. Fétis, *Biographie Universelle des Musiciens* (2nd ed., 8 vols. in four, Paris, 1864). Vol. VI: pp. 410–12.

Partch, Harry. *Genesis of a Music: Monophony* (Madison, Wis., 1949), p. 58.

Courtesy of The University of Wisconsin Press.

Payn, James. *Some Private Views* (London, 1881), pp. 40–43.

Peacock, Thomas Love. *Gryll Grange,* ed. George Saintsbury (London, 1896), chaps. XIV and XV.

———. "Mangled Operas and the Star System," in *Works* (Halliford ed., 12 vols., London, 1926). Vol. IX: pp. 225–50.

Poe, Edgar Allan. *Letters,* ed. John Ward Ostrom (2 vols., Cambridge, Mass., 1948). Vol. I: 257–58.

Courtesy of the Harvard University Press.

Prodhomme, J.-G. *Les Symphonies de Beethoven* (Paris, 1906). On "Beethoven's 'Third' and 'Fifth,' " pp. 113–14, 206–207, 220, and 221–22.

Prokofiev, Sergei. "Statement," in American-Russian Institute publication, *On Soviet Music: Documents and Discussion,* (Hollywood, 1948), pp. 9–11. Translated by Alexandra Groth.

Prunières, Henry. *A New History of Music,* trans. by Edward Lockspeiser (New York, 1943), pp. 119, 242, and 260.

Radcliffe, Ann (Ward). *The Italian: or, The Confessional of the Black Penitents,* in *Novels, to which is prefixed a Memoir by Sir Walter Scott* (London, 1824), chap. XV.

Ravel, Maurice. See Renard, Jules.

Renard, Jules. *Journal* (5 vols., Paris, 1927). Vol. V: p. 1343.

Richter, Jean-Paul. *Werke,* ed. Eduard Berend (5 vols., Berlin, 1923). Vol. V: pp. 778–79. On artists hating the world, see Hoffmann.

Rimsky-Korsakov, N. *Principes d'Orchestration,* trans. by M. D. Calvocoressi (2 vols., Paris, 1914). Vol. I: p. 2.

Rogers, Samuel. *Recollections of His Table Talk,* ed. Alexander Dyce (2nd ed., London, 1856), pp. 223–24.

Rolland, Romain. *Jean-Christophe à Paris.* Part II: *La Foire sur la Place* (Vol. V of *Jean-Christophe,* Paris, 1908), "Making the Rounds," pp. 65–69; on Bach, pp. 259–60.

Courtesy of Henry Holt and Company, Inc., and Editions Albin Michel.

Rousseau, Jean-Jacques. *Oeuvres* (17 vols., Paris, 1830). Vol. VI: *La Nouvelle Héloïse,* Part II, Letter 23, pp. 332–35.

Sand, George. "Lettres d'un Voyageur," No. IV, in *Revue des Deux Mondes,* June 1835, pp. 698–736.

Saint-Saëns, Camille. "The Composer as Psychologist," in *Portraits et Souvenirs* (Paris, 1903), pp. 206–17, and *Ecole Buissonnière* (Paris, 1913), pp. 116–19.

Santayana, George. *Reason in Art* (New York, 1917), p. 51.

Sarasate, Pablo. Letter, in Marc Pincherle, *Les Musiciens peints par eux-mêmes* (Paris, 1939), p. 182.

Schopenhauer, Arthur. *Sämmtliche Werke,* ed. Julius Frauenstädt (2nd ed., 6 vols., Leipzig, 1877). Vol. V: *Parerga und Paralipomena,* Part I, "Aphorismen zur Lebensweisheit," chap. v, pp. 450–51.

Schubert, Franz. *Briefe und Schriften,* ed. Otto Erich Deutsch (2nd ed., Munich, 1922), pp. 32–34 and 97.

Schumann, Robert. *Gesammelte Schriften über Musik und Musiker,* ed. F. Gustav Jansen (4th ed., 2 vols., Leipzig, 1891). Vol. I: pp. xxiii–xxiv and 3–5; Vol. II: p. 178.

———. *Leben aus seinen Briefen* (2 vols. in one, Berlin, 1887), under date.

Sessions, Roger. "The Composer and His Message," in *The Intent of the Artist,* ed. Augusto Centeno (Princeton, 1941), pp. 123–24.
Courtesy of the Princeton University Press.

Shaw, G. B. *Love Among the Artists* (New York, 1910), chap. ix.

———. "Sir George Grove," in *Pen Portraits and Reviews* (London, 1931), pp. 106–109.

———. *Man and Superman* (New York, 1904), Act III, p. 99.
Courtesy of The Public Trustee and The Society of Authors.

Smith, Sydney. *A Memoir of the Reverend Sydney Smith by his daughter Lady Holland, with . . . Letters,* etc. (2 vols., London, 1855). Vol. II: under date.

———. Anecdote, in George W. E. Russell, *Sydney Smith* (English Men of Letters series; New York, 1905), pp. 206–207.

Spinoza, Baruch. *Ethica ordine geometrico demonstrata,* in *Opera,* ed. C. Gebhart (4 vols., Heidelberg, 1926). Part I: Appendix.

Spohr, Louis. *Selbstbiographie* (2 vols., Cassel, 1861). Vol. II: pp. 77–88.

Stassov, Vladimir. See Moussorgsky.

Stendhal [Henri Beyle]. *Vie de Rossini,* ed. Henry Prunières (2 vols., Paris, 1922), chaps. xvi and xl; on the nations, in "Raison, Folie," Vol. I, p. 230, ed. Henry Martineau, *Oeuvres Complètes* (Le Divan), 79 vols., Paris, 1927–37.

Stewart, Donald Ogden. *Perfect Behavior* (New York, 1922), p. 94.

Swift, Jonathan. *Works,* ed. Sir Walter Scott (2nd ed., 19 vols., London, 1884). Vol. XIX: pp. 254–57.

Tchaikovsky, P. I. *The Diaries,* ed. and trans. by Wladimir Lakond (New York, 1945), pp. 247–49.
Courtesy of W. W. Norton & Company, Inc.
Copyright 1945 by Wladimir Lakond.

Tolstoy, Leo. *War and Peace,* authorized trans. into French (3 vols., Paris, 1885). Vol. I: Part I, chap. iv, Sec. xv, pp. 378–81.

———. *What is Art?,* trans. by Aylmer Maude (World's Classics; London, 1930), chaps. i and ii.
Courtesy of the Oxford University Press.

Turgenev, Ivan. *Smoke,* French ed. by Charles Sarolea (Paris: Nelson n.d.), pp. 125–28.

Turner, W. J. *Berlioz, The Man and His Work* (London, 1934), pp. 133–35.
————. *Orpheus, or The Music of the Future* (London, n.d. [1926]), p. 9.
van Dieren, Bernard. *Down Among the Dead Men and Other Essays* (London, 1935).
"What Gives Us Pause," pp. 96–99, aphorisms, pp. 247 and 267. Mozart anecdote, in *Berlioz . . . the report of a discussion* (London, 1929), p. 25.
Courtesy of Mr. Bernard van Dieren, Jr.
Verdi, Giuseppe. *I Copialettere di Giuseppe Verdi,* ed. G. Cesari and A. Luzio (Milan, 1913), under dates.
Vernon, P. E. "Non-Musical Factors in the Appreciation of Music," in *Musical Times,* Feb.–Apr. 1929, pp. 123 ff.
Courtesy of Mr. Vernon.
Voltaire [F.-M. Arouet]. *Le siècle de Louis XIV,* ed. René Groos (2 vols., Paris, 1929). Vol. II: pp. 330 and 348–49.
Wagner, Richard. *Gesammelte Schriften und Dichtungen* (3rd ed., 10 vols. in five, Leipzig, 1883 ff.). Vol. I: "A Pilgrimage to Beethoven," pp. 90–114; Vol. III: on Meyerbeer, p. 300; Vol. IX: Beethoven's Day, pp. 96–97.
Weber, C.-M. von. *Sämtliche Schriften,* ed. Georg Kaiser (Berlin and Leipzig, 1908). Letter, pp. 404–406; novel outline, 439–510; on Italian music, p. 510.
Wolf, Hugo. *Musikalische Kritiken,* ed. R. Bakta and H. Werner (Leipzig, 1911), pp. 222–24, 228, and 334.
Wolzogen, Hans von. *Guide through the Music of R. Wagner's "The Ring of the Nibelung,"* tr. by Ernst von Wolzogen (2nd ed., Leipzig and London, n.d. [1882]), pp. 45–79.
Wotton, Tom S. "Drums," in *Musical Times,* July–Sept. 1930, pp. 602 ff.
Courtesy of Mrs. Florence M. Wotton.

Index of Authors and Composers

Numbers in italics refer to the passages, short or long, by which a writer is represented in this volume. Numbers not in italics refer to the mention of a writer, a composer, *or his works*.